YUKIO MISHIMA'S
REPORT TO THE EMPEROR

RICHARD APPIGNANESI

YUKIO MISHIMA'S REPORT TO THE EMPEROR

SINCLAIR-STEVENSON

LONDON

First published in the United Kingdom in 2002
by Christopher Sinclair-Stevenson
3 South Terrace, London SW7 2TB

ISBN 0 9540476 6 4

Typeset by Rowland Phototypesetting Ltd., Bury St Edmunds, Suffolk.
Printed and bound in the United Kingdom by
St Edmundsbury Press Ltd., Bury St Edmunds, Suffolk.

鏡

玉

刀

CONTENTS

Part One: THE MIRROR:
A Financial Rebirth

1 Made in Japan — 3
2 Madame de Sade — 12
3 The Reverse Course — 28
4 Buster Keaton — 45
5 A Subterranean Bookeeper — 56
6 By the Waters of Sumidagawa — 82
7 Selling the Dead — 90
8 A Game of Noble Losers — 99
9 No Surrender — 117

Part Two: THE JEWEL:
Anatomy of a Bestseller

1 Transcripts of Yukio Mishima's Interview — 121
2 A Basket of Broken Legs — 143
3 The Unassailable Article of Faith — 148
4 *Second Day in Benares*:
   Remembering the divine Marquis — 159
5 All in White — 164
6 *Benares*: the Manikarnika Ghat — 168
7 Last Words of a Realist — 177
8 *Benares:* The Widows' House — 186
9 The Kiss — 190
10 Riding the Tiger — 206
11 Fernando Pinto Mendes — 216

12 Incident on a Station Platform   233
13 *Benares:* A Mass for the Dead   245

Part Three: THE SWORD:
Treason

1 Letter to Baroness Omiyeke Keiko   275
2 At the Back of the Mirror   278
3 Again, the Sumidagawa   285
4 The Patriot   293
5 The Entombed Lovers of Gakijima   307
6 A Shadow Boxer's Head   326
7 The Tough Guy   344
8 Ikigami:– Recognizing the Living Goddess   382
9 A Tea Party for Assassins   402

Restore the Emperor

The posthumous script of a Modern Noh
Drama by Yukio Mishima   437

Part One

THE MIRROR
A Financial Rebirth

1   MADE IN JAPAN

UNDERSTAND THAT I, Yukio Mishima, was born on New Year's Eve, 1947, two weeks before my twenty-third birthday. Time had ceased for us and 1947 equalled 0 + 2. What strange arithmetic is this to account for a birth that makes no sense? It is a true accountancy which needs explaining to a generation that cannot recall the meaning of Defeat, Unconditional Surrender and Occupation.

1945 was Year Zero. That year, on August 14th, the 124th divine successor to the Imperial Throne, the Showa Emperor, accepted Unconditional Surrender. The initials of those two fatal words in English are by coincidence US, and it was under supreme US authority that the Occupation of Japan proceeded for the next seven years. What did time matter then? The sun had gone out and the progress of time counted for nothing in our day of endless eclipse.

Unconditional Surrender is my true beginning. The fact that such a beginning might similarly have preoccupied millions of other unconditionally surrendered persons, did not concern me, since I was no concern of theirs. In short, I was not famous yet. And wishing to be famous was my one sincere consideration at the time.

A particular kind of irony lies in store for a people defeated in war. It is the inevitable fate of the vanquished to seem two-faced in the eyes of the victor. Only gradually did we come to see that our Janus-faced monstrosity was a deformity shared by vanquished and victor alike. But I am anticipating a painful enlightenment which remains to be described. I did not know, and could not have known, that on New Year's Eve, 1947, I was born into a new era of *Nipponsei*, Made in Japan, a trademark of shame which broadcast our goods as poor and shoddy throughout the world. These were the mirage years of our national economic recovery. I wandered into this mirage with spectacular naivety and bearing a double identity, my own two faces, or at least two names, my civic one Hiraoka Kimitake, and the pseudonym of a writer. Hiraoka Kimitake had to disappear without trace so that the writer known abroad today as Yukio Mishima might gain notoriety. Nothing so glamorous or wholesome as a murder tells how this substitution of one by the other occurred. As I said, it is a matter of unnatural parturition.

I first adopted my pen-name Yukio Mishima at the age of fifteen, when it is also the custom of apprentice Noh actors to put aside the garments of childhood for those of their adult careers. But my teenage choice of vocational identity had to go underground in 1947 when I exchanged my university uniform for the masquerade of a banker's three-piece suit.

In conformity with my father's wishes and the stipulated creed of filial piety, I had graduated from Tokyo (formerly Imperial) University with a first-class law degree. That post-war demotion of the university from imperial to humbler civil rank was only one small consequence of the US Occupation purge and its democratizing zeal. I too considered myself a casualty of the new democracy. Following my graduation, I took the arduous higher civil service examination. I overcame this obstacle too, with complete success, but in violation of my true nature. I was accepted by the Ministry of Finance, and on Christmas eve, 1947, appointed to the National Savings Section of the Banking Bureau. My father was immensely gratified to see me enter the most prestigious Ministry, in the enviable position of elite bureaucrat, a career advantage that he had never enjoyed as a former civil servant.

I felt considerably less than pleased by my apparent success. I reckoned that my advancement had been due to unfair circumstances, partly because competent graduates were scarce after the war, and no less important, because my services as a third generation bureaucrat were especially welcome. I had even more reason to feel despondent, because now my double life began, writing as Yukio Mishima by night in hiding from my father who abominated literature, and by day relying on masquerade to see me through my office routine. I dared not imagine what effect my sleepless, moonlighting nights would have on my daytime performance.

On New Year's Eve, I celebrated my desperate situation at a nightclub in Akasaka. At the time, there were scarcely half a dozen such off-limits nightspots amid Tokyo's ruins, licensed for the exclusive pleasure of Occupation officers and their Nipponese harlots, male and female, but also frequented by a circle of wealthy young aristocrats of the Peers' School set. My access to the club was permitted on the strength of being an alumnus of the Peers' School, an Imperially founded academy for the nincompoop sons of the Meiji peerage and *nouveau riche* upstarts, and I had graduated among the very few who belonged to neither class.

I imposed on myself the social discipline of attending clubs like these on Saturday nights, although I detested the rowdy, vacuous Peers' set. I could neither afford nor stomach the black market whisky, and the brash GI-style sexual promiscuity offended my sensibilities. Out of place among these Kansas gargantuas and their whores, I was a puny, sickly weed in danger of being trampled to death by rioting carnivores. I stood below average in height, 5-foot 4½ inches. My health was poor. I suffered from chronic gastroenteritis and persistent migraines. In other words, I was the perfect specimen of the defeated Japanese, the fearsome enemy, the invincible demon of Asia, unmasked as an undersized and sick thing.

I often used to recruit my younger brother Chiyuki to accompany me, a complacent, sturdy lad on whom I relied as my talismanic protector. The agonies of sleeplessness, blinding headaches and my constant intestinal spasms did not help to make these odious nights pleasant. On this fateful night, I went bravely on my own. I forced myself on to the dance floor to exhibit my uncoordinated performances of the jitterbug, struggling against my utter lack of natural rhythm, in an effort to appear the very image of spontaneous grace and zest. I managed to produce a credible simulation of ecstasy, driven by my Nietzschean longing to dance with maniacal Dionysian enthralment. I came painfully face to face with my own innate awkwardness. Every episode of physical mastery in my life, whether it concerned dancing, martial arts or body-building in my later years, has never been more than a studied triumph of mimicry. Never once have I lost my sobriety or known pure selfless rapture. Pretence dogs me even in my flights to embrace what is natural, physical, normal. Everything physical I do bears the scars of a forceps delivery; all my doings are unnaturally accomplished acts of desperation.

On that particular evening in question, as I danced in my usual state of feigned blindness, I noticed someone engaged in a truly admirable foxtrot. I recognized him at once. There could be no mistaking his distinctively striking appearance, though I had only ever seen him in photographs – the wan leper's complexion, the rats' tails of long hair whipping his cheeks, a Christ-like face that acknowledged every symptom of physical and spiritual dissipation, the icon of despair worshipped by countless readers of the new generation – Dazai Osamu – with a series of bestselling novels to his credit.

Here I was sharing a dance floor with the most dazzling writer of our time, our Prince Myshkin of Unconditional Surrender, our spokesman of the post-war malaise, the abhorrent caricature of *Nipponsei* pessimism. I respected Dazai's rare talent, but he filled me with violent revulsion. His dark-ringed eyes indecently proclaimed all his vices. He surrendered helplessly to depravity of every sort, alcoholism, drug addiction and sexual truancy. He glorified despair, self-hate and destruction. An attempted *shinju* love-pact suicide with a prostitute had resulted in her death but left him alive and covered in shame, disowned by his family. Dazai Osamu was the perfect exemplar of a generation forsaken by death. He was a well-stocked emporium of vile excesses in a time of rationing, a clearance sale advertisement of Japan's bankrupt culture. My contemporaries made him their hero. Nay, more, he was canonized a saint. Anyone who volunteers to befoul and villainize himself to such a degree will inevitably be sainted. His outcry against life is so extreme that the onlookers are shocked into blessing him. He is our excremental scapegoat, a sacred monster when sacredness has entirely perished. His open wounds remind us of the wound within us that our normality wishes disguised.

I hated Dazai Osamu. I envied and feared him. He held up a mirror to me in which every one of my concealed lusts stood exposed, but that I shrank from committing through weak-kneed timidity.

I elbowed my way closer to my loathsome idol. He danced his rapturous foxtrot with a tawdry bargirl, her face veneered with cosmetics, clad in a strapless cocktail dress of turquoise organza refashioned from a 30s gown. The pair moved like demented somnambulists, their eyes shut, reminding me of the religious hysteria which claims Matsuri festival dancers. I was jealous of Dazai's intoxicated submersion. I tried in vain to relinquish conscious power over my legs and become like him indistinguishable from the mass.

Dazai's partner turned her plump, naked back to me, its muscles rippling like spume on the surface of a bottomless ocean. I was astonished to see Dazai's ragged fingernails gouging into the girl's back, raking furrows of blood across her fleshy omoplates. A mole in the niche of her spine had been partly ripped out. It hung by a purple root, a little decapitated mushroom bleeding copiously. She did not feel it. Nor did she feel my fingertips dipping into the rivulet of blood on her back.

I wished it were Dazai's blood dripping between my fingers. Envy overwhelmed me in a sulphuric flood of bile, scorching my nostrils and bringing tears to my eyes. I burned with fanatic desire to assassinate my rival. Only his murder would relieve my insane covetousness. Like a child locked in a murderous tantrum, for whom the entire world shrinks to a single imperative cry, I kept on repeating – I want Dazai's crown, I want Dazai's crown.

I could bear it no longer. I had to flee.

The cloakroom girl seemed to look pityingly at me as she handed over my overcoat and gumboots. A Japanese bouncer in a smart wing-collared tuxedo, with a bonze's shaven head, winked conspiratorially at the girl as I struggled to pull on my boots. My mother Shizue forbade me to go out in winter without this ridiculous footgear, her precious gift scrounged from the black market.

The frosty night air and clean new-fallen snow refreshed my senses. I hoped to find a taxi. I enjoyed the hard-packed snow's crepitation as though on my palate. In the parking-lot adjoining the nightclub, I saw a young woman quarrelling fiercely with a tall GI lounging against a jeep, one foot raised on the step. I should have turned away at once. I fell captive instead to my disquiet. Something of courtly beauty in the woman's face upset and held me. A face imperially aquiline, slashed by a concubine's red mouth. She was draped negligently in an ankle-length coat of Russian sable, her legs exposed magnificently bare to the cold. Red toenails, accenting the gap of paleness, sank pinioned by high-heeled sandals into the snow. She teetered, a statuesque derelict, crashing against the blonde GI titan on whose chest she rained defiant but useless blows. He laughed in her face, creased in fury round the crimson mouth and hawk's nose – a laughter that seemed produced by her thumps on a cavernous chest. I had never seen two people more insanely drunk.

She gave up pummelling him at last and ran off unsteadily on her high heels. In two swift, long-legged strides, the GI had overtaken the fugitive and was gripping her by the arm. He demonstrated an immense strength by lifting her with ease clear off the ground. Then he turned and saw me.

'Hey you – Mickey Rooney in the boots,' he called. 'Yeah – you, shrimp. Come over here.'

The snow, like dense granular flurries of moths, whirled into the magnetic blue haloes of the street-lamps overhead. I too was drawn unresistingly into the force-field of the soldier's blue eyes. He let go of his prey and she fell in a heap at his feet, her coat spilling open in a pool of aquamarine silk on which her thighs gleamed white.

'Do you speak English?'

I nodded.

He spoke gently, without menace. I stared up at an incredibly baby-like face on which a white stubble of beard seemed foreign. The age of Westerners is something I find difficult to estimate; but his features of perplexing youthfulness apparently disguised a man of middle age. He smiled sweetly like a benign nursery giant. The alcohol on his breath enveloped me in a medical ether smell.

'Do you know me? I'm Satan,' he confided, and, as if further to amuse us both, he added, 'Why don't you stand on her belly?'

I understood the words, but couldn't believe what they meant. 'Don't you get it?' He gripped my shoulder encouragingly. 'Go on, Tojo, you heard me. Climb up on her fucking belly!' I raised my booted foot, disbelievingly, and sought confirmation of the order in those merry blue eyes, so innocent, so lyrically remote from any trace of cruelty.

I put my foot on squelching laundry. What must I expect to feel as I pressed down? Her lips tightened in surprise of pain, but her face seemed to come apart like the petals of a wilting chrysanthemum. She groaned the GI's name, Shep, Shep. 'Harder, for Chrissake, step harder!' With impatient good humour, he hoisted me up by the elbows, forcing me to regain my balance by resting both feet on her stomach. What is it like? It is the attractive snare of mud. Many years later, in 1961, my dance teacher Hijikata Tatsumi would say to me, 'If you put your foot in mud, you'll find a child's face in there.' Infected by the GI's child-like murderous insobriety, I could taste jubilation arising in my throat like black phlegm.

'All right, you've done your Sermon on the Mount,' and Shep pulled me away by the waist.

I looked down at the prostitute's stricken face and held my breath. Never had I seen a face like it. It was the moon spirit's frighteningly beautiful visage, ghost pale in a black aura of hair. History had stopped in that face; a face such as one might see in the cross-section of a felled tree, exposed in the miraculous grain of the wood.

Her eyes gaped, bulging open still in response to my weight, but unseeing. Her face, bright as the sterile moon, looked severed from her body, motionless like the fallen trunk of a tree, peeled of its bark, white. Shep lit a cigar and contemplated her body. 'We've killed her,' I thought.

Her lips stirred at last and she gasped out, 'I'm pregnant.'

I did not have to translate. I knew Shep understood the meaning.

He helped her up now, with a diligence reserved for elderly invalids. He brushed the mud-stained snow from her legs and guided her back to the jeep. He left the sable coat were it lay. Everything stood bathed in that unearthly dominance of blue as though sunken into Shep's eyes. I saw him looking down quizzically at the little black drops falling on the snow between the woman's footprints as she reached the jeep. Did I imagine these tiny blossoms growing from the snow? Would these too disappear into the vacuum of Shep's gaze?

I saw him wrap the prostitute in a khaki army blanket and deposit her like a doll in the jeep. Her head lolled back over the seat like a corpse's.

I stared at the petalled script in the snow and the idea came to me: 'I have written a poem of evil tonight better than ever you could, Dazai Osamu.'

I knelt in the snow, and my stomach heaved up its poisonous content. My vomit appeared the decayed hollow of a tooth. A pair of immaculately polished military boots entered my perimeter of vision. I heard the GI say, 'Here, kid,' as he handed over the woman's sable coat. I shook my head. 'Take it. She's not going to need it.' He draped the coat over my shoulders and left me in the wake of his cigar.

'Thief –' I heard the woman say plainly, before the jeep drove away.

I remained where I was, kneeling, embraced by the fur and the prostitute's aroma. For how long, I cannot say; but suddenly another pair of soldier's shoes occupied my downcast view. These were not GI boots, however, but custom-made shoes encased in low, sole-fitting galoshes. The uniform too was not standard issue but handsomely tailored, I observed, as my eyes mounted to the stranger's face. Instead of the normal army greatcoat, he wore a long cape, ankle-length like the girl's sable, officially khaki in colour, but of cashmere lined with splended red fox fur. One hand fastened the mantle snugly close to him; while the other held his cap by the visor, turned inside up as though to catch the falling snow. His insignia gave him the rank of US army captain. He was a young man of ordinary height – not a giant like my GI – and of decidedly odd looks. His uncovered head seemed aflame with wavy, bright red hair. He was strikingly snub-nosed, and his cleft chin tilted up emphasized an enormous humped Adam's apple, pulsing and white as a frog's belly in his long lean neck. He stood peering up into dark space whence the snowflakes fell on his colourless eyelashes, or perhaps searching for stars with eyes of astonishing green. The freckles on his pallid skin looked blue in the light. His choice of fox to line his cape had been appropriate, for his face too had something of the fox in it, an impression supported by the glistening teeth laid bare to the gums as he grimaced in response to the sting of snow on his eyes.

There was an air at once attractive and repellant about this eccentrically costumed officer. He had the demeanour of someone bold, ironic and ruthless. A certain trait of the demonic in him made me think of the *kitsuni-tsukahi*, the 'fox-possessor', a legendary and feared species of magician. These people gained their magic powers in a very odd and cruel way. They bury a fox alive with only its head left free. Bean-curd, the fox's preferred delicacy, is placed tantalizingly out of reach of its mouth, so that the animal strains after the food in frantic but vain efforts. In the last agonies of starvation, and just at the crucial point of death, the fox is decapitated and the head lunges to seize the food it has been denied. The fox's spirit passes into the food, which is then mixed with clay and shaped into the animal's form, and this charm becomes an infallible guide to foretelling the future.

In my distracted state, the red-haired captain looked to me like the very embodiment of the fox-spirit turned visible. With his head twisted back, thin neck straining and teeth bared, he portrayed the agonizing fox awaiting the axe. Slowly, I realized that his pulsating throat did not indicate agony, but a silently restrained laughter.

He put on his cap and met my rudely gawking stare with his enthralling green eyes.

'You must be feeling distinctly cold,' he said, in a slow academically precise Japanese. 'Please accept the accommodation of my car, and I shall be happy to drive you home, if that is your wish.'

'It is my wish.'

He helped me up from the snow, and at his gesture, a vast black Packard came to meet us on the spot where the GI's jeep had stood.

What a bizarre couple we must have made, an officer in queerly custom-tailored uniform, and I in a prostitute's fur coat.

'Where would you like us to take you?'

'Midorigaoka.'

The captain's chauffeur replied with a glance in the rearview mirror, 'I know it.'

9

I was grateful for the Packard's grey plush seats and its heat smarting on my gelid cheeks. Rose-scented cologne emanated from the captain as he bowed towards me. 'Sam Lazar,' he introduced himself. He offered me an English cigarette in a gold-lined ivory case – the carving was Japanese. 'Spoils of war,' Captain Lazar said, in answer to my look.

As my limbs thawed, my mind too awakened to the situation. Captain Lazar's arrival at the parking lot could not have been an accident. It was very likely that he had witnessed the entire incident. I wondered why, as the GI's superior, he had not intervened. His green fox's eyes seemed to read my thoughts. 'You are fortunate to have escaped unharmed,' he smiled, caressing the sable pelt, 'and, as I see, generously rewarded.'

'The GI was not interested in me.'

'Perhaps not, Hiraoka-*san*, but he is no ordinary GI. That was Major General Charles Willoughby, chief of Military Intelligence G-2 – and I think this should amuse you – head of the Public Safety Division.'

I wasn't particularly amused by his revelation; but I did wonder why Captain Lazar so nonchalantly disclosed the Major General's identity to me, a vanquished Japanese under Occupation law. I glanced at the chauffeur, a Japanese too, with a military man's close shaven skull and massively bull-necked like a sumo wrestler, whose thick, protruding ears could not fail to overhear the conversation.

'Oh, don't worry about Masura,' Captain Lazar perceptively commented. 'As a former *kempeitai* lieutenant, he benefits from a long habit of discretion. I rescued him from indictment as a war criminal. I cannot imagine any more reliable person. Do you know what General Eichelberger, commander of our Eighth Army, has said? "Japanese soldiers are a commander's dream. They're the kind who stay on a ridge-top until they die."'

'Nevertheless, we surrendered,' I said.

A trace of irony seemed reflected in Masura's eyes in the mirror.

Captain Lazar fell back languidly in his seat, his chin raised and frog-bellied Adam's apple quavering in another demonstration of his stone silent laughter.

'Is it normally your duty,' I asked with intrepid frankness, 'to keep an eye on the major general's nocturnal activities?'

'A sort of rearguard? Oh dear, no, Willoughby's quite capable of fending for himself. He often resorts to GI masquerade for his more outrageous night time revels. It's just that tonight, he became fearfully drunk at Count Ito's party – do you know Count Ito? No? Well, perhaps you'll meet him one day – and I thought it advisable to keep old Schlep under surveillance.'

'Schlep?' That was the name – or its version – the prostitute had used. She had elided the 'l', a letter rebarbative to the Japanese tongue (just as the captain's own name must inevitably be pronounced 'razor').

The captain came to the aid of my evident puzzlement. 'Of course Schlep must sound odd to you. You see, Willoughby's real name is Tscheppe-Weidenbach, or at least that was his father's name, a Prussian officer. Willoughby's quite a Prussian character himself. Wrote a book in 1939 defending Mussolini's Abyssinian campaign. He's one of General MacArthur's old cronies – a right-hand man in our Supremo's Prussian guard. All of us "Prussians" in SCAP have one job to do – to make damn sure that the Occupation becomes our generalissimo's ticket to the presidency of the you-knighted states of ah-merica.' Captain Lazar fidgeted in his seat, in a seizure of mute laughter. 'And so, I've nick-named Willoughby *schlep*, a Yiddish word meaning "to be burdened, to haul". Suitable for MacArthur's factotum, don't you think?'

This philological elucidation did not explain why a prostitute should call her tormentor by Captain Lazar's own personal nickname for him. I took another line of enquiry. 'So you are not Prussian yourself, then, but Jewish?'

Captain Lazar stared at me with his bold, rapacious green eyes. 'Prussia is now occupied by communists and therefore imaginary. Besides, I'm an Eisenhower man.'

I looked out of the car window, at the flurries of snow hiding the ruined city.

'A famous Zen master of the T'ang period,' I said, 'one Joshu by name, is reported to have solved a Zen riddle in a most enigmatic way.'

'I know the Zen problem you refer to,' Captain Lazar interposed. 'It is Nansen's riddle of the kitten. When two groups of Nansen's disciples began to argue over who should rightfully keep a kitten as their pet, he seized it from them and said, "Tell at once why this kitten should be spared, or else I shall kill it." They failed to answer, and Nansen beheaded the animal with his sickle. Joshu arrived after this event, too late, but with the right answer that would have saved the kitten's life.'

'The very one,' I nodded. 'Joshu solved Nansen's riddle by placing his sandals on his head. I too have solved a riddle tonight – the sterile enigma of war – by placing my feet on a prostitute's belly.'

Captain Lazar considered this for a moment, then replied, 'Your solution is interesting, but mistaken in one small detail. The lady who served as your pedestal is no harlot, in the normally accepted sense of that term. She is the Baroness Omiyeke Keiko, widow of a naval pilot and a kamikaze martyr, and our hostess this evening at Count Ito's party.'

Captain Lazar perceived my confusion, and changed the subject. 'What work do you do, Hiraoka-*san*?'

'I begin this week in the Banking Bureau of the Ministry of Finance.'

'Is that so?' Captain Lazar's eyes narrowed in amusement. 'We have something in common. I too am a banker – a banker in uniform, formerly with the Chemical Bank and Trust Company, Manhattan. There are quite a few of us investment bankers camouflaged by uniforms these days.'

We had arrived at my parents' house in Midorigaoka. 'We bankers should stick together,' Captain Lazar said, in reply to my thanks. 'I shall call on you in a few weeks' time, if I may.' As I prepared to alight from the car, he removed the Baroness's coat from my shoulders. 'This would look better on its proper owner, don't you agree?' And he handed me a carton of Chesterfields in exchange for my lost prize.

2 MADAME DE SADE

PENS, BRUSHES, a replenished ink-well and a fresh supply of paper. My writer's paraphernalia, laid out on the desk with Euclidean precision by my mother, a service she dutifully performed for me every night, awaited the sleepless double agent Yukio Mishima at the usual hour that brings him to work, midnight.

Midnight is the hour at which I have habitually commenced writing for over twenty-five years now, ever since my teens. Midnight, the hour of sickroom crisis, the dreadful hour that brings the secret police knocking at your door, the hour beloved by interrogators, the dice-thrower's hour inviting temptations of suicide. Midnight is the negative appearance of time in the mirror, the hour of deceit, because it is at *mid*-night precisely that day begins. For all these years, my life has passed in a sort of equinoctial mirage, made up half of night and half of dawn. Are these not the upside-down banker's hours of a thief? Some thieves have been known to work in broad daylight, true, but night is their proper domicile.

Thief, as the Baroness had proclaimed me. And my black-petalled poem on the snow – what was that but a triumph of stillbirth.

On that particular New Year's Eve night, I was struck as never before by the real existence of a thief, alias Yukio Mishima, who would preside till dawn at the clinically ordered desk. An illimitable, ink-black sea without horizon stretched away to a future of endless nights like these. I cannot begin to describe the nausea of intense excitement that seizes me at the start of yet another night's excursion to fill yet more pages, an intoxicant, a despairing giddiness with which I am fatally in love.

'You're a thief, and a miserable one at that . . .'

I must have spoken my thoughts aloud, because my mother who entered my room just then with a steaming pot on a tray, my usual dispensation of tea for the night's journey, replied, 'A thief? Why make such a degrading comparison?'

'A thief, *chère maman*. A nocturnal tradesman. A shameful figure entirely appropriate to me.'

We spoke as we always had, and still do, with a grand old-fashioned lovers' formality irritating to others, but in hushed voices at this wolf's hour, so not to wake the sleepers in the house.

I lit a cigarette from my trophy of Chesterfields.

'Who gave you those American cigarettes?'

'An officer I met at the club,' I replied, lying with the truth.

'A thief steals from people,' my mother pursued, discerning my unease. 'From whom do you steal?'

'I steal from life. The only difference between a thief and me is that I leave an inventory of what I steal. I leave words on a page behind me, books, a trail of forensic evidence.'

'Surely, your words have a value of their own as a reflection of life, something which adds to life rather than subtracts from it?'

'I am like the fairytale princess who spent her night weaving straw into gold. Except in my case, I am the reverse alchemist, turning the precious stuff of life into waste paper. My life has been one long night of sickroom confinement which has given me a diabetic craving for the sweetness of reality that now corrodes my blood.'

I warm my hands on the teapot. Shizue touches my forehead. 'I recommended you not to carouse on such a rowdy night as this. Something has disturbed you tonight.'

'I am not more disturbed than normal.'

'You look dreadfully off colour. Perhaps you shouldn't work tonight.'

'Just imagine what colour I shall have when I begin working at the Ministry and there is still *this* to face every night.'

The expression of helplessness that my complaint furrowed on Shizue's brow, I confess, gave me pleasure. I kissed her hands. 'Don't upset yourself, dearest mother. I did not mean you to grieve over this habitual offender, a thief meant in that sense only. I have chosen to go on offending, this night, tomorrow night and every other night. There is nothing else for it, since I cannot choose not to write.'

And that too, kissing my mother's hands with lips tasting rancid still of vomit, I confess gave me reassurance. Someone of parasitical ugliness in me recognized that I had never once spoken with my mother except artificially, as I can only suppose all sons with mothers do. My poor, scanty peacock's tail of manhood opened in me, securely lodged in the evil nostalgia that never failed to see me safely home.

I wanted more than the solicitude of my mother's tea. 'Is there any alcohol in the house? After all, this is New Year's Eve.'

'Your father finished the last whisky before going out tonight. There are some remains of gin, if you like.'

I did not like. Gin is a drink repugnant to me, not the taste so much as its odour, which has the mysterious effect of bringing back an image of my grandmother, Natsuko, the Madame de Sade of my childhood.

My mother brings me a half bottle of de Kuyper's Geneva gin.

As I write, I sip a dosage from the medicinal green flask. An eerie familiarity emanates from the colourless liquid. I see Madame de Sade again, staring down at me with the terrifying eyes of a shamaness, as her maid Tsuki deposits some burning pellets of moxa at the base of her naked back. The peculiar, herbal incense of those moxa embers on Natsuko's flesh is decanted for me in the smell of gin. I see her in late middle age, a horse-faced lady of no beauty (in whose equine features I see my own adult ones reproduced), her hair in the old-fashioned *igirisu-maki* style, the short English cut that became popular among upperclass married women during the Meiji period. Now, with her kimono peeled back, the overripe womanly handsomeness of Natsuko's torso contrasts oddly with her virile face. But the wildly poetic gaze of her eyes, inflamed by the agonies of migraine and sciatica, speak to me of a time when she enjoyed a certain tyrannous beauty.

My grandmother's nudity is hidden from me, in a moment's decorous afterthought, by a screen that Tsuki arranges in front of the occidental bed. I was born in that bed. And the screen too tells the story of a birth well-known to me from Natsuko's treasury of legends. The panels show the Sea-God's daughter Toyotamahime★ approaching the shore on a great tortoise. She enters a 'doorless shed', a birthing hut thatched with cormorant feathers. She begs her husband Hohodemi not to look at her. But his curiosity is too much for him. He peeps in, and sees his wife transformed into a *wani* sea-dragon, eight fathoms long. Outraged by her dishonour, Toyotamahime abandons her new-born son to the care of her sister, and returns to her palace deep beneath the sea.

And so was born the father of Jimmu, the first human Emperor of Japan. On a certain day, twenty-six centuries before my birth, the sun goddess Amaterasu granted the Mirror of Divinity to our first Emperor Jimmu. With him begins Japan's Imperial dynasty. Our ancient chroniclers speak of *ama-tsu-hi-tsugi*, heavenly-sun-succession, terms which piously forecast the endurance of an Imperial line without break from that day to our own.

The date traditionally professed for this fabled Imperial Sunrise is 11 February 660 BC. That sounds impossibly remote. I still prefer Natsuko's

★ 'Rich Jewel Maiden'

account of the Emperor's pedigree in which twenty-six centuries seemed hardly any separating us from the legendary origins of Japan. Counted like that, twenty-six is but a short span the Age of the Gods regained across the Floating Bridge of Heaven.

During the years of my childhood, in my grandmother's sickroom, I crossed that Floating Bridge with her almost every night. But the one story she never recounted was the true one of my birth, which involved the Toyotamahime screen. I did not learn of it until I was nine years old, when finally my mother Shizue confessed to me the extent of Natsuko's cruelty. 'Just after you were born,' my mother said, 'Tsuki put up the Toyotamahime screen around my bed. She placed the screen upside-down, which is the sign that a person has died. When your father observed this, he paled and became furious with Tsuki. She said that your grandmother had ordered it, because the bed had been defiled by the occupant's *kega*, meaning my wound of childbirth. This was your grandmother's way of claiming the bed on which you were born for herself, and which has indeed remained hers ever since.'

Natsuko claimed far more than the bed. On the forty-ninth day of my life,★ I was snatched from my mother's side and for the next twelve years kept under Natsuko's strict custody. Her act of kidnapping exceeded even the immense scope of tyranny that a mother-in-law traditionally enjoys over her son's wife. Natsuko was an excessive character in everything, including this. My mother's role was reduced to domestic wet-nurse on the upper floor, my feeding times with her precisely regulated by Natsuko's pocket watch.

Is there anything significant in the number forty-nine, the chosen day on which I was forcibly transplanted to the hothouse climate of Natsuko's room? None that I can find in our traditions and folklore. Natsuko was obsessed by some crank idea of 'pediatric numerology' that she discovered in a German textbook on eugenics, from which she adopted her chronometric viligance over my breast-feedings and her subsequent notions of diet. I was the object of Natsuko's single-minded experiment. I know this for certain, because when my sister Mitsuko and my brother Chiyuki were born several years later, Natsuko showed not the slightest interest in them.

From the very first day of my twelve-year period of quarantine in Natsuko's sickroom, it became my family's dogma that I was a weak, sickly child threatened by death. Natsuko must take the blame for this 'unassailable article of faith', as my father Azusa sarcastically named it.

I do not believe that my grandmother's edict of isolation was motivated by her over-zealous love for me, but by arrogance that verged on insanity. I have suffered most in my life from cold-hearted passion, the

★ Yukio Mishima was born 14 January 1925.

effects of icy maternalism which have inhibited all subsequent possibility of pleasure. I can only understand pain as the verification of existence. My sincerest agony is reserved for what I cannot feel, which paradoxically arouses me to extremes of imaginary feeling. I am bound in service to the goddess of the unreal as her cold cerebral lover for whom pleasure is unrealizable in human beings. This was Natsuko's legacy and I am unable to regret it.

An average person – if such a statistical figment exists – might be driven to ask me: 'What, *no* regrets? Surely it is a rationalization to boast that you do not regret the absence of normal love?' Psychology should not begin with the normal, but with the 'enigmatical exception', as Nietzsche correctly diagnosed. Besides, there is a danger here of lapsing into psychological apologetics, which if I am not attentive will soon offer 'reasons' for why I am a writer. The paradoxes that make a writer are not finally referable to biography which does not explain our most eventful uncertainties, even if one is writing the biography of oneself. What explanation do I gain in revisiting the sickroom of my earliest years? Everyone has a childhood, happy or suffocated to whatever degree; but not everyone is a writer. To say that I blame writing on my grandmother does not succeed to explain much. Nevertheless, there is something in it, as in the peacock's eerie cry.

What I choose to say about my childhood will appear as inhumanly cold as dry-ice. I am perfectly aware of that. There are many probable explanations for my anaesthetized inhumanity, but I am not interested in any one of them. I will however propose one analogy as a sort of explanation. Children who have experienced winters in which the temperature falls below freezing all know of a certain trick that is played on unsuspecting juniors. The littlest one will be commanded by his elders to place his lips on some piece of frozen metal, a brass letter-slot, for instance. Such a kiss will of course result in the victim's lips becoming glued fast to the metal, a cohesion that can only be painfully ended by tearing off the skin, much to everyone else's hilarity.

This trick, old as Emperor Jimmu himself, was played on me – as I, in succession, played it on others. But I grew so fond of the painful sensation that I would perform it on myself, repeatedly, until my lips were skinned to a bloody pulp. 'Look at this child,' Natsuko would shout against the entire household when I arrived home from the Peers' School. 'See what a constant fever has done to his lips!' Those raw lips were Natsuko's proof of my congenital inclination to tuberculosis.

At supper, on a winter's evening in 1931, Natsuko announced her decision that I would attend the Peers' School in April. There was no question but that I must satisfy Natsuko's ambition and enter the *Gakushu-in*, the Peers' School, privately established in 1821 by the ex-Emperor Kokaku for the sons of the Imperial family and aristocracy.

Nothing less would do. A fearsome pitched battle between the adult com-
batants at the supper-table was sure to follow the proclamation of Natsuko's decree; but it would do no good. My fate was sealed. I stared at my
plate of food, always the same bland constituents – the poached white
flesh of halibut or turbot, strained and mashed potatoes. I was allowed no
chocolates or bean jams, only wafers, dry biscuits and peeled, thinly sliced
apple. My grandmother's personal maid Tsuki herself prepared my meals,
and they were like the nutritionless ones served by the monstrous cook in
Strindberg's *Ghost Sonata*, with all the strength boiled out of the food. I
watched Natsuko's fine manicured fingers skinning a mandarin for me,
carefully removing the white pellicule from the segments, my dose of
Vitamin C stripped of its essential bioflavanoids. I could see the elegant
fingers of my grandfather Jotaro, the disgraced former governor of Sakhalin, arranging orange pips on the slubbed quadrangular patterns of the
linen tablecloth, playing his solitary game of Go. I saw my father Azusa
fidgeting belligerently with a cigarette he was forbidden to light in my
presence, because of the frailty of my lungs.

I dared not look up and see my mother's face. My mother Shizue's
beauty had assumed an air of violated fragility from the moment that
Natsuko had seized control of my destiny six years ago. Each one of
Natsuko's further victories seemed to enhance this sad, bewitching quality in my mother. Natsuko's announcement had brought a pallid bloom
to Shizue's cheeks, a colour like that of flowers which open only in the
chill, forlorn light of the moon. I could feel it radiating on me, a
sorrowing compassion that made my heart swell painfully in the grip
of secret bliss.

'Is it no deterrent to you, mother-in-law,' Shizue said, 'that your
grandson will suffer many unpleasant years of exposure to the snobbery
of his uppercrust classmates at the *Gakushu-in?*'

'Exactly,' my father Azusa broke in, 'those idle, arrogant, imbecile
sons of dukes and barons.' He stuffed the cigarette in his mouth, remembering just in time not to light it.

Natsuko's hand shook as she fed me a segment of mandarin. She
addressed her son, Azusa. 'Please ask the bride to keep silent on matters
that she cannot comprehend.' After seven years of marriage, Natsuko
still referred discourteously to my mother as *yome*, the bride, never as
musume, daughter.

'There is of course a proportionate rump of commoners like ourselves
at the school,' Azusa went on, disregarding his mother's irritation, 'other
social climbers, but even these can at least claim the vulgar advantage
of being *nouveau riche*.'

Azusa's venomous tongue brought unexpected assistance to my
mother, not from any real agreement between my disunited parents,
but because of my father's own deep bitterness. He resented the privilege

I would gain by attending the *Gakushu-in*; and he groaned inwardly at the financial burden of the school fees, another of Natsuko's extravagances that his civil servant's meagre pay would have to bear. These years of the Great Depression had begun to weigh heavily on middleclass minor officials like my father, and he was the only provider of the Hiraoka family.

Shizue's brave challenge had offered Azusa the opportunity he liked to attack his mother's aristocratic pretensions and her total financial irresponsibility. 'My wife is right,' he said. 'The boy's nose will be constantly rubbed in the dog's droppings of his abject condition. Look at him – no muscles, no social standing, no money.'

'Whose condition do you dare call *abject*? Your own –' Natsuko scanned the table's occupants with such fiery contempt that it forced them to lower their eyes. '– not the boy's. Noble superiority runs in his blood, as it does in mine.'

Jotaro sighed. He itched to return to his backroom parlour, continue his game of Go, drink saké and sing music-hall ballads in his fine tenor voice. Jotaro normally kept aloof from the family mêlée, indifferent to the havoc of escalating debts and Natsuko's imperious antics. For once, he spoke up. 'Woman, you are encouraging the boy to an absurd attitude,' he paused, as though too weary to finish; the rakish smile of a one-time womanizer came to his lips, '– an attitude of genealogical segregation from his closest kin. Can you not see the sad little monster you are in danger of creating?'

'I can see very well what I'm doing – sifting the gold from the pebbles,' Natsuko replied, citing a phrase from a 9th century social register of the Heian era, which justified strict demarcations of social rank.

Jotaro called the maid Tsuki to his side. 'Fetch me a bowl of saké,' he told her, and to Azusa, 'Please light your cigarette. It can do no more harm to the boy than your mother is set on doing.'

'Even you must admit, mother-in-law,' Shizue tried reasoning again, 'that Kimitake is a frail, shy lad, without notion of proper virile behaviour. How will he fare in a school that prizes martial character and sports above academic excellence?'

'He's a girl, thanks to your closeting him all these years,' Azusa threw at his mother, exhaling a fiendish amount of smoke.

'A girl, do you think?' Natsuko laughed. 'I shall live to see this *girl* at least among his own kind, at the Peers', and by way of the Imperial University he will come far nearer to the centre than ever you could.'

This was ambitious Imperial civil servants' talk. Natsuko's reference to the 'centre', with its coded allusion to the unapproachable Emperor, was a deliberate sarcasm highlighting Azusa's lack of official success.

'Of course, the Imperial University is a worthy goal,' Shizue agreed, in a vain effort to appease Natsuko. 'But I know of another route than the *Gakushu-in* that could equally well lead to the same end.'

'A school of genuine academic merit, and cheaper,' Azusa added, knowing very well that Shizue aimed to recommend the school in which her own father acted as principal.

'Cheaper? Is that your only concern?' Natsuko replied. 'As for you, bride, have you not yet learned anything in this house? There are things one should not see. It is better to feign blindness than recognize the commonplace. Do you know the story told by a certain lady of the Heian court? How she saw one day, on her way to the Kamo shrines, some oddly dressed women moving backwards across a field, bending down and then straightening up again – for what purpose she couldn't imagine? This enigmatic scene represented nothing more uncommon than the occupation of planting rice, the commonest of sights in Japan's countryside, but to which no lady of the court would admit recognition.'

'I am familiar with this anecdote from Sei Shonagon's *Pillow Book*,' my mother said.

'Ah, the bride pretends to some culture. Do you recall why Sei Shonagon remarked so disapprovingly on these particular peasant women?'

'Because they are singing a song about the *hototogisu*, the nightingale, a bird reserved for poetic themes.'

'Precisely, and hence the property of the Heian court. Rice-planters whom Sei Shonagon's decorum cannot permit her to name – nameless like your own vulgar forbears – are nevertheless recognized as infringing upon a privileged language. She has wisely counselled blindness as the adept way of avoiding calamities. Do you understand, *yome*?'

'I understand.' A single tear descended my mother's cheek.

'And you, *hototogisu*,' my grandmother smiled ominously down at me, 'do you understand?'

I nodded in silence, fearful that the undigested food risen in my gullet would spew out.

Jotaro looked pityingly at my mother. 'Don't be upset, daughter. It was always fated that your Kimitake would be a third generation civil servant.'

'A misfortune thrice repeated,' Shizue had the invincible daring to say.

An ill-advised remark, however, which detonated Toyotamahime's sea-dragon fury in my grandmother. 'What do you know of misfortune, you ill-bred worthless creature?' Now began Natsuko's litany, often heard before but nonetheless impressive for all that. Each sentence was punctuated by her cane striking the floor, like the footfalls of a Noh actor resounding across the stage as he recites his character's ancestry. She was a Nagai, of feudal samurai stock, clan supporters of the Tokugawa

Shoguns. On her mother's side, she was the heir of renowned Tokugawa court ministers, the Matsudaira. Allegiance to the Tokugawa regime had brought the Nagai into discredit with the restoration of the Meiji Emperor in 1868, and Natsuko's father was consequently denied peerage under the new system. Natsuko's embitterment was always summed up in the refrain to her litany: 'Noble fealty ends in loss and brings one to ruin as certainly as crime.' Natsuko's grievance against the oligarchs of the Meiji court would some day have to be revenged by me.

Supper over, I sat on my little courtier's stool, contemplating the Toyotamahime screen. From behind it came the smell of moxa. From my parents' ghetto quarters upstairs came the sound of Shizue weeping, the howls of my siblings, and the shouts of Azusa's unchecked anger, detailing the cut in his wages ordained by Imperial decree, a ten percent decrease for every bureaucrat earning more than a 100 yen – a mere 50 dollars a month.

Natsuko behind the screen, in the anguish of her migraine, groaned, 'Azusa, Azusa strums in my head.' A fine play on words that even at six years old made me smile. Azusa means catalpa wood, and it is on a bow of catalpa that the *miko* spirit-medium strums to conjure up the demon ghost of lady Aoi in the Noh drama of that name.

And now my grandmother took up this bow in a vengeful story. She told me that our surname Hiraoka first appeared on a temple register of Shikata village near Kobe in central Japan in 1827, and only then because of a crime committed by an ancestor, a young boy whose arrow felled a sacred white pheasant on the local daimyo's estate. Our family record thus began with a crime and the disgrace of the boy's father, Hiraoka Tazaemon, dispossessed of his home. According to Han Dynasty legend, the white pheasant is a propitious omen of rulership, and to destroy it must therefore bring misfortune upon the transgressor and his descendents. In her own erudite way, Natsuko communicated to me that our family's quest for success and respectability was ill-fated. Natsuko had spoken plainly enough. She considered herself the white pheasant brought down by a delinquent of nameless origin. Thinking back, I realize that my father too must have known this parable from Natsuko. He too was raised with a sense of inherited transgression and misfortune.

My poor grandmother. Her ambitions had shrunk to the size of a little boy whose weak shoulders she burdened with the awesome title of last samurai of the Nagai family. My duty as her samurai was to lead her by the hand on frequent trips to the toilet in the dead of night, visits dictated by Natsuko's bad kidneys. I dreaded that long darkened corridor, as I waited, shivering by the door, desperate for those companionable sounds of life that would bring my vigil at last to an end – Natsuko's groans, a hiss of urine on the porcelain, the clang and gush of a water-closet that had once been the height of fashion at the turn of the century. This corridor was for me the Floating Bridge of Heaven; but it introduced me to *yomi*, the netherworld of hades.

A disused room nearby contained the Nagai relics, the fantastic crustacean shapes of samurai armour bristling with swords like sea urchin spines, grimacing warrior masks under horse-tail wigs and pagoda-shaped helmets. I saw them wakening to movement, alive, their plated fists reaching for the door handle. I saw the handle turning, and I cried 'Grandmother', but she did not hear me or pretended not to.

It was harder still to return on my own from the toilet. The maid Tsuki would accompany me down the three turnings of the corridor and then leave me, saying, 'You are old enough now to go back alone.' Tsuki was a frightful old woman who enjoyed playing obscene tricks on me. One of her special tasks was to dust the Nagai armour. She often forced me to join her in this storeroom, out of sheer malice, in order to prey on my fears. She would warn me to beware, the maid Noriko who served at table had put bamboo splinters and rat poison in my soup. At times, she might comment on her charge of valuable Nagai antiques, 'One more missing. Sold to pay for your grandfather's debts. Soon I'll have nothing to bother dusting.' Her laughter was most unpleasant.

Tsuki was an obsessionally devout Shintoist. Her name itself has unusual Shinto associations, *tsuki*, moon, from the Moon spirit *tsukiyomi*, the netherworld reckoner of darkness. I would find her every morning, her kimono hitched up, cleaning out my grandmother's lavatory, and her greeting to me was always, *ojigi*, good manners, a reminder of one's duty to the small god of privies. She was the one who first acquainted me with the *kami* spirits that reside in all manner of things which must be dreaded and revered, the sea and mountains, trees, thunder and the dragon, jewels and mirrors, the echo and the fox. And the peach.

I remember how she once beckoned me into the lavatory to show me a secret. She sliced open a ripe peach, stuck her thumbs knuckle-deep into the cut, and prised apart the fuzzy halves of the globe. Juice ran down her wrists, and she said, 'Look closely inside.' I saw the peach stone, a reddish puckered thing with hairs of pulp attached to it in a glistening skein. 'Drink from it, little master,' she instructed. The odour of the juices I sucked mingled with the antiseptic one on Tsuki's knuckles and the latrine's effluvia. 'Ask your grandmother what it means,' she cackled, as she wiped my sticky cheeks. Tsuki said that blind spirit mediums known as *miko* in the north made rosaries of peach stones which they rattled to exorcise evil spirits.

Clean. Unclean. On this imaginary axis revolves the entire Shinto spirit world.

Tsuki acted as my nursemaid, a status which granted her privileges denied to my mother. She regularly took me on walks. On one of my excursions with her at the age of four we encountered a night-soil man who attended to the latrines of our neighbourhood. Two large buckets of excrement dangled and bounced from the yoke across his shoulder as he trotted towards us. He was a youth of cheerful moon-faced countenance, a pair of sturdy thighs emphasized by the tight workingman's denims he wore, in physique the replica and predecessor of Morita.* The pressure of Tsuki's hand communicated her excitement to me and the clack of her *geta* perceptibly quickened. She wanted a closer look to satisfy her near-sighted inspection. As he passed by us, with his tragic pungency of sweat and human waste, Tsuki averted her gaze, but the corners of her eyes sparkled with lewdness. A lizard's flick of her tongue retrieved a speck of saliva at the edge of her lips. She eased her pace. Her hand continued damply to transfix mine. She began telling me then about the Shinto latrine god who has no name, the one whom devout persons are wise to humour by nailing a card with the inscription *ojigi* on the privy door. Dunghills, latrines and all other unclean places are haunted by the souls of bad men in the diminished shapes of flies and maggots.

'Women like myself who daily clean your privies are blessed by the god. He keeps us free from diseases here—' Tsuki gestured to the area below her girdle, '—such as bedevil your grandmother.'

Was *that* the god we had just met? 'Who – the night-soil lad?' Tsuki laughed. 'Yes, that's him.'

And what was my grandmother's disease, then?

'Why ask me? You meet it every night.'

That was true. All my nights were spent as Natsuko's sickroom companion.

Our house in the unfashionable Yotsuya district of Tokyo accommodated my grandparents, my parents and I, and a costly retinue of six maidservants and a houseboy. It was a rented house. My grandfather Jotaro's career of entrepreneurial débâcles and my grandmother's extravagances had reduced the family to near penury. I remember a multi-storeyed building of Victorian semblance, of a peculiarly charred appearance which led me to imagine a ghost-tormented ruin of the medieval Onin civil war. Certainly, it was a perfect setting for Natsuko's tales of the supernatural. Looking back, I suppose it had a quality of *sabi*, a term specifying the aesthetic sense of desolation. *Sabi* expresses a love of whatever is old, faded, forlorn. *Sabi* is a craving to have the moon obscured by rain. I now believe that the reigning spirit of *sabi* emanated from my mother, alone, like a deposed queen stricken by exile.

On those rare days when I was allowed to play on Natsuko's ground-

---

* Morita Masakatsu, lieutenant in Mishima's paramilitary cadet corps, the *Tatenokai* or Shield Society, who followed Mishima's *seppuku* with his own on 25 November 1970.

floor terrace, I would feel my mother gazing down at me from the upper-storey window. I came to accept the weight of those eyes without turning to acknowledge the longing in them. What impotent dreams of revenge my mother must have nurtured in her heart. And I? I was taking my first steps as a voyeur who learns to preside by making myself invisible. I could not help but admire the ferocity of Natsuko's heartlessness.

Every part of the house seemed occupied by the viscuous presence of my grandmother's illness. In her room especially it took ectoplasmic shape visible to me as the merciless *oni* demon that came in the late hours of night till dawn to strike upon her body. She was tortured by sciatica, stomach ulcers and defective kidneys, pains at times so bad that she cried out for the relief of suicide. '*Obasama*, what shall I do?' I wept, kneeling at her side. She held a dagger to her throat, the abysmal whites of her eyes glaringly exposed, and she would beg me, 'Press it in, *anata*! My strength fails me.'

At first, in my tenderest years, I felt such scenes of horror would drive me mad. Eventually, I wept no more. I learned to endure these spectacles as though I judged them play-acted. I came at last to see her like Lady Awoi in the Noh drama of that name, whose sickness and death are represented simply by a red flowered kimono folded once lengthwise and laid at the front edge of the stage, whereupon the evil apparition of her own jealousy comes forward to strike this garment with a fan in a stylized embodiment of the lady's torment. Many years later I wrote a modern version of Lady Awoi with both Natsuko and my mother in mind.

Natsuko called me *anata*, a term of intimacy, and at five years old I was her lover, a privileged observer of the disarray of her nightgown, of a woman in the manifest extremes of abandonment. Her daylight tyrannies were acceptable as the routine demands of a jealous mistress which earned me my night-time's prerogative of ascendancy over her. I was the one alone entrusted to pour her medicine into a stemmed wineglass. I massaged her and sponged her forehead. I attended to her with all the devout allegiance of a samurai courtier.

Unhappiness would not in the least be the accurate word to describe my condition. I was so far distant from anything remotely like happiness that I was a stranger even to its opposite.

I had no understanding of the mystery of Natsuko's illness, or why it should confine me to quarantine with her, and so I had no choice but to make it my mirror. I became the model of the pale indoor invalid. The success of my accomplishment I could gauge in my mother's horrified expression, in her frenzied attempts, mostly unsuccessful, to spirit me away from the house in my grandmother's few unguarded moments, to take some air in the forbidden paradise of nearby Yotsuya park. I responded to my mother's command, run and play, with sad proof of my feebleness. I requited myself with the fantasy of being the miraculously gifted but misshapen child of the Dragon Princess Toyotamahime who lived in her palace deep beneath the sea, as described in Natsuko's story from the ancient chronicles.

In her own way, my grandmother understood that our condition was the infernal one of no hope. From her lips, I first heard the word *mappo* and of the certainty of hell. *Yomi* was the hell prophesized by the Amida Buddhist monk Genshin. Natsuko depicted Genshin's hell with its rainfall of razor-keen swords, the variety of its agonies that cannot be borne. 'Into this place fall those who have killed a living being with concupiscence.'

I trembled at the unknown sound of this word *concupiscence* which merited razor-keen swords – much to the amusement of our listener Tsuki who sniggered as she went about her duties – and how should we escape punishment in the netherworld of *yomi*?

—There is no escape from *yomi*. It is a sad place that awaits us all. Shall I tell you how it came to be?

My teeth chattered, but I nodded, yes.

How she harked back to the Shinto myths of creation that she so loved to recount.—'The ancient chronicles of *Nihongi* and *Kojiki* tell us that—' she began, and though I quaked to the depths of my being at the grave tone of her voice, yet I felt cocooned in safety with her—in this sickroom, misty with illness, evil-smelling with the decay of her body—safe from the Nagai spirits from *yomi*, those revenants in armour, who appeared reduced now to harmless beetles scuttling across the floorboards—'that the twin brother and sister deities, Izanagi and Izanami, stood on the Floating Bridge of Heaven and held counsel together, saying "Is there not a country beneath?" Thereupon they thrust down the Jewel Spear of Heaven and groping about with it found the Ocean. The brine which dripped from the spear point coagulated and formed an island to which they descended. On this island they erected a *fuseya* nuptial hut. They wished to be united as husband and wife to produce countries. Izanagi addressed Izanami, saying "How is your body formed?" Izanami replied, "My body is incomplete in one part." Izanagi said, "And mine is superfluous in one part. Suppose that we supplement that which incomplete in you with that which is superfluous in me, and thereby procreate lands."''

An incestuous union between brother and sister which entirely eluded me did not pass without Tsuki's muttered comment that I understood no better, '—good idea, keeping your plus and minus together in the family—'

'—be silent, you wicked old woman,' my grandmother said, and she named the lands that Izanagi and Izanami procreated, the islands of

Japan, and all the great numbers of gods and *kami* spirits that reside in everything that exists in our world. '—and the last god to be produced was the *kami* of Fire, Kagutsuchi. In giving birth to him, Izanami was badly burned so that she sickened and lay down—'

'—singed her private parts, the scoundrel,' Tsuki cackled in a sotto voce, for she knew these stories as well as Natsuko by heart, 'and from her vomit, faeces and urine were born the *kami* spirits of metal, clay and water—'

Natsuko carried on, blanketing Tsuki's comments, '—and when Izanami died of her labours, Izanagi in tears resolved to follow to the dark underworld of *yomi*. Izanami warned him, "Do not look at me." Izanagi paid her no heed but broke off the *wo-bashira* end-tooth of his many-toothed comb and made of it a torch to look at her. He was horrified to see Izanami putrefying, her body covered in maggots. Izanami was put to shame and she sent the Ugly Females of *yomi* to pursue and slay him. Izanagi fled and threw down many things to delay his pursuers, his comb, his headdress, garments, and three peaches—'

'—tell the little master what the peaches mean—'

Natsuko glanced severely at her, '—and thus from shame, Izanami swore eternal enmity against the living and brought *yomi*'s revenge of death into our world. After his escape from *yomi*, Izanagi's first care was to wash in the sea to purify himself from the pollutions of death. The sun goddess Amaterasu was born from washing his left eye, and the mischievous sea god Susanoo was born from washing his nose. Susanoo wept the green mountains bare and the sea and the rivers dry, howling in desperation to be with his mother Izanami in the the netherworld, and so Izanagi banished him to it. But before taking charge of *yomi* as its ruler, Susanoo paid a visit to his sister Amaterasu. They met on the Milky Way. Amaterasu was alarmed by Susanoo's fierce nature which had caused earthquakes and typhoons as he rose heavenwards. Susanoo assured his sister that he meant no harm and proposed that they produce children by biting off and crunching their jewels and swords and blowing away the fragments—'

—and this I found utterly delightful. I tried to imagine my parents on the upperfloor crunching jewels and blowing out the chewed bits like soap bubbles in their production of my younger sister and brother, Mitsuko and Chiyuki—

'—and from one of the eight children born in this way, named in the Shojiroku genealogies of noble families, our august Emperors can trace their descent from the sun goddess Amaterasu. Susanoo, however, went on to commit many impudent deeds of mischief against his sister. He smashed the divisions between her rice-fields. He relieved himself in the most shamefully infantile manner during Amaterasu's performance of the sacred rites. But the worst of his misdeeds was to flay the piebald starry colt of Heaven and drop its cadaver through the roof of the hall where Amaterasu and her attendants were busy weaving celestial garments, so alarming one of the maidens that she accidentally pricked her genitals and died.

'In great indignation, the sun goddess withdrew into the Rock-Cave near Ise and the world was left completely in darkness. Efforts were made to lure her out of her cave. A tub was placed upside-down before the cave, upon which the Dread Female of Heaven, Ama no Uzume, performed a noisy, frenzied and not very decent dance.' The vague words 'not very decent' provoked Tsuki's sour look of disgust. 'The heavens resounded to the laughter of eight hundred gods. Amaterasu, aroused by curiosity, peeped out of the cave, whereupon the great Eight-handed Mirror was held up to her and Ama no Uzume, the shamaness of Heaven, proclaimed the discovery of a new sun goddess. Amaterasu jealously attempted to seize her own image, and this gave Strong-handed Male a chance to pull her out of the cave. As for the culprit Susanoo, he was sorely punished by a tribunal of the gods who pulled out the nails of his fingers and toes, and he was banished forthwith to *yomi*.'

My grandmother's stories were intended as catechism lessons on the Imperial cult. I grew up familiar as all Japanese are – or were – with the Imperial Regalia, the Mirror, the Jewel and the Sword. I knew that these *kami*-possessed objects were divine heirlooms inherited by each successive Emperor since Jimmu's time and derived originally from Amaterasu's Mirror, the moon god's Jewel and Susanoo's dragon-slaying sword Kusanagi. I understood that the Emperor reigns in a state of *kami gakari*, spirit possession, obedient to the divine words of the *kami*. And it was this above all, the unearthly sound of those words from the ancient breviary, that spellbound me. Their fascination was *kotodama*, a term signifying the potency of spirit that resides in words, a power released by the sound of the *koto*-zither or the twanging of the catalpa-wood bow which induces ecstatic trance in the listener. The words in Natsuko's mouth sounded to me like the rattle of the blind *miko*'s rosaries of peach stones, as I imagined them, summoning ghosts back to life.

These mysteries were my playthings, my recreational antechamber to the centrally mysterious figure of the Emperor, who was also no more than my toy. Years later, when I finally visited the blind *miko* clairvoyants in their mountain retreats, and witnessed them in the violent seizures of trance during their séances, I saw them clutching *oshirasama*, crude dolls made up of foot-long sticks, cloth and a makeshift horse's head. Then I remembered how the Emperor himself had been placed like such a puppet in my hands, once, long ago.

At five years old, I began to write my first stories. It would only be a half truth to say that writing began for me with nights of story-telling like these, as the Shinto cosmos unfolded its mysteries and led me to collision with the Unnameable One, Emperor of forsaken divinity. Something else haunted that sickroom, an indefinable quality of transgression, a profound sense of sin as though great but unaccountable crimes of treason had been committed in the long ago past.

Tsuki's incessant little villainies confirmed the sense but not the true substance of the transgression that resided with us at Yotsuya. Tsuki had served my grandmother ever since both were in their teens. Rumour was that she had been apprenticed to a geisha, the truth more likely being that she was a geisha's slave purchased by the Nagai to perform as my grandmother's menial watchdog. She certainly liked being mistaken for a geisha.

The waxing and waning of Tsuki's work day could be recognized by her changes of kimono. She appeared first in a rough cotton one and an apron to cope with the heavier chores. She would change into a second one of finer cloth and pattern as night fell and her wrinkles vanished under a thickness of lunar white make-up. My grandfather Jotaro nicknamed her 'two kimonos'. She was permitted the most extraordinary rudeness without censure from my grandmother, as though long and close familiarity with her had left Natsuko insensitive to her misbehaviour. I saw Tsuki on more than one occasion late at night in her second kimono, with her artificial geisha face and hair solidly lacquered, gliding down the corridor towards Jotaro's room.

It is asserted that we Japanese have no sense of sin. Shame is what we feel, not guilt. We recognize only infractions of the social code, not the tormenting inner voice of conscience. Tsuki would ideally fit the Westerners' preconception of the amoral Japanese. Her indiscretions never offended convention, which is to say, they were simply never detected. Tsuki was the sort of old school woman who slept in the traditionally decorous manner, fixed to her head-rest all night, without disturbing a single correct fold of her night-dress. In short, she was a thoroughly practised hypocrite in every detail. When she used to bathe me, the neck of her first kimono somehow always managed to offer me a glimpse of her small girlish breasts of which she was inordinately proud. Often too she would ask herself how a poor weed of my size could boast such a long root, and she would seize my thing and tug vigorously at it to encourage its length.

Tsuki gave me a demonstration of Ama no Uzume's dance, the nature of which Natsuko had left veiled as 'not very decent'. An overturned laundry tub in the washroom provided the required resonance for her pantomime. Like a Sarume monkey-woman doing the *kagura* dance, a frenzied shamaness, or highly indecorous geisha, she banged away with her square peasant feet, inch by inch lifting her skirts past the ankles to her calves of deformed brevity, the muscles pumping up from them to the gelatinous flaps at the insides of her thighs, until at last I saw a rust-coloured goatee.

What had caused the laughter of eight hundred gods turned me to ice.

Tsuki's striptease dance was no more than a comic misdemeanour, not something I would classify as traumatic. And yet, this little act of household impropriety worked its magic on me. Tsuki had enlightened me. I understood now what scurrilous fictions our ancient chroniclers told!

I awoke prematurely from the chrysalis of childhood, an ill-formed and invincible skeptic at the age of five. What precipitated my awakening was the unreality of human emotions. Incredulity is the one strength of a weak, unprepossessing child. My skepticism matured into the unattractive virtue of immunity to others.

One night, as I knelt to pour Natsuko's medicine as usual into the wineglass, I noticed the bottle was empty. I became giddy with panic. The weight and opaque blue colour of the bottle had deceived us. I turned away from Natsuko's bedside lamp and held the bottle up to the moonlit window. A nasty voice inside the bottle coaxed me to pour nevertheless,—Why not dispense a phial of moonlight into the glass half filled with water? My grandmother would never know, if only I betrayed no nervousness. I did so, and felt I was the governor of my grandmother's life, the *bakufu** Shogun of a captive Empress in my power. I knew too that my position of authority required that I must suffer the intrigues of obscene geishas and the dangers of poisoners, but heaviest of all, the burdens of disillusionment.

3 THE REVERSE COURSE

GYAKU KOSU. I first heard the expression 'reverse course' rumoured in the corridors of the Banking Section. What did it mean? To me, those jargon words *gyaku kosu* were simply another barbaric neologism of the Occupation – *kosu* being a rendition of the English word 'course'. I did not realize that I was soon to become a victim of the *gyaku kosu* whirlwind passing through the Ministry of Finance. My life, and indeed the entire future of the nation, was in reverse course.

---

* *Bakufu*, 'tent government', the Shoguns' military regime which ruled in the Emperor's name and with his theoretical sanction until the Restoration of the Meiji Emperor in 1868.

I had given no further thought to my mysterious rescuer on New Year's Eve, the red-haired Captain Sam Lazar, and his proposed rendez-vous in 'some weeks' time'. The dull routine of the National Savings Section during the following weeks had not, however, expunged the memory of that evil incident in the parking lot. On the contrary, the torment of it gleamed ever brighter in the dark of my consciousness like poisonous beads of mercury, sometimes concentrated, sometimes dispersing unpredictably within me. These quicksilver pearls of memory ran through the banker's hours of my day, and through the upside-down banker's hours of my nights of writing, adding their load to the crushing weight of my fatigue.

On a depressing, snowy afternoon in February, my section chief, Nishida Akira, came to my desk with an urgent message summoning me downstairs to the lobby of the Ministry building. I was alarmed. A section chief does not usually trifle to act as a messenger unless con-strained by something out of the ordinary. I imagined some catastrophe at home. I hurried from the office to the lobby, and found Captain Lazar's chauffeur, Masura, waiting for me. 'The captain is expecting you, Hiraoka-san. Please come with me.' Former *kempeitai* lieutenant Masura had not lost the imperious manner of the military police which permitted no option but obedience.

Once again I rode in the Packard. The captain's rose scent lingered in the back seat. Masura did not name our destination, but, in a short while, it became clear as a familiar ominous shape emerged through the falling snow. Masura was delivering me to the former secret service headquarters, a building distinguished by its situation on the moated western flank of the Imperial Palace. In this dreaded place, Captain Sam Lazar of Military Intelligence G-2, awaited me.

Masura's eyes in the rearview mirror were stagnant pools that read my panic. As we left the car, he told me with disaffected amusement, 'Beware of Captain Lazar. He has a predatory appetite.'

I was surprised by the loud, bustling activity inside the building, which was somehow reassuringly chaotic. An unexpected number of Japanese could be seen, apparently on familiar terms with high-ranking G-2 staff officers. The sound of their laughter seemed entirely directed at me. One other impression succeeded in penetrating the iron haze of my terror. It was cold. Very cold. A fault in the heating system had brought the temperature down to arctic level: a fortunate accident, since it gave some plausible excuse for the chattering of my teeth. Masura escorted me to an office on an upper floor. He opened the door and pushed me through into the lone presence of Captain Lazar.

The room was strangely furnished. One corner boasted a small, inti-mately lit cocktail bar, with the requisite stools. A ping-pong table occupied the centre, under two green-shaded lights such as one finds in pool-halls. The net was still in place, dividing the table into two sections, both heaped high with papers. This arrangement of papers on the ping-pong table, I later discovered, was Captain Lazar's ingenious version of 'in' and 'out' trays. Each end of the table had a calculating-machine installed beside it. A tangle of cables littered the fine Chinese rugs on the floor, and two electric fires burned like footlights round Captain Lazar, seated at a baby grand piano. He shivered, although wrapped in his fox-lined mantle, and his forehead rested on the piano stand, eyes staring at the keys, as he picked out a Gershwin tune. *Embraceable You.* I remembered Dazai Osamu dancing riotously to that melody on the accursed night that brought me to Captain Lazar's attention.

'Welcome to the the morgue of the former Imperial economy,' Captain Lazar said. 'Will you have a drink?'

I shook my head.

Captain Lazar poured himself a highball at the cocktail bar, and one more that he brought back and placed in my hand. He sat down on a typist's swivel chair by the ping-pong table and motioned me to a second one beside him.

'How old are you?'

'Twenty-three,' I replied.

'You look much younger, perhaps because you're undersized. Must be the ill effect of war-time shortages.'

'No. I think perhaps the rationing is worse now.'

'Is it?' Captain Lazar smiled. He swivelled on his chair, back and forth, irritatingly. 'How's the banking business, Mishima-*san*?'

The use of my alias took me unpleasantly by surprise. Captain Lazar did not await my answer, but opened a dossier on the ping-pong table. I was stunned to discover copies of my literary work in the file he exhibited. He caught me gawking at the proofs of my illicit identity. He leafed through a January copy of *Nihon Tanka* magazine which had printed my latest story. 'Banking must be exceedingly tiresome,' he said, 'for a writer like you, talented from what I can see, though somewhat too baroque for my conservative tastes. Have you considered a full time career in literature, Mishima-*san*?'

'That would be financially very awkward,' I stammered.

'Yes, yes, I am aware that in your country a patron is an absolute necessity. The occupation of writer is indeed very risky without one.'

'Yes, very.'

'But surely, writing must interfere with your duties at the Ministry? Your section chief, Nishida Akira, complains of errors in your calculations and that he often sees you falling asleep over the figures.'

Could it be that I had been summoned here for a reprimand? It seemed unlikely that G-2 would show any great interest in disciplining an erring clerk. Unlikely, perhaps, but the threat of dismissal that Captain Lazar's interrogation presented made me quake with fear.

I could think of nothing else to do. I bowed. I bowed in apology, again and again. 'Please forgive, Captain Lazar-*san*. These are the errors of a raw apprentice which I shall truly do my utmost to correct in the future.'

Captain Lazar's body tipped back in the chair, his long neck unflexed in that horrible, silent way he had of laughing. The refrigerated circle of my highball glass perspired in the palm of my hand. The swivel frame clicked loudly as it snapped forward and the captain lunged suddenly towards me, his grinning snub-nosed face almost meeting mine. 'Drink it!' He shouted; and then again, more gently, 'Drink, you're going to need it.'

I emptied the glass as he ordered, and he went to replenish it.

'Your job is not at risk,' Captain Lazar said. '*Au contraire, cher ami*, your record of negligence at the Banking Bureau could actually serve to your advantage. Do you follow me?'

I hadn't the faintest glimmer of what was being asked of me. I knew, of course, that one's survival these days depended on a certain versatile aptitude for collaboration. But my life had always been cushioned from everyday reality, first by the aristocratic ghetto of the Peers' School, and then at university, and I was not adept at inventing answers that would please our victors. I would have to learn fast.

'What is it you require of me, Captain?'

'Your talent.'

'Surely not as a lowly employee of the Banking Bureau?'

'Dare I ask – are you an ambitious young man, Mishima-*san*?' he consulted my dossier again. 'I see that you were recently invited to join the Peerless Poetry Association. What a strange name. You people have a bizarre appetite for sloganist names.'

'That was in 1947,' I replied. 'But I turned down the invitation.'

'Your refusal doesn't interest me, but *why* the invitation was made in the first place.'

'There's no sinister mystery in that. You see, the Peerless Poetry Association edits *Fuji*, a poetry magazine, and it merely sought my literary contributions.'

'Merely? And were you conscious that the Association is supported by ex-Colonel Hattori Takushiro, former head of the Strategic Section of the General Staff and one of Prime Minister Tojo's secretaries?'

'I wasn't aware of that.'

'Weren't you. Let's take a closer look at this "peerless" bunch of yours.' Captain Lazar fished out a pair of spectacles from his jacket, glasses of the old-fashioned pince-nez type that he clipped to the bridge of his nose. It gave me odd satisfaction to see that my green-eyed fox was myopic. He studied another page from his file. 'According to this, your Peerless Poetry Association is in fact a son's pious recreation of the *Daito Juku*, the Great East Institute, founded in 1939 by his father Kageyama Shohei. The father is something of a legendary martyr, it seems. At 1 a.m. on 24 August 1945, the elder Kageyama led fourteen members of the Great East Institute to the Yoyogi Parade Grounds, and after bowing to the Imperial Palace, each one proceeded to commit *seppuku* – the whole ritual works – disembowelment and beheading – beginning with Kageyama himself. Apparently, the location of these heroic suicides is holy ground, but, unfortunately, it now lies within the compound of the US Washington Heights military base. The son, Kageyama Masaharu, would like to reclaim the site for a commemorative shrine. This is of course impossible, and indeed, the Great East Institute has been purged by a SCAP directive. So, the astute Kageyama junior has concocted the "peerless" group based on the farewell vow of his father's Institute – namely "for all eternity to protect the Imperial Palace" – a vow which he has begun implementing by bringing numbers of country lads to Tokyo to clean the grounds of the Imperial Palace free of charge.' Captain Lazar glanced at me over the rims of his pince-nez. 'You don't strike me as a country bumpkin that Kageyama junior would recruit to sweep the Emperor's pavements. So, why would he invite you to join?'

'I told you –'

'– yes, I know, for literary reasons. However, the Peerless Poetry Association styles itself *sei shinshugi-teki uyoku* – a "spiritual rightwing group", and the slogan of its *Fuji* magazine is "a restoration of the Emperor and a new national literature". With such frankly declared rightwing aims, do you expect me to believe that Kageyama's group would choose to invite someone of unreliable liberal views, or even someone intellectually neutral? No, it is patently clear why they called on you, because in the 1940s you were a respected member of an ultra-right literary coterie – isn't that so?'

'Admittedly, I once belonged to an insignificant literary group with certain romantic leanings –'

'– fascist leanings,' Captain Lazar corrected.

'Pardon me, but no, I would simply define them as nationalist. Such was the atmosphere of the times. I was no exception to the general war-time fever.'

'Ah yes, the war fever. Would you agree that the cold shower of the Occupation has lowered the nationalist temperature?'

'I would say that even the right has welcomed the new Peace Constitution.'

Captain Lazar shook his head. 'Beware that your prudence does not blind you to the opportunity I am able to offer you.' He peered at my file. 'You never served overseas, I notice – classified unfit for active military duty. Excuse me for saying so, but you are a rather poor specimen, Mishima-*san*.'

'I am not proud of my debility.'

'Don't fret, my boy. We can't all be kamikaze heroes.' Captain Lazar fetched us two more highballs. 'I've never seen any combat myself, you know. *This* is my front line –' he gestured to the mountains of paper on the ping-pong table, '– this is my autopsy table where I am the pathologist of the *real* war. The investment war. Here, exposed in front of you, are the entrails of the Imperial war economy. Are you able to read an augury of the future in these dead guts? I could train you to become like the ancient Roman fortune-teller, the haruspex – the reader of entrails. My name, Lazar, that you find unpronounceable, has earned a rhyming soubriquet within G-2 – "Czar" – I am the Czar of G-2's financial investigations. Would you like to be the Czar's special agent at the Ministry?'

'I don't understand what is required of me?'

'Listen, and consider for a moment this ex-Colonel I mentioned before, Hattori. His former boss, Tojo, has been tried and hanged. And what about Hattori? Isn't he a Class A war criminal too? Certainly he is. And yet, he hasn't been purged. Our own chief of Military Intelligence, Major General Willoughby, rescued Hattori and promoted him to head the Demobilization Bureau which has screened four million ex-servicemen. In short, a war criminal who should have been purged has instead been awarded a position which actually allows him to veto the purging of other senior officers. What do you make of that?'

'I cannot judge. But the answer must be that the war has left us very short of competent men.'

'Nonsense. Our problem at G-2 is precisely that *too* many competent men are left for us to deal with.'

'I don't understand. If you consider Hattori unreliable, why promote him to power?'

'Unreliability is a measure of no importance. Willoughby's task is to salvage Hattori and few others like him as a nucleus of the future general staff of Japan's new military establishment. No former Imperial officer can possibly be imagined 'reliable' for that position. But there is a greater problem. Chiang Kai-shek is losing the war in China, and very soon Mao Tse-tung's reds will seize power. And that will pose a communist threat to all of South East Asia. Indochina is not safe in the unreliable hands of our former token allies, the French. Remind me, Mishima-*san* – what was that marvellously inappropriate name Japan bestowed on its war-time colonies in Asia?'

'The Greater East Asia Co-Prosperity Sphere.'

'Precisely. Well, my dear fellow, *we* have inherited your "Co-Prosperity

Sphere" in Asia. Willoughby's job is to encourage a reliably anti-
communist establishment in Japan. Mine is to guarantee reliability by
making your economy a client dependent on ours, so that any acts of
*un*reliability will be economically punished. Mine is the greater and
more subtle task, for it is at heart to uncover what Japan's true cultural
desire has always been.'

'Surely you must mean *financial* desire?' I could not help saying.

'No, I mean cultural. There is only one universally real culture –
and it is of course financial.'

I began to suspect that Captain Lazar was completely mad. I glanced at
my watch: it was after 9 o'clock and my parents must be worrying by now.

'Relax, Mishima-*san*. Your section chief, Nishida, has telephoned
your parents to say that you would be working late tonight.'

'Thank you, that was very thoughtful.'

'As a matter of fact, what do you think of section chief Nishida?'

I shrugged. 'A dry stick of a man, a bureaucrat of no interest.'

'Your writer's instinct fails you. Nishida might seem a "dry stick",
but he is certainly very interesting. Did you know he acted as an advisor
to Prince Higashikuni, the Emperor's uncle, who formed the Surrender
cabinet in 1945? And before that he worked closely with your own
version of Albert Speer, Kishi Nobusuke, the Vice-Minister of
Munitions, who's now serving three years as a Class A war criminal.
Nishida himself only escaped indictment because your first duly elected
Prime Minister in 1946, Yoshida Shigeru, directly appealed to General
MacArthur. Very few top executive bureaucrats like Nishida have been
purged, only oh–point–oh–nine percent to be precise. He's been down-
graded and put temporarily on ice at the Finance Ministry. But you just
watch his star rise again when Kishi, Yoshida and the others start paying
back their old debts to him.'

'Are you saying he's not a reliable civil servant?'

'I'm saying he owes G-2 some big favours. Right now, things are
very fluid, and Japanese high finance is about to benefit tremendously
from a reverse course in Occupation policy. Don't tell me you haven't
heard the gossip in the Ministry corridors? We originally set out to
deconcentrate and dissolve the big business cartels, your so-called *zaibatsu*. A pure-minded, idealist hangover from the Roosevelt New Deal
era. I arrived here in Tokyo in November 1945, just after the Finance
Minister Viscount Shibusawa had been appointed to dissolve the *zaibatsu*. A pretty hilarious situation, given that Viscount Shibusawa is
himself the head of a *zaibatsu* firm supposedly listed for extinction, and
serving in the cabinet of Prime Minister Yoshida, who's also allied by
marriage to a coal-mining *zaibatsu* family. Out of the original number
of twelve-hundred firms scheduled for democratic de-cartelization, only
nineteen, and perhaps even fewer will be dealt with by the end of the

year. That's not my concern. I'm not here to *dis*solve but to *re*solve the *zaibatsu* affair, or you might say, to *re*-cartelize big business, industry and finance, but on a basis that Washington and the investment bankers can approve. Nishida's favour to me is to pass on any and all sensitive accounts relating to the reverse course finance programme. Nishida is a close friend of Viscount Shibusawa. Do you follow me? Because this is where you come in, son. Nishida's spoken to me of you – of your clownish behaviour, your somnambulism during office hours, your clandestine writing at night – and your *errors*. And that's exactly the cover we need. Your talent for errors. Nishida will give you certain accounts to vet, and you'll make errors – not real ones, of course, but as a distraction to avert suspicion from the copies you will be making for me. You will bring me those copies at the weekend, and I'll brief you on the revised figures that are going to be the "corrections" you will then insert into those accounts on Monday. All you have to do is follow Nishida's and my instructions to the letter. Have you got it?'

'I am being asked to serve in financial espionage.'

'I wouldn't put it quite so grandly. Just think of it as your own small contribution to the miracle of your country's economic recovery.'

Captain Lazar's briefing was interrupted by a thunderous voice roaring towards us down the corridor outside. 'Where's that goddam Kike fairy accountant?' The door flew open, and a cold blast of air announced the entry of my titan GI, or I should say, Major General Willoughby, Schlep in battle dress. 'Chrissakes, stinks like poontang in here.'

Captain Lazar gave what I thought must be the most lanquid salute ever seen in military history, curtly acknowledged by Schlep's own. 'Cap'n Czar, personnel have just brought in Colonel Tsuji from old Ishiwara's farm up in Yamagata Prefecture. Want to get a few kicks in before I hand him over to MI debriefing?'

'Have you let Hattori's demob boys loose on him?'

'Don't get all rankled, Cap'n Czar,' Schlep grinned, showing his teeth clamped to the cigar. 'No, I ain't yet, but I'll give you odds that Colonel Tsuji's already made contact with Hattori.'

'Didn't Tsuji just creep in from China?'

'You bet. Just in the nick of time to save his hide, the goddam weasel. Fact is, though, if he managed to sneak past our personnel and reach Ishiwara's place, he could also have contacted Hattori.'

'Aren't Tsuji and Hattori rivals from the old days?'

'Well, maybe so. But you know what they say, Cap'n – the enemy of my enemy isn't necessarily my friend.'

'Sure.'

''Smatter son, you cold?' The major general pierced me through with his blue eyes. I trembled in the freezing draught let loose on us from the corridor, and prayed that Schlep would not recognize me.

'Who's the runt?'

'My assistant,' Captain Lazar replied.

'Your assistant, huh?' Schlep chuckled. 'You want to see this guy Tsuji or not?'

'Give me time to brief myself, sir.'

'Move your ass, Cap'n. Ten minutes is all.' With this, he saluted, slammed the door and was gone.

'Did he recognize me?' I asked.

'Couldn't say,' Captain Lazar shrugged, warming his hands over the electric fire. 'Have you heard of our illustrious captive, ex-Colonel Tsuji Masanobu?'

'I think not,' I said, lying.

'Now there's a Class A war criminal. As a staff officer of the Kwantung Army in Manchuria, he master-minded the rape of Nanking in 1937. He planned the conquest of Malaya and Singapore in 1942, and as Chief of Operations Squad in the Philippines, he supervised the Bataan Death March. He's a specialist in tank and commando warfare, a courageous fighting man and a master of subterfuge. Don't be misled by his relatively low rank – he has, or had, more power than a lot of top brass on the General Staff.'

'A formidable man.'

'He certainly is – and this is your opportunity to help me interrogate him.'

'Pardon me, Captain Lazar-san, but I could not possibly take part in torture.'

'Torture? What are you talking about?'

'I overheard the major general instructing you to "get some kicks in" before the prisoner is removed.'

Captain Lazar buried his face in his fur mantle, and his rancid milk complexion emerged pink with amusement. 'Christ almighty, boy, it's time you learnt some American. Nobody's going to lay a finger on ex-Colonel Tsuji – certainly not on G-2's potential star collaborator in our fight against communism. Our slippery colonel evaded capture in 1945 by taking refuge in a Buddhist monastery in Bangkok. When the British began flushing him out, he turned for help to Chiang Kai-shek's Blue Shirt secret police who smuggled him away to Chungking. He repaid Chiang handsomely for this rescue by supplying him with twenty years' accumulated intelligence on China and South East Asia. Tsuji led a nucleus of Japanese former staff officers released from Chiang's prisons in the campaign against Mao Tse-tung's red army. Until now. Until it became obvious that Chiang was going to lose and he started killing unrepatriated Japanese colonists on Taiwan. You'll never guess where some of Tsuji's fugitive officers went to find new employment. With another emperor. That's right. With Emperor Haile Selassie of Ethiopia.

Well, whether he knows it or not, ex-Colonel Tsuji is now about to find employment with the new Shogun of Japan, General Douglas MacArthur.'

'Please, I do not think my English is adequate for this task.'

'Now's your chance to improve it,' Captain Lazar said, as he collected several dossiers from the ping-pong table. 'Come on, let's take a look at this prodigy.'

Captain Lazar led me down to the basement section where formerly the secret police had its cells. We entered a bare windowless room dimly lit by a single desk lamp on a table. Here was another empty cube of night, surcharged with the psychic traces of its bygone victims, their screams under interrogation and their death rattles. A darkened corner of the room was occupied by Major General Willoughby, sitting in – of all things – a cushioned rocking-chair, in the unlikely pose of another benign giant, Abe Lincoln. A bilingual stenographer sat at one of the tables, and at the other, ex-Colonel Tsuji Masanobu. He wore the robes of a Nichiren Buddhist priest, a pair of *geta* sandals, and an old mackintosh over his shoulders which gleamed with the dew of evaporating snow. The snake-necked desk lamp was turned on his face, flood-lighting his clean shaven, angular cranium and the elfin ears jutting from it. His visage was that of a samurai, blank, arrogant and utterly fearless. He gave me barely an instant's glance; but I flinched under it, in deep shame. Throughout the interview, his eyes stared straight ahead, fixed on thin air.

'Tell him he can put on his glasses,' Captain Lazar informed me. Tsuji's personal effects had been dumped on the table – eyeglasses, wallet and the contents of a small rucksack. I suspected from the way Tsuji snatched up his glasses even before I had completed my translation, that his ignorance of English was pretended. Our three-way interview that now followed was an absurd circus.

'Ask him, what's this?' Captain Lazar held up a little stoneware saké cup and a pair of silver cuff-links, all items embossed with the Imperial crest of the chrysanthemum.

'Souvenirs,' Tsuji replied.

Captain Lazar studied the cup. 'This is the sixteen-petal chrysanthemum, reserved for the Emperor's own use. Only the Emperor can make such a gift, and it is therefore part of the Colonel's secret credentials.'

'I don't know about secret credentials. But there is no crime in accepting a gift.'

'These cuff-links – are they not a personal gift from the Emperor's younger brother, Prince Mikasa?'

'Yes.'

'And was Prince Mikasa not the Colonel's protégé at the Military Academy? What was the Colonel's function at the Academy?'

'Morals instructor.'

'Fucking H Christ,' Schlep muttered, as he rocked back and forth.

'Is it not true,' Captain Lazar continued, 'that the Colonel was recruited to the Emperor's inner circle, a military cabal known as the Cherry Society in 1930?'

'There was no cabal. His Majesty only wished to honour me by showing his confidence in me.'

'Yeah, sure, a confidence to commit mass murder,' Schlep commented. 'Ask him if he knows I could have him hanged for his escapades in Nanking and Bataan.'

'Apparently, the guilty parties have already been tried and executed. That chapter is closed. Although, for my part, I do not fear the threat of death.'

'Cheeky son of a bitch,' Schlep grinned.

'You have only recently escaped from China,' Captain Lazar said. 'Why did you go at once to visit Lieutenant-General Ishiwara Kanji at his Nishiyama farm in Yamagata Prefecture?'

'Ishiwara-*san* is nearing death. It was imperative that I renew my contact with him, for he is a great teacher of Nichiren Buddhism.'

'You mean, you wished to renew contact with former Lieutenant-General Ishiwara, ex-senior officer of the Kwantung Army and the chief strategist of the Manchurian conquest.'

'I do not deny being a Kwantung Army officer.'

'An officer in an Army that was never defeated and never surrendered?'

'So you say.'

'What did you discuss with ex-Lt.-General Ishiwara?'

'We discussed the remarkable properties of yeast fertilizer for increasing crop yields.'

'Your great teacher of Nichiren Buddhism, Ishiwara, is in fact an extreme rightwing zealot who has recruited ex-servicemen into his schemes for cooperative agriculture. He has coined the retrogressive slogan, *kokumin kaino*, "all the people back to the land". His programme envisages dispersal of the cities to the countryside, village-based industry and self-denying frugality.'

'Ishiwara-*san* is a Tolstoyan idealist, a visionary like Gandhi.'

'Is it like Gandhi for Ishiwara to call for a single-party totalitarian state in order to implement his programme of ruralization? Has it not struck you that Ishiwara's programme is very like Mao Tse-tung's peasant dictatorship?'

'Ishiwara-*san* is a staunch anti-communist.'

'Horseshit,' Schlep interjected. 'What Ishiwara's trying to sell us is *Tennoism*, old-style Emperor worship in new clothes.'

'Ishiwara-*san* is respectful of our ancient sovereign institution,' Tsuji replied, 'but in a non-political sense.'

Schlep laughed.

'Non-political or not,' Captain Lazar pursued, 'Ishiwara's cooperative farming venture in Tohoku, The East Asia League Comrades' Association, was dissolved by a SCAP directive in 1946 and your teacher himself purged.'

'Yes, but not indicted. If I recall correctly, when Ishiwara-*san* appeared before the Military Tribunal, he told the United States Prosecutor that President Truman who had ordered the indiscriminate napalm and A-bombing of civilians should himself be charged as a Class A war criminal.'

'It does not behoove you to speak arrogantly, Tsuji-*san*.'

'Please excuse me.'

'I see here,' Captain Lazar said, looking into his dossiers, 'that General Tojo forced Ishiwara to resign from active military service in 1942. Why is that?'

'They could never see eye to eye on the East Asia war. I have told you, Ishiwara-*san* is a true idealist, his aim being a limited war that would create a Greater East Asia League with Japan, China and Manchukuo on equal footing.'

'You mean, he foresaw that Tojo's prosecution of the war would end in defeat. Ishiwara did not scruple to call General Tojo "a dunce" in public. I note too, that Ishiwara was appointed special advisor to Prince Higashikuni's Surrender cabinet, and in his role as a popular hero of Nichiren fundamentalism he toured the countryside blaming Tojo for the defeat. With Prince Higashikuni's permission, and the Emperor's own connivance, Tojo's head was being offered for sacrifice. Wasn't that the "repentance" plan?'

'His Majesty knew nothing of that. And besides, it was not Ishiwara-*san* who hanged General Tojo.'

'He might as well have,' Schlep chuckled.

'What does Ishiwara mean by *saishusen*?' Captain Lazar went on.

'He means the Final War, the greatest, most cataclysmic global war that mankind has ever seen, that will be fought between two great ideological blocs. He prophesied *saishusen* already in 1940, before the Pacific War began.'

'When does he prophesy this event to occur?'

'1960.'

'Very precise date, isn't it?'

'Ishiwara-*san* has calculated that date on the teachings of Nichiren who in the 13th century had forecast an unprecedented conflict in our time. Nichiren's prophecy is based on the doctrine of *mappo no yo*, "the last days of the Law", our own period of degeneracy when the Buddha's Law will no longer have the power of salvation for mankind. The cataclysm will happen twenty-five centuries after the Buddha's death.'

'Nichiren also prophesied a foreign invasion, which did in fact occur in 1274 when the Mongol fleets arrived.'

'That is correct.'

'Japan was saved at that time by the intervention of divine winds, the *kamikaze*, which swept the Mongol fleets away.'

'Yes.'

'However, this time your *kamikaze* did not succeed in preventing our Occupation of Japan. Your leader, Ishiwara has set himself up as a latter-day Nichiren who predicted this calamity. How does he hope to save Japan from the impending Final War of 1960?'

'First, by making it secure from communism.'

'How so – by rearming?'

'No, Ishiwara-*san* believes in unarmed neutrality.'

'And yourself, Colonel Tsuji – what do you believe in?'

'For myself, I believe in armed neutrality.'

'A reconstituted armed forces under the command no doubt of former staff officers of the Kwantung Army?'

'It is admittedly an interesting ambition.'

'Ask him if he's prepared to work with Hattori's ex-servicemen's unit,' Schlep put in.

'I have the greatest respect for ex-Colonel Hattori, a man of integrity and competence, but I would prefer not to be linked to his particular military coterie.'

'You mean, you'd rather not be associated with the American Occupation forces.'

'If you want to put it that way, I suppose so.'

'Will you quit buggering around, Cap'n Czar, and start getting some real China intelligence out of this guy?'

'Excuse me, sir, but I'm working up to the situation in Indochina. Tsuji is an intelligence expert on South East Asia.'

'Never mind fucking Indochina, Cap'n. Our Froggie colleagues have got that one pretty well in hand.'

The question of Indochina was nevertheless put to Colonel Tsuji, despite Schlep's impatient dismissal of it.

Tsuji's strongly chiselled lips almost smiled for once as he replied. 'It is only a matter of time before the communist Vietminh forces drive the French out of Indochina.'

'Complete and total crap,' Schlep irritably remarked. 'Leclerc's forces have pacified the south and driven the Vietminh right out of Hanoi. What's the guy talking about? Vo Nguyen Giap couldn't possibly sustain an offensive against the French.'

'Such an assessment of Giap's regular Vietminh army is at present correct but short-sighted. The French will lose for several other reasons. First, because they failed to take advantage of their victories in 1946 and prosecute the war on an irregular, guerrilla basis in the Viet Bac mountains where the communists have taken refuge – if necessary, even to push on and follow them into China.'

'China would never have allowed that,' Schlep objected.

'One does not necessarily have to ask Chiang Kai-shek's permission for everything,' Tsuji drily stated. 'Second, the French are increasingly bogged down by guerrilla harassment in the so-called "pacified" areas. Third, and most important, the French will be defeated politically. This is a war of national independence, and the Vietnamese, like other peoples of South East Asia, have learned their lesson from Japan's victories over the white supremicist colonialists. France has installed the ex-Emperor Bao Dai as puppet head of state. Please recall – it was Japan that gave Vietnam its national independence in 1945 as our collaborators within the Greater East Asia Co-Prosperity Sphere – and it was we who dissolved the French colonial administration and placed Vietnamese personnel in government – men like Ngo Dinh Diem who now refuse to work with Bao Dai's puppet regime – men who are anti-Vietminh nationalists, but who see that Bao's ineffectual rule as a French tool not only stymies independence but promotes Ho Chi Minh's claim as the only true independence fighter.'

Captain Lazar added his own voice to Colonel Tsuji's survey. 'I think our friend Tsuji is right on target with some Pentagon views. We should listen to him, especially now that Washington's about to commit us to aiding the French.'

Major General Willoughby sighed. 'I'm going to tell you this just once, Cap'n Czar – you're a banker, not a soldier. Stick to accounting and keep your nose out of my business. Got it?'

'Yes sir! It was only a suggestion, sir.'

'You know where to stick your suggestion, Cap'n?' Schlep bellowed. 'Just ask him this – is he saying that Mao's soon going to come to Ho Chi Minh's assistance?'

'No, I don't believe so,' Tsuji replied. 'We are very familiar with this Ho Chi Minh fellow – or Nguyen Tat Thanh as he was originally called. He first gained Chiang Kai-shek's support, although Chiang's Kuomintang forces held him in "protective custody" for thirteen months in 1941. He was released in 1942 to head the Kuomintang's apparently loyal anti-Japanese Indochina resistance, with 100,000 dollars and his new name. In fact, Ho's Vietminh did little to risk itself in action against us, preferring to keep its organization intact to command the situation after 1945. Ho is Stalin's man, not Mao's.'

'So if it's not Indochina we've got to keep an eye on for the moment, *where* then?'

'Korea,' Tsuji said. 'I am convinced that Mao will prepare to strike there, once he's done with Chiang.'

Schlep's rocking-chair had ceased moving. 'We're finally getting somewhere, by God!' Tsuji's head swivelled round to the left, slowly, in Schlep's direction, and for the first time, their eyes met and held. For some long moments, Tsuji's eyes of glazed obsidian stared into the major general's chillingly blue ones.

At last, Major General Willoughby rose up from his chair. 'O.k., Cap'n, I'll take it from here. This guy's debriefing is going straight to King Arthur,' he said, and then named another interpreter that the stenographer was ordered to fetch.

Captain Lazar stood, mouth ajar, in bewildered fury.

'Dismissed, Cap'n,' the major general saluted.

'Sir!'

I followed a pale, silently raging Captain Lazar back to his office. In these few possible moments of quiet, I tried to grasp what I had seen and heard. My throat was constricted, my limbs quaked, not in fear but in the grip of some unnameable sensation of evil, like a delirium. This was my very first tutorial in the special art of *gyaku kosu*, the reverse course, even before that cynical name had gained currency. One thing seemed clear. With the first snows of the Cold War, Japan had overnight ceased being a menace and a fascist state scheduled for total democratic reform, and was suddenly being recast as a crucial anti-communist ally in the Far East. To this end, the G-2 section of SCAP, whose job it had been to ferret out and dissolve all rightwing and ultra-nationalist organizations, was now seeking to employ these very agencies in the reconstruction of a conservative state. I could not understand, however, why there should be such peculiar, contradictory tensions between the economic and military strategic elements of this 'reverse course', evident in the antagonism between Captain Lazar and Major General Willoughby.

Captain Lazar headed straight for his cocktail bar and poured two Bushmills into massive half-pint glasses. In the next hour, he would refill our cut-glass tumblers with savage quantities of whisky, which did nothing to soothe him. He paced up and down, his lips animated as though by silent prayers. His fox-lined mantle fell unnoticed from his shoulders to the floor, outspread in his path like a fur carpet on which he stepped with complete disinterest. He loosened his tie and threw off his jacket. All his earlier vulnerability to the cold was now forgotten in the blaze of his agitation. My presence too seemed forgotten, except that my glass was not.

I knew neither what to say nor what to do to extricate myself from this prowling beast.

Without warning, he turned to me, his face reddened in a veil of alcoholic sudation. 'Have I succeeded to excite your interest in banking?'

'Captain Lazar-*san*, you have introduced me to so much privileged information, I am speechless.'

'You dunce. There's nothing privileged in it than is already known to every Japanese executive bureaucrat. Now you're just one more among them. This isn't a conspiracy, but merely a government.'

'Pardon me, but if you are the "Czar of banking", why does Major General Willoughby treat you like a rival?'

'Like a rival? You mean, with such contempt? You're a writer. I'll tell you a story that should interest you. And I'll begin with what interests me most. Myself.' Captain Lazar had stationed himself in front of me, very close, jamming me against the ping-pong table. 'I am the product of immigrant Jews from Vilna. There were anarchists and extreme leftwing lunatics galore among my ancestors. Bolshevism cured most of them of that infantile disorder, terminally. I was raised in the Bronx, a place as remote from you as the Sea of Fertility on the moon.'

On and on he went, into areas where I could not follow or understand him, in his meandering story of a Bronx *wunderkind*, star-crazed by ambition, bullying his way up the ladder from the mean streets to Harvard, a Rhodes Scholarship, Oxford, and post-graduate studies at Tokyo Imperial University. As he climbed, so did my slow improvement in American proceed, from lessons in dismally low English to high, from Yiddishisms and Damon Runyon's Broadway slang to Harvard jargon and Oxford affectations. So did I hear of his apprenticeship in a powerful investment firm with interests in Japan, Dillon Reed, as a protégé of William Draper, merchant banker and now a major-general charged with the 'reverse course' task of halting the de-cartelization of Germany's former Nazi corporations and of restoring another vanquished nation's industry. Lazar led me down still murkier alleyways, a vague terrain in which I was soon lost – his recruitment into Allen Dulles's Office of Strategic Services, forerunner of the CIA, and the bargaining over surrender terms with Japanese bankers in the Swiss Bank of International Settlements.

Lazar's story ended with a story. 'Only three days after Pearl Harbour, the director of Mitsubishi addressed a plenary inter-company meeting, and he already spoke to the shareholders of restoring the alliance between Japan and United States big business.'

'My father also told me a story,' I said. 'On the eve of Surrender, when it looked certain that America and not our communist adversaries would be the occupying power, my father's business partners uncorked champagne in celebration.'

'A toast, Mishima-*san*, a toast to the new industrial era and the universal culture of finance!'

Captain Lazar forced the brimming jars of Bushmills down both our throats. Rose-scent, alcohol and a disagreeable smell of burning metal oozed from him. I was squeezed against the table, under his insistent pressure, cheek-to-cheek with him. I became aware that he was fumbling with my trouser buttons. 'Holy Toledo, will you look at the knob on this guy,' he rasped, grimacing with lust as he dandled my lizard. 'Have you got a licence for this thing?'

Captain Lazar stripped off his shoes, trousers and shirt, all in one swift motion. I looked at his cast aside underpants, amazed by their silk fabric, like a lady's.

'Come on, get your clothes off,' he ordered. 'We're going to do some marathon fucking.'

He hurried over to a phonograph, loaded it expeditiously with a pile of 78s, and returned carrying a tube of something pharmaceutical. Anti-haemorrhoidal lotion. 'Put some on. Kills two birds with one stone.' He awaited me on the floor, his fur-lined mantle beneath him, the fox pelts of a lighter shade than the orang-utan's red hair on his thighs' backsides that he raised up to greet me. 'Hurry up, get that stick of dynamite into me.' He had the practised catamite's bruised anus, the lax sphincter and insides roughened by fistula scars.

One after another, the 78s drop on the turn-table, as we bang mechanically without respite against each other. Teeth clenched, snarling, blood-shot green eyes aswirl, Lazar's neck stretches to its arching limit, like the starved and tantalized fox in its death agonies. My body probing deep into his covers him like earth, like the hard-packed, imprisoning soil of his grave. The record-player's arm engraves its sounds on my skull with its tattooist's needle. All the familiar Broadway and tin-pan alley hits – tunes by Gershwin, Cole Porter, Hoagy Carmichael and Jerome Kern – all begin to sound alike to me, as though a single *gyaku kosu* orchestra were playing the 'reverse course' rhumba, the 'reverse course' foxtrot, the 'reverse course' boogie – and all the lyrics are the amuletic slogans of 'reverse course' democracy, joined together into a single, ominous poem as my mind strays and follows the words –

'You know I'm yours for just the taking, I'd gladly surrender myself to you, BODY AND SOUL ...' (and the Declaration of Independence, anti-trust legislation and the Fifth Amendment)

'The fundamental things apply, AS TIME GOES BY ...' (and Wall Street, Ford and Texaco)

'So DREAM when the day is thru' – DREAM and they might come true ...' (and the Monroe Doctrine, MGM and the Cold War)

'Don't you know, little fool, you never can win – Use your mentality – Wake up to reality ...'cause I got you UNDER MY SKIN ...' (and the Statue of Liberty, the Wobblies and the Klu Klux Klan)

'Blue skies up above, ev'ryone's in love, UP A LAZY RIVER, how happy you can be ...' (and Clarence Darrow, Betty Grable and Walt Whitman's elegy on Lincoln)

'A trip to the moon on gossamer wings, JUST ONE OF THOSE THINGS . . .' (and the Gettysburg Address)

'De tings dat yo li'ble to read in de Bible, IT AIN'T NECES-SARILY SO . . .' (Einstein, Oppenheimer and Los Alamos)

'I found a MILLION DOLLAR BABY in a Five-and-Ten Cent Store . . .' (and the 'Fat Man' A-bomb dropped on Nagasaki from 'Bock's Car' a B-29 bomber)

'So when you hear it thunder, don't run under a tree – there'll be PENNIES FROM HEAVEN for you and me . . .' (and the napalming of Tokyo, 124,000 dead in one day, over twice the total number of US battle dead for the entire Pacific War)

'Oh how the ghost of you clings, THESE FOOLISH THINGS remind me of you . . .'

4 BUSTER KEATON

MY YOUNGER brother Chiyuki began his own law studies at Tokyo University two years after Japan's surrender. I decided to treat him on that occasion to the costliest meal our derelict city could provide, followed by an American double feature at the cinema. Hollywood had been served a lucrative dumping ground for recycling its products in those Occupation days when so few Japanese films were permitted. Buster Keaton's silent film classic, *The Cameraman*, came as the hors-d'oeuvre to the main billing, *White Heat*, a James Cagney thriller.

At the end of the Keaton film, Chiyuki turned to me, puzzled. 'You didn't laugh once. Don't you find Keaton funny?'

'No, I find him true.'

Chiyuki might not be a very imaginative person, but he had the discernment to say, 'You'll never get over the times with grandmother, will you?'

I felt so intensely disturbed by Buster Keaton's face that I did not permit myself to see another of his films until many years later. What was the painful truth I recognized in his face? A mystery in my childhood had been clarified by my encounter with Keaton's strange, autistic lack of expression. Clarified, yes, but without relieving me of my past torments.

Like the erratic zigzagging patterns of fireflies at night, memories return. I did not leave childhood behind me. It remains a dark, overgrown forest ever creeping up on me, obliterating all trace of my progress to the present. What I remember does not matter so much as why I remember.

The spectre of my unhappy childhood can never speak uninhibitedly, for reasons that involve a most secret, intimate drama of love and betrayal and ethical preference. Even to this day, the story is virtually incommunicable, but I can attempt to tell it by invoking the silent film impassivity of Buster Keaton.

Natsuko's attendance at the grand premieres of the Noh and Kabuki theatre seasons was almost a religious practice with her. The annual rite demanded a costly new wardrobe of kimonos. 'I am asked to make economies,' Natsuko complained to me, late one night on her return from a Noh play. A swift glance of her eyes to the ceiling identified the miserly asker as my father upstairs. His request would not seem entirely unreasonable. The accumulation of Natsuko's past outfits appeared to me limitless, her closet vast and in its way as frightening as the Nagai armoury down the corridor. The naphthalene odour of that cedar-lined hangar, the rustle of gorgeous patterned silks arrayed under dust-cloths threatened me with ghosts no less fearful than the samurai panoplies in the other chamber. Tsuki had encouraged me to believe that the two rooms were somehow interconnected, despite their obvious distance apart.

To my mind, Natsuko's luxurious cult of new kimonos was a search to find the ideally satisfying one. My childish insight delighted me, and to an extent calmed my fears. 'Is there not one kimono you prefer above all others, grandmother?' I asked.

'One kimono for which I would sacrifice my craving for new ones, as your father wants? There is one I especially treasure, of course, but it could only be worn once. It is modelled on the Noh character in the play that I have seen again tonight, after countless times before, the Lady Awoi. Would you like me to put on this kimono and tell you the story of the Lady Awoi?'

The time was well beyond midnight, a new day beginning on the eve of my 4th birthday, in the winter of 1929. My place as Natsuko's solo audience took the usual one, at the foot of her bed where I slept like a privileged guardsman in service during all the years of my extra-uterine captivity with her, at first in a cot and now on a child's couch.

The play begins with Lady Aowi on her deathbed, after her carriage has overturned, and the betrayal of her love by Prince Genji takes the incarnate form as a beautiful demon of jealousy come to torture her. 'I came aimlessly hither,' the apparition says, 'drawn only by the sound of the *azusa* bow . . .' Loudly, from behind the Toyotamahime screen, Natsuko declaims the sepulchral bass tones of the demon. I can hear the swish of her robes as she dresses up for me. I can hear my father upstairs, groaning to wakefulness, unspared the loudness of a recitation which is meant as much for his shame as for my benefit.

Lady Awoi's apparition steps out from the screen, in an under-kimono of black satin, embroidered with small irregular circles of flowers, and the upper of stiff gold brocade shot through with purples, greens and reds. 'Who do you think I am? When I was still in the world, spring was there with me. I feasted on the cloud with spirits who shared my feast of flowers. On the evening of maple leaves, I had the moon for mirror. I was drunk with colour and perfume. And for all my joyous flare at the time, I am now like a shut morning-glory awaiting the sunshine. Now I am come for a whim. I am come uncounting the hour, seizing on no set moment. I would set my sorrow aside. Let someone else bear it awhile.' She glides in Noh fashion to the bed on which the Lady Awoi is imagined dying, closes her fan, and strikes her. 'The woman is hateful! I cannot restrain my blows.'

At this point, my role as the *miko* clairvoyant in the play is to protest. 'No, Stop! How can you, a Princess, do such a thing?'

'I cannot, however much you might pray,' she replies, and then reflectively, as if detached from her action, she describes it: 'So she went toward the pillow, and struck. Struck!'

It was an uncanny spectacle to watch Natsuko striking her own pillow, and by the force of her artistry convincing me that the head I saw on the pillow was not the Lady Awoi's but her own. I beheld Natsuko as two persons, split into the sick woman I knew from my disturbed nights with her, and this other glamorously costumed spectre of jealousy. I knew, beyond a child's span of understanding, that I was the hostage of these antagonistic beings, one sick with jealousy, the other revenging herself on reality. I knew, without the capacity yet to understand, that I was being moulded into an isolated spectator – I didn't know the word yet – a voyeur.

I slept badly with these precocious thoughts, unaware that my father in his bed upstairs was calculating his own revenge.

I awoke from my dreams the next day, and for days afterwards, with an insistent feeling of curiosity. A child reasons only from the effect felt, not at first from causes. I could not have named my feeling for what it truly was, resentment. I had become aware of a flagrant contradiction in the rules governing my solitary confinement. Natsuko prescribed a regimen of diet, dress and play which outlawed any form of stimulation. Noisy or aggressive toys were strictly prohibited as liable to over-excite me. This agreed with her 'unassailable article of faith', my weakness. And yet, she over-indulged me with stories of the most intoxicating kind, not the least suitable for the impressionable mind of an invalid child. Indiscriminately, she lavished her excessive tales on me, not only from the Japanese classics but from her favourite English, French and German authors, the decadent vagaries of Poe, Villers de l'Isle-Adam, Hoffmann and others.

Can one speak of infantile paranoia? Maybe not. But something like it preyed on my feelings as we sat one snowy morning leafing through Natsuko's collection of fashion magazines, old copies of the Paris *Vogue*, *Gazette du Bon Ton*, but most precious of all the complete numbers of *La Dernière Mode* edited by the poet Stéphane Mallarmé in 1874. Natsuko was a fine conoisseur of styles from the 1900s to the early 20s, when her interest abruptly ceased. Hours would pass in eloquent contemplation of the fashion plates from the designers and couturiers she most admired, Worth, Callot Soeurs, Lady Lucile Duff Gordon and Paul Poiret who in 1910 introduced the bright Scheherazade colours of Bakst's *Ballet Russe* to design; but above all, Natsuko's titan of fashion, the Venetian Mariano Fortuny who clothed the avantgarde beauties of Europe and America in the 1910s and 20s.

'Look at this masterpiece, little nightingale,' Natsuko indicated a black satin Delphos evening dress by Fortuny, inspired by the ancient Ionic chiton, hanging in minute pleats from the neck with a drawstring decorated with Venetian glass beads. 'See how Fortuny combines a Greek gown with a kimono-style evening jacket, hand-printed in bronze pigment.'

I had never seen Natsuko in anything but kimonos. Had she never once satisfied her gourmet appetite for any of this European finery? 'Once, yes, once I wore many such gowns, indeed for nearly thirty years from the end of the Rokumeikan period to the first years of the Taisho era, when your grandfather was governor of Sakhalin.'

'Why did you stop?'

Natsuko shook her head.

'What has happened to those dresses?'

She nodded towards the closet.

'Would you put on one of them for me, grandmother?'

Natsuko blushed. Her eyes strayed away, unfocussed, as though in some reachless dream. 'Yes, perhaps one last time.'

She went to her dresser to seek the stockings that had lain unused for fifteen years in their original crêpe paper and box from La Samaritaine. Then she placed the screen in front of the closet and vanished into it, like Toyotamahime into her feathered birthing-hut, for what seemed an endless time. The room filled with the escaped fumes of mothballs. I heard her singing one of Jotaro's ballads from the 1920s *nansensu** times. At last, I recognized those faint sighs like willow leaves that announce the exquisite pathos of a woman dressing. Soon after came Natsuko's cries of distress in her labour to insert herself in Cinderella's things. 'How broad my feet have become. These shoes are too tight.' Her exclamations of despair attracted me to look, and I crept up to the screen and peered through the slit between the hinges. Natsuko

---

* 'Nonsense', referring to the frivolous era of Taisho Emperor.

rested her foot on a stool, exerting herself in vain to button the strap of a shoe. The metallic sheen of her opaque, peach-coloured silk stockings, leashed by frilly rucked garters of similar hue, enhanced her burly legs. She wrestled with a sleeveless flat-busted evening dress of columnar shape, belted low at mid-pelvis. Transparent layers of silk voile, printed pink and green on pale yellow, embroidered with pearlized sequins and gold glass bugle beads, fell to a scalloped hem at the ankles. The slack of Natsuko's upper arms bulged flat as she strained grimly, hopelessly to fasten the dress at the back. 'I've grown too stout. My arthritis –'

She gave up the contest, sat down on the stool and laughed derisively. Perspiration glimmered through her make-up. Never more than now did she seem to me the apparition of the Lady Awoi, whose words she now moaned, 'This hate is only repayment.' She knew I spied on her, but was past caring. 'What have you made me do, little nightingale? Your love is cruel.' And then, dishevelled as she was and planted on her stool, Natsuko began to tell me the story of a *shinju* love-pact suicide. 'Japanese suicide is not the result of a blind, quick frenzy of pain. It is not only cool and methodical, it is sacramental. It involves a marriage of which the certificate is death. No pledge can be more profoundly sacred than *shinju*. Do you hear me, *hototogisu?*'

Natsuko's story told of two youngsters, Taro and Oyoshi, unable to marry, and at the end the lovers cross the ricefields and run along the railroad tracks to meet the Tokyo express. '. . . they could see the smoke coming. They grasped each other and lay down cheek to cheek straight across the inside rail, already thundering like a blacksmith's anvil to the vibration of the great locomotive. The wheels passed through both – cutting off their heads evenly, like enormous scissors. Go now and find Tsuki. Leave me.'

As I stepped from our room to the corridor, a head turbaned in cigarette smoke and two viperish eyes met me. My father stood outside the door, listening, in wait for me. I glimpsed Tsuki flitting away round the corner. 'So, now you are the beneficiary of that story too?' Azusa grinned evilly. He seized me by the hand. 'Come on, lizard belly, I'm taking you for a walk.'

I was literally dragged along out of the house and taken – or practically kidnapped – for this walk. I do not suppose my father knew where it was he headed, or cared, and I am certain what happened next was not premeditated. Azusa held my hand pinioned furiously in his and my feet hardly touched the snowy ground at the pace he went. 'Your grandmother's protective custody,' he said, speaking more to himself than me, 'segregates you from the likes of us commonplace folk. Is that already well-established in your freakish little mind, lizard belly?'

A damp, freezing pall descended from a leaden January sky. We

arrived at a railraod crossing. The barrier was down, and a great black
steam engine approached in the distance. It was a rare enough opportunity for me to see a train. Like all children, I wondered at the strange,
level, ash-strewn way, with its double lines of iron shining away north
and south into mystery. I felt overawed by the ocean of black smoke
and roar of the titanic dragon making the ground quake that would
pass so very near me. My father picked me up in his arms, a gesture of
affection to reassure a child against fright and at once give him a better
view of the monster. Or so it seemed. What I next recall is suddenly
being thrust out, in mid-air, towards the engine which loomed vast and
menacing. The wheels appeared inches away, about to devour me. I
heard my father behind me say, 'Don't flinch. No coward's tears or I'll
drop you in the ditch.'

I do not know how long the test lasted. The train vanished. Finally
I remember Azusa's face staring into mine. 'Were you scared?' He set
me on the ground and crouched down to peer closely into my eyes.
'Were you scared?', he went on demanding to know. I was in a state
of autistic shock, unable to speak, unable to move or even nod my
head.

The barrier rose. The way ahead was clear. But we two stood rooted
to the spot. After a time, a bell rang, the fence re-descended. Another
locomotive came for us – or at any rate for me, since my father once
more attempted the same trial of my courage. Azusa desired some reaction from me, of fear or protest, which my traumatized gaze could not
satisfy. The rapt enigma of a child's eyes can be most unsettling to an
adult. He mistook my blank, frightened stare for defiance – and, of
course, Natsuko's influence.

A child once traumatized like that will never again recover. His gaze
will remain fixed in an inconsolable state of mourning. Nothing will
ever appear real to it, except melancholy. I have had other lessons in
estranged male affection from my father, other trials of Spartan proof of
valour. Lessons that no woman – no mother – would ever countenance.

I could never react treasonably against Azusa's model lesson in cruelty.
I understand it. Fathers will never tire of telling their sons the same old
story, never wearying of it generation after generation, that women are
the stronger. It is not a tale ever told straightforwardly, but by subterfuge,
by clandestine indirection. It is communicated by moments of frustrated
violence. In households where mothers dominate – in Latin ones notoriously, as in ours to an unnatural degree during Natsuko's years of
gynocratic tyranny and again subsequently in my mother's reign – fathers
will revenge themselves on their sons by the cruellest acts of wayward
love. And should the son betray the indoors' pallor of frail over-
sensitivity which marks him as mother's property, he will be regarded
a traitor by his father.

I have a spent a lifetime in resentful quarrels with my father. I dislike the man. But the truth involves another secret, intimate drama. My defences surrounding my trauma at the railroad crossing gradually transformed themselves into a binding ethical model. Deep down, I have never disagreed with my father's Confucianist disapproval of literature, its mendacity, its moral delinquency. Writing is a dishonourable profession. To ask whether Azusa's Confucianism was purely principled or motivated by jealousy is another matter. The question is what I made of it, a conflict within the self that I have attempted to resolve by combining the Ways of the Sword and the Pen, and which in the end favours the first.

There is something of grisly comedy in this scene of a helpless child pinioned in the arms of a villainous father. Something out of a Buster Keaton film. In the face of peril, Buster Keaton's expression remains impermeable. It is a stuntman's stoical mask. Everything and anything can happen to him, except what really happens to him. His face never mirrors anything that mercilessly befalls him, and hence the significance of events dissolves into gags. Like the chief actor in Noh plays, the *shi-te*, Keaton appears unmasked. The naked blankness of his face achieves *hie*, the absolute beauty of coldness, a painfully true mask. My espousal of an expressionless, autistic Noh mask at the railroad crossing was a silent film comedy expedient.

Natsuko had plunged me into a sense-deprivation environment, no noise, no stimulation, only the space for her illness and my devotional spectatorship. From the start, single-mindedly and without interference from the outside world, she moulded me into a contradictory fiction – a sick child with samurai longings against the grain of nature, against the natural love of mother and the filial piety I owed my father. And when Azusa in rivalry with his mother attempted to reclaim my filial piety at the crossing, and challenge Natsuko's 'unassailable article of faith', he became her ally without knowing it. Azusa's lesson achieved the opposite of his purpose: it condemned me to aesthetics, unappealing and unheroic as that condition is.

On the evening after my railside ordeal, Natsuko alerted the house to the fact that I was dying. 'Come quickly,' she cried, 'he's stopped breathing!' I had fallen into a state of catalepsy, lying in a coma, stiff and blue on my couch. My mother summoned a cousin who was a consultant at Tokyo's St Luke's Hospital. 'The pulse is imperceptible,' he announced on examining me. He gave me injections of camphor to stimulate the heart. 'What is it?' Natsuko asked, in a calm, almost disinterested way. 'Will he recover?' 'I fear he will not,' the doctor replied. 'This is an extreme case of *jikachudoku*.'

Western acquaintances of mine have never been able to identify their equivalent to this pediatric crisis, translated as spontaneous or self-intoxication. A uniquely Japanese illness, then, and one entirely fitting to my exaggerated personality.

Several hours passed. Time enough to gather our closest relatives who came to look at my corpse. Natsuko ordered my mother to collect my favourite toys and prepare the shroud for my funeral. Jotaro would make the funeral arrangements. My grandmother paced up and down the corridor, her footsteps and cane resounding on the floor as though empty jars were placed beneath it for acoustics, like a Noh stage. Shortly before dawn, she asked: 'Is he dead yet?' Before the consultant could reply, my mother exclaimed, 'Look –', and a little jet of urine gushed from me. I stirred back to life, vomiting an amount of vile brown stuff. 'Good,' the doctor said. 'Assuredly he will live now.'

My father sat alone in Jotaro's parlour, chain-smoking and drinking tea, as he stared at Jotaro's Go board with its arrangement of pebbles. He had many hours to think about this house, devastated by civil war, by unquenchable feuds between everyone against everyone. Strange house of cleavages, of dichotomies and separations. Natsuko dominated all the compartments of this Chinese puzzle-box. She reigned by the occult means of *inzei*, cloistered rule, a strategy favoured by certain 11th century Emperors whose Buddhist vows of retirement and abdication did not prevent them from controlling the throne from behind the scenes. This was my grandmother's tactic – rule by obturation – and I was the puppet successor groomed in sealed confinement with her. 'So, would it not be better for me if lizard belly died?' Azusa concluded.

Tsuki arrived to tell him of my miraculous recovery. 'I never doubted he would live,' Azusa replied.

How could I know these things, if I was unconscious at the time? I deduced them from what Tsuki later confided, and from Azusa's subsequent reactions.

Two years later, very near the anniversary of my first cataleptic attack – followed since by others in a monthly routine – Tsuki gave me her account of that night, adding much to what Natsuko had neglected to say. And she had something more to tell me. 'Many years ago, when your grandmother and I were still innocent girls –'

'Twenty-six centuries before my birth?' I interrupted.

'Yes, that many, so ancient are we,' Tsuki's malign laughter came as a forewarning of something unpleasant. 'We are all familiar with your grandmother's unassailable article of faith. She blames your weakness on your mother's anaemia. Did you know? The fact that your mother has also produced a pair of unexceptionally healthy specimens as proof to the contrary, does not seem obvious to Madame's eyes. Take heed of what I say, little master. Sap is bled from the lacquer bush to create a veneer, a fragile crust which is a wonder of the cabinet-maker's art. Your grandmother is such an artist, and this –' Tsuki gestured at the

room, '– this is her cabinet, made to contain you, her *jizo* – her compassionate child rescuer. To her, you are also the boy Kompira, another
transformation of the Buddha dedicated to fighting the enemies of faith
– her faith, of course. She is aware that Kompira was orginally a Hindu
demon, the alligator of the Ganges.'

Tsuki's enigmas were aimed at a point that she delayed reaching.
Thinking back, I can see that she deliberately chose this particular time
and place to ambush me. Tsuki had been dusting my grandmother's
bookshelves when she waylaid me. Now she ran her fingernails along
the spines of a row of these books. 'These are all medical textbooks –
twenty-six centuries old – that once belonged to an eminent practitioner,
by origin a samurai of the Satsuma clan who took part in Saigo's 1877
rebellion in his teens. He courted your grandmother ardently, in those
days when she was still hardly more than a girl. He committed suicide
in 1893, a year before she married your grandfather Jotaro, and he left
her these books in remembrance. This one in particular –' Tsuki pulled
out a leather-spined folio volume and handed it to me, '– this might
tell us the reason for his suicide.' I opened the book which illustrated the
progressively devastating stages of syphilis. What these plates revealed, in
stiff hand-printed colours that gave the victims a wax-museum grue-
someness, overwhelmed me with fear. Leprous abscesses oozing apple-
jelly liquid, ulcerated testes, pseudo-elephantiasis of the vulva, nephritic
side-effects of mercury treatment, a torso hideously embossed with
mediastinitic varicose veins. 'At the end, they say, the roof of his mouth
and larynx were eaten away,' Tsuki's voice buzzed in my ears, like
tinnitis. 'He shed buckets of mucus and flesh every day. The stench was
unbearable.'

The book dropped from my hands, but too late. The contagion of
its pages had wormed its way into my mind. The mysterious *oni* demon
of my grandmother's illness had suddenly been unmasked, and its pus-
tulent features laid bare. I would consult that book, again and again, as
Tsuki had reckoned, attracted to it by a thrilling sensation of doom,
until its nightmare pigmentations were tattooed on my soul. The venom
of syphilis and Natsuko's corrupt romanticism were the same. I came
to believe them the necessary ingredients of genius. I was the diseased
weed favoured by destiny to occupy my grandmother's night garden.

Azusa too, in his own way, confirmed my findings by acting mysteriously. My father belonged to the breed of *shin kanryo-ha*, the new
bureaucracy in the Ministries, an ambitious rising class of civil servants
in the 1930s. They embraced an ultra-right conservative ideology
founded on Confucianist state ethics and the *kodo* or Imperial Way
mystique, a doctrine which upheld supreme moral obligation to the
Imperial Throne at the expense of the Diet's ever weakening political
parties. The goal of all young nationalist militants at the time was *ishin*

nippon. Restoration of Japan, a concept which looked back to Meiji times when the feudal hierarchy purged itself of Shogunate barbarism and by voluntary surrender of its privileges restored the Emperor to his rightful status and power. *Ishin nippon* expected the great *zaibatsu* cartel capitalists and the political parties in the Diet to restore their powers to the Emperor by the same self-sacrifice. When the Taisho Emperor died in 1926 and his successor chose Showa or Enlightened Peace as the title of his Emperorship, the *ishin nippon* movement took this as an omen and changed their name to *Showa ishin.* The nationalists of my father's generation interpreted the national structure as the unity of government and religion, and in this light it became clear to them that Japan's heaven-ordained mission was to create an ideal world benevolently supervised by the Emperor of Enlightened Peace. In essence, this looks forward to the Greater East Asia Co-Prosperity Sphere, the grandiose name of Japan's wartime empire as promoted by idealists.

Azusa was by no means an idealist. He was not the sort of man to risk himself on foolish ultra-right conspiracies against the government, rife at the time, and which gave the name *kurai tanima* or Dark Valley to this decade of extremist instability from 1931 to the outbreak of war in 1941. It is true, his admiration of Nazi ideology became unrestrained during the years leading to Japan's Axis Pact with Germany and Italy. But this was the fashionable thing, even among the more discreetly pro-Fascist ranks of minor bureaucrats to which he belonged. Azusa had found a ready-made careerist purpose in opposition to Jotaro's style of 'democratic malpractice' – in Azusa's own words – and something to arm himself against Natsuko's aristocratic pretension. This was the weapon he would turn against my passion for art.

Contact with Azusa, although restricted in my early years, gave me a glimpse into the cold uninviting reality of his world beyond the confines of Natsuko's sickroom. He came and went from a dark corridor which threatened more sinister apparitions than any of the phantoms I met in my passage from our room to the toilet. His corridor was the one of everyday life, the *kurai tanima* of fanatic violence. Both these passageways, in fantasy and reality, were fused in my mind as equally implicated in pathological ambition.

Azusa certainly did his utmost to defy his mother. He declared his own rival version of Natsuko's *inzei* rule-by-retirement by himself withdrawing to a summer hut he had built in the garden. This occurred in the summer after Tsuki's revelation, in 1931, when I first entered the Peers' School. I would sometimes contemplate Azusa's hut at night from a window next to the toilet at the end of the corridor, and I wondered what he was thinking and doing alone out there, hidden among the ilex shrubs. I envied his adventurist fortitude, a sulking Robinson Crusoe marooned by his own protest.

One night, as I lingered by that window, I saw my mother Shizue leave the house. She looked back at it as though troubled by the eyes she felt spying on her. I watched her put on garden *geta* and pass like a moonlit Noh figure en route to Azusa's retreat, her shadow lengthening giantly towards me as she receded from view. I felt beckoned to follow her.

So unusual was my rebellious act of courage that it seems to me I crept out in spirit rather than fact, that my memories of wet rough grass on my bare feet, the sharp cries of cicadas in the trees and the sighing of the cryptomeria, were entirely imagined. Through the open door of Azusa's hut, I saw the faint shape of green mosquito net flapping and swelling as if in a sea breeze round his bed. Something gleamed in the darkness. A woman's foot was thrust out from the net, but I could not recognize it as my mother's. The haunch of muscle in the sole of her foot tightened and relaxed in heartbeat rhythms, and the toes curled like fingers gripping at sheer smooth glass. No sounds reached me other than the rustling complaint of the straw mattress and the almost undetectable lapping of flesh on flesh.

I felt urged to take the umbrella leaning by the doorway and lift the net, as I have since observed a peeping Tom do one night in a park, raising a woman's skirt with the ferrule of his cane to expose the flesh between her suspender belt and panties, so expertly, so unobtrusively that she know nothing of it until the mosquitoes began biting. I knelt at the threshold, as a Shinto priest does before a shrine in prelude to the *ukei* ritual of summoning the *kami* ancestral spirits, a sanctuary no bigger than my father's hut, as dark inside and hot, filled with the drone of mosquitoes, the rustle of paper strips on *gohei* wands, and the sacred Mirror glinting faintly within the darkness.

I was a Shinto officiant at that moment, and I perceived the moon reflected in the mirror of Shizue's foot.

The next morning, Natsuko worried herself to a panic over my rash of mosquito bites. She feared mosquitoes as the carriers of infected blood from tuberculosis victims, a disease all too common in the 1930s. The old mosquito netting on the windows of our room were replaced by new and expensive copper screens, and Tsuki had orders to burn eucalyptus fumigants in the room and corridor an hour before we retired.

I remembered my grandmother's instruction to avoid calamities by feigning blindness as I sat down to record my garden vision in my diary. As my pen scripts these words again tonight, I am struck once more by the divinatory origin of the Sino-Japanese characters. In ancient times, the practitioners of *uranahi* divination used a tortoise shell and a stick of *hahaka* wood to foretell the future. This stick, about the size of my pen, was kindled in a fire and the glowing tip applied to the back of the tortoise shell. Divination was then made from the cracks produced.

Chinese ideograms are said to originate from copying these random oracle cracks. Astrological calendar-making can be retraced to this source, and so too can the habit of keeping personal diaries. A diary was originally nothing other than the astral record of auspicious or ill-omened signs of Heaven and their influence on human doings. The notorious Japanese obsession with diaries goes back to this – fortune-telling.

Japanese writers must render special homage to the Heian court ladies of the 10th century AD, the originators of our prose, who brought the 'cracked shell' of the diary genre to literary perfection. There is nothing in early medieval European literature to match the Jane Austen-like verve and wit of Sei Shonagon's *Pillow Book* or the genius of Lady Murasaki. While men exhausted their talents on ornate, sterile imitations of the Chinese classics, women were left free to act as the vernacular architects of our own domestic forms of narrative. Yet, for all their great refinement of expression, a sensibility alive to every social nuance and minute detail of nature, there is something oddly dream-like and incomplete in these women writers. We have no sense from them of the imminent catastrophe which threatened the Heian way of courtly life. They chose consciously or not to live in a splendidly sunlit and confined garden soon to be obliterated by earthquake and a tidal wave of darkness. Cracked-bone oracles perhaps still remained at the heart of these ancient writers, instructing them to shun any mention of calamities and thereby avoid them.

In my lonely night-time vigils as a diarist long ago in childhood, I was the apprentice of these genially competent court ladies of elder days. I owe a great deal to women as a writer, everything perhaps, except the one reason that has for so long confined me to writing.

5   A SUBTERRANEAN BOOKKEEPER

I TOOK no pleasure in the passage of the seasons. Snow, always for me a symbol of Japan's heroic past, had simply melted away in defeat as the weeks passed and my deliveries of surreptitious accounts to Captain Lazar continued. I could still look back in wonder at that moment in February when I awoke in disbelief, unwilling to credit the under-cover assignment that Captain Lazar had ordained for me. It had seemed incredible that a single night's orgiastic extravagance could be anything more than a vagary, a dream without meaning that I must try to shrug off, along with the morning's after-taste of humiliation that lingered undismissable like seasickness. I tried to reassure myself that my nomination to espionage had been an elaborate homosexual charade engineered by Captain Lazar to secure me as his plaything. I had been the object of a sadistic prank, an evening's delirious entertainment and no more.

I was disabused of any such egotistical notions on my return to my desk at the Banking Bureau the very next morning. I arrived late, of course, and looking more than usually destroyed. Section Chief, Nishida Akira, summoned me to his desk. I expected another one of his vitriolic rebukes, but instead he glanced up at me, his head bandaged in cigarette smoke, green-complexioned with migraine, and remarked, 'Out late again last night with the Peers' School set, Hiraoka-*san*?' His icy, saccharine smile greeted my confusion. 'You must feel as evil as you look,' he added, and indicated a portfolio of accounts for my attention. 'Do you feel up to accomplishing some work this morning, Section Clerk Hiraoka-*san*?' The note of solicitude in his tone struck false, though he apparently wished it genuine. I nodded, mortified. 'Well then, if you can restrain your inclination to errors, might I entrust you with these perfectly trifling accounts?'

Nishida's endeavour at humour was quite unprecedented. Geniality had never been his custom with anyone, least of all me. His sudden venture into bonhomie with me now, even clumsy as it was and incapable of overcoming a lifetime's practice in sarcasm, alerted me to the unexpected. I sensed danger. I looked at Nishida's portfolio of 'perfectly trifling accounts' and saw that it was stamped Classified and Confidential. I had the very unhappy feeling that my assigned mission had inescapably begun in truth.

'You seem positively ill, Hiraoka-*san*.' Nishida attempted to sustain a human warmth that violated his temperament and his grammar.

'I shall manage very well, thank you Section Chief.'

I returned to my desk and stared at the infernal dossier. What was I to do? 'By the waters of Babylon sit down and weep,' a little advisory voice of black humour whispered in the ruins of my soul.

An intellectual's first impulse is always to assess his feelings before he can properly allow himself to have them. Immediacy, to which normal people give vent, becomes sluggish in the intellectual by force of a habit that prizes clarification above the wonders of sensation. A habit of this sort tends to rob him of any real feelings at all, except those abnormal ones that come by the nastiest route of surprise. And these are the very ones he is least likely to accommodate to clarification.

In short, I was in no hurry to have feelings. And as for the clarification of the task awaiting me in that portfolio, I can only remember my frightened anticipation that still oozes dread from every pore of my memory to this day.

Feelings cannot be postponed forever, even in a person who thinks himself ethically superior to them. And so I opened the portfolio. I admit approaching this small action and its unknowable sequel with considerable excitement, with a thrill one enjoys at the moment of opening a pornographic magazine, in which the surfeit of one's curiosity is already present in all its greedy cloying sweetness. 'These pages are going to be my damnation.' That was the first clear thought I had; and with it, a flood of feelings at last released.

A courage born of desperation, a fatalist indifference to the consequences of my action swept over me, hurling me between extreme opposite poles of feeling. 'I am entombed, a blind earthworm, a vile subterranean bookkeeper ignorant even of my real master.' A slave – yes, but in whose service? Lazar had recruited me to perform a task – in whose interest? His own or Washington's or Japan's? I did not know. My role as subterranean bookkeeper at the Ministry had no sanction, no official endorsement, no status in reality whatsoever except for a purpose that I was not asked to understand.

I felt like one of those despicable clerks in Dostoyevsky's stories invested with an outrageous power that condemns them to a parasitical existence secluded from real life. In the end, such creatures become grandiose out of sheer puniness. So it was with me. I had a moment of exaltation in which I imagined my earthworm activities somehow benefiting the nation. I imagined myself somehow recognized in this millipede Byzantine mass of Occupation personnel, my name rising to the highest echelons of SCAP, to that supreme eminence occupying the sixth floor of the Dai Ichi Insurance Building in splendid isolation, General MacArthur himself, who would reward me in person.

At the next moment, my thoughts of loftiness were plunged into an abyss. It occurred to me that my dilemma – 'in whose service do I act?' – was the common one occupying the entire nation. And its solution could be found in reply to another greater enigma: 'Who is really the sovereign head of the nation? Is it the Generalissimo in splendid isolation in the Dai Ichi? Or in equally splendid isolation, and literally across the street from the Dai Ichi, the Emperor in his Imperial Palace? Whom did one serve? An Emperor in captivity or his captor?' The answer concerned service to an unforeseeable future.

Captain Lazar had been right about one thing. The military aspect of the war might be past, accounted a defeat for one side and a victory for the other; but an economic war of tactical recovery was now being fought, silently, and with grimmer ferocity than in the jungles of Malaya or Burma. I saw myself drafted into this bitterly determined, covert war. I saw my moral character being tested as never before. I saw myself torn asunder by the needs of two rival masters, tormented beyond endurance by my breach of trust, my disloyalty to His Majesty, to the Ministry and to my family, and finally driven to suicide.

Ridiculous. My imaginings only left me with the cold, unwelcome proof that I burrowed in total night.

I opened my pornographic magazine, so to speak, and found disappointment. As I glanced through these accounts, I encountered only disenchantingly blank, detumescent figures. My excitement at the prospect of crime had been invalidated. Or to use another analogy, if I had expected the blinding revelation that befell St Paul on the road to Damascus, I was absurdly mistaken. So far as I could see, the task set before me required no more skill than the pedestrian one of a bookkeeper, the routine calculations of receipts, statements, bills of exchange and discounts to be rendered on balance sheets. I was a copyist, not a grand accomplice in treason. What did I expect? Did I believe these opaque bloodless columns of numbers would at once make plain their secrets to a twenty-three-year-old, raw trainee in banking?

I should have felt relieved, indeed, grateful to Captain Lazar for landing me in the position of tame bookkeeper in which I could choose to remain ignorant of any treason, real or imagined. All that was being asked of me was my discreet unquestioning acquiescence, which no doubt would soon reap me its own profitable dividends. Instead, no; instead I felt anger. I felt humiliated by the grotesque circumstances of my ignorance, and I desired revenge that the power of knowledge alone can bring, no matter how risky such an enterprise could prove to a foolish youth. Humiliation is an unbearable condition in which the sufferer may be driven to seek relief in the very thing causing his torment. And so, rather than withdraw from the flame, I began to flirt with it.

A traditional stratagem of Japanese civil servants is to know just so much as is necessary to avert personal responsibility. There is no virtue attached to knowing more than can affect one's jurisdiction. The aim is not to shirk one's duty, but to depersonalize it. For all I know, this is a universal golden rule applicable to all bureaucrats everywhere. Whatever the truth or wisdom of this rule, I would have been better advised to persist in it with narrow Confucian rectitude, rather than attempt to subvert it by permitting myself any feelings of morbid curiosity.

There is little point in detailing the painstaking miseries, the penitential sweat expended over the next months on these recalcitrant Ministry accounts. I attached myself obstinately to the figures, like a limpet to an unyielding mass of rock. Finance is a dry, mystifying science. The mind-numbing authority of its figures can mislead one about the realities concealed in balance sheet abstractions. Financial secrets will only yield to patient scrutiny – and to a mind prepared to doubt the sacredness of numbers. What sort of mind is that? A writer's, of course. A writer whose conscience is attuned to believe nothing – a thorough-going skeptic and nihilist – should be the ideal detective to uncover the realities papered over by numerical alibis. The nocturnal writer, Yukio Mishima, came to the aid of the poor bewildered daylight Section Clerk, Hiraoka Kimitake, and together, like the psychic complementaries Hyde and Jekyll, they began to keep a subterranean bookkeeper's notebook into which they jotted every discrepancy in the records of financial transactions that might provide clues to a plot, a truly enigmatic plot, mined with sub-plots and intrigues designed to turn facts and figures into fictions.

So, this is a writer's account. Does such an account surrender objective credibility by admitting fiction? I have always believed that objectivity is perfectly useless in a writer's copy of reality, since one or the other – objectivity or reality – must perish in the attempt to render things as they are. A writer must proceed confidently in his will to transgress the laws of reality, so that existence in all its marvellous unreality can make an entertaining appearance. But how could I – a mere cipher, a subterranean bookkeeper occupying the vacant space, zero – perform a transgression of the laws constraining me to reality and thereby bestow on it the supreme existence of art?

An audacious idea had occurred to me of the means to accomplish this transformation of reality into art. It involved the convergence of two irreconcilable worlds, that of finance and of writing. Can any two worlds be more remote; two forms of calculation more alien and antagonistic to each other than finance and writing, than numbers and words? Surely, my idea was complete lunacy? And yet, the calculations of financial accounts and those of fiction share a common denominator. Both numbers and words are in the strictest sense, figurative; both are in themselves bloodless, but can make one bleed; and both *re*-compose the world. Whether it be in the mundane sphere of accountancy or in the loftier regions of mathematics, the aim of the calculator is never merely 'sums', but the recomposition of a new reality. So it is with writing.

To make myself sufficiently clear, let me put this another way, drawing once more on the incomparable worlds of business affairs and literature. There is an unscrupulous but accepted business practice known as factoring, a tactic by which one purchases at discount the bad debts owed to another, in order to profit by collecting them. This shady enterprise of factoring suddenly revealed itself to me as the very essence of capitalist finance, the real everyday means by which profits emerge from the unknown, appearing by magic from transactions of loss that disappear again in calculations of gain. Finance always works at someone else's expense; there is never a true balance, since profit and loss are always being carried forward, and progress in human affairs carries on unimpeded by this essential injustice which can never be redressed.

It became clear to me that I must profit from my own capacity to factor, in short, to turn the *numbers* of my loss into the *words* of my credit. What I mean is this. My indebtedness to Captain Lazar, G-2 Section and the Ministry of Finance amounted to the sources of my loss. How could I collect on these bad debts and turn them into the future resources of my profit? How could I earn my manumission from indentured slavery to them – to Captain Lazar, G-2 Section and the Ministry – and gain safe passage to the terrain of literature, where I wished to be? Self-evidently, my retirement into literature that I so fervently desired could only proceed by a withdrawal *now* on that future, by a withdrawal on the securities of my knowledge that my present unpromising circumstances offered at knock-down discount. My transformation from victim of finance to free enterprise speculator in the literary market depended on my extracting knowledge from these wretched Ministry accounts, sufficient to win my safe-conduct, to put it bluntly, by resort to blackmail, if need be.

Reckless, perhaps even improbable as my plan might now seem to anyone enjoying present-day affluence, I can assure you that it could only have formed in my mind as a direct result of the figures thrust under my nose day after day by Nishida, and submitted to Captain Lazar at the weekends. I am saying that my little individual conspiracy to recover my freedom was nothing other than a miniscule reflection, a tiny mirror fragment of the economic recovery being implemented on a national scale at the time of the Reverse Course. My own little plan of strategic recovery could not indeed have progressed at all unless it was generally the norm among thousands, and perhaps millions of other cases like mine, all of them copyists like me in the service of 'who-knows-what'. Never has clandestinity operated more broadly in the open. In this way, affluence appeared as if by magic from darkness, only to disappear again in the light of present-day beliefs which no longer bear resemblance to their origins.

I cannot pretend that things were anything as clear to me then as I have outlined them here. Certainly not on that early spring morning of 1948 when once more I submitted my accounts and myself to Captain Lazar's attention. The venue of our meetings had changed from G-2 Section HQ to Captain Lazar's personal suite at the Imperial Hotel. He would greet me at the door, sometimes in the nude or in a lewdly unfastened kimono, with the usual unseemly formula, 'Ah, breakfast in bed.'

A similar chaos reigned in Lazar's suite as in his office, but on a more stunning scale. I constantly marvelled at the disorderly cache of ancient

Haniwa figurines, Fujiwara pottery, dry-lacquer sculptures of Amida Buddhas of the Heian period, rarities such as Zo-ami Noh masks and Nara copper reliefs, Shinto altar gods, screen paintings and ivories – a precious trove of antiquities cast pell-mell as if in an auction salesroom. An inventory of Lazar's hoard would require several pages, eventually a catalogue, since the items seemed to increase at every one of my visits. I especially mourned for the collection of samurai armour, the fine specimens from the Kamakura and early Tokugawa epochs. I had seen ancestral mementos like these lost to pay for my grandparents' debts. And these articles seemed depressingly to turn up again here by sad magic in Lazar's suite, in a pillager's treasury – in one more looter's example of the general spoliation afflicting Japan. Lazar revealed to me that he had an exceptional broker, the Emperor's own uncle, Prince Higashikuni-no-miya-Naruhiko, former head of the Surrender cabinet, who had entered the antiques business. 'I get these trinkets at bargain prices from him, very often gratis in appreciation of my little favours to Prince Higashikuni's entourage.'

Confusion extended to the heaps of Imperial state papers, SCAP directives and other confidential documents in complete disarray on the floor and without regard for secrecy. This apparently casual debris aroused my angry suspicion. Lazar's bewildering largesse with secrets which had initially so impressed me, I now began to realize had been designed to mislead me. Nothing seriously privileged had been divulged. I reflected bitterly on this truth, for I now knew better that any real secrets were safely codified in the Ministry accounts outspread among the breakfast things.

Among these untidily stacked records of Imperial Japan's debacle, I noted a complete set of the Nuremberg Trial transcripts, a souvenir of Captain Lazar's former OSS tour of duty in Occupied Germany. Interspersed among the buff covers of the Trial's sinister records, I could see loud neon ones proclaiming comic books, Batman and Steve Canyon next to the US Chief Prosecutor, Mr Justice Robert H. Jackson's closing speech to the tribunal; Captain Marvel and Mandrake the Magician alongside the depositions of Auschwitz victims.

Bizarre, or shocking, according to one's prejudice, as this odd combination of tastes in reading might seem in a financial specialist, it was far less puzzling than another example of Captain Lazar's bookish preferences. Lazar was a voracious collector of mystical and occult treatises, these too in a haphazard babel which gave evidence of his astonishing magpie talent for languages: Shinto ritual manuals, the Kabbala and Secrets of the Torah in Hebrew, the Zohar in the original Aramaic, precious Chinese manuscripts on alchemy and incunabula of German works on that same subject (no doubt also pillaged), editions of Jacob Boehme, Swedenborg and Eliphas Levi.

What possible place could necromancy or the celestial mechanics of astrology have in a banker's calculations? I had wandered into the fox magician's burrow; a private cabinet of wonders that reduced the universe to a collector's whimsy.

My eyes strayed to the bed, itself another eccentric wonder, spread with a coverlet of sable skins originally come from the Soviet Union as plunder on the backs of Japanese soldiers. From what undisclosed stockpile of goods had these skins emerged to grace Captain Lazar's bed?

On a table littered with dregged coffee cups, toast crumbs and the hollow relics of soft-boiled eggs – among balance sheets that might suddenly yield a Dick Tracy comic book gluey with jam or a stomach-jolting photograph of corpses awaiting the crematoria at Dachau – I wrestled in the dark with Captain Lazar's revised figures for the trans-actions conducted by the Holding Company Liquidation Commission. The HCLC, a voluntary, self-appointed body of Japanese financial executives, had been approved by SCAP to proceed with the immediate liquidation of the holdings and assets of our big business combines, the so-called *zaibatsu* which included giants like Mitsui and Mitsubishi. Although approved in November 1945, the commission did not begin till the following summer to liquidate securities handed over to it by the designated *zaibatsu* and their subsidiaries: a clearance sale of divested holdings that was in theory and in the words of Occupation directive FEC-230 supposed to give 'decided purchase preference' to small entre-preneurs, new investors, cooperatives and trade unions. In theory – again, always in theory – the elimination of the *zaibatsu* monopolies and their massive aggregations of capital would put an end to Imperial Japan's undemocratic enterprises. In practice, however, ample time had elapsed in that year's time to permit the *zaibatsu*'s a self-elected liquida-tors, composed after all of unpurged Ministry of Finance bureaucrats, Bank of Japan officials and oligarch politicians, to manipulate the post-war inflation and currency situation to their advantage.

To make sense of the HCLC's transactions in sales of liquidated stock, government obligations and corporate debentures in the present, a reply would have to be found to a question which concerns the past: 'From whence does the credit now become available to purchase *zaibatsu* stocks in this national clearance sale?'

As I have already said, factoring can make a loss in the past disappear, and by unscrupulous magic take credit for it in the future. A sort of tactical factoring had taken place on a national scale, even before the ink dried on the terms of the Surrender agreement. What the HCLC records of present-day transactions did not and could not show involved precisely a loss in the past, a disappearance preparatory to the Surrender: an officially sanctioned looting and stockpiling of bullion and platinum, industrial utilities and raw materials, food and other goods – no doubt, including Captain Lazar's portion of sable skins – a rumoured 10 billion dollars' worth of materials which had melted away without trace until 1947. Loss seemed indeed to be the government's goal in the feverish last months before Surrender, a deliberate policy of sinking itself into massive deficit. Nationalizations of industries, expedited at a Blitzkrieg tempo, amounted to state insurance for private *zaibatsu* enterprises. With apparent irresponsibility, the government ran itself further into debt by hastening its surrender payments on state bonds, insurances, military and civil pensions which it financed by a 40% increase in the money supply. A pathological urgency to strip itself of its assets had apparently seized the government, a spendthrift frenzy which in reality meant that the state was amortizing itself by converting a great number of its citizens into trustees of those assets – temporary asset-holders whom it immediately wiped out by inflationary price rises of 295%.

So, the question imposes itself: with an official stock exchange forbidden by SCAP authorities till 1949 – with uncontrolled inflation and a currency of questionable value – with wartime emergency laws in the economic sphere unrepealed by SCAP which left the Japanese government entirely responsible for control over wages, prices of essential commodities, a rationing programme, regulation of the money supply and currency – where did purchase of the HCLC shares of stock figured in hundreds of millions come from?

Isn't there another question I overlook? Where is the fox magician inhabitant of this lair? Where is Captain Lazar?

Captain Lazar indulges in a 'backbone wind', a Japanese-style bath in water hot enough to scald lobsters. Our breakfast accountancy has already once been interrupted by a sexual excursus. The door of the bathroom stands open, but Lazar cannot see me. I scribble his corrections of the HCLC figures quickly into my own notebook, though unable yet to understand the real significance of Captain Lazar's double entries.

He lolls confidently in gold bath-salt tinctured water, immersed in the perusal of a scholarly book on his favourite poet, Dante. He reads passages aloud to me from Francesco de Sanctis' commentary on Italy's divine poet. 'Listen to this, Kochan,' Lazar calls, with irritating familiarity employing the diminutive of my name. 'Did you know that Dante classified some words as combed and smooth, others as hairy and bristling? Hairy ones are monosyllabic interjections, like *si, no, me, te*. Combed ones are trisyllabic, unaspirated and which quit the lips most sweetly, *amore, donne, salute*. I am struck by the number of compact monosyllables in Dante's verse, which ought to interest someone like you, in love with the syntactical compactness of classical Sino-Japanese writing.'

'I'm sorry, Captain Lazar-*san*, but I do not read Italian.'

'Sam, goddamit, *Sam*. I'm tired of hearing myself called razor all the time.'

'Yes sir, Sam.'

My concern was not with Dante's combed or uncombed syllables, but with my own decipherment of other dishevelled syllables – those which appeared as aliases in the HCLC accounts. Changes of name for professional or social reasons are traditional and routinely commonplace in Japan, but very confusing to foreigners. I have myself undergone the change in professing the name 'Yukio Mishima'. This accepted custom was now being systematically exploited by *zaibatsu* members and their appointed trustees for illicit traffic in HCLC stocks. I jotted down these falsified names too, with the intention of tracing their true owners.

'Have you heard of Dante's tactic of the "renunciative metaphor"?'

'No, Sam, I haven't. But it seems to describe my situation.'

'You bet your life it does,' Sam replied. And he proceeds in his translation of de Sanctis. 'Dante perfected a rhetorical tactic first deployed by orators in Roman times, Cicero chiefly among others, which can be defined as the renunciative metaphor. The device is simple. A description of something phenomenal is achieved by proclaiming defeat in one's ability to describe it. Dante resorts to this stratagem. By confessing that his "inspiration fails him", or by other tactical admissions of despair in his talent, Dante accomplishes the opposite of retreat before the object which oppresses his vision. He succeeds instead in bringing an object of transcendental ineffability closer to us, makes it appear familiar, real and placed upon a classical pedestal of limpid visibility. What do you think of that, Kochan?'

'I think it describes a form of surrender well-known to us.'

I could not hear Sam's laughter, which would anyway be silent. 'Are you referring to the Emperor's renunciative metaphor of non-Divinity?'

'We are not encouraged to have opinions about His Majesty.'

Sam grunted and slammed his book shut. He climbed out of the bath. I hurried to make further notes on Bank of Japan records from the winter of 1946 which – if I hadn't known Captain Lazar's foxiness better – I would think he had carelessly forgotten on the table after consulting them earlier that morning.

These were records of important transactions in stock purchases drawn against blocked Bank of Japan accounts by clients under names that were almost certainly falsified. Here was another decisive clue to the enigma of purchase power at a time of apparent non-existent funds.

In February 1946, the government had ordered an emergency block on all bank deposits, which limited cash withdrawals to fixed living expenses for each household. In March, a new yen currency was introduced. All currency notes in circulation, upwards of 5 yen, not deposited with monetary institutions ceased being legal tender. At the same time, however, the government sanctioned payments of capital increases out of blocked accounts and the use of blocked accounts for the acquisition of stocks which could then be sold for the new yen. Speculation on the new yen brought inflationary misery to society, but provided a great stimulus to stock trading. The disguised accounts of *zaibatsu* trustees began to show a bonanza recuperation of securities, just as the HCLC first came into operation.

Sam Lazar approached me, naked, the immaculate pallor of his skin splotched vermilion by the fearsome temperature of his bath. His cleanliness was spoilt by one of Major General Willoughby's large, turd-like cigars stuck in his mouth. He leaned over me, and the six-pointed Star of David drooping from the chain round his neck fell before my eyes like an occult talisman. 'I see you're taking an interest in ancient history,' he commented, his feral green eyes seeing right through me, as he shut the Bank of Japan file. 'If your appetite for financial chicanery has become so morbidly keen, I would advise you to investigate the transactions in real estate.'

Was this another of Lazar's misleadingly frank indiscretions? The expression in his eyes said not, blazing merrily with an intensity of anger that baffled me. That incomprehensible anger – if it was anger – invited me to pose a question that I would never have dared to ask until now. 'It is not my place to wonder, Sam, but there is something I find very puzzling. The figures that I submit for your examination –'

'– for my revision,' he interrupted.

'– quite so, revision. These same revised figures of last week, or last month, seem to turn up again for further revision. I wonder if these retrospective adjustments mean that completed transactions in the past are changing value.'

I had prudently optioned the question which I really had in mind: what – or whose – purpose did Lazar's revisions serve? Did these figures that I carried as unofficial postman – submitted, revised and resubmitted – really constitute a form of communication between SCAP and a former Imperial administration with *zaibatsu* interests to protect?

The fire in Lazar's eyes abated; or dulled. 'After all this time, a question of such naive proportions does not merit a reply.' He turned his back on me and strolled to the open window.

Spring warmth announced the irony of another indecently hot, putrescent summer, after another winter in a series of exceptionally cold ones since 1945 which had visited hardship and death on the homeless people in unheated shanties and parks of Tokyo. The cherry blossom season was over. Fallen petals in clusters of decayed pink and white, like ribbons of entrails, stirred in the gutters under the trailing hem of a southerly breeze.

Lazar gazed out of the window. He scratched one of his meagre, chicken-fleshed buttocks. The itch of self-dislike can grow into an eczema of the soul. I contemplated a pair of buttocks that I would be called on again to penetrate. The indecency had nothing to do with the nature of sodomy. Ignorance is a viler and more shameful pollution than a mere sterile form of intercourse. The humiliating effects of ignorance on the psychic foundations of the will are far more grave than the inconsequential abuse of the anus.

'Come over here,' Lazar said, 'and see the answer for yourself.'

Through the window, I saw the moated vastness of the Imperial Palace, a gloomy, impassive splendour, with the broccoli tips of cryptomeria visible above the fortress walls. This was the former Yedo Castle of the ruling Shoguns. Lazar craned his neck in the direction of the old Sakurada Gate of Yedo Castle, once upon a time the stately entrance of great *daimyo* feudal lords in liege to the omnipotent Shoguns, a sight now rendered less gracious by its proximity to everyday traffic, a delapidated stream of prosaic trams, lorries and cars. Lazar pointed to the the Sakurada Gate. 'That's the very spot where the Shogun's counsellor, Ii Naosuke, was assassinated in 1860 for authorizing the opening of Japan to Occidental trade.'

'It happened in the snow, that incident.'

'Ii Naosuke's treaty with the Westerners led directly to the Shogunate's fall eight years later and the restoration of the Emperor, isn't that right?'

'Yes, the Meiji Restoration of 1868.'

'And the Meiji Emperor moved from his ancient residence in Kyoto to this one, the Shoguns' Yedo Castle, also right?'

'Also right.'

'One might say that in a sense Kyoto is the Emperor's real home.'

'In a sense, one might.' What was Lazar getting at?

'Not one bomb was ever dropped on Kyoto, though it was no less vulnerable to air attacks than Tokyo or Hiroshima or Nagasaki.'

'We are told Kyoto was spared because it houses so many irreplaceable antiquities, including the tombs of past Emperors.'

'Horseshit, boy. Do you think we're a bunch of benign museum curators? Do you imagine that our bombardiers who have an enviable record in precision targeting *missed* the Imperial Palace when they took out most of Tokyo? On the evening of 25th May 1945, these clinically precise flyers brought the lesson of incendiary bombing home to His Imperial Majesty himself, when they levelled the grand villas of the aristocracy to ashes right next to the Palace walls. And that night too, the ceremonial Meiji Outer Palace burned to the ground. That was our warning to the Emperor, and if that failed – well, Henry Stimson's policy of easing up on B-29 raids had reserved a number of unblemished urban targets for spectacular A-bomb demonstrations, Kyoto foremost among them. Did you know that, Kochan?'

'No, Sam, I didn't.'

Lazar gazed at the Imperial Palace with a real estate speculator's eye. 'How many acres does the Emperor enjoy in seclusion?'

'I don't know, Sam.'

'Two hundred and forty, by God. Just imagine, all that wasted acreage at the very heart of Tokyo, a residence inhabited by an Emperor who is never seen, which is to say, *by no one knows who*. Look at it; it's like one of those sterile maria on the face of the moon, a Sea of Tranquillity.'

'Is it really any different than the Vatican, another Forbidden City within a city?'

'A city of God?'

'Formerly a god, since the Emperor officially declared himself *ningen*, human, two years ago on New Year's Day 1946.'

'Yes, *ningen*. Human all-too-human. And so now the entire city has to circle in perpetual detour round a void, an evaporated notion of divinity. A traffic nuisance. Why not demolish all of it for real estate development? I would. I'd only leave place for one monument – a tomb reserved for General Douglas MacArthur, Japan's last Shogun.'

'And who would be the foolhardy Ii Naosuke to authorize this real estate deal for the last Shogun?'

Lazar speculated and meanwhile toyed with his penis in blissful, polymorphous perverse oblivion. 'Does my irreverence towards the Voice of the Crane⋆ shock you?' Mute laughter.

'I pledged allegiance to His Majesty, Sam.'

'So did the entire nation. Just think of it as a worthless Imperial-issue war bond. But you can still cash in on the past value of the Emperor's bond. You're a writer with ambition. Why don't you write about him?'

'*Him*?' I laughed. 'That's as unlikely a proposition as your real estate dream. You should know better, Sam. No one refers to "him". Our language is reluctant to use even the most ordinary personal pronouns, it shuns them, and that is the mystery of its richness and poverty. And at the heart of this mystery? – *him*, as you say, *no one knows who* – one Voice among one thousand cranes, the Jewel Voice, the One who never speaks personally either as We, I or He, but as *chin*, the ancient Chinese Imperial character for "moon speaking to heaven". Our entire nation is composed of non-existent pronouns all referring to a central mystery, the existence of *no one knows who*, the Unnameable "I". You cannot seriously expect me to name the Unnameable in a novel.'

'The Unnameable – like the Jewish god Yahweh. God in the Ark of the Covenant, an empty cube of night carried on the brawny backs of Israelites lost in the desert.'

'There was something inside the Ark.'

'Nothing – only the testimony of a divine contract.'

⋆ One of the Emperor's many honorific titles.

'We don't even have a divine contract, only a human Emperor who declares himself our constitutional sovereign by ties of mutual trust and affection.'

'Don't go making the same mistake as simple country folk who believe the Emperor was forced to resign his divinity at gunpoint by MacArthur. The Emperor never cared a pig's arse for divinity. He would sacrifice it again, so long as he retained real secret power.'

'What power?'

Lazar merely glanced at the accounts on the breakfast table.

'Money is not a sacred power,' I objected. 'Simple country people may cling to a bygone notion of divinity, but cynics in Tokyo can see the Emperor has no clothes, he is simply "Mr Ah so".'

'You hold the Emperor responsible for the war?'

'Perhaps I hold him responsible for something worse, the peace. The consciousness of my generation was formed by a willingness to die. We were accustomed to the slogan of No Surrender, *ichioku gyokusai*, Death to the Hundred Million. We woke up one morning and the slogan had changed – *ichioku so-zange* – One Hundred Million Repent.'

'A slight change of characters,' Lazar punned. 'Would you have preferred Death to the Hundred Million?'

'Does it matter what I prefer? Is it better to perish or live a miserable zombie existence? The choice has been made.'

A deep, inadmissable resentment smouldered in my heart. I felt betrayed by my own words of disloyalty; torn by anger at the unrequited love I still cherished for the romantic principle of divinity, for an Emperor who had left us in a condition forsaken by death.

'You met the Emperor in person once, didn't you?'

'Yes, once. In 1944, when he awarded me a silver watch at my graduation from the Peers' School.'

'Were you impressed by him?'

'He didn't move a muscle for three hours during the ceremony.'

'Being stationary is a virtue of writers, not of kings.'

'Nietzsche remarked that a sedentary occupation is the sure proof of a scoundrel.'

'Then, what a pair of scoundrels we must make, hey? and *this* – what about this – the Emperor Waltz?'

I laughed in spite of myself as stark naked Sam aped the 'Imperial shuffle', the Emperor's curious shambling simian gait, the effect of a congenital motor defect.

'How can you possibly revere someone as a divinity who walks like that?'

'The man's personal faults or physical handicaps do not matter, only his connection to the divine.'

'But he's broken that connection.'

'Yes.'

'*Hasn't* he?'

'Yes, Sam.'

He lit another of Willoughby's foul cigars, adjusted his pince-nez eyeglasses, and plunged back into the accounts. I marvelled at the way Sam transformed himself into a calculating machine. A stream of numbers flowed without cease or correction from his pen in tightly knotted rows. (So too, in the dead of night, a seamless textile of words had to spill from me at unchecked speed, not as the product of inspiration, but from the spirit-killing demands of necessity.)

Sam calculated his revisions of the HCLC accounts from another ledger, as if from a book of magical formulae. It occurred to me that we were desperado necromancers, not bankers; that between us we were bringing a financial cadaver back to life.

Sam's earlier irreverent tirade against the Emperor gave me pause. I wondered if all these calculations did not in fact conceal a very particular non-presence, a black hole of immense but occult force. Just as a stone cast into a lake disappears entirely, but causes ripples of increasing dimension to radiate from its disappearance, so too did the Emperor vanish in these accounts.

Without a break in his pace, Sam asked, 'How are you getting on with your Section Chief Nishida?'

'That mummified little ghoul treats me with a formality that one reserves for competitors or those regarded with the utmost suspicion.'

'Evidence of respect in either case.'

'Respect? My situation at the Bureau is to say the least invidious. Nishida's chilling little smiles openly broadcast to all my shameful activities. Fortunately, my colleagues mistranslate Nishida's irony as a sure sign of my advancement. In the simple arithmetic of bureaucratic convention, I am assumed exceptionally well-connected and therefore guaranteed swift promotion.'

'That sounds reasonable to me.'

It was not at all reasonable. To disguise my unease, I began to cultivate a flamboyant character, a gruff nonchalance that would allow me to decline my colleagues' invitations to drinks after office hours without offence. I strived to give them the conviction that my weekday evenings were devoted to extramural office toil and my weekends pledged to carousel with the aristocratic Peers' School set. In short, my conduct had become unbearably clownish.

'Be a good fellow and put on those records, will you?' Sam pointed with his pen to an album on the phonograph.

Our monotonous routine was now graced by Richard Strauss's *Der Rosenkavalier*, a 1944 Bavarian State Opera recording directed by Clemens Krauss, featuring Viorica Ursuleac as the Marschallin and

Georgine von Milinkovic as Octavian. Strauss's rococo swirls and tone clusters – Mozart rendered in Viennese whipped cream – added a curiously proper dessert to our bourgeois menu of accountancy.

'Do you ever think of suicide?' Lazar casually inquired.

'I don't think of impossibilities.'

'Not entirely true, Kochan. I see you've just written a little essay in your leisure, "A Lethal Weapon for the Seriously Wounded".'

Even my nocturnal writings were submitted to Captain Lazar's investigation. I burned with exasperated shame to think of my privacy violated like this. And now, Lazar's intrusion extended even to what I should write, going so far as to propose the Emperor as fit subject matter. He wanted to manipulate my tongue itself, to bind it in puppet-strings, to weigh it down with the leaden silence of humiliation.

'I find the conclusion of your essay puzzling. You say that suicide is impossible for this post-war generation, these freak sideshow performers toughened by cynicism. Yours is – I quote – "the plight of a virtual immortal for whom suicide will never be possible."'

'What's so puzzling? I wanted to prove that suicide is logically impossible for us today.'

'Whom did you write this essay for?'

'You know very well – for *Ningen* magazine.'

'Of course, an aptly named magazine for a post-Surrender, born-again writer. *Ningen*. Very, very human. No, I don't mean for what magazine, but for *whom*? Or against whom?'

Lazar stared at me over the rim of his pince-nez. Those myopic, brilliantly indifferent green eyes mesmerized me into an answer. 'I had Osamu Dazai in mind.'

'Ah yes, your rival. The writer who flirts ineffectually with suicide.' Lazar smiled. 'On occasion, I think it would have been more interesting if Japan had won the war. Don't you agree?'

'What an extraordinary notion for an American army officer.'

'A banker. But surely the notion isn't unfamiliar to you? Wasn't it your own *Roman-ha*★ Japanists who expressed a similar irony – that it would be perhaps more interesting if Germany won the war?'

'An irony, because stated when defeat looked certain. Mass annihilation, not victory was their aim.'

'I am passably aware of *Roman-ha* philosophy – Karl Marx and Shinto, Goethe's *Faust* and Manchurian conquest. A school of thought into which you were enlisted by your teacher, Hasuda Zenmei – died in the garrison at Baharu Johor, Malaya, 1945 – shot his commanding officer for accepting Surrender and then himself. Am I right?'

'He was a friend, not my teacher.'

★ The Romantics, a 1930s' school of ultra-nationalist intellectuals.

'Very well, a friend. A literary patron, one who prefaced your first book of stories with remarkable claims – that "at nineteen, Mishima is a youthful version of ourselves – a jewel, an heir to Japan's everlasting history – from ourselves he is born" etcetera. Was this Hasuda's prophetic last instructions to you before he went to seek death in Malaya? Was it he who instructed you to refuse the "lethal weapon" of suicide, to stay alive and polish the jewel of romantic literature?'

'Despite all of Hasuda-*san*'s flattering remarks, where am I? Who am I? An unknown writer.'

'Nonsense. You are favoured by the exemplary patronage of *Ningen*'s editor, Kawabata Yasunari, one of the country's foremost writers, and by other influential chieftains of the literary clique who are securing your career by publishing your stories –' Lazar slapped the accounts with the flat of his palm '– and why not, since you can see with your own eyes how much they have in the bank – or how much they *shouldn't* have.'

'That's entirely unjust,' I exclaimed, my voice rising in a soprano quaver, like Octavian's in *Der Rosenkavalier*. 'I would never use blackmail to advance my career.'

'You'd be a damn silly fool not to,' Lazar shrugged, his eyes fastening again to the numbers. 'You're beginning to outlive your usefulness.'

'That sounds like a threat, Sam.'

'Not a threat, a fact. By the end of this year, there won't be any record left of what we're doing here.'

'These figures will be destroyed?'

'Sort of. Like history consuming itself in the making. You dimwit – *we* are the ones in the process of destroying these frigging accounts, don't you see?'

I didn't see. Lazar sighed. 'What are you really after, Kochan?'

'To write.'

'*Wozu Dichter in dürftiger Zeit?*' Sam quoted Friedrich Hölderlin – Why be a poet in spiritless times? A thoroughly apt question to which I had no answer.

'I would like to taste blood, Sam. It is my fate merely to spill ink.'

'Well you'd better hustle. Time is short. I'll draw you a picture of what exactly is going to happen.' On a blank sheet of paper, he drew a triangle. 'You're dead keen to know what we're doing? Here's what it should look like in a year's time. A triangle. Let's start at point *one* of this triangle. What is it Japan lacks which could rehabilitate its industries? Raw materials. Our own US investors are going to supply you with surplus raw materials. And what funds have you got to pay for that? Apparently none, except for the long term credit available at point *two* of our triangle – the liquidated securities of the *zaibatsu* combines, here, in our HCLC accounts. They aren't much good to anyone in that shape, unless reconsolidated. As you know, the HCLC chose to evaluate stock value by paid-up capital rather than assets, a measure that would normally be disadvantageous to the seller, but not to a buyer enabled to purchase with a new yen currency of questionable value. And – point *three* – who's the buyer? Reconstituted *zaibatsu* enterprises who will benefit from US capital investment tie-ins: Toshiba with General Electric, Mitsubishi Electric with Westinghouse, Mitsui with American Can, Furukawa Rubber with Goodrich, Mitsubishi Petroleum with Associated Oil, and so on. O.k., so the triangle is in place. What's next? We are entering a world-wide recession, and SCAP is poised to remove price floors on Japanese exports. Let's go over the triangle again. *One*: the US sells you raw material, say, surplus cotton – which *two*: is partly financed by a *zaibatsu* tie-in, or US financial institution, or an oil company bank – which *three*: you manufacture cheap into textiles and sell at an undercut price to a South East Asian country, from which – round *one* again – the US buys more raw materials, tin, for instance, which finances the tin producer's import dependence on Japanese manufactured goods – and so on and so on. War in Korea looks inevitable. It will greatly speed up Japan's recovery as a US secured factory in the Far East.'

Our double entry diet of balance sheets and *Der Rosenkavalier* had succeeded to unhinge Lazar's maniacal lechery. In a fury of crazed geometry, he now wished his hindquarters bisected by an iron-clad priapic theorem. And so, to fulfill his erotic Euclidean fantasy, he assists in harnessing my torso and thighs to plates of aesthetically pleasing samurai armour. Appropriately enough, he has chosen red-lacquered armour, the colour of waxen faded roses. It strikes cold on my flesh where the leather inner casing has worn away to the patina gleam of copper. This is ceremonial toy armour incapable of deflecting a sword or arrow or a bullet from the gun-sticks introduced by the Portuguese *nambanjin* seafarers, 'barbarians from the south', who brought miraculous things in the holds of their caravels, canon and harquebus, Jesuit mission-aries, Holy Eucharist and sponge cake, and the first blacks ever seen until masses of GI ones reappeared with MacArthur. The *nambanjin* art of the Portuguese has influenced the style of my armour, which is not in the samurai's plainer barrel shape, but moulded into clenched Herculean pectorals on the breastplate, with side latchworks of projecting ribs above a muscled epigastrium, and a back of embossed omoplates cleft by a spinal indentation: a style of armour itself reminiscent of Imperial Rome, of bronze carapaced centurions in command of invincible legions.

The fit is uncanny, Lazar says, butter-fingered with excitement as he hitches up my shoulder straps. The original samurai owner of this rosy-shelled integument was probably of normal size for his times – and I am small.

I look at myself in the mirror. This armour is proof that my 17th century predecessor had grown effeminate in the court of the omnipotent Tokugawa Shoguns. I am costumed in the ceremonial tuxedo of a *daimyo* warlord, worn once yearly on those formal occasions when he would be forced to attend the Shogun's court at Yedo. The sagacious Shoguns had instituted a hostage system, under which the *daimyo* lords were compelled to leave their wives and children permanently in Yedo, a costly obligation which promoted luxury, ostentation and indebtedness. Potentially rebellious *daimyo*, many of them already converts to Christianity, provided with firearms by foreigners and enriched by overseas trade threatened a scenario that the Shoguns could not possibly tolerate. And so, in 1639, the third Shogun, Tokugawa Iemitsu, proclaimed the Edict of Seclusion, *sakoku*, literally 'closed country', by which he expelled the barbarians and confined Japan to strict quarantine for over two hundred years – until Pinkerton arrived to dishonour Madame Butterfly – sealed, entombed, as surely as I am in the armour that Lazar has now completely buckled shut.

My thoughts on the former Rose Cavalier of two hundred years ago have a certain dire legitimacy in my situation. I too am reduced to the caricature of a samurai, defiled and pornographic. I too am a hostage, presently of the Shogun MacArthur who has once again ordered *sakoku* in his reign, allowing no visitors into the country and no Japanese out.

Finally outfitted to his pleasure, Lazar says, 'You look like a lobster with a hard on,' as he tests the temper of my stiffness with a blacksmith's expert grip.

Although my rose chrysalis clings snugly to my flesh, and friction between them incubates my perspiration, I lose all sense of my body's existence. I feel the armour cocoons an empty hollow. My coital exertions take place in a vacuum, without pleasure or displeasure, as though my proboscis jammed in Sam's anus were narcotically dissociated from me.

Through the visor slits of my helmet, a Portuguese-style pointed casque, I can see the exposed teeth, of a matchmaker, the marriage broker of big business alliances, his fingers clawing at the sable skin bedspread. His cries of delight or pain strike hollow on my helmet. I see a triangle, an occult shape formed at the base by two sexually coupled bodies, and at the apex, a divine non-presence – *no one knows who*.

Sam Lazar's triangle had demonstrated a financial theorem. Once again he had misled me with the eroticism of numbers, which kept the real substance of their meaning hidden from me. I understood the real common denominator that numbers and words share. Eroticism. The economy of eroticism for its true connoisseur is not the vulgar sum of coitus, but rather the dissection of an object of desire, in order to recompose reality according to an imaginary model. Eroticism is just another means of factoring the bad debts of life.

Our second congress of the morning dredges the semen out of me like burning granules of sand. Lazar pulls away from me. The passage of his buttocks over the bed leaves a snail's lustrous track, a glistening slime of haemmorhoidal ointment, semen and blood on the sable skins. He goes to turn the platters of *Der Rosenkavalier*. His foot strikes against a book on the floor, which he picks up and opens. A copy of the Zohar, and he reads aloud from it: 'Who is the beautiful virgin who has no eyes? and a body concealed, yet revealed – concealed in the daytime, revealed in the morning? – and is bedecked with ornaments which are not?'

I begin to unfasten the armour. 'Hold on there, chum,' Lazar calls. 'I'm going to take some pictures.' He stations me in front of a ponderous Hasselblad camera on a tripod, equipped with a news photographer's flash at the side, like a big icecream scoop. He fetches me a samurai sword to hold, a black-and-white chequered handle and a yard-long razor displaying a watered-silk tempered pattern on the steel, the most dangerous blade ever forged by man. 'Be careful with that. It's a 16th century sword made by the master craftsman Seki no Magoroku.'

I take up the poses that Lazar commands, a ridiculous weedy invalid, genitalia exposed, posturing with a killer's sword. 'Just imagine if your Section Chief Nishida ever saw these photos,' Lazar cruelly speculates. 'Or your parents.'

I am reduced to a pornographic exhibit under the Hasselblad's clinical eye. It reflects the parody of a classically muscled body, a rose lobster shell cavity with no one inside.

I am seized by the eerie, unnerving truth of my confinement. I find myself in the condition of reverse course to the *onnagata*, the transvestite actor who plays exclusively female roles in Kabuki theatre. In my case, an impersonated female inhabits the inner life of a male imposter whose natural inclinations to virility had long since atrophied. Outwardly exiled as a man, I had no other option but to play a masculine role to which I had never sincerely been apprenticed. I am compelled to exaggerate every effort of this poor awkward foreigner. Walled up inside me, the impersonated female gazes reluctantly, skeptically into the mirror which reflects the travestied parody of a man. She is restricted to onlooker, unable or unwilling to help correct the exiled bungler's indexterity.

How can I ever expel the woman inside me? How can I reverse the permanently inverted, and by what possible means evict her from the inside out? I am trying to imagine an unimaginable act of self-origination.

I want a different body, a body transformed beyond recognition.

Lazar's caprice, on that inglorious morning, planted the seed crystals of my future metamorphosis that would blossom in the dark of my blood, in the secret longings of my heart, to ripen one day into factual muscles on the sun-enlightened surface of my body.

Meanwhile, I would have to suffer the dark larval stage of my evolution, but, alas, with no foretaste of my future liberation. The fact is, however, that liberation can never truly occur from such evil necessity. The butterfly that must at last emerge will have wings bloodstained with the memories of its captivity.

Sam Lazar peers over my shoulder into the mirror as he helps unbuckle my travestied costume. That eerie fox's head, appearing from behind me, seems for a moment to spout from my armour. 'I don't know why on earth I like you,' he says. 'You are so repellantly ugly.'

He strolls up and down the room, his chin grasped in one hand, the other at rest on his hip, in the pose of a contemplative satyr. 'I've given serious thought to your situation, Kochan,' he announces. 'And I think I've found the solution.'

'Thank you, Sam.'

'Spare me the ironical tone. This is an entirely serious business. I've found the ideal solution for an exceptional breed of man like you, a eugenic solution, so to speak.'

'Which is?'

'Marriage.'

'Marriage, for *me*?' I could not resist laughing, helplessly, at the same time conscious of a dawning peril.

'The mystic, Rabbi Simeon, states in the Zohar that it behooves a man to be both male and female, always, so that his faith in the Divine Presence may never leave him. Why is this? Because, as Rabbi Simeon observes, male and female were already conceived as one in the Divine syllables of creation, Adam, *alef, daled* and *mem* and the female was sealed in his side, not in a rib taken from him, and certainly not Eve, but the first woman, Lilith, who is Adam's own phallic presence.'

'This is all very well, Sam, but are you married yourself?'

'Naturally.'

'But you're a —'

'— a dyed in the wool sodomite? A homosexual? I much prefer the endearingly old-fashioned term André Gide uses — uranist — I am a son of the revolutionary planet Uranus, discovered by Herschel at the time of revolutions in America and France. I am related to the birth of democracy in its most radical, sanguine and original form, a democracy which rejects the collective platitude of the average man, but one which, as Nietzsche desired, begins with the enigmatical exception.'

'I don't believe you.'

'What, about Uranus?'

'No, that you're married.'

'Because of my uranist indulgences? You fail dismally in imagination. The mystic teachings of the Zohar also state that a man on a journey is in a condition of greatest honour, because the Divine Presence journeys with him. A travelling man, however, risks imperfection by being deprived of union with the female, a lack which threatens to break off the holy union the Divine Presence itself. I am on a journey. My faith in the Presence is unshakable, because I do not permit the female within me to lack union. When my journey is done and I am back again with my earthly wife, I do as the Zohar prescribes, I go into her and rejoice her.'

'Sometimes I think you're plain crazy, Sam. First you tell me Nazi Germany's victory might perhaps have been more "interesting", and this in spite of your racial antecedents.'

'Do not commit the vulgar error of equating a Jew with the Jewish race. I speak of an exceptional breed of man, those in whom the characteristics of Aryan or Semitic or even Nipponese blood are irrelevant. For such as us, Kochan, salvation can only be morally individual.'

'And yet you propose the "eugenic solution" of marriage to me? This is entirely illogical.'

'Not in the least. For every man, no matter how inwardly feminine, there is a female who includes his male counterpart within her. Unless you find such a balance of male and female, a third element of the triangle, the Divine Presence, will forever elude you, and you will exist as half a man more dead than alive.'

'Then I'm doomed to a half life. You don't realize that the very word itself, "woman", arouses less sensation in me than pencil or automobile or shovel. Women are all the same to me, all completely without sensual content.'

'Baloney. I am willing to bet that your experience of women has been restricted to a few household ones, your mother, sister, some female relatives, from which you falsely deduce that all women are alike.'

'No so. My grandmother was a domineering, virile woman; whereas my mother exemplified the purely feminine. No two women in my life could have been more unlike.'

'Are you sure? Didn't they convince you of their similarity by devoting themselves obsessively to you? The woman you need will have to offer an intimacy that challenges the only one you've known so far, the domestic routine of service.'

'You know our customs. I could never marry according to my wishes without the consent of my parents.'

'And that's precisely the danger you face. One day, your parents will coerce you into an arranged marriage. An arranged marriage is an evil because it disregards the imbalances of male and female components in partners matched against their natural inclinations. It violates the law of democratic choice between complementary poles of attraction across the range of sexual indeterminacy, and such a mercenary marriage of convenience is worse than prostitution in which at least there is some little trace of choice. Love is the expression of eugenic free enterprise which breeds an improved species.'

'Illogical again. You condemn arranged marriages, and yet you want to arrange one for me?'

'I will certainly not arrange anything unsuitable to your requirements.'

I knew from experience that Captain Lazar's whimsies had better be taken seriously. This was no joke.

'Can you show me a picture of your wife?'

'Of course, but I'll do even better than that. I'll let you pick her out for yourself from a number of photographs of women who might all seem quite similar to you – or not. It is a well-known law that what one individual considers beautiful in the opposite sex is relative, and my chosen partner might only seem aesthetically indifferent to you, or downright ugly. Aesthetics does not deal with the grades of beauty, but merely with a conception of beauty from which the sexual factor has been eliminated.'

Lazar now produced a leather-bound album of photographs for my inspection. 'This is a collection of women who display some definite but varying proportion of femininity that responds to my sexual taste. Select the one that seems to you, by an educated guess, to correspond best to my own choice, and you will have found my wife – just as I could choose one that I would expect you to think the most beautiful, and hence, sexually compatible.'

I glanced at first reluctantly through the album, as though I were being forced myself to choose a wife from a geisha appointment book of prints. I saw the portraits of some dozen or so women, nude or in the act of undressing, and posed without apparent aesthetic intention. 'The photographs are of poor quality,' I said. Lazar nodded, staring at me with a strange eagerness in his eyes. I compelled myself to look for his wife, in despair of any success.

His choice of women did seem to me inscrutably uniform, but of a physical type that I would never have imagined appealing to him. These females were indubitably feminine – though I recognized little 'varying proportion' of it in Lazar's gallery – women generous in their excess of flesh, broad of rump, with avoirdupois pouches below sunken belly-buttons and thighs chicken-poxed with dimples. My first impression of fat was mistaken. These were simply female bodies in which the aesthetic prejudice could not take comfort. The ideal of aesthetically proportioned flesh is itself oppressively changeable and conditioned by fashions in which a variable preponderance of the male or female component will dictate beauty.

As I looked more critically at these figures, I began to see the virile Amazonic element in some more than in others, despite any distracting over-ripeness or scanty lacks in their proportions. In these cases, my eye was drawn more strongly to the fluted drapery of a pair of thighs, to the shaded triangle of a crotch which conceals (for me) the useless pottery of the vagina, the parenthesis of my total disinterest, and yet which now gave me an uneasy sense of exposure.

My unease led me to perceive a vulnerability that conveyed distress, explained by the women's unnatural condition of nudity. At last I understood what the sadness in all their faces plainly exposed. They did not *want* to be seen naked like this. They were being forced into nakedness, not as models but as victims of a criminal purpose. I recognized what these photographs illustrated. These figures had been carefully isolated from their original group contexts and enlarged into single portraits. I remembered the photographs that Lazar had shown me, taken by *Einsatzgruppen* extermination squads, of people undressing and lining up for execution, men and women both, destined for mass graves in the countryside of Eastern Europe or the gas chambers of death camps.

'This is monstrous,' I protested, more than ever convinced that Lazar was pathologically unhinged.

'Have you found my wife yet?' Lazar spoke in a hoarse voice, as though his throat had gone dry with anticipation, and he gazed steadily at me with that same peculiar beseeching eagerness.

For a chilling moment, I felt sure that Captain Lazar's wife had perished in the Holocaust, and these photographs were grotesque curios of his search for her.

'Go on, keep looking for her.'

I went on reviewing the photographs as he asked, until I finally settled on one. Why this particular one, I cannot say for certain, except that it seemed the only photograph of a solo figure not originally part of a group. Unless I was wrong and she faced individual execution against the blank wall showing behind her. She too was perhaps another dead woman. Was there anything else to convince me that this was the picture of Captain Lazar's true, living wife? Nothing, only a woman in the pose of Eve banished from Paradise, her arms raised, trying to shield her breasts and genitalia from the prodding camera; the flank of her thigh scalloped by shadowy muscles as she turns reluctantly to face her photographer.

'Yes, that's her. Well done.' Lazar relaxes into a smile. He rekindles the spent cigar stuck in his mouth. 'Do you find her handsome?'

'There is certainly an Amazonic quality to appreciate. What is her name?'

'Jael. At least, that's her code name. Do you know the Biblical story of Jael, Judges, chapter four, verses seventeen etcetera?'

'I've read the Bible, Sam.'

'Good, then tell me.'

'Jael slew the general of the Canaanites, Sisera, by driving a tent peg through his head with a hammer.'

'Bravo, my little Nipponese scholar. Do you also know the Talmudic interpretation of this story? No? It is said that Jael killed Sisera with a tent peg and hammer because Deuteronomy 22:5 prohibits the use of weapons by women. The commentators also say that Sisera had sexual congress seven times with Jael on the day he fled from battle with the Israelites to seek refuge in her tent, that she derived no gratification from this, and that she gave Sisera to drink from the milk of her breasts. The prophetess Deborah praised her as greater than Sarah, Rebecca, Rachel or Leah.'

In the photograph of Sam's wife, I see the Biblical Jael, hands cupped on her breasts, uniting in coitus seven times with the enemy of Israel, consoling him with the milk of her breasts, and when he falls asleep . . . 'Strange matters of praise,' I muttered, half to myself.

'Some texts say that Jael means "wild goat" and was the name of a man.'

'Pardon me, Sam, but she looks so distressed. Why did she permit such a picture to be taken?'

'She didn't. Her Iraqi captors took it, and she has good reason for appearing distressed. Jael was a member of the Irgun Zvai Leumi. Have you heard of it?'

'I've seen it mentioned in the London *Times* that we receive at the Ministry, yes – a Jewish terrorist organization fighting in Palestine.'

'Israel now. In 1941, the Irgun agreed to suspend activities against the British forces occupying Palestine and join in the common struggle against Nazi Germany. Irgun leaders began at once with a plan to kidnap Haj Amin el-Husseini, the Grand Mufti of Jerusalem and an arch-Nazi collaborator, who had taken refuge in Baghdad. British personnel near Baghdad, pinned down and outnumbered by pro-Axis Iraqi forces, were of no use to the Irgun. During a commando reconnaisance operation, a skirmish with the Iraqis occurred, and Jael was captured. To use the discreet lingo of police reports, Jael was indecently assaulted on repeated occasions. This photograph was sent to the Irgun by the Iraqis in order to extort a great deal of sterling for her life. But she foreclosed on that scheme by escaping. Later, in 1945, she was parachuted into Germany with the Allied liberation forces. That's where I met her.'

'She seems a woman of unusual courage.'

'Bravery is not a prerogative of gender. Nor is a taste for revenge.'

'Where is she now?'

'I don't know. Undercover somewhere in the Middle Eastern war zones, nailing her tent peg into another Sisera's skull, I expect.'

This extravagant story of Jael, the fugitive eluding her Iraqi rapists, the Amazon parachutist and commando – if it was true and she really was Lazar's wife, provided an unforeseen explanation for his bizarre conduct. Those stories I had glanced at in the *Times*, idly, without serious interest, which told of Irgun terrorism, of Britain's military humiliation by Jewish partisan fighters, those incidents so remote from Japan and my own concerns, cast a sudden light of reason on Lazar's doings. At this very moment, in this very spring of 1948, Israeli forces were inflicting resounding defeats on the armies of the Arab League. Lazar brought this home to me: the very real possibility that he was a nationalist fanatic, a Jewish zealot engaged in the recovery of racial integrity. If this was true, then he was right – he truly did journey in the Divine Presence.

I drew another triangle over the one Lazar had made, an equilateral shape like his, but upside-down, base uppermost, so that the two now formed a Star of David.

'What's this – trying to square the circle, Kochan?' A smile escaped him like the wink of a snake on his cheeks. But he allowed no further comment on my discovery.

'Do you think you will ever see your wife again?'

'I pray so. I want to end up in Haifa, a grandfather, a fat old café idler writing poetry in Hebrew. But probably I'll die a fool's death somewhere in Asia.'

'You are fortunate in having found your Lilith. As for me –'

'– you'll resign yourself to a conventional marriage arranged by your parents?'

'Such is our custom of filial piety.'

'It is the exceptional man's duty to transgress social convention.'

'Maybe so. But I am perhaps too much the enigmatical exception that you recommend for democracy. No woman could ever be sexually attractive to me.'

'Well, I've found a Lilith for you. Come on, get washed and dressed. I'm going to introduce you to your prospective bride.'

Lazar consults his wardrobe with the fretful anxiety of a middleaged lady of fashion, and at last chooses a double-breasted suit of bleached linen, a Jermyn Street tailored shirt of opalescent silk, a tie and matching pocket hanky of tarnished silver, and white pumps. While he dallies over his toilette, I open a copy of the Bible at Deuteronomy 22:5.

'It says here: "The woman shall not wear that which pertaineth unto a man, neither shall a man put on a woman's garment: for all that do so are abomination unto to the Lord thy God." Which doesn't forbid women the use of weapons except by implication.'

'But it does expressly forbid transvestism – the very thing exalted by that Viennese bluffer, Strauss.'

Der Rosenkavalier enters again into the foreground of my perception.

In it, a woman playing a man masquerades as a woman – travesty farcically compounded.

'Don't you feel we're going out disguised as men?' Sam Lazar says, as he knots his silk tie – silver, like the cavalier's rose presented to Baron Och's fiancee, Sophie. '*Mein Gott, es war nicht mehr als eine Farce,*' Lazar mimics Sophie's exclamation. Indeed, it was no more than a farce.

6 BY THE WATERS OF SUMIDAGAWA

SUMIDAGAWA, A TOKYO RIVER, also gives its name to a classic 15th century Noh play by Motomasa, son of the great founder of Noh drama, Ze-ami. The play tells of a woman, driven to madness in her search for a lost son, who learns when crossing the Sumida river that he died a year before. The news of his death restores her to a moment of dignity that supersedes madness. Madness had been rehearsal preparing her for the truth, a foreshadowed anticipation of the grief that she now expresses with unearthly lyricism.

In the winter of 1934, some weeks before the Western New Year and close again to my birthday, an incident occurred that epitomizes for me the distracted grief of a mother who has lost her son, such as the Noh play Sumidagawa describes. I recall a moment that carries all the terrifying force of the sea, representing the violence of my mother Shizue's pent up, frustrated love.

Outings with my mother were rare events, rose-coloured by a sense of the illicit, the furtive rendezvous of lovers. She always treated me to entertainments and delicacies that were unlawful at home. On that particular day in 1934, Shizue conspired with Jotaro's houseboy to smuggle me out of Natsuko's room while she slept. It was a very cold, damp snowy day, the sort that would have made it impermissable for me to go out.

Our ramble in town seemed aimless, and the expected treat did not materialize. My mother was unusually withdrawn, speaking hardly at all but communicating her distress to me by a weight of silence. On a bridge, overlooking a canal of the Sumidagawa, we paused for a long time. Shizue held my hand and looked down at the icy water. Passersby were few at that hour of the afternoon, but they glanced suspiciously at us. Why was a respectable-looking woman with a child loitering like this?

I could feel Shizue's hand moist with sweat, even through my woolen glove. Our hands, although tightly joined, were a disconnection, a disseverment.

Finally, as though making up her mind, my mother said, 'Let's go to the photographer. I want you to remember this day.'

When my picture was taken, Shizue remarked in a sad, resigned voice, 'Now that we face *inkyo*, I shall be entirely removed from you.'

The generations of a family traditionally divide into separate residences at a certain time. This practice is called *inkyo*. My father took advantage of the custom to move out of Yotsuya in February 1935. *Inkyo* solved nothing for Shizue and me. I was not permitted to join the younger Hiraoka generation at their new home in Shibuya district for another two years, in 1937, when Natsuko's deteriorating health forced her to relax her hold on me.

Back at Yotsuya, after our visit to the photographer's studio, Shizue took me to her room to show me another memento of separation. I have never forgotten the sight of a ceremonial dagger that formed part of Shizue's bridal dowry, a reminder that she must never again return home to her family, not alive anyway. I still remember the click the blade gave as it was liberated from its scabbard, like the snap of a lipstick drawn from its tube. In the look she bestowed on me then, I understood how my life had been granted by no more than the valedictory sound of a bridal dagger.

What awaited me at Shibuya finally in 1937 was a continuance of civil war between my parents: between a sensitive, literate and beautiful young woman, filled with reproaches, and a sadistic drill sergeant. Years of struggle against Natsuko that my mother had undergone, and the resentment she harboured against Azusa for having left her to endure them, had turned her into a sour combatant without hope of peace. Azusa could now exert the entire dead weight of a bureaucrat's hand on us. From his reservoir of bile, full to overflowing after years of Natsuko's exotic whimsies, he poured endless scorn on me for being a bookish freak. He set about at once to break me of my literary bad habit by routine assaults on my books and manuscripts.

On my return from school one spring day, shortly after my arrival at Shibuya, I was greeted at the door by our housemaid Mina with a summons to see my father in his study. He had come home unusually early from the Bureau of Fisheries. On such a fine April afternoon, my mother would be out in the garden with my younger sister and brother, Mitsuko and Chiyuki. Shizue had become a passionate gardener, and that somehow gave our house a reassuring sense of tranquillity. My good humour did not prepare me for the chill I felt in my father's presence.

Azusa's study has always remained with me as a place of cheerless sobriety, a clinical façade of law books and filing cabinets. A row of luxury edition artbooks acquired on a sojourn in Europe, which he never opened, stood like bottles of costly foreign liquors to impress visitors. A vapoury plume drifts into the shaded light from a cup of green tea on his desk beside a Ministry file he contemplates, pen in one hand and cigarette in the other, the ashtray testifying to his chain-smoking vice.

'Don't slouch in my presence, boy,' he says without looking up. 'Obviously they don't teach you any manners in that snob school of yours. When I think of the sacrifices demanded of me for your entertainment –' He broke off suddenly to catch me eyeing the pile of books on his desk – mine, taken from the shelves in my room. I see the trace of a malicious smile on his lips as he savours my wonderment. His fox terrier Inari lying by his chair raises an eyebrow as if to copy my father's mocking look. Azusa and I differ completely even in our preference for animals. I cannot bear dogs and their slobbering obedience, Azusa detests cats (I have one now on my lap as I write). He does not comment on my books for the moment. Instead he talks to me of Confucian precepts which clearly lay down the importance of the harmonious family as a safeguard of the nation itself. 'Any slacking in your duty to me is an insult to His Majesty the Emperor,' he declares, as he lights another cigarette on his last. 'I speak to a person of some intelligence. You are not a total dunce like your brother Chiyuki. I give up on him.'

He speaks quietly at first, a restraint which I know is a deceptive lull before the storm-god Susanoo will begin raging. He smokes Jotaro's cheap brand of workingman's cigarettes. Everything about him is deliberately Spartan, his metal-framed spectacles, the military haircut and drab clothes. These are times of phoney stoicism. Looking at him, I am reminded of the vigilante fanatics roaming our streets these days armed with tailors' scissors, ready to prune the skirts or hair that offend against national decency and the government's sumptuary regulations. Phoney, repulsive to me as the kendo cries of my Peers' schoolmates. Dangerous thoughts are being hunted down by the *kempei* military police out there. The entire country seems under police surveillance.

Azusa does not invite me to sit down. His tactics of humiliation have been perfected on clerks interrogated for misdemeanours.

'Literature –' he begins; and pauses to sip his tea and puff on his cigarette. 'Mendacity. That's all it is. Only effeminates and unprincipled no-gooders indulge in it. It's a depraved habit, like this –' and he demonstrates in the air with a brief obscene wave of his hand '– isn't it? I know, I can see how self-abuse and scribbling have turned you into a girlish bloodless little worm.'

His voice rises in a steady crescendo of fury, his lips grow pale.

Although I know that everything in his performance is calculated, it is nonetheless effective for that.

He makes a show of trying regain calm. 'You behave in defiance of commonsense,' he says in a subdued voice. 'I forbid any more waste of your manly energy on these obscenities,' at last indicating my books, fingering one of them like some unhygienic specimen. I am surprised by the careful – I would almost say tasteful – selection he has made of some of my favourite authors, Raymond Radiquet, Oscar Wilde, Rilke, Tanizaki – and Ueda, of course. 'I will cure you of your diseased taste for these hopelessly subhuman decadents. Do you know what they do with such books in Germany? They burn them.'

I can see my precious books going to a Nazi pyre in our garden, and I begin to weep.

The silence reigning in the house is suddenly disturbed by Mitsuko's piano practice in the front parlour and Chiyuki's gallop on the stairs. I see my mother peering in at the study window, her face mottled light and dark by a raffia straw hat. I realize that Azusa had commanded them to stay in the garden during my ordeal, and Shizue has disobeyed him. He motions her away from the window with a vexed, peremptory gesture. 'Stop crying like a female,' he orders. 'You should read *Mein Kampf.*'

'I have.'

My reply does not please him; but he smiles. 'Very well, then. So you won't need this rubbish anymore –' he sweeps my books off his desk to the floor '– and you can stop masturbating on paper.' Azusa opens a beribboned Ministry folder which contains the shreds of my manuscripts. I can barely recognize them through a downpour of tears. Nausea overcomes me. I wish to collapse on the floor; but Azusa is shouting at me.

– No, he is shouting at my mother. She has rushed into Azusa's study from the garden, her straw hat clutched in her hand, her face perspiring and ablaze with indignation. Shizue's affliction that afternoon drove her to trespass against her own conventional good breeding. I had grown up with the insoluble mystery of Natsuko's illness, with Tsuki's allusions to evils 'below the girdle', and my father's dark grumblings about Jotaro's feckless womanizing. Shizue's anger led her to an indiscreet accusation. Jotaro's crime had been to infect my grandmother with a disease of an unnameable sort. A taboo word from the medical textbook was on Shizue's lips. 'Your mother is a diseased madwoman. She has robbed me of my child to poison his mind.'

Azusa stood immobile for a moment, a killer's look in his eyes. He seized my mother by the hair and twisted her head round to face me. 'And there it is,' he exclaimed, 'if you want to see tainted blood. Your precious sickly genius. A noxious little weed from my mother's

85

cemetery.' He tugged at Shizue's hair, so that her face veered from side to side in a dumbshow accentuation of his words. 'I shall pull him up by the roots – *by the roots* – do you hear me? I'll squeeze every last drop of pretension out of him, till I've made him a fit servant of His Imperial Majesty.'

My mother suffered her humiliation passively. She was no match for Natsuko's demonic son. The expression on her face haunts me still, that fixed, absented look of someone completely stripped of defensive façade which leaves the innermost self shamefully exposed. Her eyelids drooped, her mouth hung open – a severed head in an executioner's fist.

Azusa released her abruptly, and she fell against the desk with the disjointed inertia of a puppet. Drops of blood spilled from Shizue's mouth on the torn pages of my manuscripts, gathering there like miniature vermilion java flowers, as she raised herself up on trembling arms. In a bemused, dreamy way she began tidying the pages in the folder. 'Leave it, and get out both of you!' Azusa ordered, lighting a cigarette to calm himself.

Like two battle-shocked wrecks, my mother and I clung to each other for comfort, with Mitsuko and Chiyuki watching us from a safe distance, cordoned off by the aura of misery we emitted. My books and papers would have remained confiscated had not Shizue taken risks in defiance of Azusa. She connived to make a duplicate key to Azusa's study and smuggled out books to me whenever he travelled overnight to Osaka on Ministry business. She did more; she spent those nights making copies in her own hand of my mutilated, blood-stained manuscripts which she presented to me early in the morning, secretly, before anyone stirred.

Azusa had come too late to extirpate the weed that had sprung up in Natsuko's night garden. But he did not cease in his reformatory assaults. Throughout my adolescence, I was constantly barraged by Azusa's Nazi propagandist literature. I doubt that young people today will know anything of Otto Weininger or understand why his book of anti-Semitic eugenics led me to read the Bible, Christian commentaries and the *Protocols of the Elders of Zion*. Azusa's dull, middle-ranking bureacrat's prescription of domestic Nazism as an antidote to art backfired. He did not count on the enjoyment that his nimble-witted freak would take from the cultural excursion. He lacked the imagination to foresee how easy the passage is from Huysmans and Nietzsche to the Nazis' criminally debased form of German romanticism. To me, Nazi doctrine was simply another branch of decadent aesthetics. Azusa unwittingly nurtured a perverse Westernized Japanism in me.

Less than a year after my reunion with my parents, my father appeared at breakfast one morning looking abnormally cheerful. Shizue and I took it as a sign of impending calamity. Our discomfort hugely gratified Azusa. 'My father often absented himself on trips abroad,' Azusa began by saying. 'He would disappear for months at a time, no doubt in pursuit of some hare-brained scheme to make his fortune. I must admit that these absences came as a relief to me, and they obviously pleased my parents. What do you think, wife?' He addressed my mother, whose downcast look indicated her mounting anxiety. 'Do you think my parents enjoyed their periodic separations? Those holidays apart must have ideally suited them, don't you agree?'

Shizue made no answer.

'You can be sure it suited them all right,' Azusa laughed. Cigarette smoke swirled from his nostrils, yellow at first and whitening to striated wisps. He stared at me. 'Well, it is now your turn to be relieved, Kimitake – and you too, wife. We shall all of us be accommodated by a separation.'

Shizue's alarm was palpable. What was he saying? Was he threatening divorce? That was unthinkable.

'Why are you gaping at me like two idiots?' Azusa's mood turned to anger. 'Is that the way to congratulate me? Obviously you care nothing about my career.'

We waited, too frightened even to dare look at each other.

'I have been promoted Director of the Bureau of Fisheries,' Azusa finally said.

We sat dazed for some moments, unable to respond to Azusa's unexpected news. He surveyed our confusion with vindictive triumph. Shizue came to herself at last and began complimenting him on his success. Azusa shrugged her off at once with an ill-natured remark. 'Spare me the effusions. It would be more honest to rejoice, since you will be seeing considerably less of me from now on.' He explained that the post of director involved part-time residence in Osaka, some 350 miles west of Tokyo, where the Bureau had its headquarters.

Until 1942, when Azusa took early retirement from the civil service, he was scarcely home several nights in a month. I had four years' respite as probationary orphan in which to acquaint myself with my mother. I fell in love with Shizue.

I had graduated as an accomplished but highly vulnerable fantasist from Natsuko's cell. I was ripe for Shizue's introduction to the treacherous malady of love. In her, I met the sea in full force. In my grandmother's sickroom I had known the sea only as a tame idyll of the mind, as a decadent voyager imagines it without ever leaving home. Shizue brought me the sea as it truly is. I remember my first visit at the age of ten with her to the seaside, my fear at its overwhelming, limitless extent. I experienced a sense of vertigo, such as the fear of heights at first inspires, but which then grows dangerously attractive.

My apprenticeship in reconnoitring the depths began in earnest with a near fatal lesson in the summer of 1937, at Shibata, a resort on the Izu peninsula where my mother and I spent the holidays with Mitsuko and Chiyuki. Azusa occasionally came down from Tokyo on weekends. This was the first opportunity Shizue and I had to enjoy an unprecedented degree of intimacy. I could place my head on her lap and lie there contentedly by her side under the beach umbrella, without fear of being upbraided for unmanliness. Nothing prevented me from gazing unashamedly at the fine-veined alabaster of her thigh under my cheek, the dimples of her knees, her depilated shanks glittering with miniscule diamonds of sand. Our little cavern of shadow resounded with the sea's insatiable whispering. I stared greedily at her foot, trying to recognize in it the one I had seen protruding from the mosquito net in Azusa's hut.

My eyes feasted with a gluttony that left me strangulated. A grieving loneliness took possession of me, like an embolus of air in my veins that descended to the loop of my thing, inflating it, so that it grated pleasurably against the wool of my swimming trunks and sparked itself ablaze on the cool irritant flints of sand eddying down my crotch. I felt enthralled by a wish to scrape my erection raw upon the goosefleshed emery board of Shizue's armpit. A poor lubricant dribble emerged from the loosened sphincter of my penis; the sides of my groin ached as though two fingers inside were plunging into my testicles. Shizue lay half dozing, one hand combing the pages of a Pierre Loti novel, the other in my hair. I eased away from her, backwards, on my elbows and knees. I had to carry this grotesquely arched impediment elsewhere, out of sight of people. The adjoining cove beyond some fishing boats and groups of swimmers on our beach had bigger rocks and wilder water. I hoped it would be deserted; and thankfully it was.

I stepped into the water, kept calm at the shoreline by a barrier of low weed-encrusted rocks like wind-bent pines. My feet stirred up a litter of broken shells and tiny transparent crabs in the shallow pools rippling between the rocks. I continued to wade out further, until the cold hair of an undertow began to lash at my knees. I steadied myself against a rock, and after a last look round to make certain of my privacy, I liberated my ponderous thing from its covering. Only a massive cerulean sky above could see me, and the sun burning on my back like a cape of stinging nettles.

The encouragement of my hand is hardly necessary. Almost at once, the miracle of blind invincible semen gushes from the depths of exultation and misery. It hurtles out of me in a release of scalding pain as though my urethra had been packed with sand.

I awoke from my reverie to face a great swell which had slipped past the rocky barrier and was headed for me at alarming speed. The level of water at my midriff shrank, vacuumed up into the vast green belly of the wave towering over me, its head sharpened to the brilliant white edge of a guillotine. It fell with a tremendous roar on my chest, taking my breath away in a cold painful shock like a heart seizure. I collapsed beneath it, a crushed lifeless bit of flotsam rolling and bumping along the sea floor, immured in a glaucous envelope that would carry me to certain death. My terror increased as each moment brought me closer to an agreeably welcoming suffocation. No sound penetrated my tomb, and yet I distinctly heard my mother's panic-stricken voice calling my name. Kimitake. Kimitake. She knew I was in peril and had come to rescue me.

The sea tired of its game with me. It spat me out contemptuously in the shallows by the beach, and with a last gurgle of laughter, left me. No one awaited me on the shore. Not a soul. The sea had whispered my name; its voice was my mother's, claiming me.

Bruised, trembling on my hands and knees though I was, I looked back at her in exaltation. She now contained within her, together with all the countless organisms and seeds of marine life, my own myriad spermatozoa. I had succeeded to impregnate the sea.

I dragged myself back to the first beach. Shizue lay just as I had left her, in carefree siesta, with a fine dew of perspiration on her limbs. 'Don't wander too far,' she murmurs. 'You haven't learnt to swim yet.' The sea drips from me, imprinting my shadow in rivulets of ink on the sand. I watch the swell of my mother's stomach, rising and falling like waves in steady pursuit of each other, and I try to imagine myself a captive foetus in that sea. I was a twelve-year-old aesthete attempting in my invalid feebleness to measure the ocean, my mother.

Shizue's tidy, apparently safe version of the sea is a dangerous illusion. The realization dawns on me, that she is after all an irresponsible and spoilt young woman. No one can be trusted. Have I escaped drowning only to choke on my own bile? My resentment compels me to take action of some sort.

Mina, our maid, is asleep with a film magazine on her face. I survey the beach, but for the moment cannot see Mitsuko and Chiyuki. I rejoice in the idea that they have been washed out to sea, right under my mother's nose, and I am left alive to take pleasure in her shock. My evil hope is frustrated by the sight of them playing at the water's edge.

'Where are Mitsuko and Chiyuki?' I pose the question rudely to the derelict sleeper. I have reproduced the accusatory ring of Azusa's voice, and it achieves the desired effect. At once, by instantaneous reflex, Shizue's torso springs upright so abruptly that she bumps her head against the edge of the umbrella. Stunned, her eyes still latched by drowsiness, Shizue cries out in desperation the names of her lost children. Poor lame-witted Mina, roused summarily from her nap, dashes shouting towards the water, the huge, muscular calves of her bow-legs pumping madly across the dunes. I can see Mitsuko and Chiyuki approaching us with the reluctant trailing gait of fatigued children.

'Don't worry, mother,' I smile. 'I've kept an eye on them.'

Shizue catches the irony distorting my grin. She cradles her head on her knees. 'I apologize, Kimitake,' she says. I am tempted to fall into step with Azusa's type of malignant remark, but I resist, because I have fallen even more deeply in love with her.

7   SELLING THE DEAD

AM I DREAMING that I stand mirrored between two worlds?

The chiselled masculinity of a face – Barbara Stanwyck's or Joan Crawford's in *Mildred Pierce*, I can no longer recall whose – on a poster outside a cinema whose name too I cannot remember, Emerald or impossibly Empire – a woman's face on a rain-soaked poster, peeling away like the transvestite make-up of a Kabuki *onnagata*, reveals a man's features beneath, Spencer Tracy's, hideously contorted in his advertised film role as Hyde in *Dr Jekyll and Mr Hyde*.

Masura had stationed the Packard outside a cinema in the ruined commercial district of Sanya. I had made Dante's journey through hell in the short time since we left the hedonist luxury of the Imperial Hotel suite, and Lazar was my guide. Was he going to lead me to a celestial Beatrice – my prospective bride – in this terrible place? This proletarian quarter, which even before its devastation by incendiary bombs, had been a region of slums, a wooden-built fire hazard, criss-crossed by telegraph wires and malodorous open sewers. Now it defied description even as a slum. Shanties thrown together from jettisoned packing crates, patched with tin; street-hawkers' stalls offering the crowds a black market flotsam of goods, under the protectionist eye of hoodlums tattooed and stripped to the waist in the springtime heat, the lowest echelon of *yakuza* scum; and in the meagre evidence of garbage, the untouchables of the Eta class disputing their spoils. This was a savage's idea of a city, a hell to which his dreams guiltily attract him. And to this place, spring had brought – as it always had – the terrifying smile of an idiot.

In that ruined corner of Tokyo, one immediately heard everything it was. A barbarous jargon resounded all about me, a language different than mine, pronounced by mouths at once repugnant and marvellously shaped by ill health and hunger. Who were these people – Siberian tribesmen or Berbers, people of an exotic race from an unfamiliar world? A slang or dialect from its first words will always socially reveal the speaker. But here, those words I heard revealed their speakers under a frightening asocial, alien aspect. I had come to a place in hell where the inhabitants had chosen a condition which is inevitable anyway: anonymity, a condition as their actual ideal which brings them no innocence. No innocence at all in their plight, but a conformism that gives their slow-motion traffic a frantic sense of running, of a crowd running behind a flag of some sort unidentified by any symbol.

Masura eases our way through a knot of ex-servicemen, ferocious-eyed demons guarding the entrance to the cinema. Inside too, the cinema audience is composed predominantly of veterans, evident in the number of missing limbs, the scarred faces, and among these, some wives, grandparents and children. The orchestra pit has been outfitted with an altar, festively decorated with spring wild flowers somehow transported here from the countryside, and surmounted by a large gold-painted Sakyamuni figure of the compassionate Buddha. Attendant priests, looking more Shinto than Buddhist in their white robes and conical black caps, squat in a semi-circle round the altar enclosure, some with gongs, drums, and one even equipped with a catalpa-wood bow that clairvoyants strum to conjure the spirits of the dead.

Captain Lazar and I take our seats at the end of a row of rickety wooden folding chairs. There is no movie screen on stage. In the cleared space, lit by early afternoon sunshine that falls from an open skylight in the ceiling above – or, since I cannot properly see it, perhaps from an unrepaired roof damaged by bombs – two Kendo teams are seated facing one another, opponent groups distinguished by the slender red and white pendants attached to their backs.

'This is illegal,' I whisper into Lazar's ear. He nods, grinning content-edly, and replies: 'You're witnessing another of Prince Higashikuni's little enterprises, a veterans' cult trying to pass as Buddhist.'

Kendo and all other traditional martial arts had been prohibited by SCAP, as also all Shinto cult practices, even down to the *kamidana* god-shelves in private households. Such directives aimed to purge Japan of fascist beliefs by striking at the ideological heart of ultra-nationalism, Shintoism itself. Buddhism had been exempted from prohibition, since it was assumed untainted by the Emperor-worship system upheld by Shinto. The outcome of SCAP persecution was to drive Shinto under-ground, whence it re-emerged, as it did here in this cinema, in bizarre populist forms that assumed the esoteric disguise of Nichiren or Shingon Buddhism. I had even heard tell of a sect called *Denshinkyo*, founded by an Osaka electrician, that worshipped electricity as its principal deity and Thomas Edison as one of the lesser deities.

New fundamentalist cults were springing up in myriads, often estab-lished round a shamanist figure of unusual charisma, the *miko* or clairvoy-ant spirit-world communicant whose origins are anciently taprooted in

Japan's rural society. I was not surprised to learn that Prince Higashikuni was the entrepreneurial speculator behind this veterans' cult. A good many of the so-called new cults were in fact directly linked to pre-war populist sects with ultra-rightwing political affiliations, an inheritance of anti-communism passed on to their present-day successors, which earned them the tacit blessing of SCAP's G-2 Intelligence Section. A revival of the old Japanese folk ethos in simplified and disguised neo-Shintoist forms was as important to national recovery as the economic recuperation now in progress. Both were linked to the secret transactions of former *zaibatsu* oligarchs and their government collaborators. A convalescence in religious fundamentalism would compensate for the loss of imperial ascendancy in Asia, won by a military dictatorship which caused the nation great hardship, but had bestowed a goal on the lowest strata of society. The new sects offered neither Buddhist deliverance nor Christian salvation, but far more important to a humiliated and purposeless nation, a tapping of Japanese spiritual potential, as lacquer sap is tapped from the *Rhus vernicifera* tree, a vitality of folk blood, an energy harnessed to economic recovery on a Messianic scale.

We were permitted Barbara Stanwyck, Joan Crawford or Spencer Tracy – the entire stockpile of Hollywood films as a democratic anodyne – but not this, not the militarist clash of bamboo fencing staves on a screenless proscenium like an open-air Noh stage. 'This is headed straight for a G-2 crack-down,' Lazar declared. 'So you'd better enjoy it now.'

I didn't enjoy it. I had disliked Kendo ever since meeting with it at the Peers' School where my cretinous classmates devoutly indulged in its practice. Martial prowess, rather than academic achievement, stood higher in esteem at that school for brainless aristocrats. There was more to my dislike, however, than the resentment a weedy intellectual bears against jockstraps. The *kiai* shout of attack, issuing from the hollow of a mask, the protective neck flaps of armour distending like fish gills on the fencers' shoulders, frightened and upset me, as though the spectral armour in my grandmother's storeroom had come alive to haunt me. Those ferocious cries and crash of staves, which left me unsettled for days afterwards, reached deep within me like the pain of a razor slicing through my innards.

I had never truly understood why my classmates' cries of easy pleasure caused me such disproportionate anxiety. And I was not pleased to be reminded of it again, here of all places, in a cinema given over to an illegal display of Kendo as prelude to some dubious magical rites.

'Look at that,' Lazar draws my afflicted mind back to the match, and to a particular Kendoist from the red team who has already dispatched two white opponents with resounding cracks on their helmets. Even to my inexperienced eye, this fencer appears admirable. He relies more on an efficient compactness of attack, a lightning daring, than skill in manoeuvres. From him, the *kiai* shout issues fiercely, nonplussing his opponent with its confident sonority. It is truly *inspiratio*, inspirited breath, a supreme cry of 'no mind' from the very depths of being in action. His cuirass gleams black as a scarab's in a shaft of afternoon light. A remarkably white section of forearm is exposed for a moment as the faded blue sleeve of his tunic slips down from beneath the cuff of his gauntlet. His feet are well-fleshed, and yet white and dainty too.

There is something endearingly fragile in the long loose strand of hair escaped from the towel folded under the mask straps. A slovenly, fugitive stray wisp of hair floats in the whirlwind draught of his bamboo staff as it descends with formidable precision – crack! – for a third time on a white opponent's helmet. The match is over. The red pendant warrior is declared champion. He unfastens his mask, unfolds the towel, and releases a great mass of black hair. The Rose Cavalier is once more revealed a woman.

'This is impermissable,' I exclaim in my surprise – one that neither Lazar nor anyone else in the cinema appears to share.

'Everything's permissable to her. She's virtually the high priestess of this cult. Don't you recognize her?'

Even at some distance away from the stage, there could be no mistaking that face, unforgettably impressed on my memory. Resurrected in that Kendo champion on stage, I met again the woman who had lain supine in January snow, a pedestal under my feet. Baroness Omiyeke Keiko.

I shivered. Lazar contemplated my reaction with a look almost of sympathy. 'Funny how you get to meet some people again.'

'Yes, very funny indeed.'

'Do you want to sit through the séance next on the agenda? They're going to communicate with the spirits of the war-dead. Could be interesting.'

'I should like to leave immediately.'

'Not before paying your respects to the Baroness, surely?'

'You're not seriously asking me to confront her after what occurred?'

'You can't always refuse the way reality is. Besides, what makes you think she'll remember you?'

'And suppose she does?'

'Avoiding to meet her won't prove she does.'

He propelled me by the arm down the aisle steps towards the backstage. An uproar began, a crescendo swell of gongs, drums, savage flute-playing in accompaniment to chanting, that sounded like my own anxiety given vent. My distress would now compensate Lazar for his own in showing me a picture of his wife Jael in naked humiliation.

We arrived at a backstage area that contained several dressing-rooms from the days long past when the cinema had also served as a variety theatre. Seats were arranged along one wall, presumably for visitors to the sect's clairvoyant, and on two of these sat an elderly couple, dressed in a sober provincial manner that identified them as well-to-do country folk.

A curtain parted, a door behind it opened, and out stepped another unmistakable personage, Imperial Prince Higashikuni-no-miya-Naruhiko, the Emperor's uncle. Newspaper photographs had made us all familiar with that portly, bullnecked figure, the pancake-flat face and a droopy mouth that added to the playboy air of insouciance he affected. His suit of light grey slub-patterned silk rivalled Lazar's dandy elegance. He grasped Lazar's hand warmly, 'Sam, *mon cher*,' and continued in a rapid flow of French. The Prince handed Lazar a flat thin gift-wrapped package. 'I've found the little book you desired.'

The door to the dressing-room had been left carelessly ajar in the Prince's exit. I glanced in. I confess to a foolish, despairingly absurd hope that its occupant would somehow have magically transformed into a male imposter, into the *onnagata* apparition of the Baroness Omiyeke Keiko I had seen on stage. I cherished this lunatic hope, encouraged by the occult din of Shinto ritual music from the orchestra pit, a Kabuki echo that brought theatrical unreality into the stifling mugginess of the backstage space.

My gaze, beseeching magical deliverance, encountered an empty Kendo costume arranged on a clothes-frame. Beside it, inclined towards a dressing-table mirror, the Baroness sat powdering her face. A kimono of sepia shades loosened below her shoulders and breasts exposed a skin of intense whiteness, a lustrous snow pliant under the fingers of a middleaged maidservant rubbing cologne on her back. Her breasts reflected in the mirror seemed cones of brilliant ice. Dazzled, handicapped as I am by a slight myopia, my eyes nevertheless made out the tiny shape of a peony tattooed on the Baroness Omiyeke's shoulder, and within the corolla of petals, a dark mole stood as though furry with pollen. The maid bent down to the flower, nostrils widening voraciously to sniff it, and the tip of her tongue grazed the mole. Strange thing to say, but I too found myself leaning forward, my lips attracted to that pollinous flower in the snow. The Baroness smiled back at the maid's reflection of praise, and then she focussed her eyes on mine, impolitely gawking at her in the mirror. My legs melted away at that look. I sat down, unmindful of my discourtesy to the Prince's Imperial presence.

'Your friend looks gruesome,' Prince Higashikuni commented to Lazar.

'The indoor pallor of the writer, I fear,' Lazar explained. 'Such is the price of literature.'

Prince Higashikuni grunted, shook hands again with Lazar, and took his leave.

Lazar steered me into the dressing-room. I prayed he would maintain his hold on my arm, for fear that I might collapse otherwise.

'Keiko, my dear, what a splendid performance,' Lazar breezely hailed, in English, as he laid a kiss on the cheek she turned to him.

Her snowy hills were by now enclosed under the sepia-patterned kimono. She inspected me with alarming, unconventional directness, a little smile lightening those glacial moon-goddess features. How could she possibly fail to recognize me? 'Is this the one?' Those words from her lips, rudely piercing through me, sealed my condemnation. I felt faint.

'My assistant, the notable writer, Yukio Mishima,' Lazar said.

Baroness Omiyeke, to my surprise, bowed. 'Forgive me, *sensei*. You are somehow unlike any of the photographs of you I have seen published.'

I took in the respectful term *sensei* – master – with even greater wonder. 'You have seen my photograph before?' I replied, in guilty confusion.

'Before?' She frowned, uncertain of what my awkwardness betrayed. She laughed. 'Well, perhaps only once before, if you insist on counting.'

'Pardon my impoliteness. I simply expressed my astonishment that you should recognize an unknown writer of no importance.'

'Oh, but that's quite untrue, Mishima-*san*. I have admired your writing ever since I read your first collection of stories, *The Forest in Full Bloom*, in 1944.'

'I am disconcerted by your praise of such a worthless trifle lost in obscurity.'

Baroness Omiyeke's recognition of me as a writer, rather than as her parking-lot assailant of so few months ago, began to allay my worst fears. A person like her, of such strength and direct frankness, would not have hesitated to make her accusation heard. Clearly, the effects of Baroness Omiyeke's intoxication at the time had entirely blinded her, and she remained without memory of my presence at the scene. My heart resumed beating in a tempo less likely to cause cardiac arrest.

'My praise is as nothing,' the Baroness continued, 'when compared to that of your teacher, the esteemed scholar Hasuda Zenmei. I well remember the exceptional status he awarded you in his postscript to your first book.'

'You knew Hasuda-*san*?' I glanced suspiciously at Lazar. Had he coached the Baroness to make this reference to Hasuda? His demeanour pleaded innocence of any such ploy.

'Not personally at the time, no, but I am happy that we have been instrumental in repatriating his mortal remains from the Baharu Johor garrison in Malaya.'

'Excuse me, Baroness?'

She turned to Lazar. 'Haven't you explained to Mishima-*san* what chiefly preoccupies the members of our church?'

Lazar admitted his lapse with a shrug.

Undismayed, the Baroness laughed in an amiably spontaneous manner, omitting to cover her mouth with her hand as is the custom of Japanese women. 'I'll wager he has neglected even to mention the name of our association – the Church of Cosmopolitan Buddhism.'

The name did not impress me as being any odder or more grandiose than others in vogue among the post-war sects – the Church of World Messianity, the Value Creation Society, the Perfect Liberty Foundation, and many more in proliferating numbers.

'You communicate with the dead, is that so?' I asked.

'Communication with the spirits of the heroic war-dead is an aspect of our practice which brings solace to our bereaved members. Our immediate and more practical task, however, is to locate the graves of the war-dead wherever possible, identify the remains, and transport them home to await enshrinement at the Yasukuni Memorial★.'

'A long wait is in store for those ashes,' Lazar interjected.

'Yes, Sam, I am aware that SCAP has forbidden us to honour our dead in a proper manner. We can afford to wait.'

'Of course, since you charge your bereaved a healthy fee in expectation of that glorious day.'

Baroness Omiyeke replied to this cynicism with nonchalant laughter.

I noticed a quantity of boxes arranged on shelves at the back of the dressing-room. These boxes of varying size, wrapped in white cotton cloth, each displayed an individual's name and military rank in black handwritten characters, a fine calligraphy that additionally invoked the Lotus Sutra, *namu-myo-ho-renge-kyo*, Hail the Lotus of the Wonderful Law.

My curiosity drew a comment from Baroness Omiyeke. 'Those are the relics of the illustrious dead that we have managed to redeem during the past six months. They will be claimed by the surviving families after the ceremony.'

I had heard rumours that a lucrative traffic flourished in the sale of war-dead remains. Now that I actually saw these ashes, pigeon-holed in their columbarium niches, they stirred uncertain feelings of disgust and wonder in me.

'This is one of our recent and most precious discoveries,' the Baroness said, as she placed a shoe-box sized container on her dressing-table. She unfolded the loose cotton wrapping to reveal a box of plain satiny white pine. She removed the lid and lifted out a skull. 'It is in exceptionally

---

★ A national memorial in Tokyo enshrining the deified spirits of war heroes who died for the 'peace of the land', *yasu kuni*, that is, for the Imperial cause, and suppressed by the Occupation.

good condition, you see,' she said, presenting us with the skull, the Lotus Sutra invocation written across its parietal and frontal bones. 'The dental work eventually led us to identify Lieutenant Colonel Kimura Takeo of the Imperial Marines. Only this evidence survived, after his decapitation by Borneo head-hunters. Did you notice the old couple waiting outside? His parents, landowners from Nara Prefecture, eager for a last look at their beloved son's only mortal remnant before the cremation rite.'

She held the skull close to her face, as though searching in it for her own reflection. The skull's defunct nose assumed shape again, mirroring the aquiline majesty of Baroness Omiyeke's nose in its hollow pools of bone. For a moment, I thought she would plant her lips on those hideous, unfleshed teeth, like Salomé kissing John the Baptist's severed head.

I studied the lady's perfection intently for some betraying marks of imperfection. I imagined that in her middle years the statuesque pro-portions of her figure would run to fat. Along one jawline, under the coiled eaves of her hair, I was pleased to detect a slight trace of discolor-ation in the skin. These freckles, rendered bluish by her makeup, I supposed were the effect of hormones secreted during pregnancy. My diagnosis only succeeded in reviving painful memories of the incident in the parking-lot, thus adding an unwelcome degree of poignancy to her beauty.

'You look troubled, Mishima-*san*,' the Baroness remarked, as she replaced the skull in its little coffin and shut the lid. 'Perhaps my enthusi-asm for these melancholy relics has upset you.'

'I was thinking of all the young men who perished in the war.'

'A sad thing to consider.'

Baroness Omiyeke's maidservant produced a tray of whiskies for us, and, miracle to behold, a pitcher of ice – in this funerary dressing-room, in this infernal district of ruins, ice. I felt tempted to seize the ice in both my hands and rub my face with it, something that might ease my burning sense of oppression.

'Kindly excuse my impoliteness, gentlemen, but I must hasten now to join the ceremony.'

'We understand, you are expected to preside on stage,' Lazar said.

'On stage? How quaintly theatrical that sounds,' the Baroness laughed, and turning to me, added: 'Please assure me that you will visit me again soon, Mishima-*san?*'

'I promise you his constant attendance, dear Baroness,' Lazar put in.

She arose, and the maid helped her don an outer kimono of taffeta with a design of primroses, and over this, another sleeveless robe of white silk displaying the sect's lotus, red-embroidered on the back. Baroness Omiyeke's attirement produced a crackling sound of electricity, louder and more startling as the maid brushed her lady's splendid, waist-length hair.

Climbing the aisle steps to the exit, I looked back once at the stage, as the instrumental cacophony augmented to signal Baroness Omiyeke's entrance. She glided in, truly the vision of a Kabuki *onnagata*, black hair bannered in a halo round the white face of an avenging ghost.

Beggars, cripples, dismal onlookers of every sort gave way to Masura's commands as he brought us unmolested to the Packard. The car's unventilated interior had become sweltering in the afternoon sun, but I hoped its safe haven would restore me to normalcy.

'Magnificent, isn't she, *notre chère* Keiko?' Lazar inquired.

I thought of the peony tattoo on the snowy verge of Keiko's shoulder. 'That performance with the skull disagreed with me.'

Lazar was more intent on opening the parcel that Prince Higashikuni had given him. He tore up the wrapping of hand-made rice paper of a fine type no longer manufactured these days, and obviously drawn from a stock lovingly preserved for many years. A slim, quarto-size artbook emerged, its cover bound in leather the colour of blanched straw and without imprint of title or image. Protective films of gauzy white paper fluttered like dove's wings as Lazar browsed through the pages of the volume. Images of dragons, garlanded roses, insects and birds flashed by, brilliantly pigmented on sheets of stiff parchment. I judged this to be a textile pattern-book of flora and fauna, with a certain naive charm, but of a gaudiness that precluded artistic value.

'What is it?' I asked.

'Take a closer look,' Lazar instructed, pressing down a sheet of the grainy parchment for me to touch. 'Hair follicles – can't you feel them? And look – blackheads still lodged in the pores. Can't you see? These are specimens of *yakuza* tattooes. Don't worry, Kochan, they were collected after the donors' expiry.'

He closed the book and handed it to me. 'Prince Higashikuni dug up these *yakuza* skins for me, but at Keiko's own insistent request, I make you a gift of them.'

Despite all my protests, Captain Lazar deposited the book in its rice-paper envelope on my lap.

'Did you not find Keiko attractive, as I predicted?' Lazar smiled confidently.

I looked at him. 'You're not proposing *her* as my bride?'

'It is for you to propose.'

'You're not serious?'

'What better candidate?'

'Oh yes, a notorious courtesan of the rightwing? Really, Sam, do you see my parents embracing her with joy?'

'You, not your parents, will do the embracing.'

'It is unthinkable.'

'Why? She's impeccably aristocratic by birth, her family is Imperially connected, and her husband was a celebrated war hero.'

'And she's also much older than I.'

'By five years. She's only twenty-eight. Next you'll complain that she's too tall for you.'

'How do you know she'd accept me?'

Lazar grinned. 'Just keep seeing her, and nature will take its own perverse course.'

There was no point arguing with Lazar. His forecast of events always seemed accurate, as his prediction concerning the fate of Prince Higashi-kuni's Church of Cosmopolitan Buddhism soon proved. A week after our visit to the cinema, the Church was dissolved by order of SCAP. This did not, however, put an end to the traffic in war-dead relics.

8 A GAME OF NOBLE LOSERS

MY SITUATION of impasse in that summer of 1948 seemed to me a humiliating regression to a time ten years ago when at the age of thirteen I suffered my first grave attack of careerism. No recovery thereafter was possible from the besetting illness of ambition.

I am left with a bizarre regret, a sort of envious nostalgia for the someone other I might have been, but am not. Do I mourn the demise of Hiraoka Kimitake? Not really. Hiraoka Kimitake, as I have already declared, was originally my given name. How I came to select my professional name Yukio Mishima is something that until now I have preferred to keep mysterious. With shameless disregard for the truth, my father told a journalist that I chose my name by sticking a pin at random in a page of the telephone directory. I have not denied Azusa's story, nor indeed other varieties of legend about me that open like a fan to reveal rather than hide a dissembler's smile. All stories told about Yukio Mishima are true; their explanations are most likely not.

I was inspired to take my vocational name from a song my grandfather Jotaro sang for me one night in December 1938, as Natsuko eked out a gradual death from haemorrhaging ulcers. That song flowing robustly over Natsuko's helpless cries of agony brought me my name, as from a clear refreshing stream.

Often in my childhood I found myself attracted to the portals of Jotaro's room. In the blackened grain of oak, a verdict seemed to me written: 'Herein is confined the disgraced ex-governor of Sakhalin.' He too was mysteriously sentenced to isolation, but of a carefree debonair sort which permitted him to entertain his cronies, the retired grandees of the Ministries, judiciary and banking, including some rogues who had hastened his financial ruin. Jotaro had a witty name for his revellers, 'shades of the old empirical Confucian school', looking back to the golden days of the Meiji era.

A fine tenor voice was all that remained to him of his times as an extraordinary gallant. Through the oaken double-doors, I would hear him singing a favourite music hall ballad or a washerwoman's simple ditty.

> Even to see the birds flying freely above me
> Only deepens my sorrow – makes me thoughtful the more.

I was not permitted in Jotaro's gaming parlour with its pestilent atmosphere of saké and manufactory discharge of tobacco. Jotaro smoked a cheap brand of cigarettes, Justice, as I recall with a pleasing image of a golden bat on the packet, popular among workingmen in the Depression years. I relied on my mother's state of grace with Jotaro – a favouritism that he readily bestowed on any woman of good looks – to salvage the empty packets from him.

On one such occasion, when Shizue had collected my illicit stock of trophies from Jotaro's accomplice houseboy, and as we crept away from the parlour doors, she began to describe the unseemly event of my *oshichiya*, the naming ceremony which traditionally occurs a week following birth. On the evening of the seventh day, Jotaro wrote my name on a strip of ceremonial rice-paper and placed it in the family's *tokonoma* shrine. Jotaro and Azusa had been drinking sake all afternoon, and my father, who had no head for alcohol, became very tipsy and belligerent. Shizue remembered with deep shame that my father accidently upset the votive offerings on the *tokonoma* altar. Jotaro tried to make light of this ill-omened mishap by commenting on my name. Kimitake signifies a person of public prominence – a name dictated by my grandmother's own preference – and Hiraoka is a common surname meaning flat hill or plateau. Jotaro made a pun, 'This is a sign that the boy will enjoy a prominence far surpassing our own level.'

'The nail that stands out gets hammered down,' Azusa replied with a commonplace proverb.

Natsuko at once retaliated: 'My son excels in the art of dwarfing pine trees.' She took me from my mother's arms and added, 'Joke as much as you like, but in six weeks' time you'll certainly see this boy raised to higher ground.'

'No one understood what she meant at the moment,' my mother said, 'but sure enough, on the forty-ninth day –'

'— I kept my word,' a voice behind us, down the corridor, interrupted my mother's story. Natsuko had come up on us silently, without the forewarning thump of her cane that usually told of her approach. She was returning from her bath, with Tsuki in attendance carrying towels and lotions. Severe neuralgia had left her unable to bathe without Tsuki's assistance. 'I remember very well what I said on that day,' Natsuko continued. 'And it's no bad thing that you should remind the boy of the pygmies who inhabit this house.'

My mother seemed a gazelle trapped in a python's coils. 'Tsuki, please confiscate those items the bride is hiding,' Natsuko ordered. 'It is improper for the boy to collect such tokens of the underclass.'

I have never known why Shizue chose that day to report on my *oshichiya* already seven years in the past. But I did know from it that my name memorialized Shizue's unhappiness. The moment of my recognition, however, was clouded by a puzzling association between Jotaro's cheap brand of cigarettes and my grandmother's love of fine port wines and English tobacco. A divergence in my grandparents' tastes somehow implied an alliance, linking them together in a shared enigma.

When I was finally permitted to join my mother at Shibuya in 1937, Natsuko extracted a solemn promise from me to spend one night a week with her. I acceded to her plea with the dubious magnanimity of a victor. At the age of twelve, I felt like Prince Genji negotiating with an old discarded mistress. Out of altruistic deference to her, and to our past amity, I complied with this once-a-week infidelity to my mother.

Natsuko repaid my sacrificed nights to her with regular outings to the theatre. Gradually, as we passed to the summer of 1938, her condition deteriorated, the strain of these attendances at the Kabuki and Noh began to tell. On returning to her room, she would collapse on the bed, too fatigued by pain even to sip the tea provided by Tsuki. Now began the moans that were soon to escalate into soul-piercing cries of torment. I administered the sedatives, and sat by her, wiping away the spittle that dribbled from her open mouth.

After a brief interval of comatose but uneasy sleep, she opened her eyes. The whites were bile-coloured. 'You are so pale, nightingale,' she said. 'Pale like the *abisha-ho* who summons ghosts.' She looked troubled, as though really seeing in me the *abisha-ho* of occult folk tradition, a child spirit medium whose face is painted white. 'Entertain me with ghosts, my *abisha-ho*,' she smiled as her pain receded. 'Does your father still write to you from Osaka?'

'With absolute regularity, every week.'

'Ah, he too importunes you on a weekly basis. And what sage instruction does he send you?'

'Always the same. The invincibility of Nazi Germany. He expects to transform me miraculously into a healthy-minded Nipponese fascist.

In his last epistle from Osaka, he quotes some lines from Oswald Spengler's *Decline of the West*.' I produced Azusa's letter and read from it, as I did every week, for Natsuko's amusement. 'Spengler says, "if the influence of this book leads men of the new generation to turn from poetry to technology, from painting to the merchant marine, from epistemology to politics, they are doing what I desire. One could wish nothing better for them".'

'Does he seriously recommend you to join the merchant marine?' Natsuko laughed.

'He demands great things from me, but neglects to specify them – except to quote from Hitler's *Mein Kampf*: "In world history the man who really rises above the norm of the broad average usually announces himself personally".'

'So, he hasn't forgotten the meaning of Kimtake after all.'

'Strange to tell, grandmother, and I am reluctant to admit it. But I must confess a grudging respect for my father's letters. I find myself admiring the severity of his prose, which reminds of me of Mori Ogai. I did not suspect my father capable of such talent.'

'The talent of Mori? You are entirely misled. Azusa only strums his bow, producing the single hollow note of a deceitful bureaucrat. Can you not hear it?'

Later, when Natsuko had fallen asleep again, I heard a scratching at the door. I assumed it was Shah, my old tortoise-shell tomcat that I raised from a feral kitten. Azusa had forbidden me to bring Shah into his new Shibuya home. I opened the door and found Jotaro, splendid in a white shantung suit and leaning atilt on his ivory-handled teakwood stick, back from a late night revel. 'Is she asleep?' He beckoned me to follow. 'Come along, lad. Tsuki has prepared some rice cakes and saké.'

Tsuki, the superannuated geisha of albino moon face, went ahead of us with a steaming tray of delicacies.

'I cannot leave grandmother for very long.'

'Assuredly you can,' Jotaro airily contended. 'I am eager to acquaint you with an event of the utmost importance which has just occurred.'

I wondered, what could be so momentous?

This would be the first time I entered Jotaro's parlour to spend any considerable span with him. As Tsuki switched on the wall lamps, Jotaro commented, 'When electric lights were first introduced in the 1870s they lengthened a working girl's day to sixteen hours.'

'Since when have you been a union spokesman?' Tsuki challenged him. 'I would have imagined you more interested in the girl's after-hours.'

'Perhaps I am more of a wild-eyed socialist, full of dangerous thoughts about our oppressed workers, than you think.'

'Don't talk such nonsense,' Tsuki scolded.

We sat down at Jotaro's gaming table. Intimacy between maid and master was openly displayed in the proprietory way Tsuki brushed a stray hair from Jotaro's collar. Tsuki's fingers were odiously contorted by arthritis. Jotaro noticed my look and declared in a stage whisper, 'She's become dreadfully gnarled, our Two Kimonos, to the point of incapacity. Do you know, these days I have to cut her toenails?'

'My incapacity is rarely any disadvantage to you,' Tsuki retorted, with a coy pout made barbarous by her red-veneered lips.

This exchange of innuendoes between the aged couple embarrassed and repelled me. At seventy-six, Jotaro was still strikingly handsome. I envied his classical features that Azusa had to a lesser degree inherited, but not I.

'What is the momentous event you spoke of, grandfather?' I felt impatient to take leave leave of this oppressively giddy atmosphere.

For reply, Jotaro indicated the Go board on the table.

This –? Could this be more important than Natsuko's illness, than the capture of Nanking or the battle against Soviet Russia for Changku-feng? Jotaro read my disappointment with a sly glance as he sipped from his bowl of saké.

'Several days ago,' he explained, 'on 26th June, a Go match began in Tokyo at the Koyokan restaurant in Shiba Park. I dare say this could prove the most crucial game ever played in the spectacular history of Go. Shusai, the present Master, now sixty-five years old, is twenty-first in the Honnimba succession of Masters, the first being Sansa who lived from 1558 to 1623. Honnimba is the name of a cell at the Jakkoji Temple in Kyoto where Shusai took holy orders and his clerical name, Nichion. All masters of Go have been clerics ever since the days of its founder Nikkai, the clerical name of the venerable Sansa.'

'I am not a player,' I broke in rudely to impress on him my disinterest.

'Oh, but you are already one,' he smiled, 'without even being aware of it. Renounce all further pointless anxiety concerning your grand-mother. Her time is up. Yours has only just begun, as will become plain in the course of this decisive tournament. Do you understand?'

'I do not. Nor am I able to be so callous.'

'Bear with me a little longer, then. Tsuki will sit by your patient, as she must anyway when you are absent. Let me advise you of what is at stake in this match. Shusai is known as the invincible Master, devious as a fox and tiny, tiny like a dwarf and apparently very frail. He is challenged by Kitani Minoru, a thirty-year-old professional of the 7th rank whose style of play is said dangerously impulsive. Two sessions have already taken place, and the positions so far are recorded here,' Jotaro bowed to the Go board, a beautiful one of paulownia wood. Two bowls of polished walnut at each end of the board held the 'stones' – respectively the white and black pebbles used in the game.

'Have you played chess or *shogi*★?' Jotaro inquired.

'I dislike the gratuitous effort that all such games require.'

'No matter. Go is anyway not the least like chess. It is not a game of moves but of pure intuitive strategy, demanding an immense power of abstraction. The placing of a stone by either the white or black player is final. A stone may be captured and removed from the board, but never moved to a second position after it occupies one of the 361 points. You see, there 19 points squared, counting from the four corners vertically and horizontally, or 18 by 18 squares. The fundamentals of Go are simple, the execution infinitely complex. The object is to build up positions invulnerable to every attack, while surrounding and capturing enemy stones. This is military architecture composed of imaginary battlefields and theatres of war.'

'I have little patience and no talent for conflicts of this kind.'

'Do you have little patience and less talent for friendship?'

'I am shy of intimacy. My nature is too wildly abstract to permit close friendship with anyone.'

'Then, believe me, this game is for you. The isolation that comes from being wildly abstract, as you say, is at the root of samurai courage. And Go is the ultimate samurai game. I shall take the Shusai Master's white, and you the reckless challenger's black. Are you willing to humour me, lad, and follow this match to the end? We shall undoubtedly discover where the antagonism between the old and new schools of samurai tactics is going to lead us in the end. Reports of the match are being serialized in the Tokyo *Nichinichi Shimbun* by the worthy writer Kawabata Yasunari. This will enable us to attempt our alternative solutions to a previous session and then check the results of the opponents' own choice in the next.'

My first lesson in Go began after 1 a.m. and lasted till dawn, when Natsuko awoke and demanded my presence. What were we really witnessing as the stones fell into place? What else but a construction of the mind resembling an ancient tumulus burial mound.

After the second session of play on June 27th, a storm brought flash floods to the east and west of Japan. On 19th August 1938, rain still glistened on the chestnut leaves. The Shusai Master fell seriously ill and was taken to St Luke's Hospital. A three-month recess now ensued till mid-November.

The summer rainstorms complemented Shizue's mood. My pledge to visit Natsuko once a week had to be honoured, as Shizue herself acknowledged, but not without reproach. 'Of what use is that old woman to you now?' Shizue protested indecorously. 'She hasn't even the strength to accompany you to the theatre anymore.'

★ A variety of Japanese chess.

'Don't begrudge her the little time she has left.'

'She has already made too much of my time,' Shizue replied, and exhibited the pocket watch she constantly wore ever since Natsuko had presented it to her as a memento of *inkyo*, saying, 'I have no more use for it.' This was the infamous timepiece which told Natsuko when to press the electric buzzer that would summon my mother from her room upstairs to my breast-feedings, each one measured to a precise duration. 'Consider how little time I have left to make my efforts before your father returns from Osaka.'

Shizue had risen from one-time salvager of my cigarette packs to the highest secret rank of literary envoy. She was my devoted lobbyist who introduced my writings to the potentates of the literary cliques, whose approval and patronage were indispensable in establishing a career. Beauty, good taste and a lineage of respectable scholars were advantages she exploited in her implacable campaign to see me admitted to one of the fashionable coteries.

'Is it necessary to confess my indebtedness to you?' I said.

'Indebtedness is a condition of unavoidable social burden that you owe your father. To me, you owe a second life – one of love that I should not expect you to feel burdensome.'

An umbilical chain nevertheless weighs heavy, even when it is lightened by a smile from the loveliest of maternal jailers. 'Look at your desk,' Shizue recommended, as she left my room. 'You will see what a dedicated thief I have become for your sake.'

I had coaxed Shizue into being my clandestine librarian, fulfilling my curiosity to see the prized Western artbooks locked away in Azusa's study. She penetrated the forbidden study and brought me the books one by one. In one of these latest pilfered volumes, like the others sumptuously illustrated with half-tone plates, individually protected by sheets of crêpe tissue paper, I fell upon a picture which had been lying in ambush for me. Suddenly, as the tissue paper fluttered apart from the image, Natsuko's sacred white pheasant burst out of the page.

A nude torso of perfect albescence, like marble in moonlight, blinds me. A young athlete leans against a tree, arms raised and bound to it by the wrists, with two arrows buried under the left armpit and between the ribs at his right. He suffers his martyrdom indifferently, as though casually taking pleasure from it. This is my fatal encounter with Guido Reni's painting of St Sebastian, a marvel of Baroque devotional art.

Among leaf shadows and ruined monuments, I found Sebastian. My eyes were raped by the arrows that pierce the saint, sprouting it seems from within him, like the tufts of hair that had begun to appear on me. Is there any more vengeful intoxicant, anything more melancholy, than to discover one's true sensual nature buried under an assumed mental masquerade? An immense self-lesioning sensuality, a fever-stricken blood lust erupts from my own underground incognizance in a murderous spasm, and it will return again and again to torment me.

I unbutton my trousers as though opening a pencil-box in search of a ruler. I aim my stiffened thing at the martyr, propped up against my desk. He gazes patiently heavenward, awaiting the shaft in my hand. I dream of a pool of red, of leper-white feathers exploding as the pheasant is struck. I hear a far off anguishing sob – mine, as a fiery poker flashes through me, hurling itself from the scalded throat of my penis. The white pheasant explodes into a maggot-riddled corpse. A beech tree outside sheds coppery red on my desk, on the ink bottle and schoolbooks spattered with the languid maggots of my semen. I am astonished, I feel executed. In aftermath of pain comes the vest ebb of dizzying nausea.

A discreet sigh alerts me in time to glance at the door sliding shut. I had glimpsed my mother's face in the space, peering at me, but with a calm expressionless disregard as though I were invisible. Did I imagine she smiled?

By its own volition, and with total indifference to my self-sickness, my thing once again began to unfurl. The senseless creature, dribbling a mucous unguent from its pouting lips, wanted a touch other than mine to assuage it. I went to the door and slid it ajar. The corridor stood empty. I waited – for how long and for the satisfaction of what miracle, I cannot say. After a time, I began to sense a disagreeable odour, one that seemed at first unreal, emanating from the pores of my memory alone. An oppressive malodour associated with the terrors of my infancy had somehow been released by my act of onanism. Or so I believed. Was it a reminiscence of Natsuko's moxapellets? No, it reeked more incisively of the naphthalene in her closet.

To rid myself of evil memories, I pushed the door shut, with the intention of squashing my erect penis between the sharp edges of the frame and the jamb. I pressed down hard, steadily, until the torture extracted a glittering mica of tears from my eyes. But *it*, it of course, took unconscionable pleasure from the bruise inflicted. Then I remembered. *Camphor*. The endless injections of camphor and glucose that I had received practically every month for many years whenever I suffered my attacks of *jikachudoka*. And the smell I recognized did not arise solely from memory, but was there in reality, coming from the corridor. I put myself in order and went in pursuit of the trace.

My quest soon ended at my parents' bedroom. I found Shizue kneeling at a table. She held an envelope between a pair of chopsticks over an incense jar in which some camphor burned. What strange ritual is this? Has she now taken to fumigating my father's letters? 'Is that you?' She asked without turning. 'Your weakness causes me much anxiety. I feel you are in grave risk of contagion from every source.'

'From my father's letters?'

'I should have the privilege of knowing what he writes to you, not your grandmother. But in fact, no, this is a letter from your friend Azuma Takashi.'

Azuma Takashi was five years my senior at the Peers' School and chairman of the school's literary club, the *Bungei Bu*, which had affiliations with a small but elite coterie of ultra-nationalist writers, the *Nippon Roman-ha*, Japan Romantic Movement. I longed to join this dedicated band of Japanese scholars and mystics, but Shizue disapproved of their extremism. Behind her back, I courted Azuma with the specific aim of being recommended to the *Roman-ha*. It seemed no obstacle to me that its members were three times my age. Azuma had recently succumbed to tuberculosis. Its swift progress in the next years would eat up his throat and larynx, until he was left mute, unable at last even to sit up. Entombed in his bed, he wrote to me by guidance of a mirror fixed at an angle above his head.

'Given your disinclination to friendship, an epistolary form of it must be the ideal solution for you,' Jotaro commented when I told him the anecdote of Shizue's fumigation.

'Isolation has always been preferable to intimacy,' I replied. In the past, I had never invited any of my Peers' classmates home to Yotsuya. How could a shabby rented house in a second class quarter stand comparison with my friends' mansions? How could I introduce anyone to our disorderly household inhabited by a vengeful madwoman, a dishonoured official, a boorish authoritarian and a victimized bride? Grotesque personages from a Dostoyevsky story. Impossible to express anything of this to Jotaro, but I knew he understood my shame.

'My mother obliged me to consult her specialist cousin at St Luke's Hospital. She too has embraced the unassailable article of faith.'

'And the diagnosis?'

'Anaemia. A confirmation of my weakness.'

'Was this after the fumigation episode?'

'It was a punishment for my independent ambition.'

'Ambition is a fine thing. A manly virtue.'

'My father's disingenuous principles of manliness have much to do with the gnawing worm of ambition, which has made him a most disagreeable person.'

'Azusa is neither very gifted, nor alas a particularly successful civil servant. I can understand the narrowness of his pragmatism which struggles against the odds of his handicaps. He has shouldered the task of redeeming the Hiraoka name from dishonour.'

'Does our name need redeeming?'

'Now who's being disingenuous? You know very well that Azusa blames me for a wanton miscarriage of *risshin shusse*, success and advancement in life, a Meiji democratic policy that once benefited anyone of ability and merit even from the underclass. Our commendable Meiji modernists introduced us to a European form of secular salvation – self-improvement.'

I glanced at a hanging scroll over Jotaro's Go board. 'My life – a fragment of landscape', an inscription in Chinese characters by Chushu, the elegant soubriquet of a 19th century sinologist, Mishima Ki. The parlour spoke of a former Meiji governor's office, stocked with bygone, awkwardly prepossessing Victorian furniture that I assumed had not changed since Jotaro's days on the Sakhalin island colony.

'I had *risshin shusse* till 1914,' Jotaro said. 'It earned me a governorship and a wife of illustrious samurai pedigree, a Nagai. But success is in fact illusory.'

Saké gave me the courage to ask an impertinent question. 'Without disrespect, grandfather, might I ask what brought you to resign the governorship in 1914?'

'Forced me to resign, you mean. Hasn't your father seen fit to tell you of this alleged irregularity in my political conduct? Nothing very spectacular, in fact, which was not customary to other officials. I channelled some campaign funds from the island's fish canneries to the *Seiyukai*, the conservative majority party in government at the time. Party politics in those days was entirely dominated by constant rivalry between the Satsuma and Choshu clans, the ruling oligarchies. I owed my allegiance and governorship to the *Seiyukai* boss, Ito Hirobumi, of the Satsuma clan. A bribery scandal involving Satsuma naval officers and a German firm toppled the government in 1914. Public opinion was outraged, severe rioting broke out, and in the general chaos I became a minor casualty of the feuding oligarchies.'

'You are saying that corruption equals normal practice, and you played by the rules.'

'I am saying no such thing,' Jotaro rejected my callow manoeuvre. 'I am trying to instruct you in the art of depersonalization, a skill essential to the ambitious man. Look again dispassionately at the game you are playing. Passionate feelings are stirring to wakefulness in you. No blame in that. Don't you see? What is properly natural to you lends itself to misguidance by the unassailable article of faith? It predominates and inspires you to play rashly, blind to the transparent beauty of the Master's game.'

I was not sure that Jotaro compared me to the Master's rival, Kitani Minoru, in a flattering sense, even metaphorically. 'You are convinced the Shusai Master will win?'

'I fear he might lose to such an opponent. He faces a player who fails to respect the truth of Go – that winning and losing are not in themselves proper calculations.'

'One thing has certainly impressed me. Counting the points in Go is extremely complicated. I lack the visual and kinetic faculties to sum up the winning and losing positions that might be self-evident even at this stage.'

'Exactly so. In this game, even to acknowledge defeat is in itself a triumph of skill.'

Towards the end of November, the match accelerated to a tempo that far outstripped my comprehension. The volume of Natsuko's cries had also increased, upsetting my concentration. Deep into the night, Jotaro carried on anatomizing the emergent pattern. 'Kitani plays with his eyes wide open, very skilfully, but totally unaware of the picture the Shusai Master is creating,' Jotaro complained. 'There is a weakness at the centre.'

'Weakness at the centre' could only mean one thing, a reference to His Imperial Majesty that startled me back to attention. Natsuko's pleadings faded from my consciousness. Jotaro regarded my shock with amusement. 'What history do they teach at the Peers' School? Tiresome banalities, I'll wager. Orthodoxy without the least flavour of reality, Do they teach how modern Japan came into being by way of *gekokujo*, the overturning of seniors on top by juniors below?'

'I have heard the term before and wondered what it meant.'

'Here is an appreciable paradox for you. Can you believe that Japanese modernism came about by means of regression to a living god? Our present Showa Emperor owes his status of divinity to Japan's mania for progress and modernism, just as I owe it my success and downfall.'

Could anything sound more outrageously nonsensical? Jotaro must have taken leave of his senses. What had the outmoded myth of Nippon's Sun God to do with progress and modernism? I prided myself on being well-informed – there was little else to take pride in, other than being an omniscient little freak. I was unprepared for Jotaro's unconventional views, indeed as I now see them, transgressive ones. In any case, I replied, 'Anyone with the least knowledge of Shinto will object that the Emperor's divinity relies on ancient and nebulous creation fables that can hardly be called progressive or modernist.'

'That's obvious, of course, but fails to consider our national peculiarity. Old and new are characteristically Japanese twins. Tradition and novelty have always been contemporaries with us. Follow closely what I say, for the story I tell of our Celestial Majesty's pedigree is also in a sense mine – and yours. I was born at the end of the period called *yoake maye*, Before the Dawn. I assume your familiar with that?'

I nodded, aware that it described the long night of transition from the mid-18th century regime of the Tokugawa Shoguns to the Meiji Restoration in the 1860s when Japan opened her doors to the West.

'A century of endless famines and peasant uprisings,' Jotaro continued. 'And when the peasants could not take up arms in *ikki* against their landlords, the unscupulous rice merchants and tax collectors, they sought rectification in messianic cults. I remember being confronted as a boy of five by fanatics of this sort – men dressed in women's kimonos, women in male attire, who invaded wealthy homes demanding food, drink and money. *Ee ja naika*, they said, any action is all right. These were the followers of the trance-inducing *ya naoshi odori*, the dance to change the course of the world. My father and his employees used their clubs most savagely to drive them out.'

'You grew up in a wealthy household?'

'My father Hiraoka Takichi was a landowner and money lender with two warehouses in Kobe and Osaka. We are not quite the "nameless rustics" of your grandmother's legend. Do you know her story of the young Hiraoka who shot the white pheasant?'

'I am familiar with his crime.'

'It was an ordinary pheasant, not a sacred white one. White is her embellishment – and do you know why? The shootist was none other than my father, Hiraoka Takichi. As a young man, my father served for a time in the police force of the Tokugawa *bakufu*. This was in 1837 at Osaka. In this year, Oshio Heiachiro, a gentleman of the samurai class, eminent scholar of *yomeigaku* Confucianism and a former police official of Osaka city, led a protest against the conditions of famine prevailing in that city. Oshio's aim was *kyumin*, Save the People, a motto emblazoned on his banners. It was the most serious uprising the Tokugawa regime had faced in a long time. But judged purely on its organizational merits, Oshio's insurrection was a total fiasco. The *bakufu* forces easily suppressed it. Oshio committed suicide, his salt-pickled corpse and that of his son were disgraced by public crucifixion in Osaka sixteen months after his death. No alleviation of misery benefited the starving townsfolk as a result of the rebellion. It is hard to see why Oshio's failure is venerated by both left and right even today. Popular legend says that Oshio escaped to China, and there, in metamorphosis as Hung Hsiu-chü'an, he led the far more catastrophic Taiping Rebellion.

'The police squad in which my father happened to find himself, captured a follower of Oshio, a lower class *ronin* samurai, who asked permission to commit suicide. To which the police lieutenant replied, "There are many samurai like us who sympathize with Oshio's action. We are officers trained to obey our overlords, the Tokugawa *bakufu*. Oshio too, until now, was a faithful state official. Can you explain to us how he resolved his act of civil disobedience?"

"Oshio espoused the way of *yomeigaku*★," the *ronin* said. "To know

---

★ Unorthodox neo-Confucianist philosophy of the Hsin-hsüeh school of intuitionism, developed by the Chinese warrior scholar Wang Yang-ming in opposition to official Confucian state rationalism.

and not to act is the same as not knowing at all. This sums up Oshio's justification."

"A time will soon come," the police lieutenant said, "when samurai of our class must wipe the mist from the mirror." Wiping the mirror clear of mist is an essential of *yomeigaku*, and by saying this the lieutenant revealed himself a secret adherent of that philosophy. What does the saying really propose? It means regaining one's innate, intuitive knowledge which can only come from identifying oneself with the Absolute, *kitaikyo*. This idea of celestial rectitude, inherent in everyone, has unexpected revolutionary consequences. Oshio understood that rectification of self in the light of the Absolute carries with it the categorically imperative necessity to rectify injustice. He argued that loyalty to the Absolute must precede fealty to one's lord. Therefore, although the government might lawfully condemn his act as a rebellious uprising, Oshio confidently named it *gikyo*, Righteous Undertaking. He claimed allegiance to the Emperor, the Mirror of eternally pure Japanese values, and refused it to the mere temporal political authority of the *bakufu*. Oshio held that the *bakufu* had betrayed the Imperial Throne. His act was a sacrificial one of remonstrance, a religious and not social revolutionary one. Purity of intention is the goal, not necessarily success. The sincere action does not require any effectiveness. Do you grasp the significance of Oshio's noble failure?'

'It is hard to see.'

'What else can wiping the mirror clear suggest but restoring the Emperor and overthrowing the *bakufu* Shogun usurpers? Oshio's pure self-sacrificial act was a model to a certain type of samurai who in thirty years time would do precisely that – create the Meiji Restoration in reality.'

'Did the police lieutenant allow the *ronin* to go free?'

'Indeed, yes, by generously allowing him his wish to die. He disembowelled himself and was decapitated by the lieutenant serving as his *kaishaku-nin* in accordance with *seppuku* ritual. His body was handed over to the authorities, who displayed it on a gallows. My father had the duty to return the head in a jar of saké to the *ronin*'s daughter. The police lieutenant had pledged himself to look after the *ronin*'s sixteen-year-old daughter. And this is how my father came to set his foot on the lower rung of the samurai class, by way of a marriage to this girl as commanded by a superior officer.'

'I knew nothing of this.'

'Do you feel gratified to have a disembowelled and beheaded samurai outlaw in your geneology?'

'I am, but how did Hiraoka Takichi feel to have him for a postmortem father-in-law?'

Jotaro laughed. 'I never had the temerity to ask him. My father was the very opposite of an anarchist, but he reminded me physically of Oshio, green-complexioned, suffering from weak lungs, a man of severe and humourless temper. Oshio had been a policeman too, renowned for his persecutions of Christians, corrupt Buddhist clerics and municipal officials. My father earned his notoriety by ruthless exploitation of the same poor folk that Oshio had given his life to defend. This unlikely pair – the unswerving idealist and the narrow realist – are the original twin cutting edges of Japan's modernism. I remember my father's comment to me once: "Modern Japan is like the strong rice wine which the ancient chronicles tell us was an invention of the mischief deity Susanoo. Oshio was the first to taste this ragpickers' wine. Now we are all drunk on it." I took him to mean that the Tokugawa regime's strictly enforced, 200-years' policy of closed country isolationism had encouraged the underground fermentation of a modernism to which a new breed of man had grown addicted. My father belonged to the first phase of samurai capitalism – a formulation that might strike you as a little odd. The Tokugawa precept which upheld samurai virtue in ideal opposition to the merchant species motivated by greed had long become a pious hypocrisy. In reality, the Shoguns' 200 years' era of peace had completely deprived the samurai class of its traditional warrior function, and it thereby brought the cult of *bushido* to life. *Bushido* was a way of maintaining practical self-respect in peacetime when the sword is impractical. The samurai thus peacefully engaged, at once practical and inward-looking, would seem to be the ideal bulwark of Tokugawa stability. In fact, these peacetime samurai carried the seeds of the Tokugawa Shoguns' own destruction. The pacification of the samurai class on which the regime stood firmly pedestalled would eventually bring *gekokujo*, the toppling of seniors on top by juniors below. One way alone could ensure that the sword did not rust in its scabbard, and this cutting edge was recognized by intelligent young samurai of humbler origin. Intermarriages between these and merchant families had proceeded apace in the century Before the Dawn. Do you see? This is the same as asking – what did the Meiji modernists modernize? Can you answer me that without reference to the pious clichés of your school textbooks?

'I am afraid that is the only answer I can refer to.'

'Well, perhaps you might consider the Meiji Restoration in this light. It restored the lands held in fiefdom to the Emperor, that is, feudalism was abolished in the Emperor's name only, but in actual fact constitutionally, to establish a uniform Westernized central government under the command of the ruling Meiji oligarchies of former samurai. The end of feudalism, they knew, would mean the liquidation of the samurai as a class and the creation of a conscript army drawn from the peasantry. Meiji reformers were very astute. Their achievement was to consolidate loyalty to the state by simplifying it to a common denominator. This they did, first, by the samuraization of the new Imperial army, and second, by a speeded-up programme of mass education which in effect Confucianized the entire population. The creeds and codes which had formerly been the minority privileges of a feudal hierarchy were now prescribed for all. This meant any citizen who served in the army was de facto a samurai enjoined to act as one; just as anyone educated, thanks to benign Imperial sanction, owed direct fealty and obligation to the Emperor, along the lines of Confucian patriarchal conformity. But real former samurai were now entrepreneurs who created our *zaibatsu* clique of financial and industrial cartels. To minimize the risks of Western industrialism, the Meiji restorationists ideologically feudalized the whole population in order to modernize it thoroughly and bring it under state control. Our industrial life employment system today is one long-term Meiji sequel which guarantees the dependence of those who benefit from it.'

'In other words, what you're really saying is that the Meiji Restoration restored *no one* – it was simply a modernist episode of Shogunism.'

'You might conclude that,' Jotaro answered, finally deciding to place a white pebble that he had much worried to a silvery polish between his fingers.

'How depressing.'

Jotaro's unconventional teaching at the time totally surprised me. It had an unorthodox but persuasive 'flavour of reality', as he put it. I imagined that Jotaro's history lesson must somehow be plain to read on the Go board, but I could not for the life of me see it in the coded message of the stones. My head ached from the effort, and from the pounding on it of Natsuko's lamentations, like the avenging furies of Greek legend who drive the guilty mad. Her world was literally scream-ing itself to death, while Jotaro revealed another and perhaps only real one in which my ambition must play from now on. I was not eager to inhabit this new practical world of cynicism. To speak plainly, I felt terrified of it. I longed for Natsuko's walls that were shrinking away to mist.

'One thing I still do not comprehend,' I said, looking for a subclause of escape. 'What does Oshio's noble failure have to do with his suc-cessors' modernism? He exemplifies a retrograde virtue worlds apart from modern progress.'

'Is there not something deeply regressive in all modernist ambitions? Regression is not a characteristic peculiar to our Meiji modernists alone. Modernism is at heart arch-reactionary because it simplifies, and thereby lands in the most unmanageable contradictions. You have not grasped that Oshio's intention, while entirely pure, was also deeply speculative. He cast the dice, intending neither to win nor to lose – and what was the result? Such a throw has the most incalculable and wildest repercussions. My generation represents the second phase consolidation of samurai capitalism. Call it merely speculative capitalism, bearing little resemblance to its origins, since all traces of the samurai have passed into mythology. And yet. And yet. We have entered the third and decisive expansionary phase of capitalism, and this is where Oshio's throw of the dice has led us. The original intention now seems remote, but its consequences are not. We will soon know if the elder and younger players of this game any longer agree on the meaning of speculation.'

Over the next several nights, I accompanied Jotaro on his past entre-preneurial adventures. The ruination of Jotaro's civil service career in 1914 had left the bosses of the *Seiyukai* party indebted to him. Compensation for his misfortune – as much a reward for his loyalty as a further mortgage on it – came from the giant industrial cartel Mitsui. This *zaibatsu* firm, a supporter of the *Seiyukai*, made Jotaro its scout, or more precisely in today's terms, an industrial spy. Jotaro travelled to South East Asia, Europe, Russia and even America in the period of the First World War which were boom years for the Japanese economy. He benefited from privileged *Seiyukai* information and purchased shares in the rapidly expanding industrial sectors. Jotaro prospered most in the brief three-year premiership of the new *Seiyukai* chieftain, Hara Takashi, the 'Great Commoner', so-called because he was the first head of government to come from neither of the ruling clans. Hara's reign was also a time of mass industrial unrest, with rice rioters out in the streets again as in Oshio's day, protesting this time against war profiteers like my grandfather. One such fanatic protestor stabbed Prime Minister Hara to death on Tokyo station in 1921, the year in which the war boom collapsed, and both these events seriously affected Jotaro's fortunes. The banking crisis of 1927, forerunner of the Great Depression soon to come, undermined the credit structure of the new firms in which Jotaro had invested. The catastrophe of 1929 had been predicted in another more occult sense, 'when the Catfish stirred.' On 1 September 1923, two years before my birth, an immense earthquake wiped out the city of Yokohama, destroyed half of Tokyo and many other towns in the Kanto area. Popular superstition has it that a giant catfish lives beneath the land of Japan, and periodically, when angered by the wickedness of fools dwelling on the surface, he arches his back in reprisal, and this explains the tremors and earthquakes that have troubled Japan through-out the ages.

Jotaro's decline in the 20s was the usual sad story of debt, foreclosure of mortgages, repossessed properties, family heirlooms auctioned, and the family home in Tokyo sold. Jotaro regretted nothing in his adventures. He showed me a survey map of rubber plantations in Malaya, laid out very like the rectilineal divisions of the Go board, with spaces here and there claimed by black patches. These were the plantations in which he still held shares. 'Rubber prices fell in the slump after the war and my shares were reckoned worthless. Now they have risen steeply again. This will be my legacy to Azusa.'

Jotaro had not been the only Japanese speculator to invest in the Malayan rubber plantations. Indeed, the network of artificially straight avenues, useful alike to rubber-tappers and transport had already become well-known to our military strategists, and would soon provide convenient routes for the Imperial Army's advance, the assault troops equipped with folding bicycles and the light-armoured columns, in their lightning strike on Singapore.

'I was unaware of this outcome of speculation, foretold by the chequered survey map. Nor did I fully comprehend the implications of Jotaro's analysis of the Go match. In the characters of the Shusai Master and his younger opponent, and in their styles of play, Jotaro could read the future. As in the game, his own Meiji style of speculative capitalism, corrupt but prudently liberal, had given way to impetuous tactics, a strange blend of planning and haphazardous élan which characterized an intuitive war economy.

'You are very like me,' Jotaro surprised me by saying. 'An avidity for life masquerading as a taste for entertainment – this has been my disguise. And yours? Have you already decided on it?'

'Mine I expect will take the form of art.'

'In that case, you will repeat the speculative misadventures of my life, but differently of course.'

Not even the experienced player Jotaro could have anticipated how long the game would take. Ten hours are normally allotted to a match between high-ranking players. This rule was relaxed to allow the Master 19 hours and 57 minutes of play, and his opponent 34 hours and 19 minutes – 14 sessions in all, serialized in 64 installments by the reporter Kawabata Yasunari. The contest stretched nearly six months to December 4th, when the game finally ended in Ito at Dan Koen Inn, and the Shusai Master declared white defeated on the black opponent's 237th play. On the morning of 18 January 1940, the Shusai Master died in Atami at the Urokoya Inn. Stone by stone, we had witnessed his tumulus built.

Our replay of the last sessions went on after December 4th, nearly to Christmas, at which time Natsuko's crisis approached its fatal conclusion. At 3 a.m., on our last night of play, Jotaro opened a bottle of whisky to toast the Shusai Master's retirement from the game. I heard Natsuko call my name several times. Jotaro did not require me to stay, but I preferred to think he did. After a pause, I heard her cry again with a dreadful, unnatural sadness, 'Mother does not love you anymore.' Natsuko had spoken the words of last resort that mothers use to blackmail little children. I could bear it no more. Jotaro understood and nodded his encouragement to go to her.

My exit from the parlour was blocked by Tsuki, carrying a white enamelled bucket in which I saw blood-soaked cloths afloat in disinfectant. 'The mistress bleeds. It is unsightly,' Tsuki informed her Jotaro. 'The young master ought to be spared.'

'But she goes on asking for me,' I objected, by now in a state of tears. 'It is cruel to deny her, unpardonably cruel.'

'Unpardonable or not, come back and sit down,' Jotaro ordered, although in the kindliest tone.

Tsuki stood sentry at the door to prevent my escape.

'Perhaps we could begin a new game,' Jotaro offered.

'The young master has no heart for that now,' Tsuki said. 'Why don't you entertain him?'

'What do you suggest?' Jotaro knocked back a stiff measure of whisky.

Tsuki began to sing: 'Things never changed since the Time of the Gods . . .'

'The flowing of water, the Way of Love,' Jotaro added the next line. Tsuki came forward to accept the drink he offered. 'A fine old song,' he laughed. 'But I have a much better one, truly unpardonable at this moment.' And this is what my grandfather sang:

> The white snow on Fuji
> Melts in the morning sun,
> Melts and runs down
> To Mishima,
> Where Mishima's prostitutes
> Mix it in their make-up . . .

These verses were far from sad. I listened to the elders improvise additional stanzas of increasing ribaldry as the alcohol warmed away inhibition.

The ballad identified Mishima, a town well known for its excellent view of snow-capped Mount Fuji, situated between Fuji and the sea to the south. My aged entertainers sang of Fuji's eternal snow, leeched away by eroticism. I had found my true name. *Mishima* – the place, which at once gave me my forename, *Yukio*, derived from the word snow, streaming down the mountainside to Mishima. The ice-cold waters of Mishima flowed down my cheeks in warm streams.

'Is this a song to make you weep?' Jotaro the affable monster remarked, marvelling at my tears.

'She can hear us,' I replied.

'As we do her,' Jotaro shrugged. 'It cannot be helped. We are waiting to see who will appear first at the door.'

'She cannot get up from her bed. How can she possibly come here? And I am not permitted to see her.'

Jotaro shook his head. 'No, you do not foresee the entrance she could make.'

'What are you saying?' I blamed Jotaro's ominous tone on his excess of alcohol. But I too began to share his expectation.

'In your grandmother's estimation, I am a music hall *farceur*, a country jester with no appreciation of higher things. She prides herself on a deep understanding of Noh and its arcane rules. Isn't it true in these plays that the main character is a ghost, often introduced in the disguise of a humble rustic person, a fisherman or reaper –' and here Jotaro seized Tsuki by the wrists to exhibit her hands to me, those deformities that culled Natsuko's blood '– or an old woman? Does the character not finally reappear in original shape, a former great warrior or beautiful court lady, the manifestation of a tormented spirit seeking to be exorcised of its past? What can this mean?'

I looked at the door, apprehensive of finding Natsuko's wrathful form visible there. I heard the approaching thump of her cane, and again the plaintive, unnaturally assumed mother's voice calling to me.

'She strikes the floor with her cane,' Tsuki said, breaking the spell and the hold of Jotaro's manacles. 'Let me attend to her.'

Yukio Mishima, the ironist and dissembler, employs the melted snow of sacred Fuji in his cosmetic. Does he wish to impersonate the white-faced, lowliest of creatures, Mishima's *joroshu*, a prostitute? Does he also intend to mimic the hideously frightening whiteness of leprosy?

9   NO SURRENDER

I BEGAN TO 'DATE' the Baroness Omiyeke Keiko, as Americans say with uncharacteristic discretion, whenever my other weekend duties left me an evening free to entertain this Kendo-practising Rose Cavalier. She became my regular partner in sorties to nightclubs and aristocratic house parties, but these companionable enjoyments never trespassed beyond Platonic limits. Duty evolved into a peculiar sort of pleasure, in which nature did take its course, but not this time as Captain Sam Lazar had calculated. Ex-Baroness Omiyeke was the vixen to Lazar's fox with her own calculating ambitions, and, as is often the case with women of independent character, she gratified her freedom by basking in the company of an exclusively homosexual male.

Some months into our odd partnership that summer, Keiko and I attended an evening fête at the fashionable Karuizawa resort outside Tokyo. 'You are aware of Captain Sam's romantic designs?' Keiko asked, as we took refreshments after our dance-floor exertions.

'What designs do you mean?'

'Don't pretend ignorance, Kochan – his matrimonial plans for us.'

'Can you imagine us married, Baroness? I did not consider Sam's fantasies even worth mentioning.'

Keiko made no reply but fished in her handbag, I thought for cigarettes. She came out with a photograph. At the sight of it, I plunged into an abyss of shame. Blood pounded in my ears. It was a portrait of me in the rose-coloured samurai armour, taken in Sam's Imperial Hotel studio.

'Looks like you're being devoured by a lobster,' Keiko observed, as she threw it on the table. 'Here, a souvenir.'

'I can be blackmailed,' I exclaimed.

'What for blackmailed? Aren't you perfectly willing to do anything Sam requires of you?'

'I am not willing,' I protested. 'I have no choice.'

'Like the rest of us,' the Baroness acidly remarked.

I forced myself not to snatch up the photograph and hide it away from the crowd of revellers. But no one paused from the swirl to pry into my contemplation of Hiraoka Kimitake, 'devoured by a lobster', the edges of the picture sticky with spilt Coke on the table.

'I would like another body,' I said.

'What's wrong with the one you have?' Keiko laughed. 'You people are so theatrical.'

You people. I felt stripped of my humanity with those words, which condemned me to the ghetto of extraterrestrial gay freaks. 'I would like that lobster shell to fasten itself to me, like coral, and become fossilized into rock-hard muscles of my own. I would like to be a perfect surface of muscles, a classically perfect Greek statue. I shall pose for the public one day, I vow it, I shall pose flamboyantly with a different body, a body transformed beyond recognition.'

Keiko listened sadly, as one might to a frightened child talking to itself in the dark. 'Appearing weak can have its advantages, *cher maitre*,' she said.

'You can say that because you're beautiful and strong. I am weak and you despise me for it.'

'What makes you think I'm any different, inwardly?'

'Nonsense, inwardly. That's only talk about the inward spirit. Next you'll tell me about my "inner beauty". I want to look the part of someone who fits in with the way you look and are outwardly.'

'You already fit the part,' Baroness Omiyeke said. She picked up the photograph from the table, tore it into bits and dropped them into her handbag. 'Anything is possible in this time of reverse course.'

Part Two

THE JEWEL
− Anatomy of a Bestseller −

FROM THE UNEDITED TRANSCRIPTS OF YUKIO MISHIMA'S INTERVIEW WITH TOKUOKA ATSUO IN BENARES, INDIA, OCTOBER 1967

INTRODUCTION by Tokuoka Atsuo, correspondent of the *Mainichi Shimbun*.

ON THE MORNING of 17th October 1967, I arrived in Benares, India, and was escorted to Clark's Hotel where Yukio Mishima lodged during his brief research visit to that city. Acting on a tip from Mishima's publisher, Nitta Hiroshi, I had flown from Tokyo to interview Mishima who, according to all accounts, looked certain to win this year's Nobel Prize.

My interview began with an obvious and rather absurd question. Did Mishima himself feel confident of winning the Nobel? Why should I, already acquainted with Mishima for many years and having practised journalism even longer, begin so amateurishly? My excuse is an unusual one. Mishima received me in his room at Clark's, or more accurately, on a couch occupying the balcony of that room. He lay on this couch stark naked, like one of those *saddhu* holy men who parade through the streets of India in total unselfconscious nudity. 'Welcome to Kashi, the Jewel,' he greeted me. The meaning of 'Kashi, the Jewel' eluded me. I was too acutely embarrassed even to ask what it meant. How could I possibly conduct an interview in this situation? Fortunately, a screen of bougainvillaea over the balcony concealed us from the view of any hotel patrons strolling on the lawn.

Clumsy with nervousness, I proceeded to set up the tape-recorder, trying to keep my eyes averted from Mishima's odalisque pose on the couch. It occurred to me that nudity was a sort of masquerade for him, an idea which contributed an edge of resentment to my agitation. I disliked being tested in this absurd fashion.

As I say, I have known Mishima for a good number of years. Along with many others in his wide circle of acquaintanceship that he has cultivated with astute self-publicist charm, I watched him transform a body that had always been sickly, and even by negligent intellectual standards, decidedly puny, into a spectacular exhibition of muscles. Four or five years of discipline this had cost him, I don't rightly remember the exact number, but beginning in the mid-50s, to achieve the stock classic look of Mr Atlas, spiritual godfather to all body-builders in those more innocent days of iron-pumpers.

There is, of course, nothing wrong or improper in desiring to improve one's body. It is admirable, in fact. Nor is athletic prowess disfavoured as a virtue in Japan. As everywhere else in the world, in Japan too, comeliness of form in a man or woman is prized. All of this is obvious. But what appeared out of the ordinary in Mishima's case, abnormal in our view, is that he made his body the aesthetic centre of attention. Year by year, we were treated to the spectacle of his progress in magazines of a frankly dubious sort, in photographs ever-escalating towards the bizarre and the morbid. He trespassed beyond the limits of taste and even eccentricity. Strange thing – the more he presented himself in muscled perfection, the greater inversely did he represent a decadent.

We saw this, and in classic Japanese fashion, turned our faces away. His readers then and today cannot reconcile, as I could not on that morning in Benares, the two Mishimas, the writer of rare and accomplished style, 'the Japanese Thomas Mann', as some have called him, and the vulgar dandy of the barbells. It seemed to us that he transgressed convention in a deliberate effort to outlaw himself from respectability. And in this, he succeeded. Perhaps the critic who identified Mishima as Japan's first Dadaist was right. Only now, looking back on the interview in Benares and the last years leading up to Mishima's suicide in 1970, do I realize what his body was *for* – what for, in his thirties and at the height of his literary powers, should he expend so much of his remarkable energy on creating that particular body? It was a machine of self-execution.

I did not understand Mishima's disturbed condition of mind at the time, how perilously near to being unhinged he was.

In any case, there he was, naked, and I suppose in a way, beautiful. He answered my uninteresting question with candour. 'Am I confident of winning? I would be a little more if UN Secretary-General Dag Hammarskjöld were still living and able to influence the Swedish Academy. He was a great admirer of my work, you know. Otherwise, it is all journalists' hearsay.' He laughed, a neighing laughter that always made him sound like a nightclub manager, and added more than I bargained for. 'Two years ago, on a visit to my publisher Bonniers in Stockholm, I was taken to a very special restaurant by one of my translators, Erik Sundström This was the Gyllene Freden restaurant in Stockholm's Old Town, where the Swedish academicians traditionally meet to celebrate their selection of a Nobel Prize winner. We ate the Academy's traditional meal, reindeer meat cooked in juniper berries and served with rowanberries, "a foretaste of the Nobel," Sundström said. The reindeer delicacy was preceded by many toasts of good Finnish vodka and a dish of blood sausages, a country variety from Ullasjö in Västergötland, Sundström told me, which before cooking are blessed with some magic words to make sure they hold together. The cook says, "Tough as the skin of cock and balls", and the sausages are smacked against the wall or the stove. "Do you think these have been cooked in the right magic way?" I asked. "I don't know," Sundström replied. "Shall I throw one against the wall and see?" I got a telegram from Sundström just before I left Tokyo last week, encouraging me, "whether you win the Nobel Prize or not, remember, tough as the skin of cock and balls." And that's the confidence I feel, in reply to your question.'

Mishima stood up to illustrate his anecdote of the sausages, aware no doubt that his movements would bring my sights to bear on his penis and testicles whipping to-and-fro in a balletic *fouette*.

Mishima offered me a glass of Chivas Regal, which I accepted, despite the inordinately early time of day. I consumed a good measure of his scotch during the course of an interview which he soon hijacked as a monologue. Much of what he said, at first, seemed incomprehensible to me. He began by saying that he would rather give a 'wordless interview', one in which he would perform a dance illustrating his childhood agonies for me, 'like the stations of the Cross,' a Noh drama 'like the Catholic Mass translated into pure Shinto gestures.' Did I understand? I did not. He then went on, telling me of the spread of Greek sculpture via the Roman Empire and its influence on the art of northern India – 'a permeation of cultural frontiers, reminding me of Japan's Buddhist origins' – which had led him to a momentous discovery three days ago. 'I am entirely convinced that St Sebastian, the Christian martyr of Praetorian rank, was in fact an Indian.'

'Are you saying he was a Hindu?'

'I am saying he was involved in a dangerous heresy – mutiny against the Emperor – which apparently took the form of Christian passive resistance, something that the Christians claimed for themselves, but which proves to me that Sebastian was a Jain warrior of the Ksatriya caste. But the really amazing thing is this, Tokuoka-*san*. I have *seen* a likeness of Sebastian here in Benares. Three days ago, in the disused graveyard of a mosque, I saw a beautiful Indian lad with the upper caste, fair-skinned, Graeco-Roman features of Sebastian. Isn't that incredible?'

It was certainly incredible. But who could comprehend it?

As I drank again of the fine Chivas Regal, Mishima remarked, 'I shall have to find another bottle for my rendezvous tonight with an Aghori that Dr Chatterjee has arranged for me.'

I took this as a reproach to moderate my drinking. Mishima corrected my misapprehension by refilling my glass, but he did not venture to explain what 'an Aghori' was.

The tape was finally in place and recording.

—You've met Dr Chatterjee, my guide in Benares? Mishima asked. A perfect scoundrel. He is the sort of rogue who thrives on the complicity of fools, like those Bangkok guides who volunteer to pimp for salacious Japanese businessmen.

Dr Chatterjee had kindly escorted me from the airport to Clark's Hotel earlier that morning. He seemed to me a perfectly courteous, learned Indian gentleman. What had the poor fellow done to merit such harsh judgement?

—What's he done? Mishima laughed. Do you know what Dr Chatterjee is doing right now? Sulking. He's sitting in his little room in the Dal Mandi red light district, sulking, because your visit today has deprived him of his last opportunity to torment me, since my three days' sojourn in Benares ends tonight.

—Torments you? Then, why didn't you get rid of him at once?

—There wasn't time on this brief research tour to find someone else, Mishima said, rolling over flat on his back, as though on a psychoanalyst's couch, and gazing up at the sun-speckled bougainvillaea.—Besides, I couldn't risk offending my acquaintance at the British Council in Calcutta who recommended Dr Chatterjee to me as the ideally informed guide to Benares.

—I cannot see how such an apparently inoffensive fellow could possibly torment anyone, least of all a man like you, Mishima-*san*.

—Exactly, a man like me, Mishima replied, suddenly become animated and sitting upright to face me, eye to eye.—He is aptly named Chatterjee, reminding me of the English words, 'chattering jay'. He is teemingly garrulous, pedantic in his explanations which I find instructive but tedious. My first impression of him, on his arrival punctually at the desk of Clark's, was a favourable one of an Indian gent in a white linen suit. You've seen, he limps slightly and uses an Englishman's ashplant stick. On closer view, his white linen proves to be badly rumpled and stained calico. Colours tend to deceive one in India. Tones which appear strikingly pure at a distance reveal themselves faded or dirty in proximity. Smallpox has left his cheeks coarsely sieved like burlap. I have become all too familiar with Dr Chatterjee's disagreeable habit of scratching his private parts with sudden frantic violence as though plagued by attacks of scabies, a performance which usually climaxes one of his ponderous explanations, ending in a fit of giggles. At our first meeting, he handed me his card which introduces Dr Anant Chatterjee, PhD graduate in Social Anthropology at the LSE.

'London School of Economics?' I comment.

'No, Lahore School of English,' he giggles, a forewarning of his chronic habit. 'A joke, sir. I do apologize.'

It further transpires that his PhD has yet to be earned. He confesses to having idled ten years in the completion of his doctoral thesis, a study of Benares. I ask, 'What aspect of Benares?'

'Death – an endlessly fascinating subject. Wouldn't you agree, sir?'

'Not endless, Dr Chatterjee.'

All of this account, in all its naturalistic detail, is mimed to perfection by Mishima. He is rightly admired as an exceptionally gifted mimic. I have witnessed him in rehearsal performing all the parts of a Kabuki play, much to the astonishment of his audience, a professional cast of Kabuki actors under his direction. Mishima's voice ranges in scale from baritone to tenor, and I have heard him use it to improvise all the singers' roles in a three-act opera libretto that he had written. A baroque splendour of words, which is Mishima's hallmark in speech as in writing, has been lavished on his depiction of Dr Chatterjee. And I am almost persuaded of its reality – except that I do not remember Dr Chatterjee's face 'sieved like burlap'; nor do I recall him either limping or using a stick. Mishima evidently retains possession of his aesthetic faculties, but despite this, I am more than ever certain that he is mentally unbalanced.

Is all of this merely a verbal foreplay to Mishima's 'wordless interview'? A dance yet to come? I dread the prospect.

Mishima has arisen from his sybarite's couch and now leans against the parapet of the balcony, indifferent to the stares of an elderly couple seated on their deck chairs on the lawn, a faded blonde Englishman and a lady whose limbs are grossly swollen by oedema.

—Look there, Mishima says, pointing to the Benares skyline in the distance.—Can you see the three hills on which the city was built?

All I see is a chaos of dilapidated buildings, an overgrown tangle which permits no unobstructed sight of any hills. I see the smoke of Mishima's *bidi* – the cheap tobacco-leaf cigarette of the Indian poor – a miniature likeness of the distant greasy plume in the sky over Benares, drifting up from the cremation ghats on the river shore. Benares is rightly named 'forest of lights', no doubt because of the cremation pyres that burn here day and night without cease.—On my arrival here three days ago, we climbed to the top of one of those hills, and looked back. 'Benares, sir,' Dr Chatterjee joyfully proclaimed. 'City of awesome holiness, known to pious Hindus by its true name, Kashi, navel of the cosmos, the Jewel –' Mishima halts, simulating the rumble of bronchial catarrh which must have impeded the flow of Dr Chatterjee's paean.

He mimicks his guide now spitting up an oyster of phlegm – 'begging your pardon, sir' – and the elderly couple below abandon their deck chairs, in retreat from this expectorating madman on the balcony. Mishima proceeds with Dr Chatterjee's oration. 'This is Vishvanatha hilltop, the middle one of three hills on which ancient Kashi first arose. To our eyes these hills are the three prongs of the Lord God Shiva's trident. Upheld by Shiva's trident – Jewel suspended above the earth – Kashi alone will survive the universal holocaust of fire and flood, *pralaya*, as we Hindus say.'

—Half an hour before, Shiva had nearly let us drown, Mishima added, grinning sardonically.

—What do you mean, *drown*?

—I refer to a totally unseasonable monsoon downpour, discharged on us from a wall of yellow clouds, like the slabs of a urinal. 'Dust from the southern plains,' Dr Chatterjee explains. The Ganges itself seemed to have broken over our heads; a diluvial torrent next followed by an icy breeze from the Himalayas, chilling us to the marrow. Can't you feel it, Tokuoka-*san*, the Himalayan chill in the air?

It is a pleasantly warm, autumn day, but Mishima's torso appears suddenly goosefleshed by a phantom draught that I cannot feel.

—'Most unusually temperamental weather for Benares,' Dr Chatterjee tells me, that rascal. 'Only in England can one expect to have all four seasons in a single day.'

'Is it an omen?' I ask.

'Here, everything is an omen, sir,' he replies. He fishes out a damp *bidi* from his jacket and the tobacco splutters in the flame of his Korean-made Zippo.

Nice detail, that 'Korean-made Zippo'. But is it true? I offered Dr Chatterjee a cigarette in the taxi on our way to Clark's, which he politely declined, saying he was a non-smoker.

—On Vishvanatha hilltop, Dr Chatterjee waves his ashplant like a maestro's baton, describing a whirlpool of circles in the air. 'A pilgrim to Kashi must circle the city seven times,' he says. 'These circuits represent the seven circles of the spine, according to Yogic anatomy, a reminder to us that Kashi is a living being, indeed the female spouse of Lord Shiva from whom he gains unsurpassed pleasure. With the gift of *divya drsti* – divine sight – one is able to perceive the real Kashi, a sacred geography of temples displaying all the precision, clarity and order of a mandala. Kashi is a *tirtha*, a crossing place between this world and the far shore of the transcendent. That is why so many old people undertake the hardships of Kashi-*vas*, residence in Kashi, because to die here will bring them immediate attainment of liberation from the cycle of rebirth. Can you see anything of this intangible Jewel, sir?' Are *you* able to see this Jewel, Tokuoka-*san*?

—I must confess not, *sensei*.

—There is nothing mysterious about India. At night, beyond the perimeter of the hotel gardens, under a cluster of pipal trees, I can see the glow-worm winks of *bidis* that a gang of coolies are smoking before they bed down on the earth. Those red dots might be the eyes of *rakshasas*, goblins that fly by night till cock-crow, the providers of Shiva's demonic sky transport. By daylight I know these coolies as transporters of another haunted type, rickshaw cyclists, impromptu porters and hirelings of the meanest caste, including a cobra charmer whose oboe bleats for rupees from every passerby, a diseased crew of gloomy and gentle wretches. I have seen them at twilight scavenging for their 'pudding' in the hotel rubbish bins. I am tempted to abandon literature and pass beyond the curtain of night in search of adventures. Every writer is drawn to flight, to dreams of exotic salvation, and sooner or later he will seek like Rimbaud to renounce his art for the unlettered paganism of some tropical land where he cannot speak the language. What adventures await me out there in the night? Only the mirage of my own spiritual weariness, a monotony of illness, the smell of poor food and death, of dusty earth-coloured villages worn out by droughts and monsoons. I feel engulfed in a sea of rags, beseiged as if by the countless refugees of an earthquake, a shadow army asleep in every doorway at nightfall. I confront a black mirror that reflects my own fultility and decay; my own imprisonment in the labyrinth of *mappo*.

I am surprised to hear Mishima use this word, *mappo*. I myself have not heard it spoken for a very long time, since my boyhood. *Mappo* is a Buddhist concept, meaning 'the end of the Law', an age of degeneracy when the Buddha's teaching loses its power over the natural depravity of man. *Mappo*, which our sect of Amida Buddhists says began in 1052, condemns us all to a time of ruin without foreseeable end. A truly frightful pessimism which I know accords with Mishima's cherished belief in the inevitability of nuclear holocaust. My feeling is, however, that Mishima has selected this word with a jeweller's cunning art to embellish his own sensationalist mood. He is too much an irreligious skeptic to put any credence in *mappo*.

Mishima observes my incredulity, and he laughs.—Do you imagine, Tokuoka-*san*, that by achieving the Nobel Prize I shall have found a loophole in the penitentiary condition of *mappo*? An escape from this endless nightmare of corruption, decadence and ruin?

—I cannot say it offers the redemption you seek.

—One's highest expectations can be a territory in which a sense of helpless disorientation prevails over ambition. Immediately on my arrival at Clark's, I was handed a telegram from my publisher Nitta Hiroshi, informing me that I had been shortlisted for the Nobel Prize. Did I have the foresight to pack my tuxedo? he inquired jokingly. Nitta appreciates my vanity, you see. I felt a desperate vitality coursing through me, like a poisonous mercury. Dr Chatterjee noticed my distress. 'You look troubled, sir. Is it bad news?' 'That will depend entirely on the outcome,' I answered. I could have been satisfied with this concise but elusive reply. Instead, some wayward impulse – my vanity perhaps, but also something more unaccountably perverse – compelled me to tell him of my candidature. The effect on Dr Chatterjee was electric. He insisted that we journey at once to Tatheri Bazaar for an immediate astrological prognosis. He overruled my feeble protestations. 'Benares is a place of no interest, sir. It can wait. A possible victory of this kind – the *Nobel Prize*, sir – a lifetime's goal, isn't it? Surely it outweighs all other considerations.' Dr Chatterjee is the mouthpiece of my own concessions to fame. I surrendered to his prurient salesmanship – weakly, resentfully, because weakness and resentment are the collaborationist twins of defeat. Unerringly, he has reckoned on my deepest flaw. Superstition. The scarecrow of my ambition. I am swept along to Vishvanatha Lane and the legendary Tatheri Bazaar. Have you seen it, Tokuoka-*san*? Brassware, ivory-handled sabres, *kinkob* brocades of silk and silver, painted wooden toys and clay figurines of the Hindu deities – all this gaudy merchandize seemed heart-rending, the sad treasury of a destitute land, which resurrects memories in me of the junk heap that Japan was after the war. Why am I confronted here, in a Third World bazaar, by images from a shameful past? I am heartsick and do not know why. An overcast sky of jaundiced clouds shuts out the light. And it thunders. Dr Chatterjee buys a *panchanga*, an astrology calendar in a tabloid format. He consults it like a racing-form to see if my horse will come up winner in the Nobel Prize sweepstakes. 'Inauspicious, sir,' he decides, 'if you do not mind me speaking frankly like this. Your expectation falls under the unfortunate spell of *chaturdasi*, the penultimate day of the dark lunar fortnight of our Hindu month, and the even more inauspicious new moon day of *amavasya* when ghosts manifest themselves.'

'What does your calendar say about my birthday, January 14th?'

His finger runs along the printed columns of symbols and Hindi gibberish until he announces, 'Altogether a different kettle of fish, sir. Most auspicious. You see, your birthday is the first day of the winter solstice which contains the lunar mansions of *uttarayana*, the daytime of the gods which goes on for six months. It is a particularly auspicious time to make a good death, as we say in Benares.'

He accommodates my laughter by promptly joining in with it.

Do you recognize what I felt, Tokuoka-*san*?

—I do, and I am flattered that you confide in me, Mishima-*san*. But aren't you tempting fate by relying on a journalist's discretion?

—Oh, but I *am* relying on it. Dr Chatterjee is my foreign correspondent, so to speak, as you are my domestic one. That's the point, you see.

I did not entirely see Mishima's point, but I finally understood the reason for his distemper of mind. A foretaste of deception had already subtly poisoned Mishima's hopes of securing the Nobel Prize. His eagerness to be a Nobel laureate would somehow conspire to deprive him of it.

We sat down again to the Chivas Regal. Mishima massaged himself vigorously against a ghostly chill, undetectable to my senses.

—Tell me, Mishima said. Have you journeyed all this way merely to interview a prospective Nobel Prize candidate?

—That is my assignment.

—Please do not lie to me, Tokuoka-*san*. You are in Benares chiefly to meet with a CIA executive, Sam Lazar.

—How on earth do you know that? I replied, genuinely startled by this revelation.

—I knew Sam when he was attached to G-2 Section after the war. That was nearly twenty years ago. Meeting him again, here in Benares, really was a matter of pure chance. Of course, nothing is so *im*pure as chance, as I realize, now that I am given a second 'chance' at the Nobel Prize.

—How did you chance to meet Colonel Lazar?

—Do you recall the disused graveyard of a mosque that I mentioned earlier?

—Where you saw a likeness of Sebastian?

—The very place. I found the mosque and its graveyard in a space shared by the Jnana Vapi Temple. Only Hindus are permitted to enter this holy inner sanctum, but, either by an oversight or by mischievous design, Dr Chatterjee led me into it, with unhappy consequences. There was something he urgently wished me to see: the *lingam* of Shiva, a phallic black stone set in a recessed altar of silver. You cannot imagine the deafening noise, Tokuoka-*san*, offensive to Japanese ears, the clanging of bells, the chanting – *Om Namah Shivaya!* – as the worshippers splash Ganges water on the *lingam* and cover it with marigolds and *bilva* leaves. Dr Chatterjee drags me over to a bidet-shaped rock, 'The *yoni*, sir,' he exclaims, and in a lewd whisper, 'the vagina, sir, a woman's *thing*,' as though unveiling the secret of the universe. My Japanese face had by now alerted a number of irate temple attendants, and we were forcibly expelled. Dr Chatterjee is full of apologies but unrepentant. He shows me a well in the courtyard, containing the *jnana* water of wisdom, 'The water first created by Shiva, dug from the earth with his trident, to cool his *lingam*. You see, the well is sealed by iron bars to prevent the suicide of enthusiastic liberation seekers.' In my mood, I would like to fling Dr Chatterjee into the well. Across a narrow strip of land, I see the white stucco cupola of a mosque, 'Built in the 16th century by Aurangzeb,' Dr Chatterjee says, 'on the ruins of the Vishveshvara Temple.' He refuses to cross this neutral zone separating the Jnana Vapi Temple from the mosque. 'Hindu and Muslim have too often murdered each other for possession of this sacred precinct.' If I want to enter the mosque, I must do so alone.

The clean, virile faith of Islam is very beguiling to me; but have you noticed something peculiar about the architecture of mosques, Tokuoka-san? Most of them seem to be obsessive copies of the former St Sophia in Constantinople – endless variations on a Byzantine theme with minarets stuck on. Muslims were perhaps keen to celebrate their greatest victory over Christianity. Aurangzeb's mosque is no exception, although one of its walls is very clearly a relic of the old, ornate Hindu temple. And what do I find *inside* the mosque? A perfect, empty cube of night. Something which for me has always represented the ultimate, absolute frigid thrill of asceticism, which is the void. Here, in this empty cube, away from the multitudinous din of Hinduism, I can *think* again, I can *feel*, I can *see*, and I can remember Nietzsche's meditation on the ascetic void: 'A will to nothingness, a revulsion from life, a rebellion against the principal conditions of being.' Yes, in this vacant space, I can see the materialized form of Nietzsche's conclusion. 'Man would sooner have the void for his purpose than to be void of purpose.'

—Pardon me, Mishima-*san*, but your encounter with Colonel Lazar?

—Don't worry, I'm coming to that. I emerged from a side door of the mosque, feeling refreshed by the science of nothingness, into a small, neglected graveyard. My vision was momentarily blinded by the incontinent flood of sunlight. I recovered my sight in time to glimpse a naked Indian lad struggling hastily to put on his *dhoti* as he fled. Was he perhaps a beggar, tranquilly sunbathing in the nude among these ruined tombs, whose privacy had been disturbed by my entrance? In those few instants, I had the breath-taking impression of exquisite beauty. I had been allowed a tantalizing glance at Sebastian, reincarnated in all the brilliance of his youth. I cannot adequately describe my satisfaction, Tokuoka-*san*, only to say, he appeared to me as a *proof*, a miraculous birth out of the void that I had touched inside the mosque. The void itself had been inseminated by my will to produce him. Are you familiar with our popular folktales of the *jizo*? He is the Bodhisattva Ksitigarbha, a Buddha deity of boundless compassion, who vowed to tarry on earth until the last soul in hell would be redeemed. The *jizo* manifests himself as a young boy who restores people to life, a protector of dead infants (and of my own suffocated years of infancy). He is in fact one of our own aboriginal Shinto spirits, a *kami*, adapted to Buddhist form, none other than the *sai-no-kami* guardian of the crossroads. Sebastian's likeness in the graveyard is my *jizo*, who signals a turning-point in my life.

—A large claim for a stranger you saw only briefly, and whom you are unlikely to see again.

—I *have* seen him again, Mishima assured me, unaware that he had grasped his penis, as small boys do when they are deeply engrossed.—Ah, but you want to hear about Sam Lazar. I contemplated the Muslim cemetery for a while, this unclean boneyard, thinking how very offensive it must be, if not indeed sacrilegious, to Hindus who cremate their dead. I looked back at the side wall of the mosque, at the details of Hindu ornament that had crumbled away to a mere façade of braille, a scripture of decay. My glance fell casually on an alcove in this wall, a Byzantine arch, and framed under its shadow I noticed another presence than my own. Someone else had come ahead of me into this place, silently observing me all the while. A man stood there, clad in a yellow Moroccan djellaba, a rucksack over his shoulder. His wide-brimmed straw hat sheltered a complexion of alarming paleness. I recognized that Mongol snub nose, the bluish freckles, the elongated Adam's apple bobbing up and down as he laughed in that hideously silent way of his. There could be no mistake. It was Sam Lazar. Wrinkles had begun to cobweb the skin round his eyes; his hair had gone from vehement red to dampened rust, but he was otherwise the same.

—Yes, that's him. Always the Peter Pan of the undercover world. He must have been greatly surprised to meet you again in such an unexpected way?

—Not in the least. I neglected to say, he had the latest model Hasselblad camera mounted on a tripod in front of him, pointed at the very spot where I had glimpsed my naked Indian *jizo*. His first words to me were, 'Mother fucker, you've ruined my picture.'

—I see, a spot of nude photography in a graveyard.

Of course, his taste for indecencies of that kind is well-known.

Mishima eyed me with amusement, relishing the embarrassment that my incautious remark now cost me.

—Not this time, Mishima replied. Apparently, Sam's interest had long since turned to photographing *deserted* graveyards, and my entry had ruined an hour's painstaking composition. What about my naked Indian boy? 'Haven't seen any nude Hindu, but if I had, I'd have told him to clear the hell out too.'

—Did you believe him?

—To photograph deserted graveyards, while on leave from the over-populated one of Vietnam, seems to me a credible form of recreational therapy. It is entirely natural that Sam should want to be another Atget, who specialized in taking pictures of Paris void of people. And his straw hat, red hair and green eyes put me in mind of Van Gogh, searching this time to capture the pure abstract effects of light in a vacant cemetery. But why did he choose to appear in the absurd yellow djellaba? 'You look like a hippy tourist just off the train from Marrakesh,' I said. 'And you, Kochan? Those ridiculous tumescent muscles, like a pneumatic doll.' My clothes were still uncomfortably damp after the monsoon rain. I took off my shirt. 'All right, Sam, you've already wasted one frame on me. Why not take some more pictures?' He replied, 'Why not strip down completely? Let's have a nude Emperor-worshipper posing in a Muslim graveyard.'

Mishima laughed rowdily and struck a few muscle man poses for me.

—Did you comply, Mishima-*san*?

—Not totally. But he took some photographs anyway, promising to visit me that night at Clark's with the results. I will show you later what Sam's artistry produced. Dr Chatterjee, in the meanwhile, had begun to fret over the disappearance of his client. Anxious lest I escape him, he had violated his own taboo and crossed the forbidden zone. There he was, holding his shoes at the side entrance of the cemetery, among a number of spectators that I felt sure he had enlisted. Dr Chatterjee watched us for a time before approaching. He greeted me with an inquiry: 'Excuse the disturbance, sir, but those gentlemen –' he pointed to the onlookers, ' – are eager to know if you belong to a wrestlers' school. You see, in Benares there are schools of a type in which the athletes – how shall I say? – hire themselves out as strong arm men.'

'In Japan, we call such hired ruffians *soshi*, the lowest rank of the *yakuza*. So then, these good citizens take me for a Japanese gangster?'

'Aren't you flattered, Kochan?' Sam commented.

'Oh, of course not, sir,' Dr Chatterjee protested. 'It is simply these people's way of complimenting you on a fine physique.'

Mishima's story, for all its flavour of truth, failed to convince me. I did not believe in Mishima's fortuitous meeting with Colonel Lazar. It was an elaborate burlesque, served up to chastize me for admitting that I had not come to Benares solely to interview Mishima. I have seen him destroy others who were deemed guilty of affronting his ego, and he would do so coldly, by a criminal masterpiece of mockery. I had no liking for the role of dupe.

—Can it be that in such an extraordinary reunion, I asked, after a lapse of twenty years, you discussed only photography?

—We certainly discussed other things, Tokuoka-*san*. Things which might indeed greatly fascinate the readers of your newspaper, and which I can presume have attracted you to make this pilgrimage to Benares. I know, as most people in the world do not, that Japanese pilots are flying in non-combat missions over Vietnam, as so-called trainee observers, and that we have top-ranking SDF officers, intelligence chiefs-of-staff and other 'observer' personnel on the ground in Vietnam.

—This is strictly classified information. Colonel Lazar would never discuss such things with a civilian.

—Wouldn't he? I told you, Sam is an intimate acquaintance of mine from the postwar G-2 Section days. I remember meeting a certain alleged war criminal at that time, Colonel Tsuji Masanobu, who survived the purge and became a member of the Diet in 1952. Ex-Colonel Tsuji is an army man in politician's clothing, and through him I have my own contacts in our present-day Self Defence Forces which make Sam Lazar's disclosures quite redundant.

—Dietman Tsuji vanished without trace in 1961 while visiting Hanoi.

—Not exactly without trace, according to friend Sam. There have been recent confirmed sightings of Tsuji-*san* behind Vietcong lines in Laos, in Cambodia and Vietnam.

—Unconfirmed reports, I said, with increasing testiness. This is all fanciful speculation. The file on Dietman Tsuji was closed years ago. He is dead.

—If so, why have his remains never been found? Why have the veterans' associations, otherwise so efficient in recovering our war dead in South East Asia, been unsuccessful in tracing him? And why has the veterans' league patronized by ex-Baroness Omiyeke Keiko and ex-Count Ito, both close friends of Tsuji, not even bothered to look for him? Because he's alive and operating in clandestinity, that's why. As a matter of interest, did you know that the former Baroness retired to a Hosso sect nunnery last year, the Gesshuji convent outside Nara?

—Just a moment. Are you linking Madame Omiyeke's unexpected retirement from the world to the unsolved mystery of Tsuji's where-abouts?

—Oh, she probably had other motives of her own for choosing a life of penitence. Sam knew of her retirement, naturally, but he confused the location. 'Isn't it the same convent near Kyoto to which she banished her maid Koyumi?' The same, but close to Nara, not Kyoto. He was displeased to find himself in error. Even so trivial a detail as confusing Nara with Kyoto offended his sense of artistic integrity, since after all a professional secret agent must be infallible in the smallest details.

Once again, Mishima was taunting me, ridiculing my efforts to bag an exclusive interview with a CIA official. Mishima had in effect 'scooped' me, and I felt terribly vexed.

—You needn't look so worried, Tokuoka-*san*, he said, laughing. I'm not a journalist in pursuit of the mystery man Tsuji. The fact is, Sam and I spoke hardly at all about Tsuji or Vietnam. Our time together was indeed brief, and for the most part confined to reminiscences of Sam's wife. You know he has a wife?

—I've heard rumours about her, yes.

—Her name is Jael, a lady of Amazonic qualities. I told Colonel Lazar of my encounter with her earlier that same day.

—What's this? You met his wife *here*, Benares? Are you sure? I wasn't informed that Colonel Lazar would be accompanied by his wife.

—I saw her, but under peculiar circumstances that I should explain.

You recall the monsoon inundation that I spoke of before. It surprised us as we began our ascent of Chauk Road to the Vishvanatha heights. The first pellets of rain became in a moment a thunderous, hammering waterfall of opaque yellow. Dr Chatterjee hurried us towards a shelter, against the muddy rubbish-littered floodstream coursing downhill. We entered a side street and found harbour under the archway of a courtyard. I hadn't regained my breath, when a naked old man suddenly leapt out of nowhere, a wizened toothless apparition in a loincloth, jabbering shrilly at us. He smears dots of vermilion cinnabar on our foreheads, which at once streak away in the rain that penetrates our inadequate refuge. Dr Chatterjee's nose drips blood-red as he leans to me and says, 'Throw some rupees into the courtyard, sir.'

'Where are we?'

'Actually, sir, I live here. The old man is my groundfloor neighbour, but he is also a priest of sorts and a respected clairvoyant. Today he celebrates a Kali service, which I presumed you would be interested to witness.'

I was outraged by his candid presumption, which left me speechless with laughter. I had no option but to view the spectacle provided by our detour. In a small, dingy courtyard, a number of umbrellas were grouped together like black toadstools, beneath which I saw a half-dozen young women of a dark-skinned low caste type, in bright saris, with nose rings and tattooed hands. They circled a *lingam*, showering this phallic pillar with Java flowers and Ganges water from brass pots. An older woman stood in the middle, balancing a statue of Kali on the *lingam*, a little replica of the original which I had seen in Calcutta's famous Kali shrine. Hers was twice the size of this one, purchased yesterday in the bazaar.

Mishima indicated a 30-centimetre statue of Kali on a coffee table inside the room. She is repellent, this goddess of destruction, black of body and a red tongue protruding between fangs. She wears a necklace of severed heads, her skirt is a waistband of human hands; dead children serve as earrings. She dances in mindless blood-lust on the prone body of her husband Shiva of exsanguinated colour like a corpse.

—Ugly, isn't she? Mishima laughs. You would benefit from Dr Chatterjee's rhapsodic lesson on Kali. 'Kali might seem to you outwardly terrifying, but to her devotees she is unsurpassably beautiful. To them, her lips are faultlessly lovely, her teeth fair as the jasmin, her face is like a lotus, her form beautiful as the rain cloud. To you, she grimaces. To them, she smiles benignly. The secret of Kali's true beauty is *shakti*, pure energy, the active female aspect of her consort Shiva. A well-known aphorism says that without *shakti* Shiva is a *sava* – a corpse. We live in a time of uncertainty and chaos when Shiva seems deprived of energy, like a corpse, and Kali's *shakti* will seem merely hideous to unbelievers who exist in fear of destruction. This is the age of Kali, according to the Hindu concept of time. The illusory *samsara* world of matter, of space and time, was not once and for all created in eternity but ceaselessly dissolves and recreates itself in cyclic phases on the Great Wheel of Being. The world first emerges perfect from the womb of Brahma, but inexorably lapses into decay, a downward passage reflected in the four ages or *yugas* of varying imperfection. The last and most frightful is Kali *yuga* which accurately describes our own time of anarchic ideologies, exterminating wars and nuclear holocaust.'

'We call it *mappo*,' I reply.

'I am familiar with *mappo*,' Dr Chatterjee assaults his armpit in a spasm of scratching, '*Paschima dharma*, degeneration. According to your Amida pietists, it is an age of unending decay. How dismal. For us, Kali *yuga* is short, only eighteen hundred years. Then again the world will emerge perfect once more as the Great Wheel turns and another cycle begins. Kali *yuga* is our expression of qualified hope. Kali *Ma*, the great Mother destroyer, is in fact benevolent, because she represents the renewal of life and freedom from the illusion of death. If I may be permitted to say without offence, *mappo* is a true reflection only of Buddhism's own degenerate condition and extinction, rightly deserved since it is a heresy.'

'You cannot offend me, Dr Chatterjee. I have no religion.'

Dr Chatterjee's barbed little jibes cannot distract me from admiring that woman at the centre of the courtyard, who hands the Kali figure over to one of her entourage. The density of rain lessens, and I am able to see her clearly. She is a middleaged lady of magnificent beauty, much superior in height to her companions, but even more remarkable for a lightness of skin that contrasts with the others' dark, like the albino colour of a leper. Her green liturgical sari is soaked through, glued to her body which appears nude, of a statuesque Rubens-like amplitude, perhaps too overfleshed for Japanese taste. Politeness would require me to avert my gaze – as one does from women rising from their bath in the Ganges – but there is such nobility in her gestures that I cannot help but stare.

Something about her disturbed me – an odd feeling of remembering someone *unnameable*. I watched her cross the yard to join Dr Chatterjee's 'neighbour', the old priest, who was dragging a little black goat to a pair of wooden posts set close together in the ground, an improvised guillotine yoke, into which he clamped the kid's head. The kid's forehead had also been daubed with red *sindur*. The old man now slices off the kid's head with one expert lop of a curved sword, and then grabs the wildly twitching hind legs of the beheaded creature and pulls it away. The woman kneels and pours water from her brass jug on the posts. I am amazed to see her crouching down to press her forehead against the blood-petalled scaffold. For a dizzying instant, I expect the executioner to come forward again with his scimitar and decapitate her. She arches back on her knees, and with fingers spread far apart and curved stiffly upwards like an ecstatic dancer, scatters tiny Java flowers and prays as the rain cascades from her head to her thighs in vermilion rivulets. And suddenly I realize the truth. She *is* Kali, transformed into the redemptive beauty that Dr Chatterjee has claimed is visible to a believer in Kali.

My thoughts rush madly in pursuit of a *name* to describe this metamorphosis of Kali; ideas that are as futile as the last ungovernable twitches of the decapitated goat. Where have I seen the prototype of this beauty? Is it in the sculptures of the late Hellenistic epoch which emphasize the female figure in clinging drapery? The comparison galls me with its resort to Mannerist decadence. But how else describe what the true shape of Kali inspires in me? I can foresee a descent into Orientalist clichés. Out of sheer frustration at the beggarliness of my description, I revenge myself on Kali by fitting her to the most absurd, rhetorical simile that occurs to me. I think of Annibale Carracci's paintings of nudes, exemplifying the eclectic Bolognese school of the 16th century. This is the apogee of icy academicism in Western art, and it ought to freeze even Kali's blood.

I laugh at my own bad joke, and then the name and its provenance become clear to me in a flash. Sam's wife, Jael, middleaged by now but still recognizable from her photograph that he showed me in 1948.

—Excuse me, Mishima-*san*, but isn't Colonel Lazar's wife an Israeli? You encountered an Indian woman who bears some resemblance to her, is that what you're saying?

Mishima neither accepted nor denied my explanation. He merely smiled.

—Dr Chatterjee overheard me naming the woman Jael. 'Do you know this lady?' he asked, and I answered, 'She is Kali's hidden likeness that I remember from another time.' My reply appeared to startle him. The rain had ceased. Jael and her cortège of dark maidens filed into the street. We followed her for some distance, as though drawn into the slipstream of those monumental, swaying hips. She arrived at the doorway of a two-storeyed house and was greeted from the balcony by the mournful ululation of more women.

'What place is this?' I asked Dr Chatterjee.

'This, sir, is one of the many brothels in Dal Mandi, the red light district in which we are presently located. Your lady of Kali is better known to me as the madam of this fine establishment.'

Dr Chatterjee's mischievous little grin was echoed by Jael, who now looked back at me with grieving eyes and a harlot's smile of allurement that exposed a gold incisor in her upper jaw.

—Any resemblance to Colonel Lazar's wife must surely have ended there?

—It might have, if Sam hadn't confirmed my description. 'Jael also has a missing upper incisor,' he said, 'and a gold replacement like the one you've seen.'

I could make no sense of this, except to believe that Mishima was playing a sinister game with me.

—Who would you say is the more inartistic, Tokuoka-*san*? The skeptic or the fanatic?

—I do not feel competent to answer you, *sensei*.

—That was Sam's response too, when I questioned him. I told him of my decision to follow *hijiri-do*, the path of sanctification, which requires abnormal indifference to pain, stress and persecution. This is the way of *shugen-do*, the mountain priesthood founded by En-no-Shokaku, exiled to the island of Izu for his unorthodoxy in the eighth century by Emperor Mommu. Sam ridiculed me, of course. 'So, now you've got the virus of sainthood? A virus of the *progressive* Asian sort, I presume, and therefore fatally Nipponese? Just concentrate on winning the Nobel Prize, Kochan. That's the nearest you'll get to canonization these days.' Admirable sarcasm, even if it is off target. I am not a 'progressive Asian' but a Japanese with entirely foreign ambitions. Sam Lazar cannot possibly understand my *dis*orientation. I have travelled westwards to India from the Far East. My passage to India has completely displaced the Oriental that I am supposed to be. I have never felt so Western as I do in India. It is unlucky, they say, for the Emperor to travel from East to West, for in so doing he must turn his back on the sun – just as it was for our Imperial Army on its declining westerly course to India. I am troubled by other bad omens, by the Ganges flowing west to east, and running north at Benares.

What was Mishima trying to express in his bizarre meanderings? The one coherent strand in all this seemed to me Mishima's ominous foreboding of *loss*, a dark, occult sense of failure that reached beyond the Nobel Prize. 'I am arriving at the stage of non-communication,' Mishima had already told me several months ago.

Mishima returned from the bedroom with a portrait-sized photograph that he handed me.

—Sam didn't keep his promise to visit me that evening here at Clark's, but he sent a messenger instead with this.

—Look at the back, Mishima said.

I read an inscription in English: 'Took this pic in France last year, a tomb sculpture of Louis XII and his wife Anne de Bretagne, c.1530, at the Abbey Church of St-Denis. The style is called *en transi*, an exact portrayal of the corpse in decay, with the embalmer's crude stitch-marks plain to see. Does that answer your question? Sam.'

—An image of appalling literalness, I said. What does it mean?

—It is Sam's answer to my question: Who is the more inartistic, the skeptic or the fanatic? The classical aesthetic of the nude body cannot be taken further than this – especially if the sculptures were commissioned *before* Louis XII's death.

I confessed my bewilderment.

—Do you know the purpose of my visit to Benares?

—To research the background of a novel, so I'm told by your publisher Nitta Hiroshi.

—I have come to Benares to drink water from Yuan Hsiao's skull.

—Excuse me?

—A story from the Tang Era in China tells of an acolyte named Yuan Hsiao on his way to Mount Kaoyu to study Buddhism. Night fell as he came to a cemetery, and he decided to sleep there. He awoke later that night with a great thirst. He discovered some water by chance in a hole close beside him. He drank, and while dozing off again thought to himself that he had never tasted water so pure, so fresh and cold. When dawn came, he saw that the water he had scooped up in the dark and which had tasted so delicious was in fact contained in a human skull. He felt sick and vomited. The experience prompted Yuan Hsiao's insight. He suddenly realized that distinctions exist because of one's conscious desire. Once desire is suppressed, distinctions dissolve, and one can drink as contentedly from a skull as from anything else.

—And you hope to find this Chinaman's skull in Benares?

—Not literally, Tokuoka-*san*. The fascination of the story for me is this: could Yuan Hsiao drink from that skull again, after his enlightenment, and still find it as pure and delicious as he first did? In other words, can one regain the experience of one's innocence after disillusionment? Commonsense would suppose not. The water of experience will taste fresh only by retrospective force of one's will. This is a key parable of Hosso sect Buddhism, representing the quintessence of its doctrine of *yuishiki* or 'consciousness only'.

—The former Baroness Omiyeke has retired to seek *yuiskiki*.

—One needn't retire to find it. *Mappo* is the condition of endless depravity that prevails everywhere, even in the convent. According to extreme Buddhist logic, impermanence is the only law, but if this is so, then even this law too must be impermanent, because nothing, literally *nothing*, is permanent. There is only one possible way out of the impasse of *mappo*. The consciousness that this *is* so. I have found tranquillity in this way of *yuishiki* 'consciousness only'.

—Consciousness only – of *what*?

—Consciousness only that the whole of the world manifests itself now in this very instant, and simultaneously in the very same moment a new one appears.

—Consciousness of illusion, therefore.

—No, consciousness *only*, Mishima grimly asserted. I am in Benares to drink the same water from Yuan Hsiao's skull, the original unclean water that will taste clean *again* to the enlightened mind. Listen, Tokuoka-*san*. Japan's aggressive modernism becomes clearer to me in the exaggerated caricature that India presents by contrast. I think, for instance, of Japan's compulsively neurotic habits of cleanliness. Shinto habits, originally? Maybe so. Ritual ablutions and the taboo of Untouchability had little to do originally with scruples of hygiene. Indians are no less obsessed by bathing, but for reasons of holiness, a ritual formality without the least regard for sensible notions of hygiene. I see thousands of pious Hindus daily plunging into the Ganges, into water that collects all the filth of a mortuary city, the cremation ashes, the cadavers of smallpox and plague victims, and the lepers. I see them diving into these sewage waters, immersing themselves, rinsing their mouths, all with perfect confidence, all performed with gestures that are mechanical, neurotic, and yet that seem natural and transcendent. Cleanliness has become a nonsensical routine and arrives at its opposite, a declension into the sordid, the atrociously unclean. *Clean. Unclean.* Not only Shinto or Hinduism revolves on this axis, but the entire concept of progress. I look into the sacred Ganges and I find the caricature image of Japan progressing towards terminal sterility, dead as a dead sea crater of the moon. Clean. Unclean. These seem to codify two contrasting worlds:

progressive Japan – backward India. What strange paradoxical relationship is there between original Buddhism born here in India and its
Japanese imitation? I look at the muddy flood waters of the Ganges,
and I think we have filtered them through Shinto's sieve of white silk.
Is it true, I wonder – have we succeeded to clarify the original muddiness
of Buddhism by means of Shinto probity to get pure clear drops of
water? A pure taste of water such as Yuan Hsiao might dare to drink
again from the skull after his enlightenment? Has our imitation improved
on the turbid Indian original by producing *yuishiki* liberation from the
filth of life?

Mishima shivers. Not with cold, but as I now begin to understand,
with the breath of fanatical conviction. I look again at the inscription
on the photograph, purportedly by Colonel Lazar, and wonder if it is
truly his or Mishima's. I do not know.

Mishima falls silent. I sit back and contemplate my surroundings.
Clark's is one of the better hotels I have known in India. Better is in
the strictest sense of the term comparative. I have grown used to counting the usual grey mosquito nets, the dead roaches in the bathtub, plush
furniture of the Raj *belle époque* marooned in vast rooms, apathetic ceiling
fans, and the atrocious English meals served in dining-rooms that always
seem populated by some funereally jolly members of the Rotary Club.
Clark's is a charming hotel which foregoes the mausoleum Raj style, a
luxury two-storey building that features garden terraces and small, clean
rooms with porticoes overhung with bougainvillaea.

—A comical incident occurred here two nights ago, Mishima said,
as I awaited Sam's visit. I sat on the verandah writing my notes by the
light of a kerosene storm-lamp after a power failure had deprived us of
electricity. Some guests took their after-dinner drinks on the verandah,
till the damp chill of night became unpleasant. One elderly English
couple remained undiscouraged at their table, with a kerosene lamp of
their own. The man was a perfect exemplar of the British colonial type,
the old tea-planter breed or retired Indian Army brigadier, complete
with white moustache and choleric complexion. This is a caricature;
but to him I am equally one. We are both of us the supremacist fictions
of two failed empires. He holds to his position on the verandah as
though it were the last disputed territory in peril of falling to the Japanese,
evidently irked by the defeatist guests who have surrendered their fortress
to me. A campaign of psychological warfare begins.

My ex-brigadier carries on a monologue intended purely for my
benefit. I know this because he speaks very slowly and loudly as one
does to imbecile foreigners. As for me, I present the mask of the uncom-
prehending Japanese, and he studiously avoids looking at me. And what
is the substance of his soliloquy? Water. The quality of the water,
unbottled, unsafe, direct from the tap, which he insists on adding to his

whisky. This is the water that comes spurting tea-coloured from the faucet into my bathtub. Ganges water, *Visnu-padabja sambhuta*, born from the lotus-like foot of Vishnu. *Mata Ganga*, Mother Ganges, fallen from heaven and tamed in the locks of Shiva's hair, Shiva's co-wife of whom his consort Parvati is jealous.

My ex-brigadier's intemperate discourse on the water (complemented by his wife's total silence) confronts me with his India, which isn't his at all, nor mine. India's water is the substitute venom of his loathing for me. Hostility stretches his English gentleman's good manners to the extreme limit, one might even say, to the end of his empire in the East. It is a gut hatred, truly visceral, a question of the *hara* as we Japanese know best of all. For us, as for the ancient Greeks and Hebrews of the Old Testament, the *hara* or abdomen enshrines the soul. One's deepest emotions are located here, courage, generosity, righteous indignation, everything conveyed by the English slang expression, 'to have guts'.

What would my ferocious old combatant make of my own personal belief about opening one's insides? It looks back to a very ancient, magical idea of ventriloquism. *Venter-loqui*, literally, 'belly speech' or stomach eloquence. What more eloquent way to express one's sincerest inner spirit, normally left impersonated, than to display the innards themselves? No doubt, he would consider it malignant proof of our criminal taste for blood. Maybe it is.

I understand that he challenges me to drink a water contaminated by his own Christian imperialism – his body, his blood – and ergo – *his* transubstantiated India. I am offered a drink from Yuan Hsaio's skull.

Ours is a duel of *hara*, a test of sincerities.

Nothing more directly affects one's guts than India, in both the symbolic and literal sense, and that is precisely why the ex-brigadier taunts me with its diseased essence in a whisky glass. One feels tormented by India, pestered and exasperated, until one's nerves succumb to a peculiar kind of hypochondria. I refer not merely to anxieties, or even to real attacks of dysentery which one risks in India. I myself fell prey to colic in Calcutta. My intestines became unruly again as they used to be in my teens and twenties before I took up physical training. Dr Chatterjee has prescribed his Benarsi remedy for a writer's cramped *hara*, a natural Indian one consisting of a spoonful of flea-seed husks in water or alternatively four drops of concentrated mint oil in water. The only uncertainty of these cures is, of course, the water.

No, I do not simply refer to fears and intestinal discomforts, but something else, like the insistent drone of migraine in one's soul. India's filth excites one to nauseated repugnance; and at the same time, one feels secretly attracted to surrender to it, to befoul oneself, to embrace the leper and finally relieve one's itch for the sewer. I experience this in the presence of Dr Chatterjee's smile of resignation which I feel somewhere inside him mocks me, mocks the ex-brigadier, mocks the entire sacred farce of India.

I do not feel any resurgence of patriotism in confronting my ex-brigadier. On the contrary, I am shamed by the crude arrogance of the Japanese salarymen I meet in South East Asia. I feel genuine sympathy for the old warrior, not shared by him, I know. I prefer his type of dinosaur to the new species of displaced Westerners in India, those Hippy arrivals on the Marrakesh Express, seekers after enlightenment and *bhang*. They are pests tolerated here along with flies, illness and everything else of sacred encumbrance. I dislike their style of going native by which they accommodate themselves parasitically to India. I recognize them as the dregs of empire, the redundant Lord Jims who formerly would have done their jobs as minor colonial administrators. This is what they still are, even as they idle like drugged crocodiles on the banks of the Ganges. Is there any difference between us in this age of *mappo*? Am I not also a tourist like them? Dr Chatterjee reassures me that whatever my motives are, I shall profit from *darshana* or sacred sight-seeing, as Hindu pilgrims call their inspection of holy places.

The ex-brigadier finally gets up from his table. He looks at me and smiles, or rather grins in a disconcerting way. I see a scurvied mouth, unexpectedly toothless, a few remaining ones in his upper jaw flash gold at me. The kerosene lamp has subdued the grimmer details of his features which now emerge as he approaches my table. His hair clings to his skull like strands of blanched straw; his face is channelled by deep lines; vapoury blue eyes swim in a rheumy liquid that threatens to spill from the enlarged orbs. He is very short and carries a grotesque paunch on inflated hindquarters. His wife, an aged woman who might be his mother, also suffers from oedematose swelling of the lower limbs. By the peculiar manner in which he steers her, I recognize that she is blind. He stops at my table and leans down, his face so close to mine that I think for a moment he is about to kiss me – or bite me. I stand up to avoid contact with those obscene, drooping lips. I know that face; but I am too startled to remember from where.

'Do not leave Kashi without seeing the Aghori,' he says.

'Excuse me, where is that?'

'Not a place,' he laughs. 'A type of person – a saint who eats corpses.'

Again he laughs and staggers away ponderously with his blind, silent wife.

2 A BASKET OF BROKEN LEGS

—ARE YOU familiar with Charles Kingsley's *Water Babies*? Mishima asks me.

—A children's book of the Victorian age, I've heard of it.

—And my brigadier story, a *Water Babies* for grown ups, did you like that?

—Why, is it a figment? Was Mishima testing me again?

He does not reply but instead asks me – Is it easier to feel pity or dislike for this? Mishima indicates his body, as one might a borrowed suit of clothes or a costume.

I look uneasily at it, at this costume of nakedness.

—Most people would feel envy, I think.

—A polite but evasive answer. I am not asking if you envy me, Tokuoka-*san*.

I am more interested in the escalade of gooseflesh that I see on Mishima's body. Why does he shiver with cold, when the temperature on the balcony seems to me perfectly warm?

Mishima reads my puzzlement.—You wonder why I shiver? How can I explain to you the cold I feel invading from Sam Lazar's photograph, a marble sclerosis infiltrates my veins as though I were lying on that marble slab and the embalmer's crude stitch marks on Louis XII's abdomen were carved on mine. Lazar has sent me this photograph to remind me of an obscene blackmailer's art.

Mishima leaves me in the dark to guess what this blackmail could possibly be.

—All my life I've wished to dance, Mishima says. My sincerest desire has been the hardest to fulfill. I had skill enough to imitate the dance, but that wasn't satisfying to my desire. How many times I begged Hijikata Tatsumi to teach me to dance. 'You are mistaken,' he would answer. 'Dance is not an experience. You have forgotten what it is to be a child.' I replied, 'Hijikata-*san*, how can I possible remember? I had no childhood.' He laughed. 'Then, learn to make the gestures of the dead. You'll learn to dance that way.' Another time, I recall, he said, 'In the old days, the darkness was crystal clear. Now there's no darkness in the night.' His remark made me think of the ancient Greek idea that originally the sky was black, yet everything appeared clear, dazzling like the whiteness of marble. Again he laughed at my intellectual reaction. 'What I do is *butoh*★. It is mud. Understanding that is hopeless. What

★ Descending dance.

has it got to do with Shinto or Buddhism or anything? I see how you walk, like all Japanese, afraid someone will steal their footsteps.'

Mishima saw my air of bafflement and stopped.

—You do know Hijikata Tatsumi?

—Of course, who doesn't? The Japanese Martha Graham, they say.

—Mistakenly. Martha Graham would never have been outlawed as a dangerous dancer by our panic-stricken Modern Dance Association.

—Hijikata is a genius of scandalous eccentricity. I cannot really grasp what he's doing. It all seems so eclectic – elements of 1920s German New Dance, the spice of flamenco castanets and American jazz, a dash of Marquis de Sade with a handful of traditional *gidayu* music.

—And the junkies' ballad from The Velvet Underground. Why not?

—What does it all mean?

—It appeals to me, this so-called eclecticism. Which it isn't really. It is a stripping away precisely of all influences, the heresy of cutting all connections with the world to arrive at what cannot be imitated, Hijikata's invention of the dark dance, *butoh*. *Butoh* is completely Japanese because it is nothing. It is mud. Hijikata came to Tokyo after the war from the poorest, most backward place on earth, cold and ever-windswept Akita in northeastern Tohoku. He found Occupied Tokyo in ruins. He remembered something from his childhood – discovering his reflection in a barrel of water and slashing it with a sickle. What lies beyond the reflection on the surface? He arrived in Occupied Tokyo with a sack of rice, a precious gift for his chosen teacher Takaya Eguchi, who had studied with Mary Wigman, but Takaya was already busy with another pupil. I know where Hijikata really first learned *butoh* – in the dance halls of the American Occupation. He bought himself a white suit from his savings as a laundry worker, and like a B-film gangster he danced with the Japanese taxi-girls who serviced American officers. That's where it begins – in Unconditional Surrender. Do you see?

Back in 1930s Akita, Hijikata's elder sisters were sold off as children to keep the adults fed. After that, he lived with their phantoms. He remembers his brothers conscripted to Manchuria, how their faces turned bright red from the saké they drank to celebrate their going, and how they came back ashes in mortuary urns. Fire and ash, that is *butoch*. 'I was forced to eat cinders as a child,' Hijikata told me, 'to prevent worms.' That is also *butoh*. *Butoh* is most of all Hijikata's experience of the wind doll, *kazedaruma*. The wind is a kimono that Akita wears all year round. Raging gusts of it would blow the villagers along the footpaths between the rice fields like children's legless wooden *daruma* dolls to Hijikata's door. Such visitors were like ghost dancers come from the snowstorm. Even in summer, people were in the habit of banging their clogs at the entrance, to knock off the snow which wasn't there. Ghosts again at the door. Infants went with their parents to the fields and were stuffed four or five together in baskets called *izume*. All day they stayed like this, ignored while the grown ups worked, pissing and shitting themselves and crying till they passed out from exposure to the freezing wind. There was plenty of time, eternity, to study the sky, but of course when you're drifting in semi-consciousness, there is really only darkness to see overhead. When night falls and a child is released from twelve hours' scrunched-up torture in the *izume*, of course he can't stand or even straighten out his legs. He is a legless wooden *daruma*, his mind filled with dark sky and wind, and the audience of adults watching him in a circle smile vaguely at the recollection of their own torments. *Butoh* has it origin in this – a basket of broken legs.

Pause, before Mishima continues his story.—In 1961, at the *bon* festival of the dead, I went to a practice session at Hijikata's studio. I remember the festival street-lanterns at early evening and the distant heartbeat of drums – and another noise too, right by Hijikata's studio, from a row of piecework electronics workshops, the little rabbit hutches of the past-nuclear age. *Jyari, jyari, jyari,* Hijikata greeted me at the door with this imitation of his workshop neighbours. 'Like the autumn sound of silkworms eating mulberry leaves.'

I watched him at practice, as often before, and envied his genuine simplicity of movement. I could never do that. Not that he did anything spectacular, nothing grand or athletic that astounds us in other per-formers. He seemed hardly to move at all. His body, stripped to a loincloth, had exactly the look of an old sailing ship's rigging, his flesh peeled away to the bare cordage of muscles and sinews, dissected like a Vesalius anatomy drawing, and as he moved, barely moving, it seemed that the exposed clew-lines of his nerves let down the sails, the vast billowing curtains of a clipper at full speed. The wind of tohoku moved him, I realized, as I watched this *kazedaruma* clipper. I saw a thirty-two-year old man with his elder sisters' long hair going back in time, becom-ing younger, twenty-five, twenty, sixteen, nine years old – progressing to the origin. And this marvel of *butoh* progression was accompanied by a Beatles' record, 'I Want To Hold Your Hand'.

At the time, Hijikata had first begun to experiment with the Tohoku movements. The dancer assumes the crouched posture of a Tohoku farmworker, bent legs, tensely anticipating the wind on his body. Hiji-kata wanted to recreate the basket of broken legs, and so the dancer must stand bow-legged with all the weight on the painful outer edges of the feet, like unsteady keels. Hijikata's wife Motofuji Akiko tried out these agonizing steps, and the only music to guide her was Hijikata striking a mahogany table of the early Edo period – a valuable piece of furniture – with a wooden clog. He stopped and lit a cigarette. 'You want to dance?' He said to me. 'Go ahead, take off your clothes now and dance. Dance completely naked.' He put on a Carlos Gardel tango, 'Madreselva'. I did the best I could, under the impassive gaze of Hijikata and his wife. 'Stop, stop, why are you leaping about like that?' Hijikata exclaimed. 'I cannot possibly copy your Tohoku movements,' I said. 'Whose asking you to copy? Just remember, if you put your foot in mud, you'll find a child's mouth in there. You don't want to step on his face, do you?' Hijikata stood and faced the wall. 'What am I doing?' he asked. 'It looks like you're urinating,' I replied. 'How do you know I'm pissing against a wall, unless the posture of my back indicates crisis? Does it?' He was right, it did. 'The acme of crisis in Western dance is to stand erect on pointed feet, to take flight, to leave the earth and become weightless. Everyone talks about Nijinsky's leaps. In Tohoku, it's different. The feet are a pair of broken sticks. How can you leave the earth? Forget all ideas of classical beauty, Japanese ones especially, because all such ideas are violations of beauty.' He picked up a little hand drum, the sort used by Nichiren priests to beat out the rhythm of the Lotus Sutra, *dondon dondoko dondon*. 'Stop!' he cried again. 'You're not listening. Anyway, the music doesn't matter.' He laughed and said to his wife, Akiko, 'It looks like he's got a flapping hen between his legs. We should tie it up and put it an *izume*.' And this is what happened.

At this point, Mishima had fetched a roll of wide, buff-coloured surgical adhesive tape. He coiled a strip of it round his penis and testicles, securing them in tight windings, like a mummy's embalming rag.

—The first time this was done to me, Mishima remarked, as he cut the tape with his teeth, it was Akiko, instructed by Hijikata.

—It looks painful, I said.

—Only when you tear it off and the pubic hair comes with it. When I was ready, Hijikata said, 'Now listen carefully. What I am playing on the drum is a language of the elements, water, rice ears, a child waking from a nightmare, ashes, leaves on a tree – listen, discover what it is, don't copy it, don't dance it – *be* it.' *Dondon dondoko dondon.*

I watched Mishima dancing the *kazedaruma* on the Clark's Hotel balcony, repelled and fascinated by the surreal narrative of his body, his penis, by nature large, magnified by the wreath of tape. I watched. What else could I do? I sipped my Chivas Regal.—Did you begin to understand Hijikata's language of the elements?

—I'm still learning the vocabulary of *butoh*. In three years' time, I shall speak it perfectly, when I comprehend that it needs no movement.

Myself, I did not comprehend what Mishima meant by 'three years' time'; but I did finally on 25 November 1970.

Mishima sat down.—Japan grows wealthier by the day, is that not so, Tokuoka-*san*? We are no longer seeing the recovery of a weakling economy but the first morning of a giant. Year Zero is forgotten. We are miraculously reborn as a successful nation. I am Japanese. I too am a success. I benefit from Japan's economic recuperation, and with the filial piety of any other loyal hard-working citizen, I contribute to it. Are not the thirty-six collected volumes of my works a shining example of Stakhanovite high-yield industrial output? Am I not one more exemplary labourer typical of our post-war efforts at recovery? Have not the world-wide translations of my novels, plays and essays assisted Japan in redeeming its cultural respectability?

I listened with something like sadness to Mishima's boardroom inventory. Before he could say it, I knew what he was going to say. This was his moment of permissable indecorousness, like the salaryman and the executive, drunk as dogs in some Ginza bar, sentimentally, tearfully lamenting their unrecognized sacrifices to each other. Drunkards' conversation, gone with the next morning's hangover. Mishima's complaint went beyond the permissable.

—What has brought me on pilgrimage to Benares, what I have come to find, what deception I have suffered – who would believe me if I said it?

—A drink of water from Yuan Hsiao's skull, I reminded him.

—Yes, and do *you* believe me? My Japanese readers have made me rich but not respectable. To them, I am a music hall *blagueur*, a boulevard comedian. How could I, a non-political man, a non-religious man convince them that my faith is serious? My public have given me success – is that not reward enough? I can be forgiven every transgression, except one. I am not permitted to sin against my own conformity to success. Faith is permissable only to simpletons who have no voice in the affairs of success. This is the crux. My contemporaries are creatures of atrophied imagination who respond only to a single conditioned reflex. Success. They are unfit to understand or accept or forgive anyone who wantonly subverts their cherished faith in success. Woe to the person who puts the ease of his success to work on self-destruction. He will face a blank wall of incomprehension which is their final revenge. He will be classified a social deviant. I am of course aware that the writer as an economic figure is negligible, if not indeed derisory. It's true, perfectly true, I am merely a writer, merely an entertainer. But for me, nothing has been added to Year Zero.

—I was just beginning my military training when the war ended.

—The same could be said of me, Mishima replied.

—How can that be, Mishima-*san*? In your *Confessions of a Mask**, you describe an episode of work in a Kamikaze aircraft plant. Was that made up?

—Ah, that book, Mishima smiles. No, it was not made up, but it

---

* Bestselling autobiographical novel, 1949, that brought Mishima to national prominence.

cannot properly speaking be called an experience of war. It was what I say it is – a purely aesthetical experience.

—I see, a fiction of a sort. I never realized before that you might have invented your autobiography. Will you allow me to print my observations?

—Go ahead, Mishima shrugs. But remember, Japanese are exceptionally literal readers. I hope you will bear that in mind when you make your observations about my inventiveness.

—*Confessions of a Mask* is the work of yours that I most admire, because it was so daringly truthful in its time.

—In its time! Mishima explodes with laughter. Nothing can be more fictitious than a writer's autobiography. I was never the person it describes, either 'in its time' or now. I am not concealing anything from you, I am not being ironical. The time I mean is the time no one understands, because it is still with us and still Zero. I will never be rid of the body I once had, although I have replaced it with another. Yukio Mishima's unnatural birth, not from a woman's uterus but by the Mirror way of *gyaku kosu*, the reverse course from Year Zero, has finally arrived at a convincing reflection – a Nobel Prize candidate! Can anyone know that for me it is still only a reflection – that for me 1967 is still only 0 + 22? Please allow me to speak frankly, Tokuoka-*san*, and I will describe for you the difference between fiction and faith, which has everything and nothing to do with the facts confessed by a twenty-three-year-old writer nineteen years ago.

I take additional notes as the tape runs.

3   THE UNASSAILABLE ARTICLE OF FAITH

YOU ARE ONLY a few years my junior, Tokuoka-*san*, old enough therefore to remember the war and to have towards it an attitude that wavers between curiosity and doubt. For you too, the Year Zero came as unexpected rebirth, but into democratic liberalism. In other words, into amnesia. You do not want to trouble your democratic amnesia by talking to me, a dangerous rightwinger, and thereby awaken memories that are no longer – in a sense – your own.

My main concern is the unassailable article of faith. Ah! you grunt with that sudden, blank and at the same time alarmed look of a pre-war Japanese who understands that I am speaking of the Emperor. I do not accept that it is mere legend or myth or a false concept that the Emperor is divine and that the Japanese people are superior to other races and fated to rule the world. I have taken the words from the Emperor's own lips, from his *ningen sengen* declaration of New Year's Day 1946, in which he officially repudiated his divinity, to state the opposite of what he declared. I am uttering forbidden words, contrary to the Peace Constitution.

I go on speaking as you grow by the second visibly more embarrassed. You feign disinterest in this much publicized aspect of Yukio Mishima's ultra-nationalist fanaticism, in Mishima's paramilitary cadet unit, the Shield Society, Mishima's private army of one hundred 'toy soldiers', Mishima's folly. I speak to you of outrageous things scandalous to a democratic Japanese public, *outwardly*; but inwardly, 'the unassailable article of faith' is a different matter, which speaks differently of the person I was in the days of a god.

My ears are filled with the roar of engines under construction at the Koizumi plant of the Nakajima Aircraft Company. How did I arrive at this Kamikaze factory in the desperate last-ditch autumn of 1944? Answer: by way of the unassailable article of faith.

I recall a sickly youth of nineteen, with black caterpillar eyebrows emphasizing a death's-head pallor, summoned to his first army medical in 1944. I remember him with the emaciated arms of a child, unable to lift a bale of rice in that medical fitness test. Peasant boys could hoist the load above their heads repeatedly with ease. I was submitted to this rustic trial of strength because of my father Azusa's dishonest ploy to safeguard me from death. He had decided that I should volunteer to take my induction test in Shikata, the Hiraoka family's *honseki* or registered place of origin where our peasant forebears had once tilled the soil. Azusa conveniently resorted to our bygone rural status. He calculated that my active military service would be postponed if I were drafted into a 'farmyard regiment' remote from Tokyo. Perhaps the war might even be over before my unit saw any action. Azusa's ruse succeeded in having me classified 2B, a borderline qualification for active service, which guaranteed me an interval of safety. Azusa's stratagem in time of war meant that my weakness — my family's own unassailable article of faith — had priority over history itself.

I was drafted in October 1944 to Koizumi in Gumma prefecture, 50 miles north of Tokyo. My 2B classification led me inevitably, I would say, a-historically, to the Nakajima plant — to the manufacture of death for others of my own age. I need not stress the irony of my situation, except to point out something else additionally humiliating in it. I was not judged fit or suitable enough for training as a builder of these suicide Zero-combat aircraft. Middleaged women and girls surpassed me even in this, and it was they in the majority, together with a nucleus of male engineers, who contributed to the endless day and night assembly-line thunder of the Nakajima plant, while I sat to one side in an office cubicle. I had not even been awarded the humblest non-commissioned rank, but was simply a draftee rations and payroll sub-clerk assigned to Quartermaster-rating Odagiri Ryotaro.

I was lucky at least in being assigned to Odagiri. He was an extremely bitter, cynical fellow, but indulgent towards my 'intellectual idleness', as he called it. I could read, I could write for long stretches of time, although hardly shielded from the manufactory roar by partitions which quaked and set the glass rattling. Odagiri would look up at me from his desk, and say, 'Do you need a hand in your intellectual masturbation?' This was Odagiri's perennial joke, one of many concerning 'former able-bodied seaman Odagiri' who only had one arm. *Dis*-abled seaman Odagiri, as he in fact was, had good reason for bitterness. He came from a distinguished line of Mito *fudai daimyo*, hereditary feudal lords and reliable vassals of the Shogun Ieyasu Tokugawa, and some these, rather than proving themselves loyalists of the Shogun regime, became the most fanatical avantgarde leaders of Emperor restoration. Mito, northeast of Tokyo, had for centuries been renowned as the intellectual stronghold of imperial historiography. Odagiri's father was himself a Mito school historian and teacher of *yomeigaku* neo-Confucian philosophy which had inspired the Meiji restorationists.

In his teens, while serving as a cadet at the Tsuchiura naval air-training station, Odagiri became involved with an ultra-right terrorist faction, the *ketsumeidan* or League of Blood. 'A bunch of provincial terrorists and neo-Kropotkin eccentrics,' according to Odagiri's present assessment, led by Inouye Nissho, a former army spy and adventurer in China, then a Nichiren sect priest at a seacoast temple near Mito. In 1932, Blood League assassins killed the Finance Minister Inouye (no relation to Nissho) Junnosuke and a director of the Mitsui holding company, Baron Dan Takuma. The peasants' Blood League plot for mass killings of top politicians, capitalist magnates and senior Court officials was uncovered, and the leading spirit at Tsuchiura station, Lieutenant-Commander Fuji Hiroshi, was posted to the aircraft carriers on active duty off Shanghai. 'And I, for my insignificant role in this lunacy, on the eve of receiving my first commission, was also posted to the aircraft carrier *Kaga* at Shanghai, where I ended up in the naval landing force. Lt.-Commander Fuji died in that ill-fated Shanghai adventure provoked by Admiral Shiozawa. The army had to come to our rescue. And, as for me, I lost this to Chiang Kai-shek's nationalists –' Odagiri waved his stump '– my shag hand. And what's my reward at the age of thirty for the heroic sacrifice of my best right arm? A petty officer rating to do the job of a female office worker. That's the navy for you, an absolute Grade A shithouse of terminal diarrhoea.'

Odagiri was a dazzling expert of foul-mouthed obscenities, a below-decks, Kyushu south-islanders' lingo, often incomprehensible to me, which I still cannot reproduce. Odagiri's loud and continuous litany of defeatist blasphemies should have attracted the interest of the *kempeitai* secret police, but no one cared. Just as no one took any notice of me, a sub-clerk bookworm and scribbler.

The quarter-master office staff numbered few, Odagiri and myself, the chief accountant, Nagumo Jiro, a retired civilian seventy years of age and former accounts section manager at Nakajima, and his two female assistant bookkeepers. Rarely did Odagiri's tirades upset phlegmatic Nagumo, and then he would remove his glasses, polish the lenses vigorously and mildly object, 'Gentlemen, please, a little respect for my years.' Nagumo's assistant parakeets, the two 'Miss Peach Blossoms', as Odagiri nicknamed them, would titter. Nagumo had trained me to perform my simple duties, but thereafter he regarded me with less interest than a functional adding-machine.

I began to form the rather disquieting notion that my scribblings, pilfered from my office hours, were produced by Odagiri's right arm.

I have neglected to add that Quartermaster Odagiri had a pastime of his own. He was a taxidermist who specialized uniquely in birds. Such a hobby would seem impracticable in his condition, but Odagiri had invented an artificial limb which compensated for his deficiency. Disabled veterans rarely benefited from the luxury of prosthetic appliances in those days of shortages, and so Odagiri had constructed one of his own, with the help of an orthopaedic surgeon. It was an ugly, awkward-looking gadget, nothing more than a sort of beaked pliers at the end of a metal armature. With this accessory, and the aid of vises and clamps, Odagiri performed miracles. He would only strap on the monster arm when stuffing his birds, otherwise it hung on the back of his chair like an aluminium branch of tendons.

Odagiri did not like being stared at while he worked. He knew very well of course that it was impossible for us not to gawk at him, and he revelled in our discomfort, a queasiness in our guts that a cripple provokes by astonishing us with the impossible. Fully aware of the spellbound horror that his virtuoso mortician's art caused in us, he would boast of 'stuffing a hummingbird in an hour', once he'd prepared the skin. Odagiri's personal quarters stank of the abattoir. Week by week, the office filled with dead, glass-eyed birds on their mounts staring back at us. Toucans, long-billed avocets, exotic and unknown species arrived from the far reaches of the Imperial Army's territories. In this way, Odagiri said, he could sample the jungles of Borneo and other Godforsaken graveyards of South East Asia without having to venture there himself. So celebrated were Odagiri's masterpieces of taxidermy that Chiefs of Staff commissioned him, dispatching specimens to him by courier. One of his latest, a large stripey-feathered vulturine guinea-fowl had been commissioned by no less than Vice-Admiral Onishi himself. 'That's why the *kempeitai* haven't shut my mouth. Artists of my genius are rare and exempted on the grounds of eccentricity. We are irreplaceable freaks, aren't we, sub-clerk Hiraoka? And we have time, a great deal of time for our hobbies, because the great advantage of Kamikaze planes is that they never come back for repairs.'

We inhabited a musty, oppressive aviary of life-like cadavers forever perched, until they would grow mouldy and worm-eaten. And what was it, Odagiri's robotic arm, with surgeon's precision fitting a glass eye to his guinea-fowl? Looking at it, I thought, 'Marcel Duchamp's mechanical bride, the marriage of a dentist's drill and a vagina.'

'What's this – reading the enemy's language?' Odagiri snatched the book I had in my hands, one day, and clown that he was tried to read from it as he held it, upside-down. Still, he managed: 'The Plays of William Butler Yeats. Surprised that I can read English, sub-human clerk Hiraoka?' He looked down at me, eyes set close together like a rat's, albino pale, greying bristly hair lengthier than regulations permitted. His nose was slender, and like his scholar's long fingers, refined, which made one regret the hand he had lost. 'You know Yeats?' I asked.

'Of course, a proto-fascist Irishman. Why are you wasting your time on him, traitorous decadent?'

Odagiri had a small mouth, indecently cherry-lipped like a girl's, pursed in a constant *moue* that never adapted itself to a smile or laughter. It was impossible to tell where his joking ended and seriousness (if at all) began.

'I read an essay of his which says that he modelled his plays on Noh drama. I am trying to translate one of his plays back into the proper language of Noh.'

'This one?' He turned the book right side up and read from *At the Hawk's Well*.

> Why do you fix those eyes of a hawk upon me?
> I am not afraid of you, bird, woman, or witch.
> Do what you will, I shall not leave this place
> Till I have grown immortal like you.

'I shall have to give it up,' I said. 'My English isn't good enough. Unless you would care to help me?'

'My Japanese isn't good enough. You haven't answered my question.'

'It is only a matter of time before I get my *akagami**** and I am sent into battle to die. I have a short while, a respite, in which to write my

---

* 'The Red Paper' – draft summons to active duty.

valedictory masterpiece. I translate Yeats for the moment to strengthen myself with Noh language, in preparation for my single last masterpiece.'

Odagiri turned his cynical rodent's eyes on me, pity or disgust in them, I could not tell. 'You expect to die?'

'It is my assurance to die in battle.'

I record my words as I spoke them at the time, unbelievably Martian although they may sound to the ears of a new generation today. We all spoke in resounding wartime phrases, believing in them, to the extent at least in which like prayers they shielded us from our own doubts. It was Odagiri's great merit of consciousness that he used the slogans demonically, making them blasphemies in his mouth, to show their emptiness.

'So, so, so –' Odagiri stared at me, then back through the glass at the engineering works of mass suicide, as though comparing us both. I wished he would smile. I wished he would laugh. 'So, apparently you share in the general Kamikaze fever. Just suppose you recovered from this fever, and were condemned to live, then what?'

'You are laughing at me, Ryochan.' I was not allowed to address Odagiri correctly by his rank, only by his diminutive. ('Not to demonstrate friendship but our common shame,' he said.)

'Am I laughing? Do you know what it's like, bayonetting a man in the guts – or better still, a pregnant woman or a child?'

'You had an experience of war,' I protested, 'that's why you can mock me.'

'An incredibly stupid thing to say.' Odagiri showed his kindness by hurling the Yeats volume at me. 'Beware, poet. You descend to the level of those imbecile mothers who collect *senninbari*.' Odagiri referred to the 'thousand-stitch-belt' worn by Kamikaze pilots. This was a waistband prepared by mothers of the suicide pilots who would go in search of a thousand young maidens of purity to contribute one stitch each to the belt, and thus bestow ritual virtue on it. 'I would give those virgins and mothers stitches all right, with this – my vaselined stump shoved up their cunts. You are like me, 2B Classification Hiraoka, an invalid. You can write your final *senninbari* masterpiece, but you won't ever die in battle, let me assure you.'

'I expect the destruction of Japan. It is inevitable.'

'Inevitable is that we're both going to live. We are the orphans of Vice-Admiral Onishi,★ the pair of us, and we will be spared to see far worse than Japan's annihilation, the complete, total and well-deserved humiliation of one hundred million cretins.'

Odagiri's outspoken cynicism thrilled me. My romantic convictions of death in the Emperor's service, of Japan's holocaust – no, it is useless

---

★ Vice-Admiral Onishi Takijiro, architect of the Kamikaze strategy, committed suicide by cutting open his stomach, 16 August 1945.

to ask if these articles of faith were sincere – they were, and could only be, the last shreds of my dignity. Odagiri spoke my mind, admittedly, yes, he stripped the Emperor's clothes of self-deception, and yet I was not left naked. Our extremes of cynicism and bad faith met in the perfect marriage of two cripples.

I would sit contemplating Odagiri through the glass, in his navy fatigues, cap askew on his unruly hair, as he charmed another 'Miss Peach Blossom' during a lunchtime recess. All women, young and old, who were apt to feed his prodigious sexual appetite, he called 'Miss Peach Blossom'. I saw him with his arm round a prospective morsel, the right arm, of course, thumping excitedly on Miss Peach Blossom's sweaty back. It made them feel sorry for him, that stump, and he revenged himself sexually on their pity with a heartlessness peculiar to cripples.

When the air raid sirens began yowling, my bladder would swell with panic and urine, and I would run for the shelter faster than anyone else. Not Odagiri. He laughed at me. 'Practising for a glorious death in battle, are you, sub-clerk Hiraoka? Or is it a scramble for the latrine?' He took sadistic delight in ordering me to wait. 'I've made an important discovery in sexual psychopathology,' he said. 'The air raid signal gives me a tremendous hard on, and similarly, our average Miss Peach Blossom goes all wet in the pussy. We're mad with passion, and when the place is cleared of runners like you, and we have all the factory to ourselves – ah, the ecstasy! I lean against a propeller, unbutton my fly, and Miss Peach Blossom performs a blow job with the hottest lips, you can't imagine. I recommend that you try it next time. Maybe one of Nagumo's twittering parakeets. All right – if you want to run, run – make for the shelter, my pathetic little hero. *Banzai!*'

I began to fear that Odagiri might be right. Suppose there was no glorious death in store for me? Worse still, suppose a glorious death in reality was no more than this – a full-bladdered, panicked flight, not away from the enemy as usual in air raids, but finally *towards* him? My glorious death would be an inglorious moment of wetting myself on the battlefield, before the enemy ran me through with his bayonet, *uh!* – ah, the shame of it, dying with your trousers full of shit. Which seemed worse? To be passed over by death, forsaken by death, or to die a trembling pissy coward? I imagined these wretched alternatives, dwelling on them to the point of nausea. *I don't want to know.*

'What's that, sub-clerk Hiraoka?' Nagumo blinked at me from his desk. In my alarm, in my self-disgust, I had bellowed out the words like someone in a nightmare.

'Leave him be, Chief Accountant Nagumo,' Odagiri said. 'He's uttering an immortal line from his last masterpiece. Can we know the exemplary topic you have chosen, *sensei*?'

'I am writing a Noh play about Saigo-*boshi*.'

'Good choice of subject – a mutineer and failure.'

Nagumo shook his head. 'So, gentlemen, even Saigo the Great will not be spared your monkey music.' It was the longest, or most pointed, complaint that Nagumo had ever lodged.

Saigo Takamori, 'Saigo the Great', was indeed as Odagiri rightly but unjustly said, a mutineer and a failure. Saigo had been one of the architects of the Meiji Restoration, and Imperial Army Marshal and Chief Counsellor of State. Saigo's actions, after the modernizing success of the Restoration, poses an immense riddle. Why did this loyalist and cynosure of the Restoration decide to lead the Satsuma rebellion of 1877, to confront his former colleagues in the Meiji oligarchy with mutiny and civil war, and thereby act treasonably against the very government he had helped to create? The answer in the end is a simple one of dissent. Dissent against the *success* of modernism. The outcome of Saigo's treasonable dissent was inevitably the total and convincing defeat of his rebel samurai army by the new Imperial Army of peasant conscripts, which he had also helped to create. Saigo, another failed hero in the mould of Oshio Heihachiro, finished as a hunted down mutineer. In a cave by Shiroyama, north of Kagoshima Bay, he cut open his stomach. There is tragic irony in Saigo's end. His slogan, like Oshio's at Osaka, was the Confucian precept, 'Revere Heaven, Love Mankind'. Saigo understood 'Love Mankind' exclusively as 'Love the Peasants', the very class successfully employed in his military defeat.

The contradiction widens. Only a few years later, Saigo was rehabilitated by the same government he had opposed, a Shinto shrine was dedicated to the worship of his spirit. He became a divinity, identified with the planet Mars, re-named Saigo-*boshi*, the Saigo star, and was portrayed as a Buddha in army uniform. Saigo the Great persists as an idol venerated equally by liberals and by extremists of the right and left. Why this veneration? Because he exemplifies belief in the posterity of success by worldly failure.

My pretension in choosing the greatest figure in the pantheon of noble failures, this hackneyed saint of folklore, obviously grated on Odagiri's nerves. He sat there, glaring into space, lips tightened into an acidic *moue*, his rat's eyes seeming to move closer together. 'What a loathsome, conceited little aesthetical snake you are, sub-human clerk Hiraoka, to choose the last samurai for your model. Saigo misled the samurai into a foolhardy rebellion that destroyed them as a class, and in so doing played right into the hands of the Meiji government by wiping out all future potential of organized resistance to it. And why did Saigo do it? Why did he commit class suicide? Because the Westernizing materialism of the Restoration offended him? Because he was denied the invasion of Korea? Because he longed for a martyr's death? No, none of these – no, it was simply because he found life tedious. And because of his whimsy, we have come to this. This is the legacy of Saigo the Great – *this*,' Odagiri waved his stump round at the Nakajima aircraft plant. 'The manufacture of exploding coffins for those eager to die young, honoured by the name of Divine Wind, but called idiot bombers by the Americans. Our superiors are playing the last trump card of noble failure, and they give it the slogan *yamato damashii* – the victory of the Japanese spirit over the material superiority of America – but it is really the nihilist, imbecilic whimsicality of Saigo-*boshi*.'

Odagiri threw his fountain pen across the room.

Nagumo peered over his glasses. 'Gentlemen, please –' Nagumo's Peach Blossom assistant returned the pen to Odagiri. 'The nib is ruined, I fear,' she said.

'Give it to Hiraoka,' Odagiri pushed her away. 'He can write his epitaph with it.'

I took the pen Kiyoko had been ordered to surrender to me, and looked at the squashed nib. Odagiri's fury deeply humiliated me. The shallowness of my faith was mirrored in him, in the profound sincerity of his beliefs which had suffered deception. Odagiri still remained at heart an idealist of the Blood League type.

'You are unjust, Ryochan,' I replied. 'My play is not about the Satsuma rebellion, nor is it concerned with its failure or Saigo's glamorous disembowelment in the Kagoshima cave. It is about – well, it's about the very thing you asked me to consider, the necessity of having to live, if I am really going to be denied a preferable death.'

'What on earth are you prattling on about, you earthworm?'

'My play is introduced, in classical Noh fashion, by a tormented ghost, that of Count Okubo Toshimichi, Saigo's rival and victor, his former boyhood friend, Saigo's betrayer, assassinated in his carriage in the spring of 1878 by a group of ex-samurai.'

'Come to the point, sinister invalid,' Odagiri rolled a cigarette, another amazing skill for which he needed but one hand.

I outlined my idea of the plot, based on W.B. Yeats' *Hawk's Well*.

When the *daimyo* of Satsuma, Shimazu Nariakira, died in Saigo's thirtieth year, he wished to follow him by committing *junshi*, ritual suicide of the attendant on the death of an overlord. He was dissuaded from this course by his friend, Gessho, a priest of the Hosso sect at the Kiyomizu in Kyoto. Gessho argued that Saigo must live for the nation. Gessho was a loyalist exponent of Emperor Restoration, a crime of treason against the Shogunate which soon made him a fugitive from the *bakufu* police. He fled to Kagoshima. Saigo and he planned to escape by boat, their idea being to drown themselves in Kagoshima Bay on a night of the full moon. Saigo was rescued, but the priest Gessho died. It remains an unsolved mystery why Saigo failed in his suicide. He celebrated the anniversary of Gessho's death every year with a Chinese poem to the spirit of his beloved friend. Can it be that Saigo was twice rescued from suicide by his friend?

'What miserable analogy are you trying to draw?' Odagiri broke in. 'Are you trying to cast me into the role of Gessho, by any chance? I am not your rescuer from suicide, my knee-high duodecimo version of Saigo.'

'Saigo's great size interests me very much.'

'He was huge as a sumo wrestler. What's size got to do with it?'

'Everything, according to the discovery I have made.' My answer was cut off by the shrieking of the air raid alert. That fearful noise had an immediate Pavlovian effect on me. I wanted to dash for the shelter. Odagiri's mouth relaxed into a smile, almost. 'Dying to scuttle off on your little insect legs, aren't you, my little Kamikaze poet?' Shame kept me nailed to my desk.

Nagumo responded to the siren by first methodically tidying up his desk, sighing all the while. 'Never a moment's tranquillity,' and then shooing his two Peach Blossoms out of the office, away from Odagiri's predatory reach. Nagumo paused at the door. 'It is forbidden to remain behind during an air raid alert, may I remind you, Quartermaster Odagiri and sub-clerk Hiraoka?'

'We shall arrive presently, Chief Accountant,' Odagiri replied.

'Of course,' and Nagumo closed the door. We were left with the spectatorship of birds.

My bladder ached exquisitely, to the point of overspill. 'What's that?' Odagiri stood over me, looking down at a colour-plate illustration in a medical textbook on my desk.

'A microscopic enlargement of the filariasis worm,' I said, 'a blood parasite common in the Pacific Islands and parts of China. Filaria worms cause anaemia of the chlorotic type and elephantiasis of the legs and genital organs. Elephantiasis is caused by the mechanical obstruction of the pelvic lymphatics by the mature worms – such as you see here.'

'And so what?' Tobacco fibres spilt on the page from the cigarette Odagiri rolled, wriggled like some filaria coming alive from the picture. 'And so, I have discovered that Saigo's colossal obesity was the result of filariasis.'

'You are a charmingly evil-minded bastard, Hiraoka. A nasty piece of work.' Odagiri's mechanical claw thumped me on the back. 'You've dug up our legendary hero and found him riddled with these disgusting worms. Elephantiasis of the genitals, is that right? In other words, a fat fag with an enormous cock.'

'Enormous, and very painful.'

'Do you think he sodomized his little friend Gessho with that ele-phant's afflication?'

'I cannot say.'

'No, you wouldn't. But I can guess. Ten to one, you've got the same implement, my mannikin fairy. A painfully big cock that you haven't had the balls to use yet.'

Odagiri struck a match with his thumbnail and lit his roll-up. He did not blow out the flame but pincered a banknote from the heap that I had begun stacking for pay packets, and set it afire, a blue 100 yen note with the Emperor's portrait on it. Odagiri watched it burn away to a wisp of ash.

'What are you doing? Are you mad?' I exclaimed. 'How am I supposed to explain the disappearance of 100 yen? Nagumo will think I've stolen it.'

'Don't worry. Inflation doesn't make it worth the paper it's printed on.'

Odagiri ground the ash between his fingers and sniffed the greyed tips. 'Value is a strange thing. No smell, not even of burnt paper.'

Odagiri took out his wallet and found a note to replace the one he had destroyed. I thanked him. 'Fool,' Odagiri said. 'How do you know it's not counterfeit? Worthless, but as good as the one it's replacing. Better, in fact. Go on, get out of here. Run for the shelter before you piss yourself.'

I fled, pursued by Odagiri's birds that could not fly, feathers moulting like exploded chrysanthemums.

You have given me a new 100 yen banknote, Tokuoka-*san*. This one too portrays the Emperor, but it speaks of our affluent time. You have watched me light it with my Zippo and seen it flame away to nothing in my fingers.

'You've burnt yourself, Mishima-*san*.'

Why do you sound pleased.

'I am burning incense in remembrance of my wartime instructor, Quartermaster Odagiri Ryotaro. A very odd fellow. On the day of Surrender, he was still at the Nakajima plant, although by then it had ceased production. He brought a prostitute with him and enjoyed her on the premises, before ingesting 90 milligrams of prussic acid, a massive dose which apparently left his corpse hideously swollen. I wonder what became of his fine collection of stuffed birds?'

I rub together my scorched thumb and forefinger. On my first trip to Greece, in the spring of 1952, I learned for the first time – to my surprise, because it pricked me – that the lemon tree has thorns. I wanted to sample the perfume of the lemon blossoms, you see, because I had in mind Goethe's famous line, 'Land where the lemon blooms . . .'. Of course, he meant Italy not Greece, but never mind, the point of my experiment was to discover if the values we cherish have any physical reality to them, any trace of smell, and are not absolute nothingness, just ash.

'And you got a thorn in the flesh for your pains.'

'Precisely. A thorn which remains the same, but not the flesh.'

4 *SECOND DAY IN BENARES:* REMEMBERING THE DIVINE MARQUIS

DR CHATTERJEE limps into the hotel diningroom at 4:30 a.m., where I await him to begin our tour of the riverside ghats. He stares at the scrambled eggs on the chafing-dish that taste of fish to me, the rack of toasts that seemed dipped in paraffin, the pot of strong Indian tea that I cannot stomach with milk and find too bitter to drink plain. 'You haven't touched your breakfast, sir,' he states regretfully.

'You are welcome to it, Dr Chatterjee.'

He sits down and helps himself to the whole lot. 'We must hurry to catch the best of dawn,' he says through mouthfuls of toast heaped with egg and marmalade.

A cycle rickshaw stands waiting for us outside, the driver wrapped in a blanket, a *bidi* stuck in his mouth and muttering lugubriously. 'There is no finer and more economic way to travel,' Dr Chatterjee declares, as our driver propels his machine along with tubercular wheezes and coughs. 'We are going to Dashashvamedha ghat, and from there we shall hire a boat to take us downstream to the Malviya Bridge.'

We pass a *saddhu* crouching in the roots of a great banyan tree. The holy man is entirely naked, covered in ashes, grey like a corpse in the chill greyish light, his hair solidly matted with dung, a stripe of vermilion *sindur* across his forehead. He stretches out his arms and follows our passage with shrill repeated cries, as though our rickshaw had crushed his foot underwheel.

'What is he saying?'

'He says he's cold,' Dr Chatterjee grins wryly. 'All Indians are beggars, sir.'

I feel I am a blind sightseer coasting down sombre, walled alleyways to which Dr Chatterjee gives names of landmark significance, Chauk, Godaulia, Jai Singh Observatory. A market street in the pre-dawn penumbra appears like a vivisection gash, with shops joined together in a gutted entanglement at the upper-storeys, and over the open drains running beneath them perch two-sided latrines in which I see Indians squatting to urinate.

On pavements slick with ordure, the beggars are stirring, hands extended for alms. I look into lepers' eyes blinded by trachoma, at limbs monstrously swollen by elephantiasis, a tide of misery lapping at the wheels of our rickshaw. Throngs of pilgrims are already on the move, some carrying their dead on litters or handcarts, all of them headed for the sacred waters of the Ganges.

Water – ah yes, my interlude with the ex-brigadier last night. I vividly recall his etiolated blond hair, rheumy blue eyes, swollen flesh and convict pallor. And now I remember who you are, my dear ex-brigadier, *mon semblable, mon frère.* You are the Marquis de Sade, flesh mildewed by a dozen years of prison, blonde hair turning albino pale, blue eyes oozing mucous, as you write your masterpiece of pornography on tiny sheets of paper glued together like a toilet roll 39-feet long, 4⅓ inches wide. And your oedema-inflated, blind wife, is she not Laure Madeleine Marquise de Sade, for many years blind and obese before she died at Echauffour Castle, 7th July 1810? You too became bloated like a Gargantuan foetus in your cell, my ex-brigadier Marquis de Sade, and on 2nd July 1789, you improvised a megaphone from a sewage drainpipe, and with this night-soil funnel, you summoned the mob to your window in the Bastille, arousing the Paris *canaille* to storm the prison. Stirring the shit. Inciting the people to murder a Sun King. What have you come back from the grave to tell me, Divine Marquis? 'Don't leave Kashi without seeing the Aghori.'

'What can you tell me about the Aghori?' I ask Dr Chatterjee.

'The Aghori?' He giggles and squirms in a frenzied itch of amusement, so turbulently that I fear the rickshaw will overturn. The driver grumbles and looks daggers at us over his shoulder. 'And who please told you about them?'

I can hardly reply, 'the Marquis de Sade', and so instead, 'An English ex-brigadier at the hotel.'

'Ah, of course, it would be from such a one. The Aghori, sir – necrophagous ascetics, mortuary cannibals – the infamous eaters of the dead. Are you seeking for a little more chutney to spice up your notebooks, sir? Aghori *avadhuts* have been said to wear the rotting skin of a porpoise, or to sit on corpses floating in the Ganges. Some poor devils identified as Aghoris by British magistrates were hanged for the alleged crime of cannibalism. Don't believe a word of it, sir. All untrue. Colonial fables. An invention of the British Raj to slander Hinduism.'

An outburst of loud, joyous singing greets us from a nearby house. 'Shall we see what all the merriment is about?' Dr Chatterjee says. We dismount from our rickshaw and approach a window with shutters thrown open. I look inside.

A corpse lies ignored in the corner of a room. I can see the corpse of a woman outlined in wrappings of jaundiced white cotton, on a rickety bamboo litter. Splashes of lustration water on the rags seem the products of her own sweat. Garlanded with marigolds, the body awaits delivery to the cremation pyre at Manikarnika Ghat. I think of my grandmother Natsuko dead of haemorrhaging ulcers in 1939 at the age of sixty-four. Twenty-eight years have since passed, and this room with its unknown cadaver is thousands of miles from Japan. Memories come to me of the Yotsuya house and Tsuki's erotic ingenuities staged in a washroom. No two spaces could be less alike, and yet I am keyed up with the expectation of a recurrent event.

This room in Benares is the antipode of Japanese cleanliness and austerity, indeed, apparently like everything else in India, it is dirty, barbaric in the excesses of its decoration and noise. A choir of some thirty or so people are packed into the room, squatting and singing to the accompaniment of two musicians, one drumming on a timbrel in a whirlwind of fingers, the other strumming the melody on a zither. They face a little altar partitioned off by a rail and heaped with gods, bright pastel-coloured ones like Disney caricatures, and in the middle Ganesha the elephant-headed god looking for all the world like Dumbo. A grey choking mist of incense from clusters of joss-sticks on the altar blankets the room.

Marshalled out of the cloud of incense, an unimaginable creature begins to dance in front of the altar rail. Tsuki's apparition as Ama no Uzume, Dread Female of Heaven, leaps vividly into the present. My reaction is to flee at once from this ill-omened reminder of the past, but I am curious to know what it means. This is a travesty of a different sort. I see a figure decked in woman's clothes, in a yellow silk bodice and long green skirt, bracelets piled at the wrists and ankles, necklaces and massive earrings, and with castanet-like cymbals attached to the fingers. Despite the long hair and female apparel, this is unmistakably a man. He spins quickly to the jangling rhythm of his cymbals, on agile, prehensile toes that grip the fractured marquetry of the floor. The soles of his feet are daubed vermilion. His gyrations cause the skirt to float round him like a vast green lily pad which reveals the twisted yellow stems of his pantaloons. There is Tsuki's expression of malign obscenity in that leering face, but grotesquely amplified by verdigris eyelids and hectic touches of rouge on the lips and cheeks. Unlike our Japanese *onnagata*, he does not strive for perfect impersonation of the feminine, but on the contrary seeks to mock both himself and his audience with it.

This is Tsuki's washtub Ama no Uzume transformed into the enigmatic god Shiva, and the fervent chorus of mourners in this room sings his praises – Shiva *avinasi*, the indestructible, Shiva *mahamritunja*, Conqueror of Death, who alone among the gods will survive the dissolution of the cosmos – Shiva of ambiguous dual natures, preserver and destroyer, ascetic and lascivious satyr, phallic and androgynous – and this now is Shiva who roams in cemeteries like a dishevelled madwoman, lord of beings whose nature is essentially darkness.

I consult my guide, Dr Chatterjee. Is this a sacred requiem dance in honour of the dead woman?

Dr Chatterjee assures me not. It is merely an erotic entertainment, but one which argues to the wealth of the deceased's family.

I cannot see evidence of wealth in this room. I look in through a window at street level, under a portico freshly painted green, one of those bright pastel tones that Indians so love. The street at my back is really a steep alleyway jammed with cycle rickshaws, bullock carts, cows and countless beggars; and this house like so many others in central Benares is made of wood, two-storeys high, a burgeoning accordion at the top, with rounded corners and fretwork crenellations.

The intrusion of my Japanese face at the window bothers no one, except to attract unembarrassed fits of laughter. I am merely a comic addition to their funeral merriment.

His dance over, the transvestite approaches me. He offers me pastel-coloured sweets on the palm of his hand which is also smeared vermilion, and he says something. 'Welcome to Kashi,' Dr Chatterjee translates. I can see that he is far from young. His hair is dyed, and the vulgar impasto of his make-up arouses an unpleasant sense of crudely disguised age. He does not impersonate a female so much as the sinister lusts of an old woman for a young man, an insatiable lewdness that is contrary to nature. I recognize the nauseating taste of my disappointment once again. There are no gods. We are all the sad scientists of a magic that does not work, that succeeds everytime only in deceiving us. Have I travelled so far merely to encounter the reflection of my unaverting skepticism? Must everything always end up adding to the accounts of my disbelief, preserved like moonlight in the empty phial of my writing? I wish I were as cheerfully resigned to ineffectual faith as the Hindus seem to be.

Now, as I look again at the transvestite's horse-faced lineaments, an unpleasant discovery forces itself on me. These are not at all the features of Tsuki, but someone else's. I am confronted by an unsightly burlesque of the *onnagata* Utaemon, the most refined and genial of Kabuki female impersonators. It has taken this unexpected meeting with a Hindu entertainer to show me why I had written my modern Kabuki plays for Utaemon. Utaemon's great talent had not been the sole or chief reason that attracted me to him, but the unconscious magic of the *onnagata*'s face, his elongated equine features that mirrored Natsuko's.

A breath from beyond the grave assails me. I see Natsuko's haemmorhaging mouth in the transvestite's rouged lips.

And what am I to do with his gift of sweets which I am convinced are infested with amoebas?

He says something else – a blessing according to Dr Chatterjee's interpretation. 'In Kashi, they say, the great *samsara* tree of desire is cut down with the axe of death and grows no more.' My well-wisher grins hugely and shows me lengths of white teeth planted haphazardly in gums of inflamed purple. He turns his face aside and I follow his gaze to another entertainer now occupying the space in front of the altar rail. I am astonished once more by an extraordinary being, but as different to the aged mime as noontime is to midnight. A young acrobat is performing some contortionist feats. It is not his agility which surprises me but the marvel of his exquisite beauty.

Indians are the most graced and disgraced people in the world. They are at times graced by the most stunning beauties I have ever seen, and disgraced by the greatest number of hideously deformed cripples on earth. My gymnast belongs to the first species, a masterpiece of beauty enhanced by the predominant frame of the second. Hair in a raven's-wing sweep falls to his coccyx as he releases his limbs from nimble double-jointed coils and stands upright. He is far paler-skinned than his spectators, a shade of coffee-stained ivory that suggests distant Aryan forbears. The delicate slimness of his figure, its absence of developed muscles, identifies an adolescent of perhaps fourteen years. His face benefits from a profile in the classical Greek manner, the brow and nose descending in one line, but the nostrils sweep into wide Oriental crescents. The generous sensuality of his mouth reminds me of Caravaggio's angelic urchins from the Roman gutter. Under the steep ogival arches of his eyebrows, the eyes appear unnaturally large, exophthalmic, the result of a hyper-anaemic constitution, a diagnosis suggested by the unhealthy blue glaze of his teeth.

I ask for Dr Chatterjee's verdict on this phenomenon. He peers over my shoulder into the room, but my acrobat has already vanished in the swirl of departing guests. He shrugs and gives me one of those radiant smiles that I have come to expect from every Indian I meet, from the humblest Tamil rickshaw cyclist to high-caste Brahmins, a smile which I cannot quite decide is either ingratiatingly acquiescent or impudent. 'You have entered the forest of *artha*,' he comments, 'as we say of Kashi. *Artha* is the profit motive, you know, and death is big business here in Benares. Behind every corpse there is a cortège of merchants of every sort, including of course entertainers such as you might imagine.'

Imagine? I have not imagined seeing that young acrobat before, I tell Dr Chatterjee, unwisely. Yesterday, in the graveyard of the mosque.

'I wonder, sir. Was it after we tracked the madam to her brothel, the woman you call Jael?'

'Yes, after. And you think I am mistaken about this boy too?'

Dr Chatterjee's head undulates in a gesture of agreement, in that curious way Indians have of expressing yes that in other countries would indicate no.

5 ALL IN WHITE

MY GRANDFATHER JOTARO died, aged eighty, in the August after Pearl Harbour. The expense of maintaining the large Yotsuya house only for him, his houseboy and the maid Tsuki, would now cease. I saw Tsuki for the last time at work packing Natsuko's kimonos into trunks, a collection more than sufficient to outfit an entire Kabuki troupe.

'Your mother wants nothing to do with them,' Tsuki said. 'They will be auctioned.'

'What will become of you?' I asked, conscious of the unhappy fate that awaits an old servant who has outlived her purpose.

'The masters have kindly provided for me.'

I had an idea that Tsuki's provision might depend on the auctioning of Natsuko's wardrobe.

'Did your grandmother show you a picture of herself as a young woman?'

'No, never.'

'Then have this one as a keepsake.' Tsuki gave me a grey-marbled cardboard folder. I opened it and saw a teenaged Natsuko in the fashionable ball dress of the Rokumeikan period. It was a shock to find a romantic débutante of the early 1890s in a décolleté gown with bustle and exaggerated bouffant shoulders, gloved to the elbows, her long hair permed to a scroll held by jewelled clips decorated with heron feathers. Even then, she was no beauty. Her photograph had something of that wonderfully remote, legendary quality of the daguerreotype, which explained its fascination. But there was something else attractive in the young Natsuko, not simply defined by the marvel of the antique, and it radiated from her eyes – a beauty, an appealing tenderness that I had never recognized in her gaze before.

'You have the same eyes,' Tsuki affirmed, and it was indeed obviously so.

Natsuko sat artfully posed at a little table, and at her right stood a full-length painting of an army officer, accompanying her as though by proxy. The officer's portrait reflected the naive, Occidentalized heroic style of the Meiji era.

'Is he the one?'

'Yes, that is Major Teruachi Inejiro, an army doctor,' Tsuki replied. 'He interrupted his medical studies at the Imperial University to join in Saigo Takamori's rebellion. The major followed Saigo-*boshi*'s example in all things, even refusing like him to have his photograph taken. Hence the painting.'

The photograph carried the date 1893, when Natsuko was eighteen, the year of her marriage to Jotaro.

'How did my grandmother come to know Major Teruachi?'

'After the defeat of the rebels in 1878, Teruachi-*san*, who was only nineteen at the time, found sanctuary with some cousins of the Nagai clan in Mito. He gained an Imperial pardon soon after and returned to his medical studies at the University, and there he became friends with your grandfather, although Teruachi-*san* was four years his senior. Were you ever told that your grandfather served as the Nagai's lawyer in their battle with the government to reclaim some lands lost in the abolition of the fiefdoms? A long, very long, hopelessly entangled contest which was part of the Nagai fight to win admittance to the new Meiji peerage.'

'I know only that my grandmother bitterly resented the Nagai fate.'

'As for *her* bitterness, that is not only a matter of a lost peerage. She was the eldest of twelve children, sent away for fifteen years to be raised by the Matsudaira branch of the family. You didn't know that, did you? Her father's circumstances meant she had little prospect of a good marriage – a surplus female, therefore, and one who besides had always been considered mentally unstable. After a severe breakdown at the age of thirteen, her kinsmen consulted Major Teruachi, an authority on nervous disorders. Although the major lived by Saigo's old-fashioned precepts of *yomeigaku*, he was a progressive in his medical views and a man of considerable culture. It was he who introduced your grandmother to European literature – something she was eager to pass on to you.'

'Did he also introduce her to the fashion of ballroom dancing, as this photograph suggests?'

Tsuki laughed. 'He would not be seen dead in the Hall of the Barking Stag★. Indeed, the picture was taken soon after his funeral rites. It was your grandfather's idea, this picture, a celebration of his friendship with the major, in a manner of speaking.'

'I begin to understand. Major Teruachi's last wish must have been for his kinswoman and pupil to marry his friend. Am I right? How strange. This seems almost a repetition of Hiraoka Takichi's earlier marriage to the *ronin* samurai's daughter, also because a superior had wished it.'

Tsuki shrugged. 'It was an ill-advised marriage, in any case. I know. I was adopted in my early teens as your grandmother's maid for life. I saw her bereft of the one child she might have had, with the one man she preferred. And that was *his* wish. Major Teruachi passionately admired her, but he did not love her.'

★ A building in Tokyo of the 1880s to entertain foreign dignitaries, in Japanese *rokumeikan*, which became the symbol of accelerated Westernization.

Was I being told, guardedly but nevertheless clearly, that the photograph recorded an evil moment? A memorial wilfully contrived by Jotaro, in which Teruachi's effigy and Natsuko appeared together in formal Western dress, bidding each other farewell after his death and her abortion? It would have been pointless to ask for Tsuki's confirmation. She had revealed as much as she ever would.

Fantastic possibilities ran wild through my mind, given life by the one original seed − that of being the replacement of *someone other*.

I looked closely at Major Teruachi, a progressive with a taste for modern science and European culture, but also an outmoded samurai whose creed forbade him to be photographed. In him, I deciphered my true ancestor − the immense, baffling contradiction of the modernist hero who had followed his overlord Saigo into doomed mutiny.

Tsuki contemplated the photograph for a last time, gripping it in hands monstrously twisted at right angles to her wrists, like the branches of pines sea-swept to one direction. My repulsion gave place for once to compassion, but far more, to a vision of beauty sadly impaired and blighted.

'Is it possble, Tsuchan,' I addressed her in the diminutive, an unprecedented endearment that startled us both, 'is it possible I was grandmother's saviour, but failed to act as one?'

Tsuki's face seemed to come apart, like paper chrysanthemums in the rain. 'Forgive us, master, for having loved so badly.'

I saw Tsuki no more. Three years later, on 10 March 1945, incendiary bombs destroyed whole districts of Tokyo, including the one to which Tsuki had retired. The devastating path of the napalm, the high-speed volcanic draught that asphyxiated and incinerated its victims, was named the Dragon's Tail. I happened to be on leave from the Nakajima plant, and I decided to investigate Tsuki's district, although without hope of finding her still alive.

The Dragon's Tail had left countless acres of smouldering rubble in its wake, ash heaps partitioned by what had once been streets and alleyways. On my way back, I crossed the ruins of a better-class neighborhood, nearer the Imperial Palace, and chanced on a mass of people focussed on a point of interest that I could not see. Some unlikely event had provoked a festive mood in this crowd of moles digging in the ruins. Did they rejoice at someone's unexpected rescue? No, came the reply, but something equally unexpected. 'His Imperial Majesty has come personally to inspect our condition.'

Only those placed fortunately close to the Heavenly One could see him and hear the pronouncement of the Jewel Voice. Just as baskets of rubble are passed along a chain of rescue-workers, so too were the precious few words of that Voice conveyed by whispers from the inner ring to the last fringe of onlookers. A sooty face turned to me, reflecting the collective spirit of insane jollity, and repeated what by now had become audible like the ocean's hiss on shingle. 'Apparently there has been some considerable damage here.'

The message from Heaven's Son could travel no further, since I stood at the outermost edge of listeners. Faces turned to me, as though expecting my reply to echo back to the Emperor.

I cannot forget those faces. Written on them was the total destruction of all evidence that they had ever previously existed as human beings. Before their eyes, all loves and hatreds, history, reason and property, all had disappeared in the holocaust. Their eyes appeared blank, submerged in apathy, and yet they emanated a radiant discontent, as though harbouring the possibility of rebellion, as they carried on with their quotidian moles' business of digging. I too shared this strange, dull-witted excitement. It was easier to imagine the annihilation of our entire families without dismay than to conceive of things that had once been, things that belonged to the distant and forbidden past. Our imagination had confined itself to easier paths, narrow ones of least resistance without stamina and without trace of cruelty or coldness of heart. Our minds had grown lazy, tepid with the anaesthesia of defeat.

How utterly meaningless the amuletic slogan now sounded, *ichioku-gyokusai*, Death to the Hundred Million! No surrender! And yet we all bowed to these words. Each day we renewed our pledge to die for the Emperor. No one expected to survive. No one knew, except the military oligarchs and the Emperor himself, that the senseless bombing of civilians would be allowed to continue as part of an official strategy of Surrender. Eventually, a reluctant Emperor would appear to accept Surrender out of compassion for his people, a celestially serene way of implying that the people had failed him. The blame for Japan's defeat would thereby rest on the shoulders of an irresolute, undutiful population. We were being prepared by incineration to feel at once grateful, defeatist and treasonable.

The sky was absurdly blue. In the carrion heat of noon, I seemed to perspire worms. I had ventured out in search of Tsuki dressed all in white – white shirt and shorts, immaculately laundered by our housemaid Mina, white knee-length golf socks and canvas plimsolls. My unsoiled whiteness excited a disquieting look in the faces turned to me. Was it hostility in their eyes, murderous envy directed against an intruder exempt from their nightmare – or was I instead a salvationist beacon for them? I could not tell. My perspiration turned stone cold. Tsuki's body may have been entirely consumed by flames, but her spirit had come to meet me here.

I was probably in no great danger. The presence of His Majesty had to be guaranteed safe by numerous policemen who would react against the least disturbance. Not reassured by this, I prepared to retreat. A woman nearest to me laid her hand on my arm, condemning the white to its first smudge of diggers' black. Did she mean to impede my flight? I could not tell, and so remained motionless. 'I am a worker at the Nakajima aircraft plant,' I said, in a foolish attempt at confederacy. 'My son would be your age,' the woman replied. 'He was a *kikusui*.' Kami-kaze pilots had this honorific name, *kikusui*, floating chrysanthemum. The woman's son was dead. I was alive. And that was signal enough to turn these black folk into a lynch mob.

Another voice behind her said, 'Bring him through!' The crowd lurched forward, drawing me in like a wave that swallows a bit of flotsam and then ebbs away. A tunnel opened through the mass, a uterine channel hardly wide enough to admit me. I was squeezed down this rippling passageway of bodies, in terror of being walled up, but not subject to any real violence. My delivery ended at the mouth of an extensive crater, where the road had collapsed into the sewers. The tips of my canvas shoes jutted over the edge of the crevasse. One more shove would have plunged me into a cesspit of corpses. I saw carbonized statues in the attitudes of crouching, running, sprawling, in whatever posture the fire had left them. The victims of Pompeii petrified by lava were found in shapes like these – but not with the infernal miasmal stink that overpowered me. Intestines had exploded through the black-calloused flesh, a raw, decomposing pink mess infested with flies. The bodies floated on a sludge from ruptured sewage pipes. I was looking into my own grave.

A handful of policemen had begun to disperse the crowd. 'Go home, schoolboy,' one of them sneered at me. 'You've gotten yourself all dirty.' His sarcasm was entirely justified. He saw right through me, just as the crowd had – not to a schoolboy but a twenty-year-old law student, a prematurely wizened old man, a fraud, a liar, a traitor forsaken by death. They knew, I had conspired against the Emperor's draft summons.

6 *BENARES:*
THE MANIKARNIKA GHAT

WE HAD LEFT our rickshaw and were negotiating a steep flight of limestone steps to the Dashashvamedha Ghat, one of the seventy-four terraces lining the west bank of the Ganges. We squeezed through a gauntlet of beggars moaning plaintively in chorus, an inhuman susur-

ration, their fluttering hands seeming to applaud our descent to the
river. Boatmen competed for Dr Chatterjee's fare, even before we had
finished our climb. He ignored their shouts and selects to haggle with a
taciturn old fellow who leans on his oar in a pose of complete indolence.

The scene is eerie, with figures shrouded in white flitting patches of
mist bone-yellowed by the sun's vague disc rising from the Ganges,
drenched in it, as the water races past, a colour of oily tea. Our ancient
boatman at last permits us aboard, like Charon reluctantly accepting
dead souls to ferry across the river Styx. I suspect that Dr Chatterjee's
choice of boatman had been pre-arranged. I resent being hoodwinked
by my guide.

Our vessel glides easily on the downstream current. Some twenty
yards from shore, it strikes against a soft weed-covered object. Dr
Chatterjee pushes the malodorous thing away from the bulwark with
the tip of his cane. I recognize it as a bloated corpse, face up, its flesh
become putrescent sponge. Pigeons flying out from a line of trees on
the foreshore settle on the cadaver as it speeds past us into midstream.

'How can anyone bathe in this water,' I remark, 'or have the courage
to drink it?'

'Courage isn't necessary,' Dr Chatterjee shrugs. His cane trails in the
water, a weed from the cadaver still clinging to it. 'Our laboratories
have studied the Ganges and found minute radioactive substances in it.
It is a curious fact that the microbes of cholera and dysentery left to
incubate in Ganges water are completely destroyed in a few hours.
Modern bacteriology confirms what every pious Hindu already knows
– the Ganges is *shakti*, the curative female life-force of Shiva.'

'Would you drink it?'

'Most willingly, sir,' and he leans over the side to scoop up some
water – much to our gondolier's disgruntlement as the shallow craft
lurches and threatens to capsize. Dr Chatterjee drinks a mouthful of the
shakti life-force and offers me the remains trickling from his cupped
hands.

'I do not share your faith in modern science, Dr Chatterjee.'

He laughs, finishes the water and wets his face. We pass the Nepalese
Temple, a wooden building famous for its erotic carvings, screened
from our view by pipal trees. Cries of distress attract my gaze to a bare
stretch of clay on which a pack of savage pariah dogs are tearing a puppy
to shreds.

'Look –' Dr Chatterjee says, and I turn in the direction he signals.
Columns of blue smoke rise into the haze which is now turning powdery
gold in the dawn. We have come to the Manikarnika and Jalasai cremation ghats. Ahead lies the Adi Keshava Ghat hidden below the girders
of the Maulviya Bridge, alongside the main sewage drains of the city.
I look back – and I am captivated by a light which is saffron and

rose-coloured, the sun glowing opal above the last miasmatic clouds of night. The mist shrivels away and the rays penetrate the recesses of the cave-like riverfront shrines, flashing on the gilded spires and red-domed temple of Durga, on the eight temple spires soaring above Jalasai Ghat, on the brass and copper pots of the recumbent bathers who now rise together and enter the water in a great worshipping mass, as if commanded to move in unison by the sudden outbreak of chanting, the crescendo noise of drums and bells which announces *sandhya*, the dawn.

I am seated in a golden amphitheatre, two miles in circuit, which is one vast sun temple. For the first time in my life, I experience the true meaning of sun worship, that great Mirror and Void at the heart of Shinto. For a moment, everything makes sense. Everything is in order.

My mood is shattered by Dr Chatterjee. 'Isn't it picturesque, sir? Truly, one is reminded of Venice, as in a painting by Turner. Did he not paint a city like this one, Venice evaporated in mists, as though hiding the decayed beauty of a woman under a veil of lingerie? By his time, Venice was the mere shadow of a once great maritime power, in which no doubt he foresaw the twilight ruin of the British empire. Death in Venice, death in Benares. He should have come here to paint the true fulfilment of his prophecy.'

The false note of Venice in Dr Chatterjee's anti-imperialist diatribe irritates me. I am especially vexed because I recognize a certain truth in what he says, like a nagging speck of grit in the eye.

My vision of a great sun temple has disintegrated. Turner's 'lingerie' of mist has now been stripped away, and I see a city in bright sunlight restored to its modest, rustic proportions and decay. The ghat staircases and terraces are in ruins, capsized in the water; the splendid Durga Temple has sunk deep into the river; the mosque of Mogul Emperor Aurangzeb, dominant on its rocky promontory at Panchganga ghat, has lost one minaret and its remaining one leans crazily out of true like the tower of Pisa; seasonal floods have left a stripe of alluvial mud all along the walls of the ghats like a ring of dirty bath-water. Women bathers, puffing and snorting, surface from the waves, their hair a mass of black eels, the thin white cloth of their loosened saris glued to their flesh as they clamber back like dugongs on the ghat steps. Sagging breasts and potbellies are in the majority everywhere, and the temptation to stare is not compelling. A huge billboard at Bhosla advertises a colossal marzipan-pink muscle man and the slogan, '85 Years of Human Service', which seems oddly inappropriate here.

'This isn't like Venice,' I reply to Dr Chatterjee's guidebook exegesis, and I point to the stockpile of corpses and the drifting smoke of the cremation fires which carries the odour of roasting meat in our direction. 'I am reminded of Auschwitz.'

Dr Chatterjee is not offended by my rudeness. 'Your eyes mislead you, sir. Kashi is not the Benares you think you see. Only those gifted with *divya drsti*, divine sight, can perceive the real Kashi. Its soil is gold, its buildings jewels, not subject to the ravages of Karma. That is why so many old people move to Benares, because to die here will bring them immediate attainment of *mukti*, release from the cycle of rebirth.'

'I believe what I see, and to my eyes Kashi is in ruins.'

'Belief in physical reality is like reading a medical textbook, the effect of which is to end up certain of having all the symptoms it describes.'

We disembark at Marnikarnika Ghat. I am tipsy, my legs unsteady from the drunken reeling of the boat that has cradled me for the past while. A dizzying nausea assails me, as though I had spent the night intoxicated. The rolling of the Ganges is not to blame for my disequilibrium, I realize, but the unruly waves of my own memories that leave me barely capable of following Dr Chatterjee's commentary.

I am shown Vishnu's footprints, set in a circular marble slab, on the ghat. Dr Chatterjee explains that Vishnu is a divine product of Shiva and *shakti* – the combined energies of spirit and matter – instructed by his progenitors to create everything on earth. We ascend a broad flight of stairs, just north of the Jalasai cremation ground, and arrive at a large pool, sixty-foot square, with stairs on all four sides narrowing down to water level. This is Vishnu's Lotus Pool, fed by an underground river that flows from Gomukha, the Cow's Mouth, far in the Himalayas, a glacier whence the Ganges originates. The story is that Vishnu dug this pool with his discus and sat here like a stone for 500,000 years performing *tapasya*, fierce austerities. From the great heat generated by Vishnu's ascetic *tapasya*, water began to flow, the sweat of his own limbs which overflowed the Lotus *kund* and inundated the void. Vishnu slept like a lotus on this sea of milk and brought forth the Cosmic Egg of creation from his navel. So it was that Manikarnika Ghat became known as *nabhi*, the navel of the universe. During the floods of creation, Shiva upheld Kashi on his trident, which will remain supported upon it when the mortal world perishes in the holocaust fire-and-flood of *pralaya*.

I see Vishnu's pool through the frosted glass of my giddiness. Dr Chatterjee's voice sounds muted, transformed by the echo chamber of a conchshell, so that I seem to hear Natsuko's recitation of the Shinto creation myths. Shiva's trident becomes Izanagi's Jewel-spear of Heaven fishing out Benares from the depths of the ocean. 'Shiva was so delighted with Vishnu's great devotion,' Dr Chatterjee says, 'that he shook with rapture, and his jewelled earring – *manikarnika* – dropped from his ear into the pool, and so gave this place its name.'

'Isn't it true,' I ask, 'that the jewel was originally a snake?'

'How do you know that?' Dr Chatterjee looks at me in wonder. 'You are absolutely right. Nagas or serpents were worshipped in aboriginal times, before the advent of Hinduism, as the guardians of underground treasures. Their names often begin with *mani*, jewel, as do the *yaksha* underworld demons.'

'I know this, because snakes and jewels have similar attributes in Japan too, related in ancient times to the moon as an underworld demon.' I do not mention Tsuki to him, my serpent instructor in matters of the moon.

Shiva's wife, Parvati, doe-eyed, with pinched hourglass waist and swelling breasts, smiles at me invitingly from a painting on a freshly whitewashed wall across the pool.

'Can one have sexual feelings for Kashi?' I ask. I want to climb over the cast-iron railings and join the bathers descending into the *kund*. Dr Chatterjee seems to guess at my distracted impulse and places a hand gently on my forearm to restrain me. 'You are perhaps growing sensitive to the incarnate reality of Kashi.'

'Maybe it's the radioactivity in the water.' My words are slurred, and soon I shall begin raving if I am not careful. I can see my alarm reflected in Dr Chatterjee's gaze. 'They say, Shiva burned with the fire of *viraha*, love in separation, in his desire to be united with Kashi. Nothing could relieve that heat of his passion, not even the moon which shrivelled to a crescent when he held it like ice to his forehead. He drenched his head with the heavenly waters of the Ganges to lower his fever. This is the revenge of Kama, the God of Pleasure, who was burned to ash by the ascetic power of Shiva, and who was condemned from that day on to live only in the spirit, not the body. And now Shiva, who burned Kama, was in turn burned by Kama.'

I sit down on the platform of the pool, trying for a moment to stop the world from spinning. Eroticism, vanity and deceit – all the stories of divinity tell the same things, everywhere.

'Are you unwell, sir? Perhaps we should return to Clark's?'

'No, no – please continue.' I invite Dr Chatterjee to sit and share a cigarette with me.

'The essence of Hinduism is this,' he says, after a time, showing me the ash on his cigarette. 'Everything comes into being not because of desire, but in spite of it, in the consuming fire of ascetic practice. The heat of Vishnu's austerities literally sweats the world into existence. This primal act of creation is also known as self-dismemberment.'

'We have the ritual of *seppuku*,' I interrupt. 'Have you heard of *seppuku*, Dr Chatterjee, hara-kiri as Westerners mistakenly call it?'

Dr Chatterjee shakes his head. 'Suicide is impermissable. Do you know of any religion that allows it?'

'No, not even Shinto. There is a universal taboo against bloodletting.. But every religion encourages sacrifice to the point of self-extinction.'

'That is the secret of religious faith – the difference between sacrifice and suicide. This is my point, sir. It is the sacrificial labour of the ascetic, the world renouncer, which is truly creative – not of those who labour in the field, the "black folk" as serfs were called in Tsarist Russia. Reality is produced by the sweat of ascetic sacrifice, not by the sweat of peasants who produce food and children and thereby increase life. The aim is the controlled diminution of life – of less food, less sex, less breath – which are in essence the yogis' disciplines.'

'To the point of self-extinction?'

'No, to the point where enlightenment becomes possible, because it is no longer an encumbrance.'

Dr Chatterjee's dismissal of the 'black folk' to a negligible status, to invisibility, sounds very much to me like Sei Shonagon's unwillingness to recognize the peasant rice-planters. Natsuko's admonition to feign blindness returns in the form of ascetic superiority, here, at Vishnu's pool.

'Are you feeling better, sir?' Dr Chatterjee smiles. 'Let's see if we can find some more chutney for your notebooks.'

We leave the Lotus *kund* for the nearby cremation grounds. A disused temple stands there, ugly, hulking and four-postered, blackened by centuries of smoke. Wood is stacked in the crannies between its turrets. The dark, charred appearance of the temple reminds me of our old family house in Yotsuya. There is a higher bulkhead for flood season cremations, and a lower part on which a number of fires are burning. Corpses strapped to bamboo litters lie at the water's edge, awaiting the last dip in the Ganges before passing to the flames. The place is considerably less impressive than I had imagined, a crude platform of rough concrete like the floor of an abattoir on which the pyres are built.

'Cremation is not simply a means of sanitary disposal,' Dr Chatterjee says. 'The cremated corpse undergoes its own individual *pralaya*, the end of time holocaust, destruction by fire and flood. Cremation is known as *antyesti*, the last sacrifice, because finally the flesh sweats like Vishnu's, burns to ash, and rejoins the flood waters of the Ganges. Cremation recapitulates Vishnu's cosmic act of of creation. The deceased is both a sacrificial oblation and a foetus assigned to rebirth. What I am describing is a theological form of obstetrics. Do you see him, sir?' Dr Chatterjee points to a tonsured young man in a liturgical ochre-coloured garment circumambulating the pyre before lighting it. 'He is the dead person's chief mourner, probably the eldest son. During the ritual period of mourning, he too becomes a temporary ascetic, not shaving, not washing his hair, sleeping on the ground, fasting and abstaining from sex.'

We approach the blazing pyre. A cow nonchalantly chews the bast cords on the ground that were used to lash the body to its litter. I cannot identify the gender of the corpse, until the pellucid haze of flame from the dry wood consumes the white cloth wrappings soaked in ghee, and the charred flesh of a man is revelaed in obscene nudity. A steam-kettle hiss escapes from the grey body as the heat grips the sinews, compressing them, and producing a torsion in the muscles which arches the dead man's back and compels him to sit up. He is bedded down again by a cremation attendant who prods him unceremoniously with a bamboo rod.

'This is incorrect,' Dr Chatterjee complains. 'Men should always be placed face down on the pyre, women face up, for that is how the sexes come into the world.'

'Are men always wrapped in white?' I ask.

'Yes, they should be. Red is for women.'

So I was mistaken earlier this morning. The cadaver I had seen bound in white at the dawn entertainment was that of a man, and not as I thought, a woman. And indeed, I recognize some of the mourners from that funeral merriment. I wonder if my beautiful gymnast is still in the party; but I cannot find him.

We are driven back by the heat, the flames leaping up invisibly, a shimmering mirage from which a greasy smoke billows and curls in the breeze. I can hear the sizzling of roasted intestines as the fire devours the abdomen. The smell is not more disagreeable than that of an outdoor barbecue.

This burning ghat is appropriately named Jalasai, which means 'sleeper on the waters'. The activity here is constant, busy, and yet at the same time apathetic. Funeral parties stand or sit nearby, watching the cremation attendants of the Untouchable caste doing their work. There is no indication of sadness among the bereaved, only a prosaic indifference, waiting listlessly for the bonfire to finish. The scene has all the uncanny familiarity of a *déjà vu*, audited by Dr Chatterjee's inventory of the funeral entrepreneurs of Manikarnika Ghat under the mushroom clusters of umbrellas. He points out the *ghatias* who mind the bathers' clothes and belongings; the *panda* priests who daub the *tilaka* crimson spot on pilgrims' foreheads; the barbers, the *ojha* spirit mediums and the boatmen; the *karm kandi* ritual technicians and the Mahabrahman funeral priests. Cremations are exclusively supervised by *doms* of the Untouchable caste who operate the grounds in a complex profit-sharing rota system. *Doms* sell the wood, collect a corpse tax and tend the ever-burning sacred fire from which all pyres must be lit. These mortuary ancillaries from every social category gain their living, in one specialist form or another, from the dead.

'Suppose I described an industrial system of production,' I remark to Dr Chatterjee, 'a vast, efficient assembly-line run on the principles of modern scientific management, applied to the manufacture of one thing – death – what would you think I was describing?'

'You would certainly not be describing Kashi, sir, but, as you said before, Auschwitz.'

'Auschwitz, of course. But also the factory in which I worked, dedicated to producing the Zero-model combat plane for suicide squadrons. Auschwitz would not be possible, the Kamikaze would not be possible, except for belief in the spirit, what we called *seishinshugi*, the victory of the spirit over material things. Just as I see is happening here.'

'An amusing but far-fetched comparison, sir,' Dr Chatterjee giggles.

'Is it, Dr Chatterjee? What I encountered at the Kamikaze plant, as I do here, I can also find in the modern Hitachi copper mine on the Kanto plain. Everything the Hitachi miners and their families will ever need, from barbershop to cremation – from haircut to funeral – is contained within the company perimeter. It is their only home, their only native land.'

'Are you a friend of Marxism?'

'I am its loyal enemy. I do not need it to tell me that the advanced manufacturing techniques which produced death twenty or so years ago are the same ones that make us wealthy today.'

Our barbecued corpse has lost its entrails by now. Its abdomen is a cavity. I see the *dom* inserting his pole like a pitchfork into the thorax, casually raising the charred remains of the chest from the embers and dropping it where the flames burn steadiest.

I raise my eyes to an upper tier of the ghat, above the umbrellas which hide most of the lower steps. I am surprised to find a half dozen young men in loincloths, superbly muscled, engaged in exercises. One of these athletes manipulates a pair of *varzesh*, heavy mahogany clubs that Persian body-builders traditionally employ. I wonder who these men can be. In reply, Dr Chatterjee grimaces disparagingly. 'These are specimens from our many wrestling schools. I have told you, sir, death is big business in Kashi, and competition is very fierce between rival groups of priests. They hire these muscle men to protect themselves against competitors. Violence is not uncommon, and sometimes results in deaths.'

'So then, even the victory of the spirit over matter requires the assistance of gangsters?'

'Petty criminals, sir, of no interest. They follow Vindhya Vasini Devi, goddess of destruction, worshipped in olden times by those infamous highwaymen and stranglers, the Thugs. You can see her shrine at Bindhachal on the Ganges – a very ugly goddess she is, all shrunken and black and standing on a black rat. They call her the Black Mother.'

My gaze lingers on those wrestlers. I see them joined now by a young lad, emerging like a swimmer from the sea of canopied pilgrims, an adolescent of gracious figure and hip-length hair. I can distinguish him at once from all the rest by the light skin, the exquisite features, which identify my acrobat performer at the foredawn entertainment. I had lost him; but here he is again, my will-o'-the-wisp boy rescuer. My *jizo* of the crossroads. He is welcomed by the strong-arm men. He obviously belongs with them. Perhaps he is their mascot, perhaps a miraculous gift of their rat-pedestalled Black Mother. My acrobat is probably nothing more than a wily street urchin, one more Benarsi orphan among countless others, a survivalist who plays catamite to these wrestlers. I try to imagine who he is, how he lives, as I watch him combing his long hair with a large wooden comb. His hair is black flame, the netherworld torch of Izanagi's many-toothed comb.

I envy him. Is there any greater sanity – any healthier disdain for the imagination – than to sit as he does, chewing betel nuts and sipping a frothy drink of yoghurt, here in this death factory. He is idle, sensual and totally indifferent to the transactions of Manikarnika Ghat. No one could better incarnate my rescue. I point him out to Dr Chatterjee, but his eyes are stung blind by the smoke drifting over us from the pyre. He is in any case uninterested in my new addition to the rabble of posturing wrestlers.

My wistful contemplation of the boy ends abruptly with a strange noise. One of the *dom* cremators has used his bamboo staff to crack the skull of our incinerated corpse, the only part not yet reduced to smouldering ash. He pokes his rod through the shattered top of the skull and the crunching sound reverberates against the temple walls. Dr Chatterjee winces and shakes his head. 'The rites are so often performed incorrectly these days,' he sighs. 'This is the most decisive moment of the ritual, the *kapal kriya*, cracking open the skull. Until this happens, the *pran* or vital breath has not left the body, and it must still be considered animate. After, it is a *preta*, a disembodied and polluted ghost dangerous to both priests and mourners. The chief mourner himself should have performed *kapal kriya* halfway through the cremation. This is most improper.'

We had already seen the chief mourner throw the clay pot of Ganges water over his shoulder onto the pyre in a farewell gesture, and without looking back, walk away with the funeral party. The cremator was left to douse the embers with milk, a liquid prescribed to cool the ashes of the fiery sacrifice, before consigning them to the river.

I search the summit of the ghat for my *jizo*. But he has vanished again. Salvation once more eludes me.

7   LAST WORDS OF A REALIST

WHEN I REACHED the draft age of eighteen in 1943, my superiors at
the Peers' School expected me to undertake officer training. Being an
officer was not merely an entitlement of my Peers' status, but a duty
to His Imperial Majesty whose ancestor had founded the school. Pressure
to assume my duty went on till May 1944, when the summons to my
first induction test arrived, and a choice had to be made.

The choice was Azusa's, as I have said, and I was registered for service
in a farmyard regiment at Shikata. The army doctors' 2B borderline
verdict was communicated to the Peers' School principal, with the
desired result – the acceptance of my unfitness as officer material. I
could pretend myself innocent of any collusion to obstruct the draft.
I could blame the deception on my father. But the truth as always
surpasses a mere recitation of the facts, being in this case an entanglement
of doomed love and perverse ambition. The truth is a maze of footprints
in the February snow. It is my burden now, after twenty-five years, to
retrace these footsteps.

The summons to die could not be indefinitely evaded. On 15 February 1945, my *akagami* did finally reach me. I faced a second routine
medical test that might well overturn the judgement of the first. Did
I feel ready to die? Yes, if one believes what my last words said, as I
wrote them on the night of the 15th February. It is time to bring this
embarrassing document out of twenty-five years' sequestration. I refer
to my *isho*, the traditional farewell note composed when I got my Red
Paper notice. The envelope still contains the nail and hair clippings
which custom ordains should be included with the *isho*.

> Father, Mother, Mr Shimizu, and my other teachers
> at the *Gakushuin* and at the Tokyo Imperial
> University, who were so kind to me, I thank
> you for your blessings bestowed upon me.
>   Also, I shall never forget the friendshp
> of my classmates and seniors at the *Gakushuin*.
> May you have a bright future!
>   You, my younger sister Mitsuko and younger
> brother Chiyuki, must discharge your duties to
> our parents in my place. Above all, Chiyuki,
> follow me and join the Imperial Army as soon as
> possible. Serve the Emperor!
>   *Tenno Heika Banzai!*

Simple words. Ones that could have been my last.

I have cherished this mouldering souvenir, like a mother treasuring her offspring's mummified piece of umbilical cord. My little note is like a pawn ticket still valid today.

What remarkable claim do I make for these few banal words prescribed by convention? My *isho* is a carbon copy likeness of countless others written by youths of my age. I can say it took me several hours to compose these 10 lines, an excessively long effort spent on a right choice of words. Why did I, who enjoyed considerably more education and literary skill than the majority of draftees, submit to empty platitudes? Is there something inapparent in my *isho* that makes it different from all others? It is my postponed suicide note, a lifeless, senseless formula to which my death must now finally give meaning.

Did my *isho* perhaps conceal my cynical dandyism? At twenty, I understood that form alone was sufficient to satisfy a mere formality. Such understanding would suffice to make a cynic. Is there any truth at all in these 'last words'? I certainly did not believe what these words said at the time I wrote them. And yet, what truth of my own did I possess, what standpoint to determine them as entirely false? None.

The one simple answer to all these questions, raised by my farewell note, is *realism*. I deliberately chose realism as the style in which to write my last words.

My answer will sound gratuitously aesthetic, I know, and yet it is true. Only those who experienced the acute irreality of the final months of the war can understand the sense of my realism. The mood of the times provided a conviction which has since lost all its force to explain anything convincingly. Besides, I am not relying on any past conviction to explain why my *isho* is still valid now. My last words stand at the beginning.

I am aware that I risk falling into the most virulent form of decadentism: hyper-literalism. Its terminal phase is the Boeotian condition, a philistine literalism of the sort to which bureaucrats like my father are steadfastly committed. No doubt, I adopted Azusa's literalism in writing my goodbye to him and the world.

'What is a Boeotian?' I asked my *sensei*, Hasuda Zenmei, a beacon of the *Roman-ha* school. Since 1938, I had campaigned by every means of literary effort and subterfuge to gain admission to this Romantic circle of ultra-nationalist scholars and writers, and by 1942 my perserverance had been rewarded.

'I shall tell you what it is,' Hasuda replied, 'if first you can answer me this. What is culture?'

Hasuda Zenmei, a classical scholar of deep erudition, retained the harshness of his native Kyushu and the fierce gaze of the Nichiren priests in his ancestry. His eyes transfixed one with unendurable intensity. He did not like careless or tame answers.

'How can you ask me what culture is?' I said. 'The question is as senseless as asking what permits me to put these very words to use.'

'Not a foolish answer. You are right, of course. To question culture is to put the very words we use into question. Two people conversing in the most ordinary way *are* culture. They do not require to think that what they do is culture, or even that culture permits them to say trite things. Nevertheless, let us think rash futilities, such as, what is culture?'

A scar on the right of Hasuda's prominent cheekbones appears cresent-moon white on a face that shines bright red, like Hijikata's brothers, from the saké we drink in ceremonial cups. Hasuda does not normally imbibe alcohol, but in a week's time he will join his regiment in Malaya. This is our farewell salute as he 'goes to seek death' – another typical wartime formula, one of the many so-called amuletic slogans.

Hasuda is slender to the point of gauntness. His freshly shaven head like a Buddhist novice's gleams as blue as the late winter sky of 1943. At thirty-nine, he cannot be said young to serve the Emperor again, given that he had already been seriously wounded in 1938 during the Manchurian campaign.

We kneel facing each other across a lacquer table on which are placed the saké jar and cups, a stand of ink and brushes, and the five instalments of my novella first published two years ago in the *Roman-ha*'s literary journal. I was the single guest at my teacher's farewell ceremonial, a great honour, but one which I profaned by caring more to discuss the fate of my novellas. I desired them published in a single volume. My stories already benefited from Hasuda's fervently nationalist preface, an imprimatur that easily assured me the censors' own, but the far greater obstacle was the wartime shortage of paper. Now, with Lieutenant Hasuda Zenmei's imminent departure, of what use would he be to me?

'What is culture?' Hasuda repeated. 'Perhaps I should be clearer. Do you truly understand in what peril the question of culture puts you? Risks are undertaken by the mercenaries of industry, by politicians and military experts. These are risks everyone recognizes. But culture? Whom does culture threaten with any serious risk?'

'Everyday practical wisdom confirms what we both know,' I said, 'that despite pious lip service to the arts, we have a civilization conceivable without culture.'

'And it is already in operation,' Hasuda interjected. He lit a cigarette. My teacher might not be a drinker, but he consumed a fearsome amount of tobacco. 'The pre-Socratic philosopher Heraclitus said it – *ethos anthropo daimon*. A man's character is his fate. *Daimon*, fate, is rich in other significations. It can mean one's allotted genius or fortune, a dead person's shade, or skill or simply death. One could therefore understand Heraclitus to mean that a man's character is his "skill at death", as fate implies. One's death is a disclosure of irony in which culture manifests its truth or hollowness.'

'The meaning of culture is therefore death,' I replied.

'An outlandish but perfectly obvious conclusion, yes.'

'I have already come to see this in the impasse to which writing leads me.'

'What do you mean?' Hasuda's face brightened even redder.

'I mean simply that I too await my Red Paper. No work of mine should be anything other than a monument raised on the absolute assurance of my death in battle.' I bit my tongue to keep from saying further ' – and the only impediment is not the Red Paper but a shortage of paper.'

Hasuda was a man of romantic irony – that is, a man of humourless religion. He could never have guessed at what I was really saying between the lines. Or so I thought in my naive ambition.

'Have I named you the blessed child of ancient history for nothing?' Hasuda's redness now became incandescent, as he burst into one of his frequent, inexplicable rages.

'You have lavished a preface on my worthless stories from the immense bounty of your scholarship,' I bowed. 'I am eternally indebted to you, *sensei*.'

My apology enraged him more. 'Is this how you repay me, then? With no understanding of the classics? You speak of the bounty of scholarship without understanding what it means. The tenderness of my feelings for you is my acknowledgement of the classics. What have you acknowledged in them?'

The sword's length of table between us shrank to the size of a dagger. Its menace was the dazzling weakness I felt. A pheasant's white wings churned up from my guts to my skull: the sweet, morbid whiteness of Sebastian probed by arrows.

Was this my acknowledgement of the classics, an obscene weakness? Hasuda had spoken of tenderness, *bushi no nasake*, the warrior's com-passion that the classics teach. Eroticism has its rightful place in the samurai code, but not the ungenerous evil thing that preyed on me.

My teacher's choleric look acknowledged only the rectitude of love. I would have to make good the betrayal of that love. My eyes fell on the *Hagakure* at my side, Hasuda's precious farewell gift to me, an 18th century copy of the book annotated in his own hand. It had been his breviary for many years and should by rights have accompanied him into battle. The *Hagakure*, Yamamoto Jocho's masterpiece of samurai thought, has since remained my constant companion for the last twenty-seven years.

When I try to imagine the sort of writer I could have been but am not, I think of the samurai priest Yamamoto Jocho, a writer purely by effect of chance. Jocho had determined to follow his liege lord Mitsu-shige Nabeshima into death by committing *junshi seppuku*. But the lord had issued an edict before his death expressly forbidding loyalty suicides. And so, in the 13th year of Genroku (1700), Jocho then 42 years old, shaved his head, took Buddhist vows and lived a hermit's existence for the next twenty years in a hut secluded within a forest. From this retreat comes the title of Jocho's great work, *Hagakure*, 'hidden among the leaves', a transcription of oral discussions compiled by a young samurai, Tsuramoto Tashiro, who spent seven years arranging the master's recorded words in eleven volumes. Tashiro disobeyed Jocho's order to burn the records.

Jocho foresaw that his book must one day be consigned to the flames – those ignited after 1945 by shamefaced embarrassment at Japan's defeat. *Hagakure* was the militarists' adopted Gospel of the 1930s, the Bible of Bushido. Vast numbers of the book were popularly distributed. Kami-kaze pilots confirmed their resolve to die in *Hagakure*. Consequently, after surrender, *Hagakure* fell into the subversive category of *Mein Kampf*, proscribed and abandoned to the pyres of oblivion. Whosoever today retrieves this book from attic mouldiness will stand glaringly identified as a fanatic, conspicuous as a Chinese Red Guard flaunting Mao's Little Red Book. Jocho's thoughts are not to be compared to Mao's, and certainly not Hitler's inchoate fulminations, but can be likened to La Rochefoucauld's ethical maxims.

Of course, the defeat of 1945 was unforeseeable to me in 1943, although Hasuda's irony foretold it at our last meeting. I was too shallow to comprehend him.

I opened the *Hagakure* and read aloud Jocho's famous injunction which sounds as offensively barbarian to our times as it did to his own effeminate and corrupt Shogunate era of peace. 'I have found that the Way of the Samurai is death.' And I added, 'Is this not the perilous question of culture – and the right answer to it?'

'Jocho also says that the chances of a correct death are rarely given,' Hasuda replied, his anger now giving way to a strange melancholy. 'He advises death only in a fifty-fifty life or death situation. By what criterion can we judge when a situation is in fact "fifty-fifty"?'

'The Red Paper will give me a better than fifty-fifty chance of dying.'

'Understanding death does not in the least reconcile one to life, if that's what you think,' Hasuda smiled like a father to a wayward child. He quoted a famous haiku of the medieval Heian period. '*A scattering of cherry blossoms, ah, the sadness of things*. These perfect lines, fallen into cliché from over use, speak of Arima no Miko, tragic prince of the 7th century, son of the 36th Emperor Kotoku. Do you not recall my essay on him? His only fame is to have been executed at the age of eighteen on a false charge of treason by his opportunist cousin, Prince Naka no

Oe. Arima no Miko sanctified life by being the innocent object of political villainy. This alone sufficed to attract the praise of our classical authors.'

'You said in that essay, *sensei*, that "to die young is the culture of my country". Heroes are always those who atone for progress, and progress is known by its opposite, loss. Noble failure atones for the impossibility of resisting progress successfully. Your essay has helped me to understand the secret the classics teach, *sense*.'

'You can best honour the classics by resigning yourself to be one. Such is the lesson in humility that Arima no Miko exemplifies. Jocho advises likewise: do not immodestly court death, but earn it. Safeguard yourself against immature destruction. And if you love me, do no less and no more than your father commands.'

Hasuda's instruction came as a shock to me. 'I cannot do otherwise than obey him. But how can you ask me to submit to a philistine out of love for you?'

'Now I can tell you what a Boeotian is,' Hasuda smiled, not in a way that I had misread as paternal, but like someone already dead. 'Boeotian is the same as philistine, but posited as the absolutely non-creative man, the realist, the complete antipode to the artist. The dilemma is that Boeotianism is coextensive with certain qualities of realism to which artists are compelled to adhere. Think of it. Sincerity before the object — and therefore to oneself — are ethical exigencies which confront all artists and render them inevitably realists. The problem is, can a degree of transcendent idealism survive the test of realism? Does realist art itself not also suffer from flat-footed materialism? Or should one agree with Mann's hero, Gustav von Aschenbach, that philosophy of any kind leads to skepticism and the certain ruin of art? But doesn't this end in a disingenuous "flight from thought" which succumbs to a Boeotian realist anti-philosophy?

'The trouble with realism is that of being an automat of values which reduces all things to the same mechanical level of significance — state and civil liberty, patriotism and resistance, peace, war and technical progress are all equally significant and real necessities. Realism can assert a platitude likeness between values that are in conflict, because as the spirit of conservatism it can claim to be their creator. It represents itself in essence as the memory of generations, of the aptitudes proper in the struggle for the survival of nation, state and race, and has hence created everything: liberal sympathy and racial conflict, the individual and the people, variable life styles and fixed institutions, social mobility and stratified classes, and all other familiar antinomies. Boeotian realism makes an absolute imbrication of thing, concept and word, a mechanically imposed harmony in which one overhears the grinding of cogwheels.

'Therefore, the Boeotian realist of strict observance is "nothing more" than the memory of a generation, best recognized in the horribly adult addict of crossword puzzles.'

'The puzzle is, *sensei*, that you advise me to put my faith in such an unprincipled realist. I cannot see any truth in this.'

'The truth is a maze of footprints in the snow,' Hasuda answered.

Hasuda's last words to me on the platform of Shinjuku station contradicted the prudence he had seemed to recommend. 'Life as it is, is unacceptable. *Shichisho hokoku* – Serve the Emperor for Seven Lives!' He looked angry, but there were tears in his eyes as he conferred the *Hagakure* on me with hands that trembled.

Have I made my realism clear? Realism as I understood then – in conditions that are no longer understandable?

Early in the morning of my departure for Shikata on February 16th, a dishevelled madwoman appeared in my room. My mother Shizue, driven to hysterics by the arrival of my *akagami*, beseiged me with two watches in either hand. One of these was the Emperor's award, my silver graduation watch, presented to me six months before in September 1944. The other was Natsuko's pocket watch. 'Look –' she cried, 'look! Do you see? They tell different times. Different times! It is impossible!' She went on shouting *impossible, impossible*, deaf to my father's pleas for calm. Even he looked unusually distressed.

Shizue threw herself on her knees before the Buddha image in our household shrine. She sank into a trance there, like the statue of a heart-pierced Mater Dolorosa one finds in Mediterranean churches, imploring heaven with outstretched arms. At the sight of her, I felt gripped by sea-sickness, unbalanced by a sensation of icy embarrassment. I recognized this feeling as a cover for my exhilaration, my sense of relief, of joy even, at thus seeing my mother distraught, because it was evidence that she was losing me. 'Saved from women at last,' is what came into my mind. I was witnessing the proof of my death, my own funeral rites in Shizue's prayers. I admired myself for the alarm which this feeling of cold-hearted satisfaction gave me.

My father and I boarded a train for the Kansai district. Azusa found seats for us beside a window in need of repair. A glacial February wind whistled through the broken glass. Exposure to this draught over a 300-mile journey would aggravate the cold I had caught at the Nakajima plant. I suggested that we move, but Azusa refused to hear of it. 'What ails you?' Azusa scolded. 'Pull up your scarf. A conscript in His Majesty's Army must endure more than a little discomfort.'

An hour's refrigeration sufficed to leave me shaking with fever, aching in every joint. In my state of misery, I did not grasp Azusa's question, suddenly addressed to me out of the blue. '*I said*, can you understand why your teacher Hasuda-*san* holds you in such exaggerated esteem? For I cannot.'

I could not believe my ears. Was I suffering a feverish delusion? My father's gloating little smile was proof that I heard correctly. 'You were in contact with Hasuda-*san* before his departure?' I asked.

'It was my duty. Lieutenant Hasuda invited me to see him.'

I had nothing to lose now in expressing myself freely. 'This is incredible. You'll go to any length to block my literary career.'

'Now that's gratitude,' Azusa laughed. 'Tell me, did you not petition the government last year for paper to publish your book? And you were successful. Do you imagine the favour was granted by a miracle? I still have some influence in the Ministries, you know. What a fool my dear wife and son must take me for. Am I supposed *not* to know you are a celebrity, *not* to know who Yukio Mishima is, when all my colleagues congratulate me on my son's achievement? Admirable book, unusual success in wartime, etcetera. Oh yes, but only your Lieutenant Hasuda knows what is owed to me for having secured the paper to print it on.'

'Is that why he invited you to see him?'

Azusa shrugged. 'Would you like a report of our conversation?'

'It isn't necessary.' I turned my face to the cold blast as winter darkness fell.

By the time we arrived at the home of some friends in Shikata village, I had become almost too weak to stand. My father declined his friends' offer to treat my high fever with traditional febrifuge remedies, insisting that these would do no good, and that some analgesic tablets and a good night's sleep were all I required.

I am in no doubt that my father deliberately schemed to keep me ill, in order to mislead the army doctors next morning when I had to report to the barracks. His plan might not have succeeded without my collaboration. My fever ran high the following morning, and this combined with my deathly paleness and a dry rattle in my bronchial tubes could easily be mistaken for incipient tuberculosis. My vague answers to the inexperienced young army doctor misled him to make exactly that diagnosis. I was declared unfit for active service and sent home that same day.

Once safe outside the barracks, Azusa took my hand and broke into a euphoric run across the snow, down the slope to the village. We left a crisscross mêlée of footprints in the snow, my father's, mine. Who can tell them apart?

Our return home to Shizue was a triumph for Azusa. He had rescued me from the Emperor's fatal Red Paper, though not even he would have dared to put it that bluntly. Rice cakes and saké materialized, a potlach within the frugal limits imposed by wartime rationing. Shizue appeared in her best stored-away kimono. Azusa's laughter that evening was not one normally heard within our family, a brand reserved for his lawyer cronies, a raucous falsehood emitted in sushi bars and restaurants which signals a 'deal' concluded. His laughter betrayed a certain unease, felt whenever his eyes strayed to meet mine. My gaze reflected nothing, neither the jubilation of my younger sister and brother, nor unhappiness. It was an expressionless blank, like a visor pulled down over my eyes.

No one could have guessed the disorder reigning in my thoughts at that moment. I dwelt with some perplexity on my father's evident relief. I could not reconcile this celebrant of affectionate fatherhood with the dead-handed bureaucrat who had relentlessly persecuted me. Why should Azusa rejoice to have saved a 'freak'? Who was this strange fellow, whose bonhomie verged on bragging that he had cheated the Emperor of his rightful prize? Was this the same believer in Nazi ideology, the loyally pledged servant of His Imperial Majesty?

Azusa could no longer bear my impenetrable gaze. He was experienced enough in bureaucratic stoicism to know I was being insubordinate. Between putting out one cigarette and lighting another, he remarked to Shizue, whose eyes sparkled with a gaiety she had not demonstrated for years, 'Our little asparagus (Azusa's injurious nickname, not used for years, but here revived in a show of jocular affection) reveals nothing of his true feelings, as usual.' Azusa laughed, and now addressed me. 'Surely you don't regret our escape? I'd say we had a pretty narrow squeak through the valley of death.'

'I am certainly fortunate,' I replied. 'Thank you.'

My father averted his eyes at the utterance, 'thank you', almost wincing to hear it.

I contemplated Azusa. I saw a well-preserved man of fifty, whose hair in trim military fashion sparkled silver, a retired civil servant of middle rank who now operated a private law practice. I discovered a sleek, smug man who had no power over me. My self-assured discovery brought me no pleasure, only a downcast sense of regret as I viewed my mother. Shizue's intense joy served to emphasize her diminished beauty. She was a lean matriarch of forty, with that wolfish look women acquired these days as the hard-pressed provisoners of their families. Her face and arms had turned leathery brown from the hours spent labouring in our vegetable patch.

Shizue handed me back my silver graduation watch. 'You see, not even *he* could rob me of my love,' she proudly announced to the family. I glanced across the table at my sister Mitsuko. Shizue had boastfully declared her preference, not for the first time, which elevated me in her love far higher than my sister and brother. What did they make of it? Mitsuko, in her Sacred Heart School uniform, held Chiyuki's hand. They seemed genuinely happy to have me back, saved from death. Mitsuko smiled at me. Her plain, honest features, radiating simple tenderness, the comic little gap in her front teeth, touched me strangely. I remembered Mitsuko smiling like this many years ago when I shamed my mother by appearing before a roomful of guests, travestied in Shizue's make-up and best kimono. 'Don't look so downhearted, brother,' Mitsuko said. 'Things are returning to normal.' And she blew me a kiss on the palm of her hand. Shizue at once reproached her. 'Don't do that! Are young ladies at the Sacred Heart encouraged to such vulgar displays?'

Mitsuko's innocent airborne kiss entered my heart like a virus.

8   *BENARES:*
THE WIDOWS' HOUSE

'OBVIOUSLY, he's attempting to drown himself.'

Dr Chatterjee's words did not make sense to me at first, lost as I was in Mitsuko's kiss.

A pair of boatmen some distance from the shore were tugging at an object in the water. Their colleagues and a number of onlookers shouted encouragement. It dawned on me that the *mallahs* were struggling to haul out a body from the river, an old man. I saw him being dragged over the gunwale into one of the boats.

A strange notion convinced me for a moment that the man's corpse, whose cremation we had just witnessed, his ashes thrown into the Ganges, had somehow been miraculously restored and made incarnate again by the sacred waters. I laughed at my own credulity. Dr Chatterjee smiled too, believing that I shared in the general merriment aroused by the old man's rescue and his continued protests against salvation.

'Why have they rescued him?' I asked. 'Does one not come to Kashi precisely to die?'

'I have said, suicide is impermissable. It is not a good death.'

'What is a good death?'

'One to which the individual voluntarily submits.'

'Isn't that a reasonably satisfactory definition of suicide?'

'You are playing with words, sir.'

'Yes, you're right, Dr Chatterjee. One shouldn't trifle with words. They have an immense power of realization, I know.'

'I could show you the Kashi Karwat Temple. A great saw, the *karwat*, hangs from the ceiling, and in a less corrupt age, it is said, the saw would fall on the petitioner whom Shiva chose to bless with death. Shall I take you there? You might receive Shiva's blessing, if this is your fate and your time has come.'

'Suicide is not a matter of blessing or fate, but of choice.'

'Anyway, it would do no good. Nowadays the *karwat* no longer falls spontaneously. But I can show you a good death, if you so wish.'

We leave Manikarnika by one of the myriad steep alleyways that pigeonhole the massive flank of temples and buildings overhanging the ghats. At a street corner level, we encounter the jolly scene of some children aboard a tiny, hand-powered merry-go-round. Their cries of joy as they ride on gaily painted midget horses, earnestly watched by their mothers clad in bright festive saris, seem to exist in another world miles apart from the skeletal figure of an old beggar, writhing and moaning in death agonies, only a few yards away. He lies unnoticed, dying beside a wall steaming with urine, on a foul bed of excreta and rubbish in which a lone pariah dog roots for morsels.

A crowd pays heed instead to another figure, a naked *saddhu*, crawling along the narrow street. He inches forward on his belly, using his elbows and knees to make progress through the surrounding mass of street hawkers, goats and beggars. Lepers accompany him on his *via crucis* to the Ganges. His hair trails on the ground in long ash-covered strands, knotted with dung; his nude body slithers past our legs, coated in filthy grey scales, his eyes and gaping mouth repulsively red and moist. He disregards the alms thrown in his path, which the lepers scoop up like sparrows pouncing on crumbs. I am certain he is the same creature we met before dawn near Clark's, the imposter *saddhu* quaking with cold under the banyan tree. 'What difference does it make?' Dr Chatterjee shrugs.

'Do you believe any of this, Dr Chatterjee?'

'I am only your guide, sir,' he answers with uncustomary solemnity. 'A poor scholar in the age of Kali. My opinions are worthless.'

Everywhere I see idleness and indifference, but Dr Chatterjee calls these an accepted art of living, *phakkarpan* or carefreeness. Shopkeepers and rickshaw cyclists sip their yoghurt drafts of *thandai*, containing the intoxicant *bhang*, or chew betel nuts wrapped in *pan* leaves. The streets are red-flecked with the spit of betel-nut chewers, like the floor of some unsanitary TB ward.

'You could see it another way,' Dr Chatterjee claims, 'as perhaps the redness of *lac* painted on the feet of *devadasis*, the beautiful courtesans whose footprints mark the streets.'

'Fine poetry, which overlooks the squalor and waste.'

'Hindus abide by the four aims of a life well and fully lived, the *purusharthas*. We do not deny ourselves the *kama* of pleasure, or reaping the *artha* of wealth and power, or fulfilling the religious duties of *dharma*. But there is no rush to achieve the last aim, *moksha*, liberation.'

We entered a garden compound from the street and approached a two-storey building along a path flanked by sacred *tulsi* bushes. Little signs posted among the florae enjoined the visitor to pray, advertising such mottoes as, 'Ram, Ram, Remember the Name of Ram'.

'This is the House of Widows. Here you will find the seekers after *moksha*,' Dr Chatterjee declares, thoughtfully chewing on a *tulsi* leaf picked on the way.

We cross a prayer room with altar and deities and a record player that communicates nothing else but *Hare Krishna*, chanted over and over again, day and night. 'I know the director of the hospice,' Dr Chatterjee assures me, as we pass some dour, unfriendly-looking attendants. A centre courtyard awaited us, sunlit at the end of a passage, and round it on two floors are the small bare rooms inhabited by the old women who have come here to die.

Dr Chatterjee led me into one of these damp, gloomy cells. The occupant lay on a narrow pallet. It seemed she wanted to rise, but as though petrified in a nightmare, she could not. Only her head rolled freely from side to side: the rest of her was agonizing stone embossed with contracted sinews. Her dress of blazing, lurid green silk fell completely open, exposing an emaciated ribcage and the breasts of a pubescent girl. I felt drawn to this woman, pitiably shrunken and yet sublime, and stepping nearer, noticed an amazing feature. Her long loose hair had turned white a few centimetres from the roots up, but was otherwise steadfastly jet black. This gave one the impression of a black halo floating some little distance apart from the head. From close up, I saw that the chewing motions of her mouth, which had seemed those of anguish, were in fact shaping the words, or at least the sounds of a dirge. The dying woman was singing. Grief, fear, torture had crystallized into a melody.

Every hour or so, two or three attendants would pass from one cell to the next, chanting, banging on a gong and blowing a conch-shell trumpet into the ears of the dying.

'This is hardly a peaceable way to make a good death,' I commented on the undignified din to which the poor lady had just been subjected.

'She isn't here to be comfortable,' Dr Chatterjee smiled. 'Did you hear? They already address her Hara, Hara Mahadeva, the salutation proper only to Shiva or a corpse.'

'Does she receive no treatment?'

'None of a conventional medical sort. Only some Ganges water and *tulsi* leaves every few hours.'

'So, in effect she'll starve to death.'

'You still harp on suicide?'

'In Japan we have *mokujiki* or tree-eating austerity, a thousand-day fast undertaken by ascetics, which is in fact a prolonged death by starvation. The process results in natural self-mummification in the end.'

'Our good lady is engaged simply in purification, not self-extinction.'

'I cannot see the difference.'

'The difference is a *good* death,' Dr Chatterjee replied, sternly, with evident exasperation. To illustrate his meaning, he used the dying woman as his model, like a non-sentient specimen in an anatomy class. 'In a bad or untimely death, *akala mrtyu*, the last breath emerges contaminated by excrement through the anus, or by vomit from the mouth, or through some other unclean orifice. It is best to die on an empty stomach, purified of all faecal and waste matter.' He poked his finger into the woman's mouth, palped her hindquarters and thighs, and at last pressed on the top of her skull. 'In a good death, the vital breath is released here, through the skull. She fasts in order to weaken her body, so that the breath may leave it more easily.'

During this tour of her physical parts, the woman eyed me, apparently conscious, and repeated some words.

'What is she saying?' I asked.

'She says, "My teeth are strong. A fire in my heart refuses to go out." She regrets the slowness of her death and the cost to her family.'

'How long has she been here?'

'Nearly four months.'

I could not restrain a smile. 'She has no choice but to overcome life by choosing to die.'

'It would seem so. Pardon me, sir. I have failed to show you a good death.'

'Apologies are unnecessary. I am already convinced that to know how to die is a matter of practice. But how does one practice *that?*'

As we pass between the *tulsi* bushes again on our way out, I pluck a leaf and sample its bitter taste. I imagine the old woman chewing on it, with strong white teeth, the reminders to her of an unsubdued hunger for life, like a sexual tapeworm of endless length.

The absurd deathbed scene has left me elated, though Dr Chatterjee seems downcast. Without cause, I feel assured of meeting my beautiful athlete, my *jizo* saviour, again for a fourth time. My expectation cuts a fire trail through the crowded streets as I search for him. Why should I expect to gain the *jizo*'s compassion when I denied it to Natsuko? My hope is based on treason. Hardly knowing why, or even what I am doing, I snatch a brass jug of Ganges water from a passer-by and wash the *tulsi* leaf down in a swallow.

9   THE KISS

MY REPORT TO the Emperor disappoints me. These foregoing pages have assumed a cold-blooded mechanical grandeur that defeats the small truth I am attempting to tell. I am soon going to die, but my courage to admit the petty, awkward truths of life has not grown a millimetre in stature. An unflinching autopsy of the creature who in 1945 nurtured ambitions of being a world-class author should in fact result in exposing the motivations of a domestic pygmy. I speak of a creature who imagines universal conquests with all the impotent rage of a drunkard, as he stretches out after dinner on the family's parlour sofa. I speak of a diminutive conquistador who cannot succeed to leave the front door of his home without feeling a traumatic lump of nostalgia in his throat, choking on his own fright like an agoraphobic. I speak of a romantic idler in the domain of dreams, a small household monster of resentment whose gigantism poses a nightmare threat to humanity, should chance ever marry him to real power. I speak of a closely guarded domestic secret, a virtuoso fiend sheltered in every bourgeois home. This is the small truth I should tell. All poets, great and minor, have from time immemorial dreamt their vengefully unfulfilled dreams of this front parlour messiah, have dreamt of nothing else but of his coming, the revenging anti-Christ of idleness. Have you guessed how he is? I speak of Hitler. Yes, him. The small truth. Hitler, the petty and grandiose enigma who remains incognito in our poets' dreams, until one day the excruciating, weed-choked idleness and humiliation of poets at last explodes into action.

So much for the small truth! On with the autopsy of the small teller of truths!

With the assured clarity of a blind man's touch, I can still identify the vertebral links that raised me from obscurity to best-selling celebrity status.

I was idle in 1945. Inconceivably so. A totalitarian war effort looks immense from the outside, and for those who have not experienced it, would seem to occupy every inch, every second of one's life. Wartime in fact provides unusual scope for idleness, ideal for the poet's extravagant abuse of time.

In the final months before Unconditional Surrender, I was transferred with my small number of law classmates at the Imperial University – all of them, incidentally, to some medically legitimate degree at last more physically unfit than I – to the naval dockyards at Koza, some thirty miles southwest of Tokyo. There, I was given the properly invalid job of librarian, a position so absurd that it would be tiresome to comment on it. Most of my effort went into digging more latrines than seemed necessary for the depleted personnel at the dockyards, or scurrying to the flimsy air raid shelters on the hillside. We had even ceased to comment on the massive air raids that annihilated entire cities but left military targets like our own dockyards untouched.

They say that having a cold is really a disguised or symbolic form of weeping. If that's so, then I spent the summer months of 1945 in an endless symbolic flood of tears. Bronchitis, flu, tonsilitis beset me in all minor varieties, and whether these colds were the effects of undernourishment or melancholy, I cannot say.

I was at home in Shibuya at the end of July, on leave from Koza and recuperating from another cold. The dreadful air raids of March had finally persuaded my father to evacuate the family to the relative safety offered by some cousins at Gotokuji, on the countryside outskirts of Tokyo. Azusa remained behind in Shibuya, a resolute sentinel armed with a revolver in constant vigil against bands of looters whose depredations were becoming increasingly common in those chaotic last days. He seemed far more occupied with surreptitious calls to his financial cronies, when the telephone lines functioned, in shady dealings conducted in whispers and grunted code words.

I lay outstretched on the parlour sofa, when Azusa entered the room after one of his grunt-grunt calls. His eyes widened in startlement, no doubt having forgotten my presence in the house, and not pleased to discover me in it.

'You should go to your cousins' in Gotokuji, the air might do your cold some good.'

'Did you know our houseboy is selling our stock of food item by item on the black market?'

Azusa shrugged. 'He's useful to me in other ways,' eyeing me in a way that connoted my utter uselessness.

'Do you still carry your gun with you?'

He grunted and patted his jacket pocket. 'I have an extra one in my desk drawer, just in case.'

'This is just like the *yoake maye*, the upside-down days Before the Dawn.'

'Huh? What?'

'Grandfather told me how his father Hiraoka Takichi had to defend the household from the anarchist looters of the *yoake maye*.'

'Trust you to find some outrageous cultural parallel.' Azusa poured himself a large scotch. Where on earth, at this time of shortages verging on famine, did he get priceless scotch?

'What are you reading?'

'Marquis de Sade.'

'A fine patriotic choice of reading matter, as the world comes to an end,' he laughed, with disagreeable absence of humour. 'You're a sick person.'

As he approached the parlour door, glass of scotch in hand, Azusa turned. 'Please take yourself to Gotokuji. Your presence seems more to your mother's injudicious taste than mine.'

I wished a B-29 would drop its tonnage of napalm on this house, on my father's hoard of scotch, on his vigilante revolver, as he grunt-grunted on the phone. Let the heavenly blue sky of summer guillotine the bastard!

To be precise, it was not Marquis de Sade I read, but an essay on him by Georges Bataille. And more precisely still, a certain passage in Bataille that I knew by heart and which had become central to my meditations 'as the world came to an end', in my father's words. I had first met the Divine Marquis in a selection of his works hidden among the other books that Natsuko's death had bequeathed to me. He had impressed me then, and increasingly with the years, as the only philosopher worth listening to. I suppose what first gained him my immediate affection, after my own twelve years in quarantine with Natsuko, was Sade's near lifetime in prison. Something else, though, fascinated me in this quaint jailbird's record – another mysterious, secret form of occlusion additional to his real prison cell, as it were, another inescapable cell *within* him, like a Chinese box puzzle. This lifetime's condemnation to an inner cell had everything to do with pleasure – or rather, the impossibility of pleasure.

Sade's inferno of twenty-seven years' confinement to various prisons and insane asylums first began with the criminal charge brought against him by Rose Keller, a beggar prostitute he tied face-down on a bed and severely flogged on Easter Sunday, 1768. Mademoiselle Keller's testimony stated that the Marquis did not have sexual relations with her, but that his repeated attacks with a cat-o'-nine-tails upon her buttocks finally brought him to 'loud, very terrifying cries'. Could these howls really be the satisfied cries of pleasurable orgasm? I very much doubt so. Bataille also confirmed that other witnesses at Sade's orgies had spoken of his frantic ululations, testifying to his agonized impotency of pleasure.

Sade's predicament – I would name it the anaesthesia of pleasure – drove him to indefatigable excesses in fantasy and fact, to Satanic destruction motivated by an incapacity to discharge his semen pleasurably except at times of deepest, excruciating displeasure.

My own secret share in the Marquis' frustration had been exposed to me in my early teens. My onanist's bad habit had gained such mastery over me that it forced me to surrender myself to its commands in the strangest, most inconvenient and risky places. I remember more than once retreating to the Peers' School toilets to indulge my insatiable glutton's lust. And there, one fine summer's day, as I practised my shameful exercise came the practice sounds of teenaged Kendoists through the open windows of the gym. Revulsion drove me to tug faster at my accursed supernumerary limb, stiff and resistant as the handle of a Kendo staff, *prestissimo* to get it over with. My wrist ached, but the damn thing wouldn't vomit up its contents. And when finally it yielded its gob of liquor, with an extreme ill will that sent an electrocutionary shudder through me, it did so in unexpected concord with a soul-stirring *kiai* from one of the Kendoists in the gym. It could have been – it was, in a sense – my own deep outcry, but not of soul or satisfaction. It was the same 'loud, terrifying cry' of Sade's displeasure, suppressed by biting my lips, for fear of being discovered in my act by one of the school prefects.

A simple discovery made. An axiom demonstrated. QED, as the geometricians say. Harm did not come from my classmates' innocent expression of martial virility, but from the nihilist ghost of my own displeasure resident within me and summoned up by their cries of easy pleasure. I knew then what my true nature was. I could gain some small amount of real pleasure only by causing harm or pain or death to another.

I lay on the sofa, in a delicious state of malaise that a slight fever induces in one, like a summer's breeze from a great river, chill in the midst of warmth, gently ruffling the hair of one's head. And I thought, 'Yes, for once my father advises well. My destination is Gotokuji. I will go there.' I would go there because my sister Mitsuko had been very much on my mind lately.

Mitsuko's innocent kiss, blown to me from the palm of her hand, had remained disturbingly vivid in memory ever since that ignoble February evening's celebration of my rescue from the jaws of death. There had to be a reason why such a mischievous whimsy, ethereal as dandelion fluff or pollen on a butterfly's wings, should have left me with a bad case of spiritual hayfever. And, of course, my analytic turn of mind found a reason. The kiss had been infectious because my mother's reaction to it had made it so. I could still hear Shizue's reprimand, 'Don't do that! Are young ladies at the Sacred Heart encouraged to such vulgar displays?' Shizue's voice betrayed the over-enthusiasm of jealousy.

But then, as it must be clear by now, my parents' intemperances could be explained as being nearly 100% focussed on me. I was the Hiraoka elders' centre of gravity. Everything – or almost everything in this household universe – was centripetal to me. Mitsuko and Chiyuki were excluded from my parents' unhealthy fixation, or more accurately, they were redundant personages outside it. I never seriously considered what feelings of resentment they might quietly harbour, but Mitsuko's wafted kiss now made me realize how fortunate she was not to be a satellite. Beyond reach of my dark magnetic field, she existed in her own safe-keeping, an admirably weightless being who gave indications of a future of unknown simple marvels denied to me.

Mitsuko's homely features, her tomboy character, aroused a sense of attraction in me, of the sort that makes a convalescent idealize his nurse. I fell in love with the idea of having a sister, only for the first time recognizing that I already had one. Mitsuko, alone among the Hiraokas, had always enjoyed a unique privilege. She could tease me out of my most aggravated moods. She had pursed her lips in a kiss on that dismal February evening of 1945, intending no more than a goodhearted jest to lighten the black nadir of my depression. Shizue, on course within the field of my gravity, had responded with jealousy. But there was more to it this time. Shizue's rebuke had alerted me to the erotic pout of my sister's lips, the result of slightly protruding front teeth with a funny little gap between them. Something almost resembling a human spark had ignited the dry autumn leaves of my soul, and in the next months it would become a consuming obsession to feel the pressure of Mitsuko's lips on mine in a real, physical kiss.

Seeing Mitsuko after my month's interval away at Kozu came as a shock. My imaginings had pictured her in the Sacred Heart School uniform, a girl with the coquettish airs of a nun. I was not prepared for the young woman seemingly older than her seventeen years, tanned beyond recognition, in a V-neck sweater riddled with holes that made her breasts appear mountainous. Nor could I have predicted the farm woman's bloomer-style denim trousers she wore, which blazed a pair of legs into my mind, a disclosure of womanly beauty that cut through my sight like scissors.

'Don't look so apprehensive, Tom, it's me,' Mitsuko laughed, referring to my private nickname for me, Tom, the chimneysweep boy turned water sprite in Charles Kingsley's *Water Babies*, her favourite and most treasured childhood book. She took my hand. Hers felt ridged like a lobster's back, and mine depressingly dainty. 'That's from working in the vegetable garden these last three months.' She looked at the crescents of dirt under her fingernails. 'I don't suppose these hands would be much good for a Chopin étude anymore.'

'You were never exactly going to be Wanda Landowska, were you?'

Mitsuko cared greatly for the piano, and my remark wounded her. I hadn't meant to sound so caustic, but the attempt to recover my balance left me clumsy. 'Is this the delicate and complimentary route to her deepest affection, fool?' I rebuked myself. 'Is this how you'll insinuate yourself into the girl's favour?'

But there in fact the problem stood – Mitsuko was no schoolgirl

194

within easy grasp of my fantasy but a young woman with independent desires of her own, remote from me as the height of a cliff face. How could I possibly scale that reality with my beggarly imaginings? It was hopeless.

'I'm glad you've come, Tom,' Mitsuko said. 'It's unsafe in Shibuya.'

'Who knows? An air raid might put an end to my useless life.'

'Don't say that,' a distressed anger flashed in her eyes, and I understood (of course, of course) that her anxiety did not limit itself to me, but included Azusa.

I so wanted to convince her of my desire to die, something so incommunicably impressive to me which apparently impressed only me, something less credible than demanding from her outright, here and now, on the spot, the kiss I desired.

'Cheer up, Tom. The war will soon be over, father says,' and she pecked me on the cheek, a sisterly-fraternal kiss that doomed the other imagined one to extinction.

B-29s showered us with leaflets outlining the Allies' surrender terms on 14 August 1945. I was in bed with tonsilitis at our Gotokuji relatives' house. The next day, the Hiraoka family complete in number gathered to hear the news. At noon, on 15 August 1945, the radio broadcast the sacred *gyukuon*, the Jewel Voice, heard for the first time ever on air across the land, surrendering.

How strange, how sinister that Night's emblematic voice, the Jewel of moon-brilliance, should be heard at noon, and to announce what? That the Imperial Mirror lay shattered and the sun fallen into permanent eclipse. Unfamiliar to His subjects, the Voice crackled like soft and ghostly flames that devour decayed wood, speaking in an antiquated, erudite language unintelligible to the commonfolk. '. . . the war situation has developed not necessarily to Japan's advantage,' at those words I saw, or believed I saw, a smile dart fleeting as a lizard across my father's lips. Azusa stared carefully at me, intent on my reaction. '. . . We have resolved to pave the way for a grand peace for all the generations to come by enduring the unendurable and suffering what is insufferable.'

'What can it mean?' Was it Chiyuki or one of our Gotokuji cousins who commented?

'Ask the scholar,' my father suggested.

My reply, volunteered from a throat painfully constricted, sounded not unlike the Jewel Croak. 'It means our Showa Emperor is finally living up to the title of his reign, Enlightened Peace.'

'It means –' Azusa said, lighting a cigarette, '– that now we enter an age of culture.' Drily, contemptuously he spoke these words to me: 'So if you still want to be a writer, go ahead.'

Azusa gave us time enough to let the words sink in, like one does in watering a houseplant whose soil has shrunken to an arid crust after long neglect. And then, because he knew how much everyone in the room could see deep into the gap between my thirsty, calcified earth and the sides of the pot – knew how much his permission to write meant to me – he withdrew it in a perfectly judged anticlimactic throw-away: 'In the meantime, finish your law studies.'

I went back to my sick bed. After a time, long enough at least that would appear discreet with regards to Azusa, Mitsuko came into my room. I expected her. She carried the excuse of a febrifuge beverage concocted from the Gotokuji herb plot. 'I'm so sorry –' she broke off, and simply handed me the infusion.

'Awful stuff,' I complained, sipping the tea and very much enjoying her discomfort. 'It isn't for you to apologize.'

'I felt shamed.'

'Shame for whom? Me, yourself, Pater Noster?'

'Pater Noster – really, Tom, you can be quite as extravagant as father sometimes.'

'The comparison does not excuse him. You know very well it was a deliberate and inexcusable cruelty.' She looked more invaluably beautiful than ever, because more unattainable than ever. 'And don't call me Tom anymore.'

'Father spoke in the great emotion of the moment.'

'What great emotion of the moment?' I laughed – a crow's tonsilitic squawk. 'Am I the only one with some sense of honesty left in this family? Shall I tell you what I felt upon hearing the Jewel Voice declare Unconditional Surrender? No great emotion, no grief, not even a sense of deliverance. My life has already been cut in two by being spared. Surrender brings me only the vaguest, uneasy promise that my isolation will now end and I must do something in life for which I am totally unfit and prepared. I should commit suicide like General Anami, Vice-Admiral Onishi and the five hundred officers who have at least taken responsibility for the surrender –' I thrust the cup into Mitsuko's hands. 'Why don't you put some rat poison in this? Or has father already instructed you to do so?'

'Don't talk like that.'

'Why not? You would be doing everyone a favour by putting an end to my life.'

Mitsuko knelt beside my mat, her back curved by the gravity of my outburst. I marvelled at the persuasive effect of my histrionics. So genuine in tone did my despair sound that Mitsuko's consequent reaction seemed entirely natural and expected. I watched her rise from her heels and travel in a crouched arc towards me, a progress that seemed to occur in slow motion, until her head came to rest on my lap. It had dropped there, swiftly in fact, as though decapitated, and I could feel the weight and its warmth spreading over my legs like blood.

'So this is the way to Mitsuko's heart?' I thought. She was unacquainted with the nihilist expression of sentiment, and therefore vulnerable to it. Cynicism, the one element entirely foreign to her nature, provided me with the secret means to overpower her innocence. Mitsuko was no longer 'Mitsuko my sister' but an independent stranger fallen victim to me. If I went slowly, in time I would make her feel a real inhabitant of my fictitious inner world of inconsolable despair.

In the meantime, my father took to smoking the new Peace brand of cigarettes. So did others still alive and able to smoke. As for me, there could be no alternative but to soldier on normally with my law studies at the re-named Tokyo University. I donned the Peers' School uniform again, a shabby hand-me-down of a senior student. I invested myself in my law books with single-minded dedication that baffled Azusa, who wondered if I might not be striving to deceive him. He was wrong to suspect me, at least for the time being, of clandestine scribbling. Even he could not possibly have imagined the revulsion I felt for writing at that moment. He could not guess how I scourged myself for my wartime record of aestheticism and outright literary opportunism, unmitigated by any excuse of imminent death. I embraced the dry abstractions of the law with genuine relief, convinced that my salvation from a fictitious life would be won by enduring the austerities of jurisprudence. This too was a fiction. My penitence was simply another form of aestheticism.

It never occurred to me to ask what virtues would come from study-ing outmoded laws, derived in Meiji times from the Prussian legal system, that General MacArthur's Occupation programme of reforms had set out to change. Everything would be reconstructed to accommo-date peacetime democracy and anti-communism. Such a concept of change was beyond my feeble grasp of reality. I cared nothing for the fact that MacArthur's backroom Jeffersons at SCAP Headquarters were busy concocting our Peace Constitution in a hurry to meet his deadline of Lincoln's birthday.

Before my classes began, I often went out in my preferred costume of white shirt and shorts to explore the devastated capital. 'Death affects us more profoundly under the pompous reign of summer.' So said my tutor in arch-decadence, Baudelaire. And it was true. Midsummer seemed to extend its reign of putrefaction from 1945 to 1948, punctuated by winters of utmost severity. Tokyo was a graveyard of rusty, inciner-ated junk. An outlaw vegetation of impressive exuberance had taken over, crabgrass like a wilderness of cabbages in the midst of rubble and molten bakelite, outsized arsenic yellow dandelions and tangled bindweed erupting from concrete. A vermin plantation had sprung to life in vast greenhouses of derelict steel girders twisted into eerie ogival shapes against a sky of such dazzling azure that it all seemed a mirage.

A perfect rectilineal hedge of cinders outlined acres of vanished buildings and in the very middle of nothing stood a safe, the one object secured from destruction, a reliquary empty inside but seething with fantastic Venusian convolvulus.

A work like this by a modernist cretin would gain the praise of connoisseurs nowadays. Tokyo entire was a cretinous modernist exhibition. I thought: there is nothing so admirably beautiful as ruins. Nothing appears so fresh as the first day of creation than freshly created ruins.

I experienced an intoxicating, savage lyricism in the midst of sub-human dereliction. I celebrated an intellectual victory of ancient things over the irrelevance of the present. Was it not true, I asked myself, that Noh drama and the tea ceremony had arisen unexpectedly like moon-nurtured flowers from the devastation of the Onin civil wars? Did not the ghost-tormented mysteries of Noh reflect the cemetery that Japan had virtually become by the 15th century? The lucid, economically restrained gestures of a tea master or Noh actor are stylized moments of 'no action' which have the suspense of the elemental in them, but which betray their origin in darkest pessimism, in the appalling war and famine conditions of medieval Japan. What we experienced even now looking at them is the sense of enclave, momentary and threatened refuge, in a world prepared to do murder. These antiquated and useless things – the quietism of certain objects, the sparseness of the tea hut, the slightly flawed coarse dull brown or black pottery of the tea utensils, the patch of rust on the tea kettle – all of this art, preserves what was already antiquated and useless at their first appearance. It is a withdrawal into things subdued, veiled, which elude the menace of extinction by anticipating harmony with it. This is *sabi*. *Sabi* is a craving to have the moon obscured by rain.

I found this moonscape peopled by savage breeds of folk. Troglodyte park-dwellers exposed to the decimating rigours of winter. Repatriated tatters of the Imperial Army, now maimed and dejected beggars – the younger, hardier ones naturally gravitating towards the black market. And among these primitives of the Year Zero, I saw the newcomer missionaries of Democracy in crisp, off-duty khakis speeding past in their jeeps, the Occupation Bibles of chewing gum, contraceptives and penicillin stuffed in their kitbags.

I considered all of this with the brutally elegaic eyes of a clinician. And it enlightened me as to a Law more fundamental than any I would find in my irrelevant compendia of laws. *An admission of defeat is perjury.* I realized that these multitudes were no longer Japanese or anything, but a barbarian encampment from who-knows-where, beyond reach of the missionaries' War Crimes Tribunal, because they might as well have been themselves victors overrunning the fallen city from some unknown place. I realized, too, that nothing could ever be reconstructed to take the place of the beauty I now saw. Rebuilding anything on these ruins would be condemned to ugliness that neither time would redeem, nor any aseptic loss of memory would expunge. Ugliness, with sudden immense panic I foresaw, a boundless nightmare ugliness, was stirring to life, like those maggot weeds in the putrescent sun.

I wanted everything to remain as it was, at a standstill, fresh as the first day of creation. A voluble silence screamed inside to find expression, and I did not on any account *want* it expressed. A return home to my desk filled me with dread. Writing had never before frightened me so. I did not know why. Nor did I want to know why.

I walked. I walked, hoping to awake as one more homeless madman, at home in this place. One of them, but not one of them. I was a different species of alien. Street corner racketeers lounging in the fierce sun, bare-chested, muscular, swaddled in bellybands, frightened me with their tribalist earrings and tatooes.

I often headed for a lonely bridge, which for some time had been my favourite haunt, offering I don't know what secret allure. There I would lean on the parapet, in the full noontide glare, staring into the river's clear-flowing current on which the debris of war still drifted seaward. One day, I noticed something that had escaped my attention. On an escarpment below the bridge, half hidden by acacias, stood a urinal of rusted iron and concrete. I felt attracted to go down and explore it. I found nothing inside but a yellowed slab of *oya* lava-stone furrowed by dripping water. It was surprisingly cool within the cubicle, shaded by the bridge overhead. A sharp, insistent stench of ammonia brought back memories of Tsuki, and I, deeply excited as though about to commit a crime, prepared to urinate for the first time in a man's public toilet. I suddenly heard voices approaching, and two men entered before I could flee. There was no alternative but to remain planted there, my head bowed in shame, between the two men urinating with immodest grunts against the slab. 'Look at the man-sized tool on this minnow,' one of them said to his companion at my left, an ex-serviceman hoodlum dressed in an open Aloha shirt and baggy pin-striped trousers rolled up at the cuffs. I gazed up at the speaker, into a scarred face, one eye a crazed slit twitching in a curl of smoke from the cigarette wedged between his lips. He was a swarthy complexioned youth in his twenties, without a shirt, the tensely knit bulging muscles of his torso imprisoned in a grey soiled bellyband. Black tufts stuck out from the paler cracks of his armpits, under the gleaming pads of his shoulders. A peony was tattooed on his chest. He wore a single earring, a US penny with its familiar, benign profile of Abraham Lincoln engraved on copper. What better symbol of the Year Zero than Lincoln turned into a bauble on a black marketeer's ear. The muscles on his neck became thickly knotted as he threw back his head and laughed.

'You keep on staring like that, kid, and you're going to piss on your shoes.'

When I came to myself again, alone at the bridge parapet, I felt inundated by palpitations. I had not been able to prevent my thing from arching in maverick response to the peony tattoo on the gangster's stiffened pectoral. He had seen it prance, and his laughter of complicity had given my immature, *virgo intacta* modesty a violent shock, but one which I found profoundly pleasurable. Pleasure came from an ungovernable thrill of pain, razor-keen as the singe of ammonia in my nostrils, pain that the gangster might inflict on me, and more profoundly yet, the visionary ecstasy I would feel to pierce his beautiful carcass with steel. I began to realize, in my spasmodic, breathless agitation, that the shock of encounter held far more compelling attractions to be exploited than my solitary mirror vice had represented till now. I began to seek practical ways of renewing the offence to my modesty.

A plan immediately formed in my mind. I would pretend to gaze at the river as usual, until someone went into the urinal, and then I would enter too. For several weeks, I devoted whatever free hours I had to my noonday vigil on the bridge, plotting my course from that urinal to other ones I had discovered. Many days were spent at the altar of urine-drenched slabs, in the company of buzzing horseflies and stray wasps. I often lay awake at night, my eyes wide open, propping myself up on my elbows. I would stay like this, perhaps for an hour, staring at my thing, trying to see perfectly, in every detail, all the indecencies it might commit, exposed in the awful subterranean light of the urinals.

My underground expeditions did not lessen my resolve to win Mitsuko's kiss, as perhaps should have been their effect. My first adventures into the region of homoeroticism were essentially figments. My curiosity was real, my intentions real, but the results of my explorations were not. So also Mitsuko's kiss existed in ideality, having nothing to do with the corporal embrace of a woman or sexual desire in any practical or even abnormal sense. I searched out Mitsuko's lips, without desire for them, but for the entertainment of an idea. And the idea was destruction.

Mitsuko arrived home from the Sacred Heart School later than usual one evening at the start of October term in 1945. She came to see me in my room, her face soiled and perspiring, her hands dirty after some labour. 'I've been helping them reshelve the books at the school library,' Mitsuko declared. But it did not explain why she chose to appear before me in this state. A disquieting sense that she had tunnelled through my dreams to arrive begrimed like this, overcame me for a moment. I soon regained tranquillity by submitting her to pitiless examination. How unattractive she looked in her school uniform, plump knees demurely joined as she sat down, her bare dumpy legs not disguised now into nimbly beautiful ones by farm woman's bloomers. Her lips did not pout erotically enough to rescue a schoolgirl with jutting teeth from mere homeliness.

She set her glass of water down on my desk. This would have been impermissable, a desecration of my inviolable writer's altar, had I not permitted Mitsuko these regular visits to my room which encouraged an assumption of familiarity. A glance at my desk told her that the papers on it had not been disturbed in weeks. 'You've given up writing these last months, Tom,' she said, a question posed as a statement.

'I've told you before, don't call me that.'

'Why don't you write anymore?'

'What's the use? I'm going to be a lawyer.'

She frowned, and then critically alerted to the unconscious humour in my words, broke into sunny laughter. 'Even father does not expect you to take a career in law all that seriously.'

'And what do you suppose – that he'll accept my scribbling behind his back?'

'I think he does, and probably always has.'

The possible truth of Mitsuko's remark deeply upset me. And entire world of fantasy evaporated in the dawning light of realism that she casually suggested. Had it been true all along that I *preferred* the myth of Azusa's implacable enmity towards my writing? Did I not rely on his animosity to support . . . Support what?

'I've danced my life away to an imaginary Emperor's Waltz,' I exclaimed, and began loudly to hum Strauss's tune, *one-two-three*.

She motioned for silence, finger across her lips – and how ravishingly beautiful those lips were again!

'You're not the only one with a secret, you know,' she earnestly contended.

'Oh really? And what sinfulness are you hiding from our head of family?'

'Not from him only, but from mother too. I don't know how I can possibly tell them.'

I suppressed my eagerness to mock, not in order to spare her, but to conceal from us both the selfish annoyance I felt. I would have resented any distraction from my own towering burden at this moment, and she now asked me to participate in a solemn fellowship that I did not share.

'Do you want one of these?' Mitsuko offered me a cigarette from her pack of Lucky Strikes. I knew from what illicit source they came, an upperclass virago at Mitsuko's school. I accepted one, though not grown yet to like smoking, it nevertheless made us feel participants in the fashionable devil-may-care mood of the times. I furnished the ashtray for such ritual occasions as this, a seashell in my desk drawer.

'Are you going to tell me now?'

'Yes, quickly, before I lose my courage even with you,' Mitsuko sipped from her glass of water and puffed amateurishly at the cigarette. 'I've decided to be baptized this Christmas.'

I skated over my astonishment with a bantering remark. 'So, the first *kirishitan* Hiraoka. Now that's something. And what Christian name will you take, Mary Magdalene?'

'I'm being completely serious, but you're right – I do feel myself to be a fallen woman.'

'It will pass,' I replied, in a surly way. 'In the name of reason, what makes you think you're fallen?'

'That's not something I feel able to tell you,' she drank again. 'Least of all you,' she added, her voice dusky from a throat parched by some recondite anxiety. Was I imagining a coquettish plea in her words that disclosed a secret open to both of us, and for that very reason perfectly absurd?

She brought herself to confess something more. 'That's why I am so grateful to you. I thank you, brother.'

'Thank me for *what*, if you please?'

Her lips pouted on words that wouldn't come out. Wonderful those gasping lips, so despairingly did I crave them, and yet so unattached to the womanly rest of her – legs that seemed awkward sexless pieces of furniture to me, breasts, uterus, mere anatomical nullities that excited nothing other than my disinterest.

'Well? For what do you owe me any gratitude? You're saying exactly the opposite, aren't you? You mean *I* owe you something, that's what you're really saying.'

'This is hard for me, please don't laugh. In these past two months, something has happened. You have been so open with me, and I never realized before – what I'm trying to say is, I understand your despair, really, for the first time – please don't smile like that – I can only understand it with my affection, I don't have the words you do. And it troubles me that you cannot sit at your desk and find satisfaction in those words anymore.'

'I am sitting at it now.'

'Don't make a joke of it. What troubles me is that you seem to have turned against writing now, ever since – well, ever since I began taking up your time.'

'Do you think I've given up writing on your account?' I exploded into laughter. 'Is that how you understand my despair? What's this – Christian psychology at its crudest and most inept? Ah, of course, now I do see. You want deliverance from my sudden interest in you that you think comes from my despair – or from what else? sacrifice? is that the right word, a kind of self-immolation? Why not call it what it is – a preparation for suicide?'

'You are not far wrong,' she murmured, her eyes dilating into tears.

'Since you fancy yourself a Christian, then you should identify what I suffer from by its proper clinical name. I am a passable expert on the Christian diagnosis of spiritual sickness, which enables me to report expertly on my own pathological condition. It isn't even a year ago, you must recall that grotesque February evening? Father, my saviour from death, triumphant on saké and treachery, and mother, like a she-wolf who's rescued her cub by eating it – and you – do you recall? I escaped death by a lie. Did you realize that?'

Mitsuko nodded. 'I didn't at the time.'

'And you still don't. I wasn't only relieved to be discharged as unfit, I felt pleased. Can you imagine that, *pleased*? Pleased to be what, forsaken by death? Isn't this the condition of the sinfully despairing man, accord-ing to Christianity? What would it prescribe for the atonement of this sin? My cowardice on that February day was no worse in fact than the expeditious resignation which seems to have overtaken the majority of the nation when confronted by defeat. They too were relieved, who knows, maybe even secretly pleased to surrender? I might as well say that the entire Japanese population was forsaken by death, and therefore assume upon myself a regret of unspeakable arrogance. And why not? Why not take on the entire burden of messianic regret? How else atone, when everyone else refuses to? Writing is certainly not the way to do it.'

'What are you going to do?' Mitsuko put to me, wide-eyed, a tear clearing a line down her smudged cheek.

I had no idea, and no answer. In my confusion, I went to stub out my cigarette in the shell, and with my usual doddering old man's clumsiness, upset its balance, spilling the ashes. The jerky recoil of my hand next succeeded in knocking over Mitsuko's glass of water. I watched dumbfounded as the water ran down, blotting into my papers, into the script of a story left incomplete, the chapter of a new novel begun.

Mitsuko reacted with immediate presence of mind by springing to my side of the desk and mopping up the spillage with her hankerchief. I took the wet pages from her and fanned them in the air. Our actions brought us into close touch. I felt the yielding pads of Mitsuko's breasts on my shoulders. I turned my face to hers, and the kiss I had craved for so greedily these past months happened like an afterthought – a clash of mouths from which I at once attempted to withdraw, but could not, because Mitsuko's damp cold hand held me at the nape. I yielded to her pliancy, a marshy sensation like that of her breasts on my shoulders, and I felt the worm's head tip of her tongue nudging at my lips. For the briefest instant, my tongue crept out to meet hers, to taste the strangeness of another's taste, the slight foulness of commingled breaths. A spider's yarn of saliva lengthened and broke on our chins as we parted.

Mitsuko wiped away mine with her fingers; and I cleansed her face with the soaked handkerchief. 'Now you have a story to write about,' she said, eyeing me in her tomboy way, but with a perplexing severity in her look.

'Not that I could.'

'No, not that you could.'

A story? There is indeed one to tell, of subsequent and unforeseen nightmare.

Two days after our kiss, Mitsuko fell ill with the aggravated symptoms of flu, and by evening she passed from high fever to coma. Typhoid was diagnosed at Keio Hospital. She was at once transferred to another hospital for infectious diseases in Okubu, a grim, desolate place that struck fear in our hearts.

Mitsuko had always been the robust picture of health. How could this possibly happen? Shizue wondered. Azusa gave characteristic vent to his anxiety in an outraged monologue, a reconnoitring of his own good conscience as a good family provider – 'could one have wished her in a safer place, supervised by the duennas of the Sacred Heart?' – 'and her diet, as indeed for the entire household, was it not superior to the below par rations doled out by the Occupation authorities, at best insufficient, which brought illness and starvation to those unwilling or unable to trade on the black market?' Yes, he had provided for Mitsuko. 'Then how could this happen?'

Infected well water at the school was to blame, apparently.

I had my own idea about the real source of infection. Yuan Hsiao had scooped up water unsuspectingly from a skull beside him in the darkness, and Mitsuko too, I felt, had been misled in her innocence to drink from the black, polluted waters of Japan's cemetery. Misled by whom? Wasn't I the skull from which Mitsuko drank uncleanliness? My deviant search for humiliation by the riverside had finally emerged from darkness to contaminate Mitsuko. I imagined my corruption seeping like diseased waste from the urinals I frequented into my sister's entrails. My sinful incapacity to love had delivered Mitsuko to *yomi*, that vague, grey underworld of tears and maggots.

The hospital in Okubu was understaffed. My mother and I took turns nursing Mitsuko. I would arrive from the university with my law books to keep an all-night vigil at her bedside. Mitsuko's spirit maintained the frailest thread to life; but I did not accept that she could die. I forced myself to concentrate on dry as dust legal formulae, which had a curiously anaesthetic effect on me. I felt numbed, as if weaving a soundproof cocoon, through which Mitsuko's delirious murmurs reached me like the distant rumour of a stream.

I sat, eyes focussed on the pages of my texts, but in peripheral vision beyond their margins, I sensed what I could not dare turn to and see.

A picture of my guilt, the tormenting uncertainty of *yomi*, lay just outside the halo of my page.

The little I still retain of my desultory law studies, I remember most from those hospital hours in Mitsuko's attendance. I remember Sir Henry James Sumner Maine's *Ancient Law* and the work of another legal historian, Vinogradoff's *Outlines of Historical Jurisprudence* – 'agnation, cognation, corporation, matriarchy and patriarchy . . . these are the key concepts of anthropology which have their origins in historical and comparative jurisprudence.' I think – I can never really be sure of this – but I think, often in the hours after midnight, in a delirium of my own, I communicated with Mitsuko, I spoke aloud my crazed ideas to one who could not hear them. I say she couldn't, but of this too I cannot be sure. Her eyes were sometimes open, and perhaps what I saw in my mind and said, she could see and hear.

Narrowed to the page, like a mule in blinders, I could nevertheless see down that tunnel with more dazzling clarity than ever. I could see towards my eventual, fully matured nemesis, voyeurism. '– so you see, in my own speculative jurist's way, I too am an anthropologist. My social disgrace as a voyeur makes me a fitting social scientist able to recognize the juridical underpinnings of our ancient legalist customs, the weight of the socially obligatory in Japan and its archaic system of indebtedness. And I shall be compelled to expose the *dis*obliging underside, the margins of illegality in these venerable but irrational customs. I exist as a spectator contrary to history . . .'

'Now I shall never be baptized.'

I looked up. Mitsuko's teeth jutted from the small open O of her mouth like a rodent's. Had she spoken those words? Whether or not she had, did it matter? Wasn't I duty bound to fulfil her wish, since I alone knew what it was? I considered the likelihood of inviting a GI chaplain here to baptize Mitsuko. How could I do that without arousing the curiosity of the hospital staff or my parents' suspicion? Baptism is simple to perform. I knew the formula. Was it permissable for a non-Christian to administer baptism? 'Anthropologically speaking, what harm could it do?' I glanced speculatively – anthropologically – at the bottle of distilled water on the bedside cabinet. It was too late now for its purity; or too soon yet for Yuan Hsiao's retrospective drink of water. I could not bring myself to say the obligatory words, 'In the name of the Father . . .'

As I sponged Mitsuko's forehead and fed her spoons of sugared water, I remembered my nights at Natsuko's side. Once again, my grandmother's sickroom closed in on me, this time in the squalid quarantine conditions of a hospital. Natsuko had died of haemorrhaging ulcers. And now, in her turn, Mitsuko's end was hastened by intestinal bleeding.

'Not long now,' the doctor stated at a glance, too overworked and fatigued to notice the cruelty of his words. And still I could not believe she would die. Her eyes were open, her breathing stertorous through a little rodent's opening, fixed in surprise. I approached that hole – no longer a mouth but the paralyzed aperture soon to geyser up blood from her viscera – and I kissed its parched rim. I would hear forever Mitsuko's last words to me, spoken clearly in her last unexpected instant of lucidity. 'Thank you, brother,' she said. She thanked me for having killed her.

10 RIDING THE TIGER

THE MIRROR   THE JEWEL   THE SWORD

THESE ARE the Imperial regalia, the sacred heirlooms of 124 Emperors in succession for 26 centuries, recognized not as mere symbols but as the realities of divinity. These three emblems divide my report to the Emperor into three sections. I do not need a book. I should need to declare no more than this – the Mirror, the Jewel and the Sword. Three words, the most enigmatic trinity in the world, because they are the dialectic of divinity. Instead . . .

'Are there not moments, Tokuoka-*san*, few perhaps, when you can sorrow over Mishima's desperation, when you can find him genuinely poignant? Poignant and ridiculous. For isn't it true, Mishima exemplifies better than most how far one must go to restore faith? My excesses in this direction measure just how utterly remote we all are from religion, how hopelessly lost and irretrievable faith is, precisely in the sorry and ridiculous spectacle I make of myself in my futile efforts to regain the unregainable. In this, I am almost admirable.

'Sorrow passes. One is left with an incorrigible fantasist who concocts a Nipponized Oscar Wilde fairytale of an Emperor on a white horse who rides among his squadrons of faithful young men kneeling in the snow, and benignly encourages them to cut their stomachs open for love of him. Is this the religious fantasy Mishima would have us accept?'

Pretence. It is all pretence. This is not the interview I gave to the *Asahi Shimbun* correspondent, Tokuoka Atsuo, but the one I would like to have given. Yes, there was a factual interview with Tokuoka Atsuo in Benares on the morning of 17th October 1967, but not as I desired it. My desire to dance the after-life sense of my life for my interviewer was neither insincere nor fictitious. I did not have the courage to act out my desire, proving once more how tragically comic the human spirit is. One can resolve to commit suicide and yet still be unable to relax the inhibitions attached to the life one is surrendering.

I know only too well why Yukio Mishima's performance has exhausted him. How much longer can he go on doing what he has done for too long, riding the tiger? How much longer can he keep his balance as a reasonably sane, responsible author with a popularity to maintain, a success threatened by an irresistable temptation to force outright fantasy upon a public that will at once renounce him? How often in these twenty-five years of nocturnal travail has my skepticism been the ballast against the wild listings of Mishima's self-intoxicated egoism which inclines him to every sort of folly? There are moments at night, at the writing desk, when the fever of aesthetic quarantine raises the mind's temperature to vertiginous delirium, to a superhuman conviction that could mislead the writer to test what should never be tested – the faithfulness of his readers.

Mishima's unabated fever since February 1945 has, so to speak, left its footprints in the snow.

It does not matter. After all, I am writing the book that I am writing, the same as all the others, except in one particular. I have come to the end of writing. I have planned my conclusion so that the ending of this book will end my life. The end of my life will coincide with the stitching shut of my writing wound forever. I ought to feel relief, perhaps even a sense of triumph that I have come to the end of so many years' immense labour at last. There is neither relief nor satisfaction at last in being able to say apprehensively, at last. The exhaustion of finality is what I feel, vacancy, a void. Writers know very well this feeling of being eviscerated, of giving everything that is best in oneself to one's best and conclusive work, only to discover that it too succeeds inconclusively. It too falls below the bottom line of what is without purpose in this world – another work of art. Fatigued, bitterly distracted by so much that remains uncertain and inconclusive in my life, I would almost wish not to end. I feel like a lady's glove turned inside-out and discarded. It is no comfort, even if one could be absolutely sure, to have written a masterpiece. The very word masterpiece itself is an imprimatur of irrelevance. It is an ugly word when one finally understands what it masks.

With death so close – who was I? What sense had my life?

My teacher Hasuda Zenmei marked these lines in *Hagakure*. 'One cannot accomplish feats of greatness in a normal frame of mind. One must turn fanatic and delevop a mania for dying.'

In a book of mine written over twenty years ago, I confessed that '. . . my heart's leaning toward Death and Night and Blood would not be denied.'* While pretending to reveal something about me, what did these three words 'Death and Night and Blood' conceal? They were

* In *Confessions of a Mask* (1949).

code words. They stood for three things that might seem very different: the Mirror, the Jewel and the Sword – in other words, the Imperial regalia. For they are the same: the Mirror reflects the Sun's Void, Death; the Jewel is the Moon, reflection of Night; and the Sword is the lightning flash of Blood. These emblems can also be transposed to read as Religion, Aesthetics and Ethics. A little poem of trinities sums up my life.

death	死	night	夜	blood	血
mirror	鏡	jewel	玉	sword	刀
religion	宗教	aesthetics	美学	ethics	倫理学
sun	太陽	moon	月	Uranus	天王星
Emperor	天皇	Chin	朕	treason	反逆
mind	精神／知	voice	声	action	行動
suicide	自殺	writing	書	homosexuality	同性愛

Like a Greek *stela*, this threefold column is the gravestone memorializing the entire development of my life.

Death and Night and Blood . . . Between this first profitable line I wrote and the last I shall ever write, stretches twenty-five years of riding the tiger.

I can date the time precisely when I set off on my hazardous ride. In a second radio broadcast, on New Year's Day 1946, the Son of Heaven declared himself human. The Mirror fell from heaven and shattered into one hundred million democratic pieces. One piece cut me in two, like an earthworm, and the two halves looked at each other in surprise and disgust. I chose this moment for my critical rendezvous with the senior writer Kawabata Yasunari. To put it in the plainest Machiavellian terms, I needed a literary protector of unblemished repute to champion me in a risky time of democratic sanitation. Kawabata, now in his mid-forties, had navigated through the war years on an apparently innocent course which brought him safely through the Occupation purge. He was judged a blameless liberal by MacArthur's authorities on the subject. An essay of his which appeared in November 1945 had decided me to approach him. 'I have the strong, unavoidable feeling that my life is already at an end,' Kawabata wrote. 'For me, there is only the solitary return to the mountains and rivers of the past. From this point on, as one already dead, I intend to write only of the poor beauty of Japan, not a line else.'

I sent Kawabata my published work and the best of my manuscripts in a bid to win his patronage. He responded to them with discouraging coolness, writing back that he was 'already conscious of this young writer's literary merits'. I endeavoured to woo him by correspondence, to which he replied that 'our little coterie is nothing more than a lending library, registered with the SCAP authorities, for the use of reclusive and elderly scholars, which, I fear, in its humble provinciality offers restricted scope to a young writer of ambition in these times'. My persistence was finally rewarded with the laconic promise: 'Let us see what the New Year brings.'

I did not wait for the New Year, with its tidings of the *ningen sengen*, but forced myself shamelessly on Kawabata on the very day of its pronouncement.

An hour's journey by train south from Tokyo brought me to Kamakura, Kawabata's home, in the morning of the scheduled New Year's Day radio broadcast. A voyage to Kamakura, so near to devastated Tokyo, impressed me as a return to a Japan that was no more, truly, 'the mountains and rivers of the past'. I saw a fairytale place coming into view through my window, an unspoilt winter scene of hills covered with unbelievable trees, glimpses of temples and traditional villas discreetly screened by evergreens. Wartime had not existed in Kamakura. It was, as it still is, an enclave of the wealthy disturbed by nothing harsher than the swish of kimonos on the hillside streets.

I felt like a plague carrier sent from the netherworld as I stepped off the train. 'It is entirely fitting that destiny has led you to Kamakura,' I chided myself. 'Remember, this is the ancient feudal capital of the Literary Government.' In 1185, Yoritomo, head of the victorious Minomoto clan, established his miliary dictatorship at Kamakura, winning the supreme title of Seii-Tai-Shogun or Barbarian-Subduing Generalissimo, from the cloistered Emperor at Kyoto. So began the form of military regime known as *bakufu*, 'tent government' ruling in the Emperor's name, which laid the foundations of the later Shogun system. Disgruntled scholars like Oe Hiromoto whose family had served the Imperial house for centuries, deserted Kyoto and flocked to Yoritomo's encampment of rough semi-literate samurai. A colloquial written style of Sino-Japanese was hammered out at Kamakura in military despatches and regulations, and in its court poetry. The name 'Literary Government' was accordingly given to Yoritomo's regime by soothsayers and astrologers.

Would not an astrologer of my own time have said, rightly and properly, in the Year Zero + one, 'the discontented *ronin* scholar, Yukio Mishima, abandoned the capital for the Literary Government of Kawabata Yasunari . . .'?

Kawabata welcomed me at the garden gate of his villa. I handed him my tribute, a bottle of French brandy and a dozen Havana cigars, a gift, need I say, requisitioned from Azusa's provisions. 'How very thoughtful,' he thanked me. 'You have hit upon my favourite vices, and my mouth waters. Will you join me later for a glass and a cigar?'

'Forgive me, I neither drink nor smoke.'

'Nothing to forgive. In a time of famine, one might as well fast.'

A fat marmalade tomcat brushes round the hem of his quilted kimono, meows its greeting, and slinks into the cedar hedge. A good omen. Kawabata points to a rise of snow-burdened trees on the neighbouring hill. 'You can see a Zen *dojo* over there.' An immense hush of silence glides past me, like the cat's ghost circling my legs.

'One hears the sound of the mountain in Kamakura,' I said, quoting the Zen epigram.

'No doubt the sigh of trees in the wind.'

Kawabata looks like a heron. His forehead slopes back sharply from a ridge of beaked nose to a crest of black hair turning white, and the scraggy flesh of his long neck resembles soft plummage. The better I became acquainted with Kawabata over the years, the more did his likeness to the white heron increase. He walks ahead of me with slow, unctuous, priestly steps of a heron. Dry snow crackles underfoot like granulated sugar. A flurry of loosened snow descends from a cryptomeria and stings our faces. The icy blue sky dims as we pass beneath the shadows of cedars and emerge at a rock garden flanking the villa.

A group of men stand round a cherry tree. Kawabata introduces me. I know most of them, at least by repute. This one is a Catholic novelist from Nagasaki who survived in clandestinity for fifteen years. The misfortune of a rural exile spared him the far greater one of the A-bomb. Another is a dissident professor of Kantian moral philosophy, hounded by the *kempeitai*. Others include a retired politician of the old pre-war liberal school, celebrated for his verses in imitation of the early Kamakura style of the *Hyakunin Isshu*. An art historian, specialist in the *emakimono* picture scrolls of the Kamakura period, engages me in a conversation on the miniatures illustrating the battle scenes from the military romance, *Heike Monogatari*.

This quintet of men twice or more my age, the principals of Kamakura lending library and my jury, were the sad revenants of a time that is no more. Dry, rustling husks of former men. Ghosts in a brilliantly transparent winter landscape.

An elderly maid came out to us from the villa with a tray of steaming saké cups. Susanoo's warm brew revives me. A rough, surly old fellow in hempen-laced gaiters and badly patched quilted jacket, leaning on the handle of a mattock, eyed the cherry tree as though measuring it for firewood. Hajime is his name, gardener to Kawabata these twenty years and another thirty previously to the family. It seems I am not the only one out of place among the spectres of the Literary Government.

'Our cherry tree is past its prime,' Kawabata says. 'It has not blossomed the last two years. We are trying to decide whether to cut it down or spare it.'

'It's time, sir,' Hajime said.

Kawabata glanced at his watch. 'You're right.' He instructed the maid to open a screen window at the side of the house. A radio has been placed on a table by the window, its volume turned up to reach us by the cherry tree. The last notes of an anthem cease, a time signal is heard, and a voice announces that His Majesty will now read the Official Rescript of this day . . .

An eternity ended in the few minutes it took for the Emperor's *ningen sengen*, his 'human declaration'.

Saké was again served, now with sweet rice cakes. The mood could not be said celebratory. In good stoical Japanese fashion, no one offered an opinion. Or rather, no, it was not quite the usual turning one's face away from the unpleasant, the out of place, the unusual. Faces were turned to me, I felt, in expectation of my opinion. My induction into the Kamakura circle had begun.

'Who could venture to say what has been irredeemably lost today, or perhaps gained?' Kawabata declared.

But I was being subtly pressured to venture myself on a statement. 'One hundred million have apparently benefited today from one more human,' I said.

The Catholic novelist faintly smiled. Heron priest Kawabata in his black soutane of down-quilted worsted, raised his saké cup in a toast. 'Who can doubt it?' he replied.

Hajime peered up at the blue sky. It had lost nothing of its clinical brilliance; nor had it fallen on us. Hajime wept. Kawabata, the gentle undogmatic realist, looked hurt, as we all were, by the loyalist tears of the gardener. 'Come now, old fellow, come now,' was all Kawabata could manage to say.

Hajime began singing, in a rough broken voice, a nationalist anthem of the 1930s. '. . . the form of towering Mount Fuji is the pride . . .', but the words faltered into a sob. The connoisseur of *emakimono* miniatures visibly winced.

I proceeded where Hajime had left off, in the middle of the well-known verse, '. . . the pride of our flawless like a golden chalice, unshakable Nippon . . .'.

'The flawless chalice lies entirely in pieces, Hajime,' Kawabata said, but quietly reproaching me.

'It is regrettable, sir,' Hajime answered, wiping his eyes. 'To hear what I've heard today, and on such an improper instrument.' He meant the radio.

'Let's make up our minds about this unfortunate cherry tree,' Kawabata said.

'A tree of this age might skip a year or two before it decides to blossom once more,' Hajime proposed, his hand stroking the tree's mottled bark.

'A postponement of fate is not a decision,' the Catholic novelist remarked. I imagined what it was like for him, sifting through the radioactive ashes of Nagasaki for his kin.

I shivered. Not having foreseen that my initiation to Kawabata's circle would take place in the open, I had dressed formally but too lightly for the cold. Memories of standing naked for my medical exam at the Shikata barracks came back to me.

The comparison was not a promising one. My first hour of probationary investigation by the Literary Government seemed to me a disaster, because of my failure to mind my tongue.

Hajime unexpectedly drove the sharp edge of his mattock into the trunk of the cherry tree, It shuddered, and snow fell on us from its branches like spring blossoms. 'What are you doing?' complained the art historian, as though one of his precious scrolls had been defaced. 'A shock might bring it back to life,' Hajime said. He left the mattock buried like a question mark in the tree and slouched off round the house. 'I suppose he will get very drunk now,' the Catholic novelist remarked.

Hajime's action saved me from desolation. I felt revived. What did I care if the Kamakura spectres dismissed me from their sanctimonious coterie?

'It has been a day of grievous emotion,' Kawabata said.

'Or perhaps one of anticlimax in our emotions,' the retired politician added, looking at me, 'for which our youth is not prepared.'

'We have endured a miscarriage of history,' I replied to him, no longer caring to bridle my tongue. 'The truth is, cynicism weighs light as a feather on the sadness of youth, because it soon forgets both. As for me –' I faltered, but without Hajime's permissable grief.

'As for you?' inquired the Kantian moral philosopher. 'Please go on.'

'I feel terribly old,' Kawabata sighed, 'without confidence in the future. Will we recover? I cannot conceive of it.'

'My father assures me that we will see capitalism healthier than ever before.'

'A commendable faith,' the politician drily observed.

'You were saying, Mishima-*san?*' the Kantian encouraged.

'As for me, I meant to say, there is an unbridgeable difference between experience and reality.'

'Please explain what you mean by this peculiar opposition of experience and reality,' the philosopher asked, intrigued by the distinction.

I briefly described my tour of duty at the Nakajima aircraft plant, which had consisted mostly of leisure to work on my translation of the Yeats play. 'I had begun to transcribe this play into the language of Noh a year earlier, before my teacher Hasuda Zenmei was posted to Malaya. Together, we had composed a letter to the American poet, Ezra Pound, at that time in Rapallo, Italy, and directed it to him via the Italian Embassy in Tokyo.'

'Ezra Pound? How very enterprising,' the politician said. 'The Americans have caged him up as a fascist collaborator.'

'Why did Hasuda-*san* advise you to write to Ezra Pound?' Kawabata gently asked.

'The idea was mine. My English was faulty, Yeats was dead and beyond consultation, and Ezra Pound seemed my next best course. Events interrupted my work, until Nakajima afforded me considerable time to resume it.'

'Hm!' the politician grunted.

I could read disgust on the faces of my jury. My extreme hyperaesthetical creepiness could only strike them as sickly, as perhaps I intended. I don't know. My feet had turned into ton blocks of ice, and I had lost any capacity to judge reactions, even my own.

'I agree with you, Mishima-*san*, about the paradox of considerable time,' Kawabata said. 'Totalitarian war is strangely porous, honeycombed by secret little enclaves of freedom in which time seems infinite, unlike anything in peacetime. I remember an occasion in April 1942, just after the first American B-29s appeared over Tokyo. I went into a bookshop in Gotemba to consult some legal texts – something to do with my wife's complicated inheritance of a property, of no interest here – and the air raid signal interrupted my researches. Everyone rushed out of the shop, as is perfectly natural, but I was in no mood to be hurried. "The mobilized mob," I thought, in a somewhat ungenerous frame of mind. I noticed a young man at the far end of an aisle, deeply engrossed in a large textbook propped up on the shelf, totally unmindful of the noise and stampede. My curiosity was aroused by his concentration. I stole quietly down the adjoining aisle and peeked at him through a gap in the bookshelf. He wore a soiled gabardine coat and looked famished and ill, the stereotype of the penniless student. He stood very rigidly, I would say, monumentally tense, his left hand extended and holding the book open on the shelf. I could see a deep hollow clefting the muscles at the back of his shaven neck above a knob of spine. Was he perhaps frozen in panic, as sometimes happens to people in an air raid? Then I noticed the page he was staring at, a medical photogravure of a woman's vagina probed by an unpleasant array of urological instruments. The woman's face in foreshortened perspective was barely visible beyond her thighs, possibly a dead woman, a specimen of the anatomy class. The steady, pumping movements of the young man's right hand, hidden from sight under his coat, indicated that he was masturbating. I regretted my curiosity and left the shop at once. The air raid turned out to be a false alarm, in any case.'

'A dreadful story,' the philosopher said.

'Not at all, not at all,' Kawabata insisted. 'I was disgusted by the sad vision at first, certainly, but then I reconsidered. I began to admire the young man's determination to create an enclave of pleasure for himself in public, so to speak, in the eye of the storm, bizarre as it might be to find gratification in a surgically explored vagina. A space of freedom, visible to all and yet not, in a condition of total mobilization – is this not what we intellectuals in wartime called "inner emigration"? Was not my young man the very model of the inner emigrant?'

'Nietzsche's pale criminal,' I muttered to myself. Kawabata's story could just as well have described me.

'Nietzsche's what?' said the art historian to me. I thought of Odagiri Ryotaro, leaning back against the propellor of a Zero-model combat plane to enjoy fellatio by Miss Peach Blossom during an air raid.

The Catholic novelist laughed disapprovingly. 'Onanism is not a flattering comparison to make with our efforts to dissociate ourselves spiritually from the war.'

'Why should we flatter ourselves?' Kawabata responded.

'Your teacher Hasuda Zenmei committed suicide, did he not?' the politician asked, eyeing me strangely.

'That's correct. When the commanding officer of the Bohor Johor garrison in Malaya ordered his troops to lay down their weapons, in accordance with the surrender terms, Hasuda-*san* stepped forward and accused him of treachery. He drew his pistol and shot his commander through the heart, and then himself in the head.'

'A fanatical act of insubordination,' the politician shook his head.

'Hasuda Zenmei was an exceptionally fine scholar of the Heian classics,' the art historian said. 'Do you approve of his act?'

'His act was inscribed in his philosophy. It is not for me to approve or not.'

'Nevertheless,' Kawabata gently demurred, 'will you attend the memorial service that is rumoured in preparation for Hasuda Zenmei?'

'A service will not occur till the return of his ashes from Malaya.'

'It would be inadvisable, don't you think, Mishima-*san*, to celebrate the memory of someone who rejected surrender?'

'What would you have me do? Deny my association with him?'

'There are some,' Kawabata said, 'who accepted unconditional surrender long before the war inevitably led us to it.'

'I suppose I must count myself in that number, among the "inner emigrants", as you say.'

'It is neither wise nor necessary,' the moral philosopher added, 'to insist on what everyone already knows, that Hasuda Zenmei was your teacher.'

'*Was* your teacher,' the politician put in for redundant emphasis.

'I see.'

'And so, therefore, will you attend?' Kawabata asked.

'I cannot do otherwise.'

Kawabata stared at Hajime's mattock buried in the tree. 'No matter.'

The early twilight of mid-winter had crept up furtively on us. A light snow began to fall. Kawabata led me back to the garden gate. On our way back through the sombre passage of cedars, I said, 'I have made a fool of myself.'

'What makes you say that?'

'By appearing a fanatic.'

'I don't believe the others are much worried about that.'

At the gate, Kawabata said, 'We have decided to launch a new literary journal called *Ningen*. A name of opportune resonance, don't you agree?' He smiled. 'We would be delighted to receive your contributions.'

'There is a problem, indeed an all-too-human one.'

'Ah –'

'What shall I write about, *sensei*? I feel coldhearted towards any enthusiasm. I have nothing left to say.'

'I have shared that feeling. Might I advise, why not write about yourself? Your generation would seem to require a confession of truth.'

'But that's my problem. What can I write about *me*, if I don't exist? It would be a masquerade.'

'You quoted Nietzsche earlier, "the pale criminal". Then you must know his saying: "The poet able to lie consciously, willingly, alone is able to tell the truth."'

Trudging back through the snow in the darkening afternoon, I began to recognize what my encounter with Kawabata had really signified. We had played our parts in a fable of The Crane★, the heron and the fox cub, which might have been entitled, 'A Test of Humanity'.

★ referring to the Emperor.

11 FERNANDO PINTO MENDES

ON THE EARLY afternoon of my third day in Benares, I bade goodbye to the real Tokuoka Atsuo in a taxi outside the Central Post Office. I had journeyed there to contact my publisher Nitta Hiroshi by telegram, but the message was never sent. A startling creature on the post office verandah diverted me from my errand. A man's vast naked carcass, sleek as a porpoise, encumbered the entrance way. A smile of utter self-contentment acknowledged the titillation that his enormous sexual organs excited in the band of onlookers as he rolled over lazily on his side.

I assumed him to be another naked *saddhu*, unusual only in his obesity and the insanely debauched look of his face. We watched the holy man devour a stuffed *paratha*, while a young attendant massaged his mountainous back. This masseur I recognized at once as my trickster acrobat, my *jizo*, whom I had expected to meet yesterday after visiting the House of Widows. He turned up here instead, a chain of funeral marigolds round his neck, smiling beatifically as he ministered with several others to the cetacean *saddhu*. Closer inspection of the lad, so tantalizingly near, was impeded by the densely packed number of spectators.

'You are wishing a closer look?' a falsetto voice proposed in my ear. My solicitous inquirer, and the perpetrator of this slapstick Indian turn of phrase, was none other than Dr Anant Chatterjee. 'The guided finds the guide,' he said, as the concourse pressed us into near embrace. 'How providential and poetical.' Dr Chatterjee's normal costume had been supplanted by a cotton blouse of the Indian sort and capacious khaki shorts. His breath had an odour of repulsive innocence, which tells of guts anaesthetized by alcohol. He was, in short, drunk.

The *saddhu* had risen to his feet now and was sipping a liquid from one of the half-dozen tins on the porch ledge. Dr Chatterjee tapped the shoulder of a nervous young Brahmin in front of us with his rolled-up Bombay *Times*. 'What is occurring here, please?' my guide asked, adopting a mock Indian cantilena. 'That is an Aghori,' the Brahmin explained. 'He is drinking his own urine, you see. Very healthy for you.' The urine drinker next splashed the crowd with the remnant liquor in his tin. 'People are coming here every day for this blessing.' I considered myself lucky to have stood out of range of the Aghori's benediction, which also brought his daily stage appearance to an end. He descended the Post Office steps, a colossus of shuddering jelly, with his followers in tow. My *jizo*'s eyes and mine met for the first time. His smile confirmed my original impression of unhealthy bluish teeth, a symptom of phthisic anaemia, the one blemish in his astounding perfection. My longing to pursue him was thwarted by Dr Chatterjee arguing with the Brahmin. 'That preposterous sideshow freak, an Aghori? No, no, he's a fake.' The young man looked offended.

At the next moment, the crowd disassembled into its constituent market strollers, but not before the dubious Aghori and the boy had vanished. 'Would you return with me to my lodgings in Dal Mandi,' Dr Chatterjee said, 'and join a poor scholar in a farewell drink? Allow me that great pleasure, sir.'

'Since this is adieu, Dr Chatterjee, I accept. You can repay me with a favour. Let me try to find my own way to your house, without your guidance.'

I suffer from a poor sense of direction, but perhaps chance guided my steps that day. With uncanny assurance, like a sleepwalker on intimate footing with this city of the dead, I succeeded in reaching the pastel blue archway that had sheltered us from the rain two days ago. 'Well done, sir, but not the shortest route.'

We encountered Dr Chatterjee's neighbour, the old priest, damp still from his dip in the Ganges and sprinkling water from a brass pot onto the *lingam* in the courtyard as he chanted *baba, baba*. Dr Chatterjee's arrival threw the elder into an immediate fit of giggling, and a cruelly exact pantomime of my guide's tics, his limp and a well-known repertoire of itches. The old man's laughter followed us up the staircase.

'Why do you allow him to mock you like that?'

In reply, Dr Chatterjee pronounced some incomprehensible words for each step that he mounted. 'Non coerceri maximo, contineri tamen a minimo, divinum est.'

'What's that?'

'Latin. It means, not to be encompassed by the greatest, but to be contained by the smallest, is a divine thing. Are you familiar with Spiritual Exercises of St Ignatius of Loyola?'

'By repute only.'

An upper-storey porch led us to a door, the once gorgeous hand-carvings on its panels and frame now mouldered to silvery grey.

Dr Chatterjee slumped into an Edwardian wing-chair. 'Have some gin,' he invited, at once pouring me an uncontrolled amount from a bottle of Gordon's. 'There's quinine water in the jug – perfectly safe even for the indisposed guts of a sahib. How are they, incidentally, after yesterday's impulsive draught of Ganges water?'

'Perfectly fine.'

Dr Chatterjee's slouching posture had hitched up his loose shorts. The reason for his limp was now clearly on view. His left knee presented me with a scarred deformity. 'This –?' he said, intercepting my gaze. 'A souvenir of my encounter with the Calcutta police during a riot some years ago. I was a Marxist of a sort in those great days of protest.' He picked up a book from a Regency side-table. 'Even the weariest river winds somewhere safe to sea,' he quoted, without opening the volume. 'Swinburne, from the *Garden of Proserpine*. I've intoxicated myself with his poetry all morning, which has put me in a somewhat delinquent mood.'

An odour of the intoxicant *bhang* from Dr Chatterjee's cigarette suggested another vice besides Swinburne. Dr Chatterjee read my thoughts perfectly. 'You must think me a typical Benarsi idler.'

'More British than typical.' I glanced round at his surroundings. Not a single item anywhere in sight gave hint of India. English landscape watercolours, a shelf of Loeb classics, a cricket bat in the corner – I refrain from adding more to this shameful catalogue of Anglo-Indian idolatry, except to observe that a fine granular dust, most likely human ash swept in by the breeze from the cremation ghats, coated everything.

'Do my quarters displease you?'

'I am surprised.'

'Why on earth should you be? Can you think why my anglophiliac preferences should cause you such unease? Might I suggest a reason why? This room could well be the study of some English provincial headmaster – indeed it could – but here, in view of Benares through the open casement with the Ganges visible in the distance – why, of course, how perverse it must seem, a complete withdrawal into an enshrined fantasy of the British Raj. Am I right in my diagnosis?'

'You exaggerate.'

'Is it really an exaggeration to diagnose a sense of Asian superiority outraged by the look of this room?'

'Pieces of furniture do not threaten my Asiatic pride, Dr Chatterjee.'

'Then you should not appear offended. After all, haven't you preferred to surround yourself with imitation Rococo furniture? Did you not boast of sitting to watch television on a Louis Quatorze chair, in Levis and aloha shirt? What sort of house did you build for yourself in Magome eight years ago? A colonial-style Victorian mansion reminiscent of America's deep South, something vaguely Palladian, an eccentric house such as you once saw in Brazil or in Guildford England. Something fancifully scandalous that only a Westernized Asian could dream up – or live in.'

'Where did you hear this?'

'Why, from your own lips – wasn't it?'

Dr Chatterjee's description baffled and astonished me. He would have to be very well-acquainted with the Japanese gossip columns to know such details.

'I don't remember telling you anything like that.'

'Bad conscience tends to a selectively poor memory.'

I became aware of an absence in Dr Chatterjee's behaviour. His nervous tics had entirely vanished, no fidgety scratching, no obsequious 'sir' perpetually on his lips. The volume of Swinburne had remained propped on his lap, his forefinger wedged between the pages. 'Memory is at best unreliable, which makes it all the more poignant,' he said, and opened the book. 'Look at this flower pressed between the pages. A species of wild tulip I found in a Suffolk marsh, how many years past, I don't even recall. Isn't it appropriate? A specimen of memorious bloom in the garden of Proserpine, goddess of the dead and forgotten.' I was shown a flower of pyramid-edged petals, its violet colour faded to mothwing transparency. 'I used to be quite a botanist in my Cambridge days.' He flicked through the pages, naming other bookmark relics of the English countryside. 'I never found what I was perhaps truly seeking for – the amaranth, the imaginary unfading flower, no matter how many samples of the genus amaranthus I collected, prince's feather and love-lies-bleeding.'

'Dr Chatterjee, if you please, can we leave Proserpine's garden for a moment and return to the question?'

'What question is that?'

'Your source of information about me.'

'Shall I acquaint you with a little secret? When by chance I heard of your scheduled visit to India, I lobbied the British Council in Calcutta to appoint me as your guide.'

'Why such eagerness for the job?'

'Not for the job. I have never been anyone's tourist guide – and not this time either.'

'Nevertheless, why?'

'Did you see an Aghori this afternoon?'

'Not according to you.'

'Exactly. Why be misled by a fake? You have already seen the real thing, several times in fact, without recognizing *what* you saw.'

'Strange about-face, Dr Chatterjee. Now you're claiming this mythical creature not only exists, despite all your previous denials, but that I've seen him?'

'You have denied until now the real purpose that has brought you to Benares, and I have simply reflected your pretence. To research a book – is that the excuse you plead? As a writer you should know better than most, intentions are reality's original little misfits. What are you really writing? Is it – or will it – end up being what you originally intended?'

'A fiction will convince us if it seems to pre-exist in our recognition – is that what you're getting at? I know very well, an illusion of reality is not achieved simply by the writer's skill, but as the result of our own inexpectation.'

'You have expressed my idea better than I could. With the same clarity, can you now see that witnessing the Aghori is the true purpose of your coming to Benares?'

'How can that be? I had never before in my life even heard the name Aghori, until a guest at the hotel mentioned it.'

'Why should the casual mention of a name by a stranger excite your interest – unless the stranger himself made some unusual impression on you?'

I thought of my Brigadier on Clark's verandah, Marquis de Sade returned from the grave – and I laughed. 'I was thinking, life is an exception to the rules that are much stricter in art.'

'As is only natural, since life is not something we can possibly imagine.'

As we spoke, the declining afternoon sunlight fell on a picture I had overlooked in the shadow between two bookcases, a colour lithograph of a Brahmin holy man. 'Is that your guru?'

'In a manner of speaking,' Dr Chatterjee replied, smiling wistfully at my sarcasm. 'He's been dead some three hundred years. That is Roberto de Nobili, a Jesuit missionary of the 17th century.'

'A Jesuit missionary in Brahmin dress?'

'You would not be the first to be surprised. De Nobili created a unique marriage of Brahmanism and Christianity, known as the Malabar rites. Christianity had made little headway in the Portuguese colony of India before de Nobili's arrival. Christian neophytes were compelled to take Portuguese surnames, to eat, dress and behave like Portuguese. These converts became *parangis*, outcast of Hindu society. De Nobili upset European arrogance by joining the Brahmin caste. He adopted the *kudumi* hair tuft and shoulder thread, the wooden clogs, saffron robes and vegetarian diet. A stripe of *santal* on his brow marked him as a teacher, a *sannyasi*. When his fellow Brahmins learned that de Nobili's father was a count and a general in the Papal Army, they gave him the aristocratic title *Raja Sannyasi*. His success as a missionary overcame the Vatican critics opposed to his scandalous idea that being a Brahmin and Jesuit were not incompatible, until 1744, when Pope Benedict XIV outlawed the Malabar rites in a sixteen-point decree.'

'If I understand you rightly, you are a follower of these Malabar rites?'

'To answer you rightly, yes, I am a follower of the rites, but no, because I am forbidden to practise them. A Jesuitical answer, which might perhaps suggest something else to you?'

'You don't mean to tell me you're a Jesuit?'

'I am.'

'Is this true, Dr Chatterjee, or another of your practical jokes?'

'It is a perfectly genuine enigma concerning my life, and the Aghori's place in it. You see, I was not born with the name Anant Chatterjee, but was originally christened Fernando Pinto Mendes in the cathedral of Goa in 1930. My father, Vasco Pinto Mendes, emigrated from Goa to Bombay in the 1920s and made his fortune there as manufacturer of confectionery. He was a *mestizo*, one-quarter Portuguese, a degree of blood which would therefore make me an octoroon, according to the stock-breeding calculations of the old slave traders. I am, I suppose, a not so uncommon Anglo-Lusitanian Indian. Vasco Pinto Mendes figures powerfully in my memory as a cavalier type, very stout, as befits a maker of sweets, of almost dwarfish stature, very ugly but with remarkable grey eyes, the only characteristic, as you can see, that I inherited from him. He married a girl half his age, a high caste beauty from Purva Pradesh, the heartland of India. She came without dowry, because her family had of course disowned her, and with another severe liability, tuberculosis, which had already put her life at risk. Medical specialists, in those days before antibiotic treatment, advised her against conception, as pregnancy could prove fatal. My parents ignored this judgement, and, if I am to believe the nursery tales of my Goan *ayah*, I was conceived in a weekend of passionate abandon during one of my mother's visits to a sanatorium. Contrary to medical opinion, my mother not only survived my birth but seemed for a time to flourish. Only a few years, alas, and then she had a lung removed, and all her teeth were pulled out, a routine part of the treatment at the time. Her beauty was gravely attained, and so too was Vasco Pinto Mendes in his heart and conscience. His guilt, as I imagined it to be, drove him to the alternative solace of drink and vice, and as for me, I saw little of either parent, one often back in the sanatorium, the other out carousing.

'Total misfortune struck when I was aged five and my father died suddenly of a brain tumour. Vasco Pinto Mendes passed away bankrupt, and we found ourselves virtually destitute. Finished the upper-class life of Bombay, the summer retreats to the Western highlands of Khandala, my private tutors and all that. We scraped by on the charity of some Mendes cousins, but my mother's own kin remained unsympathetic. I do not flatter myself when I say my mother hung on to life as long as she could for my sake, until I was six, at which time, in desperation she wrote to an uncle in England, begging him to come to my assistance. This uncle, Anant Chatterjee, whose name as you can guess I later adopted, was the junior of a clan of brothers, and himself considered something of a black sheep. He had not followed in the Chatterjee tradition of magistrates and bankers, but went to England in his early twenties, where apparently he had become the wealthy proprietor of a chain of chemist shops – drugstores, Americans call them. Anant

Chatterjee surprised his niece by graciously offering to pay for my passage to England, whereupon he would assume responsibility for my education. My mother was relieved. She imagined my future secured as a pharmacist in remote and unimaginable Birmingham. The reality would prove something very different.

'I was permitted my first sight of Anant Chatterjee at Sunday lunch, in the winter's eve of 1937, ten days after my arrival at his Chelsea home on the Thames. His young manservant Amit had seen to my needs during my uncle's mysterious interval of absence. Amit was a very goodlooking fellow, but he paled to insignificance beside my intimidatingly handsome uncle. I could see my mother's sadly deteriorated beauty renascent in his features – beauty, but with a disconcerting element of menace. Amit had warned me, "Consider yourself an Untouchable in the presence of an English lord, and you won't go far wrong."

'Anant Chatterjee was indeed, and to an insufferable degree, English, an adept of the high-handed, cruel mannerisms of the Bloomsbury freaks, a circle in which he was in fact welcomed. His own first words of welcome to me were, "He looks like an overstrung Brahmin with the eyes of a Portu*goose*." And I was always thereafter "that Portugoose", and always indirectly addressed as "him" like someone transparent. "His mother died three days ago, incidentally," he announced, speaking to Amit as he served lunch. "A bad death, by the reckoning of Hindoo superstition, but I've attended as best I could to that miserable lady's funeral rites – and for pity's sake, Amit, tell him not to snivel like that!"

'My uncle introduced me to my first traditional English Sunday lunch. He himself, of course, not Amit, undertook to carve the roast – "you can't trust wogs to carve beef properly", and God help me, what a chilling, abysmally sinister laugh accompanied that remark!

'I had never before seen beef, let alone eaten it – and there it was, a haemorrhaging slice of flesh handed to me on a plate, awash in some fluid the colour of excrement – gravy, and for heaven's sake, Yorkshire pudding. The abattoir menstruum from my mother's lungs – that's what confronted me on that plate, and if that wasn't enough, I had a glass of turtle's blood to go with it, my uncle's best vintage claret. "You'd better tuck in, sir," Amit whispered his encouragement, my uncle certainly overheard him, and with a glance at his master, adding, "He's eaten the dead, you know." I paid no attention to Amit's remark, thinking it a rather childish means of frightening a child into obedience.

'Strange. What I most remember of that cannibal lunch is the taste of King Edward potatoes – as though the very earth itself of this dark, unfriendly land were entering my soul.

'My uncle said nothing more, until we came finally to the dessert, treacle tart, which I consumed with real enthusiasm, its sweetness an antiseptic that cleansed my mouth of blood and earth. "He speaks Hindi like a Bombay brat, English like a coolie, and I'll wager he's infected with Portugeese too," my uncle suddenly commented. "This won't do, definitely won't do. A year's strict tutoring should improve matters a little, and then – well, Gordonstoun, I suppose? Yes, certainly Gordonstoun. That should succeed to civilize even a half-caste Portugoose."

'Anant Chatterjee spoke to no one in particular, at least, no one present in the room. It occurred to me for a moment that my uncle might be insane.

'A year's "strict tutorials", as threatened, thereupon proceeded. And so too would the public school, Gordonstoun, at the end. In that year's house arrest, I became familiar with the strangeness of my uncle's entertainments at his Chelsea domicile. Strange, but not in any way manifest beyond the normal grandee eccentricities of the time, a specifiable Englishness of advanced opinions, a 1930s avantgardism observable in the election of guests, a number of artists and connoisseurs, City speculators, Fabians and converts to Freudian psychoanalysis – but also civil servants in the Ministries and in particular the India Office, those clever bright younger ones, it seemed, not unfriendly to the independence of the sub-continent. A strangeness especially in this last, not that I could properly identify it yet, except that our young enthusiasts from the India Office seemed curiously redundant in a house which banished India, and all things to do with it. Mosy unusually, I was permitted to this round of teas and cocktails and soirées, introduced as "my Bombay orphan", rather like some product of my uncle's past sexual indiscretion.

'I endured daytimes of interminable study, under the guidance of implacable drill sergeants, my tutors – a parade of them – interspersed with other callers, as I began to notice, the bright young men from the Ministries on solo visits who would disappear upstairs in private tête-à-têtes with my uncle. Sometimes, I would hear laughter from above; sometimes too, a cry of what sounded like pain, or its confusing twin, joy. On such an occasion, Amit came into my room with an afternoon tray of milk and shortbread biscuits whilst I studied geography, and at the sound of ahh! from up there, he grinned and pointed to a map in my book. "India appears pink in the map of the British Empire," he said. "Your uncle upstairs is repainting it blood red."

'I hadn't the slightest notion what Amit meant – nor what the procession of young and always well-favoured men were doing in my uncle's room – nor had I yet even grasped that Amit too was one of a large hareem of my uncle's catamites.

'Gordonstoun – what should I tell you concerning that school? It is located on the Scottish coast, which most fittingly matches the school's rigorously austere regime, devised by a refugee German Jew, Kurt Hahn, a personal acquaintance of my uncle's. Would it give you some flavour of the place, if I said that Prince Philip, the Duke of Edinburgh, had preceded me by four years at Gordonstoun, and was leaving it for naval college as I entered? A flavour, perhaps, but a misleading impression. I was happy there. Or, let me phrase it another way. My years at the school meant that I saw very little of my uncle, and that was Anant Chatterjee's greatest kindness to me.

'The turning-point in my relations with Anant Chatterjee occurred in the Easter term break of 1945, during one of those ritual interviews in which he expected a progress report from me. "Have you anything in sight for the future, after you leave Gordonstoun?"

"I should like to read anthropology at King's College Cambridge, if you will permit me."

"You have my approval. But there's a war on, you know?"

"I know, and if I were of age, I would enlist for service in India."

"What – go back there to join a wogs' army? Don't even consider it. I would veto any such foolishness."

'He spoke with such unusual heat that for a moment I felt he might be admitting concern for my safety. Foolishness indeed.

"I see they've turned you into a patriot of some sort. You have a great deal to learn about patriotism, my lad, and everything yet to face concerning our Indian homeland."

"Our Indian homeland?" Curious turn of phrase from someone like him. "I don't understand you, sir," and that was certainly true.

"Don't you? Perhaps this is as good a time as any to ask you – why on earth do you think I brought you to this wretched country? Why did I send you to Gordonstoun's? Have you never questioned my kindness, examined it for the ulterior motive it might conceal? A purpose?"

"I have never questioned your kindness, uncle."

"Don't expect me to believe that," he laughed. "Nonsense. You know me, or think you do, as a coldhearted bastard, and far worse to your way of thinking, an impeccably Anglified traitor to India. Have I struck the right chord? Go on, in all frankness, admit it."

"I have never asked why you detest India so."

"You would badly miscomprehend passion if you relied on its exhibition alone for proof. Do you still imagine that I rescued you from the miseries of India, out of what – kindness or kinship feelings? On the contrary, my aim was to remould its miseries in the likeness of your spirit. You are in my custody spiritually for a purpose, to acquaint yourself with the enemy, and thereby appreciate his weakness. Gordonstoun, Cambridge and all that should succeed in doing just that, but there is a risk, however. It is said, familiarity breeds contempt. Not so: familiarity breeds affection dangerous to the oppositionist. Why do you look at me with such puzzlement?"

"What are you asking of me, sir, that I become an Indian emancipationist?"

"Something like – and something more."

"You foresee my return to India, then?"

"I not only foresee it, I shall require it, when *I* go."

"Perhaps you are wrong about me, uncle. My nostalgia for home should not be overestimated as a firm enough basis for nationalism."

"I know your true nature," Anant Chatterjee's smile confirmed him as my unassailable authority. "Nothing much of the Portugoose in you now, is there?"

"It was bled out of me."

"A colourful expression – meaning what?"

"I read an account of some 17th century Portuguese Franciscan missionaries, who voyaged far beyond the known coastal fringes of Africa to the interior. Each day these Franciscans would cut open their veins, so that their blood would mingle and blend together with the earth of Africa in mystical transubtantiation."

"Is that what you suppose yourself to be – a Lusitano-wog mystically transubstantiated by England's heart of darkness?"

"Neither that nor its opposite, as you would wish me to be. My purpose is clear to me. I have a vocation for another sort of army, one in which I shall enlist after I graduate from Cambridge. I am resolved to enter the Society of Jesus."

"Resolved to be a Jesuit?" Some moments' pause, and then a demonic fury of laughter exploded from Anant Chatterjee. The windowpanes rattled, I do not exaggerate, and the fearful power behind that laughter seemed intent on reaching into me to tear the soul from out of my body.

'Abruptly, the killer storm ended, but the words that followed equally tore at the roots of my soul. "My little highstrung Brahmin with eyes of grey – I know your true nature to the very bottom of its secret. You are no Brahmin priestling but like me a descendant of the Ksatriya warrior caste – a soldier, indeed a soldier, in half-breed mutiny against his own kind. Bloodspawn of my treasonable niece. She deserved a bad death. And such a person who dies such a death forfeits her spirit to the control of such a one as me. Do you understand? I have eaten her soul. And you, quisling half-thing of miscegenated nothingness, you will not escape from my command. I have not yet begun to haunt you, but you shall come to recognize in your increasing terror the form of your mother's agony. You have this to look forward to, Jesuit."'

Dr Chatterjee fell into a remote silence.

I guessed that his uncle had said more to him than he cared to tell me. He truly did look a haunted person as he sat drinking glass upon glass of gin, till he came to himself again. 'I have come to believe, Mr

Mishima, that people are everywhere the same, only their cultures differ. Everywhere, we struggle to realize the instinctive sameness of our human nature, but find ourselves at odds with the differences of culture, and this collision between the two forces unleashes a chain reaction of nuclear proportion.'

'The world is becoming the same everywhere, Dr Chatterjee, and cultures are sadly dwindling forces unable to prevent this happening.'

'I do not speak of artificial sameness, a levelling of human nature to the American denominator of hamburgers and motorcar corporations. I mean a deep sameness, a universal state, in which we will be spiritually *different* as human beings.'

Dr Chatterjee's hands fluttered like sparrows in a dust bath over the things environing him – the Edwardian armchair, the Swinburne volume, the Regency table. 'Everything you see in this room belongs to my uncle Anant Chatterjee, everything, including this room itself and this house are his, and even my name is his. My uncle returned to India in 1947, a year before independence, and he settled here in Benares.'

An explanation suddenly accounted for the insulting way Dr Chatterjee had been greeted by his neighbour downstairs. 'That old man in the courtyard, he isn't –'

'– the real Anant Chatterjee? An interesting idea, but no, my uncle resided only a short while in this house before moving to Magahar, on the eastern shore, across from Benares. You can just make it out through the window. Does anything odd strike you about that eastern far shore?'

'I've wondered why it has been left underpopulated, when Benares is so crowded on this side.'

'Tradition says that anyone dying on Magahar's eastern shore will be reborn an ass.'

'Why should your uncle choose to live there?'

'Our great Hindi poet of the 15th century, Kabir, once said – "Going on endless pilgrimages, the world died exhausted by too much bathing." He was an impudent fellow, Kabir, from low-caste Benarsi weavers, the Julahas, recent converts to Islam. But no one knows what Kabir's religion was, since he delighted in mocking Hindus and Muslims alike. On the point of death, Kabir, like Anant Chatterjee, chose to defy liberation by leaving Kashi for Magahar. In negativity alone does one find God, you see? Let me try to explain what it took me considerable anguish to understand about my uncle, Anant Chatterjee.

'Before our decisive interview in 1937, I had no way of knowing that Anant Chatterjee was a supporter of Subhas Chandra Bose, the Bengali ultra-nationalist. Chandra Bose was a martial Kayastha of the Ksatriya caste, a devout believer in the primeval force of *shakti* represented by the goddess Kali. My uncle admired Chandra Bose's advocacy of bloodshed and his antagonism to Gandhi's policy of non-violent civil disobedience. In the early 30s, Chandra Bose was a contender for the political leadership of the Indian Congress Party, his only rival being Jawaharlal Nehru – both of them Cambridge graduates too, as a matter of fact. Gandhi favoured the skeptical, urbane and compromising Nehru as his heir apparent, and he very astutely outmanoeuvred Chandra Bose and drove him into the political wilderness. My uncle detested Gandhi for this, "that ugly little spider spinning his khadi cloth", and his joy at Gandhi's assassination was unbounded.'

'I know this Chandra Bose of yours – or should I say ours? He attended a Tokyo conference in the 30s, at which the idea of a Japanese-led pan-Asianist liberation movement first gained credence. This was the beginning of our plan for the Greater East Asia Co-Prosperity Sphere.'

'My uncle also attended that conference. In 1940, Chandra Bose escaped from British arrest and fled to Berlin. Hitler sent him by submarine to Japan. Your High Command provided Chandra Bose with an excellent idea that he eagerly accepted – to recruit Indian prisoners-of-war taken at the fall of Singapore and form them into an Indian National Army that would fight alongside Japan against the British, the final aim being to recapture India from the imperialists with Bose's help.

'Madness. Total blind madness. Did Bose consider the reality for one minute? Twenty-thousand Indian PoWs accepted his idea, but forty-five thousand did not, and they were made to suffer greatly for it. Two and a half million native Indian troops were engaged in fighting against the Axis forces, which made them the biggest volunteer army the world has ever seen. Not a single one of them was a conscripted man. Just think what that means. God knows if these men considered Germans, Italians and Japanese as their enemies, but they had certainly volunteered to side with the British. Only a great fool or a fanatic like Chandra Bose could overlook such evidence. Bose's fantasy of ruling India under the umbrella of the Co-Prosperity Sphere was exactly that, a fantasy. Luckily for him his plane crashed on Formosa in 1945, or he would have ended on the gallows as a traitor – and he would not have gained either the sympathy of Congress or the status of martyr. My uncle also shared his blind fanaticism. He still blames Gandhi and Congress for depriving India of genuine Hindu nationalism, by which he meant an all-out blood-drenched holy war in the name of Kali.'

'All these absurd English things, this house – pardon me, Dr Chatterjee, but why do you accept to live like this?'

'Like a ghost, you mean? I must, you see. I must. I am not free to do otherwise. You cannot understand that Anant Chatterjee *possesses* my mother's soul. How can this be, you wonder? How can an enlightened Cambridge graduate, a Jesuit, believe in such nonsensical superstition? Because I have *seen*, Mr Mishima. I have seen with my own eyes.'

'What have you seen, Dr Chatterjee?'

He shook his head, refusing or unable to explain.

'Something else I did not know until 1937 was that Anant Chatterjee practised the Aghori rites.'

'That non-existent being I am supposed to have seen? What is an Aghori? You have always refrained from telling me what rites they follow.'

'These are known as the left-hand rites – do you see?, the *sinister* rites? It is Hindu practice never to eat with the left hand or to employ it in rituals, because that is the unclean hand reserved for washing after excretion. The left-hand route of foulness and vice is the chosen one of the Aghori ascetic. He turns the world upside-down. Everything is permitted. The aim of all yogic disciplines is to achieve *samadhi*, a timeless state of non-duality, beyond birth and death, a motionless unity in which all is the same and one thing is not different from another. Unity and non-difference are also the Aghori's aim, but he attains *samadhi* by literally experiencing the identity of opposites. That is why the Aghori can permit himself alcohol, taboo foods and sexual intercourse. Everything he does is in the strictest sense mortuary – he sleeps on a bed that served as a dead person's bier, he clothes himself from the shroud of a corpse, wears a necklace of human bones like Kali, he smears himself with ashes from cremation pyres and cooks his food on charcoal stolen from them, he eats from a human skull which is also his alms bowl, and at least once, at the outset of his career, the Aghori must eat the flesh of someone who has died a bad death, hence the Aghori are known as necrophagous ascetics, eaters of the dead. Acquiring a skull is in itself central to Aghori meditation. First, he obtains a corpse – easy enough, since all who die bad or untimely deaths are not cremated but simply cast into the river. The point however is to get the right corpse. That of a trader is prized because traders are sly, or oil pressers because they are deemed stupid and their spirits easy to control. He binds the corpse by the ankle with a silk thread fastened to a stake, and draws a circle round it to keep away the evil spirits of the cremation ground, since this is where the ritual of *sava-sadhana* or sitting on the torso of the corpse takes place. These spirits will try to entice him into dialogue that he must at all costs resist, until they give up and accept the offering of food he has provided for them outside the circle. Now the corpse's mouth will open, and the Aghori feeds it a little *khir* rice-pudding. Next he decapitates it to obtain the skull, by which total mastery over the deceased's spirit is won. Remember, the *pran* or vital breath has not been released by cracking the skull at the cremation ritual, but is trapped and accessible to the Aghori who restores it to life to do his bidding. In this and other ways, the Aghori amasses *siddhis*, great magical powers. You see, by scavenging all his needs from the dead, the Aghori gains absolute autonomy from life, and that's why he's named *arbhangi*, care-free, mad and divinely whimsical like the god Shiva himself.'

'How did he get control of your mother's soul? You're not suggesting he returned to India during his ten days' absence to sit on her corpse?'

'He did not have to leave England for that. The Aghori can transport his spirit anywhere he chooses. You look skeptical. But what would you have felt in my place to learn about the true nature of my uncle's arrangements for my mother's funeral? I heard from him that her body had been sent to the ashram of his guru, Kina Bhagvan Ram, where it underwent *sava-sadhana*. My uncle's return to Benares in 1947 coincided with his *avadhut's* death – not of course that a true Aghori can really be said to die, but rather he takes *samadhi*, a perpetual condition of suspended animation before the beginning of time in which he meditates. Anant Chatterjee himself arranged Kina Bhagvan Ram's limbs in the meditational lotus posture by breaking the spine, then burying him in a clay jar in the grounds of the ashram. My uncle inherited the *mahant* status of guru of the ashram, a leper colony over there on the eastern shore.'

'He runs a leper colony?'

'He does, under his *mahant's* name, Baba Krin Ram.'

'I begin to see. Anant Chatterjee is no more – and *you* are Anant Chatterjee. But the Jesuit, Fernando Pinto Mendes, what's become of him?'

'There is only Anant Chatterjee, outcast member of the Society of Jesus, SJ – initials that should please you – Samurai of Jesus. My superiors in Rome have forbidden me to administer the sacraments under pain of excommunication, until Anant Chatterjee forswears the Malabar rites of Roberto de Nobili and resumes being Fernando Pinto Mendes SJ.'

'You are a *ronin* samurai, Dr Chatterjee, as we say of vagrant samurai without an overlord. Is there some sort of contest between you and this Baba Krin Ram?'

'Some sort – yes. I congratulate you on your mastery of the English understatement. Some sort,' he repeated, laughing bitterly the while over this. 'And as for my being a samurai without an overlord – *extra ecclesiam nulla salus*. Outside the Church there is no salvation. I have undertaken a duel with the *mahant* with both hands tied behind my back.' Dr Chatterjee stared into his glass of gin, a potion which held the captivating aroma of ghosts for me. 'What do you make of this? Say frankly.'

'Frankly? I can deeply sympathize with but not intellectually assent to eaters of the dead, soul possession and ghosts. Frankly, there is a mirror-likeness between the *mahant* and you, a reflection of East and West of unreal axial symmetry, because, after all, you are both eaters of the dead. Do not Catholics eat the dead when they consume the Eucharist?'

'I do not care to debate theological niceties, but, yes, you are right to be skeptical. You are right – as an Asian – to gloat over the dilemma of a Westernized Asian.'

'Now you are mocking me.'

'Why mocking? Do you share my dilemma?'

Dare I admit, for the first time the foreign greyness of Dr Chatterjee's eyes impressed itself on me? I had not really seen them before. He stroked the glossy pale, pockmarked expanse of scar down his cheek and neck. 'This is the form my tuberculosis took after my mother's death – and external lupus of the skin.'

Again, I cannot say why, but that caress and the exposure of a disease shared with his mother demonstrated to me the truth of all he said.

'Tonight is the *mahakal ratri*, one of the moonless nights of Shiva, destructive Lord of Time. An evil moment that favours the Aghori's sacred rite of *cakra-puja*, in which sexual intercourse is performed to incarnate Shiva united with his consort. Would you care to see this?'

'Forgive me if I offend you, Dr Chatterjee, but in Bangkok one is often invited by pimps to witness displays of athletic intercourse. I am not inclined to voyeurism.' (What a persistent liar you are, Hiraoka Kimitake!)

'The resistance of your skepticism does you credit, Mr Mishima, and is not offensive to me. The truth is, you see, I am not personally inviting you to anything pornographic. You are expected.'

Strange, and yet entirely obvious, that we should burst out laughing in unison. The lie had been confessed without being admitted. 'It is true, it is perfectly true,' Dr Chatterjee said. 'Your steps have taken you to where you have already succeeded in arriving.'

Sunset approached. Dr Chatterjee yawned as though waking from a trance-like slumber, and he reverted to his habit of nervous jitters. 'There is an urgent errand I must attend to before dark,' he said. 'Please accompany me, there is a taxi rank nearby.'

We descended to the courtyard, where I saw Dr Chatterjee's old neighbour again, praying to the setting sun. I glanced at him, to assure myself that he was not by chance the real 'Anant Chatterjee', but he paid neither of us any heed this time.

October twilight in Benares is prodigious, and like fires of dawn, justifies the city's title of 'forest of lights'. It inspired me to ask, 'Have you been to Japan, Dr Chatterjee?'

'Are you still wondering how I came to know those little details about you? Your curiosity has led you to guess correctly. Yes, I've spent time in your country, all of last year in fact, researching the Jesuit missionaries' record of success in the 16th century. It was not my first visit. A preserved relic of St Francis Xavier, his right arm, was brought from Rome to Japan in June 1949 to mark the 400th anniversary of his arrival there. That year was the second of my novitiate in Rome, and I had been invited by a Jesuit descendent of Roberto de Nobili to join with the anniversary delegation bearing its strange gift to Japan. I was permitted to spend the rest of the year in study with the Rinzai sect of Zen monks at the Kinkakuji Temple.'

'– the Temple of the Golden Pavilion?' I broke in, astounded by what he said. 'But that is the one burned to the ground by a Zen novice in 1950.'

'Yes, a great treasure reduced to ashes, some months after I had returned to Rome. And I first became interested in your work, then in you, when you published a novel about this Zen arsonist in 1956.'

'But last year, when you were back in Japan, why didn't you come to see me?'

'No need. I knew we would eventually meet in Benares, when the time was right. Oh, I am not being mystical. Not at all. I am only thinking of what my researches into 16th century Japan told me – of an encounter between two élite feudal miltary castes, the Jesuit soldiers of St Ignatius of Loyola and the warriors of the overlord Oda Nobunaga. We were missionaries welcomed at first by Zen monks as "fellow monks from Tenjiku", from India, the cradle of Buddhism. I weep, Mr Mishima, I weep the passionate tears of the Spaniard Loyola to think of the sadly missed opportunity of a marriage between the élite shock troops of the Baroque Counter-Reformation and the samurai of esoteric Zen Buddhism. I can imagine the Catholic Mass celebrated in the way of Shinto – something in the spirit of de Nobili's Malabar rites.'

'We might have conquered the world under a different banner.'

'It all depends on who you mean by "we".' Once more, we laughed together.

We had walked some distance, when I began to sense a familiarity in my surroundings, a quality less remarkable in the buildings than in the shiftiness of the men parading the streets, a complicity of gaze, a certain perfume in the air, and low caste girls all spangles and bright saris calling from lighted doorways.

We came to a house I knew, of memorable pastel shades, its second-storey verandah ranged with filagreed shutters over-bellying the ground floor. This was the brothel in Dal Mandi to which my avatar of Kali, Jael, had led me two days ago. And there she was again, the whorehouse madam, slumped motionless in a wicker chair in the doorway, her stately mass of flesh turned to stone, like the despondent Niobe of Greek legend, snakes of dishevelled hair coiled on her lap and *kohl*-stained tears running down her cheeks. From the passageway behind her, burnished to redness by oil lamps that concealed better than giving visibility, a figure approached, a young man of feminine grace, who stooped over the grieving woman and threw his arms round her neck. A tide of his own hair swept across her shoulders and breasts, and petals from his necklace of marigolds dripped orange speckles onto her lap. She remained impervious as stone, unconsoled by his embrace. But I, I felt moved to call out to him – by what name? *jizo*, the only name I knew? For it was my truant *jizo*, the gymnast always somersaulting into view when I least expected him – this time with his arms round the neck of a dolorous brothel-keeper. He gave up his hold, defeated or repulsed by the boulder of sadness, and I distinctly heard him whisper a name, Shiva, as he rose up to go, but whether he named the destructive Lord of Time or himself, I could not tell. I glimpsed phthistic blue teeth, purple for a moment in the sinister lamplight, before he retreated into the house.

'You can get a taxi back to Clark's over there,' Dr Chatterjee said, pointing to a crossroads.

'Why have we come back to this place?'

'Nothing to do with you, sir. Simply the nature of my errand.'

At the sound of our voices, the woman looked up, greeting me with a repetition of her gold-incisored smile, a sight made more disagreeable by those clown's black markings of tears.

'What sort of errand could that be?'

'To book the right consort for the *mahant's cakra-puja* tonight. His sexual partner in this rite must be a prostitute of low caste who has the curse – ah, you don't know that English expression, the curse? Menstruating. She must be menstruating. The Aghori requires a female doubly polluted – a whore and one with the curse – and what better way to show his contempt for life and procreation than by copulating with a female in her period of infertility? This act must indeed be guaranteed barren, for if the Aghori fails to retain his semen or reabsorb it into his penis after ejaculation, he risks paying the penalty of madness and death. He will become *aughar-masan*, a malevolent ghost who resists all exorcisms.'

A whiff of festering human matter from an open drain jangled on my nerves. My exasperation ebbed away into sickly weariment. 'I don't follow you at all, Dr Chatterjee. Is this the way you duel with your uncle, by serving as his pimp?'

'Oh yes, oh yes, I understand your distaste for the malodorous condition of my person. But there is only one way out of my impasse. To become an Aghori myself.'

I had no stomach left even to question such a flagrant contradiction, except to laugh. 'I think the only real Aghori in existence is you, imagining that you could be one.'

'You can decide for yourself if he is the figment of my imagination tonight. Present yourself at my house at 9 p.m., and a car will take us to Magahar. And if you do accept, please bring a bottle of whisky. The *mahant* is very appreciative of whisky.'

12 INCIDENT ON A STATION PLATFORM

THE JEWEL VOICE had warned us to 'endure the unendurable and suffer the insufferable.' So did a former God speak on behalf of humanity, his own and ours. The unendurable and insufferable began for me at the Ministry of Finance as a junior bureaucrat supernally elevated from the miseries of the millions less privileged. My foot was set on the quagmire path of repentance, of becoming human, in the same direction as national economic recovery. My real motive for clinging to a job I detested was very far from being idealist. Although I slaved like a demon every night to increase my literary output, I knew that such efforts would not provide me with secure income. Poverty frightened me, and so I maintained the pretence that my cowardice enforced.

There is something else I should confess. My psychological disposition did not render me all that ill-suited to the civil service, despite my protested aversion to it. I possess qualities that might well have made me a successful government functionary. I am gregarious enough to camouflage my personality under the superficialities of team spirit and present myself as an amusing colleague in the barracks environment of the Ministry. I have disciplined myself to tolerate any amount of routine – in any case, a precondition of being Japanese – and I am exceptionally gifted at organization. These bureaucratic virtues had as little real life in them as paper flowers. My hours of literary moonlighting were gradually seeping into those of the Banking Bureau. I consistently failed to arrive punctually for work. Hiraoka Kimitake's mimicry began to sag with weariness. It was only a matter of time before the complaints of my superiors would reach my father's ears. I felt myself evaporating like the steamy circle of a teacup on black lacquer. Something had to be done, and urgently.

I awaited some miraculous intervention from heaven, without any hope of it, and meanwhile went on contriving my paper flowers. One such venomous little flower that bloomed from my pen, an essay published in March 1948, had the title *A Weapon for the Seriously Wounded*. Reference to this essay has already been made, which, if it is recalled, gave Sam Lazar one more reason to scoff at me. At that time, as I have described before, all my self-corrosive envy had come to focus on the successful writer, Dazai Osamu, my rival, so little aware of my existence that he could not even repay me with the acknowledgement of his contempt. I wanted to make him aware of my intent to strip him of his crown. I wrote with the intention to murder. I could not bear the immense popularity Dazai had reaped from his pitiable, bungled suicide.

It seemed to me perfectly clear that our post-war survival had left us like sideshow freaks, calloused, cynical and immune to suicide. I had said to Mitsuko – oh, and with such terrible irony that became self-fulfilling prophecy – that we were a generation 'forsaken by death'. Our plight was the tragic one of virtual immortals for whom suicide is impossible – or, at least, that was my own plight, one that I must strive to exalt into the cultural condition for all. I wrote with the aftertaste of death in my mouth, an invulnerable zombie, but tormented at night by the festering poison of *yomi* in my guts.

I showed my essay to Kawabata Yasunari. He knew very well that my assassin's aim was Dazai Osamu, but he avoided mentioning him. Instead, he chided me in his gentle, abstract way. 'Our writing should be like a ladder of swords invisible to others. Elucidations of the risks we take are of no use to anyone.' And he quoted Wittgenstein's famous dictum: 'What we cannot speak about we must pass over in silence.'

Kawabata smiled comfortingly when he saw the embarrassment his words caused me. 'If you believe yourself right, then write about the reality that only you know, without fantasy.'

'That's my trouble, *sensei*,' I said, now thoroughly downcast. 'I fear that my only experience of reality is fantasy.'

'Then write that,' was again his advice, as it had been two years ago at our first meeting in Kamakura.

My essay was a blunder, a misfired imbecilic effort to harm Dazai who was beyond my range. I still had some way to go in my *via crucis* before coming to the discovery that reality is the commonplace miscarriage of fantasy.

My heaven-sent intervention came unexpectedly five months later, on 19 July 1948, as I left the Ministry premises at the end of another day's routine violence to myself. My hopes of escape from the nether-world were disappointed by the shining face of the moon. I mean, of course, the moon-goddess visage of my beautiful companion, Baroness Omiyeke Keiko, the presentable face of corruption. She hailed me – 'Kochan' – quickening her steps to reach me after we had passed a safe distance away from the Ministry and the eyes of my Bureau colleagues. It was inadvisable to be seen together. Why had Keiko decided to risk this imprudent encounter? She looked the very picture of impulsiveness, a rosy freshness beaming from her, as it did whenever I had seen her returned from Kendo practice. Keiko took my arm. My dainty limb in her robust grip sank me into despair. To look at her required immense effort. My gaze itself felt like the breath of dried-out compost.

'I've heard of an interesting new gay bar in Kando, the Elysée,' Keiko said.

'I can't this weekend. Lazar expects his pound of flesh.'

Though she pretended to humour me in our frequentations of 'interesting gay bars', sordid places where our Occupiers disclosed their backsides, metaphorically and literally, these explorations indulged her own unhealthy interest as much as mine in the gutter life. 'Is a new gay bar really a matter of such urgency?'

'Have you seen this?' Keiko put a copy of the *Asahi* evening news in my hands. And there it was – my heaven-sent sign – a report of Dazai Osamu's corpse fished out of a canal. His disappearance from home, together with his mistress, in mid-June had given weight to rumours of suicide, but no trace of him had been found. So, he had finally succeeded in killing himself, once more choosing the *shinju* love-pact exit in the mode of his previously failed attempt. He drowned himself with his mistress in the Tamagawa canal near Mikata suburb, tied to her by a red kimono sash. I imagined them found stuck together like cheap paper flowers.

I read the news item several times as we journeyed on without regard to any destination. On a bridge over a Sumida river canal, I paused, looked at Dazai's photograph one last time, and dropped the newspaper into the foul, unappetizing water below. Salarymen in suits like mine, hurrying past, glanced disapprovingly at me. They could not have guessed what happiness I felt to see that grey patch of drowned face.

I exulted in the death of my rival, convinced that my essay published five months ago, in which I had demonstrated myself immune to suicide, in which I had elevated myself to prophetic spokesman of a generation so nihilist that even suicide was a comfort denied to it, had been the last nail in Dazai's coffin. I congratulated myself as Dazai's secret executioner, a subterranean bookkeeper turned murderer, as though I had myself pushed him into this polluted water.

'Will you kiss me, Baroness?'

Keiko laughed, as often before, at my use of her defunct title. What a sight we must have made for the gawking passers-by, not your usual young couple embracing but a puny weed osculating a lady of heroic splendour from the pages of Balzac.

She pulled away from me, amused but off balance and breathless. 'Does the suicide of your rival excite you to such unnatural passion?'

'Tell me, does your mouth taste poisoned?' I asked.

'You're a strange one,' but involuntarily Keiko's tongue tested her lips.

'Surely you realize what this means?'

'You've given me more of an idea than I expected, Kochan.'

'Hiraoka Kimitake is no more. There he is,' and I pointed to the Sumidagawa canal into which Dazai's features had submerged. 'I am going to resign from the Ministry.'

'A courageous notion, my dear poet, but an idle one. Captain Lazar will not permit you to quit.'

'What does he have to do with it?'

Keiko glanced pityingly at me. 'Boast if you like about poor Dazai's comic ending, but don't act the fool yourself.'

'I feel very tempted at this moment to ask you to marry me.'

'And I would agree at this very moment – and what? do you think marrying me will get you off the hook with G-2 Section?' She eyed me with uncomplimentary amusement. 'Anyway, you're just the husband I need.'

'But you find me attractive, don't you, at this very moment? Repulsive as I am to you, I know, I *am* attractive because I've killed someone. Don't pretend not to understand. Absurd, megalomaniac as the idea might sound to you, I believe Dazai responded to my challenge. I have successfully tampered with reality. Dazai's suicide does not in the least disprove my theory of invulnerability to suicide. On the contrary, he has simply removed himself as the obstacle to my verification of it in reality. He has exhausted the pay-dirt vein of romantic futility, without discovering the richer deposit of absolute enlightened hopelessness that a resolute positivist like me can claim. He has abandoned the exploitation of that precious ore to me. His suicide directs me to the analytic dissection of a hopeless fantasist, a youth forsaken by death, whose abnormality is a masquerade of normal everyday prescription – in short, me. All I have to do now is confess it publicly, and it will guarantee me the spokesman's crown in a time of selfish virtues devoted to economic convalescence.'

'What on earth are you saying?'

'Watch me, just watch, and you'll find out exactly what I mean. Not only Dazai, but Sam Lazar's G-2 Section bunch of swindlers have put a lethal weapon for the seriously wounded into my hands.'

'Beware you don't shoot yourself with it.'

Does the silkworm scream as it spins its cocoon? I could hear the gnashing of my teeth, *jyari, jyari, jyari,* like the silkworm endlessly busy chewing on mulberry leaves. My mother did not seem to hear this noise. She had begun hinting too frequently at marriage, something logical, inevitable, normal, now that I was established and my future apparently assured. My literary ambition had fallen to second place, even in Shizue's estimation. *Jyari, jyari* went my teeth at the prospect of matrimony spun out from the masquerade at the Banking Bureau. Sam Lazar's warning not to be stampeded into marriage by force of convention had come to premature fulfilment. Just wait, dear parents, and I will confront you with a marriage that will put an end to all talk of marriage!

I returned home one August afternoon from a meeting with Sam Lazar at the Imperial Hotel. I had lied to Shizue, telling her that my day had been devoted to a restful countryside outing with some office

236

colleagues. It took no great effort to appear even more ashen-faced and stricken than usual. I collapsed on the parlour sofa. 'You don't seem to have benefited much from this holiday,' Shizue said.

'I witnessed the most dreadful scene on the way home from G—. A freak accident claimed the lives of two young people.' I impressed Shizue enough with this introduction to offer me a glass of my father's brandy. 'I could certainly do with it. I still can't believe what I saw with my own eyes. We were all jammed together on the G— station platform, a crowd of day-trippers waiting for the train back home. This couple at the front – newly weds in their early twenties, arm in arm, both office workers I took them to be – were returning like us from a pleasant Sunday excursion. Suddenly, quite without warning, they were jostled onto the track. They fell, arms linked, dragging each other down in the path of the incoming Tokyo relay. The wheels of the engine sliced right over their necks. The train went into reverse, too late for the couple's rescue, and this caused their heads to be deposited side by side on the pebbles between the rails – a bizarre trick of chance, so precise, so neat that I thought our docile pack of holiday onlookers would begin applauding the engineer's skill.'

Shizue listened to my tale with an appropriately shocked expression. 'How terrible for those poor youngsters.'

'Terrible, yes, but a lesson for me of what is terrible. I had an impression of conformism, of stifling routine and healthy mediocrity which predestined those two office workers to a farcical death, a vendetta that threatens my own existence. I go cold to think of the execution that a commonplace life holds in store for me.'

I had read an account of a similar accident in an Osaka newspaper, embellished with the further untruthful detail recalled from Natsuko's story about the suicide-pact lovers decapitated by a train.

'Is this a story you have contemplated writing?'

I insisted it was true; to which Shizue rebutted, 'We'll see what the papers have to say.'

'It is railroad policy not to publicize incidents of this kind, suicides, and so on.' My reply was not entirely a perjury. 'It is a warning, this accident, a clear omen of what must happen to me if I carry on like this much longer.'

'I foresee little chance of that,' she replied sourly. 'You have grown very selfish lately, with no concern at all for my failing health. You do not care to respect my desire to see you well placed in society before I die. You will not allow me to die at peace with the world.'

Jyari-jyari-jyari

Weeks passed. I had resolved to act on that July day of exaltation at the Sumidagawa canal, but I delayed till my blackmailer's portfolio was complete and could be implemented against all my opponents.

On a September morning, I went off to work as usual. As I waited for the train at Shibuya station in a crush of fellow salarymen, trapped in a mass that moved and heaved like a polypous gelatin, I saw my time had come. I stood back as all the others rushed into the train. I did not board it. I was left behind. Now there was no turning back. The station guard stared questioningly at me as I knelt on the platform, jabbed my elbows into the dust, and finished off by rubbing dirt on my clean white shirt. Satisfied that I looked genuinely bedraggled, I made my way back home.

My parents were alarmed at my unexpected return and the shocking condition of my clothes. 'What's happened? Are you ill?' My extreme pallor and bloodshot eyes, the results of months of sleep deprivation, gave added credibility to my appearance. 'I fell off the station platform,' I announced resolutely, 'and was nearly killed by a commuter train.'

Azusa looked startled. 'What's this you say – fell off?'

'Yes, at Shibuya station. Practically under the wheels of the train.'

I stared at him with the fixed gaze of a person on the verge of complete breakdown. I gambled on the hope that Azusa had not forgotten the incident at the railway crossing some twenty years ago, when he had experimented on me like a Nazi.

'He risked his life,' Shizue exclaimed, glaring at her husband. Ah, excellent, I thought. She has scored with the perfect reminder to unsettle Azusa. The malicious gleam in Shizue's eyes plainly revealed her willingness to comply with my subterfuge. But I had an unpleasantness in store for her too.

Azusa examined us both with scientific composure. 'That's nothing to the risk he has now decided to face. You spend all your nights writing. Is it my fault if you stumble off railway platforms like a sleepwalker?' He shrugged. 'You must choose between one thing or another. Either the Ministry or literature. Which is it?'

'Writing.'

'It's like that, is it?' Azusa smiled, for the last time the holder of all the aces. 'Stay home today. I will call the Bureau and make excuses. But don't think your charade has impressed me.'

'I have something else to announce,' I said. 'I am getting married.'

I did not expect Shizue to be pleased. And she wasn't. 'What news is this? I haven't been consulted.'

'It's news that I expect should please you, mother.' I toyed with her a little longer.

'What are you hiding from me?' she declared, and with applaudable timing, grasped at her stomach where an imaginary cancer had resided for some time. Shizue's talent for histrionic mimicry could rival mine, at times. I wanted to see her in real pain.

'I wanted to make sure of the lady's affections before speaking up.

She is a woman of impeccable noble origins. Her husband, a naval pilot, met a hero's death.'

'A widow?' My mother went genuinely pale as she uttered 'widow', as though sighting a fearful ghost. 'What else are you hiding from me?' In a voice, juddering with sobs, she keened, 'Oh, I shall die, I shall die from the anguish you are causing me.'

Azusa had become flushed, but for a moment too stunned for words. 'That's enough,' he exploded, aiming his wrath at Shizue. 'You don't realize what he's doing.'

'I know very well what he's doing,' Shizue wept, 'but I cannot believe it possible from the one I cherish. I can see it now. You are keeping from me what the doctor really said.'

'There's nothing in the least wrong with you,' Azusa growled. 'Only hyperacidity and an over-active imagination, like your son.'

'Hasn't father told you something about this lady?' I added, as though surprised by the lack of pillow talk between my parents. 'Strange, I would expect him to know all about it, since he has an ear to the ground at the Ministry, so to speak, and is acquainted with all my doings.'

A dumb-struck Shizue turned indignantly to her husband for confirmation. 'Don't listen to him,' Azusa brought his fist down hard on the table, upsetting his teacup. 'He'll say anything to gain his way against me.'

'Do you think I'm making this up too?' I said, taking the portfolio of my secret transactions with Sam Lazar from my briefcase and handing it to Azusa. 'Well then, just imagine if I had really been killed this morning, and they found *this* on me.'

Azusa put on his glasses and started to leaf through my blueprints of financial chicanery. Almost at once, he recognized what they meant. He glanced up at me, marvelling at the unsuspected person who was his son. 'What is it? What is it?' My death certificate in Azusa's hand could not have distressed Shizue more, as she tried in vain to peer over his shoulder at the Cabbalist figures on the page. 'You're like a flea in my ear, woman. Stop jabbering!' Azusa waved her away, the smoke from his cigarette trailing blue gossamer in the morning sunlight. 'Please allow me a little time to consider this.'

'Take all the time you need,' I said, intending that my triumphant largesse should rankle him.

'Let's go to my study,' he offered, and as an aside to Shizue, 'Be patient. I'm sure we can resolve the entire affair this morning.'

I remember very clearly thinking as I entered Azusa's study, 'Since the Emperor is human, the only alternative is to be *in*human. This is the right tragic course.'

'I know you're in trouble with your Section Chief Nishida Akira,'

Azusa began. 'It's not too late. I could use my influence to patch things up, if you are willing to reform.'

'Things have gone far beyond that. I offered Nishida my resignation.'

'What did he say?'

'He said, Section Clerk Hiraoka, your resignation would be unseemly under the circumstances.'

'Of course, I can see what he means. But in spite of these circumstances, you are determined to resign? Is that so?'

'My mind is made up.'

'It is folly.' Azusa poured himself a stiff scotch, and for the first time, one for me too. I had become a business crony – my soiled clothes notwithstanding.

'May I speak candidly?'

'I think you had better.'

'Folly, you say? Let's be clear. Do you mean the immediate risk I might face by resigning? Or the folly of surrendering a brilliant career guaranteed by the progress I have so far made at the Ministry?'

'Both, obviously.'

'But suppose, just suppose, that my retirement not only posed no risk to me, but on the contrary would be gratefully welcomed by my superiors, thanks to my little bookkeeper's diary of recent financial events?'

'A safe-conduct from the Ministry? Maybe so. The specific merit of your diary, as you call it, is that it need never be made public.'

'Exactly as you say. Never made public, but known to *some*, as delicacy requires.'

'Did your lady friend advise you on these underhand tactics?'

'The former Baroness Omiyeke? Certainly not. She strongly advised me against resignation.'

'And quite as she ought. Why then should I assist you to give up a perfectly respectable career?'

'Because, as I've said, I will seek by whatever means to make my retirement desirable.'

'You presume much on the power you think is contained in these documents. Give me some moments to reflect on them, if I may?'

'Please do.'

Another scotch later, after less than a half-hour's scrutiny of the dossier, Azusa turned from it to contemplate the garden through the window. 'I see,' he said. 'You have been misled.'

'Are you telling me it's worthless?'

'I wouldn't say worthless. Just simply that Section Chief Nishida is acting under different instructions than one might suppose from looking at these accounts.'

'I don't understand.'

'Only a fool would fail to understand,' Azusa said, with an irascible return of confidence. 'But since you've come this far – leave the dossier with me.'

I hesitated. Azusa's eyes clouded over with exasperation. 'Don't you trust me with them?'

'Naturally I do.'

'Am I supposed to believe that you haven't made a second copy of this thing?' Azusa's lips hinted at a smile. 'It wasn't necessary to strengthen your case with me, since, as you might as well know, I have consented to your aspiration.'

'To let me be a writer?'

'Very well, then – yes, to be a writer,' he sighed.

'Why the change of heart?'

'Because the gamble is permissable.' Azusa raised the scotch to his mouth; but he had already drained the glass. 'Promise me this – swear to it – that you will make sure of becoming the *best* writer in this country.'

'I will.'

Azusa closed the dossier. 'Now, can you leave this with me?'

I nodded.

'And the Baroness?' he put in as a seeming afterthought.

'I have no intention of marrying,' I answered, but thought it advisable to add, 'not her, anyway.'

I found Shizue in the parlour, lighting joss sticks to the Buddha image in the family shrine – the Shinto *kadana* god-shelf had been packed away in accordance with SCAP directives.

'I have been granted my wish,' I told her, in reply to her distraught look of inquiry. I chose to announce my news in this ambiguous way to see the effect on her. 'You can light more joss sticks in thanksgiving.'

'Your wish?'

'Yes – permission to write. Aren't you pleased?'

'I am relieved, if that is the end of the matter.'

'Rest assured, it puts finis to any misguided notion of marriage. We shall never mention that again.'

I was tempted to laugh.

I had lasted only nine months at the Banking Bureau, from January to September of 1948. I was twenty-three years old and now irrevocably committed to an economically hazardous profession. 'You fool –' a dawning realization cut short my laughter. 'Don't you see what a copy of the Ministry dossier in Azusa's hands amounts to? It's an exchange of contracts! A covenant!' I had set out to hoodwink Azusa, but he had proved considerably shrewder than I imagined. He had already decided to relent and thereby neutralize any real attempt on my part to defy him or my superiors. This left me indebted to him for his generosity.

He had gauged my character astutely enough. He knew me to be thoroughly conventional deep down, a veritable paradigm of our traditional *on* system of social obligation. No son had been more dutifully obedient than I; no worker more disciplined and industrious; no one more exemplary of sacrifice to conformist obligation. When my father said 'best writer', he clearly intended financial success. He had merely shifted the onus of careerist success to my new profession. I had agreed to a form of industrial authorship on that day of 13 September 1948, when I pledged myself to write primarily for money. There are consequently two Yukio Mishimas, the Siamese twins of literary and commercial endeavours. Western readers of my works are very unlikely to encounter the second Mishima. This one is the indefatigable purveyor of serialized potboiler novels, the confectioner of lightweight articles for ladies' magazines. The scrivener of tawdry commercial output. I had obligated myself to guarantee the public success of that figure.

I ventured into the business of writing at a post-war time of the shoddy trademark, *Nipponsei*, Made in Japan. Much of my writing would be ephemeral *Nipponsei* goods, produced in obligatory fulfilment of Azusa's contract. I transposed my former double life to the hours of my writing, now dividing my nights in two, half for quick sale entertainment, half for my serious composition. I travailed in the low class suburbs of literature, labouring for a freedom that eluded manumission. I strove like a coolie to earn the financial security of my privileged twin, Yukio Mishima. Campaigners on behalf of my Nobel Prize candidature have no doubt overlooked this embarrassing wholesale side of Mishima, the *Nipponsei* Mr Hyde.

The marvel is that I have somehow preserved my art in hermetic isolation from my production of bargain commodities. But is it really so? Have I avoided the seepage from commercialism? Am I certain that the glib *Nipponsei* entrepreneur has not insidiously prevailed? Is it possible to sustain art impermeably against the corrosive effect of mass consumerism?

My piecework method of writing to earn money might appear similar to the industry of certain 19th century European writers, Balzac, Dickens, Dostoyevsky, prolific authors who thrived in the compromise atmosphere of commercialism and literary genius; but the likeness is superficial. The pursuit of mass popularity that in former times engendered the novel in its classic form is no longer a route the artist can travel. Commercially inspired writing has become totally incompatible with aesthetic perfectionism in the accomplishment of a masterpiece. A dichotomy of this sort, in which commercial and aesthetic values are irreconcilable, makes the very possibility of a masterpiece unlikely in our day.

I can see the entire questionable terrain of modern fiction opening up here, with all its vagaries and pitfalls. I have neither the stamina nor interest to explore it. One thing I do know. I unhesitatingly preferred to be a popular, best-selling writer even in my serious work, than to be an original novelist. My literary careerism in the last years of the war and its chaotic aftermath has given me cause for guilt; but remorse did not impede my urgency to succeed. The author who connives in his own popularity does not even merit the bad name of artist. Fortunately, or not, our public does not recognize success as a sin.

Everything I have said is to an extent true, but it is still in a sense a confession in the grand manner. It avoids telling the small truth, which is simply this. I had once again made Azusa my excuse for an Emperor, reigning over what I could not help being. I found myself once again classified 2B – this time as a twenty-three-year old writer declared unfit for active service in history – and this time again with the permission of my own domestic Emperor, Azusa.

My vassalage to Captain Lazar and G-2 Section would seem on the face of it to have terminated with my resignation from the Banking Bureau, as the country itself steadily progressed towards independence. On 28 April 1952, the eve of the Emperor's birthday, the Occupation would officially come to an end. In reality, however, my situation was not unlike Japan's, with its freedom apparently restored in 1952, and yet continuing to be a self-administered fief of the American empire.

I longed to escape from Japan. An impossible dream for someone like me, the client of my own ruined guts, the sufferer of chronic abdominal pains and sudden unpredictable attacks of diarrhoea which left me in dread of travelling any distance. My bowels conspired to keep me quarantined at my desk and the household perimeter. But travel I must; seek health I must, away from my penitentiary desk. Swimming, horseback riding, and a punishing regimen of boxing lessons – nothing so far had worked to relieve me of my incurable debility, my condemnation to ill health that had no satisfactory diagnosis.

By chance, my omission from history displayed itself to me with grotesque comic force in the spring of 1951, when I visited the Shingon temple of Kaikoji in Sakata. I went there with my night-clubbing partner, the Baroness Omiyeke Keiko, to see the mummies of two renowned 'tree-eating' saints. These saints of the 18th century, ascetics of the Mount Yudono order, had subjected themselves to a terrifying ordeal known as the tree-eating austerity, a fast which begins with a diet of nuts, bark, berries, and sometimes pine needles or grass. This food is gradually reduced to none over a long period lasting from one thousand to four thousand days. If the fast has been properly calculated, the aim will have been achieved, which is to die from starvation in the upright lotus posture on the last day of the discipline, and by which time the body of the hunger artist will have shrunken to skin and bone, with all its flesh and viscera long since vanished. After a three-year period of burial in a stone sarcophagus, the hunger artist will be found to have naturally mummified into a dry, scaly brown leather without resort to the embalming process of the Egyptians. These saintly hunger artists are said not to die but to 'take *nyujo*', a condition of suspended animation in which they await the coming of the Buddha Maitreya, millions of years in the future. The mummified tree-eaters are displayed in the splendid costume of Buddhist abbots and venerated as Buddhas by their worshippers.

On the day of our arrival at Sakata, we found that our two saints, Chukai and Emmyokai, had been removed for examination by a team of Tokyo University archeologists. We were permitted to see the mummies, however, in the archeologists' temporary laboratory set up in an outbuilding of the Kaikoji temple. The disrobed relics lay on their sides, gruesomely rigid in their cross-legged posture, like those cadavers left petrified by lava in the ruins of Pompeii.

Keiko remarked irreverently that they looked like 'two roasted Peking ducks'.

X-ray examination of the mummies had shown the cavities of their torsos moth-eaten and infested with rats' nests, one archeologist told us, and they would have to be cleaned and restored. Keiko wrinkled her perfect aquiline nose in disgust, and a beauty spot sank into a dimple on her plump, exquisitely white cheek, just below her left eye. 'How awful,' she exclaimed to me. 'Just imagine, Kochan. Will they put moth balls inside them, like I do with my fur coats?'

Her comment made me feel that my own innards had been X-rayed and found rat-infested.

'Don't take my jokes to heart,' Keiko said, in response to my look of afflication. Did she guess at the depth of my self-repugnance, in which I identified with these fossilized hunger artists?

'I am resolved to leave Japan,' I replied, as we toured the grounds of the Kaikoji Temple. 'I must undertake a voyage in quest of health. My impulse is to board the first antarctic whaler I can find and seek my cure by a test of hardship.'

'An Edgar Allan Poe fantasy of polar adventure, very romantic, but not very practical. You will need Generalissimo MacArthur's permission –' Keiko stopped short, and laughed. She had forgotten the great topic of the day in this April of 1951 – the disgrace and retirement of Japan's last Shogun, General Douglas MacArthur. President Truman had forced the egotist general to yield his suzerainty over SCAP and Japan. Matthew Ridgway replaced him in the last year of Occupation. Until now, no one had entered or left Japan without Shogun Mac-Arthur's permission. 'A travel permit might be easier to obtain now,' Keiko mused.

'Even so, I still face a medical exam to get one.'

'What do you fear, Kochan, they'll find rats nesting in your stomach?'

'Would it surprise you?'

On Christmas day, 1951, I set sail from Yokohama harbour to begin my five months' world tour that would end as my heart desired in Greece.

13   BENARES:
A MASS FOR THE DEAD

'*Quasi modo geniti infantes, alleluja . . .*'

In jolted, stuttering syllables, Dr Chatterjee's words tumble loose from him, as he clutches defensively for a handhold in his corner of the back seat. Our transport to Magahar is an ancient Dodge sedan, a war-time relic of bone-fracturing, defunct suspension. It appeared outside Dr Chatterjee's house, like a personnel carrier of matt khaki hue, shortly before 9 p.m. Our chauffeur is a certain 'Major Das, retired', a name which I take to be an incognito; a taciturn elderly Indian army type with mutton chop whiskers, turbaned and smartly outfitted in a beige linen safari suit. Major Das's eyes are as I imagine the Aghori's to be, red embers glowing at us in the rearview mirror – not a standard car mirror but a round shaving-glass fixed to an elbow bracket over the windscreen.

With juddering voice and teeth a-rattle, Dr Chatterjee attempts a translation. '. . . from the opening of the Missa in Albis, taken from St Peter's First Epistle, chapter two, verse one, "As newborn babes desire the sincere milk of the word" . . .'

I hold to the one familiar word. Quasimodo. The hunchback of Notre Dame in Victor Hugo's novel?

'The same,' Dr Chatterjee agrees. 'Quasimodo, the hunchback foundling so named from the first word of the Eastertide mass by the priest Claude Frollo who adopted him.'

'Why this reference to the mass?'

'You are in peril,' Dr Chatterjee answers.

His unusually laconic reply promises a night of rare strangeness. A black leather satchel reposes in safekeeping on his lap; on mine, the requisite gift of scotch for the Aghori.

I glanced at my watch – not yet midnight – as the Dodge recrossed the Maulviya bridge on its way back to deposit me at Clark's Hotel. I had spent little more than two hours with Dr Chatterjee's uncle, the *mahant* Krin Ramji Baba (a variant of his name Baba Krin Ram). I could not quite accept that the interview had been a total disappointment. But then, why had I fled? A mood of lightheaded amusement disabled my critical faculties. I felt unfocussed, incapacitated to judge whether a sense of let down in the presence of a charlatan had convinced me to leave after a few hours' visit, or that something so fantastic, so prodigiously threatening if I stayed, had urged me to take flight.

What I had seen tonight, even so little as I had permitted myself to see, had undoubtedly been strange. 'But it is well-known,' I told myself. 'The extremes of strangeness affect us in inverse ratio less than commonplace events, which take us longer to recognize as genuinely strange. I've had my fill of strangeness, which in the end simply reveals the monstrously commonplace.'

Major Das, who, without complaint or comment, chauffeured my escape from the Magahar shore, stared at me in his rearview barber's mirror, red-inflamed eyes skewering through my dubious, equivocal and perfidious thoughts.

'*I dated a girl who's now engaged to Crown Prince Akihito.*'

'I felt like kicking him in the shins,' Azusa replied, slumped and drawing angry pulls of a cigarette in his corner of the taxi.

'Who, the Crown Prince?'

'No, your prospective father-in-law, Sugiyama Nei,' Azusa glanced daggers at me. 'Why didn't you stick with her – what's her name, Miss Shoda, the Crown Prince's fiancée? Her father was rich and without Sugiyama Nei's pretensions. Nothing could be worse than a nouveau riche upstart who fancies himself because he's a painter of the traditional school "What?" I said to him. "What? You boast of success? My son is an international celebrity, and we are descendents of feudal *daimyo*."'

'She was a celebrity hunter.'

'Who?'

'The Crown Prince's fiancée. That's why I broke with her.'

'Do you have any idea of the dowry Sugiyama wants us to settle on his cherished offspring? It's unthinkable.'

'We can afford it.'

'*We* can, can we? You should have held hands with Sugiyama while he lectured me about "your son's respectability being somewhat in question", that pompous fake! That's when I should have kicked him in the shins.'

'Strange, from the sound of your voices in the next room, I imagined the arrangements were proceeding quite nicely.'

'You were far too preoccupied with the Sugiyama girl to take any notice of my exasperation. Besides, what's her great fascination? Your mother was at least a great beauty, while she, well, she strikes me as entirely commonplace.'

'Commonplace as plum blossoms?'

'As you say. But why on earth this sudden urgency to marry?'

'Before going into hospital for her cancer tests, mother said to me, "You are thirty-three years old, a successful writer and still unmarried, and I am an old woman soon to die. This must be resolved." I am resolving it.'

'But that was months ago. All suspicions of cancer have proven unfounded. Your mother cannot plead imminent death anymore. So what's the big hurry? She's just as puzzled as I am by your headlong rush into this Sugiyama business.'

'She's threatened to kill herself.'

'Your mother?' Azusa's eyes widened in disbelief.

'My intended, Miss Sugiyama Yoko, if her father poses any further obstacles to our marriage.'

Azusa grinned sardonically. 'Now that would upset old Sugiyama. Of course, she's not serious.'

I shrugged.

'Is she?' Azusa peered at me.

'Who knows? She's a very determined person.'

'That's the last thing we need, another headstrong female in our household.'

I am trying to reach a considered, objective view on the Aghori *mahant*, Krin Ramji Baba, and these reminiscences of my courtship and marriage obtrude, beyond my control. Perhaps some form of association exists between one thing and the other, but if there is, I cannot for the life of me see what it is. This is a dispersal of my mental energies, explained by fatigue.

> 'My whole life have I wasted in Kashi,
> But at the point of death I have risen
> And come to Mahagar.'

Dr Chatterjee quotes the ironist poet, Kabir, as we bump across the Maulviya bridge. 'Welcome to the ass's shore,' he says, 'and the *mahant*'s leprosarium.'

A low mud wall and pipal tress screen Krin Ramji Baba's leper colony from view. Within, it appears composed of some dozen buildings, a number of them open-fronted, made of corrugated tin and breeze block, so far as the occasional gas lamps permit me to judge. Pigeons roost in niches under the roofs. Dr Chatterjee shows me round the place. None of the residents seems to me to display any symptoms of leprosy, not even the tell-tale albino pallor. 'The *mahant* uses Ayurvedic medicine to treat them. Medical researchers from all over the world have come here to discover the *mahant*'s remedy, but he keeps it secret.'

'You mean, they're cured?'

'Only so long as they remain in the colony. Outside, they would fall ill again.'

Very strange.

Pariah dogs wander freely about the compound, entering through a gap in the flood wall at the back that overlooks the Ganges.

As we speak, a jeep ancient as our Dodge transport pulls up in front of a porched, mud brick dwelling. A clean-shaven man of uncertain age clambers out of the vehicle, dressed in khaki shorts, patched V-neck jersey and ankle-high desert boots without socks. He glances back at us from the porch, in the light of a kerosene storm-lantern.

'The mahant Krin Ramji Baba,' Dr Chatterjee says. 'In a moment, the *cakra-puja* ceremony will begin.'

We enter the *mahant*'s house, into the main room illumined by a single pendent lightbulb. I can hear the cough of a diesel motor outside which supplies the electricity. Krin Ramji Baba has finished undressing, and he occupies his throne – a low hempen-strung bed on a sort of little dais some two feet above the floor, both levels composed of hard-packed mud. On the dais wall behind the *mahant*'s bed is a fresco, a naive bright thing which shows the characteristic form of Aghori meditation, the *mahant* himself (for those are his features) seated in Lotus posture on the torso of a stark white corpse, which seems to be his own, and accompanied at his right and left by two peculiarly inappropriate figures, that of a crucified Jesus and a Lenin with fist outstretched in heroic salute.

The naked man sitting cross-legged on the bed, Dr Chatterjee's uncle, lives up to his nephew's description of him, remarkably handsome, though he must be over seventy, and with the frightening eyes of a madman. He too, like the mammoth Aghori pretender on the post office verandah, wears that smile of repellently obscene smugness. And I too, like his devotees seated round him on reed mats, cannot bear for long to look him directly in the face – the bloodshot eyes and rigor mortis smile soon unnerve one. I gaze instead at the termite pits in the bed's framework.

The followers of Krin Ramji Baba are an unlikely set of respectable-looking folk, and Dr Chatterjee does not scruple to describe them in a perfectly audible voice. He points out an overweight matron with gold pince-nez, 'The headmistress of a girls' public school in Bombay,' and that gentleman, 'a Delhi police inspector,' a civil servant, an accountant, and so on, six or seven persons of estimable rank, as far as I can make them out in the grey penumbra of this shrine.

Over by another doorway, ajar at the far side of the room, a woman sits preparing food on a sunken brazier in the floor. I recognize our Dal Mandi brothel madam. 'Matrika, we call her,' Dr Chatterjee says. 'It

means "mother", one of the divas of the pre-Hindu *yaksha* cult.'
Matrika, in a halo of greasy smoke from the cooking fire, has the same
tearfully grieving air that I had seen earlier. A girl of swarthy low-caste
features, looking equally despondent, huddles against Matrika's broad
back for comfort, a wing of her festive sari draping her head, the firelight
winking on her jewelled nose stud, silver toe rings and ankle bracelets.
No doubt, this is the prostitute in menses, selected for that reason by
my guide to partner the Aghori in the *cakra-puja* sexual rite. She seemed
terrified by the honour. Matrika piled an unappetizing mess of substances
from her cooking pot into a bowl and handed it to the girl. 'Take note,
sir,' Dr Chatterjee poked me in the ribs. 'That's the skull from which
the Aghori dines, do you see?' The bowl, cut from the upper part of
the cranium, could easily have passed for yellowed procelain, had not
my guide remarked on it. I felt tempted to ask if the food in the skull
might not be curried corpse, but I did not, preferring to observe closely
the waitress serving the Aghori's mortuary dinner. She could not have
been more than sixteen, and her downcast, sulking look of terror, I now
decided, was nothing of the kind. I perceived a brooding anticipation of
lechery in her eyes, matched by a flash of Krin Ramji Baba's pearly
white predator's teeth.

A strange low whine escaped the Aghori, a growl from deep in his
thorax, which summoned a pariah dog into the room through the side
door beside the cooking fire. It slinked up to the dais, yellow, like a
crouched-back hyena, and began snouting into the skull's contents that
the Aghori offered to share.

I could not stomach to watch the Aghori scooping up his befouled
stew – 'with the left hand,' Dr Chatterjee commentated, nudging me
in the ribs again – which suggested the putrescent jelly of a human
brain. 'This shows the ascetic's contempt for human necessities,' Dr
Chatterjee piped up.

I wondered if my guide's *alto voce* commentary would oppress me
throughout the evening's entertainment. No one else seemed to mind.
Nor, as I looked round, did anyone seem to take any umbrage at my
foreign presence. Then, at the shadowy rear of the assembly, I noticed
another foreigner, an enormously fat elderly white woman, the only
person accommodated by a chair. Her bloated limbs, the indistinct
straying movements of her eyes, were familiar to me, but I could not
place where I had seen her. At this moment, my attention was recalled
by a belch, and a thunderous clap from the holy man's backside that
proclaimed the meal's satisfactory end. He stared heavenwards, a vein
on his neck swelled, and, coming to view at my eye level, I saw the
interrogative curl of a turd as it drooped and fell through the string
meshes of the *mahant*'s bed. We all stared at it. Dr Chatterjee mercifully
quiet, for once. A sigh – I presumed reverential – came from the

headmistress with the gold pince-nez as she struggled to rise. Matrika had come forward with a makeshift dustpan – a potsherd of adequate shape – extended to the headmistress whose broad beam delayed her ascent. Someone nimbler on his feet seized the utensil from Matrika's hand, hurrying to claim what I presume again must have been the privilege of cleaning up the *mahant*'s excrement. This individual, hidden from my sight before, had progressed swiftly from the back of the room, from beside the memsahib lady's chair – and in fact he pulled her along commandingly by the hand, a pale, wet sea-cow, slick with the perspiration of hyperatrophied obesity. I knew him. My ex-brigadier at Clark's who preached his water sermon and recommended the Aghori to me, it was he, the revenant Marquis de Sade with his blind oedematose wife.

'Do you know this gentleman?' Dr Chatterjee tapped my shoulder. 'He puts up at Clark's on his visits here from Darjeeling. James Gilholme Blair, a Scottish lord and former colonel in the Britsh Raj days. Blotted his copybook, as they say, and was forced into retirement. A little over-enthusiastic about Indian independence, it seems, poor fellow.'

Could this corpulent, rheumy-eyed wreck, living in expatriate disgrace, once have been a pert young man recruited to uncle Chatterjee's entourage of lovers more than thirty years ago? His hair, thin and pale as blanched straw, might once have been flaxen, and like the Marquis de Sade in his blonde and blue-eyed youth, before prison transformed him into a toothless, hideously swollen foetus, he too might have boasted dainty and cherubic features. And there he was, on his hands and knees, scooping the Aghori's dung, a supplicant in pursuit of the holy man's favour. When his latrine duty was done, he posed a brief request to the Aghori, to which the latter replied curtly with an order to hand over the blind woman's cane. I did not need Dr Chatterjee's interpretation to understand this exchange. The petitioner's wife was thereupon asked to turn round, and the Aghori struck her across the kidneys three times, hard enough to make her wince. 'Now she can have children,' Dr Chatterjee translated the *mahant*'s proclamation of a miracle. A miracle which evidently dumbfounded ex-colonel Blair, whose expectation had been a cure for his wife's kidney compliant, not Sarah's prodigy of delayed fertility in old age. The *mahant*'s laughter ended this cruel jest, and the couple returned to their place. As he passed close by me, with fecund wife in tandem and the potsherd of excrement still in his hand, I greeted him. 'I've taken your advice,' I said. He glanced down at me, unseeing as the sightless being he guided, conveyed into darkness by the shard of earthenware lamp in his grip and its unsightly relic. 'He carries the broken lamp of Diogenes,' I muttered, for no other's amusement but my own.

I surveyed the Aghori's followers again, and apparently they too were in a peculiar state of blindness, unable to see me either. Was I invisible? I felt dismayed, but with a sense of wonder more comical than alarming. 'They seem drugged or hypnotized – or am I dreaming?'

'No one's drugged,' Dr Chatterjee assured me, with almost a giggle. 'Is that what you feel?'

'I should leave – that's my feeling.'

'You would regret it. Patience, sir. Why not see what effect your gift will have on the *mahant*?'

I offered the Aghori my bottle of Chivas Regal. It displeased him to find the bottle already started. He had not shown himself quite so fastidious about his food. Nevertheless, he uncapped the scotch and gulped down a fair amount of it. He signalled to Matrika and she dispatched the girl with a cup for me. Nausea overpowered me once I took the cup, with its antler stumps of broken handle, and saw the black zigzag fracture running through it, alive, impregnated with the virus of leprosy. I had received Yuan Hsiao's skull – or its more perilous facsimile in this china cup.

My head sagged. Am I going to faint? How strange, the prostitute's ringed toes, so diminutive, and the nails minimized to sunken little crescents, the results more normally seen of inveterate nail-biting. Was she addicted to nibbling her toenails? Her footprints on the humid floor were outlined in blood. No, not blood, traces of the courtesan's ver-milion *lac* on the soles of her feet.

'What do you think of my nautch girl?'

A far off voice, the sound muted as though by cotton wool, reached me. The Aghori had addressed me, a wink, a nod at the prostitute, as he poured Chivas Regal into my plague-infested chalice. Alcohol would sterilize it, I hoped.

What is a nautch girl? I turned to Dr Chatterjee for enlightenment, but my reliably tedious guide was not to be seen. When once I need him ... My ingestion of scotch began to work as an antidote to the blackout fog of giddiness into which I had temporarily lapsed. My guide's unexplained disappearance gave me the resolve I needed to leave. I had no desire to witness the *cakra-puja* re-enactment of Shiva and Parvati in coitus, which promised the Aghori in ugly blood-sport intercourse with his 'nautch girl'.

At this precise instant of my decision, the Aghori, who retained the blind woman's cane, struck a sudden violent blow with it across the back of the harlot's knees, a hamstringing impact that toppled the girl to the floor. 'She will bleed when I need her to,' he said in English, those madman's eyes like incandescent drills penetrating the thoughts in my brain.

The hair on my head rose up, ruffled by a whoosh of air, as the *mahant* slashed his cane with swordsman's precision barely millimetres over my head. '*Uragirimono! Kutabare!*' he exclaimed, in passable Japanese. Traitor! Go to hell! And he carried on, eloquent enough in my language, denouncing Japan for its betrayal of Chandra Bose's Indian National Army – all those patriots misled and subsequently abandoned in Burma, confined like animals in barbed wire cages, tormented by Gurkhas until the British hanged them.

I kept an eye on his cane, hammering against the bedframe to accent his tirade.

'I am not responsible for the failures of the Japanese High Command,' I said, when at last he finished. I stood up. 'I would appreciate some transport back to Clark's.'

'Running away condemns you to the same place,' the Aghori said. He leaned his chin on the handle of the cane. 'Major Das will escort you.'

A chill breeze outside blew in from the Ganges. I heard bat cries in the darkness and the dry rustle of pipal leaves. Our walk to Major Das's car took us past one of the open-fronted huts, brightly advertised by a pair of storm-lanterns hung in the eaves. I was presented with a strange tableau – Dr Chatterjee, standing before an improvised altar, apparelled in a black chasuble, IHS emblazoned in gold on the back. He raised his arms, the thumbs and forefingers of his hands pinched together, eyeing the chalice on the altar cloth – '*Introibo ad altare* Dei.'

'*Ad Deum, qui laetificat juventutem meam,*' the response came from ex-colonel Blair, in place behind Fernando Pinto Mendes SJ, at the threshold of the cramped hut. The altar attendant Blair turned slightly to me and in a hush said, 'Will you stay for this ceremony?'

At the back of the hut, I saw the brothel keeper Matrika squatting on the floor beside a corpse bundled in a white shroud, lying festooned with marigolds on its litter. A requiem mass was in progress.

I watched for some moments. Until, at last, Major Das rattled his car keys and stared at me with his usual dourness. 'Are you staying, sir?' And that – that unimportant detail of my chauffeur's impatience, a rattle of keys, and his deadpan sobriety that found nothing unusual in anything, nothing worthy to get excited about – those small facts returned me to a sense of the comical unreality of the real, to a truthfulness which was no mere vagary of my mind. Even I, a lifetime practitioner of fiction, an extremist habitué of the unusual on paper, could not have invented the perfect truth of Major Das's keys; while instead the jingling little altar bell in Lord Blair's hand, real in itself, yet differently real, lay within my writer's compass.

Yushiki consciousness-only apprehends instantaneous reality only. All else is illusion. I experience the truthfulness of *yushiki* now; but because it is now only, it is provisory like Yuan Hsiao's drink of water. Enlightenment cannot possibly occur once (instantaneous reality forbids any possibility of 'once'), but must be an endless series of repetitions prolonged into one consciousness only. Ethics, in the extended dimension of such consciousness, must inevitably make one an outlaw. I can see that in the Aghori, in the accomplishment of his absolute self-befoulment, a topsy-turvy saint even if he is a fake; and I can see it in his nephew, the spiritual abolition of limits.

The leather satchel I saw on Dr Chatterjee's lap on our way here had contained a priest's regalia. A battle for spiritual dominion went on between Father Fernando Pinto Mendes SJ and his uncle Anant Chatterjee. Against the Aghori rites of *cakra-puja*, the Jesuit defied his superiors in Rome and performed the prohibited Malabar rites, a requiem mass – but for whom, I wondered?

No, my interview with the Aghori has not been disappointing. It amuses me to have discovered, in the oddest of extreme circumstances, an unrepentant ultra-nationalist fanatic. The former millionaire chemist and Chelsea gent, Anant Chatterjee, now the Aghori miracle-worker in a leper colony, naked, violent, defecating before an audience of believers, is undoubtedly an aberration. But what is really aberrant about him? Strangeness is not the interesting thing. I have not encountered anything more bizarre in this hour of spectacle than I experienced in one of Hijikata Tatsumi's dance classes when as a naked and legless *daruma* doll, summoned like a Tohoku wind spirit from a basket of broken legs, I perform impossible movements to the rhythm of his little Nichiren hand drum. Hijikata's art is an outlaw condition of being, not even art, recognizing no orthodoxy, not Shinto, Buddhism or anything. So then, what is aberrant about the Aghori? Those few moments of his diatribe against Japan's treason, the expression of an ultra-nationalist's outraged faith – *that* is the aesthetically, religiously and ethically justified aberration for which he has turned himself inside-out – and that is also the meaning of Hijikata's mutiny against art, against religion, against ethics, and it is mine. We have come to deny what is superficially judged strange.

Jostled and concussed at the back of Major Das's Dodge, I am pleased enough to have chanced upon another outlaw artist. I look into the shaving-glass and meet my chauffeur's eyes. I apologize for dragging him away early, at the entr'acte of the ceremony. But he does not welcome my smile – a smile that lingers on from my reminiscence of another time and place.

Azusa too had found my smile vaguely mysterious as we journeyed home by taxi from my interview with the Sugiyama maiden. 'I don't understand your satisfaction,' Azusa complained. 'The girl is ordinary, the dowry preposterous, and as for the father, well, I fear I shall come to blows with him before this is over.'

'I am satisified.'

Azusa shook his head. 'Your mother will be horrified.'

'Isn't that reason enough for satisfaction?'

My sarcasm took Azusa entirely by surprise. He could not imagine me at all cynically disposed towards my mother, and so he misjudged the intention of my irony. 'It does not gratify me that your mother has been excluded from these marriage transactions, conducted by you with such unseemly haste.' His attempt to exculpate himself revealed how little he appreciated my motives.

At winter's end, in 1958, when my mother had been presumed fatally ill, incorrectly as it soon turned out, I had enlisted Azusa to begin canvassing for eligible girls. Trusted members of the family and inter-mediaries were to assist him in arranging *omiai*, formal meetings in which the parties initially size each other up for compatability. *Omiai* are, so to speak, traditional screen tests. At this time, I wrote an article for a popular magazine in which I described the writer's ideal wife that I had in mind. I stipulated her size, looks, temperament, family pedigree, education and domestic skills with the exigent and detailed precision of a police missing person's report. My final impossible demand was for a wife who must devotedly serve a writer, but must not in any sense consider herself married to the public figure Yukio Mishima. All appli-cants would have to submit written evidence of their suitability, undergo preliminary examination by my intermediaries to spare me the waste of time, and provide full-length colour photographs of themselves.

My approach to arranged marriage, though perhaps over-finicky in detail, seemed entirely in keeping with tradition. I relied on my pro-gramme of stipulations to deter candidates and prolong the business of *omiai*, long enough at least so that Shizue's funeral would intervene and put an end to the entire farce. I had not counted on the avalanche of applications that my (Lazarian-inspired) fantasy would detonate. 99% unsuitable, of course, with scores of indecent proposals and lascivious photographs. I felt compelled to take stock of this unexpected response. My method had proven itself more realist and effective than my trust in its failure. What did it teach me? What did I find in all these unsolici-ted, intimate self-revelations from so many unknown correspondents? I discovered Yukio Mishima statistically profiled, reconstituted as though by some opinion-poll questionnaire. I discovered speculators, an anony-mous public of speculators, prepared to gamble on a figment of their dreams. Our roles had become curiously reversed. I was *their* candidate, and not the other way round.

Truly, for the first time, I was given the evidence to see myself as others imagined me to be. Strange way to see yourself, as you are perceived in reality, yes, but at the wrong end of the microscope. And the majority of my public perceivers were overwhelmingly in favour of electing me to unrespectability, someone not entirely an outlaw yet, but certainly an undesirable. 'If I am such an undesirable, what on earth is the meaning of all this desire aimed at me?' The answer was self-evidently, power. I recognized its unshaped, inchoate potential in my hands, if only I had the courage to manipulate what others seemed eager to offer me.

I had endured enough misfired *omiai* by the time I arrived at the nineteen-year-old Peers' sophomore, Sugiyama Yoko, to recognize what she offered. Yoko had taken infinite pains to transform the Sugi-yama's livingroom table into an exquisite altar, complete with English silverware, bone china service on a spread of linen, and a Western-style floral arrangement as centrepiece. A votive display of choice hors d'oeuvres showed off Mademoiselle Sugiyama's *cordon bleu* skills, caviar canapés and pheasant vol-au-vents, terrines, patés and confectionery, a superabundance that the few of us could not possibly consume.

'Is it to your liking?' Mademoiselle Yoko asked. 'I read in an article that you appreciated French cuisine.'

'Stories of that kind can be misleading. Personally, I'd much rather have a simple *chasuke* of cold rice and pickles.'

Mademoiselle Yoko frowned. I liked her independence of spirit which did not smooth over the annoyance she felt under any conventional bluff.

I made a joke about the Peers' School not being co-ed in my day.

'Fortunately, things have moved on since then,' she replied, her annoyance still evident.

'You are fortunate indeed to have only a distant childhood memory of wartime,' I laughed – my upstaging, nightclub manager's laugh, deliberately over-hearty, crude and unnerving. 'I see you aren't one of those who regrets the new ways of democracy.'

'I remember enough not to regret.'

Excellent beginning. I began to form an idea of this Sugiyama damsel as one of the new beings anthropologically remote from me, efficient and ambitious, like our upcoming generation of managers.

We left our elders to their discussion and tea – scotch on the rocks for Azusa – and adjourned to the privacy of a little sitting-room, or one so designated for the purpose of *omiai*. 'What else have you read about me in the press?' I asked her.

'Please do not form a mistaken impression of me. You are a great deal in the news, but I am not especially influenced by gossip.'

'I wonder if you had seen a recent questionnaire in a popular magazine addressed to young ladies, inviting them to rate various eligible bachelors. Apparently, I scored the lowest attraction rating, a distinction that I share with Crown Prince Akihito.'

'I supppose it wasn't very flattering for you to be compared with Crown Prince Akihito,' she smiled.

I laughed – and next door Azusa and Sugiyama *père* were also laughing. Everything seemed to be going smoothly.

I contemplated the girl. Small – in exact correspondence to my specifications and perfectly formed, her legs crossed in relaxed Western fashion. I esteemed her pretty (an evaluation which later stood the test of being 'Azusa proof'), her mouth attractively wide, sensual, the lips slightly thick and Mongol. Was she 'pretty' for me in a way that satisfied Lazar's complementary degree of masculinity? I tried to see what could possibly be attractively *un*feminine about her.

'You haven't really answered my question,' I said, 'which is, if I might put it frankly, this. What has attracted you to this meeting?'

'I don't understand the question,' she pouted – and that was a marvel to behold, for she pouted not with her lips, which became wider and more sensual, but with an odd pucker of her forehead. 'What attracted me? You have, of course.'

'How can that be, since we've never met before, and since, as you say, you aren't influenced by press gossip about a celebrity? I am confused.'

'I think you are trying to confuse me with questions that should not be asked at a meeting like this.'

I overlooked her legitimate complaint about my indiscretion. 'Have you read my books?'

She knew this too was a trick question. I sought a wife devoted to a writer, but this is not the same as an invitation to meddle in my career. 'I have read only a few. *A Misstepping of Virtue* impressed me.'

She chose well. I would not have been flattered had she said, 'Yes, all of them,' and would not have believed her if she said 'none'. Better still, she had chosen to name one of my best-known, most commercially successful 'pink romances', a potboiler that had given currency to the common expression for an adulteress, 'Lady Misstep'.

'Did you like the book?'

'I did not care much for its gloomy prediction of a world holocaust.'

'Interesting you should say that, which precisely sums up the accusation of critics – "even in his minor works Mishima still promotes the wartime nihilism of the *Roman-ha* school".'

'I do not know what the *Roman-ha* is.'

'But you read the critics?'

She nodded, as though confessing to a grave crime.

I laughed, more and more with a delirious sense of being in love – love of my commitment to power. 'Interesting, Mademoiselle Yoko, very interesting.'

'Why do you call me mademoiselle?' Cautious of some affront concealed by the title, she rubbed unawares at the sheeny grain of nylon on her knee. Plump fingers, dainty and trim like the firm moulding of her calf which did not suffer the malformed stubbiness usual among Japanese females.

'Mademoiselle, because you are such an excellent French chef.'

'How can you know? You didn't try anything I prepared.'

'I shall have plenty of time for that, after we're married, when the marvels of your superlative cuisine will astound and be the envy of our guests.'

'I beg your pardon?' She laughed. 'What are you saying?'

'Don't you agree we should marry?'

'Are you serious?'

'Entirely. You have my word on it.'

Her smile might be ironically circumspect, but the gleam in her eyes conveyed an agreement already signed and sealed. Yoko's eagerness set her crossed leg in jerky motion to and fro. Her shoe slipped free of the heel and dangled by the instep. 'Why this sudden conviction out of the blue?'

'My conviction is rock solid. Do you know William Blake's fine maxim? "In a wife I would desire what in whores is always found – the lineaments of gratified desire".'

'Translate please.' My apparent ungallant test of Yoko's English peeved her. As she bent down to refit her shoe, a tendon dimpled the flank of her knee. This moment's vision of Yoko adjusting her shoe, an aggrieved scowl on her face, contained all the domesticity of our years to come, perceived in a flash. 'Why are you rushing headlong into this?' An irrelevant voice pleaded commonsense too late. I had already succumbed, not to wedlock with this alien being, but to the bewitchment of my curiosity. I felt drawn to peer into a tunnel, enchanted by what I saw as the approaching image of myself in a telescope. I saw myself in the narrowed focus of the ordinary, through which others had the normal social advantage of seeing me. The only sure way to overcome the ordinary is to test it, which means estranging it. In such an exceptional case as mine, an effort to transcend the ordinary is wasteful and redundant struggle. Wiser to let the ordinary become a feature of the exceptional, in other words, to take a wife as proof of my strangeness. Matrimony would abet me in being ever more alien to myself. My curiosity would serve me as the accomplice hand at my own self-vivisection.

'Are you having second thoughts about the rashness of your proposal?' Yoko breezily declared, arousing me from my interval of meditation.

'Forgive me. I've been sidetracked by my reference to the English poet. I was simply trying to find other words to express my conviction.'

'Rock solid, I believe you said?'

'It is – but are you as certain? You understand, a wife of mine would have to accommodate certain of my eccentricities.'

'It sounds as though you require a courtesan, more than a wife.'

'I'm sorry if I make it sound improper –'

Yoko cut in, 'You needn't worry on that account,' and leaning forward, unexpectedly touched my hand. 'I am descended from geishas on my mother's side.'

'I see.' Yoko allowed me to hold the tips of her fingers. The palm of her hand resting on my knuckles perspired. The humid flesh excited a clinically disinterested sexual wonder in me. 'Aren't you alarmed by my unconventional proposal?'

'Do you hope to panic me into refusing?'

'I confess myself surprised to find you so determined.'

She pressed harder against my hand. 'I would kill myself if our marriage were not permitted.'

'Now – are *you* serious?' I laughed. 'I don't imagine it will come to that.'

'Just listen –' Yoko nodded to the flimsy partition separating us from the elders – and through it I could here Azusa's monotone grumble, a recognizable warning to me of his anger. Negotiations between the Hiraoka and Sugiyama factions were not going at all smoothly, as Yoko's antennae had been quicker to register.

'I have one defect that I should tell you about,' Yoko confided in a whisper, although she could not be overheard by our parents. 'I sometimes sleep with my eyes open. Do you find that very repulsive?'

'Better than having your eyes closed while awake, which seems to be a more common imperfection.'

Major Das had parked the car and opened my door before I knew we had come to the entrance of the Clark's Hotel driveway. His mustachioed face beaconed grimly over me in the flicker of some passing rickshaw lanterns. Coolies were stationing themselves outside Clark's for the night. 'Payment is not necessary,' he stated as I dug absent-mindedly into my pocket for some rupees, the impoliteness only then dawning on me.

Major Das returned to the driver's seat and lit a cigarette. 'Should you change your mind about Magahar and wish to go back, I shall be waiting here.'

'There is no need.' The offer struck me as odd. 'Are these the *mahant*'s instructions?'

'The *mahant*?' Major Das laughed. 'The only *mahant* whose orders I follow is Anant Chatterjee.'

I did not probe further into the ambiguity of which Chatterjee, uncle or nephew.

I needed a drink, but my surplus bottle of Chivas Regal had gone to the Aghori, and the hotel bar had closed. I asked the night porter to find me something drinkable. He came back in a while with the manager's compliments and a bottle of 'very fine old Famous Grouse, sir, excellent whisky'. 'Very fine, I'm sure. Put it on my bill.'

I had several drinks on my balcony. The night air was pleasantly cool. A subdued light from a bedside lamp within the room lent a morbid puce colour to the bougainvillaea, like contused flesh, shivering against a moonless pall of sky pinpricked by stars. A piece of woman's lingerie had been draped over the lampshade, muting the light to a dull red. Mosquito netting, unnecessary at this time of year, curtained one side of the bed, and poking out from under the folds, I saw a woman's foot. I contemplated this foot, as I drank my scotch, and recalled the sight of my mother's own, three decades ago on a moonlit, mosquito-infested night in Azusa's garden hut. My mother's sexual vassalage to the ruffian overlord exiled in that hut had seemed a great mystery to me then. But since, I had secured a wife of my own, and all the claustrophobic narrowness of domesticity that I had foreseen in Yoko's adjusting her shoe at our *omiai* had come to pass, otherwise than my naivety imagined, substantially demonstrated to me now by the sight of Yoko's foot protruding from a bed in a Benares hotel room.

'Discalced domesticity,' I laughed to myself, perhaps slightly intoxicated. 'The wonder is not that Yoko exists and is here with me in Benares, but that Sam Lazar's Jael has manifested herself to me in a brothel madam. The theatre of my imagination is what peoples reality, always naively prescripted as real beings.'

I had built a Victorian-style mansion in Magome for Yoko, our two children and myself, truthfully caricatured this afternoon by my Jesuit guide. I had constructed separate quarters for Shizue and Azusa in the Magome grounds, planned on the *inkyo* principle of segregating the generations, an architectural apartheid. Yoko presided as the chatelaine of my fantastical Elsinore. But if she passes from our front verandah to a little patio-sized garden with its zodiac tiles, sundial and statue of Apollo, she will confront a smaller unconnected Japanese-style bungalow at a right angle to our dwelling which houses my parents. It is so placed that no one can leave our house or enter through the front wrought-iron gate in the surrounding high white wall without being perceived from the elders' sitting-room window. I have obeyed the *inkyo* tradition, but left a loophole, an eavesdropper's annexe to our own home. I have approximated the conditions of female tension that prevailed with such internecine ferocity in my childhood.

Whose foot is it I really see, Shizue's or Yoko's? Does it matter to the decadent dreamer in his upper-floor writer's studio?

Yoko lies unstirring on the bed. I approach her from the opposite uncurtained side, by the lamp, and look to see if she feigns sleep. A book has fallen from her hand to the pillow, appropriately enough Kawabata Yasunari's

Gazing up admonishingly at me from its cranny between the two pillows, sits my old stuffed lion, a toy companion that has always been with me since my first attack of *jikachudoku*. Yoko's eyes are open. The sluggish droop of her lids, the mouth slack and breathing calmly, indicates repose on the ocean floor of sleep. Sleepers emit a peculiar brakish odour of the sea.

It is much warmer and humid inside the room than on the balcony, and the lamp clothed with Yoko's underwear radiates low heat like a feverish cheek. Yoko lies on her back, limbs akimbo, one leg and part of her torso covered by a sheet. I pull the sheet away, with slow, almost imperceptible evenness. The cotton sighs across her flesh – deafening it sounds to me, like the ebbing swish of a wave on pebbles. But it does not wake her. I ease myself up onto the bed, flat on my belly, propped on my elbows between the sprawled open brackets of Yoko's legs. I can see in minute detail the depilated pits on her shanks, tiny black grains of sand, the soft mounds traversed by undercurrents of blue veins. The sloping dunes of her legs lead to a wedged enclosure, the sea anemone's shut mouth, hidden by a quiff of fine black tentacles. I stare at it. At this moment again, as in times before, I think what a very strange alien universe the vagina is. It has nothing of the sad, comical appeal of the male undercarriage, cactus organs that look like intestines left vulnerably orphaned outside the body, a careless afterthought. The vagina is present, overwhelmingly, without being there at all. I had witnessed my wife's vagina twice giving birth, a daughter and a son. I had seen it burgeon, distend till it ripped at the seams, bleed vastly as though arterially slashed, and bring forth, and all of my close attendance at the *auto-da-fé* of birth had not solved the vagina's metaphysical enigma.

The vagina is a heresy. To men unlike me, of more or less 'normal' character, the female thing is a glutinous slough of attraction. To me, it is nothing, a hole associated with the mystical horror of the Void.

I have tried to rid myself of this absurd, oppressive sense of Nothingness that the hole gives me. I have experimented with attempts to take in, to feel what it is, with the same feeling of actuality that affirms all other ordinary realities, a tree, a chair, someone drinking tea in a moonlit landscape, a toothache.

I remember an experiment of that kind, inconclusive as the rest, when my baby daughter Noriko was first brought home from the hospital. For a few days, I spent all my time caring for her. No one who has changed a baby girl's diaper will fail to have noticed her awkwardly outsized vaginal cleft, in disproportion to the newborn's tiny figure. Strikingly, at the very beginning of life outside the womb, the immature vagina appears larger than life. The entire body must grow to accommodate what it is – or isn't – at the start.

I washed little Noriko, applied lotion to her scaly cradle-cap, played with her – so much as one can with a week-old pygmy – and I wondered, as all parents wonder, how much those intensely serious eyes could see of the world. But always, when I came to change her, that prominent relievo bulge of Venus intrigued me. Gently, apprehensively, I prised the lips apart with fore- and third fingers, and exposed the tiny pink clamped bud of mollusc. I am no paedophiliac monster. At that moment, I was simply a meddling, inquisitive child, a primitive scientist marvelling at an infibulated snarl of tissues, delicate and yet resiliently elastic as octopus flesh.

What did I learn? Nothing. More accurately, less than nothing, because each further exploration of the vagina's mystery is a subtraction from the prejudice that originally assumed itself confident of knowledge. An accumulation of minuses, so to speak, which amplifies the hole's nothingness to absolute Zero and swallows up the inquirer into the Void.

The attraction to look, to enter, does not decrease with each further minus to one's knowledge. On the contrary, it augments insatiably. I found myself on the bed, slithering lizard-bellied towards Yoko's orifice, reaching out to pry it open with two fingers like a pair of calipers. An urge to penetrate that gelatinous mouth seized me, a power that cramps my neck muscles at the nape, yanking me up on all fours. The mattress trampolined under my hands and knees, see-sawing the sleeper beneath me, but not quite waking her. I posed no weight on her, but as I broke in, the volume of my ingress caused her eyelids to flutter. Saliva clicked on her dry palate, 'ah', she complained, and her lips below accepted my penis with a slippage of effluent clicks, *trrsk!* She muttered something about finishing to pack our suitcases – senseless words from deep within sleep. 'That's all right,' I whispered.

There are moments like these when an over-urgency of pleasure betrays itself, when the semen wishes treasonably to escape and leave one hollow with regret. This is the result of unnatural lubricity, attended by nausea. Passion and annihilating emptiness are closely related, as such accidents of miscalculated pleasure will demonstrate to one's horror. I resisted exactly that prevision of horror, that deceitful onrush of desire hurrying the semen from me, promising immense gratified relief, but with less real satisfaction in store than a mere glissando of urine. I drove a stake through the heart of this vampire of desire; I shut my ears with bolts of volition against the siren song of the hole, which lures its prey into the abyss of minus.

For how long resist? Time is not calculable from zero, a maximum that remains the same and in the strangest way, infinite. My resistance failed. I had no sensation at all of having discharged, only that of its overflow trickle along my thighs. I withdrew, and as I slipped back down to my stomach, my eyes grazed past a splash of red on the bed. Yoko's blood had sluiced out of her, tranquilly, without causing her any apparent disturbance. She slept, eyes finally closed in epilogue, a dewy freshness of bloom on her skin. With somnambulist hand, she drew a sheet over her and turned on her side. No trace of me, no signs of a thief's invasion. Nothing had trespassed her dreams, only an unverified, shadowy visitation in briefest passage through her dreams which had left an aborted splash of blood.

An acute soreness, my testes' epididymal ducts swollen hard by impacted semen, gave burdensome verification of my existence. I went to the bathroom to cleanse myself. 'Wash off the afterbirth of dream – ', rusty tresses of water dribbled from the taps, a bang bang in the pipes, and then an explosive gush of cleaner water – *Visnu-padabja sambhuta* – the sacred, restorative water of the Ganges. A longing came over me to bathe in the river, an unreasoning homesickness opposed by a shudder of dread at the prospect of infection. I feared the Ganges' pollution, and at the same time thirsted for its embrace.

I snatched up a towel, retrieved what was left of the Famous Grouse, and left the room. As I emerged from Clark's driveway to the main road, the rickshaw coolies under the trees hailed me, alert as scavengers in vigil for a meal. Major Das had kept loyally to his sentinel post, in his Dodge parked across the road, and he too was awake. 'Magahar?' he asked. 'Can you take me somewhere else, please, to Manikarnika Ghat?' He nodded. 'Are you quite sure, not Magahar, sir?'

I climbed into the car. 'Positive. How long do we have before dawn?'

'Two hours, maybe less,' he glanced at the late night sky. 'You realize, sir, I can only drive you part way to the ghat, the rest you must walk?'

'I don't mind.'

Without the daytime congestion of traffic, our journey was swift. 'This is as far as I am able to go,' Major Das said, wrenching up the handbrake. He pointed off to the right. 'That way, sir, and you will find the steps to Manikarnika Ghat. I shall wait for you here.'

'Do you still expect me to return to Magahar?'

'I cannot presume to doubt it,' he smiled, but I could not be sure he did as the lights went out.

Enough doorways and windows disseminated light, supplementing the unreliable street ones, to make my way clear. Benares slumbered at this hour, and yet I had an eerie sense of its constant wakefulness. I thought of Yoko, asleep during coitus – or had she too been like these houses, watchful, in a state of detached repose that is neither sleep nor waking?

I arrived at the great Manikarnika stadium as the last flames of a cremation on the river's edge sparked up into the night, and gradually subsided. Was it the poorer class of funeral that took place in the less attractive hours of the dark? Logically, it would seem so, but this fair-sized conclave of mourners did not impress me as poor.

I sat down on the middle rank of steps. There were a few others here, perhaps early birds waiting to bathe at dawn, or insomniacs like me, or mere homeless idlers. No one took any notice of me. Empty though it was, the ghat still felt populated by throngs of worshippers and mortuary retailers, their ghostly echoes alive in this vastness magnified by unbounded dark. I lit a cigarette, but felt no craving for the whisky I had sitting at my side. Directly below me, vaguely outlined by lamps at the boatmen's quayside, I saw the *ghatias'* empty stalls, the invigilator paid to keep watch on the bathers' clothes. From this direction, as though disembarked from the river, a figure mounted the steps towards me. An elderly Indian, elegantly attired in an English business suit, approached and asked me to light his cigarette. Odd, to find such a well-dressed person at this time and place. But then, what was I doing here, a Japanese tourist in an Italian silk suit? In the flare of my match, his features appeared for a moment to resemble the handsome, predatory ones of the Aghori in Magahar. 'Are you waiting to bathe in the river, sir?' He seemed to accept that I would, as if it were a perfectly natural thing for a foreigner. 'I should warn you, the current is swift, and although less dangerous now than in the monsoon season, it is advisable to keep hold of the chains in place for the bathers' safety.'

I thanked him.

'Permit me to add a further caution, sir. Beware of thieves and pariah dogs. Both are particularly bold at night and have been known to attack persons on their own.'

I thanked him again, a little too brusquely in return for his courtesy. My attention was distracted by a figure I saw among the last few stragglers at the cremation. A young man, clad only in *dhoti* trousers, carrying some objects in one hand, hastened away from the cremation ground. He mounted the ghat steps and was swallowed up by the dark. I very nearly called out to him, dismayed to have glimpsed my beatific *jizo* again, and to have lost him once more. I had risen to my feet, peering against hope to catch sight of him in the blackness. Nothing, the shrill cry of a night bird ascending the lofty terrace. My hireling acrobat haunting the endless celebration of funerals, truly he had become a will-o'-the-wisp who tantalized and frustrated me every time we crossed paths.

I cursed my bad luck, and turned with apologies to my helpful advisor; but he too had vanished.

A breath of river cold suddenly tingled on the back of my neck. My entire body shivered. A musty smell drifted past me in the wake of this chill draught, an unpleasantly sweet, rancid smell. I remained with my back to this presence, knowing without having to look round that my longed for *jizo* stood behind me. I sat down, and cautiously stole a glance at my right, anxious lest I discover nothing real beside me. My arm grazed against something – a little brass pot on the step, and next to it red chilli peppers tied in a bunch. And as for the boy, he was certainly there, perky as a mendicant sparrow, twittering to me in a sing-song jargon that I understood not at all, but which clearly demanded tributes from me. A hand fluttered at his mouth, like a yawn being exaggeratedly stifled, indicating his request for a cigarette. I provided one; but neither this gift, nor a share of my Famous Grouse straight from the bottle, sufficed to counteract the insistent flow of his gibberish. Until one particular sound at last began to penetrate my obtuseness, and I understood that he was repeating his name. Shiva. 'Shiva' on his lips was not as I imagined it spoken. And I gave him my name in return, Yukio, which he echoed in his way, not as a Japanese might recognize it. I tried speaking to him in English, but the negative shakes of his head pronounced him ignorant of it.

I had stalked a mystery for three days, and now in close proximity it seemed mysterious no longer. The reality named Shiva, scrounging my Chesterfields and drinking my whisky, was a malodorous Benarsi guttersnipe with sickly ashen skin and blue rotted teeth. These adjectives are meaningless. The *jizo*, avatar of the all-compassionate Buddha, can appear in the form of a decaying angel. And this notion too merely conceals in transcendent adjectives the desire I felt for a boy who existed entirely at ease with his beauty, undiminished by sickness and poverty. I perceived him as if through superimposed lenses of completely different optical refraction, one which focussed on his sordidness, the other on his sublimity. I tried to recognize myself in his magnificent unself-consciousness, in the certainty he had shown tonight by directing himself straight to me, proof that he had acknowledged my watchfulness from the very start three days ago. 'How could you have seen me in the dark, Shiva, let alone recognized me? Do you have the eyes of an owl, my Bodhisattva Ksitigarbha?' I spoke to him in Japanese, and who knows that perhaps he did understand my ruinous skepticism, because he smiled.

Shiva took a marigold garland from his neck and placed it round mine. He showed me his night's poor takings, an entertainer's fee paid in chilli peppers, *pindi* riceballs in his brass pot, a frayed cotton shirt (probably the deceased's). I say 'poor', but for Shiva these funeral left-overs were small treasures. He bit half a riceball and offered me the rest. Now came the moment of my test. Was I really prepared to bathe in the Ganges? If so, I would accept the morsel of rice from Shiva's diseased mouth. He saw me hesitate – I opened my mouth quickly, and like a devout communicant received the eucharist from his fingers. We cele-brated my contamination with more whisky.

Shiva hopped nimbly onto the step from a sitting position, and with gymnast bravura arched backwards, his great peacock's tail of hair upside-down sweeping the pavement. He gripped his ankles and formed a serpent's perfect circle. His head, at this angle, looked decapitated, afloat on a wave of shimmering black blood, the face extraordinarily white and beautiful. I stepped up to him and passed my hand along the svelte oval drum of his belly, over the protuberant umbilicus, and slid under the waistband of his *dhoti* to the crêpe fern of hair and his tenoned ridge of penis.

He uncoiled with startling agility, swifter than the eye could follow, and like a pirouetting ballerina, he tendrilled himself round me. One leg pegged on tiptoe, the other embracing me tightly about the small of my back, Shiva filled my mouth with his tongue. Then, before my dazed wits could recover, he had snatched up his trophies and fled. I heard Shiva's laughter fast receding, like the passage of the night bird's cry up the storeyed bank of the ghat.

I clambered after him, trying to guess at the uniform intervals of the tiers as best I could in the dark, without causing myself an injury by a misstep. My progress appeared to me immeasurably slow, as in the restraining quagmire of a dream. I came to a pigeon-hole exit at the top that opened into an ill-lit web of alleyways. I saw him, waiting for me in a slice of light, just long enough to encourage my pursuit.

Down a pitch black corridor I went, on Shiva's trail, and I blundered into a row of wood stacked against a wall at my left. A window blinked into light, showing me the rickety strips of lumber from which the litters of the dead are made, scattered on the ground by my foot. The noise aroused a man's angry challenge from behind the lighted window. I hurried on, as other windows blazed and a medley of awakened protests brought the alley to life. I had time to think – 'this is the bier-makers' street' – as I observed Shiva ducking in through a gateway ahead.

Shiva awaited me on a colonnaded patio, open to the sky above, within an amply proportioned building. An oil lamp on the floor revealed him sitting at the bottom of what looked like a narrow pool, two steps at each end leading down to it, but drained of water. The empty pool and surrounding pavement of the arena had the pitted, scalloped and yellow glow of ancient marble.

Shiva had already made himself at home, seated naked on a rush mat in his shallow trench, propped up on one arm and cradling the upraised apex of his knee with the other. His black mantilla of hair spilled over his shoulders and back to the ground. This, I reckoned, was the vagabond boy's bedroom.

Calmly, eating his riceballs and chilli peppers, Shiva watched me undress and stow my clothes on the ledge of the pool. He hopped to his feet in a weight-lifter's low squatting position, and this way he took my penis into his mouth. He twisted his cape of hair into a ponytail and guided both my hands to clasp it tight by the end, bridling him by the moorings of his scalp, while his tongue corkscrewed wildly round my lizard. He sank his teeth into the sensitive nose of the glans. In a seizure of agony, I pulled frenziedly on his sheaf of hair. with blind urgency enough to uproot it, as he seemed to want me to do. His body went entirely limp, a deboned deadweight of jelly, that I held up by the hair, suspended clear off the mat from which his feet had withdrawn. He hung like this, without apparent discomfort, an equilibrist defying gravity on the resolute scales of my arms.

I eased him down to the floor. Shiva crouched there like the Sphinx, lapping his tongue against his lips with the rapid staccato trill of an emptying drain. He raised a forefinger to waggle my lizard's fallen head – dwindled to limpness after its bruising – coaxing from it what he desired. I released my urine, and he directed the gargoyle's cataract into his mouth.

After, he nibbled daintily on a red chilli pepper, to purge the taste of urine or perhaps add more savour to it. Innocently, it seemed, he began tugging at my lizard's collar, testing the prepuce's elasticity. *Bahut bara*, he said in Hindi, which I assumed to mean a compliment to the gradual heavenwards' assumption of my thing. Still he manipulated the ruff of skin, and I unsuspecting, did not guess why he clamped the butt-end of the chilli pepper between his teeth like a little red whistle. Shiva's eating hand was now freed – and deftly, with a circumciser's skill, he used the ragged blade of his thumbnail to cut round the neck of my penis, next rubbing the chilli pod into the incision.

The gymnast already grappled himself to me, before I could complain, and had intromitted anally. The slick molten unguent of his rectum did not assuage my scorching wound but inflamed it to an extreme which deadened the flesh and froze it to a novocained stump.

All the promise of sexual acrobacy briefly foreplayed at Manikarnika Ghat fulfilled itself on the patio of this unknown house. We re-enacted the thousand sacred delinquent erotic postures sculpted on the façade of the riverside Temple of Love. Do I imply an idealized passionate intercourse? Nothing like that. I duelled with a phantom, a Protean vapour, at times a boy of such malnourished skinniness that I feared his delicate bones would snap in my arms, and then he seemed not a boy but incredibly old, transfigured into the old woman starving herself to death in the House of Widows, her poignantly beautiful face pressed against mine, the taste of bitter *tulsa* leaf on her lips, the small black figs of her nipples erected obscenely to life on my chest, and then she evaporated, leaving a sensation of clammy scaliness as a metamorphosis into a Ganges crocodile took place, and I wrestled against the creature's saw-lengths of teeth, cold belly and swishing tail, its foul breath immersing me in the digestive tract of the Ganges, watery sepulchre vomiting up its spongy cadavers, ashes and cholera, and as its opaque current flooded over me I saw other faces and bodies mirrored, one by one in a succession of passing moments or hours or days, Yoko, Shizue, Natsuko among them, engaged in coitus with me – an endless, insane, cinematic tapeworm of apparitions in constant metamorphosis.

How long a time, I cannot say, but I saw the sky's forehead above us beginning to grey into dawn. I lay on my back, Shiva riding astride my hips, drowned in a pleasure of which I possessed no feeling – a pleasure I cannot describe, unless to call it sodomized consciousness, if that made any sense. The marble at my back leached its freezing lymph into me, turning me to stone. Shiva cantered relentlessly on my pelvis, buoying up and down on the shaft impaling him, his lips drawn back in a cat's snarl. His head seemed miles distant from me, as if banging against the night sky, and yet I could see clearly a hairline of blood along the necks of his clenched teeth, squeezing out from the corrupt gums.

Surrendering, at last, Shiva's torso drawbridged onto mine, his fore-head knocking my collar-bone in the sudden fall. An incontinent ooze spilled from his rectum on my belly and thighs. I extended a hand down to his buttocks and dipped my fingers in it, and looked. An issue of dark blood, flecked with pus and excretum. I poked two fingers through the spasmed purse of his anus and discovered a massive fistula, almost passage enough to admit a finger into the wound. 'The agony he must have suffered . . .', my last thought as I fell into exhausted sleep.

Only moments later, it seemed, someone was trying to wake me. A very irate Indian stood over me, prodding me with the handle of his broom. *Sha! sha!* he hissed, as one might to put a loitering dog to flight. I sat up. Another man, smoking a *bidi*, contemplated my situation from the patio level above me. My nudity greatly amused him. He stood beside a litter on which the naked corpse of an old man lay awkwardly sprawled – a recent death, by the look of it. Certain pieces of evidence led me suddenly to realize where I was – these two men with their *dhotis* hitched up, their buckets of water, the naked corpse, this pool with its outflow scuppers. Shiva had made our bedroom in one of those Benarsi hospices where old folk come to die, and this pool was the bath in which the dead were washed.

And where was Shiva? He had absconded, and with him – as a glance quickly confirmed – all my clothes, and my money. 'Beware of pariah dogs and thieves,' the warning of my elegant Indian at Manikarnika Ghat came back to me, too late. Shiva had allowed me a small charity, his own *dhoti* and the dead man's shirt he had earned last night, left in place of my clothes. I hastened to put these rags on, under the watchful scorn of the two hospice attendants. To them, I was one more case of the drug-crazed hippy tourist who will sleep anywhere, even in the bathhouse of the dead.

I fled. But where should I go, dressed like a barefoot pauper? Scales of dried blood veneered my midriff. I needed to wash. Manikarnika Ghat seemed the answer. I made my way there, an object of much curiosity among the dawn pilgrims thronging into the ghat.

I descended the steps to an area of the shore unfrequented by the bathers, a mudbank beyond the boat-moorings which afforded me some retreat from embarrassment. I had no choice but to enter the Ganges as I was, fully clothed. I sank to my ankles in the quaggy mud, and fearing what horrors I might encounter in it, I plunged at once into the icy water.

The bank sheered away precipitously, and as I now discovered to my alarm, I had no footing to counteract a current whose power surprised me. It pulled me swiftly out from the bank, further than I liked. I am a competent swimmer, but this current resisted my best efforts to regain the shore. Further and further out it dragged me, while I struggled to no purpose. I could see boatmen on shore pointing at me. I cried out to them for help, but no one moved to rescue me. Was it possible they could neither hear nor see me? How monstrously vast the Ganges looked to me, as I raced helplessly along, a puny, insignificant bit of human flotsam speeding seawards. I felt myself weakening, being sucked down by an invincible undertow. The water closed over my head, engulfing me in black.

I gagged on an intake of water and, convinced that I would drown, struck out desperately with my arms. My action knocked a cup from Dr Chatterjee's hand, a tin cup filled with water that he attempted to make me drink. 'Are you feeling yourself again, sir?' Spluttering, drenched by the water I had upset, I demanded to know what was happening.

'I'm afraid you blacked out some hours ago,' Dr Chatterjee replied.

I was sitting up on a pallet on the floor, dressed in the same *dhoti* and used shirt as I remembered from my adventures. 'You were sick,' Dr Chatterjee explained, indicating my suit, damp still from a washing down, suspended from a wire hanger on the wall. 'I hope you don't mind the change of clothes.'

'Whose are they – a leper's?'

Dr Chatterjee's head undulated, conveying equally yes and no.

Dawn, full and golden, flooded into the hut, an open-fronted one such as I had seen the night before, when I thought I had left the colony. A mood of disorientated aggressiveness troubled me, as often follows after an episode of lost consciousness. I felt angered by the simpler mystery of having been nowhere else but here during the entire time of my unconscious travels. 'You've put me next to a corpse,' I exclaimed, in my dissociated rage. And it was true. Behind me, against the back wall of the hut, lay the man's corpse bound from head to foot in a white shroud.

'Not to worry, sir,' Dr Chatterjee lit a *bidi*. 'He's ready for a trip down the river.'

'Is it Christian to dump him in the river?'

'Why Christian?'

'I saw you performing a requiem mass for him last night.'

'Did you?' Dr Chatterjee smiled. 'I am forbidden to say mass. Besides, a mass would not be allowed in his case, poor soul. A bad death, you see. That's why he goes into the river uncremated.'

'Ah – a leper?'

Dr Chatterjee went over to the body and uncovered its face. 'See for yourself how he chose to die.'

I rose weakly to my feet for a closer look at the deceased.

A seam of coagulated black jelly necklaced his throat, evidence of a deep gash from one side to the other. Flies immediately settled on the dried blood. And the smell – that sweet, evil, stifling, dizzying stink of the dead. 'When they told him he had leprosy, he despaired, and so – *chkk!*' Dr Chatterjee swept a thumbnail across his throat.

The suicide was a young man, hardly more than a boy, the bleached whiteness of his face corrupting to a stagnant shade of plum. His death agony had frozen to a hideous grin, exposing his teeth clenched in such maniacal fury that the pressure had squeezed a fine thread of blood out from the rims of his gums. Even in extreme disfigurement, even as rotting carrion, the delicate beauty of his features could still be recognized.

I sank down on my pallet. A black nausea threatened to drown my consciousness again. 'Shiva,' I said.

Dr Chatterjee glanced at me, the *bidi* dangling from his mouth, as he secured the flaps of cloth over the face with twines of bast. 'Do you call him Shiva?' he asked.

'I can't explain –' the words were ashes in my mouth. 'When did he commit suicide?'

'Three days ago.'

'The day I arrived in Benares?'

'Yes.'

I tried to count the times I had seen the dead boy in the past three days – was it four, five? What did the number matter? I had seen him. My eyes had not been deceived.

Dr Chatterjee and I stared at each other. Had he been aware of these manifestations of the dead? And my encounter tonight? Hallucinations. What else could they be? My obligingly explicatory guide was silent, a disquieting stillness in which he left me to decide what I understood. I remembered Dr Chatterjee's assertion, incredible at the time – 'the Aghori can transport his spirit anywhere he chooses'. I tried to form a picture of Dr Chatterjee's uncle seated on the boy's corpse this night, performing the Aghori rites of spirit possession.

The blood, I thought, *there must be signs of blood.* I raised up my cotton shirt, loosened the *dhoti*, and peered at myself. Except for the sweat of terror raining down my abdomen to my crotch, nothing, not a trace of blood. Not Yoko's. Not Shiva's.

'We washed you, after you were sick,' Dr Chatterjee said. A matter of fact remark well-timed to have the opposite effect than putting my mind at ease. I laughed.

Two men entered the hut, the pallbearers who would take Shiva's corpse to the river. The brothel keeper, Matrika, ran in after them, and with mad shrieks, flung herself on the litter to prevent them lifting it. 'Those are the mortal remains of her son – her only son, you understand,' Dr Chatterjee said. 'He committed suicide in her establishment three days ago, and she refused to let anyone take the body away. The *mahant* had to go there himself personally last night to fetch it, after Matrika had been persuaded to leave Dal Mandi.'

'When we saw him arrive by jeep, he had the body?'

Dr Chatterjee nodded.

The funeral cortège progressed slowly towards the river bank, impeded by episodes of Matrika's attempts at tug-of-war with the pall-bearers. Daylight made clear the symptoms of leprosy that had seemed inapparent to me last night. Both of the litter-carriers and others attending the procession had faces and limbs mutilated by the disease. Suicide impressed me as far preferable to a life like this.

We came at last to the shore below the flood wall. The body was placed in a narrow skiff fastened at the stern to a long tow rope. A crew of two lepers onboard manoeuvred the light craft into the stream with poles, while others on shore let it out on the rope. 'The current is very dangerous here,' Dr Chatterjee said. 'It is unwise to venture too far out.'

'I know.'

Matrika watched quietly as the boat retreated from the bank. It jerked to standstill, guyed by the rope some fifty feet offshore, and steadied by one of the lepers digging in his pole up to his forearms. The other crewman slid the body off the litter into the water, which sped away rapidly into the distance. Matrika, with heart-piercing shriek, tore herself away from the women restraining her and dashed towards the river. She slipped in the mud, fell, and lost a sandal in her haste to gain the river. In a moment, she stood waist deep in the water, her green sari floating round her like a lily pad. She fell again in the treacherous mud and sank under the current.

'Is no one going to stop her?' I exclaimed.

'No need for panic,' Dr Chatterjee stoically replied, lighting a fresh *bidi*. 'The boatmen will see to her on their way back.'

I made a move towards the river, but Dr Chatterjee held me by the arm. 'Don't trouble yourself, sir. Look –'

I saw Matrika, a Venus of patinated bronze, gasping and coughing, hauling herself out of the water by the tow rope. She stooped to pick up her sandal, brandishing it against those who offered to help her up the slope.

Matrika passed by me, wet to the skin as I had first seen her in Dr Chatterjee's courtyard, the revealed beauty of Kali and Jael, as she appeared to me then. She paused to glance at me. '*Chor,*' she said. 'Thief,' my guide confided in my ear. 'She says, thief.'

Part Three

THE SWORD
Treason

1   LETTER TO BARONESS OMIYEKE KEIKO: *APRIL*, 1952.

LEMON TREES are in flower. Goethe's celebrated lemon blossoms, which to him meant Italy, have welcomed me painfully to Greece. I learned for the first time, to my surprise, because it pricked me, that the lemon tree has thorns. I wanted to sample the perfume, and now I have a slightly infected finger. My poor weak constitution – how unpoetic!

Easter season bells echo in a metallic blue sky. A curious tinniness in the sound of these bells of Byzantine type reminds me of those in our own Buddhist temples back home.

I write at a café near the Acropolis, a dish of octopus on the table, a bottle of Metaxa brandy to drink, which does not affect my weak head for alcohol because it is already whirling in a spiritual brain fever. Athens is a disappointingly provincial Balkan town, but there is the Acropolis over my head, and all those ruins, evidence of a spiritually superior bygone age, and again I think I am home, in misty view of Mount Fuji, proof of a legendary age of heroes that seems at once both far away and near. I have a sense in Athens that Europe ends here, and the East begins just over there, which is also right here at my table.

I have spent several mornings in the museums of Athens and Piraeus, empty except for me in these lemon-scented April holidays. The visiting hours are erratic, to say the least, and have given me difficulties. I came back regularly to the Athens National Museum to look at a series of marble sculptures of long-haired, smiling youths. I am told these smiling young men of stone from remote antiquity are called *kouroi*, archaic statues from the 6th century BC, just before the dawn of the classical era. The *kouroi* seem to me like phantoms imprisoned in sleep, their arms rigidly glued to their sides like sentries on duty, cocooned in the inelastic stillness of Egypt. In the next century, these *kouroi* lads would suddenly awaken to the most wonderfully mobile, athletic poses that herald the era of Greek classicism. The enlightenment of their bodies, freed and made anatomically perfect, had somehow deprived the *kouroi* of their enigmatic smile in which all their mysterious, phantom life had previously resided, dormant but potent, to be replaced instead by heads with blank, expressionless faces that typify classical purity. I compared these *kouroi*, animated by a smile but otherwise frozen, with the neighbouring classical athletes, animated in body but with idealized faces of ice – and gradually I realized the truth. The smile had been relocated, it had spread throughout the anatomical flexures of the classical figure as a whole, and had left the face totally indifferent. I remembered a sonnet by Rainer Maria Rilke in which he had expressed a feeling like mine. In his poem, Rilke contemplates an archaic *kouros* torso of Apollo: its head is missing, and yet, 'in the gentle turning of the thighs, a smile keeps passing and returning towards that centre where the seeds converge'. The archaic smile, glowing like a lyric chandelier, vanishes from the head and reappears in the greater enigma of virility.

I can hear you saying, 'Ah, that's Yukio Mishima, the Nipponese Johann Joachim Winckelmann, in complete Graecophiliac homoerotic flight of fantasy!' My homoeroticism, for once, is quite innocent of the idea that forced itself on me. I saw the Orient in those *kouroi* cocoons, the East dawning into heroes, metaphysical, hyper-real, but at the service of a *real* history.

I sit at my post-historical café table in Athens, writing this, and you think me mad. Worse than unbalanced, you think me a sad case of degenerate pathology. A decadent, yes, I am, but I can see a metaphysical Oriental cure for it. There is a copy of André Gide's essay on Dostoyevsky at my side, in which he quotes a letter by Dostoyevsky. It has set my mind on fire.

> To be happy, must one be impersonal? Does salvation lie in self-effacement? Far from it, I should say. Not only must there be no self-effacement, but one must become a personality, even in a degree beyond what is possible in the West. Be clear as to my meaning: voluntary sacrifice, offered conspicuously and without constraint, sacrifice of the individual for the good of mankind, is, to my mind, the mark of personality in its noblest and highest development, of perfect self-control ... the absolute expression of the will. A strongly developed personality, conscious of its right to be such, having cast out fear, cannot use itself, cannot be used, except in sacrifice for others, that these may become, like unto itself, self-determining and happy personalities. It is Nature's law, and mankind tends to reach it.

Dostoyevsky was an Oriental, resolutely anti-Western in his heart. His love of humanity is explained by the deep reverence he felt for his Emperor, the Tsar, the vertical term of self-transcendence. Dostoyevsky earned his simplicity of unrequited love for his Tsar through great hardship, in Siberia, with ten-pound chains on his ankles. Dostoyevsky's penitent reverence is surely no more inscrutable than Japanese Emperor worship.

My problem concerns a love denied by 'no one knows who'. I am a fictionist mirrored in a fictive land. I seek vainly in fiction for what is obdurately fact. My contention is this. What does the Oriental emperor-worshipper, Dostoyevsky, mean by 'personality', by its 'voluntary sacrifice for mankind' which surpasses anything Western?

The objects of my shamanist contemplation are the Mirror, the Jewel and the Sword, which will in the end bring my enlightenment.

I understand the Imperial insignia of Mirror, Jewel and Sword as the aboriginal archetypes of religion, aesthetics and ethics. Religion, aesthetics and ethics are the recognizable triune properties of culture. My question is whether these properties of culture today are vitally alive or morbidly in decay. This much I think is reasonably obvious. Less than obvious however is to acknowledge that these same triune properties pertain to the Imperial Triple Emblem of Mirror, Jewel and Sword. Nothing is more opaque to Western observers of Japanese culture than our mysterious Triple Emblem. And I too have posed myself the same conundrum. Does the contradiction of the Mirror (religion) and the Jewel (art) resolve itself dialectically in the Sword – in ethics?

The answer for me is found in the unitive identity of ethics and the Sword.

I arrive at ethics not by bloodless abstraction, but by way of the heart's longing. Ethics demands more than Stoic fortitude or quiescent self-sacrifice to obligation. The concept 'ethics' has become repulsively dull to moderns, the byword of unimaginative conformism and repressed emotion. How very hard it is to understand that a culture unmasks its morbid decay in the debasement of ethics to complacent serviceability. It exposes ungenerosity. More, it reveals total impossibility of love in conditions of decay.

Ethics presupposes unrequited love. Herein is the identity of ethics and the Sword resolved, in romantic idealism. It is impossible for pragmatists in a decayed culture to understand this too! Unrequited love strives after the irreproachable ideal in which the equation of passion is dialectically resolved. Love must be elevated to a Third Term, a synthesis of deep feeling and action. We Japanese have developed a special traditional concept of *ren'ai*, romantic love, based on national faith. This concept of love, which makes no distinction between sexuality and devotion to one's ruler, was called 'falling in love with the Imperial family' (*renketsu no jo*) at the end of the Tokugawa period and laid the emotional ground for Emperor worship.

Ethics is at heart anarchic. This is evident in the presupposition of unrequited love. Love always imperils. Passionate, disorderly idealist love risks being a punishable infraction of convention. This would seem particularly so in rigidly conventional Japan. Japanese are said born into a lifelong system of indebtedness, a regulative code of obligation known as *on*. Conduct is endlessly subject to unrepayable debts of honour owed to one's parents, superiors and colleagues – and highest of all in the hierarchy, beyond all quittance – to the Emperor. An infraction of obligation brings inexpiable shame which in certain cases demands apology by suicide from the transgressor. Ours is a culture of shame; the Occident instead, one of sin. Westerners are privileged to expiate sin by repentance. Evil is therefore a temporary and reparable condition. Japan's obligatory system of *on* is permanent, it knows only the antithetical terms honour and dishonour which do not leave the Western option of a penitent 'change of heart'. Our two cultures thereby rest upon totally and mutually exclusive conditions of social being.

Two inhibiting obstacles must therefore be cut down in oneself to make way for a living cultural sense of ethics. One is the shame of unrequited love; the other is fear of transgression. One must love culture greatly to possess it. In this maddest, most unrelenting struggle to gain possession of the beloved, one must be prepared to love beyond one's means.

Idealist anarchic love is the Japanese option of a 'change of heart'. Intuition of the Void alone can rid one of obligation, the heart's unerring impulse to action, just as neo-Confucianist *Yomeigaku* enlightenment teaches. My belief in unrequited anarchic love is not the product of Mishima's uniquely eccentric notion but is conventionally Japanese. Traditionally in Japan, love is viewed with sympathetic compassion as a misfortune. It is also judged a misfortune in the West, but with cold-hearted cynicism. Our advantage is to dread anarchic love as the awesome possibility of tragedy, an idealist sacrifice of self which there is no doubt enhances the self to larger than life. Dostoyevsky's comment on this paradox of self-fulfilment seems to me perfectly accurate.

2 AT THE BACK OF THE MIRROR

WHAT POSSESSED me to write a letter exposing my innermost spiritual longings to such a person as the former Baroness Omiyeke Keiko? I deeply regretted my foolishness when, on my return to Japan in mid-May of 1952, I re-read the letter. It has always been my habit to make copies of my more important letters. Nothing I write is ever entirely personal and 'off the record'.

My indiscreet epistle to the beautiful courtesan Keiko was the culminating irritant, the acme of all the ill humour and frustration I felt at being back home in Shibuya. I looked in the mirror and saw the back of my head – as in the well-known painting by the surrealist René Magritte, a poor joke. But it was no joke to me. My five months' absence from Japan, my simpleton's world tour, had been with few exceptions a trail of debacles and fiascos. Nothing much of my pride could be salvaged from it, aside from the brief satisfaction of Greece and a delightful affair in Brazil with the son of some wealthy first generation Japanese coffee plantation owners. I had expected to feel so crushed by loneliness. Not that, strictly, I was homesick. The pain of loneliness that I experienced had to do with being confronted by my definitive incompetence for living. I knew before I set sail from Yokohama harbour on Christmas eve, 1951, that my physical weakness was not a traveller's asset and that I would suffer trials and stresses. I imagined myself able by discipline of mind to conquer these hardships and discomforts. Like all those who are deskbound cripples, I believed myself possessed of a strong-willed imagination, without realizing how much the power itself of that imagination depended on physical limitation. Away from my desk, I wasn't only disabled and ineffectual, I was no one. The loneliness that inhabited me, literally *was* me.

Looking into the mirror and finding the back of one's head – this poor joke – seemed an impairment afflicting the entire nation in 1952. My return, after a disillusioning period of truancy, gave me the unpleasant sensation of stepping back into tepid, dirty bath water, but it made me see things with surrealist clarity.

I did not believe what commonsensical folk maintained, that Japan had 'temporarily gone off its head' in the first week of May. What had happened? On the eve of the Emperor's birthday, 28 April 1952, the Occupation had officially ended. Several days later riots broke out in Tokyo on the annual May Day celebration. What had driven a peace-loving people to such unseemly behaviour? Sympathizers and critics of the riots alike agreed on the cause: the Occupation was over, but it wasn't over. American troops, UN personnel on leave from Korea, US air bases and training camps were still as much in evidence throughout Japan as before the Treaty of 28th April. The unrealistic expectation had been that all signs of the Occupation would melt away overnight. That was the simple diagnosis of the anti-American riots. But I didn't believe it.

I returned too late in May to witness the street-fighting. One might almost have welcomed the madness as an overdue return to a pre-war, anarchic Japan and its spontaneous *ikki* uprisings. In my state of anger, even I, a sickly intellectual unfit for action, longed to hear the refreshingly medieval sound of breaking bones. But I had no faith either in my nostalgia for the *ikki* chaos of the past.

I devoured the past issues of newspapers which had reported and photographed the events. My appetite for the pornography of violence was, strangely enough, fulfilled less by these pictures and articles than by the inadequacy of the journalists' analyses. With indrawn breath and throat dry, I scanned the papers to discover if anyone had guessed the truth that only I knew. No one had. Even the leading editorials and magazine features did not rise above conventional pieties. Communist-inspired students and the Left generally were blamed for the worst clashes with the police. I knew that ultra-rightwing provocateurs behind the scenes and on the street had orchestrated these confrontations. The liberal press apparently lamented the shame that misguided radicals had brought upon democratic Japan, 'an international loss of face' after all these hard years of struggle to rehabilitate itself in the eyes of the world. But, between the lines, any reader might easily construe a dissatisfaction with the aliens who went on occupying our territory. The days were not far off when this early forewarning grumble would turn into an avalanche of stories detailing every misdemeanour by a foreign ser-viceman, spicy accounts of Black GI rapists, incessant portrayals of American bases as neighbourhood cesspits of degeneracy. Nor indeed was the day far off when Vice-President Nixon would make his famous 'black is white' speech at an official banquet in Tokyo, declaring that the inclusion of Article 9 in the Peace Constitution, which strictly forbade the rearmament of Japan, had been a mistake, thereby openly condoning the unconstitutional existence of our 'Self Defence' armed forces. I had already forecast something guaranteed (non-political being although I am), that a pattern was set for the next decade in which leftwing and anti-communist conservative elements would battle over the issues of Japan's constitutional neutrality, enshrined in Article 9, with absolute, hideously corrupt, two-faced hypocrisy.

This still wasn't the point. Anyone could have arrived at the same conclusion that I had. It would take another year before the 'Bikini Atoll' scandal erupted, when the accidental fallout from an American H-bomb test poisoned the crew of a fishing vessel and caused the widespread panic that all our fish had become dangerously radioactive. Then, of course, it should have become crystal clear – at this very zenith of hysterical anti-Americanism – that the real toxic and terminal pollution had already occurred in the seven years' Occupation since Year Zero. Other deadlier elements than the unassimilable ones of uranium and plutonium had invaded our spiritual bloodstream. In short, we had fallen in love with our Occupier. His withdrawal, quite the contrary of being resented as too gradual, had been felt as too sudden, and it produced a vacuum of disappointed fury like a tight-grappled vagina prematurely evacuated.

This is what I saw. A nation looking at the back of its own head, because there was nothing else to see in the mirror, nothing but a vacuum in front of it, when it desired nothing other than to find the face of its rapist again, the familiar deadweight of his penetration grown desperately pleasurable. The vacuum had to be filled by something, and it was, by loneliness in which I recognized myself. I had encountered the loneliness abroad – and I could only have come to see it for what it is, outside of Japan.

My avid leafings through all that newsprint brought me face to face with another means to fill the vacuum. I chanced upon an item in a commercial supplement publicizing the inauguration of a new lingerie manufactory in Osaka, the 'Heavenly Body' Ladies' specialists in brassi-ères, girdles and corsets. A photograph showed a number of the celebrant dignitaries at the Heavenly Body's grand opening, but, most eye-catching, a black-capped Shinto priest blessing a commemorative Zen-style boulder raised on a plinth in the ultra-modern lobby of the factory. 'What's this?' I exclaimed, amazed by the caption's description of the stone. A company slogan inscribed on the plinth read, 'My Bra Forever'. The caption also startled me by indentifying one of the guests as Madame Omiyeke Keiko, representative of the Conservative Member of the Diet, Ito Kazushige, political racketeer and financier of this and many other post-war industrial reconstruction projects. Keiko – to whom I had foolishly confessed myself – Keiko, the protege and hostess of that rogue, the former Count Ito Kazushige. And here she was, Ito's stand-in at a brassière manufacturer's travesty of the Shinto rites. What did I expect? No sooner had the Occupation ban on Shintoism relaxed, than it was payrolled in this shamefully absurd way. 'This is the last straw!' I shouted, with such vehemence that my mother feared I'd lost my mind.

But it wasn't yet the last straw. Soon after, and totally out of the blue, a complimentary ticket to the Shimbashi theatre arrived by post. I was cordially invited to a gala performance at the Shimbashi. And my mystery host? None other than former Colonel Tsuji Masanobu, whose interrogation I had attended five years ago as Sam Lazar's translator in the cellars of G-2 Section HQ. Tsuji presented his invitation on Diet notepaper, since in fact he had recently been elected to the lower chamber of our national assembly.

The past, they say, is another country. I felt marooned in that non-existent country. I had the grotesque impression of seeing my rival's corpse, Dazai Osamu, risen like a putrescent sponge from the bottom of the Sumidagawa canal to grin at me. I had hoped that my interval abroad would succeed to cut, or at least, erode the links of collabor-ationist intrigue that Lazar had forged during his regime and which bound me still to unidentified twilight forces. I hoped that these links had been temporary ones conditioned by the Occupation, and that with the change and speed of events after the Occupation, new forces of loyalty would emerge to replace the murkier liaisons of the past.

These were the lonely, wishful notions of a person forever condemned to exile in the past – a loneliness that I shared with all my countrymen. 'It is time I paid Baroness Omiyeke a courtesy call,' I decided, and this would be my first step towards freeing myself from the past.

My moon goddess, the beautiful hetaera of political corruption, had just moved into a new suburban house near Koganei Park by the Itsukaichi highway, built for her by her protector, Count Ito Kazushige.

It was a warm, humid May afternoon, and we sat in the garden drinking chilled martinis. Drops of an earlier rain shone on the leaves of pampas grass and ilex trees, powdered white with the dust of recent construction. Keiko wore a pale green willow-patterned kimono of China crêpe, and as she fanned the column of her neck, a Chanel-perfumed breeze reached me.

I began, unwisely, by expressing my distaste for the photograph I had seen. 'Abusing our sacred rituals to immortalize a brassière, well, what can I say? It seems typical of the ugliness of our times.'

'Why are you getting so worked up over a trifle?' Keiko replied. 'Is it any more absurd than the wild romanticism you expressed in your letter to me?'

'Obviously I cannot trust you to keep my confidences secret.'

'And I, instead, did not expect that your first greeting after five months would be an insult.'

She fanned herself and awaited my apology; but I gave none.

'Have you received an invitation to attend the Shimbashi Theatre?' Keiko at last inquired.

'A ticket arrived yesterday, and it comes most unexpectedly from ex-Colonel Tsuji Masanobu. Why on earth does he want to see me after all these years?'

'You will accept, of course?'

'No. I shall decline, though I cannot imagine doing so without appearing rude.'

'You would be ill-advised to offend Tsuji-*san*. He enjoys considerable power at the moment, as you must have heard, since his election to the Diet.'

'I will take that risk.'

'One that you cannot afford. Dietman Tsuji's influence will guarantee your advancement. It would be criminally irresponsible to reject that opportunity now. This is what you've been working so hard for all these past eight years, Kochan.'

'How do you know for certain what he offers me?'

'In matters of this kind, you should know well enough to trust me unquestioningly, *sensei*.' She employed the title 'master' with a playfully mocking air of superiority.

'Please be sincere, and tell me who has really brewed this idea in Tsuji's mind. Not your benefactor, Count Ito, I hope?'

'You must give up the undemocratic habit of calling him "Count". Ito-*san* is a respected property developer. I cannot see why you feel so ill-disposed towards him.'

'In these past four years of our acquaintanceship, you will no doubt have remarked that I avoided meeting Count Ito even once. I am proud of my achievement, because I know what sort of "property development" your Ito-*san* has been engaged in – a person notorious for vile blackmailing practices.'

Keiko laughed; but she fanned herself more vehemently. The heat of anger, barely under check, showed in her eyes and mine. 'A person who has served the purposes of Captain Lazar and G-2 Section,' she began, her voice maliciously lowered as though to conceal a secret from eavesdroppers hidden in the garden, 'a person whose espionage activities for G-2 Section equipped him with financial information that can only have blackmailing value – can such a person be a fair judge of morals?'

'Such information as I do possess was never intended for blackmail, but rather as my insurance against being blackmailed.'

Keiko's indiscretion was deliberate and not a misjudged slip. She made it plain that others in her entourage knew of my 'financial blueprint' culled from the Ministry records of 1948. I was not disturbed to learn of this, on the contrary, since I wanted her to know exactly what benefit I expected from my possession of illicit data.

'Is this the reason why newly elected Dietman Tsuji wants to meet me? Count Ito put him up to this, hasn't he?'

'I think, Kochan, you overrate the value of the information Captain Lazar granted you. Can you not imagine how many other ambitious young civil servants in those days were like you, equally or even better informed? Dietman Tsuji does not seek a meeting with them, however, but with you.'

'And why does he, according to you?'

Keiko shut her fan and scoldingly tapped my forearm with it. 'You try my patience, *sensei*. Your publisher advertises an edition of your collected works for next year. How many other authors aged twenty-seven can you name who enjoy such an unprecedented honour?'

'Very flattering, *ma chère Baronesse*. However, Dietman Tsuji's interest in my success is precisely what causes me anxiety. I consider myself a person spiritually dead, my inner world is a frightful wasteland, but I wish to accomplish my destiny in my own way, alone, without obligations to anyone.'

'You dream of making your way individually, a lone woodcutter cleaving a solitary path through *this* forest?' She laughed; but then her lips froze into bitter lines. 'My late husband, Naval Air Commander Omiyeke Takuma, left me a great many service decorations. Not all of those medals put together could have bought me a single riceball for breakfast after the war.'

'Nor a Dior outfit.'

'Quite,' she smiled acidly, and her fan snapped open again in a peacock tail fanfare.

'I appreciate the point you're making, of course. But you don't sufficiently appreciate the true nature of my fears. I do not care to become a literary *ronin*, a pen-for-hire appropriated by rightwing entrepreneurs like Count Ito or Tsuji, no more than I care to be a tame creature of the leftwing cliques. I am and wish to remain apolitical. As the poet Dante said, an artist is a party unto himself.'

'Dietman Tsuji is above such vulgarity. He does not require a literary hireling.'

'Let me make myself perfectly clear. I am determined to break with the ghosts of the past, once and for all. I recognize no obligations to the petty scoundrels either of the right or left.'

'And do you place me too in the category of the past?' Keiko looked at me with melancholy presentiment.

'I value your friendship, dear lady, but I sense a coercion in your advice which is motivated by Count Ito's own shady ambitions, and if this is true, I am tempted to see you no more.'

'Does it matter what quarter my advice comes from, if it is sound? Is any area of life today perfectly clean and wholesome?'

'No, nothing is wholesome, that's true, but as they say, between two evils I choose neither. I must begin to practise some form of personal hygiene. Everything is so like quicksand. With the end of Shogun MacArthur's reign, did my serfdom to Sam Lazar and G-2 Section also come to an end? Don't you think, Madame Omiyeke, that Sam, the Eisenhower man, had a role in General MacArthur's disgrace? Sam's promotion to lieutenant-colonel, immediately on President Truman's dismissal of MacArthur, and his transfer to Indochina as special advisor to the French colonial forces, looks very suspicious to me. What if he did have a hand in it? The result was the one we all desired – goodbye Generalissimo MacArthur. But, but.'

'This is absurd, Kochan. Do you think Lazar over in Indochina is still pulling your strings?'

'My strings, as you rightly call them, are in a tangle, a web of many strands that every force unknown to me can pull, unless I cut them all.'

'Am I included in these paranoiac forces? Before you decide against me, please do me this last favour – and for yourself too – of meeting Dietman Tsuji, at least to indulge your curiosity.'

My agreement left a strange lack of impression on my mind.

3   AGAIN, THE SUMIDAGAWA

AND SO, on an afternoon in late May 1952, I found myself watching the classic 15th century play, *Sumidagawa*, at the Shimbashi Theatre, which by coincidence also happens to be located on the Tokyo river, the Sumidagawa. A first-rate Osaka puppet company was performing Ze-ami's drama of a madwoman in search of her dead son. The spot-lit, smaller than life-size figures of the madwoman and boatman are animated by shadows behind them, by the discreet silhouettes of humans who are in reality their manipulators, the Bunraku puppet masters. Seen, yet unseen, these puppeteers are like the masked and black enveloped shades of Kendo fencers whose expert wizardry of action eludes the eye. In their skilful hands, the lifeless mechanism of dolls transmits an infinity of grace that is inaccessible even to the greatest actors. Perfect grace of movement is achieved by mechanical extension, as though human beings require a prosthesis to claim the perfection they lack.

Watching these inanimate beings endowed with a mechanically extended life-force gave me cause to reflect on my own existence. I was aware of a similar mechanical extension in my life, the shadowy interference of manipulators in my actions. The strangest form of mechanical extension in one's life is coincidence, a predestined rendezvous with events that assumes an uncontrolled but recognizable perfection. Why was I here, in the Shimbashi Theatre on the Sumidagawa watching a play called Sumidagawa? Coincidence.

On our way out of the theatre to the riverside garden at the intermission, ex-Colonel Tsuji commented on the excellence of the Osaka puppet company. 'A poet might succumb to the domination of a marionette,' I replied, 'for a marionette has only imagination.'

'Curious notion,' Colonel Tsuji remarked doubtfully.

'Not mine – a quotation from Rilke's essay on dolls.'

He grunted.

Colonel – or rather, Dietman – Tsuji Masanobu – I could not get used to his new title, and I constantly slipped back to his former rank – was very elegantly clothed. Did I expect to see him dressed as I had last time at G-2 Section HQ, in the robes of a Nichiren monk, like a *waki* spirit-wrestler in Noh theatre? I felt like a fleshless coat-hanger inside my suit, with its lapels narrowly styled in the new fashion of the early 1950s.

We found a little table in the garden promenade of the Shimbashi Theatre overlooking the Sumidagawa. Azalea and camelia blossoms had already begun to decay in the summery heat. The afternoon was fine and clear, its warmth moderated by a light river breeze.

I admired the ladies' sumptuous kimonos and an ostentatious sprinkling of the latest Dior costumes. Rationing appeared a thing of the past here. Fabrics had become more opulent and brighter as the memories of the war inversely faded. Dietman Tsuji's liveried chauffeur, a young man with the jolly open mien of a country lad, presently brought us a bottle of Imperial brut, Moët Chandon champagne of pre-war vintage, a service complete with bucket of ice and glasses on a silver tray. I could not resist an observation on the turn our fortunes had taken. 'Isn't it strange that since our last encounter, Colonel Tsuji-*san*, we have both become best-selling authors?'

Tsuji bowed curtly. 'My worthless memoirs, that by chance rather than any talent seem to interest the public, cannot be said to merit the success that your writing truly deserves.'

'Such praise from a person far worthier than I, renowned for deeds rather than mere words, honours me beyond measure.'

Tsuji obviously, and to my relief, did not wish to talk of the past. I sipped my champagne from the fluted crystal. Tsuji removed his eyeglasses and wiped his perspiring eyelids with a monogrammed pocket handkerchief. He stared up at the cobalt blue sky, as the moment wore on into embarrassing silence. I studied Tsuji's classical warrior's features, a sturdy compact figure, square face with jawlines flaring prominently towards elfin ears, stamped in the mould of his Ural Altaic ancestors, those Siberian horse-breeders and shamans who invaded our islands in pre-historic times.

'What are you doing these days, Mishima-*san*?' he brusquely inquired, as though returning from his memories of that subterranean interrogation room at G-2 Section far in the past.

'These days I am enrolled in a course in Greek at Tokyo University.'

'You have taken your trip to Greece very seriously.'

'I was greatly impressed by that spiritually virile culture.'

'No, pardon me, I meant what direction do you consider following, now that your success is certain?'

'The fact is, I prepared myself a long time for success, without recognizing that it would bring me the one thing I was not prepared for.'

'And what is that?'

'Unhappiness.'

Tsuji faintly smiled. My reply had offended him. Tsuji was a man of decidedly contradictory temperament. His rare flashes of humour indicated an extreme of anger ready to spill into violence; and appearance of anger, which would darken his already dark complexion, meant instead that he was indulging in a bizarre sort of amusement.

I glanced at the waters of the Sumidagawa. 'I remember Tokyo's rivers not so long ago in which the corpses of those killed in air raids drifted by like mere flotsam. Factories had ceased production, and the rivers became ominously cleansed, reflecting a perfect blue sky that is seen at the moment of death. Now the rivers are stagnant again, reoccupied by barge traffic and garbage instead of corpses.'

'I was in Burma at the time,' Tsuji replied, 'and therefore prevented from witnessing the restoration of cleanliness that you speak of, Mishima-*san*.'

'The polluted water of the Sumidagawa is the symbol of our renewed prosperity.'

'Prosperity is the very thing His Majesty has willed for us all.'

'Then I am doing my duty by prospering.'

We drank several more glasses of champagne in silence. The chauffeur soon arrived with a fresh bottle. Our rendezvous had led to a grim, hostile impasse, and I felt rather pleased with myself.

A considerable number of geishas paraded in this delightfully sunlit garden. I fixed my eyes, glutinous with overmuch champagne and springtime longings, on a pair of exceptionally pretty geishas, superbly outfitted, scented and powdered, with diminutive feet impeccably clad in custom-made *tabi*. I enjoyed their coquettish glances; I basked in the idea of my prosperity that might now allow me to patronize one of these expensive dolls. They smoked imported gold-tipped cigarettes as they leaned elegantly against the riverbank balustrade and gazed across the water. My two geishas were looking furtively at the opposite bank on which stood the former Imperial Japanese Naval Hospital, now made over into an American military hospital for the casualties of the Korean war. I realized that the girls' surreptitious glances, their shrill affected exclamations and malicious smiles were intended for the maimed young soldiers in wheelchairs under the cherry trees on the other shore. These lads were silent, without heart for the cheerful American wolf whistles that such exquisite creatures would normally have attracted.

My pair of geishas gloated viciously. I overheard one of them coldly remarking, 'Well, they're finally going home.' 'Not too soon,' the other added, 'and look in what shape!'

Tsuji listened to these two disagreeably chattering parakeets, his head bowed, smiling in maniacal fury. He would gladly have put both of them to the sword. It was not possible for him to rejoice in the discomfiture of those young soldiers, even though they represented a former enemy. The geishas's mockery stirred unpleasant memories of defeat in him.

I pointed out to Tsuji that one of the geishas' carnelian *obi* clasps alone would cost an ordinary worker a month's wages. 'So it would, alas,' Tsuji replied. 'A recovery of wealth always seems preceded by the barbarism of conspicuous waste.'

His comment brought me back to the grey times of the 1930s, the shaved heads, government-issue eyeglasses and the Thought Police. This was authentically Colonel Tsuji, the fanatic morals instructor from another era, the zealous puritan celebrated for an act that occurred one night in 1939 when he personally and single-handedly burnt down forty Shanghai brothels which he considered were sapping the morale of his troops. This same man, anchored in samurai rectitude, had condoned the bayoneting of children in the 1937 rape of Nanking.

Tsuji offered me a cork-tipped English cigarette from his case.

'No thank you, I'm addicted to my Chesterfields.'

'If you will permit me a casual observation, Mishima-*san*, does it not seem to you that your success and talents might lead to a new direction in your career? You should at least consider that possibility.'

'Please make your suggestion, Colonel Tsuji. I am perfectly content to listen to you. However, I must be entirely frank with you. I confess that our meeting would not have occurred without Baroness Omiyeke's insistence, and I suspect that the lady was coached to persuade me by Count Ito, a person whom I regard with deep-felt misgivings.'

'Baroness, Count, Colonel – you cling to the old titles no longer credited these days, Mishima-*san*. I am not a colonel now, but a civilian member of the Diet in the service of a constitutional monarch.'

'Democracy is all the fashion, but perhaps I have a nostalgia for the way things were.'

'Democracy is the way things are, Mishima-*san*, and it affords us exceptional opportunities. Have you never thought of a political career? Your credentials for that option are absolutely perfect, a graduate of the Peers' School and Tokyo University, a lawyer by training with experience of the civil service, added to which, a writer of considerable popularity. You enjoy the advantage of beginning in politics already well known.'

'I am a non-political man, Dietman Tsuji, with an instinctive mistrust of democratic advancement. I remember a passage in *Mein Kampf* – a book my father forced on me in my teens, against my inclinations, although I ended up liking it – in which Hitler says: "Sooner will a camel pass through a needle's eye than a great man be discovered by an election. In world history, the man who really rises above the norm of the broad average usually announces himself personally."'

'A schoolboy should not have been permitted to read *Mein Kampf*,' Dietman Tsuji stated.

'I read a good many forbidden authors at the Peers' School – Hitler, Karl Marx, Kita Ikki, Otto Weininger. Our reading was never supervised.'

'Discipline at the Peers' School was intolerably lax. I remember the scandal in 1936 when it was discovered that princes of the Imperial blood were attending Marxist study seminars at the school.'

'Yes, I certainly remember that episode,' I laughed. 'War Minister Araki's allegations of "Red Princes at the Peers' School" were deliciously absurd.'

'But not quite so funny at the time.'

I shrugged. 'Dietman Tsuji, you haven't yet dispelled my anxieties concerning Count – pardon me, Ito-*san*'s participation as grey eminence in all of this.'

'I am not too well acquainted with Ito-*san*. He served briefly under my command in Malaya. His involvement, or I should rather say, his flirtation with the mutineers of February '36 earned him the punishment of frontline duty, an undeserved honour it seems to me, because he was fortunate in being a protégé of Prince Konoe. He acquitted himself bravely enough, however, and was severely wounded as we broke through the Gurkhas' defences at the Jitra line on the road to Singapore. After his convalescence, he was again accepted into Prince Konoe's political circle. I had no further dealings with Ito-*san* until last year, when he volunteered to fund raise for my election campaign.'

'Do you trust him?'

Tsuji hesitated. 'Men like Ito-*san* who made immense fortunes after the war are seldom reliable. My election to the Lower House would not have succeeded without the votes of ex-servicemen. I can rely on them with total confidence, but the truth is, I am in the vanguard of former army officers who are beginning to enlist as politicians. I am hopeful of persuading many other ex-officers to do so, once they can overcome their ingrained suspicions of politics, finance and civilians in general. We are embarking on a mission to rearm and reconstruct the nation's armed forces, despite the formidable obstacle of Article 9 of our Peace Constitution which makes that goal illegal, and we cannot possibly succeed in this without the aid of powerful civilians who are sympathetic to the army's rehabilitation.'

'Democrats like Ito-*san*, in short.'

Dietman Tsuji grunted his assent.

'I see. And you are also looking ahead to create a civilian school of younger generation politicians dedicated to the encouragement of military aims. Am I right?'

'Precisely,' Tsuji warmly concurred. His face blushed darkly as the second bottle of champagne took effect. Neither Tsuji nor I had much head for alcohol, and I began to feel my high spirits running dangerously out of control.

Tsuji's eyes sparkled with optimist fervour as he asked: 'I believe your family's registered place of residence is still in a country district outside Tokyo, is that so?'

'Yes, our official *honseki* is Shikata in the Kansai area. Why do you ask?'

'Because election to the Diet is virtually effortless from a rural base. You see, Mishima-*san*, several factors from the past have combined to gain us favourable access to the rural mandate – the ex-servicemen's majority vote, our association with populist Nichiren Buddhism and our armed neutralist brand of nationalism. In a year or two, we could groom you as a candidate guaranteed a safe rural seat.'

'This is all very interesting and flattering and perhaps even tempting, Dietman Tsuji-*san*, but I repeat what I said before. I am uninterested in politics.'

'Even if it is in a good and honourable cause?'

'Even if it is. I am personally set on a dishonourable course. Literature, the "metier of mendacity" as my father once described it, the avocation of subhuman decadents that he forbade me to embrace – I cannot tell you of the persecutions he inflicted on me in his efforts to brainwash me against literature – literature is my chosen and dishonourable profession for which I may be admired but never respected.'

'We were all educated like that, Mishima-*san*.'

'Fortunately, the Occupation has given us a practical new teaching – that a peaceful cultivation of the chrysanthemum is preferable to the Way of the Sword.'

'What a cynical young man you are.'

'Yes, perhaps cynical. Or perhaps enlightened by the difficult art of survival which has proven all too easy. What should I do, Dietman Tsuji-*san*? Should I offer prayers to the spirits illegally revered at the Atami shrine, to General Tojo and the five others hanged as war criminals? Should I thank them for a defeat which has yielded prosperity from its fertile uterus?'

'It is not unusual for men of the younger generation to blame their unhappiness on the older. This has often been a powerful motive in Japanese history. Does not the ancient Book of Changes, the *I Ching*, name this principle *gekokujo*, the overturning of seniors on top by juniors below?'

'I cannot forget certain words broadcast at noon, on 15 August 1945, by the Jewel Voice – those wonderfully discreet, noncommittal words of Surrender. "The war situation has developed not necessarily to Japan's advantage." Today, we need only change the last word to "disadvantage".'

'In your haste to sound disrespectfully clever, you overlook something, Mishima-*san*: two words that the Jewel Voice never pronounced – defeat and surrender.'

'I am aware of the irony that exists in the absence of those two words. The irony is that *we* exist, the survivors who should not have survived.'

I sailed close to an impertinent reprimand. My reckless comment had virtually accused Tsuji of failing to commit suicide, as the code of Bushido properly required to expiate defeat.

Rather than with the anger I expected for my cheekiness, Tsuji answered with a radiant smile. 'Should one have died, Mishima-*san*? I considered it, naturally, but felt a greater duty being imposed on me by His Majesty's edict of survival. I remembered the prophecy of our formidable teacher, Lieutenant-General Ishiwara Kanji.'

'You still believe in his Nichirenist concept of *saishusen*, the final war, the universal holocaust that will begin in 1960?'

'I believe it has already started.'

'Surely, you can't believe in Ishiwara-*san*'s "rural purification" of Japan, a nation committed to industrial expansion? This is not Mao Tse-tung's peasant China.'

'Old school nationalists like Ishiwara-*san* and myself can recognize Chairman Mao for the deep-dyed Confucianist that he truly is, and for that reason of ethics, truly dangerous. A race war, under the shadowy menace of the A-bomb, will inevitably occur on apparent ideological lines. Mao knows this; and Nichiren foresaw it seven hundred years ago.'

'Nichiren was termed *ikko* in his day, a single-minded fanatic, a narrowly nationalist simplifier of Buddhism who reduced all doctrine to a mere recitation of the Lotus Truth slogan, *namu myo ho renge kyo*. Can you see me, Dietman Tsuji-*san*, intoning this formula as I proceed on my way to the Lower House of the Diet? Perhaps I should accompany myself on the drum, as Nichiren and his followers did –' I snatched up the silver tray on the table and began to beat out the Nichirenist rhythm with my knuckles, *dondon dondoko dondon*. My performance attracted the stares of bewildered onlookers, the pair of geishas, the spectators filing back to the theatre as the intermission ended. Alcohol had gained the better of my commonsense; my anger, my frustration spilled out in disgraceful exhibitionism.

Tsuji remained perfectly calm. With blank equanimity, he replied to my tirade. 'Nichiren portrayed himself as the lowliest of sinful creatures transfigured by the Lotus Truth. "The body is nothing but a common human body, sharing beastlike life, nothing but a combination of the two fluids, pink and white, the products of flesh and fish. Therein the soul finds its abode, something like the moon reflected in a muddy pool, like gold wrapped up in a dirty bag."'

the moon reflected in a muddy pool . . .

The Shimbashi garden promenade had entirely emptied. Everyone had gone, except for Tsuji and me, and hovering uncertainly and alarmed behind a cedar tree, Tsuji's chauffeur.

'I would like to show you something, Dietman Tsuji.'

'What is it?'

'I don't have it with me, but it is a horoscope of His Majesty, the Showa Emperor.'

'I am not a believer in astrology.'

'Astrology is an exact science far too ahead of its time to require our belief. If you were able to read the heavens' map, I could show you the position that the revolutionary planet Uranus occupies in the Emperor's birth sign and its exact connection to the sinister planet Pluto. These two represent nothing less than the catastrophic elements, uranium and plutonium, and we know what can be manufactured from them – a bomb "brighter than a 1000 suns" to eclipse a Sun God. Japan's defeat by the A-bomb was written into the Emperor's own destiny.'

'What madness are you talking?'

'I cannot follow you back into a past, Dietman Tsuji, in which you see Japan's future salvation naively foreshadowed. Nor is it your goal of armed neutrality, though it contravenes the laws of the Peace Constitution, that especially worries me. Armed or unarmed neutrality, it's all the same. My generation's neutrality really signifies that our capacity for *any* faith is neutralized. I agree with Ishiwara-*san*'s prognosis of nuclear holocaust. I also believe that the atom bomb is a phenomenon entirely consistent with Japanese aesthetics, natural to us, in the same way that our culture seems natural. I have often reflected on the utmost, natural simplicity of the utensils employed in Shinto rites. A three-legged stool, a peach branch pared down to a stick on which strips of *mino* paper are fastened as sacred pendants. So precious little will bring us into the presence of the sacred. A shrine is no more than a perfect empty cube of night resonant with mosquitoes, the glint of a mirror, and a priest on his knees. One's attention is most forcefully drawn to the naturalness of the means used by Shinto. A place is designated sacred merely by roping off a certain tree. So too with the empty space of a sanctuary, or a pared stick, or some bits of paper. But if one withdraws a little from the enchanted spell cast by these means, what does one note? It is paper of a certain type cut in a certain way; it is rope of a certain hempen kind tied in a certain way; it is a gesture prescribed in a certain way. One is greatly mistaken to think these means closest to nature. On the contrary, they are closest to *human* nature, the ultimate form of artificiality.

'Japanese culture has constantly misled us into the impasse of our own ignorance. Japan's closeness to nature is a marvel of miscomprehension. What precisely is it we feel in contemplating the raked pebbles of a Zen garden, the shabby utensils of a tea ceremony, the harshness of Noh? The experience is one of total remoteness from nature, which speaks of our loneliness in being so far removed from it. Our aesthetic terminology is uniquely remarkable for its single-minded insistence on what is forlorn, fragile, evanescent. On the sadness of things. It is an avowal of the unreality of being human, something which truly calls for compassion.

'I restate an aesthetic truism long familiar to Western thinkers. Why is it that a piece of marble contrived by someone's hand to look like Venus can never again be seen as stone, even if it is mutilated? Stone literally has become semblance, itself disappears, and instead Venus is recognized in its place. The craftsman can be said to have defaced nature. So also, our most sophisticated machines, including the atom bomb, are contrivances no different than a rough-cast ceramic cup used in the tea ceremony. Unnatural though it may appear, A-bomb technology is but another aesthetic means to convey us hence from this fragile, evanescent and dying world. Who can say in his heart, without doubt, without uncertainty, that the nuclear bomb is mistaken? The human spirit is too great – and too artificial – to preclude its own annihilation, no matter how dreadful this seems. A ceramic cup too is a dreadful thing, like the A-bomb, if considered in its de-natured naturalness.'

Tsuji stood up and bowed.

'I apologize for my unforgivable rudeness, Dietman Tsuji-*san*. My thoughts are not commendable, but they are sincere.'

'I accept your apology, Mishima-*san*. But a day will come when you will regret your own eloquent and unnatural words.'

I left the Sumidagawa that day without regret. And, in the mistaken belief that I was really a freedman, alone but beyond the reach of the obligations of history, unhappy and yet independent, I sat down to write a story. '*The Patriot*' was the story I composed from the knowledge I possessed of Count Ito Kazushige's youthful involvement in the events of 26 February 1936, the *niniroku* mutiny. I sent copies of the manuscript to Dietman Tsuji, to my estranged friend Madame Omiyeke Keiko and another to Ito Kazushige himself. With this story, which follows, I signalled my retreat into unassailable freedom.

4 THE PATRIOT

UNDERSTAND THAT I, Ito Kazushige, was a simple lieutenant in the 7th Company, 3rd Regiment of the Imperial Guards, appointed by the advisor to the Throne, Prince Konoe Fumimaro, to participate in the conspiracy of 26 February 1936. Understand also that mine are Prince Konoe's family and kinsfolk, allied since the 11th century by landholdings in the Shimadzu domains of southern Kyushu. Obligation to a superior, to clan and blood ties compelled me to do what I did. There is more. Prince Konoe's father and my father, Count Ito Shige-masa, were both closely associated with the foundation of the Black Dragon Society in 1901. This elite secret society from the first nurtured pan-Asian ambitions were deeply hostile to Russia, and it encouraged a 'Strike North' attitude, in other words, a strategy of war with our rival Tsarist Empire. In conspiring for this end, the society defied the Imperial Throne itself, and was therefore assumed a natural ally of the Strike North (*Kodo-ha*) that steadily gained powerful adherents in the army command. And this too was another reason why Prince Konoe and his General Staff cabal picked me to infiltrate the circle of *niniroku* mutineers.

Prince Konoe had a third and other good reason to recruit me in his counter-insurgency action. One of the rebel chiefs, Captain Nonaka Shiro, a commander of the 3rd Infantry Regiment of the 1st Division, had been an acquaintance of mine at the old Ichigaya Military Academy. I remember a late night drinking session with Nonaka and some of our former classmates at a geisha house in mid-August 1935. Often, in the past, such meetings would end in bitter complaints about the new breed of military technologists from the War College who enjoyed preferential career advancement over our Military Academy traditionalists. Nonaka and his dissident Academicians raged impotently against the 1927 Volunteers' Act. 'It's criminal. Anyone these days with a secondary school education can bypass the Academy and get himself an officer's commission.'

'Of course, they are welcome at the War College. This is what our modernist reformers call professionalization of the army. Economic planning and technology are more important to them than samurai virtue.'

'It must stop!' Nonaka came to the point. 'These reforms are strengthening our opponents in the *Tosei-ha*★ faction.'

The villain they most blamed for these anti-traditionalist reforms was Major-General Nagata Tetsuzan, Chief of the Bureau of Military Affairs, an Imperial appointee, in charge of reorganizing the top echelons of the army by restaffing them with War College graduates. But on that night, shortly after 12 August 1935, our meeting was a festive one. We had come to celebrate the assassination of Major-General Nagata, put to death by the sword of Lieutenant-Colonel Aizawa Saburo.

'A masterstroke long overdue,' Nonaka said, toasting the event. 'Aizawa's court martial will be a showcase trial, just as he planned. He will air all our grievances in public.'

Of course, this public airing never took place – but, no, I don't want to anticipate events before they happened.

★ The 'Control School' rival of the *Kodo-ha* ('Imperial Way School') favoured the Strike South policy – expansion in China and the South East Asian colonies of the Western Empires.

One other guest dignified Nonaka's geisha-house celebration this night, a noble person of the Imperial household itself, Prince Chichibu, the Emperor's younger brother, who had served with Nonaka's 3rd Regiment from 1922 to 1935. I recall Prince Chichibu's warm words of sympathy for Nonaka and the Strike North's aims of war with Bolshevik Russia. 'My friends, your ideals are not displeasing to me, and I am able to go further and advise you that others close to the centre look with favour on you. Indeed, I feel gladdened enough tonight to disclose that His Majesty's own uncle, Prince Higashikuni, is such a one.'

Later on, when Prince Chichibu had left and our evening's robust carousel drew to an end, Captain Nonaka spoke to me privately of his doubts. He looked to me like a man amused on hearing his own death sentence pronounced. 'Intimacy with these exalted members of the Imperial family makes me feel lightheaded about the dangers we run. I know, I should be wary of insincerity even at the highest level, but I am convinced that the August One himself will soon recognize the justice of our cause.'

I reported these gleanings of loose talk from the Imperial circle to Prince Konoe. My ears served with many others in a conscripted army of informers. How can I explain the bizarre nature of the situation? Captain Nonaka and the others, although duped and misled by flattery, were perfectly conscious that spies were reporting all their activities back to Prince Kanin, the Chief of Staff, in charge of bringing their insurrection to nothing. Their plans for top level assassinations were already communicated in detailed police reports to Marquis Kido, Secretary to the Lord Privy Seal, who entered them in his diary at least three months before the mutiny – a list of victims that the palace chamberlains got to know almost by heart before 26 February 1936. How can I explain – a suffocating atmosphere of intrigue, a fictitious air impossible to breath, an implausible comic opera plot – and the plotters themselves now desperate to act, because their regiment and the entire 1st Division had been scheduled for imminent transfer to Manchuria.

Prince Konoe impressed on me the urgency to make contact with the Strike North ideologist, Kita Ikki. My attempts to cajole Nonaka into arranging an introduction to Kita had so far been resisted, and the deadline of the February mutiny approached. 'Do you realize what it means?' Nonaka said. 'You aren't up to your neck in this affair, but if you meet Kita Ikki, that's it, there's no turning back. You can't change your mind.'

On the night of February 24th, I was taken blindfolded to meet Kita Ikki at his headquarters in some outer suburb of Tokyo. A farcical precaution, since my guide was Captain Ando Teruzo who posed as a *niniroku* ringleader, but was in fact an undercover agent of Major-General Yamashita Tomoyuki, directed by the Palace to infiltrate the Strike

North movement. The moment my blindfold was removed, Kita Ikki greeted me with a crafty smile. 'Ah, Prince Konoe's spy,' he said, and at once two young non-commissioned officers reached for their pistols. 'Put your guns away,' Kita laughed. 'I knew this young man's father in the Black Dragon Society, a dependable radical who helped finance Sun Yat-sen's revolution. Like me, Lieutenant Ito's father detests the *zaibatsu* scoundrels who have done all they can to undermine the Chinese republic.'

I recognized Kita Ikki's powerfully intellectual face, the aggressive chin, thick eyebrows and wide saturnine lips under a droopy Chinese-style moustache. His gold-rimmed spectacles sat on an ill-matched pair of conch-shell ears and a pugilist's nose. The dandyishly parted hair, stiff wing collar and tie gave him the air of a Bolshevik conspirator in a Western diplomat's three-piece suit. Kita Ikki had served with Sun Yat-sen's revolutionaries who toppled the Manchu dynasty in 1911. Kita's ideology was a curiously ultra-Japanist confection of pan-Asianism, Leninist Marxism and National Socialism.

At this moment, Captain Nonaka arrived with a draft copy of the rebels' manifesto that they wished to present to the Emperor in two days' time. Kita read it over several times with barely restrained amusement. I remember, he sat at a desk with a radio transmitter, and right beside it, a Mauser pistol, a souvenir of the Shanghai uprising. Over the next days, he would use that radio to transmit instructions and encouragement to the rebel headquarters in Nagatacho, and the pistol was always there at his side, not for self-defence but suicide. Kita never doubted for a moment that the outcome of the insurrection would be failure and death.

It was oppressively tropical in Kita's den. A coal-fed pillar stove maintained a constant high temperature that he seemed to love. A subaltern poured us glasses of strong Russian tea from a samovar on the stove. As for Kita himself, he drank steadily from a stoneware jar, Dutch gin I believe it was. He hadn't yet invited any of us to sit down or remove our coats. Kita's spell in China had made him a radical with decidedly mandarin views of courtesy. Captain Nonaka stood in a pool of melted snow, like the rest of us, sweltering in his greatcoat. We waited in suspense and considerable embarrassment while Kita perused the draft manifesto. At last, he addressed Captain Nonaka. 'This is barrack-room prose, Captain. An expression of blunt, honest sentiments, as behooves good soldiers, but hardly the proper thing for His Majesty's ears.'

'We have come to beg respectfully for your help, Kita-*san*, in polishing our crude efforts.'

'It is less a matter of polishing than of orthopaedic surgery.' Kita now turned to me. 'What are the Lieutenant's views on the manifesto? Surely, as an apprentice of Prince Konoe, he must have some advice for us on bridging the distance between the good intentions of our junior officers and the Celestial Throne?'

Everyone was looking at me. And I looked away, at three framed pictures on the wall over Kita's desk, the first, a photograph of Lenin at the foundation of the Third Communist International, dated 1919, and signed by Zinoviev; at the centre, a photograph of the Meiji Emperor in Western military costume (I could see a likeness that Kita shared with the old mustachioed Meiji Emperor); and lastly, Ernst Roehm, the former Sturmabteilung chieftain, murdered two years ago in Hitler's Blood Purge of 1934.

I knew that Kita recognized me as a spy, and that my life depended here and now on the correctness of my answer. The sincerity of my reply did not concern Kita, who was in fact using me to reprimand Captain Nonaka for his naively careless recruitment of wayward individuals like Captain Ando and myself.

'It seems to me,' I said, 'that the young officers of this movement are neither fascists nor conscious leftists, nor even in the strictest sense partisans committed to the *kodo-ha* (Strike North) faction of the army. They are not interested in conquest or external policy, but in domestic reform. I believe they are pledged to a restoration of the Showa Emperor⋆ as the only direct means of achieving a renewal of the nation. We are living in the harsh times of a world-wide economic depression. The agony of Japan's countryside is something that our young officers know at first hand. Peasants supply the army's core of recruits, and especially excellent ones come from the North, the poorest and most depressed of all our stricken areas. Junior officers at platoon level are all too familiar with the afflications reported by the rank-and-file. Starvation at home is frequently, but only temporarily, averted by the sale of a daughter to white-slave merchants who scour the rural areas on behalf of city teahouses and brothels. Officers of this breed, exasperated by corrupt Dietmen and their *zaibatsu* financiers, feel driven to save the nation by involving themselves in a revolutionary programme of Showa Restoration. However, as we all know, politics of any sort has been strictly forbidden to all regimental officers under pain of court martial by an old but still enforceable Meiji Imperial Rescript. And so, these young officers are flirting dangerously with treason.

'For a moment, in 1932, salvation appeared possible in Manchuria. The pioneer utopia of Manchukuo was seen by many as a practical means to solve Japan's problem of over-population and rural pauperism. Rebellious officers of the Kwantung Army vowed that *zaibatsu* giants like Mitsui and Mitsubishi would never be permitted to exploit the

---

⋆ Reference is never made to the Emperor's name (Hirohito) but to the title of his reign, in Hirohito's case, Showa.

Manchukuo colony in China: it must be kept quarantined, a model of national socialism that would later serve the Showa Restoration in Japan. These idealist promises will come to nothing, since new *zaibatsu* monopolies like Nissan are likely to be promoted by the army Chiefs of Staff when the war in China continues.

'So, what's to be done? There seems no alternative left to us but the risk of mutiny. Everyone knows what happened only last month. An entire company of infantry crossed the Manchukuo border into Russia and surrendered to the Red Army. Never before have Japanese soldiers defected to an enemy power. Their message was clear. The nation cannot afford any more adventures in military expansionism.'

My account was virtually the catechism of a discontented minority of junior officers, and everyone present nodded in agreement. Everyone except Kita Ikki: 'Any repudiation of further military expansionism in Asia, no matter how sincere, will contradict His Majesty's own desires.'

'His Majesty's thoughts are beyond anyone's ken.'

'Come now, Lieutenant, do you pretend ignorance of an Imperial menu that includes China as the hors-d'oeuvre and the decadent colonies of South East Asia as the next main course? Surely you must know something of Prince Konoe's own appetite for this proposed banquet?'

'I am far too junior to know anything of such plans.'

Kita laughed. I could see he was drunk, but under it, a terrifying sobriety kept him lucid. 'I notice that you are looking at my photograph of the SA leader, Ernst Roehm,' he said. 'Look at it, all of you, and consider our own fate. The sympathy that our rebellious young officers feel for the oppressed peasants and workers naturally inclines them to the extreme left of nationalism, a position of socialist radicalism and militarist activism not unlike that occupied by Roehm's SA Brownshirts within the Nazi Party. A hopelessly avantgarde position in which the Brownshirts found themselves marginalized, just as our young zealots are now likely to discover. We too as utopians will find ourselves outmanoeuvred by the same sort of level-headed conservative forces congenial to Hitler's real purposes, by the élite majority faction of the German army and big business tycoons like Krupp, and in our own case by the Strike South faction and the *zaibatsu* manipulators. The purge that befell Roehm's SA Brownshirts on the Night of the Long Knives two years ago is what we too can expect. Isn't it perfectly clear? Hitler's purge of the domestic reformers within his own party is a preparation for war. I leave you to imagine what our destruction signals.'

Captain Nonaka understood only enough of Kita's analysis to pout, but not enough to contradict the master ideologist. Nonaka's dishevelled idealism was not of the type even fractionally conscious of the 'socialist' element that Kita attributed to it, and that was probably brought to Nonaka's attention for the first time.

'Go wait in the next room,' Kita waved us all out. 'I'll compose a manifesto such as you need, the truth for deaf ears.'

'The truth in these circumstances?' I dared remark.

Kita smiled wearily. 'The truth is always best told when it is certain not to be heard.'

'Are you convinced the insurrection must fail?'

'Entirely,' Kita briskly replied. 'But if you are asking me, is this a moment when I think it might succeed, the answer is yes.'

In the early hours before dawn of February 26th, I witnessed the rebel units securing their main objectives with ease, speed and precision. Within half an hour, the main buildings of Nagatacho district had been occupied by the columns of the 1st and 3rd Infantry Regiments from the Azabu barracks and my own comrades from the 7th Company of Imperial Guards stationed within the Palace itself. Rebel pickets surrounded the Imperial Diet, the General Staff offices, Metropolitan police headquarters and other ministries neighbouring the western wall of the Palace. We had effectively paralyzed the nerve centre of the Imperial capital.

Now then, as Prince Konoe's spy or not, I was, in Nonaka's warning phrase, 'up to my neck' in the mutiny. Assassinations were next on the mutineers' agenda. Do I have any blood of the old conservatives on my hands? I have that peculiar distinction, yes, as I will now tell.

Shortly before 5 a.m., I reported to Captain Nonaka at the rebel field headquarters in the Sanno Hotel. Captain Nonaka said, 'Our regimental commander shot himself when we disobeyed his orders not to leave the Azabu barracks. And Colonel Ishiwara Kanji, that *Tosei-ha* loyalist, has escaped from General Staff offices by shooting his way out.'

'Not a very propitious beginning,' Captain Ando Teruzo said.

'It couldn't be helped.'

I was detailed to Captain Ando's assassination unit which had been assigned to kill the Grand Chamberlain, Admiral Baron Suzuki Kantaro. A policeman on duty at the gate of Baron Suzuki's home delayed us in a skirmish until he fell wounded. We forced an elderly maid at gunpoint to lead us to the Grand Chamberlain. Captain Ando and I found him sitting up in bed with his wife. 'What is the meaning of this outrageous violence?' The old Chamberlain was frightened, but he maintained remarkable composure.

'We have come to shoot you, Excellency,' Ando replied.

'Can you at least give me some reasonable explanation why, before I am put to death?'

'Where were you last night, Grand Chamberlain?' Ando roughly inquired.

'Why, at the residence of US Ambassador Grew, isn't that so wife? We were shown a new film of the musical, *Naughty Marietta*, with Jeanette MacDonald and Nelson Eddy.'

'Yes, it was very entertaining,' the Baroness confirmed.

'A frivolous evening,' Grand Chamberlain Suzuki said, 'but hardly reason to murder me.'

To my amazement, Captain Ando sat down by the Grand Chamberlain's bedside and began discussing the aims of the *niniroku* movement with him. Their exchange of views went on interminably. I glanced at my watch, 5:30 a.m. and our mission was already running 15 minutes late. At one point, the Baroness turned to her maid, trembling in a corner of the room, and said, 'Don't just stand there, woman. Go fetch some tea for the Grand Chamberlain and his guests.' Ando would no doubt have permitted this additional folly, had I not intervened. 'She'll raise the alarm, Captain, if you don't stop her.' Presently, Baron Suzuki complained of a certain discomfort. His wife interpreted this more literally: 'Please allow the Grand Chamberlain to visit the toilet.'

'I'm sorry, I can't permit His Excellency to leave the bed,' Ando replied. 'Don't feel embarrassed, sir, it's only the fear.'

'At my age, it is more likely my bladder,' the Grand Chamberlain answered.

I could stand no more. I drew my revolver. 'Are you going to shoot this cunning old devil,' I said, 'or shall I?'

'What do you say to that, Grand Chamberlain?' Ando equivocated.

'I think that Prince Konoe has chosen an impetuous young man for his emissary,' Baron Suzuki replied, looking at me. 'Oh yes, I recognize you, Lieutenant. As a true Ito, I am sure you cherish higher political ambitions than are represented by this foolish enterprise.'

'I have no particular higher ambitions for the moment, except one.'

'Don't be so hasty. Understanding the motives of the rebels does not necessarily mean compliance with them.'

'Understanding our motives won't be of any help to you in the next world.' I aimed my gun at Baron Suzuki and felt absolutely confident of pulling the trigger in the next seconds. Ando now stood over Baron Suzuki with his own revolver unholstered and pointed down at him. 'What should I do, Excellency?'

'Do? Why, you must shoot me, of course. But aim at that embarrassing part of me which will not cause too serious an injury.' And with that, the Grand Chamberlain turned his back on the muzzle of Ando's gun. Ando fired three times – the noise startled the Baroness. I could see the bedclothes jumping each time, and the powder burns suddenly blossoming on the counterpane over the Grand Chamberlain's hindquarters. 'Ah, it hurts more than I imagined,' he groaned, and then fainted. Ando winked at me and reholstered his gun. 'Our job's done,' he said. I walked up to Baron Suzuki's body and felt his throat for a pulse. 'He's still alive,' I said. 'Finish him off with your sword.' Ando drew his sword most reluctantly, and the Baroness, with admirable sang-froid, held out her hand: 'If you think that's necessary, give me the sword. I shall do it.' Ando cursed us both under his breath and put away his sword. 'That's enough. Let's go.'

Outside the house, Ando informed me that he was not reporting to Sanno Hotel headquarters. 'Where are you going?' I asked. He pointed with his jaw, 'A restaurant over there, the Koraku. I'm going to hole up for a while, till they come to arrest me.' 'What shall I tell Nonaka?' 'The truth, if you like, or some rather less depressing version of it.' As he walked off, I felt very tempted to shoot him in the back of the head.

The only conservative blood I saw that morning came from a villain's backside. Other designated targets were not so fortunate, Finance Minister Takahashi Korekiyo, Lord Privy Seal Viscount Saito Makoto and Inspector General of Military Training, Watanabe Jotaro, were all savagely cut down. Prime Minister Okada Keisuke survived because his assassins mistakenly shot his brother-in-law, Colonel Matsuo Denzo, in his place; while outside Tokyo, Count Makino and Prince Saionji were fortunate to escape with their lives.

I knew nothing of these assassinations until later, when they were reported at Sanno Hotel HQ. I imagined a series of farces like the one I had witnessed in the Grand Chamberlain's bedroom. When finally these executions of high officials had been confirmed, I felt puzzled. How could this be? If the intended victims were already known to the Court chamberlains – almost by heart – why did the mutineers catch them out by surprise? Nothing puzzling at all, I realized. The victims had been lulled into a false sense of security by repeated assurances that the rebels would be neutralized before any harm could seriously threaten them. The pre-emptive arrests of other would-be assassins in past conspiracies of this kind had already demonstrated the effectiveness of the Imperial authorities. The truth must be that on this occasion, a real mutiny with real victims had been considered necessary – more real amount of blood than could flow from an elderly Grand Chamberlain's buttocks. But considered necessary by whom?

I noticed a peculiar atmosphere of disorientation when I visited the Imperial Palace with Prince Konoe on the morning of February 27th. All along the corridor leading to the Emperor's study in the Imperial Library, the chamberlains' cubicles were open and a disorderly mass of aides-de-camp, elderly Cabinet ministers, Generals and Imperial Household courtiers, all puffy-eyed and jaundiced after a sleepless night, bustled around or sat drinking tea on open stretches of floor-matting, the majority of them detained here under virtual protective custody. Not one of them seemed to know what was happening. I overheard Privy Seal Secretary, Marquis Kido, in conversation with Baron Harada, secretary of *genro* Prince Saionji, saying, 'His Majesty has requested a family council of *shinno** rank princes this evening. Prince Chichibu cannot possibly refuse.' To which, gossipy old Harada, added, 'Ah, but rumours say the rebels mean to kidnap Prince Chichibu when he arrives at Ueno Station.' Meanwhile, I could marvel at Imperial Household Minister Yuasa Kurahei's discussion of the Emperor's golf handicap when His Majesty played against Edward, Prince of Wales, in 1921.

A hush fell on this assembly of babblers, as His Majesty emerged from his study with Prince Konoe, Chief Aide-de-Camp Honjo Shigeru and the Strike North General Araki Sadao. His Majesty appeared in the same army uniform he had first worn on the morning of February 26th, somewhat rumpled now, and he spoke quietly but distinctly. The intonation of the Jewel Voice heard in actual proximity is unforgettable – like a *koto* with a missing string. 'I will not hear anything more on the rebels' psychological motivation, General Araki,' His Majesty said. 'They have murdered my right-hand elder vassals. I simply cannot accept that these vile insurrectionists as yet survive unpunished.'

Chief Aide-de-Camp Honjo replied, 'Sire, the rebels are cordoned off, safely quarantined and unable to infect others with the germ of their madness.'

'Do not speak to me of a *cordon sanitaire* when these loathsome traitors have posted sentries at the very walls of our inviolable residence.'

General Araki, grey with anxiety, nevertheless had the courage to speak plainly. 'Sire, although a violent suppression of these misguided lads would seem the exemplary thing to do, I fear deeply for the morale of Your Highness' troops. The spirit of this mutiny must be allowed quietly to bleed itself to death.'

'Oh, must it, General Araki? And how shall I, *Chin*, placate the unquiet spirits of my vassals who have already bled to death?'

Prince Konoe met my eye with an indecipherable smile of cheerfulness as I bowed down to the Imperial Presence. 'Who is this?' The August One inquired.

'My agent at the rebel HQ, sire.' Gaunt, camel-like, with his little Himmler moustache, the Prince remained impeccably dapper in spite of sleeplessness.

'Ah, very good. See that he does not fail.'

When the Imperial cortège had passed, Prince Konoe steered me away by the arm out of the courtiers' eavesdropping range. 'His Majesty wants to take command of the Imperial Guards and crush the insurgents personally.'

'All appearances to the contrary,' I said, 'it would seem His Majesty is enjoying himself greatly.'

'There is reason to believe so,' Prince Konoe chuckled. 'His Majesty

---

* Princes of the highest rank, including the Emperor's three brothers.

has now taken to signing his communiqués Heavenly One rather than Supreme Sovereign.'

'The army has adopted a policy of inaction towards the mutiny, which can only benefit the Heavenly One, wouldn't you say?'

'No doubt of it, kinsman. His Majesty reaps the advantage with every passing hour, without having to overplay his hand. He can demand immediate action, knowing that the General Staff will not risk bloodshed, and thereby cause maximum embarrassment to his Strike North critics within the army. My chief fear at present is that I might be appointed War Minister when this comedy is over and the purges begin. Under no circumstances do I wish to preside over the humiliation of the army. My elder kinsman, Prince Saionji, will not forgive me for the rebels' attempt on his life, and he will certainly revenge himself by advising His Majesty to offer me that appointment.'

'What will you do, Excellency?'

'Plead illness, what else? You must know what a person of delicate constitution I am.'

'I would say, of gravely endangered health.'

'Prince Chichibu is expected to comply with his duty to the *shinno*-rank tonight,' Prince Konoe added. 'He will compose a note to his friend, Captain Nonaka, requesting him to surrender with his troops. Please see that you deliver this note personally to Captain Nonaka tomorrow morning.'

A most unpleasant duty that I foresaw could result in Captain Nonaka ordering my summary execution. I was instructed by Vice-Chief of Staff Sugiyama Hajime to tarry in my delivery of Prince Chichibu's note till noon, when the Martial Law Headquarters would decide or not to proceed with their attack on the rebels.

It had stopped snowing on the 28th, but when I arrived at Captain Nonaka's headquarters, flurries of roneographed leaflets urging surrender snowed down on the rebel precincts from low-flying aircraft. Advertising balloons overhead carried similar messages, expressing the grief of wives and children and promises of forgiveness to the rank-and-file. Loudspeakers on trucks and radios blared out continuously day and night: 'Surrender or be destroyed.'

Captain Nonaka did not appear particularly surprised to see me. He read Prince Chichibu's note, and said, 'And what if I'm not prepared to surrender?'

'You know the loyalist reputation of the Martial Law Chief of Staff, Colonel Ishiwara Kanji. He judges you traitors in the simplest of fundamental religious terms – you are soldiers of the Throne in armed rebellion against the Throne.'

'He must know our allegiance to the Throne is entirely selfless.'

'He knows no such thing. Colonel Ishiwara-*san* has ordered the Ist

Division, the Konoe Guards and bomber squads to stand by for attack.'

'Our own comrades? No, that's impossible. I believe that those scoundrels in the Palace have kept His Majesty in the dark about the true nature of our protest. Kita Ikki transmitted a prophetic message from his wife last night, a clairvoyant of infallible occult power, who dreamt that the Heavenly One will listen to us in the end, if only we resist the evil counsellors who surround him.'

'Kita's wife is mistaken, and Kita fears for his life if you surrender now. You should know that the Heavenly One will assume command of the Konoe Guards in person when the attack commences.'

'How do you know that?' Captain Nonaka's will power visibly collapsed, as though I had boned him like a chicken.

'I heard it from the Heavenly One's own lips yesterday when I attended Prince Konoe at the Palace.'

'Will you relay a message from me to Prince Chichibu?'

'His Majesty will not permit any communication from you to the Imperial Prince.'

'My message is very simple. We, the officers of *niniroku*, beg His Majesty's permission to commit *seppuku* as a pledge of our absolute fidelity to the Heavenly Throne.'

'I will strive to convey your request to Vice-Chief of Staff Sugiyama.'

That very afternoon, Major General Yamashita himself went to the barricades to discuss *seppuku* terms with Nonaka's junior officers – in vain. His Majesty categorically refused to acknowledge the rebel officers' *seppuku* offer by denying them the presence of an Imperial witness, as they requested. Vice-Chief of Staff Sugiyama pleaded for an hour unsuccessfully with the Emperor, even going so far as to impede His Majesty's exit by lying down on the threshold and asking the Heavenly One to trample on him.

I witnessed the outcome of this farce, transfigured at last into a closing scene of tragedy, when the rebel troops had begun meekly to surrender at 10 a.m. on the 29th. Shortly before noon, I arrived at the Sanno Hotel with a party of Imperial Guards officers to arrest Captain Nonaka. 'Gentlemen, give me a moment,' he said. He drew his sword about halfway from its scabbard and tried to snap the blade at its weakest point, but it refused to break despite his best efforts. 'Do you see? Its will is greater than mine,' and saying this, Captain Nonaka unholstered his revolver and shot himself in the mouth.'

I conveyed the news of this suicide to my kinsman, Prince Konoe. I could not restrain myself from expressing sadness. Prince Konoe was unimpressed. 'It has ended satisfactorily, as must be.'

'I cannot understand His Majesty's denial of the officers' wish to die loyally by *seppuku*.'

'Lieutenant, you stray in Alice's wonderland, desiring fictions in place of realities. Acknowledgement of *seppuku* would have legitimized the officers' cause and given them the posthumous status of heroes.'

'I realize that, certainly. But, no, I am saddened by the Emperor's denial of a compassion that has always been the minimum prerogative of noble failure. I have heard it said that His Majesty is at bottom a modernist who disapproves of the *seppuku* tradition, and for him, spiritless technology takes precedence over the heart.'

'Are you inquiring into His Majesty's heart on the *niniroku* officers' behalf, or your own, kinsman Ito? What do you want me to confirm? That our Divine Sovereign is indeed heartless, but also a convinced traditionalist only too aware of the transgressive potential of *seppuku*? Is that why you inquire?'

'That is precisely why, Excellency.'

'Beware the seductive illness of heroism, Lieutenant, which can delude one into treason.'

I had one last unpleasant duty to face in the aftermath of the *niniroku* affair. Martial Law Chief of Staff Ishiwara Kanji himself ordered me to attend the executions of the mutineer officers, including that of Lt.-Colonel Aizawa, tried and condemned in camera and denied his showcase appeal to the nation. And why, I asked myself, why was I being made to attend at these deaths, six or more months after the events of 26 February 1936, at a time when no one even took notice of them? I understood. It was the introduction to my chastisement.

I saw Kita Ikki in his cell before he went to the firing-squad. The guards treated him indifferently, but without brutality. He had just finished shaving and a sad awkwardness obstructed his attempts to fasten his wing collar, and I felt I should volunteer to help him. He declined my offer politely, just as he had refused to wear the ceremonial kimono his wife had supplied for his execution. He would die in European mufti, neither a soldier nor entirely a Japanese civilian. His hands trembled as he lit a cigarette, not out of fear but in reaction to the damp prison chill, though it was August. 'I'll soon be warm enough in the courtyard,' he joked. I felt sorry for him, knowing how much he loved the warmth.

'Did you see how the others died?' he asked me.

'Bravely.'

'Oh yes, with a curse against the Imperial Army, but loyal *banzai* for His Majesty. There is no chance of revolution in this country, either from the left or right, because the very few like us with a stomach for it will always sacrifice ourselves to the Emperor principle in the end.'

'You cannot be accused of that, Kita-*san*.'

'Indeed I can. I could have followed Captain Nonaka's example – I *should* have – but I didn't. And that's because I naively expected to be given a final hearing in court. Fools, all of us, deprived even of a last moment's audience with the Heavenly One.'

'Deprived by whom, Kita-*san*?'

'By our acceptance of the principle, which makes us all dead men.'

When he was brought before the firing-squad, Kita Ikki demanded the privilege of standing, and not die humiliated by having to squat as though 'on a latrine', as he put it. He was nevertheless made to squat, and he cried out, 'So, the upright position of Jesus Christ and the memory of our own crucified patriots is no longer tolerated!'

My own punishment had only just begun.

After Kita's execution, I found myself transferred from the Imperial Guards and posted to Korea. This was a fate I shared with Major-General Yamashita, who suffered worse by being demoted to the command of a brigade in Korea. Both of us were left 'beyond the China Wall', as they say, anxiously wondering whether our exile had been justly or unjustly merited, whether we had overreached ourselves by interpreting our orders from the Palace too broadly or too narrowly. I recall endless evenings of saké and fruitless soul-searching with Major-General Yamashita, with the unexpressed temptation of suicide preying on our minds. Yamashita was eventually relieved of his anxiety by a personal note of encouragement from the Emperor; and I was reinstated and put on active duty in China when Prince Konoe's government finally declared all-out war on Chiang Kai-shek's Kuomintang and Mao's Reds in December 1937.

I met Yamashita again in Malaya, when he was by then renowned as 'The Tiger', conqueror of the South east Asian peninsula – hanged as a war criminal in Manila in 1946 – an unchivalrous act of spitefulness on MacArthur's part who never forgave The Tiger for the humiliation in the Philippines.

General Yamashita assigned me to the vanguard 5th Division under the command of Colonel Tsuji Masanobu, pushing swifly down the road from Bangkok towards Singapore. We struck the Jitra Line, the last-ditch British defences. I had eagerly sought to place myself at the head of Colonel Tsuji's column. Over-fuelled with repentance and samurai bravura, I encountered several empirical reminders of reality from a Gurkha's Bren-gun. I lost two ribs and a kneecap at Jitra. Our present-day Dietman, ex-Colonel Tsuji, personally carried me on his back to safety on that occasion – no doubt a piece of flamboyant knight errantry calculated to gain him further prestige from his troops.

I have become cynical in my middle years. Perhaps I judge our worthy Dietman too harshly, and whatever his faults, I impute to him a calculation of the sort which does not accord with his passionate nature as it does mine.

This, then, has been my progress from the *niniroku* mutiny to the Jitra Line and finally to our present time of economic recovery.

5   THE ENTOMBED LOVERS OF GAKIJIMA

LOVE, THEY SAY, can put out the sun. A strange occurrence of this kind is reported in the first year of the third century era of the Empress Jingu. Jingu travelled eastwards over the Yamato plain, across the straits connecting the Gulf of Ise with the Pacific, and arrived on the island of an elder kinsman of Ki. Darkness endlessly prevailed in this place, as though midnight hung immovable over the island, and it had been like this for a great many days. The Imperial retinue spoke of 'Empress Jingu's voyage through perpetual night'. Jingu enquired of her kinsman: 'What is the reason for this unprecedented wonder?' 'Not entirely unprecedented,' the old man replied. 'For we are told that in remote times, at the origin of all things, the sun goddess Amaterasu retired to a rock cave at Ise in anger at the mischief of her brother Susanoo, the deity of the netherworld, and the entire earth was plunged into total darkness.' 'Indeed, the entire world once suffered Amaterasu's anger,' Jingu said. 'But why should this island alone be singled out for such punishment again?' Jingu's kinsman told her the following story. 'I have heard it said that two priests who officiated at the temple here were known to enjoy unlawful intimacy. A preference for their sin exceeded the devotion rightfully owed to the goddess Amaterasu whom they served. When one of them fell mortally ill, the other was deeply stricken and said, "We have shared everything while alive. Why should we not share the same grave in after-life?" And so, having resolved to die at the same time, they tied themselves together with the sashes of their robes and leapt from the headland crest of the island into the deep sea below. Thereby, they surrendered themselves to the pitiless god of the netherworld, Susanoo. They were found like this, sealed in each other's arms, and so they were entombed together. From that day, the sun ceased to shine.'

Jingu at once ordered the exhumation of the lovers' tomb, and she saw with her own eyes that the story was true. Then she commanded that the bodies each be laid in a new coffin and reburied separately in different places. Immediately, the sun began to shine, and night was again divided from day.

Such is the legend of Gakijima – Ghost Island – as told to me by Ikeda Shigeru, the island's lighthouse keeper.

'In my teens,' I said to Ikeda, 'I read an official, though slightly different version of your story in our ancient chronicles of the 8th century, the *Nihon Shoki*.'

'There are as many versions,' Ikeda replied, 'as there are inhabitants on Gakijima. Twelve hundred, at the last census.'

Former naval lieutenant Ikeda Shigeru is a true-hearted native son of Kyushu, a veteran in his mid-thirties. He appears prematurely aged, a man afflicted by the death he was spared at the battle of Midway. He has endured ten years on Gakijima, ever since he deliberately chose the inferior status of lighthouse keeper, in order, as he put it, to secede from ambition. Ikeda is a recluse of impregnable civility. I envy him his retirement from the world, but the anarchist courage on which it depends is intimidating.

I came to Gakijima in the spring of 1953. My father, a retired director of the Bureau of Fisheries, had used his influence at the Ministry to gain the official endorsements that would make me a privileged guest on Gakijima. My purpose on Gakijima was aesthetic: to record the islanders' ways as background to the novel I had in mind. And lighthouse keeper Ikeda was the islander my father advised me to seek out first. 'He is an eccentric fellow, reputed to have taken the vows of a Nichiren monk; but he should prove cooperative.'

Ikeda's lighthouse at Maiden Point, on the north-western corner of Gakijima, stands on a natural pier of rocks. At high tide, Ikeda is cut off from the island. There are countless submarine reefs on the western, Pacific side of Gakijima, noticeable merely as jigsaw puckers on the surface of the water. Against this threat to shipping, Ikeda tends his solitary guardian light. Good tobacco and fine imported whisky were the only indulgences that relieved the ascetic monotony of Ikeda's existence. These luxuries, I presumed, were provided by the fisherfolk's sideline in smuggling. Ikeda's comment on my suspicion was characteristic: 'Poverty needs a little seasoning to be digestible.' He is not the sort of man to report the islanders' moonlighting misdemeanours.

Books are Ikeda's other weakness. He has amassed a considerable library in his otherwise dismally Spartan tower. I grew fond of Ikeda's company, the hours spent drinking his excellent whisky and discussing literature with him, classical Japanese, German, and especially French in which he showed himself exceptionally well-read. An exchange of views on Camus' *The Stranger* one evening brought us inevitably to the subject of post-war nihilism, a mood everywhere in vogue at the time. 'Isn't it peculiar, Mishima-*san*,' Ikeda said, 'that economic recovery should find its authentic voice in the pessimism of the idle? I am interested in your diagnosis of these *nouveau riche* nihilists who have rejected all our traditions.'

Ikeda spoke of a certain fashionable set of youths, only a few years my juniors, named the *taiyozoku*, the 'sun tribe', notorious for their pleasure-seeking zeal. On this topic, I felt reluctant to express other than prudent opinions; but, under Ikeda's level gaze, I could not be less than candid. 'I have been accused myself of sharing the case-history of such people. I am perhaps not the best diagnostician you could find.'

'Your books do not necessarily incline me to share that view,' Ikeda replied, with circumspect courtesy.

I wondered how much Ikeda knew of all the blustering noise that my first successful novel had provoked four years ago, and all the attendant bizarries of publicity that had since become attached to my name. Did he know that Yukio Mishima was a celebrity of dubious repute? On this island, far removed from Tokyo's excesses, could he know that self-aggrandizement was a career necessity and survival itself a vice? The public part of my life had become that part of myself that did not belong to me, like a hideously distorted Kabuki mask on loan, a monster that must correspond to what the public wants it to be. Things were no longer in my control. I had become an automaton of the illustrated magazines, reflecting me like an illness. I felt tempted to confess to Ikeda, 'Look, success is a horrible thing for one's moral and emotional life. That's why I cannot properly condemn the sun tribe people, since my talent makes me morally uglier than any of them.' Ikeda was a good enough judge of men not to need my boastful soul-searchings. Instead, I said, 'You have lived a long time sequestered from the cities.'

'If you mean I missed the instructive years of the Occupation, yes. Hardly anything has affected this place.'

'Defeat is a terrible thing,' I said. At once, I regretted the formalist cliché.

'I have not surrendered,' Ikeda declared.

I realized what species of man I faced. 'Have you never felt tempted to return to the mainland?'

Ikeda made no reply.

'What has become of your family in Kyushu?'

Again, no reply.

I could hear the sea outside, whispering like a treacherous old coquette. Every hour, despite the quantities of whisky imbibed, Ikeda would mount the tower stairway like a monk to service the salvationist beacon that plied the circumference of night. He stood up now, and at last spoke. 'My superiors want me to take on a helper. I refuse a helper. I know what's said about me – Ikeda, the Buddhist master of Maiden Point. A master without acolytes. What nonsense people talk.' He laughed. 'They say I'm mad. What does your father say?'

'Please don't be offended, Ikeda-*san*.'

Silently, Ikeda refilled our glasses. He stuffed tobacco into the brass-lined bowl of his pipe, a slender traditional one of paulownia wood.

I felt attracted to this strange man and wished earnestly to impress him, as though I had regained a father, and yet the imp of perverse arrogance deep within me could not resist patronizing him. At twenty-eight, I was emotionally jejune, ludicrously ill-equipped for the simplest things in life from which I believed myself excluded.

Questions that seemed uttered at midnight, slipped away unheard, like the hours, until suddenly we found ourselves on the little parapet of Ikeda's lighthouse, with glasses of whisky unsteady in our hands. I did not recall climbing up there. Had I helped Ikeda to shut down the beacon at first light? No doubt, I must have accompanied him on his last nocturnal tour of duty; but I could not remember.

Over to the east, we could see the lovers' fatal promontory screened by a gloomy mass of cryptomeria. Within this grove, atop the headland crest, the Hundred-Mirror Shrine had been built to honour Amaterasu and expiate the priests' double crimes of suicide and *lèse-majesté* affront to the sun goddess.

'There's something eerie about that place,' Ikeda muttered, reading my thoughts.

'What do you mean?'

'*Gaki*, hungry ghosts – so is the island named. They failed to placate the lovers' spirits. Gakijima is small, three miles of coastline. I cannot explain it, but somehow the climate round the shrine differs from the rest of the island. It always seems colder there, no matter the season.'

'Might it not be a phenomenon of the currents or winds?'

'Go there and see for yourself,' Ikeda grinned shrewdly. 'It fascinates you, doesn't it, this tale of love-pact suicide? Is that why you've come to Gakijima, to write the lovers' story?'

'No, not their story,' I replied. 'But, yes, a love story of another kind. I am determined for once to see passion achieve a happy ending.'

'Happy endings are most unnatural things, it seems to me,' Ikeda stated. 'Tragic endings are always more instructive. The more fatalistic the end is, the more hopeful it leaves us. It creates a need in us to search for an idea of utopia, something we can live with, even if it is unrealizable. Death is emancipation, not as the word is commonly used, but in the sense that ideals must be found necessary.'

The explanation for this curious notion, I thought, must lie with Ikeda's romantic profession of lighthouse-keeping.

'You encourage me to confess a certain utopian hope of my own,' I said. 'The happy ending that you profess to despise, Ikeda-*san*, is what I have journeyed all my life to meet. I hope for my own happy ending.'

'You expect to find that by writing a love story?'

'I hope to find a happy, innocent love story here, like the Greek one of Daphnis and Chloe, a sea pastoral discovered among the plain fisherfolk of Gakijima. I hope in this way to greet my own liberation from an incurable illness.'

Ikeda frowned. 'Ah, you are seriously ill, Mishima-*san*?'

'Only with the disease of romanticism. I hope to encounter the

reflection of my health, which has always eluded me, which the dam-
nable feebleness of my body has never permitted me to enjoy for a
single moment in twenty-eight years.' I laughed, embarrassed by this
awkward confession of my infirmity.

'Physical weakness is not a crime,' Ikeda said.

'Nor is homosexuality a country,' I blurted out.

'True, but an impractical form of exile,' Ikeda countered, as always
imperturbable.

We joined together in a moment's carefree laughter.

'Shall I tell you something else that will make you laugh?' I said.
'Ever since my return from a visit to Greece last year, I keep on finding
the evidence of Greek things everywhere, as though I'd brought back
the Aegean archipelago with me to the Sea of Japan.'

'Strange hallucination,' Ikeda remarked, 'to discover the Pelopponese
here in our "reed-plain, 1500 autumns – fair rice-ear land"★.' But he
did not laugh, as perhaps he should have.

'In my study of the Greek language,' I said, warming to my subject
with childish enthusiasm, 'I have found many similarities to our own.
For instance, *obe*, the Greek word for clan, is very like our *be*, also
meaning a clan division. Our *haniwa* clay figurines found in burial
mounds of the neolithic period resemble Minoan terracotta ones from
Bronze Age Crete. The designs on our ancient textiles resemble certain
geometric patterns on ancient Greek pottery. I could go on.'

'Do please go on,' Ikeda civilly allowed. 'But surely you do not mean
to suggest that we are a lost tribe of Athenians?'

'That's not my point,' I replied excitedly. 'I am no scholar, but these
little discoveries of mine simply confirm a feeling I had when I saw the
Greek *stelae*, you know, those sculpted tomb-markers. These monuments to the dead struck me as being admirably free of any spirituality.
I recognized that the superior, pessimist Way of the Greeks is related
to the Japanese Way of Death. Both of us share an infinite thirst for
the finite, which is beauty limited to the perishable body. Neither the
Greeks nor we have ever known the despairing illness of Christian
spiritualism in its duel with materialism.'

'I see,' Ikeda said, drawing reflectively on his little pipe. 'So you have
come to Gakijima to manufacture a Greek imitation of sensual delight.'

'Not an imitation merely,' I objected.

'Well, maybe not. But you have overlooked something, Mishima-*san*.
This absence of spirituality that you think we share with the classical
Greeks is denied on Gakijima, by the lovers who have never found
repose within the finite boundaries of death. It appears to me that you
are seeking to cast your happy Greek story of Daphnis and Chloe in

★ The old poetic name for Japan.

311

the features of those two unhappy suicides, but you will not succeed in the end to exorcise their unassuageable sadness.'

'I accept that your lovers' tragic story has a certain classical perfection of its own,' I said, somewhat let down by Ikeda's dispiriting opinion. 'Our great Chikamatsu, who specialized in *shinju*★ dramas, would no doubt have created one of his marvellous puppet plays from an incident like that. But the story is flawed by being one of love between two men, which dooms it to remain an anecdote.'

'This is the second time you have dragged up the shadow room,' Ikeda remarked frostily.

He used the old-fashioned word *kagema*, 'shadow room', which once referred to male homosexual practices. Ikeda's vexation was a protest against my irrelevant and puerile efforts to shock him.

'I am sorry to sound conventional, Ikeda-*san*, but I do believe that a love story cannot aspire to classicism unless it involves a boy and a girl.'

'So much for Homer, then,' Ikeda shrugged impatiently.

'As a man of literary taste, answer me this – for the problem I am about to put to you is my true dilemma. Can another story of merit ever come from one already finished, already enclosed in its own perfection like a pearl in its shell – or indeed like your lovers' story?'

'I don't understand. Are you worrying again about illicit imitation?'

'Yes, the problem of imitation, in a sense. But also in another more eerie sense that I often feel as a writer; a sense that what I am writing, I have *already* written, as though I were copying myself from an original but totally forgotten past life. This is the ultimate penalty of a writer who knows himself decadent – the punishment of writing again what he has already written but forgotten.'

'Or what he has never written but remembered,' Ikeda interjected, with implacable humour. He thought for a while, and then said, 'Over there,' pointing with the stem of his pipe to land's end, and beyond it to the gulf and the far off, mist occluded shore of Ise, 'over there in Ise Shrine, they say, is housed the original and most revered symbol of divinity inherited by an unbroken succession of Emperors. I mean, of course, Amaterasu's great eight-handed Mirror, the one bestowed on Jimmu, our very first Emperor in 660 BC, as the chronicles tell us, and in which the sun goddess herself is reflected. Do you believe that this Mirror of Divinity, continuously housed in Ise Shrine, is truly the original one?'

Ikeda had posed me a Zen master's riddle in which two contrary possibilities nested one inside the other. One held the key to my problem of what is original; the other, totally contrary one raised a spectre – the

★ Two persons' love-pact suicide.

taboo subject of *Tennoism*, the pre-war concept of Emperor worship. 'It is generally accepted,' I began cautiously, 'that Jimmu's original mirror no longer subsists. Its replacement, however, is believed equally sacred.'

'What matters therefore is not the original, but one's attitude to its successor. Intention is what persists.'

'You describe reverence.'

'No, I describe the correct attitude.'

The empty whisky glass slipped from my fingers and broke on the lighthouse deck. I looked down stupidly at the pieces by my feet. The glass had not dropped far, only the distance from the chair on which I sat to the floor, and not from the height of the parapet. Again, I failed to recall descending to Ikeda's living quarters, unsure by now whether I had really witnessed the dawn over Ise Gulf or sat here the entire time.

I slept away the early hours of the morning on a palliasse furnished by Ikeda. I arose shortly after nine and set out at once for the Hundred-Mirror Shrine on the north-eastern headland.

I cannot say if it was last night's spirituous after-effects or the influence of Ikeda's warning, but it did seem to me unseasonably colder at the headland. Elsewhere on the island, the peach blossoms had fallen, the red spring seaweed had shown itself and its soft-lace variety had already been culled by divers, the octopus traps had been replaced by ones for squid at the vernal equinox, wild crinum lilies on the cliffsides and the leek-coloured flowers known as beach-cotton had made their appearance, and now the abalone divers were ready to try their luck many fathoms down on the sea-beds of Gakijima. All these assurances of summer seemed not to affect the precinct of the Hundred-Mirror Shrine on its isolated crest above the troubled sea. The pines here still wore a coat of dull wintry green, their trunks hunchbacked by the winter monsoons that blow cold from the north-west direction of Tsu, the needles corroded to rusty mats under the boughs by the constant saline breath of the open Pacific at my right.

One hundred stone steps ascend to the shrine from a *torii* at the bottom, that familiar 'sacred bird-perch' shaped like the Greek letter π, sentried by a pair of stone temple lions. Two pines once formed another *torii* at the top of the steps, but these sacred evergreens had perished and been replaced by the customary pillars and crossbeams. Gazing up through these two gateway apertures at the sky framed within them, I could imagine how they might once have served to calibrate the sun and stars in astrological reckonings of the seasons. I am reminded of those great stone calendars, the Druids' trilithic henges erected for the same calculative purpose. Across the gulf, at Ise Shrine of the sun goddess Amaterasu, one can see the original model of the *torii*. Two high and neighbouring rocks stand on the shore of Ise. These twin rocks are joined together at their peaks by a rope of woven rice-straw, thus creating a natural *torii* through which the worshippers at Ise can view the sun rising above Mount Fuji. I glanced to the north-east, and far away across the channel I could see the distinct floating cone of Mount Fuji.

I began my climb. The steps at first edged along the precipice, but then more cautiously banked away from the awesome drop, as I too in my dread leaned askew from the sea. A dangerously opaque sea, confined to the embrace of jutting rocks below, formed whirlpools that spun like clay between a potter's fingers. 'Here, on this promontory, my life is exposed,' I thought. I am threatened by the sea's assault, compelling me to abandon my insecure footing to its unconscious will. I understand only too well the sense of my vertigo. A fear of heights anticipates the suicide's contrary and fatal attraction.

I force myself to stand at the very brim of the abyss, the toes of my shoes in empty space, and stare down unflinchingly into the beckoning void. Every fibre of my being is assailed by a cowardly immense scream of bankruptcy, which turns to laughter, because at the same time I welcome suicide with the pure delicacy of malice. It is this secret thrill of malice that now whispers to me, 'Why do you abstain from death? Haven't you succeeded long enough to contaminate beauty by familiarizing it with its own destructive power? Why not make an end of it now?' What can I reply? that the suicide of a feeble pen-pusher is meaningless? It is worse than meaningless; it is unconvincing. What choice have I? None, except to postpone suicide, as one delays the luxury of slumber to delight a little longer in the pleasurable excess of fatigue.

I look up at the sky, which seems to mirror above me the sea itself in turmoil. The expanse of shadow cast by a massive alpine wall of cloud ends abruptly over the shrine. A scree of sunlight plunges down the vertical end of the cloud in dazzling shafts to the sea. In response, the surface of Ise's waters gleam like a mirror of hammered white copper. This sudden, unexpected vision brings me relief, as though the sun goddess Amaterasu herself had given evidence of her compassion. I take it as a sign of hope.

I shake all over. The calves of my legs twitch uncontrollably as though I had descended a steep mile-long gradient. I resume my climb and finally reach the terrace of the Hundred-Mirror Shrine. The shrine is a disappointingly small dilapidated 19th century building. An old priest sweeps the lichened paving stones of the forecourt with a worn-out broom of reeds. The sight of a visitor appears to astonish him; but he approaches me in welcome. His robes are of jaundiced white, covered by the local fishermen's type of padded cotton jacket against the cold. Wrapped round one emaciated hand, he carries an unusual Buddhist rosary composed of Indian *rudraksha* or 'Eye of Shiva' berries, large lumpy brown things dried into beads. These rattle magically as he raises his hands in greeting. He is consumptive and piteously thin, as though he had not seen food in weeks, and each of his dry coughs threatens to send him out of this life. I note that he continues to wear war-time government issue eyeglasses.

'I have heard much about the shrine's great treasury of mirrors, reverend sir.'

'I see,' he replied, as though contemplating a ghost. 'There are in fact thirty-three such mirrors. One hundred is something of a local exaggeration.'

'Thirty-three? But this is the number of years it takes a soul to achieve final peace, *jobotsu*, is it not?'

'Indeed, sir, it is. Or, according to another calculation, forty-nine years.'

'Perhaps the thirty-three mirrors represent an effort to placate the spirits of your ancient predecessors.'

'One might conclude so,' he accepted, looking down gravely at his *geta* platform sandals and the much repatched woolen *tabi* covering his feet. 'A collection of thirty-three ancient bronze mirrors is a very great responsibility. There are some dating from the Han period, including a remarkable willow-patterned one of Chinese make.'

'Please excuse me, but isn't it odd to find a treasure of this kind in such an out of the way place?'

'It is certainly odd,' he agreed, with a beatific smile. 'In my long ago youth, I assisted at a shrine in Kyoto dedicated to broken needles.'

'Broken needles?'

'Exactly so; ordinary domestic needles. Broken ones. The shrine was maintained by an illustrious family, the Arisugawa, cousins of the Emperor Meiji. But they have probably ceased collecting broken needles now, I would think.'

'This is an amazing coincidence, reverend sir,' I exclaimed. 'In her youth, my grandmother resided for several years with the Arisugawas, her distant relatives.'

'How very interesting. Auspicious, I would venture to say,' he nodded, and then enquired with polite formality if my grandmother Natsuko had died. 'Has the lady passed to recovery?'

'She has, and now I shall never know if she left any broken needles in your Kyoto shrine.'

I gazed at the Hundred-Mirror Shrine, a sadly run down place, and wondered aloud, 'Have the fisher people neglected their sacred rites in these difficult years?'

'Oh no, sir. They are pious folk,' the priest assured me with child-like candour. 'It is simply that they have found the new god of prosperity.'

'Would it inconvenience you to permit me entry to the shrine, reverend sir, so that I might admire its treasures?'

'Regrettably, sir, all the mirrors but one were removed to a museum in Osaka last year.'

'I wasn't told.' I cursed my father for leaving me uninformed of this.

'But, please, you are very welcome to inspect our shrine,' he said, leading me to the porch. 'I need not accompany you. The shrine is small, but I think you will find it in a certain sense infinitely spacious.'

I removed my shoes on the unevenly worn cedar planks. I clapped my hands, rang the porch-roof bell, and entered through the open screen on to soft cushioned matting. I passed another, more elaborately embossed bronze ceiling bell and a lacquered reading desk on which I see an open scroll of the Peacock King Sutra, the most arcane of Buddhist scriptures. The rituals of this shrine were rooted in 9th century Ryobu or Dual Shinto, a marriage of esoteric Shingon Buddhism and Shinto spirit worship. Before me, I saw a wall of paper screens from floor to ceiling. I slid back one of these and penetrated the dim, incense-haunted inner sanctuary. I discerned the faint glimmering outlines within of the *mibashira*, the sacred red-lacquered central pillar, and a colossal bronze lamp with a lotus-shaped peak and grimacing dragons coiled round its stem. My shoulder disturbed a festoon of tinkling little bells suspended from the lamp as I groped my way forward to the altar. I slid back screen after screen, like peeling away the pellucid skins of an onion, and sunlight pouring in from the headland sky distinguished the forms of gilded brasses, wall inscriptions on silk pennants, and the altar groups of convoluted candelabra.

One would seek in vain through all these onion layers for an image of the deity. There is only one presiding spirit here – only the void of a great, round mirror of polished white copper hanging in front of me. I gaze into this pale trembling disk, and I see – nothing – only the reflected phantom of the sea far behind me.

What's this? Am I transparent? Vanished into thin air? An illusion?

I look again, and see a mockery of me far worse than any illusion of nothingness.

'What you find reflected here' – a sea-carried voice reaches me – 'is a parish of the crossroads, one who scatters unhulled rice to dispel the darkness of the eclipse, one of the breed of *tsuchigumo*, the earth-hiders, who live in sunken underground dwellings. What you see is a despised *hinin*, a non-man, an outcast strolling player, a mountebank showman at village fairs.'

This is what I see. A pair of black caterpillar eyebrows prominent on a death's-head face, a pale horse-faced Ginza boulevardier with his stylish Hollywood crew cut, absurdly, pathetically, synthetically 1950s in his Tobu department store summer suit, his garish chrome-silk tie (but mercifully today, without his Aloha shirt), his narrow pointed shoes with heels worn down at the outer rims by dint of his shambling, short-legged simian gait, a prematurely middleaged writer of the post-war 50s with the puny unfleshed arms of a child who strives farcically for a boxer's look, a mannikin hollowed out by the tapeworm of a lifetime's masquerade, a sad, worn-out, skeptical child grinning back at me – the aspiring emperor of Japanese literature in the mirror of the sun goddess.

On my exit from the shrine, I found the touchingly frail old priest awaiting me with a bowl of tea. I sat on the porch, put on my shoes (and gaped at them in astonishment, for the mirror had shown them in precise detail, an impossibility), and accepted the refreshing drink the priest offered me. As I sipped, he asked me, 'Have you found suitable lodgings on Gakijima?'

'I have a pleasant enough room in the village. Although, last night I slept on lighthouse keeper Ikeda's not very comfortable floor.'

'Oh yes, the Marquis Ikeda, a very interesting gentleman.'

'Marquis Ikeda, you say?'

'Indeed, sir. He is descended from one of the oldest samurai families of the Satsuma clan. Didn't you know?'

I kept silent, furious again with my father. This was another of his calculated oversights, one more of his cryptic little misprisions and ironies by which he had always furthered the cause of his sabotage against me. Ikeda, whom I took to be a rough diamond of Kyushu, a self-educated man of humble origin, was by right a marquis. I had grievously mis-judged him. *Well, well, Yukio, you're slipping* – I could hear my father chuckling as he relished this blow to my vanity.

My years at the Peers' School, among the worthless sons of dukes and barons, had not prepared me for Ikeda's practice of true aristocractic self-effacement. Indifference to rank is an awesome and shattering virtue.

Over by the *torii*, I now noticed Ogata Masao, the island pedlar, perched on his suitcase of wares and eyeing me irritably. I had forgotten my promise to meet him before noon at the lighthouse. Ikeda must have instructed him to find me here. Ogata plucked a fleck of cigarette paper off his lip, exhaling smoke like a guardian temple dragon by the *torii* pillar, and furtively counting the number of yen notes I offered the priest. The priest unwound the rosary from his hand and revealed a web of lines on a dessicated palm, and a new one across it, a line of piety etched by his beads. 'Might I be so bold as to ask you for a cigarette, kind sir?' I presented him with my pack of Chesterfields, but on second thought anxious that I might be handing him his death warrant. 'Oh no, sir. I require only one,' and he plucked out a single cigarette with frail, delicate fingers, the nails grey with impending death.

He sniffed the tobacco's bouquet, savouring it with all the innocence of true pleasure. 'I shall save this for tonight, before I retire.'

I joined Ogata at the *torii*. 'We'll have to hurry, Mishima-*san*,' he grumbled. 'What kept you so long in there? The shrine is totally without interest.'

We took the path leading to an open stretch of the Pacific, south of the lighthouse, and a sheltered cove in which the abalone divers congregated at noon. I wished to meet these women divers, celebrated for the amazing depths they plumbed without aid of any breathing apparatus. I felt intuitively certain that I would discover the young heroine of my novel, my ideal Greek Chloe, among the abalone divers of Gakijima. Ogata had eagerly elected himself my intermediary. 'Without me,' he boasted, 'they'll shy away from you like baby crabs into sand.' I met the itinerant pedlar, Ogata Masao, on the ferryboat to Gakijima. At once, he began ingratiating himself with me as an indispensable specialist in the Gakijima mentality. He drew his expertise from years of salesmanship on this island and others like it. Ogata's career had begun in the underworld of black market street hawking after the war on his return from Manchuria. Though, of course, he did not admit it, I knew that his pedlar's concession on the islands had been granted by the *yakuza*, Ogata's mafia comptrollers in Tokyo. He represented several shops in Sanya, Tokyo's proletarian commercial district, and touted their notoriously shoddy goods to the islanders at higher than retail prices.

Ogata was tall and gaunt, and although not more than forty, his face bore the desolate lines and decayed jowls of a man over sixty. A double-breasted brown pinstrip suit sagged round his scarecrow frame. His ill-kempt, stringy hair was swept back over a bald plateau, his nylon shirt hung open at the neck over the loosened knot of a dazzlingly broad flower-patterned tie. A smile from those broad, thick lips revealed a picket row of ochre teeth seeming about to fall from his shrivelled gums. Ogata's full suitcase of cheap trinkets – typically those post-war products that had branded *Nipponsei*, Made in Japan, a trademark of junk throughout the world – banged and rattled against his knee. With his free hand, he jerked out a cigarette from a pack of New Life, lit it, and puffed away contentedly as we marched briskly on, out of breath, towards our rendezvous.

'Do you know,' Ogata suddenly declared, 'I was a high school director of athletics before the war?'

I looked at him skeptically.

'Surprises you, eh?' He laughed. 'Let me tell you something else. I was a sergeant in the Kwantung Army, and the whole lot of us over there in Manchuria, we were never defeated. Do you realize that? They had to send us a member of the Imperial family in 1945, Prince Takeda Tsuneyoshi in person, to persuade us to surrender, because, you see, we weren't defeated. But nowadays it's all right for neutralist intellectuals to despise the Imperial Army.'

'I don't despise the Imperial Army, Ogata-*san*.'

'That's entirely to your credit,' Ogata nodded. 'I felt angry, you see, but not defeated. Except when I returned to Tokyo – to a pile of cinders – no family, nothing – and people in the streets spat on my uniform – then I was good and truly defeated.'

'And that's when you joined the black market racketeers?'

Ogata gave me a look, part offended, part reflecting pride in his non-conformity. 'Frankly, I prefer the *yakuza*'s company to the defeatist gangsters who run our country these days.'

'I'm inclined to agree, there's not much difference between them.'

'You are too young and too privileged to talk cynically like that.'

I considered how ridiculously swaggering the pair of us must seem to an onlooker. The only semblance of victory went to the American style of our clothing: Ogata, in his James Cagney hoodlum's gear, and I, the replica of a Hollywood drugstore pimp.

We plodded on for a while, and then Ogata turned to me with a lewd smile. 'Tell me, Mishima-*san*, is your interest in these abalone mermaids purely literary? If you're after a little extra-curricular sport, well, I would advise you not to trifle with the young maidens. Go for the mature ones, the widows especially – they'll teach you something about diving for molluscs – and *such* thighs, ah, so devastatingly athletic, more than anything I ever saw on my white-pantied high school girls, I can assure you.' He howled with laughter. Ogata's breath on my cheek stank of saké and dog-like foulness; but I guessed mine must be equally unsavoury.

Ogata excelled himself in pornographic poetry; but I began to doubt that he was the reliable spokesman I needed to win the abalone divers' confidence.

Ogata guided me down a narrow sandy path, through a fortress maze of limestone crags and boulders which concealed the abalone divers' cove from view. We stopped at a final screen of rocks encrusted with the dry, blackened remains of algae, before the white sand of the beach stretched away to the sea. Here, Ogata settled himself down on his suitcase, lit another cigarette, and motioned me down to another eaves-dropper's perch some fifteen feet below his: 'Stay out of sight. We'll wait here first and see how things go.' I understood that Ogata wanted to see evidence of the divers' catch, a good money-crop of abalone, before presenting himself with his merchandize. The abalone season had only just begun.

I took up my lower, less advantageous position for spying. The noonday sun blazed down from a cloudless, cobalt sky. Some hundred and twenty or so feet distance from me, a half-dozen women knelt, hunched round a driftwood fire, these being evidently the older, mature ones of Ogata's recommendation. Padded jackets thrown across the divers' shoulders hid their breasts, mature or not, from view. I could not see the contents of their baskets, but judging from the women's despondent look, the catch must not have been too encouraging. They spoke – I think perhaps one or two of them were singing – but the crash and withdrawing sighs of the waves drowned out any sound of voices.

Over to the east, vast banks of summer clouds dominated the far horizon, blackening the distant sea beneath. The water nearer this beach appeared deceptively tranquil, blue and invitingly warm, but even now, at the start of the rainy season, it would still be freezing all those fathoms down on the abalone beds. I shivered just to imagine the numbing, leaden suffocation that must grip one's body in the breathless dive to the sea-floor. I was relieved to see the embracing cove secure around me.

I looked again at the beach, and thought, how can you possibly imagine Greece in this place? A southerly breeze harrowed the sand drifts between the shafts of rock, so that the beach looked now like one of those Zen gardens of raked gravel and stone, barren of vegetation. At the sea margin of this garden, the abalone divers ate their frugal *chazuke* lunch of cold rice, pickles and tea. The picture was uniquely, indelibly Japanese. Why did I wish to see it differently?

Noon waned, and presently a boat approached the shore. Six or seven returning divers nimbly disembarked. From their agitation and the manifest weight of their baskets, it was safe to guess that the haul had been rewarding this time. These rejoicing newcomers squatted by the drying-fire, with jackets on their backs and divers' goggles still pendant round their necks. The fire's cheer, and the adrenalin of triumph, soon had them shrugging off their jackets. Their dishevelled hair like glistening strands of wet black seaweed fell across their breasts. Maidenly torsos, in varying honey tints of light mahogany and coppery sheen, were exposed to the brilliant sunlight. The divers massaged themselves roughly to dispel the last shivers of gooseflesh, grasping their breasts and palping them carelessly like globes of unripened fruit insensitive to their touch.

I envied these young, athletic specimens. A lustre seemed to emerge from deep within their flesh, as it does through the dusky, pruinose skin of a grape held up to sunlight. Their labours beneath the sea had broadened their shoulders and pectoral muscles, thus lending buttress to their breasts that in the best cases hardly drooped. Their calves and thighs were gracefully compact. Enviable bodies. And yet, a vain wish overcame me to see these marine Amazons suddenly, magically transformed into my own gender.

I sat down in the shade of my rock, and, averting my eyes from the obdurately real abalone divers, focussed on my memory of those smiling young men of stone, the *kouroi* of remote antiquity. I saw Ogata stationed above me. He stood, mouth ajar, spent cigarette-butt stuck to his lower lip. He shaded his eyes against the noontide glare with his left hand and feasted greedily on the spectacle of near naked females, while his right stealthily and continuously fluttered deep inside his trouser pocket. He was masturbating.

I turned away in disgust, sickened, but at the same time gratified by this shameless exhibition of voyeurist onanism. I leaned my cheek against the rock, on its surface of finger-sized pores from which there crawled sea-lice and transparent infant crabs. Clusters of mussels stood planted like black lacquered teeth in the spongy lichen patches. I embraced the rock, yes, I hugged it, out of gratitude, out of love for its vast maternal sloven's disregard for all things corrupt and fertile. I looked again at the abalone divers, and laughed sardonically, disgusted and yet jubilant that my vision of them was a falsehood. I had remoulded them in the features of an ersatz, decadent classicism, seen through a Prussian monocle, through the misplaced German romantic myopia of Winckelmann, Goethe and Nietzsche which had shaped my generation's vision.

Ogata passed by me, and in a stage manager's whisper instructed me to follow close behind him. We filed in tandem towards the divers, into the wisp of smoke from their fire, our absurdly inappropriate city gents' shoes capsizing in the sand. For the first time, I could distinguish the women's voices clearly, 'Masao! Masao!', they greeted him with delighted cries of kindergarten children. As we neared their circle, a gruff voice enquired, 'Who's that young fellow you're hiding, Masao?' Padded jackets were hastily shouldered as I peered round Ogata and met the questioner's gaze, the group's elder and spokeswoman, whose canny grin showed a number of missing teeth.

'Ladies, you are greatly privileged today,' Ogata proclaimed. 'This fine young man is Yukio Mishima, a world famous writer.'

'Does he write for the Tokyo newspapers?'

'Of course, auntie, for them and even foreign papers. And just imagine, he's come all the way here especially to interview you.'

'What's he want to interview us for?'

'Don't be so modest, auntie,' Ogata replied, eyeing the baskets of abalone and assessing their cash value. 'Your diving skills are renowned the world over.'

'Auntie' grunted suspiciously, but accepted Ogata's wink with her own smile of complicity. There was some hint of a pact between them, erotic or commercial, or maybe both.

'Please sit down, Mishima-*san*,' she offered. Unlike the others, 'auntie' had not bothered to conceal her nudity, nor did she avert her eyes from me, a restraint that the other women practised, along with the conventional amount of giggling and nudging of elbows. She met my inspection with even-humoured indifference. On her, the scars of a diver's hard life were in evidence. Though her hair remained youthfully abundant and jet black, her face had become seamed like the uncaulked keel of a boat, her breasts shrivelled into flat conicals, tipped with the dark fig-like areolae of her nipples, and her muscles were picked out in sinewy detail. Her toe-nails were misshapen, twisted like horn, her soles calloused with sand-clogged scars, the life-long result of a diver's habit of kicking off powerfully from the razor-shelled sea-floor in her swift ascent to the surface.

'My name is Iwai Natsuko,' she finally said, interrupting my contemplation of her.

'How extraordinary,' I replied, startled. 'My grandmother's name was Natsuko too.'

'Huh, this young fellow thinks I'm his grandma,' she chortled, to my embarrassment and everyone's laughter.

'Beware of this grandma's ardent embrace, Mishima-*san*,' Ogata interjected.

Attention was diverted from me now, as Ogata opened his suitcase like a fairytale casket overflowing with wonders. The divers' faces shone, as though the brilliance of jewels were suddenly reflected on them from Ogata's box of treasures. In a flurry of excitement, the women rose up and surrounded Ogata, uttering cries of desire and distress that so much on sale was surely beyond their means. All I could see was the shoddy wares of the Sanya district – vulgar costume jewelry, kimono materials of the cheapest tawdry cotton and rayon, velveteen padded *geta* thongs, plastic shopping bags and other gimcrack novelties – all these worthless, over-priced shop goods in exchange for the divers' small gains from their precious abalone.

'Lighthouse keeper Ikeda has told me about you,' Natsuko said.

'Marquis Ikeda?'

'The very one,' she replied, taking a cigarette from my pack of Chesterfields. I lit Natsuko's and another for myself. One pull of her diver's powerful lungs reduced half the cigarette to ash.

'Ikeda tells me you're writing a novel about us.'

'That is so,' I admitted.

I noted that Natsuko remained stationary by my side, the only woman to show complete disinterest in Ogata's fripperies. I wondered whether it was from polite scruple, requiring her to keep me company, or because she was in league with Ogata as I suspected.

'Our lighthouse keeper told me something else very disturbing. He says that others will come here next summer to make a film of your book.'

I had boasted to Ikeda of Toho Studios' bid on my novel, even before its scheduled completion.

'Yes, it is possible. A big film company in Tokyo has expressed such an interest.'

'And this big film company belongs to very rich businessmen? How do they propose to do this film? Gakijima is a small island,' Natsuko laughed, her eyes impassively reading mine. 'Do you think, Mishima-san, they will rent all of it, like a hotel room?'

Natsuko's attention passed from me to Ogata. She surveyed the divers' yen being exchanged in a favourably brisk trade for Ogata's commodities. It was a disheartening sight, preying on my conscience, for it struck me that my own objective on Gakijima bore uncomfortable resemblance to Ogata's. Was I imagining that Natsuko herself had made this link between the pedlar's commercial vampirism and mine? Was I too, in her mind, just another exploiter and cheat come here to suck the islanders' life-blood? Ogata seemed a comparatively harmless vanguard. Far worse harm would follow in the wake of my visit. Was that in Natsuko's thoughts?

In a pained, melancholy mood, I turned to the sea for comfort. Natsuko had not been the only one to remain unmoved by Ogata's goods. One other diver, the youngest it seemed, and as I now recognized, the most beautiful of them all, had stuck quietly to her place just behind me at my right. Had she been listening silently to Natsuko and me conversing? Her jacket had slipped unnoticed from her shoulders as she contemplated the sea. There was a remarkable stillness about her, as she crouched on the sand, like a bronze sculpture of the Bathing Venus from Hellenistic times. The girl's lower part of the body and legs faced in my direction, while her torso twisted back in another, towards the sea at which she gazed. She resembled a squatting caryatid, burdened by the weight of the sky. The torsion of her pose stretched a drapery of flesh across her abdomen; her wide, generous breasts were upheld by the prominent deltoid and scapulary pull of her shoulder muscles; her crouching thighs revealed the massed bulges of femoral tensors. I had found my Chloe. An impression that a smile on the sweet, virgin blankness of her face confirmed, as she turned and met my eyes. I asked her name, half expecting to hear 'Chloe'. Instead, she replied with an old, unusual name, Aoyagi, 'green willow'. Her name was extraordinarily apt, for in Greek Chloe too means 'green shoot' or 'blossoming', just as her unhappy lover's name, Daphnis, the shepherd innovator of Greek bucolic poetry, refers to Apollo's sacred evergreen, the laurel. I felt like the archeologist who had discovered Troy. I wished Ikeda was here to share my wondrous find.

My spirits were dampened by Natsuko's remorseless stare which put me down as a city-bred lunatic.

Aoyagi was eighteen. How many seasons had she already known as a diver? 'This will be my third season,' she replied. 'But I still have terrible dreams at night, dreams of bottomless water and a surface that all my efforts cannot reach.'

'At my age,' Natsuko commented, 'you'll stop having dreams of that sort.'

Two seasons of diving had not yet toughened and deformed Aoyagi's feet like Natsuko's. Several of her toes bled from cuts inflicted by the barbed sea-floor. Flakes of red seaweed were pasted on Aoyagi's limbs. Sea water dripping from her body had left a shadow imprint like ink on the sand beneath her. Aoyagi held out her hand to me, shyly, but with candid invitation. I took it, not knowing what she intended. I felt the damp touch of Aoyagi's palm on mine, wet not from the sea, but with a sweat welling up from the nightmare depths of her anxiety. Gooseflesh arose in a sympathetic crop on Aoyagi's arms and sides as she relived her deep sea memory.

'It's no use holding her hand,' Natsuko chuckled. 'She's already got a sweetheart.'

'What's this I find, Mishima-*san*?' Ogata put in, returning victorious from his trading post. 'Are you flirting with another man's fiancée?'

Aoyagi looked back again at the sea, sadly, entreatingly.

'Her boyfriend's not a fisherman out there,' Natsuko said, replying to the question my expression conveyed. 'He's in Tokyo, working in a restaurant – where *these* will end up –' Natsuko demonstrated an abalone in her hand, snatched out from one of the baskets. The abalone sea snail was bigger than Natsuko's hand with ear-shaped whorls and a series of blow-holes along the dorsal hump of its shell. She turned it over, and swiftly, expertly, with a short chisel-like blade, prised out the squirming black-membraned carcass of the snail. The shell's mother-of-pearl interior was laid bare. Natsuko sliced off the snail's foot, a muscular disc that she trimmed to the white flesh and cut into strips. She returned these edible slices to the shell and placed it like a dish before me on the sand. Beside it, she put the remains of pickles and seaweed in her *bento* lunchbox, and poured me some tea from a raffia-encased thermos bottle.

'Please help yourself,' she gestured with a nod of her head to the food. 'You've spent an hour up on those rocks without anything to eat.'

Ogata's mouth fell open, idiotically, and I too looked down abashed at my meal.

'Look here, auntie, it's like this –' Ogata vainly began his plea.

'Be quiet, Masao,' Natsuko interrupted curtly. She took a cigarette from my Chesterfields lying on the sand, lit it on one of the fire's dying embers, and stared at the storm clouds massed on the Pacific horizon.

'I know what Mishima-*san* wants. He wants to go out there with us.'

Ogata, in a jittery state, prowled the divers' circle. 'Bull's eye, auntie! You've hit right on it. Mishima-*san* will reward you handsomely for this chance to accompany you on your expedition.'

'It is not permitted,' Natsuko stated.

'Come on, auntie. That's only a superstition.'

'It is not permitted,' Natsuko calmly repeated, and she draped herself in her jacket, as though suddenly cold. The other women did likewise, and at this moment, a last vestige of the island's modesty had been regained.

Ogata slapped his forehead, gesticulating wildly like an actor in a *Kyogen* farce interlude between Noh plays. He looked up at the heavens, beseeching them for inspiration.

'Perhaps, if Ogata-*san* were to offer these ladies some fine gifts – ' I said. Ogata at once understood. He winked at me, threw open his suitcase, and pulled out a plastic shopping bag patterned like the cheapest washroom tiles. 'At the greatest sacrifice to himself, Mishima-*san* will award each and everyone of you ladies with these remarkably fine, highly attractive specimens of modern workmanship.'

Natsuko was immovable; and none of the others dared speak.

Ogata glanced despairingly at me, but tried one last time to excite Natsuko's interest. He laid before her his chief article, an eye-catching lady's handbag of machine-patterned crocodile skin in plastic, with an imitation gold clasp of plated brass. The women sighed for such a treasure. 'I'm going to ruin myself – if my shop in Tokyo ever heard of this, I'd be sacked – but I'm offering it to you, auntie, gratis, a free gift.'

'Keep your gifts, Masao,' Natsuko said.

A roll of thunder was heard, and a view of rain falling black and aslant far out on the ocean could be seen. A great swell crashed on the rocks of our cove, rising with a hiss skyward in a fine golden powdery mist.

'This time, I'll take the stern and do the sculling,' Natsuko said. 'Who's ready to go out?'

Aoyagi was the first to spring to her feet. She had taken hold of my hand again and pulled me up with her. Natsuko looked at us, but said nothing as she rose from her knees.

Aoyagi led me by the hand to the shore. The paired sweat of dread on our palms felt like a kiss, transfixed, as I remember my mother's hand squeezing mine, urging me against all my fearful reluctance to enter the sea for the first time at the age of eleven, terrified that she was delivering me to the jaws of death. I had an undersea vision this time of Aoyagi, indistinct at first, blurred by a limitless elevation of water, her breasts rising towards me like beautiful jellyfish from the aquamarine depths, her hair like black tentacles of algae floating around her, and I saw myself tumbling down towards her, my arms glued to my sides like an archaic *kouros* figure, sinking willessly, a disfigured torso without legs plummeting down, my head detached from me—

6   A SHADOW BOXER'S HEAD

A MIRACULOUS HEAD, spinning away from me and brusquely advancing again, with its enigmatic smile. I am confronted by Yuichi's head, mobile on his shoulders, my vision of him blinkered by the leather flaps of my protective headgear. A prismatic veil of sweat falling like tears into my eyes from the hot, clumsy forehead band, obscures my view of Yuichi's movements. Yuichi thrusts out his boxer's mouthpiece between his lips like grotesque rubber false teeth, or a tongue sticking out at me. He grins and offers me the target grip of his fine teeth on the mouthpiece, defying me to hit him.

My arms feel weighted down like trawler's nets, though it is only the second round of our sparring match. Interred in these strange, heavy bundles of leather, my hands do not seem part of me; my limbs are painfully fatigued, but non-existent. Yuichi's actions are darting and graceful; mine are like a gawky fledgling bird's, hopelessly intent on victory by mimicking Yuichi's skill. I resent being Yuichi's graceless shadow-boxing copy that he can torment with ease, and my punches become even more disorderly as my anger grows.

'Boxing might look like slow-motion Kendo,' Kojima Tomo, Waseda University's boxing coach, had told me. 'It seems to give the boxers more time to think, as they feint and skip about. But a boxing match is really a series of little matches. Each one, in a decisive split second, can be as precise as the art of Kendo.'

Coach Kojima's advice came back to me from my past weekly training sessions with him at the Waseda University amateur boxing club. My visits to the club had been irregular during the year and a half since my return to Tokyo from Gakijima. My shaky amount of technique had badly deteriorated in that time. My adversary, Yuichi, had frequently performed as my sparring partner. Yuichi, however, had kept in practice; besides, he was naturally able-bodied. I tried to regain my calm to withstand Yuichi's superior talent.

The little I knew of Kojima's science of pugilism had been intellectually earned, without my having any real native aptitude for it. My mind was far too intensely alert to a distracting crowd of sensations – the sweaty perfume of leather, the dry, almost chalky ozone smell of the ring itself – these and other mentally enhanced perceptions could only serve my undoing. I was not capable of a sacrifice of the intellect that is necessary if a physical skill is to become instinctive and perfect. My mind was an invincible obstacle to instinct which, in consequence, starved and withered away.

I could see Yuichi's helmeted warrior's head cocked to one side, in the direction of his coiled left arm, as he prodded me tactically with his right. I knew that Yuichi was not a natural southpaw, and so I did not anticipate any threat from it. His left jab struck with some force, as I had foreseen, and I parried it with a reasonably adroit manoeuvre that gave me the immediate advantage of a good right hook. Yuichi's lunge had left him exposed. I could see the little mole on his cheekbone just below the left eye. This mole was a beacon in the open, inviting me to strike. In the split second that I did so – in Kojima's admonitory 'deadly and precise' split second – I realized my mistake. Yuichi's head wasn't there. I had fallen for one of the most basic schoolboy feints in the annals of amateur boxing. Thin air, in which Yuichi's head had deceptively stood, suddenly became a black sky dominated by a blood red sun. My knees for a moment sagged; but I had enough defensive sense left to crouch and shield my head with my gloves. This didn't save me from Yuichi drumming rapid-fire blows on my abdomen, on the sickly innards that he knew were most vulnerable to his resentful, sadistic punches. I could feel the trampoline pliancy of the ropes on my back, sawing at my spine like pumice, as I reeled and bounced under Yuichi's attack.

'Stop! Stop!' I heard coach Kojima shouting. The beating at once ceased. I fell back on the supporting ropes, dazed, humiliated and completely pulverized. But now, a peculiar feeling stirred inside me, like leaves at night stirring in the wake of a breeze. A tranquillity descended on me, a cocooning vacuum like the menthol caress of coolness that passes over the surface of exerted muscles at rest as the sweat vanishes from them. I felt my entire being dissolving into pure transparency in which the throbbing of my lacerated eyebrow and even the pain of my humiliation were changed as if by magic into a delicious sensation of pleasure. I delighted in the unfamiliar sense of pain.

Former lightweight champion Kojima, in his white T-shirt, slacks and gym shoes, catapulted through the ropes into the ring. 'What's wrong with you, boy? This isn't a championship fight,' he berated Yuichi angrily. Kojima's sarcasm rekindled my humiliation. Yuichi lounged in his corner, elbows sprawled on the ropes, with a most unenigmatic smile of triumph on his handsome face. Kojima's real anger was reserved for me. It was a matter of shame for him to have a national celebrity in his safe-keeping, bleeding all over his nice, hygienic university ring. 'You should give this up, Mishima-*san*,' Kojima growled, 'I've never seen anyone so uncoordinated.' Kojima's anger was bafflement. He could not understand why I insisted on having my brains beaten out – the only part of me worth preserving. How could he understand? Kojima has no conception of the true nature of my weakness. Weakness confirms itself in the fear that any act of independence will bring down vengeance on one's head.

Pity softened Kojima's frustrated ire when he observed that I was on the verge of tears. 'Don't worry, you'll improve,' he gave my chin a rough, paternal tap. Kojima had the gentle indifference of a man secure in his strength. 'Let's have a look at that eye,' he said.

'It's not Yuichi's fault,' I stammered, wincing in anguish as Kojima jabbed at my cut with his styptic chalk, which came away reddened like a lipstick. 'I didn't fasten my headgear properly. My eyebrows are a nuisance, the way they stick too far out.'

'Looks like you've already got an old scar here.'

'I fell down the stairs when I was one.'

'Well,' he smiled, 'the old and the new should heal together fine.'

Kojima decided I wouldn't need stitching. His assistant brought him a first-aid kit, and he patched me up with iodine and adhesive plaster. It pleased me to see drops of blood on Kojima's clinically white T-shirt. Kojima pushed Yuichi and me together for a conciliatory handshake – the pugilists' traditional butting of gloves – but Yuichi avoided meeting my eyes.

To show Yuichi that I harboured no ill will, I invited him to a steam bath in Roppongi, and then later, supper in a good restaurant in Shinjuku. He felt compelled to accept my invitation, but with the same display of taciturn reluctance that had kept his gaze averted from mine. It seemed that a solemn, perhaps tiresome evening was in store for the pair of us.

My friend Yuichi is a *ronin*, a term which in past centuries denoted a masterless samurai for hire. Nowadays, *ronin* means a student who has failed several times to enter university, in particular one of the prestigious former Imperial universities. All the usual niceties, the abstruse honorific codes of indebtedness to one's god-like teachers which normally rule a student's behaviour and leave him virtually non-existent as a person, are compounded in the *ronin*'s case, since he must also endure the humiliation of his family to which both his failure and prolonged financial dependence on them have contributed. Suicide is not infrequent among the *ronin*.

Yuichi keenly suffers from the burden he imposes on his father, Shikata Ichiro, a respectable grocer of the Jiyugaoka district in the vicinity of my parents' house. My father's patronage of Shikata's shop had brought them into acquaintanceship. Shikata Ichiro, my father told me, was one of the lucky few hundred survivors of a death march that occurred after Japan's surrender. Shikata recalls that occasion in his nightmares when, among 6,000 other Japanese prisoners in British North Borneo, he was ordered by Australian captors to stack his arms in Pensiangan and march with the others 150 miles to Beaufort for internment. The column of disarmed PoWs suffered the unchecked vengeance of Borneo coast tribesmen, head-hunters deliberately let loose on the Japanese in repayment for the Imperial Army's alleged past misdeeds. Fortunately, Shikata senior lived to produce his beautiful son, Yuichi. That was in 1946, thus making Yuichi nineteen years old now.

Shikata senior was by no means a poor man, as his standing in the Jiyu-gaoka Merchants' Association certified. Through his contacts in a veterans' league after the war, he had formed profitable commercial alliances with the ultra-right underworld of black market bosses, thereby achieving his present respectable eminence. Shikata's affiliation to conservatism had extended itself in a curious fashion to Yuichi's activities: Shikata had recruited his young son in a baseball cheer-leading squad, in support of a popular Tokyo team favoured by a certain brand of rightwing aficionados. Yuichi's practice in this cheer-leading chorus would provide a foundation for chanting the simple-minded slogans of the right.

On my father's recommendation, I had volunteered to groom Yuichi for his next bout of university entrance exams. I refused payment for these tutorials. Shikata senior attempted to pay off his debt to me by presenting my family with numerous gifts: baskets of oysters, lobsters and the choicest fruit, saké in handmade ceramic ware beautifully wrapped in rice straw, confectionery of every sort and *kasutera* sponge cake that my mother especially likes. Each of these deliveries sank Yuichi further into dishonour, deeper into the circles of indebtedness constricting him like the system of Dante's hell.

Yuichi had two goals in life. One, of course, was to slake his father's ambition by graduating from a first-rank university. The other, postponed one, was to please himself by becoming a career officer in the *Jieitai*, the Self Defence Forces, as the newly reconstituted army was named. By night, Yuichi struggled despairingly with his books; by day, he donned the uniform of a tram conductor, a profession recently taken up that annoyed Shikata senior, but which at least partly relieved Yuichi of his sense of being parasitical and allowed him to indulge in his love of uniforms. Yuichi did indeed look very fine in his tram conductor's uniform. He had come directly from work to the Waseda gym still in uniform.

'A tram conductor's work seemed very attractive to me, when I was a child,' I said. 'I classed it among the tragic professions that I found deeply compelling. I remember how splendid the trams looked, decorated with flowers on festival days.'

'Everything for you is aesthetic,' Yuichi complained.

'I'm afraid that's true, Yuichi.'

Yuichi glanced impatiently at me.

Our supper in Shinjuku had turned out, as I expected, a gloomy business. I myself enjoyed a mood of rakish high spirits, proud of my cut eyebrow; but Yuichi's former victorious elation in the ring had fallen by rapid degrees to morose hostility.

'Mishima-*san*, please do me the immense favour of not coaching me in my studies anymore,' Yuichi formally advised, almost stammering with anger. 'The cost is something I cannot bear.'

'I'm sorry you feel that way.'

'There's something else I can't bear,' Yuichi added, eyes fiery with indignation, his lips spitefully twisted. 'Your cynicism, your disgraceful intellectual neutralism – this breath of corruption. I can't bear the unprincipled existence in which you take such pleasure. It's an infection everywhere present these days, like a flu epidemic.'

Yuichi's accusation was not a novelty to me. I had heard speeches of that kind rehearsed before. His recourse to the amuletic slogan, 'intellecual neutralism', was a cliché denunciation often lodged by right-ists, and one which sneered at a fashionable, disaffected sort of liberal. Many intellectuals had indeed found it prudent after the war to take refuge behind a non-committal façade of liberalism. Yuichi believed that such a label was credible in my case. I did not think it worthwhile to disabuse him. I preferred Yuichi to remain ignorant of my past.

Only to tease him, I said, 'One of the martyrs of the far right, ex-Lieutenant-General Ishiwara Kanji, preached non-violent neutrality, just like Gandhi. What do you say to that?'

'That's different,' Yuichi objected. 'Ishiwara was a Nichiren priest, a saintly man of great rectitude.'

'A saint, perhaps; but he was nearly indicted for war crimes.'

'What difference does that make? Besides, he died in 1949. Things have changed since then.'

'They are certainly worse,' I said. 'And what action do you propose, in order to combat this omnipresent plague of cynicism?'

Yuichi looked down earnestly into his empty saké bowl. 'I must *do* something,' he replied; and, after some moment's hesitation, he reached inside his tram conductor's jacket and took out a pamphlet, folded at a particular page, which he urged me to read. I held in my hand the journal of an eccentric ultra-right association, the *Nihon Kikuhata*, 'Japan Chrysanthemum Flag', and the paragraph indicated for me to read described their philosophy of *Kikuhata*-ism, referring to the Chrysan-themum as the traditional Imperial symbol.

> The attitude of Kikuhata-ism at the present stage is aimed at a
> revolution on the model of the Glorious Revolution in England;

330

our social policies bear a close affinity to those of the British Labour Party; for our stand on fisheries we look to Norway, on agriculture to Denmark, on the precision-industry to Switzerland, on culture to France, on philosophy to Germany, on the Emperor-system to the royal families of England and Sweden, and on political organization we find our pattern variously in Switzerland, England and the United States. Moreover, since Kikuhata-ism aims at surmounting present-day bourgeois society with its focus on greed, we resemble the former German Nazis in our hatred of Marxism, the liberals in our rejection of Fascism, the communists in our determination to purge capitalism; and our activity is modelled on that of the English Fabian Society.'

'What on earth do you call this?' I laughed at the end of it.

'Ideology,' Yuichi grimly divulged. 'Does it make any sense to you?'

'Sense? Listen, it would take a scholar to unravel this farrago of references – and a twice greater idiot to believe any of it.'

'You're the intellectual. Explain it.'

'And you? Pardon me, but aren't you knocking for admission to the university?'

'Beating my head bloody, more like,' Yuichi blushed. 'Go on – you're the law graduate of Imperial University – explain it.'

'What would you like me to explain? This is all right wing *haragei* – belly talk.'

'What does "Glorious Revolution" mean?'

'It refers to the deposition of King James II of England and his replacement on the throne by his son-in-law and nephew, William, Prince of Orange. A sort of bloodless *coup-d'état*, depending on one's point of view.'

'I'm not entirely stupid, Kochan. I *know* the history. What I don't understand is whether it's called "Glorious" because it was a revolution or because it was bloodless, as you say. I don't understand why the Kikuhata group refers to such an event.'

'I would imagine it is a veiled, recondite allusion to our own Imperial Restoration.'

'A return to the Emperor-system, in short?'

'I expect so.'

Some people in the restaurant had begun looking at us. Yuichi paid no heed to this, but settled back with an expression of wonderment on his face, and seemingly contented at last.

'Now, kindly explain to me,' I asked, 'what satisfaction you get from ideas you don't fully comprehend?'

'Exactly because I don't completely understand the concepts,' Yuichi replied. 'I feel excited by them. They appeal to something within me that I am not conscious of, something that I can only recognize when it is stimulated.'

'Perhaps, like the sensation you felt as a baseball cheer-leader?'

Yuichi glanced suspiciously at me, but he nodded. A trace of a mischievous smile appeared on his lips as he half closed his eyes and replied: 'When I read words like that – words like "chrysanthemum" – I feel I could happily sacrifice myself for something that is hidden behind them.'

'You mean, you would willingly die for something you don't understand?'

'If you want to put it like that, yes.'

'And why not the words of the great communist sages, Marx, for instance?'

'Crass materialism, fit only for the lazy, mean-spirited minds of workers.'

'But you are a worker too, Yuichi.'

'I might be a worthless *ronin*, that's true. But I'm no ordinary worker.'

'Have it your way. I meant no reproach.'

'Have it *my*, way, you say? Oh yes, I should like that, for a change,' Yuichi exclaimed, attracting more spectatorship from our neighbours. 'Shall I tell you how I would *really* like it? To die with inspired courage like the *Sonjo Doshikai**. Do you know what they did when the Surrender came? They planned to assassinate the Prime Minister, his cabinet and a bunch of other defeatist politicians and financial scoundrels.' Yuichi ticked off these killings on his fingers as though itemizing a list of dirty laundry.

'In reality, they failed to do anything of the sort,' I said. 'Your heroes ended up cornered by the police in a building in Shiba – and then what? They blew themselves up with hand-grenades.'

'So what? At least they died resisting the Surrender.'

'Indeed, and in so doing they defied the Emperor's own specific order to surrender. They died committing treason. And *that* is what really happened, Yuichi. Criminal treason against His Majesty.'

My onslaught had left Yuichi stunned, his mouth open, but with no convincing retort to fill it.

I glanced at my watch. It was time to look for a discreet gay men's hotel, so that I could enjoy Yuichi's body for a few hours before our expected return to the bosoms of our respective families. Yuichi stared at the floor in aggrieved resignation. A black-glazed water jug on our table reflected my face and its raffishly bandaged eyebrow. My vague, dark-mirrored image could be mistaken for a boxer's, a victor celebrating his match.

---

* Revere the Emperor and Expel-the-Barbarian Comrades Association.

Several months passed before I saw Yuichi again, this time by accident in Ginza. He was accompanied by two other young men. All three wore the dark blue uniform of the *Junkoku Seinentai*, the 'National Martyrs Youth Corps', emblazoned with the Imperial Chrysanthemum crest. 'Yuichi,' I called, startled to find him in that paramilitary uniform, but he passed by me with only a curt nod in response. 'Who's that?' I heard one of Yuichi's comrades ask. 'A famous writer,' he replied. 'A friend of my father's.'

I stood there dumbfounded, watching as he melted away into the crowd. So, he had finally done it. He had finally taken that step into the enveloping night of violence. I should not have been so astonished. Yuichi's journey into ultra-right fundamentalism had been ineluctably predestined for him from the start. Nevertheless, I could not help but wonder, for Yuichi had now entered into a mysterious region, a mist enshrouded underworld ruled by the grand dragons of clandestine politics, a fanatic breed of activists like Inoue Nissho, a Nichiren priest and terrorist organizer, whose Blood Pledge Corps in 1932 had assassinated a Finance Minister and a Mitsui director. Yuichi's paramilitary cadet corps, although of recent post-war vintage, had its roots in Inoue's type of pre-war conspiratorial organization and was now one more chapel of violence among others like it in a larger church of the anti-communist unification movement. Reports of crimes committed by these groups remained uninvestigated by the authorities; but ordinary citizens were well enough acquainted with them, with acts of intimidation at election times, with strike-breaking attacks on union picket-lines, with criminal methods of fund-raising that included loan recovery enforcement, protection and other forms of extortion.

I wondered, too, how much Yuichi really knew about these gangster activities. Was he able to recognize that his patriotic samurai chieftains were in league with labour bosses, racketeers and corrupt politicians? Or would fanaticism succeed to keep his beliefs blind and virgin?

My anxieties were really expressions of my desire to see Yuichi again. I had grown weary of the sort of gay boys one meets at parties or in bars, and worse still, the trade encountered in parks and other insalubrious places. I longed passionately for Yuichi's virile cleanliness that sustained its virtue on a diet of obstinate, narrow-minded convictions.

I tried several times unsuccessfully to reach Yuichi at home. At last, before my telephone calls became too embarrassingly numerous, I heard his voice. I did not have to plead for a meeting, since he apparently welcomed it. 'I am required to sleep in the Corps' dormitory,' he said. 'But I will be on leave next weekend.'

I booked a hotel room in the Tsukiji district near the port, a not very savoury accommodation, but one that guaranteed discretion.

Yuichi arrived in plain civilian clothes, but with a sensational cut across his left cheek festooned with a ladder of six stitches. 'My, aren't you a sight,' I said. 'What happened?'

Yuichi explained that together with some cadets of his Corps he had engaged in a sword-fight with a gang of Koreans – *daisangokujin* – 'third country nationals' as he called them in the jargon of the right.

'Did you enjoy having your face stapled like that?'

'It's all part of cleansing the nation,' Yuichi remarked, smiling, but not boastfully.

'When did this fight occur?'

'Yesterday.'

Our hotel room was stifling, steamy hot on this evening of high summer. The fan blades churned in vain against an atmosphere that seemed coagulated. We stripped off our clothes, not in the urgency of passion, but for sheer relief. I observed a reluctance in Yuichi which was not shyness exactly but a withdrawn faraway air. In these last three months, Yuichi had visibly changed from a quick-tempered, morose youth made unnaturally wretched by his *ronin* condition, to this indefinable person sitting naked before me but unfathomable, as though fully clothed by the leaden weight of air. Yuichi's surface of tranquillity provoked my malice, like a fine-polished veneer tempts one to run a fingernail across it.

'So, you've faced death,' I said, trying to keep my tone neutral, without sneering. 'Doesn't it worry you, now that the threat is real?'

'No.'

'Tell me sincerely, was it a rapturous feeling, that proximity to death when you fought your duel with the Koreans?'

Yuichi smiled as if at a child. 'You make it sound theatrical. There is nothing to say about it. I didn't feel near death, but simply – well, without sounding too grand, inside it.'

'*Inside* it? I must say, it does sound rather grand. Is it this the National Martyrs Youth Corps has taught you – a greater appreciation of death, as it were, seen from the inside?'

'Have you invited me here to insult me, Kochan?'

'Certainly not. Please forgive my remarks, but permit me some amount of legitimate curiosity. After all, you have been converted to a life out of the ordinary, and this is highly intriguing to someone like me.'

'An unconvertible nihilist?'

'Precisely, a staunch nihilist, as you say. But tell me, what has the Martyrs Corps really taught you?'

'We are taught the methods of farming –'

'– ah yes, the Nichiren Buddhist "return to the land".'

'If you know, why do you ask me?'

334

'Please go on.'

'We are given body-building and martial arts instruction. A cadet must weigh at least 150 pounds,' and here, Yuichi attempted to keep himself from looking at my weakling body. 'All cadets must refrain from alcohol, Western-style dancing, films and jazz, and games of mahjong or pachinko pinball are forbidden.'

'What about baseball?'

'It is not permitted.'

'There's a departure from your cheer-leading days.'

'I was only fifteen then.'

'In other words, no forms of dissipation allowed. They demand a very high standard of moral conduct.'

'It is simply Japanese conduct, which is naturally moral.'

'I see. But then, why have you accepted to come here?'

Yuichi made no reply. He contemplated the fan's blurred, whirring blades, the likeness of a huge chrysanthemum in a cage. 'You have a soul stiff as dry leather,' Yuichi finally declared.

Yuichi's rejoinder was clever and painfully accurate. I felt pathologically numbed, it was true, like a shrivelled wine-skin of brittle leather containing diseased innards. All this week, my guts had been acting up, and I prayed that a severe attack would not occur to embarrass me in front of Yuichi.

'And how do you suggest we pass our time this weekend?' I asked.

'As friends, Kochan. For once, in the harmless enjoyment of friendship.' Yuichi retrieved his briefcase and took out from it a large wooden box. 'Do you play *go* or *shogi*?'

'I don't waste my time on games,' I replied irritably.

'No, I'm not surprised. You play a game with life instead.'

'Have I booked this room for nothing – to play games?'

'So what? I don't feel especially grateful to find myself in a cheap gay fleabag.'

'Oh, you prefer the high moral plateau of the Martyrs Youth Corps, I suppose? And where does it get its money from? I'll tell you. From gangsters like the *sokaiya* – those amusingly named "general meetings experts" – who extort millions of yen from intimidated shareholders.'

'I know there are outright crooks who pose as sincere nationalists. But that's not our way. All our additional funds come from nature itself, from the profits of a single mountain, the Beppu sulphur mines.'

'Is that what you're told?'

'We are told the truth. Others fabricate malicious lies about us.'

'You are misled. What do you think is the true nature of your task?'

'The renewal of the nation.'

'Oh, well said, bravo! And you are proceeding to "renew the nation" by hooligan attacks on Koreans?'

'Do you dare call me a hooligan?'

'Hooligan, yes – and far worse, a gay boy posing as a manly samurai, while in fact being the minion of gangsters.'

My venomous tirade had finally realized the effect I desired to see – Yuichi's tranquillity shattered. My fingernail had scratched beneath his finely polished veneer, and it drew a ruffian's blood.

Yuichi went again to his briefcase on the bed, rummaging in it, and affording me a view of the wonderfully tight muscular haunches of his buttocks. I shivered, anticipating the violence that my rancorous words had merited, at the same time admiring the nobility of the body that would next mete out my punishment – and I grinned, I grinned like a fool, as I considered our two briefcases, Yuichi's and mine, for we had come here equipped with them rather than overnight luggage which might have alerted our families' suspicion.

Yuichi turned sharply round to me – and found an idiot grinning up at him passively from an armchair, a person disarmingly prepared to receive injury. Yuichi gripped a samurai's long *yoroidoshi* dagger in both hands, tightly, so that his forearm muscles bulged, with his arms extended, straight out. Slowly, his right hand drew out an inch of blade from the wooden scabbard, its sharp edge refracting the rays of neon lights outside the open window. The blade's cutting edge stood an inch or two's distance from the tip of my nose, as more and more of its threatening fang gradually became exposed. Yuichi's torso and neck muscles swelled pneumatically, as though he were exerting tremendous force to dislodge a magnetic ton of weight, and meanwhile the blade crept nearer to my nose, as if attracted by a will of its own, until it pressed on the bridge of my nose just below the cartilege. 'Did I really hear you call me a hooligan?' Yuichi growled.

'Now who's being theatrical?' I smiled, but fearing to move a hair.

Yuichi snapped the dagger shut, almost clipping some flesh off my nose, and he began singing: '. . . the form of towering Mount Fuji is the pride of our flawless like a golden chalice, unshakable Nippon . . .' He stood at attention, his dagger pointed south in salute to Mount Fuji.

'Stop singing that at once,' I exclaimed. 'You have no proper understanding of those words.'

Yuichi was surprised by the forcefulness of my protest. He seemed baffled by the quickness of my recovery from fear. 'And I suppose *you* have a proper appreciation of them?' He threw his dagger on the bed and sat down beside it.

'Words are my profession, and because they eat my flesh away, because they corrode my very bones, I fear and respect them deeply. Words have a terrifying power of realization. Those amuletic phrases from Imperial times that you mouth – phrases like *kino muketsu*, flawless like a golden chalice – such words are like the compacted matter of stellar black holes, a spoonful of which weighs tons. They are the foundation of our culture, that you handle so lightly.'

'I know that, professor,' he eyed me skeptically. 'That's why they command my faith. Do you admit to any faith?'

'You cannot seek to renew the nation unless you have studied the classics.' I was getting dangerously close to betraying myself.

'Yes, and see what studying the classics has brought you to – a lack of any faith.'

'I have a writer's conscience,' I said, in an effort to extricate myself, 'which is to believe nothing.'

He laughed. 'And you presume to admonish me about words in which you disbelieve?'

I offered Yuichi a cigarette. He hesitated to take it. 'Is smoking also forbidden? You are on leave, go on.' I lit our cigarettes with a match, and then poured us some whisky. This too he accepted, reluctantly.

I held out the spent match. 'What do you call this object which I've just used to light our cigarettes?'

Yuichi stared uncertainly at me, but replied, '*Matchi*.'

'Yes, our normal word, *matchi*, our Nipponized term for the Western match. During the war, it was thought unpatriotic to say *matchi*. We were instructed to use *kaichu toridashi hitsukegi* – pocket-extraction kindling-wood.'

'What exactly has this got to do with me?'

'Nothing and everything. If you seek moral purification, don't say *matchi* like any common, unenlightened man in the street.'

'Have you forgotten, Mishima-*san*? I dismissed you as my tutor three months ago. Your gifts still remain unwelcome.'

'My gifts were wasted on a cretin.'

Yuichi grimaced – the stitched lips of his cut folding into an additional smile crosswise on his cheek. He began to sing again, loudly to drown out my words, the anthem of the National Martyrs Youth Corps.

> Though we are but simple and honest fellows,
> We love Japan . . .
>
> Oh, let us weep bitter tears
> As we pray for our country!
>
> Aye, the hot blood burns in our breasts
> And we seethe with youthful rage!
> At the battle-cry of 'Rebuild the country!'
> We youthful patriots burst into tears . . .

Could anything be more absurd? More absurd even than the words of Yuichi's battle hymn, so tear-jerkingly, pop Nipponese that they

337

attained a certain ludicrous authenticity? (That wonderfully kitsch tough guy phrase, *guchoku no mono*, 'simple and honest fellows', acclaiming the guileless honesty of the outspoken patriot so much prized as a samurai virtue – that was surely absurd enough under the circumstances to make me burst out laughing.) No, the real absurdity was the two of us. Two men sitting naked by an electric fan, glaring at each other in repugnance. At moments like these, I bitterly resented my homosexuality. I felt it was something added to me, an enemy alien by my side, not something I felt to be within me. Ever since my adolescence I had lived in suspicion, under the obscuring shadows of its demands. I wanted to break free of the chains that bound me to the past by an act of pure Will. I wanted to kill that hypersensitive, sick adolescent who went on trying to pollute my life as a man, a life already quasi-moribund, to annihilate him with cruelties, even though in fact I loved him because he had been my life until now. I had never asked for his unnatural companionship, this creature of erudite malignance, who had arrived from who knows where to put my entire life in parenthesis (quarantined within them, as though between hospital walls, I can hear myself screaming as daily, relentlessly, the bandages of my masquerade are changed, falling from me like violet, pus-laden petals) who had turned my innermost desires into insubstantial words, waste paper and a diabetic craving for reality that sickened at my touch.

Yuichi had stopped singing and was looking at me, and I too was looking at me – or at a certain part of me, a thing with its own volition, ugly, squat, and rising like some pre-historic lizard without limbs, poking its domed, blind-eyed Cyclops' head through the collar of my prepuce. We stared at it, both of us – and there was nothing else for it – we laughed, we laughed at the shameless blind instinct of my thing.

'Look at you,' Yuichi taunted. 'You're just a rag doll with a big prick.'

'You never complained it was too big for your needs.'

I had retaliated with bile against Yuichi's scorn, and pushed him beyond endurance to fury. He jumped up from the bed and threw himself at me. I managed without thinking to resign my vulnerable position on the armchair, rise swiftly to meet him, and with even more unthinkable luck, serve him a good right hook squarely on the face. I heard my knuckles crack as they struck Yuichi's cheekbone. My punch borrowed more power than I had from the force of Yuichi's own propulsion. Blood gushed in a mass from the reopened cut on his cheek. We fell to the floor in a clinch – and I trying to safeguard my protuberant thing from jeopardy – knocking over the armchair, a night-table and lamp in our clumsy struggles, but without much credibility left in our punches. Yuichi's bad luck and my good one had drained us both of strength.

The room had grown dimmer. Light, in a curious spot-beamed angle, rose from the upset lamp in a diagonal slash across a corner of the room and part of the ceiling. Yuichi knelt, propped up on his hands, mesmerized by his blood dribbling onto the carpet. I caught this dark velvet spill in the palms of my hands, I too fascinated by the thrill of it, and carried it up to my nostrils to inhale its fleshy bouquet. I dipped my tongue into the blood cupped in the umbilical crevice of my palm. Yuichi, watching me, tried to utter something, but only a strangled sigh emerged from between his blood-stained teeth. I held out my hands to him, and he copied my ceremony, his head dipping down like a thirsty bird's into my palms. He watched me, the pupils of his eyes iridescent from the neon lights outside, as I anointed my lizard with his blood, reviving it to greater expanse now, the pouting lips of my urethra already beginning to lubricate.

In a returning upsurge of energy, I helped Yuichi to the bed, threw him on it on his back, and positioned myself over him, on my knees. I folded his legs apart and back, pinioning them under my arms. The compacted muscles of Yuichi's calves pressed hard against the stringy undersides of my upper arms. My hands under Yuichi's back could feel his kidneys pumping, as though exposed to my touch. The lizard butted against a tight enclosure. Yuichi's head was submerged over the side of the bed: he raised it into the light, a vermilion-stained *kouros* face, the enigma of its smile revealing displeasure. He thrust his fingers between my lips, between my teeth, prising them apart, in desperate urgency to reach inside my mouth and cull its saliva, once, twice, transferring this wetness, because his own mouth was too dry, to the lizard's bulbous head, anointing its passage inside. In, in, deeper, the little loose curds of excrement rubbing amorously against the lizard's sides, deeper, until my pubis rested between the flared muscles of Yuichi's buttocks.

This was the rider's position in *coitus a tergo* that I preferred, face to face with my lover. Never before had Yuichi allowed me to enjoy it, always offering me his back, turning away as though bashfully not to see the blood-flush of pleasure on my face – or not to let me witness his own – or his pain.

'Why have you never let me fuck you like this before?'

Yuichi grimaced, his eyes opening, terrifyingly blank. His tongue clicked, in release from the arid palate, as his lips formed a reply. 'Why – never – before? Your mind stinks in your guts, like a sewer.'

Again, he jammed his fingers into my mouth, deep inside, poking to the back of my tongue in his effort to reach my uvula. I gagged. Yuichi was trying to make me vomit. He wanted me to spill the foul contents of my mind-rotted guts, as he cried, 'Harder! Harder!' I struggled against the sickness welling up in my oesophagus, my stomach heaved and released an evil, bilious tasting gorge, as I bit down on Yuichi's fingers to stop myself from retching. 'Harder! Harder!' My command over myself shrank away by the instant as the image came to me of rats nesting in the mouldering cavern of my belly. The lizard's snout struck against a cartilege like lump that quivered as Yuichi's back contracted in an arch, and he groaned and ejaculated.

I lay flat on my stomach to stem the molten column of queasiness burning my insides. In this way, I fell asleep. Sometime later, before dawn, I was awoken by the sounds of moaning. I opened my eyes to find Yuichi seated at my side, on the edge of the bed, his back tattooed in the colours cast by the neon rays. 'Are you going to croak, you bastard?' Yuichi said. I realized that those moans of pain were mine. My guts were in agony, like haemorrhaging ulcers. The bed stank. I had vomited in my sleep. 'Look inside my briefcase,' I instructed Yuichi. 'You'll find something like an eyeglass case. Please bring it to me.' The case Yuichi handed me contained a hypodermic syringe and several ampoules of morphine in a camphor solution. My injection brought immediate relief, as though – in Yuichi's phrase – my mind in my guts has returned on a dizzying wave from below to its proper place.

'Are you a drug addict?' Yuichi asked. He held up one of the yellow ampoules against the light. 'Maybe I should try one.'

'Better clean the needle first,' I said giddily. 'You can never tell, I might have syphilis.'

'Very funny,' Yuichi jeered, as I staggered into the bathroom.

Ripples of steam faded on the bathroom mirror, like the weakening breath of a dying man, as I finished washing. My image floated there in mildewed patches, confused with Yuichi's as he approached me from the darkened bedroom and began massaging the nape of my neck, pressing into the occipital tendons as though relaxing them for the guillotine. I saw the reflection of a pale stunted invalid of literature. And in my rapt admiration of Yuichi's well-muscled figure, I foresaw the romantic connoisseur of my own refashioned body, myself as the future custodian of a classical sculpture that I could become – that I *had* to become – that I must will myself to be at all costs.

My *ronin* friend Yuichi could not have imagined the decision taken in that head jolting precariously under the stabs of his thumbs on my neck. I needed to make a body proportionate to the single outsized muscle that hung grotesquely dissonant between the legs of a weakling. I needed a monument fitted to the demands of that massive plaything imposed on an unfit scribbler of novels. The gods played a cruel joke on me. They did not marry me below to some nibble little twig, quickfire in its coital volley, but to a heated stake which is the slave of its own enormity. Do you understand how it is for me, Yuichi? After a spasm of bittersweet displeasure, my semen cast, the world takes on the intolerable colour of a sky after an A-bomb blast, the fall-out colour of black rain that drowns Hiroshima in plague, and a silence that things regain from devastation.

I was thirty years old. All my previous attempts at physical rehabilitation had failed. It seemed too late to reverse an incurable debility by the dictates of my will. But I was determined to construct an enviable body, such as one sees flaunted in body-building advertisements. Exactly like that; exactly with that simple-minded ambition that to the fastidious taste of an intellectual must appear pathetic, if not repulsive and degrading.

People take all sorts of decisions – to stop smoking, to diet, to beautify themselves by plastic surgery. Such apparently trivial decisions are life-affirming acts of will, not to be despised. They are attempts to compel one's mirror to yield the desired image. To the psychologist of unsentimental vision, however, these acts of volition are really the evidence of a deeper, inadmissable weakness. Every input of will in human beings inevitably produces a contrary and involuntary idea. And to this extent, all human beings are intellectuals, unable in their acts to escape the impoverishing shadow of their minds. I am not saying this to excuse myself, but only to state a theorem of everyday psychology in which, alas, I found myself enmeshed.

It was with this sort of mental repugnance, predisposed to defeatist irony, that I picked up the body-builder's weights for the first time in the Korakuen gym. As I worked with these obdurate, aptly named dumb-bells, against all odds – against the pitying glances and head shakes of the other trainees – as I tortured myself, day after day, I began to understand in my agony that these lumps of steel were the condensed essence of my own mental repugnance, the distillation of all my writer's poisoned nights corroding my viscera. I understood that these adamantine weights were in themselves nothing, only the reflection of the antithetical self I was labouring to create.

The results of a year's indescribably hard work were gratifying, but hardly spectacular. True, my gastro-enteric troubles had entirely vanished, but something wrong or missing in my attitude impeded further progress. I had come to the summer of 1956, and an opportunity now presented itself to test the strength I had so far won. The summer festival day of August 19th approached on which a select number of young men would shoulder a massive portable shrine and carry it in procession through the streets of our neighbourhood. Forty or more stalwarts were needed to bear the crushing weight of this two-ton shrine, known as the *omikoshi*, and I fervently wished to be counted among those chosen ones. I confess that my motive was no more than a childish wish to display the sinewy improvement in my figure. Yuichi's father, Shikata Ichiro, was the committee president of the Jiyugaoka Merchants'

Association which organized the *omikoshi* parade. He responded positively to my wish, since his debt to me was still unsettled.

August storm clouds thundered and rolled away from a propitious blue sky on that day. Strips of paper lay damp and limp on the forest of *gohei* sticks brandished by the crowd. I wore the Association's costume, an inscribed *hakama* jacket off one shoulder and its sleeve tied back with a pinkish-yellow cord, a *hachimaki* headband, a loincloth and belly band of bleached cotton, and tight knee-length trousers. I was stationed at the front left of the *omikoshi*, preparing to take hold of one of its two lengthwise wooden bars that would rest on our shoulders, when I glanced up once more at the formidable structure with its several tiers, its wreath-sculpted pillars and rails of ebony and goldleaf, and a golden pheasant crowning its summit. My intention of showing off appeared foolhardy as I shrank before that awesome object.

Among the *tengu* demon masks worn by the Shinto priest's assistants, one in particular appeared to be sizing me up: this mask, covering the chief priest's own face, was the golden-eyed effigy of a fox, the fox attendant of the rice god Inari, patron deity of good fortune. The priest raised his jingling, metal-ringed staff in signal, and with a tremendous *kiai* shout in unison we hoisted up the shrine.

I felt as though the entire weight of the blue sky had suddenly descended on my shoulders. The *omikoshi* lurched and dipped perilously earthwards as each one of us experienced the surprise of that fearful colossus on our backs, as though for a moment each of us had been left alone to bear it all in isolation. As my legs sagged, I remembered the golden-eyed fox measuring me up for the task, and I wondered if I could endure the hours of travail ahead of me.

We struggled to gain coordination, to achieve the single-willed tonnage capacity demanded of us by our cargo. As the sweat of panic dried cold on my chest and forehead – as it also did on every other bearer – and the tendons in my legs stiffened into pistons, I shouted, I shouted in chorus together with the others. Our cries became a sort of battle hymn, torn from us by necessity, that gave voice to our singular resolve. Our cheer-leader scurried round us, waving his fan, and shouting instructions and encouragement like a racing-boat coxwain. The din was ferocious as the procession took on momentum, with our rhythmic bellows merging into the priests' ceremonial chants, the clang of bells and the tumult of drums. Ahead of us went the miniature *omikoshi* carried by children, a mock replica of our own load, a reflection of consoling lightness.

My companions' faces expressed Dionysiac frenzy, savage masks stripped of individual identity, without consciousness. Our bodies and the *omikoshi* were fused together in a single, drunkenly swaying, black and gold caterpillar supported by a tangle of legs.

And what inconceivable, sacred thing did we hold up to the noon sky with such back-breaking effort? What precious object did the shrine conceal behind its locked doors? Nothing. Vacant darkness. A void. A perfect cube of empty night. The sacred value of the *omikoshi* was no more than the sum total of its weight, nothing else.

The apparent emptiness and futility of our drudgery gave me an unexpected insight into my wrong-headed notions of body-building. I asked myself: what is the purpose of weight-lifting? Is it not to render things weight*less*? Yes, exactly. It is to make the resistance of weight itself weightless. I must strive to be weightless – and also shadowless, a noontime sun-encased being.

I began dimly to see that muscles were a preparation for another, higher category of visceral sensation. Muscles rendered possible a voluntary acceptance of pain – pain that no longer resulted from a mere dysfunction of one's organs, a diseased liver, a toxic colon – but that could be courted with aesthetic objectivity. Only with a body fit to kill or be killed could one seek true culture – visceral equanimity – which is the samurai Way of Death.

As we toiled along Jiyugaoka's thoroughfares, at a slug's pace, every muscle aching, sun-hammered and drenched in sweat, I began to understand what the *omikoshi* really contained. Our perfect cube of empty night enclosed the secret of weightlessness. Only by the collective fusion of our manhood, by a toil that left our bodies smelly, dirt-caked and exhausted – only by such a drowning of one's individuality in the mass could one penetrate the enshrined Void and become oneself weightless. *I am myself the weightlessness that I carry.* This was the secret I finally learnt that day.

I speak of an intense, blurred duration of time. I speak of intense pleasure, far surpassing the keenness of homoeroticism in which my mind had always intervened, had always persisted, separating me from the core of my pleasure. I speak of participation in happiness, which is always uncomplicated and tragic.

Yuichi, at my side, must have read this moment's uncommon ecstasy on my face. 'Enjoy yourself,' he hissed in my ear. 'But you'll never be one of us. Never.'

Never. That spiteful word of banishment on Yuichi's lips opened my eyes to my exclusion from the life of others.

7   THE TOUGH GUY

I LOCK the door of the shadow room. I want no more memories of the past. Let them evaporate like mist on a mirror. My wish is to enter the future, the perfect empty cube of night, which is the mirror at last clarified.

  •   Not yet. There is still a trace of vapour on the mirror, one more imaginary reflection out of the past, from the damp smouldering days of June 1960. I remember a summer ghost, a B-movie tough guy nicknamed *karakkaze yaro*. He is a blustery fellow, the *karakkaze yaro*, literally, for he takes his name from a pestering *karakkaze* autumn wind that blows the smog of Tokyo away south over the bay and presages winter. Idle or empty threats are also popularly called *karakkaze*, and it is therefore an appropriate epithet for a *yakuza* hoodlum of minor rank.

So then, what is the story of this boastful tough guy?

A rain-blistered poster outside a cinema in a low class quarter of northeast Tokyo advertizes the film, *Karakkaze Yaro*. The beetle-browed face of a ruffian scowls down from the film poster, a convict's shorn head, his black leather jacket open over a pneumatically muscled torso bronzed by exercises in the prison yard. A sword is poised across his chest, as though the gangster were cutting his way through the paper. The poster hangs in shreds. Four months have passed since I starred in that *yakuza* film produced by Dai-ei Studios. *Karakkaze Yaro* opened at the end of March 1960, and in May, riots on a more ferocious and protracted scale than in 1952 erupted again in protest at the renewal of the security pact with the United States. Prime Minister Kishi Nobusuke ordered the police to remove by force the Socialist members of the Diet who had occupied the corridors of the Chamber in a sit-down strike.

Once again the streets of Tokyo were slick with excitement. Blood flowed, as it did in medieval times of the *ikko ikki*, fanatic uprisings, when faith was no tolerant peaceable affair, when unruly warrior monks of Esoteric Buddhism frequently clashed with each other and with the authorities. Tendai monks would sweep down from Mount Hiei into Kyoto carrying aloft the Shinto god Sanno to meet in open pitched battle with their Hosso sect rivals bearing the sacred Shinto tree of the Kasuga shrine. In the Communist slogans of the 1960 rioters, in their chanting appeals for the death of the traitorous Prime Minister Kishi, I heard the war cries of the Pure Land extremists of former times: 'The mercy of Buddha should be recompensed even by pounding flesh to pieces! One's obligation to the Buddha should be recompensed even by smashing bones to bits!'

344

That summer, I felt the old, disorderly riotous Japan breaking free of its modern shell of conformity, as it does periodically like the islands' wayward earthquakes and volcanic explosions, and I wanted to take part in the anarchy.

There is only time for a moment's pause before the poster of *Karak-kaze Yaro* which reflects me like a mirror in tatters. My leather jacket flaps open as I run, my black string-fronted shirt loosened in the June heat. Round my left arm, I wear the armband of a *Mainichi* newspaper reporter. I fasten the chin straps of my protective helmet against the rioters' flying debris and the batons of the police. Twilight gathers under a blush of storm clouds to the West.

Since early morning, I have been following the demonstrators as they assembled outside the Ministries and the Imperial Palace, from the Kanda district to this poorer outlying quarter, an acephalous mass that gathers and disperses, the same one and yet constantly different like the river of Heraclitus. I go with it like a piece of flotsam in a current that flows by will or by chance to this cinema.

I hurry to join the crowd, the treasonable crowd, as it swells caterpillar-like round the corner and blocks all the streets ahead. The crowd has its own peculiarly muddy odour of closeness, one which suddenly turns chokingly crystalline, piercing one's throat. A thick granular swarm of moths seems to issue from the accordioning flanks of the caterpillar, as the crowd squeezes together for a moment and then expands, and a cloud of unbearably stinking ammonia rises from the street. Cannisters of tear-gas on the pavements are kicked away in desperation; but the fumes lie heavy in the torpid air. The caterpillar falls apart into segments, devoured into smaller and smaller portions by hungry brown ants. Policemen in helmets and gas-masks, under riot shields, are striking out mercilessly with their batons. I hear the crack of breaking bones, the groans of those fallen with split skulls and ruptured kidneys. I fall back with a retreating knot of demonstrators under the cinema marquee. As I duck into a side-street, away from the wave of attacks on my fellow refugees, a policeman with his baton raised like a practiced Kendoist confronts me. Instinctively, I take up a Karate posture, left leg bent forward in a crouch, my right flexed to deliver a counter-attacking kick. I raise my left forearm defensively, the sleeve of my leather jacket affording some minimal protection – the reason for wearing such apparel on a hot day like this. The policeman notices the journalist's armband. His grip on the baton relaxes, and he lowers his tear-gas mask. The perspiring face of a young man glares at me from under the helmet. 'Move on!' he bellows.

I look round. The street is deserted. Not a soul remains, not even a trace of the wounded. It is a strange phenomenon of riots that so vast a crowd can dematerialize so quickly. Tomorrow, the *Mainichi* will print my thoughts on the riot. Tomorrow, the newspapers will report the government's officially approved casualty figures, less than the ones I have counted today.

Beads of rain sparkle iridescently on my jacket. I hadn't even noticed the shower passing over us in a black squall. I stand alone on a forlorn back street of a commercial quarter. No one knows me here – a *karakkaze* hoodlum among eerie, seemingly abandoned proletarian shops. The air is pestilent with smog and the stench of open sewers. Houses of slum matchwood have a grey rural look of misery. This is the humble Japan I see in 1960 as we progress full speed towards the heights of manufacturing glory.

From the opaque, pustular sky, a ray of twilight sun falls pink on a mud puddle at my feet. I see the hazy opal ghost of the full moon reflected on slime. In this illumined pool of foulness, my heart finds what is scarcely credible, remorse, betrayal, the impossibility of love. In that negligible mirror of rain water at my feet, I feel my heart constricted, my soul's tiny abode as the prophet Nichiren had long ago claimed: 'Something like the moon reflected in a muddy pool, like gold wrapped up in a dirty bag.'

The sun declines in the West, for a few last minutes radiantly luminous on shop windows and mud puddles. There was a time, before the war, when people would have emerged from their houses to offer prayers of thanks for the sun's reappearance after a thunderstorm. No one comes out now. The sun's divinity has been extinguished in their hearts. Am I the only one assailed by a foolishly constricted heart, by the pangs of melancholy that an unrequited lover suffers? A face gazes back at me from the resplendent puddle which seems a fragment of mirror dropped from the sky. That piece of reflected heaven on the road bears the imprint of my face, a stranger's face drowned in filth. Unwelcome thoughts arise from the confined reflection, a claustrophobic nostalgia filled with images that are erotic, sad, resentful, like a closet that discharges a suffocating tear-gas flurry of moths.

I peer into this closet, as though entering fearfully again into my grandmother's musty storeroom of samurai armour, as I used to in my childhood. It is a bygone place of terror and enchantment, filled with the fancy dress of notions that are moth-eaten and decayed, haunted by the memory of a particular sunrise that now seems faint and absurd. On a certain day twenty-six centuries before my birth, on 11 February 660 BC, the sun goddess Amaterasu granted the Mirror of Divinity to our first Emperor Jimmu. With him began Japan's imperial dynasty. Our ancient chroniclers spoke of that fabled Imperial Sunrise as *ama-tsu-hi-tsugi*, heavenly-sun-succession, terms which piously forecast the endurance of an imperial line without break from that day to our own.

Where is the Mirror of Divinity today? It is here, lying at my feet. A puddle, sunset pink, like the insides of flesh or fish. A mirror fallen from the sky – the bright sun of divinity eclipsed by the earth's own uranium force, by the A-bomb 'brighter than a thousand suns'.

What happens to those who live in eclipse, after the sun has gone out? They exist in perpetual midnight, like the inhabitants of Gakijima in the days of Empress Jingu, when the sun goddess Amaterasu withdrew her mirror from sight. They are bewildered, grimacing comically as people do when passing from sunlight into a darkened interior.

Today, 15 June 1960, I have found a single little piece of the Emperor's solar looking-glass – a mirror shattered into many millions of fragments, one piece for each eclipsed citizen of this nation bereaved of divine light. By a strange, fatal irony, the Imperial eclipse has brought the fulfilment of the war-time prophecy, *ichioku gyokusai*, Death to the Hundred Million, not as the slogan anticipated in heroic last-ditch resistance to the Allied invasion, but in the mass entombment of souls in darkness.

I retrace my steps that earlier carried me here. An object left discarded on the street by the fleeing rioters catches my eye in the falling dark. It is an article of woman's lingerie. I contemplate the thing incredulously for a while before daring to touch it. What I see, beyond any doubt, is a woman's brassière, black in colour, its cups forming rotund twin peaks on the asphalt. I pick it up gingerly by the shoulder straps, half expecting to find the haemorrhaging, amputated cones of the owner's breasts inside the cups. They are vacant, of course, but of an impressive depth and circumference that testify to a large bosomed female. And yet, the side straps provide evidence of a petite torso. Even more baffling, these straps have remained securely fastened by the clasp at the back. How on earth could such a snug-fitting harness possibly drop off from the wearer? I examine the brassière more closely: heavy black silk, unfrilly and severely utilitarian, old-fashioned in its sturdiness, its cups braced by strips of whalebone. I raise the cups to my nose. Again, like a release of pale moths in the twilight, a faint whiff of ammonia that comes from a stranger's unknown flesh, repugnant and mysteriously attractive, fills my nostrils.

I glance round. Am I being watched? I feel like a guilty husband shopping for his mistress. Or a transvestite purchasing the last items of lingerie that he will wear tonight when he plans to hang himself. Should I throw the rag back in the gutter? I decide to keep it, as though I were appointed to find its original owner. I fold the brassière away in my rucksack, together with my *Mainichi* armband, helmet and reporter's paraphernalia.

Night falls. Streetlamps bloom suddenly into life. I begin walking, directed vaguely towards the city centre. I do not know where my feet will carry me, or my thoughts. Thoughts of a nature that pass without leaving any clear impression, like the frames of a film rewinding at high speed, exhaust me more than my seemingly endless route through the city. A sense of futility overcomes me, an evil taste that suffuses my mouth.

In this bleak, self-lacerating mood, I arrived at the Ginza. A bright, oppressive clutter of neon signalling the Ginza's unlimited nocturnal entertainments, convinced me that I had entered a region of the inferno that punishes vice by eternally glutting its victims with it. I stared at the neon-ignited faces of the Ginza strollers as though I were witnessing again the air raid casualties of B-29 incendiary bombs that devastated Tokyo in May 1945. These apparently cauterized, napalm-singed faces were smiling, some were even laughing and gossiping – I overheard one passer-by commenting on the death of a girl that occurred earlier today in the unsuccessful storming of the Diet by Communist students. Today is 15 June 1960, not 24 May 1945.

I cannot rid myself of a memory of death which has never occurred. I can never be certain of reality or that anything is permanent. Total destruction is the only thing I feel sure is unavoidable.

I found myself seated at a table in a Ginza stripclub. I recall neither its name nor having chosen to enter it nor asking for the gin Tom Collins – a drink I cannot stomach – which is placed before me. The club is dark, but its mass of inhabitants distinguishable in a marine phosphorescent glow. This was one of the plural nightspots of the water business, and here the defunct souls of our present-day salarymen appeared in their office after-life, surrendering all dignity to barfly drunkenness. I saw a Mitsui company executive, reduced to infantilism, weeping unrestrained tears of complaint on the bosom of a Thai hostess. I looked round, persuaded that this was indeed the rock cave at Ise into which the sun goddess Amaterasu had withdrawn and plunged the earth in everlasting night.

What did all these men seek here? Had they crept into Amaterasu's cave – jammed together in this sleazy plastic and strobe-lit version of a Shinto shrine – in the hope of enticing the sun-goddess out of her sulking refusal to shine? A ceremony was taking place on stage, in which striptease artistes prepared to mimic the recuperation of daylight. My fellow males were assembled here for the excitement of the *tokadashi*, the 'open event', the vaginal aperture that the naked girls on stage exhibited as they crouched down, leaning far back like Caribbean limbo dancers, their legs spread wide apart. They offered for view that hypnotizing, fleshy carmine cave, inches away from their clients' unblinking eyes. A man in a golf cap held up a magnifying glass to the vagina that a girl prises open for his scrutiny, and he perspired and grunted, turning his bug-eyed gaze this way and that as though sizing up a birdie putt on a golf green.

Our company executives' gynecological inspection will not succeed to entice Amaterasu from her cave. The laughter was forced; the performance impotent. Our days will remain just as they are, dark.

I left, wandering aimlessly on the Ginza until my fatigue prompted me to enter a bar that seemed invitingly tranquil, a place where I might convalesce from my disorderly imaginings. I had no sooner ordered a Chivas Regal, lit a Chesterfield and begun to relax, when I recognized that my distraction had misled me into another impasse of the inferno. The few couples on a miniature dance floor, smiling inanely at me as they performed to an outdated Xavier Cugat rhumba, were all male. My instincts had unconsciously brought me to a gay bar. I resolved to get out once my drink was finished: but I was too tired even to summon the energy for escape.

Everything about this place irritated me beyond measure. The waiters selected for their empty-headed pretty airs, the clients discreetly kissing like exotic tropical fish in the bar's aquarium penumbra, but especially the dancers – why did they have to simper like that? Why all the narcissist affectations, the phoney smiles that advertised their natural inclinations as unnatural? Why should men who love each other lack dignity? Why must they appear doomed to absurdity?

'Oh, Mishima-*san*!' I heard myself called, as one is at a crowded cocktail party, with a special note of surprise in the voice that alludes to a relationship interrupted for some time or abandoned or become sadly clandestine. I was less than pleased to be recognized in this gay men's cupboard, but I could not ignore the greeting. A voice that I remembered, a woman's voice, seemed to descend on me from the ceiling. I looked up, and in the depth of an eye found the poignant distance of eight years. Baroness Omiyeke Keiko towered over me on the little balcony of the staircase leading down to the bar. The elegant sweep of her hips appeared vast from below, like a titanic green-glazed vase of the Sung dynasty, enhanced by a narrow-waisted Balenciaga suit of celadon colour. The exquisite cornice of a knee, a perfectly fluted calf, flashed under the pearly gleam of her stockings as she lifted her tight skirt to manoeuvre the stairs. Each thud of her heels on the steps was like a blow on my head.

From the waiters' flurries of respectful bows, I judged that Keiko was the proprietress of this bar. 'How well you look, Madame Keiko,' I said, bowing too.

'And how different you look – more like a sports' coach than a writer.'

'I've changed in eight years; but you haven't.'

'Our meeting is really fortuitous,' Keiko declared. 'This isn't the night I normally reserve for my tour of inspection here.'

'Are there other such places that claim your attention?'

'Several others.'

'That you own – or Count Ito?'

She laughed at the mention of Ito's title. 'We resume a conversation left unfinished for eight years.'

'Or one finally unfinished, as the artist Marcel Duchamp said of his masterpiece.'

'What are you doing in this place?'

'Like you, I'm here by chance – for a drink.' My reply sounded unconvincing, as I observed in Keiko's predatory smile of amusement.

'Which of your two swords are you bearing tonight, *sensei*★?'

'Neither one, tonight.'

'Both safely at home with your wife, are they?'

'You've heard of my marriage?'

'Naturally I heard. It was an event reported in the national press. You contrived to marry at the same time as Crown Prince Akihito.'

'Again by chance. It is true, however, that Crown Prince Akihito married a girl I used to date. Strange, that I could have married someone who will be our Empress one day.'

'If Shoda Michiko had married you, she would not be the Crown Prince's wife, logically speaking.'

'Fantasy isn't logical'

Champagne in an ice bucket had appeared, and Keiko offered me a glass.

'I'm happy to continue with scotch, thanks.'

'Are you equally happy with your marriage, Mishima-*san*?'

'I am perfectly content.'

'I find that hard to believe, pardon my rudeness for saying so. You frown, and that makes me recall the funny little V between Captain Lazar's eyebrows, you know, when his haemorrhoids were acting up? Have you forgotten the poor fellow's match-making efforts? He had a bizarre idea about the consummation of our union, didn't he?'

'Was it so bizarre? I sometimes regret that we were not united.'

'What, in marriage? Devious fellow,' Keiko exploded in raucous laughter, 'is that why you married someone else? Flattery will not succeed to distract me from the truth, and the truth is, the topic of your marriage makes you uncomfortable.'

'I would prefer another topic.'

'Men who come here generally do prefer something else.'

'I meant, another topic with you.'

'Of course, with me. And what topic is that?'

Keiko spoke in her old customary way, in a voice of loud aristocratic hauteur that cared not a damn about eavesdroppers. This place was no safer than others from black-mailers. Indeed, gay bars like this one were the notorious haunt of black-mailers. I looked round. Everything here, the dance floor, the space under the bar stools and even rising above in storeys to the sky, the very air itself we were breathing, only existed

---

★ In Japanese, 'a bearer of two swords' refers humorously to a bisexual.

as the figments of Count Ito's real estate dealings. My conversation with Keiko would no doubt appear in his inventory tomorrow.

Keiko was tipsy and combative, and I too, embarking on my fourth scotch, began to feel a peculiar transformation, a change from fatigue into an aggressive contempt for my surroundings.

The jukebox by the dance floor now began a familar number, Xavier Cugat's *Night Must Fall*. 'Listen,' I said to Keiko, as I shed my leather jacket. 'We often used to dance to that. Shall we try it once more?'

I helped Keiko out of her suit jacket. Beneath, a chiffon blouse of matching willowy green revealed the black lineations of her brassière. I peered through the gauze in quest of the mole in its peony tattoo on Keiko's right shoulder, but I could not find it.

Our arrival on the dance floor caused the other couples to retire from it. Keiko and I were now openly the centre of attention, sprinkled with applause and respectful compliments like a bridal pair with rice. Irony in our onlookers' tactful appraisal made itself felt in a curious way, as though the parents of these gay men were represented by the two of us on stage. In this climate of filial surveillance, Keiko and I danced to one number after another replenished by the jukebox. My fingers went on searching for the mole on Keiko's shoulder, even prying under her brassière strap; but the tattooed floret eluded me, seeming never to have existed.

'The way you fondle me, *sensei*,' Keiko said, 'could give our spectators the wrong impression.' She tweaked the spider legs of hair creeping out of my string-fronted shirt. 'You have an abnormally robust crop of hair on your chest, very un-Japanese.'

'I fervently petitioned the gods for an abundance of it in my childhood.'

'And these too were petitioned?' She caressed my biceps, affirming by her touch the existence of muscles totally absent eight years ago. 'These muscles you've acquired, Kochan, are impressive but somehow theatrical. I preferred the Mishima of bygone times, physically weaker but moulded by a certain inner beauty of the spirit.'

'The heroic martyr of the desk?'

'Yes.'

'You knew me then as a prematurely ugly old man. I was not so much moulded by spirit as riddled with it, a corpse emaciated by spirit, by an excess of soul. The inner beauty you prefer is admired by those who prize above all the heroism born of weakness. The only beauty I recognize is one that perishes with the body.'

'You are eloquent in defence of virility, and yet I seem to overhear a woman who regrets being forty.'

'I'm thirty-five.'

'But I *am* forty.'

Keiko had touched painfully on a nerve. My bad conscience nagged me. What did my muscles amount to, if not a Peter Pan vanity, a prolonged nostalgia for adolescence? A craving for youth, confirmed by an unageing, eternal and primitive Japan that existed only in my imagination. Muscles were a fairytale, a forgery of what eluded me inwardly, the religious will to act against my own skepticism. To act religiously meant to act from the purest, spontaneously unmotivated impulse – a description which did not fit me. I was unfit for the pure selfless action that I had struggled manfully to imitate by my outward appearance.

We returned our table. I dug out the black brassière from my rucksack and explained to Keiko how this implausible relic had come to me. Our entourage of onlookers almost gasped in astonished delight as I presented Keiko with the anonymous rioter's piece of lingerie.

'She must have been Houdini to get free of this,' Keiko remarked. She too sniffed the enigmatic hollows of the cups, as I had been attracted to do. She made a face: 'The lady's perfume is not to my taste, in any case.'

'Would you like to keep it?' I felt I was returning the errant brassière to its rightful owner.

'Excuse me, whatever for?'

'A memento, perhaps.' I then began, for no reason and without knowing why, to recite my complaints about the disagreeable face of things that I had encountered on my evening's walk through the Ginza. I spoke of Amaterasu's eclipse, the fragmented Mirror of Divinity, without actually naming them as the source of my malaise. I mentioned the 'open event' at the striptease club, and from this went on to list all the other symptoms of irreversible and pathogenic changes since 1945, legible like those of a terminal disease. 'Striptease Kabuki and Noh drama in the nude may have some flavour of appeal these days – but to whom and why? Perhaps I indulge in nationalist paranoia, but there is really something amiss when an *O-bon* Festival of the Dead is danced to the cha-cha, or Shinto rites are accompanied by rockabilly music. This is not a further episode in our customary mania for modern things. As you know, *ima meku*★ was an expression of praise already current in the 10th century Heian Era. I cannot see this as a cultural eccentricity which accompanies our progress in electronics, higher ship-building output and radical assembly-line tactics. No, this is something altogether more sinister. This is a new and terrifying sort of progress conditioned by an absolute spiritual vacuum. I do not simply blame the over-rapid importa-tion of things Western for this blatant incongruity of mixed symbols. I blame a spineless nation that is permitting its culture to die.'

★ 'To have a modern air', the craze for novelty.

'Is that what your article on the riots will say tomorrow?'

'What good is there in writing?'

'I don't know, *sensei*. What other good do you expect?'

My answer should have been, 'action', but I dared not state it. 'One thing I do expect. A month of prolonged demonstrations, rioters' blood on the streets, the rowdy impropriety of Socialist Dietmen and policemen violating the sanctity of the Diet Chamber – nothing of this matters, because in some days' time, quietly and with complete indifference to popular protest, the Emperor in his palatial seclusion will place his seal on a ratified new Security Pact with the US.'

'What else did you expect?' Keiko folded the brassière, one cup inside the other, as some women do when tidying up a drawer of lingerie. She glanced down at the *Mainichi* armband in the open rucksack. 'So now you're a reporter?'

'Only for this assignment.'

'It's hard to keep up with you, *sensei*. You are a restless whirlwind of activities, novelist, dramatist, theatre director, and recently even a film actor.'

'Oh yes, my scandalous performance as a *yakuza* rogue.'

'Scandalous is precisely the word. You risked the unforgiving disapproval of the literary establishment to appear in that film. Why take such a risk?'

'I enjoyed my death scene on the escalator. What do you imagine I risk?'

'You ask me that? I remember very well your complaints to me about the literary clique's venomous puritanism, its intolerance of mavericks. Has your tight little mafia changed its code in these last eight years?'

'No. If anything, things have grown worse. That mafia of literary non-entities has long awaited the opportunity to lavish its vengeance on me.'

'Exactly. You know very well what to expect – condemnation to death by silence, by vicious rumour, by exclusion – these are the clique's mortal weapons. You cannot dismiss them as laughing matters that will have no effect on a writer's career. Respectability may be conformist humbug, but it is a fact of life perilous to trifle with in our day.'

Her concern was genuine, as though my own mother were severely upbraiding me; but it was concern fuelled by a deep, glowering anger that arose from her own situation.

'All my efforts to achieve respectability have been in vain, Keiko. I can therefore sacrifice it in a gamble, because I don't really benefit from it.'

Keiko's face for a moment turned ugly with deep, long withheld resentment. Ugliness, or a grand terrifying beauty. Once again, I beheld

353

a cross-section of history like the exposed grain of a tree on her face, as I had on that night twelve years ago in the parking-lot.

'You suffer far less from disrepute than some others – those especially who risked everything for the sake of economic recovery in the first terrible years after the war. They gambled away their reputations on ventures that were by necessity unclean, a passage through the sewers that has left them contaminated and forever outcasts from present-day respectability, such being the ingratitude of those who risked nothing. I think of former Count Ito, an astute, ruthless man perhaps, but one to whom the nation is obligated.'

'Or perhaps former Baroness Omiyeke?' Keiko did not respond to my taunt. 'I see that former Count Ito has recently been made a Diet member of the Upper House, an honour that does not speak of the nation's ingratitude.'

'You don't understand anything,' Keiko spitefully retorted. 'Honours of that kind will not make amends for what respectable folk really think of him.'

'Yes, yes, I know. Respectable folk. My own father-in-law, Sugiyama Nei, my wife's high-minded, traditionalist and hypocrite father, will always consider me disreputable. A dubious individual unworthy of his daughter.'

'Knowing this, why did you go out of your way to defy convention even more by appearing in that ridiculous *yakuza* film?'

'I shall tell you exactly why. The *yakuza* B-film genre, although it glamorizes the underworld and its complex codes, its loyalties and cult of the sword, is a populist fiction that preserves a last link with the vanished world of the samurai, a way of life genocidally eradicated a hundred years ago when Western modernization began. *Yakuza* film-making was strictly prohibited by the Occupation authorities; but it has survived American persecution and the disapproval of Japanese liberals, a resilient folk art which defies Americanism, post-war liberalism and spiritless modernism. I convinced myself that by participating in the revival of this genre, I was taking my first political step. My intuition proved entirely correct. One month after I completed the film, the people were rioting in the streets. My own small rebellious gesture had anticipated popular discontent with the sell-out to American big business and military interests.'

'An empty gesture, unless supported by political action,' Keiko said, with a smile that now restored a degree of friendliness. 'But why wait till 1960 to make this film?'

'For an obvious reason – I lacked the physical qualifications.'

I watched Keiko's plump, competent fingers stroking the peaks of the brassière's cups gloved one inside the other. 'Do you still compete in Kendo matches?' I asked.

'Not these days, except on those rare occasions when I train.'

'Your performance on that cinema stage twelve years ago remains unforgettable. There is something I always intended to ask you, but never had enough courage to do so, concerning your role in the Church of Cosmopolitan Buddhism.'

'I can guess what it is. You wonder if my religious belief in the sect was genuine or feigned.'

'If you want to put it like that.'

'Let me ask you, do you have any children?'

'Yes, a daughter, Noriko. She's one year old this month.'

'I had a daughter who died at that age.'

'I didn't know you had a child.'

'In a sense, I did not know it either. At the time, I resented her birth as an unwelcome intrusion in my life. I had no room in my heart for her, the poor creature, and I often found myself wishing her dead. Do you remember my maid Koyumi? I surrendered the child entirely to Koyumi's care, an expedient that was prompted by evil intention. No person could be imagined less suited to care for a child than Koyumi. Koyumi was a former geisha, a true man-hater if ever there was one, and a deep-dyed lesbian zealously attuned to my every whim. She seemed to guess what was in my heart.'

'This is monstrous, Keiko — you mean she abused the child?'

'Yes, by an excess of devotion. I would sometimes find her covering the child's little body with kisses, slobering over her, suffocating her with unnatural affection. Koyumi would bathe her I don't know how many times in one day, lavish cologne on her, feed her on sweets rather than proper nourishing food. Had she lived, my daughter would have grown into a diseased monster. Koyumi's attention guaranteed an early death for her, perhaps mercifully. And it finally happened because Koyumi never stopped hauling the child around with her everywhere, even in areas of potential hazard that commonsense would not have permitted. One day, while in the kitchen preparing dinner, Koyumi dropped a kettle of scalding water on the child. When I returned home on the following day, it was too late, and I saw my child a last time in the hospital morgue, so cruelly disfigured, so ugly, and then my heart broke, but my contrition came too late. You ask me if my faith is sincere? Sincere as my repentance which torments me without end, which drives me to visit all the chief temples of the land, to attend every great religious festival, to seek out *miko* clairvoyants, so that my daughter's offended spirit will cease haunting me.'

'This is dreadful, Keiko, I'm sorry. When did it happen? Since I last saw you?'

'Yes, since.'

'And what became of your maid Koyumi?'

Keiko smiled, as though relishing some delicious vengeance. 'She undertook to commit suicide, of course, but the accursed healthy cow survived the attempt. I ordered her to shave her head and enter a convent of the Hosso sect near Kyoto, a place renowned for its extreme austerity. There she will remain confined till her death, praying at all hours for the repose of my daughter's spirit. Once a year, on the anniversary of the child's death, I visit Koyumi at the convent. Once a year, I present myself in her cell, and then she can wail and shed tears, rip her breasts and bang her head on the floor till blood flows, as I allow her to gaze on my scar.'

'Scar? What scar do you mean?'

'That I cannot say. No one has ever been told how I came by it.'

'Not even your closest admirer, Count Ito?'

Keiko shook her head. A strand of hair escaped from its plaited bundle and fell across her face. The vagrant strand ran like a crack through fine white porcelain. The crazed expression on her face, the sharp contrast of her hair and delicate skin against the bar's dusky silk background, gave Keiko the frightening air of a Kami spirit in one of Mitsunobu's black and white scroll paintings. Keiko was unbearable to look at, and I averted my eyes. Around us, the bar's patrons seemed figures calcified by lava; waiters passing solemnly between the tables were like ushers at a funeral. I wondered if Keiko's power might be so great over these onlookers that it would oblige them to keep our conversation secret.

'Is your baby daughter Noriko in good health?'

'I pray so,' guardedly I conceded, in superstitious dread. Superstition is an ingrained defect in my mental complexion. I dislike the unreasoning, childish fears it causes in me, but I cannot resist superstition's hold on me. And now I could feel my flesh beginning to creep, as though my daughter Noriko's safety were threatened by the unquiet, jealous shade of Keiko's dead child. I could almost feel the presence of her ghost turning the close atmosphere of the bar to ice. I wished Keiko would say no more.

'I shall tell you the story no one else has heard,' Keiko began. I turned to stop her, to tell her, no, enough, when I saw the unspilled pools of tears that her eyes contained, and I kept silent. 'The death of my child, Noriko –' Keiko halted, her expression returning the appalled reflection of my own. She buried her face in her hands. 'Forgive me, Mishima-*san*. My sorrow makes me clumsy. You see how it is? My tongue refuses even to pronounce her name. Reiko. Reiko was her name.'

'You don't have to continue.'

'I must. It is so important that I finally tell my story, and thereby finish with it. Reiko's death, you see, was anticipated by the unhappy circumstances of her delivery. My obstetrician, Professor Maruyama Shunichi at St Luke's Hospital, had decided on a Caesarean section. He would hear of nothing else. Professor Maruyama favoured the old school prejudice that women of the upper-class should not suffer in delivery like peasant women in the rice fields. Professor Maruyama was typical of that smug, pompous clique of dealers in gynaecology. Clinical access to women's genitalia seems to attract men of fascist disposition. He promised me a painless delivery. "You'll go to sleep, experience no distressing labour pains, and you'll wake to find a healthy child produced as if by magic." The scar would be no embarrassment to my looks, for he planned to make an incision horizontally at the base of the abdomen. "All very discreet. You need not throw your bikini away, if you are a follower of that fashion."

'I felt very tense on the morning of my operation, and things seemed destined to go badly from the start. We arrived at the theatre doors and found them locked. Mine was the first operation of the day, scheduled for 8 o'clock. Professor Maruyama became disagreeable with his staff over this matter of mislaid keys. His temper was not improved when he discovered that his usual anaesthetist was ill and had been replaced by a very nervous young man.

'It was nine when the operation began, after the delay. I could see the theatre clock on the wall facing me. The anaesthetist inserted a needle in my left arm and asked me to count backwards from ten. I reached seven and fell into deep sleep. The next thing I remember – two things, in fact, which led me to panic – was seeing the clock again, and its hands apparently had not moved, a dream, obviously a dream, I told myself; but a tube stuck down my throat, some piece of breathing apparatus choking me, was not a dream. Then I heard the anaesthetist exclaim, "Professor, her eyes are open!" Professor Maruyama glanced down at me, and replied irritably, "Nothing so unusual in that. Madame Omiyeke can neither see nor feel a thing." And he proceeded with the operation.'

'– your eyes were *open*?' I interrupted.

'Open. And worse than open, I could not shut them again. I was completely paralyzed by the injection of general anaesthetic, unable to make even the slightest movement, but able to see and to hear, and as I next discovered to my terror, able to feel. I had woken up immobilized, but with all my other senses keenly alert, just as the operation commenced.

'I tried to focus all my will on moving some part of my body – an eyelid, a finger – or to summon up a whimper – something, anything – to tell them I was awake. Stop! Stop! I was imprisoned inside myself, entombed, buried alive in a catatonic lump of flesh. I screamed without producing a sound; I cried without shedding any tears. I would die, I knew I would die like this – and worst of all, die in agony while having to face a clock that seemed to drag out the time to eternity.

'Then, suddenly, an excruciating pain, something I could never have imagined, a red hot poker burning through me. This was the knife cutting into me. I knew, because a spray of my own blood covered the aprons of Professor Maruyama and his assistant with little dots. The knife was hidden from me, behind the mound in which Reiko stirred, as they began to jerk her out.'

'You really experienced the pain, despite the anaesthetic?'

'Yes, I truly felt it.'

'Can you still remember the pain to describe it?'

Keiko looked at me. Tears had channelled lustrous paths through her makeup. 'I can recall it intellectually, in a certain sense, but my body does not retain a memory of it. Only the body could properly speak of the agony, but fortunately it does not have the words to do so. It was indescribable pain.'

I tried to coax a description from her, without appearing too morbidly inquisitive.

Keiko's testimony was precious. What she was uniquely enabled to describe, startled and fascinated me. She could give me an account of consciously experienced vivisection performed on herself. Another comparable form of vivisection had come to mind as she spoke, but one that does not leave a survivor to describe it. I mean the self-disembowellment that takes place in ritual *seppuku*. Not a single book I had ever read on samurai history or the code of Bushido, not even the great teachings of *Hagakure* on the samurai Way of Death by the 17th century priest Yamamoto Jocho, gave the slightest real indication of what one endured physically during the ordeal of *seppuku*, because, as I have said, those who performed it in earnest – even incorrectly – would not survive a suicide ritual that ends with decapitation by the *kaishaku-nin*, the appointed beheader. There was, of course, an absolute difference between the accident of Keiko's involuntary consciousness and the *seppuku* ritualist's self-conscious will to die. *Seppuku* demands the perserverance of one's will to live in the effort to die. However great the difference, Keiko could at least offer me the witnessed savour of that pain, minus the volition.

Keiko's tears of pained memory gave way to a veiled, mischievous smile. She seemed to plumb my thoughts. 'Someone said, "It's a girl." All I could see, with helpless terror, was that clock and Reiko's head suddenly appearing beside it like a blood-stained spider. You ask me to describe the pain? It is loneliness like none other. You are alone in a universe that reveals itself for what it really is, dead, and no one hears you scream for the release of death. The pain intensified again as Professor Maruyama began to stitch me up. I could see the needle in his butcher's fingers, rising and falling, and meanwhile Professor Maruyama lectured his assistant on French cookery. Can you imagine that? In my endless agony, I had to listen to an amateur of French cuisine discussing his recipe for *pâte sablée*.

'At last, when it was all over and the anaesthetic had completely worn off, I began to scream and flail my arms like a madwoman. They had to tie me to the bed. I refused to hold the child or feed her or even see her. It wasn't until after Reiko's death that I found an American book on psychiatry that explained my condition as reactive depression.'

Keiko had opened her compact and was powdering her face as she spoke. An array of different faces crowded into her mirror, each one colliding with the other as her description proceeded to its end, in that shameless way females have of pouting their lips, arching an eyebrow, tilting their cheeks side to side as they rehearse a series of dissatisfactions in the mirror. A painter able to capture each of her facial expressions in the mirror would end up with a hell's canvas of grimacing, tormented women.

'Pardon my impertinence, but can you tell me who the child's father was?'

Keiko stopped making up her face. 'Certainly not Ito-*san*, if that's on your mind.'

'Someone unknown to me, then?'

She shrugged. 'For all the difference it makes, he wasn't Japanese.'

'Would you permit me to see your scar?' I asked on an impulse.

Calmly, snapping her makeup-case shut, Keiko replied. 'It is hardly a complimentary wish to see a woman's disfigurement.'

'My request sounds odd, I know, but I cannot imagine a more suitable end to your story.'

After a pause, Keiko nodded. 'Very well. I accept, on one condition – that you will agree to meet Ito-*san*. He gives a monthly tea party, a semi-formal occasion often attended by political luminaries, such as Prime Minister Kishi Nobusuke. Will you come?'

I agreed.

A taxi delivered us to the upper-class section of Azabu and a house set behind an English garden with a spacious driveway curving up to the front entrance. The building had an impressive façade in the art nouveau fashion of the 1900s, a stained-glass door mullioned with the curlicue tendrils and lily patterns favoured by that style. The house spoke confidently of the Meiji era's last golden decade, a rare pre-war relic that miraculously survived Tokyo's devastation, like the Marunouchi Building.

'Have you moved here from Koganei Park?' I asked Keiko.

'Oh, I cannot yet afford anything so grand. This is Ito-*san*'s residence. Don't look worried, Kochan. He's away on business in Switzerland till the end of the month.'

The interior of Count Ito's house was commandingly splendid. A lobby with a chequered black and white marble tiled floor, hung with Flemish tapestries and Dutch still life canvasses, had the chaste and severe grace of a Vermeer painting. Here and there, a Japanese antique stood discreetly placed to accord with the mood of the decor, a simple line drawing of Otsu folk art or a clay figurine of the Asuka period. Every room appeared uniquely furnished in the style of different periods, always in a delightfully matching blend of European and Japanese artefacts that revealed a connoisseur's unerring taste.

Keiko led me into a Louis Quinze drawing-room, the rococo magnificence beautifully supplemented by scroll paintings of the Higashiyama period. 'This is a museum,' I exclaimed. 'Ito must be rich as Croesus.'

'Rumour has it that Prince Higashikuni built this house for a mistress, a French Comtesse, who never resided in it. Ito-*san* got it from the Prince in lieu of his winnings in a bridge game.'

Keiko served me bourbon in a Venetian cut-glass tumbler. 'Give me a little time to prepare for my exhibition,' she said. 'In the meantime, you might enjoy glancing at a *chigo* story.' Keiko indicated an *emakimono* roll painting on a console side table, as she passed to an adjoining room. The manuscript roll lay open at the first illustration of a story. 'I know this,' I called out to Keiko in the next room. 'This is a treasure of the Daigo-ji Monastery, the *chigo* notebook. Ito is a collector of impeccable elegance.'

'Ito-*san* modelled himself on his preceptor and idol, Prince Konoe Fumimaro,' Keiko replied through a door left ajar. 'Do you know the story of Prince Konoe's suicide? On the night before his indictment as a Class A war criminal, he entertained some friends at his villa, and then took poison. On a table beside his bed, a copy of Oscar Wilde's *De Profundis* was found the next day, open at a passage he had marked. "I must say to myself that I ruined myself and that nobody great or small can be ruined except by his own hand." In this way, he apologized to the Emperor.'

'You know the quotation off by heart in English?'

'I've heard Ito-*san* repeat it often enough,' Keiko laughed. 'Prince Konoe lived and died in the style of a true ancient sybarite, like the Roman poet Petronius, *arbiter elegantiae* of the Imperial Court. The *emakimono* in your hand belonged originally to him.'

Prince Konoe's manuscript of illustrated *chigo* stories were of a frankly homosexual nature. A *chigo* is a boy, a priest's sexual favourite. I began to read where Keiko had left the roll painting open. 'A story tells of a highly venerated abbot at Ninna-ji Abbey, a very old man of incomparable virtue, but still devoted to boy love. He had many favourites at the abbey, but there was one beautiful *chigo* above all whom he slept with most often. He was far too old for anal penetration, and had to satisfy himself with intercrural intercourse, "rubbing his arrow between the hills". His favourite *chigo* found such a practice ungratifying and deplorable, and so every evening he prepared himself in a special way that would give his abbot true and proper satisfaction of lust.'

'Speaking of Oscar Wilde, incidentally,' Keiko interrupted my reading, 'I attended a performance of Wilde's *Salomé* that you directed at the Bungakuza Theatre in April. I went with Madame Sato – you know, the wife of Prime Minister Kishi's younger brother, Sato Eisaku? Sato-*san* will one day succeed his elder brother as an LDP prime minister.'

'You move in a very exalted circle, dear Keiko.'

'A circle that will open to you, once you've met Ito-*san*.'

'What did you think of my *Salomé* production?'

'Oh, Madame Sato was very taken with it. She will certainly want to pester you about it, when you meet.'

'And were you also taken with it?'

'Perhaps less. The stage sets, the costumes – everything in monochromes of black and white – did seem to me a trifle indulgent.'

'Hyper-aesthetical?'

'Yes, I suppose that's it.'

Keiko reacted like someone faced with the choicest sweet on a luxury confectioner's tray: uncertain that it will taste quite as richly as it looks.

'My choice of monochromes, as you put it, adhered strictly to Aubrey Beardsley's black and white illustrations to Wilde's *Salomé*. You know, I was greatly tempted to take the role myself of John the Baptist. That would have given my critics in the literary establishment another chance to vent their Lilliputian rage.'

Keiko laughed. I could hear the swish of the garments she donned, as though our conversation emitted an electric crackle. 'I think, coming only a month after *Karakkaze Yaro*, your 'hyper-aesthetical' *Salomé* must have looked to them like an excuse.'

'Very likely so. A lame apology on my part to atone for the exhibitionist bad taste of *Karakkaze Yaro*.'

I returned to my *chigo* story. '. . . every evening, the abbot's *chigo* would summon his servant, the son of his old wet nurse, and ordered him to "work with his fingers" on his anus. Next, he got the servant to introduce an enormous *harikata* dildo in his rectum, which was then filled with warmed *choji* vegetable oil. Lastly, he warmed his pretty buttocks over a charcoal brazier.

'As for the poor servant, devotedly operating like this on the beautiful *chigo*'s nether parts, he could not prevent himself from getting an erection and masturbating.

'Suitably prepared as he then was, the Abbot's beloved *chigo* would go to his master when he called out for him in the early hours before dawn, and the Abbot would succeed in penetrating without difficulty.

'The *chigo*'s affectionate ministrations are of incomparable value to men even in old age.'

I had just finished the last illustrated frame of the *chigososhi*, when Keiko's voice summoned me to her room. 'Please come in now, Mishima-*san*, if you will.'

I entered a bedroom furnished in the neo-classical style of the early Regency period. The use of marine subjects as decorative motifs on the furniture – the dolphins, shell-patterned mouldings and sailors' knots carved in wood – celebrated England's successful naval campaigns against Napoleon's armada in the early 1800s. These examples of the Regency maritime style were marvellously airy pieces, in highly figured mahogany veneers, cross-banded with inlays of boxwood and gilt brass stringing.

Keiko sat with her back to me on a delicately curved chair in the classic Henry Holland manner, the mahogany back-rest designed as an open scroll supported by two Roman fasces. A pedestal-end sideboard of richly figured satinwood with a rose marble top had been adapted to serve as her dressing-table. On the wall, over the bottles of scent, hairbrushes and cosmetics, a large oval mirror stood framed by Trafalgar motifs in gilded wood, the knotted cables emerging from anchors and stylized waves at the base. Keiko's face stared at me from this mirror as though from a decorated porthole.

An odd, uncomfortable notion suddenly came to me that all this picturesque naval adornment was a tribute to Keiko's late husband, Naval Air Commander Omiyeke Takuma.

With a petulant smile, Keiko addressed me in her looking-glass. 'How typical of your breed, Mishima-*san*. You prefer to admire the qualities of the furniture in a room rather than its female occupant.'

'Please forgive me, but this room makes me think of Admiral de Villeneuve after his defeat at Trafalgar. He chose a method of suicide in apology to his Emperor that is even more commendable than Prince Konoe's for its sheer elegance – a long needle through the heart.'

'You think of suicide at this moment? How very flattering to me!'

Keiko stood up. Her loosened hair swept like a waterfall to its full length down her back. She wore an under kimono of cream-coloured brocaded silk on which sprays of cherry blossoms were so delicately embroidered that they seemed dyed in the textile. Her blue *obi* was clasped at the back by a cicada of transparent white jade set in amethysts.

It would be useless to pretend that Keiko's outfit had escaped my notice. I had feigned a certain devious preoccupation with the room's furnishings in order to hide my embarrassment. From the moment I first entered the room, her costume had struck me with its oddity, no less strange in its way than meeting a circus performer in full regalia on a busy thoroughfare at midday. She wore a wedding kimono. It is normally the custom even among the best families to rent a gown of that sort for the occasion, and very unusual indeed to have it in one's possession after the event. Some extraordinary circumstance must have dictated the reason for its creation in the past and its continued presence as a souvenir in Keiko's wardrobe.

My increasing disquiet was plainly evident to Keiko, and I could not go on with my show of inattention.

'This is the gown I wore at my wedding,' Keiko said. 'My husband, Baron Omiyeke, disapproved of it. Kamikaze planes were named cherry blossoms in those days, and he did not care to be reminded of that.'

'I know. I helped manufacture those exploding "cherry blossom" coffins at the Nakajima aircraft plant.'

'I had this gown embroidered with cherry blossoms to commemorate the number of Kamikazes fallen at that time.'

'With the same number?'

'With the precise same number, according to the officially declared list. The final blossoms were added on the very last evening before the wedding, to make up the correct number reported that day. Baron Omiyeke had been twice seriously wounded in combat before our marriage, and again shortly afterwards, which left him nearly blinded in one eye. But he still insisted on flying to the end.'

'I understand.'

'Do you?'

I did not have to count the number of blossoms to know what Naval Air Commander Baron Omiyeke would also have known on the day of his marriage – that his bride's gown mocked him with an officially untrue accountancy. The true number of dead, not only of Kamikaze but in all the armed forces, was far greater than the civilian population imagined.

I suddenly had a picture before my eyes, clear as a photograph, of a bride and bridegroom in those distant feverishly hallucinatory days of 1944. I could see Baron Omiyeke, a career officer of bravery and recti- tude, but by no means a narrow fanatic, confronted on his wedding day by a naively fanatic bride, wearing the balance-sheet of a lie. I could see beautiful young Keiko, confident that her little patriotic surprise would gratify her warrior spouse.

'Would I be correct in supposing that you employed girls of unblem- ished virtue to embroider your gown?'

'You would be entirely correct.'

'I feel sorry for the bride who wore this gown,' I said.

'So did the bridegroom, upon reflection later, but too late. I have not looked at this gown since then.'

'Why do you honour me by choosing to wear it again on this occasion?'

Keiko's eyes narrowed defiantly. 'Perhaps an occasion that might in a sense be called a postponed marriage? A revindication of the past?'

'The past weighs heavy on us all, dear lady, and without remedy.'

A certain ferocious determination in Keiko's look unnerved me. Her face, amid a magnetized sheaf of hair, appeared pitifully small, fragile, and yet frightening. Her fine neck, as yet unblemished by age, was suffused by a dark blush that conveyed a passion beyond the extremes of sexual arousal.

Keiko struggled to regain control over herself. 'A step is sometimes taken which changes everything. Did you not confess that tonight, Mishima-*san*?'

'You refer to my appearance as a fictitious villain in a *yakuza* film?'

'No, as a villain that you could be in reality.'

I laughed; but more and more, my impulsive request at the bar exhausted itself in nervous reluctance. 'I expressed a desire to see something that shouldn't be seen.'

'And now you're afraid to see. Are you one of those proud souls who can only enjoy the fulfilment of a desire when it is commanded?'

'Perhaps I am.'

'So be it.'

Keiko now raised the hem of her gown, and lacquered toenails appeared like small red tulip petals, and as she pulled on the hem some more, the tensed sinewy arch of her bare foot in a bedroom slipper edged out, and higher still it rose to reveal the forepart of a naked shank.

'Kneel down, Kochan,' she commanded. 'Begin with what you see. Prove to yourself the humility of your own courage by kissing my foot. That's it. Go on, go on – you shall have to continue in quest of my scar till you find it. Pardon my reticence which does not allow me to stand entirely naked before you.'

My lips traced the corrugations of bone on the arch of Keiko's foot, like the dainty, supple valleys of a marble balustrade that led to the plinth of her ankle and a column that receded into mystery above. I crept beneath the silken canopy of her gown that began to swell and hiss as my shoulders rose from their kowtowing position on the floor. A crepuscular light enveloped me, ethereally transmitted through the cherry-petalled fabric, a patchy network of redness twinkling like a shattered mirror. I had crawled into the sun-goddess Amaterasu's cave, a place fragrant with the scent of hibiscus and another perfume, a fungous sea-smell that filled my nostrils as my head slowly mounted upwards. My fingers ascended a pair of smooth, faintly veined pillars that trembled slightly under my touch. I climbed up higher in a stoop, until at last I faced a nebula of glimmering spidery black rays.

My hands had reached Keiko's hips and were prying up the *obi* sash that padlocked the kimono firmly to her abdomen. I could feel Keiko's movements as she unpinned the *obi* clasp at the back to loosen the sash. It fell away with a swish, and my cave was suddenly flooded with visibility as the kimono flaps came asunder. I gasped at the inundation my eyes received of a ripe, majestically proportioned body that would have gladdened the judicious eye of Titian himself. A deity serenely contemplated the worshipper at her feet. I studied her abdomen just above the coarse braille-line of hair, my fingers pressing into the ledge of flesh as though I hung from a cliff-face. I stared at every millimetre of that white, blank precipice, and it was flawless.

'I cannot find the slightest trace of a scar.'

'You haven't searched thoroughly enough,' Keiko replied.

I laid the balls of my thumbs on Keiko's radiant black pubes. I pushed down firmly on the soft mounds, as one does to the middle pages of a book on which the print has dribbled illegibly into the margins of the gutter.

Keiko drew back from my hands with a laugh. 'You seek in the wrong place.' She turned round to face the maritime looking-glass again. 'The scar you are to find is in the mirror.' With one knee poised on the chair, she leaned forward over the dressing-table and hitched up her kimono, unveiling her buttocks which invited me to see for myself. I approached her and prised apart the magnificent white boulders of her hindquarters. A glistening pink mollusc in the crevice pouted at me. The sly vixen! She had already glycerined her anus in preparation for my visit.

Perfume flacons, cold cream jars, a silver-framed photograph of Baron Omiyeke — all the stock on the dressing-table clattered to the floor, swept away as Keiko lurched violently forward and seized hold of the marble top to regain her balance. 'Ah *sensei*, you are so hugely talented,' she proclaimed with a husky sigh of pain.

I clung to the arch of Keiko's back, my arms barrelling her torso, my hands fixed on her pendant breasts that nuzzled my palms with their grainy nipples. 'Have I found it now?'

'Not yet,' she smiled through gritted teeth. 'Go on.'

We continued to stare at the two inhuman masks of displeasure in the mirror. Keiko's arms twitched spasmodically as they upheld our weight; an excrescence of sweat pelleted her forehead; her teeth clamped down on a tongue pregnant with a suppressed outcry. Two faces were reflected in grimacing partnership on the glass.

At last, Keiko lowered her head, a dishevelled cascade of hair tumbling onto the rose marble. I stepped back, leaving her hunched across the dressing-table, the kimono still upraised over her hips. A hand cautiously reached behind her in a languid, somnambulist gesture, to discover a trickle of blood weeping down from her buttocks.

'I've hurt you.'

'Yes,' she replied. She turned, her eyes imperiously quizzing the blood on her fingertips, a lesser shade of red than on her nails cupped together like a tulip. 'You make love without feeling anything,' Keiko declared, 'as though your organ were injected with novocaine.'

'Why did you say you had a scar, when there isn't one? Was the whole story a lie?'

'Come with me,' she replied. 'I want to show you something.'

I followed Keiko out of the bedroom into the passageway and through the door of an adjoining room. We entered the cramped space of a photographer's developing room. 'This was once a bathroom,' Keiko explained. 'Since the war it has served quite another purpose.'

Tiles were still fixed to the walls, but the bathroom fittings had been replaced by studio accessories. Fresh prints and contact strips hung clothes-pegged to wires over a row of trays on a sink unit. A pungent, citric aroma of developing agents, the sleepy trickle of a faucet into a basin of photographs, gave signs of recent activity.

A familiar shape next caught my eye. There, poised on a tripod and facing a curtain on the wall, stood a big 35mm Hasselblad camera. Unpleasant memories came back to me of my sessions in front of that camera in Captain Lazar's Imperial Hotel suite. 'Sam Lazar used to have a camera like that,' I said, and immediately regretted my indiscretion.

'I know. But rest assured, this one is our own.' Keiko modestly fastened her loose kimono with one hand, and with her other free one tugged at a cord which threw open the curtain. I saw into the bedroom that we had just left. Only an oblong glass partition separated us from the room that stood framed before me. The maritime glass over Keiko's dressing-table was indeed a porthole, as I now realized, or in fact a two-way spying mirror.

The bedroom lighting, which had seemed so persuasively subdued, as though issuing from candelabra, from this new perspective demonstrated a cunningly disguised force, a clarity of tone directed by vasiform art nouveau lamps on the walls and ceiling that could well suffice for pictures on high-speed film.

Keiko peered into the bedroom. 'I feel that we are still in there, Kochan, don't you? I can see us so clearly, the two of us looking into the mirror.'

'A very ingenious blackmailer's apparatus. Is that why you deceived me into coming here, to trap me? Did you act on orders from that scoundrel, Count Ito?'

'Don't be so foolish,' she laughed. 'Had I really wished to blackmail you, Kochan, I could have done so long before now.'

'What do you mean by that – Sam Lazar's little confidences, perhaps?'

'You needn't fear his tricks,' she replied, staring at me in that level, imperious way that she used to examine her blood-smeared fingers. 'I have felt your weight on me for a second time tonight. Next time, I hope it will be in a more customary fashion.'

All this time, since that January night in the snow twelve years ago, Keiko had known the identity of her other assailant in the parking-lot. I shied away from those eyes harpooning me; those eyes, like the omniscient moon impassively stalking me. My downcast look fell on a row of little objects that had survived in place on the dressing-table top. There, on the rose-veined marble surface, stood five little porcelain figurines of a dog, a rabbit, a squirrel, a bear and a fox, which escaped the destructive sweep of Keiko's fall.

My forehead touches the deceitful mirror. I can feel the superciliary ridge of bone pressing through the skin on my brow. How frail, how surprisingly thin the flesh is, pulped between the cold kiss of bone and glass. I stare down at the animal figurines, like a child clasped to a toy shop window. A vague reflection appears from behind me on the glass: the hazy opal ghost of a full moon – one small moon, and another beside it – as the kimono falls away in sea-spume hiss from Keiko's shoulders and her breasts emerge from the mist like the twin rocks at Ise. Keiko's overcast image floats up to me as though from oceanic space: blurred underwater face amidst black algae tentacles of hair.

The more she appears to surface – with each step approaching me from behind – the more faint her image grows on the treacherous side of this mirror. I must prevent the materialization of physical contact that would eventually succeed the vanishing of Keiko's reflection. She must not touch me; not yet. Our slightest contact would jeopardize the great miracle that had befallen me. I had passed through the looking-glass. This is what had happened in Keiko's bedroom only moments ago – I had trespassed to the other side of the mirror, to a place where the woman exiled within me could at last be seen. I had recognized the dark side of the moon; an impossibility had been made possible – that of seeing the woman trapped and hidden within me, who could see me, but who had always remained herself invisible. Perhaps this is what Keiko had meant by the 'scar in the mirror'? Perhaps she had been my midwife, my Caesarean sectioner? Not yet. My delivery was not yet completed. I must now incise the scar in the mirror, reopen it, and expel the woman imprisoned inside. I must separate her from me at last, and at the very instant of her birth, entomb her permanently outside me.

A fever blazed up within me in the split second that gave voice to my decision. At once, the temperature of my forehead rose to scorching, the wafer of skin pressed against the mirror radiating a heat intense enough to melt the glass. I could feel Keiko's breath on the nape of my neck; without turning, I could see her hand reaching out to touch me. My dizzying fever was ignited by the voice of self-disgust screaming inside my head, a voice raised in mutineer protest against my cowardly hesitation, against my skeptical reluctance to embrace the fantasy without scruple. I must not surrender to my usual pathological timidity and allow my instinctive craving to pass unsatisfied, ending up with inaction, poisoned dreams and regret. A religious moment is achieved by the unhesitating, fearless realization of one's deepest impulse.

'Those figurines on your dressing-table,' I said, 'are they English porcelain?'

'Wedgwood,' Keiko replied, her breath like the stray caress of a flame on my cheek.

'Would you give them to me?'

Now it was her turn to hesitate. Over my shoulder, I glimpsed the waning of Keiko's doleful smile.

'I cannot,' she said. 'They are Baron Omiyeke's gift, brought from Singapore immediately after its capture.'

'Items of sentimental value.'

'Yes, a souvenir of our one all too brief moment of happiness – the only value these poor objects have. Why do you want them?'

'The figures are essential to a story I am going to write, conceived at this very moment.'

'Isn't it enough that you've seen them? Why the need to possess them?'

'Because it is essential to my story that you willingly surrender them to me.'

'Surrender is a rather violent way to express a whim, don't you think?'

I did not reply, but instead pointed to the installation of a microphone in the wall and transmission cables leading to a tape-recorder beside the tripodal Hasselblad. 'I assume the bedroom is wired for eavesdropping. But can you also transmit sound from here to the bedroom?'

'Yes, it is a two-way system.'

'And this room is sound-proof?'

'Of course. Why do you ask?'

'Another whim, perhaps. You can give me infinite pleasure.'

'Infinite?' Greed briefly showed its teeth in Keiko's smile. 'Your wishes tonight seem to exceed the limits I can satisfy.'

'You will find this a very easy wish to fulfil.' I turned round to face the glass again and pressed my hands flat on it. 'Mirrors have constantly obsessed me since my earliest childhood. How does the mirror engineer its reflection? That is a magic construction deeply disturbing to me, beyond reasonable explanation. I remember a sailor suit I wore when I was three years old, and the name, *Katori*, a battleship from the Russo-Japanese war, written on the band of my cap. I shall never forget the day I looked into the mirror and saw *irotaK*, the ship's name reversed. I cannot describe the nausea that overwhelmed me on discovering the phenomenon of mirror reversal. I became ill with anxiety. It had not occurred to me until then that a mirror does not *see* but merely reflects – a simple enlightenment which had quite the opposite effect of reassuring me, indeed, it shocked me and profoundly upset my entire notion of reality. To this day, I still feel the presence of evil in mirrors. A mirror tempts me to see what it can never actually reflect, that is, to see me as only another person can. I want to stand before a mirror one day, and when I raise my right hand, my reflection too will raise his right, but in a copy of reality – diagonally at my left. I want the mirror to read *Katori* as *Katori*. I want to appear in the mirror as my true double: myself as others see me, turned inside-out.'

'Your thoughts wander, *sensei*,' Keiko grinned with drowsy sarcasm. 'No one sees you turned inside-out.'

'I am trying to describe a condition of soul very difficult to convey. I am confessing the secret of my nature which aspires to appear like a crystal, not superposable on its mirror-image.'

'You aspire to the condition of a crystal?' She laughed. 'I still do not comprehend.'

'Fulfil my wish and you will be the first to see me as I wish to see myself.'

'What do you wish me to do?'

'Stand as you are before this two-way glass. I will return to the bedroom and take my position facing you in the mirror. Switch on the microphone so that I can hear you in the bedroom. Then, command me to perform whatever actions you like. Whatever comes into your head.'

'Absolutely anything?'

'Without exception.'

My reckless consent astonishes me. As I retrace my steps to the bedroom, I am staggered by the cross of absurdity I have accepted to bear, by the fool's crown of thorns that I have placed on my own head like ass's ears. I have delivered myself wholly to Keiko's revenge, I have given her *carte blanche* on which my doom is already featured, as though the prefiguration of a script now materialized in

MIRROR WRITING

as I approach the boudoir looking-glass compassed by maritime allegories, and I peer into its responsive surface, a vacant sheet of paper that awaits the imprint of my own hazardous musings.

'Put everything back on the dressing-table.' Keiko's first electronically transmitted command startles me. And yet, her wish is the remote echo of the action I am already performing: the rearrangement of her cosmetic utensils on the rose marble top. I am a lady's faultless maidservant, an efficient prisoner of her will, fulfilling the expressions of her disorderly ambition.

My unseen, emancipated mistress urges me to hurry, 'quickly, don't fuss so,' hastening impatiently to her next command. 'Undress.' I feel like a lady's glove, turned inside-out and tossed carelessly on the floor. But again my actions are clairvoyant; I am already stripping off the clothes that she wants removed.

I must neither precede nor lag behind her instructions, but like patient clay that anticipates the corrections of a potter's thumb, I must take the instant shape of her wishes. Everything crucially depends on knowing what comes next, without any possible foreknowledge of the words that shall come next.

'Sit down now and apply the makeup exactly as I say.'

Her desire gurgles from the electronic conduit like impure water from a waste-pipe. Do I detect a comic element in her voice, a note of self-derisive hesitancy? Does it offer me one last chance to withdraw from absurdity? No, it is pitiless, without sympathy for my predicament. An intravenous drip-feed of sarcasm penetrates my being. 'Eye shadow first. Yes, that's the one, in your hand.' Velvety, bruise-coloured daubs of cosmetic appear on my eyelids. A tiny blackamoor toothbrush deposits impasto flecks of mascara on my eyelashes.

'There is nothing of the samurai in you,' she taunts. 'Your eyes have always betrayed you. An assumed air of tough guy has never concealed from anyone the feminine softness of your gaze.'

'Do my eyes seem any less feminine now that they are made up as you want?'

Laughter: 'You are free to choose against fantasy and not submit yourself to it.'

'Choosing not to free myself of illusion has become my freedom.'

'Only a link of pretence exists between us: I, the instructress behind the glass, and you, the malleable volunteer. Sheerest fantasy envelops us, like the gauzy filament of a stocking that artificially beautifies a woman's leg and invites temptation and mystery and prurience.'

'Or perhaps another sort of envelope – the chorion, the outermost membrane surrounding a foetus.'

'This is absurdly theatrical. A mirror gimmick of disembodied voice and puppet. A mere illusory, mechanical submission to unreality. You risk being totally farcical. Aren't you afraid of ridicule?'

'Of course it is ridiculous. Mystery always attracts ridicule. Timidity, self-conscious embarrassment and skepticism, all must be transcended. A complete, deliberate surrender to artificiality is the only way to achieve the victory of pure intention. The grimace of farce turns into the dreadfully complicit smile of tragedy.'

'Something as immensely fragile as "purity of intention" demands immense conviction.'

'A will is needed that is like compassion or the corrosive effect of nostalgia.'

'Do you have the stomach for it?'

'I don't know. I feel paralyzed by my own intense sexual excitement, dizzied and numb at the climactic peak of egoism, below which an engulfing, dragon-infested ocean of unreason awaits me.'

The same laughter again, enclosing our words (spoken or imagined) in parenthesis.

My travesty proceeds relentlessly, instructed by a constant, obscene dribble of commands from the faucet in the wall. A foundation cream of morbid tan is next decreed, paving my entire face from hairline to jaws and throat. Rouge highlights on the crests of my cheekbones, on the bulging pockets of my cheeks, are blended centrifugally with finger-tips into the undercoat of brunette veneer. Lipstick of Tyrian red gives my mouth the awesome look of a sliced, bleeding liver. I rub my lips together, lubricating them with saliva like a trumpet-player, to bring out the desired liquid effect.

'Outline the edges of your lips with a darker shade of eyebrow pencil – carefully, just a hint of black round the area of gloss.'

A final brushing of lilac-white face powder subdues my unnaturally rubescent colour; but I am left with a curiously grim pruinose tone, like a made-up cadaver.

I am a wild, extravagant sunset awash on the mirror's Dead Sea, my decapitated head shedding rays of blood on its surface. My brightness penetrates to the other side of the mirror, to the perpetually dark hidden back of the moon. And the virgin moon, ruler of tides and blood, takes possession of my viscera.

An uncanny sensation of accomplishment has indeed taken possession of me, an absolute certainty that my lips reflected in the glass, although immobile, are the ones really forming the commands that I obey. I am in fact the concealed ventriloquist animating my own image with a woman's voice.

'You have always wanted to know what the *onnagata* discovers in his mirror,' her voice or mine says. 'Now go ahead and look.'

'I have always known what the *onnagata* sees, as he powders his shoulders like a woman and sweats like a man. I know what he feels, the Kabuki female impersonator who has played all the stage roles of heroically proportioned love, as he now prepares himself for the final masquerade, a real life emotion in the streets, a real lover who awaits him outside at the stage-door under an umbrella in the rain.'

'You are looking at a *tableau vivant* of crime in which the old-fashioned instruments of torture, the whip, the knife and the rope, reveal themselves for what they really are – pornographic fossils, sad human inventions, no different from the instruments we women use to beautify ourselves, powder, lipstick and perfume. These are all looking-glass means of hiding one's terror.'

'Or the means of facing one's terror. There is only one crime: failure to appear beautiful, even and especially in death. I am obeying the precepts of the samurai priest, Yamamoto Jocho, who expressed the essential *bushido* creed in a single maxim: "I have found that the Way of the Samurai is death." Jocho prescribes the use cosmetics to hide the bad colour of a samurai's hangover. So also, rouge should be applied to one's cheeks before committing ritual disembowelment, because a warrior must always have the colour of cherry blossoms, even after he is beheaded. It is shameful and immoral to die without preserving the appearance of robust beauty. Consequently, seeing my face artificially painted like this, does not make me feel absurd or ashamed or in the least effeminate. The *onnagata*'s female mimicry, Zen ascetic practice and the art of suicide are all equally expressions of the same principle. What is moral is of necessity beautiful. Energetically beautiful.'

'Shouldn't you rather say, *artificially* beautiful?'

'No, energetically. But the strain of artificiality must never tell.'

'Stand up. Go on, stand further back in the room, so that we can see you entire.'

'How very little is known of woman,' I muse, in wonder at the figure we both see.

'Physically, nothing. Or everything there is to know.'

A pause, as the trickling faucet of the microphone ceases. An interim of gazing; long moments of silence in which I overhear a pulse, a heartbeat, the caress of flesh on flesh, a sigh. Ruthlessly as any commandment, this prolonged silence fills the room with darkness: a possessive, constricted uterine night, leaving only the bright umbilical opening of the mirror in which to focus myself.

'You are using me to give birth to yourself,' my discontented instructress reproaches me.

'Rebirth, from the imaginary.'

'It doesn't interest me to see you naked. Look inside the dressing-table, find something, anything to conceal what is unappealing to me.'

I approach the dressing-table. As the drawers slide open, items of lingerie stir and ripple in puffs of escaping air, shuddering like plummage on the throats of doves. Among these pearly satin wisps of fabric, what choice of garment do I have?

A slip crackles and seethes, vivacious as a serpent uncoiling in my hands; the epidermis of a woman's torso placed against mine, with small drooping hammocks where the absentee breasts should lie.

An indecent, assailant odour is released from the swarm of under-clothes, the stale relics of perfume, but something else more hauntingly insistent, a muddy odour of decaying seaweed that permeates my body and begins to transform it. The delicacy of a woman's things insinuates itself within me, like a subtly totalitarian virus. An infectious, utterly persuasive sense of contentment overcomes me, as though I were basking contentedly in a warm bath of milk; as though I had become acclimatized to a temperature of blood in the pleasurable inundation of a bath, instead of blood confined to the sealed precinct of a masculine body.

My sense of contentment baffles and mystifies me, but already my ability to question it begins to elude me, as I experience the far greater strangeness of an opening, a vastness without familiar horizon, yet in which everything appears closer and intimate, in which time has no single committed perspective, but loses itself in that indescribable sense of intimacy with things, a flowing rhythm of things, a woman's things, small, familiar, beautiful, gentle things in which the world vanishes. And I now belong to a woman's things.

I have crystallized her. I have captured her in my reflection caged in glass. I have succeeded. *I am a woman.*

A woman, yes, but of a monstrously hermaphroditic sort. I have not crossed safely from my gender to hers in a voyage of complete transfiguration. A hybrid metamorphosis has occurred, in which male-ness survives, poignantly intact as it testifies to a woman's shape. We are the incestuously paired cohabitants of one and the same body, she and I, but joined in mortal competition for it. Our eyes are Siamese twinned: both of us see a body that is the other's, while struggling to reclaim one's own. The flat plane of my stomach – object of my body-builder's jealous pride – swells and gains adipose rotundity, its navel unrecognizably knotted like a child's balloon. A chromosomal mutation inflates my haunches and expands my pelvis to accommodate a uterine crevasse, and extensile chamber tunnelled by ovarian ducts. My pectorals are burgeoning and bulging shamelessly, the ellipses of muscles turning into gelatinous breasts, pliant, pendulous, delicately veined like orchids with large venom-tipped purple areolae. Weights of a spatially foreign quality are being added to me; weights altogether different from any I have ever lifted in the gym. I know now what the earth suffers – the aches of immense fertile arthritis – as it fuses the roots of plant life through its surface, enduring the weight of countless living pillars that seek to defy gravity, rising like lovers from her in muscular growth towards the sun. But most bizarre of all, the more undeniably feminine I appear, the more intensely male I feel.

I have surrendered myself to an illusion, consciously substituted fic-tion for reality, intentionally transgressed against the invincible laws of nature – and my reward is a criminal work of art in which I achieve unlawful existence. And *she* – she is not a mere figment on glass, a mirage of my own criminal imaginings – she has truly vanquished the schism of difference between us, and I feel her predominance as *my* visible triumph. No adequate description is possible of this feeling, except to call it an inseparable union of pleasure and pain. One of us – (she or I, it doesn't matter who) – endures unendurable pleasure that the other enjoys as martyrdom.

A spillage of underclothes litters the floor, a creamy shimmering ooze of finery that I have ransacked. Unaware until now of what my hands were doing, I have knotted together several petticoats to form a single length. I am improvising an eccentric species of *fundoshi*, the traditional loincloth normally composed of immaculate white cotton. A trial inspection in the mirror reveals a comical sight: shoulder-straps dangle in loops from the makeshift *fundoshi*, like the gaudy fringe on the G-string of a striptease artiste.

As I begin the process of wrapping myself in this deviant loincloth, I am interrupted.

'One moment, before you start tying the Gordian Knot. There is something else you must do first. Fill your anus with cotton wool.'

'Why must I do that?'

A reply is preceded by ghostly laughter, like the last cricket at autumn's end or the sussuration of willow leaves on a moonless night. 'Look in the bottom drawer of the dressing-table.'

That is the one remaining drawer I haven't examined yet. My efforts to tug it loose are resisted at first, but then it comes unjammed, shuddering open. The drawer contains only a single mysterious object, long, narrow and wrapped in a sack of bleached canvas. Its weight, its shape and distinctive feel in my hands give me warning of the fatal thing concealed within the swathe of canvas. Carefully, I unfasten the wrapper and find, as I had suspected, a samurai sword together with its smaller replica, the *yoroidoshi* dagger. The hilts and scabbards of the two weapons display a familiar diamond-shaped, black and white chequered panelling, inlaid with mother-of-pearl. These are superb, rare examples of antique manufacture. I unsheath the *yoroidoshi* with a click, like the snap of a lipstick liberated from its tube. A protective film of grease obscures the steel's pattern of wavy, watered-silk tempering, known as *sambonsugi*. I wipe the blade clean with a pair of frilly panties. It gleams menacingly, in razor-edged pristine condition.

'Do you recognize this sword and dagger?'

'I do. They are the work of the sixteenth-century master craftsman, Seki no Magoroku. I have seem them once before, twelve years ago, in Sam Lazar's collection.'

'Do you finally accept what Seki's masterpiece requires of you?'

'I do.'

I scan the dressing-table for a stock of prescribed cotton wool; but I find none. Only the waste basket provides me with discarded wads of the stuff, make-up crusted clots of earth. I fish them out in a handful from among the tangled strands of hair, the tissue papers imprinted with bites of lipstick and eye-liner smears.

'Turn with your back to the mirror. I want to watch you doing this.'

When I have finished packing my anus, and fastened the loincloth, I retreat far enough back into the room so that my image in a kneeling position will appear completely visible in the mirror's optic. I anticipate the next command, 'Kneel,' just as I have reflected all the others. I have incarnated all my spectator's desires, everything she secretly confesses. And her secret wish has disclosed a blade on which is written – 'Make thyself a woman.'

I expect one final utterance, her first and last expression of pure desire —

I WANT TO SEE YOU DIE

—at last, those words I have waited all my life to hear. An entire nation has come expectantly to look at me; an entire, anonymous spectatorship awaiting a pornographic apparition in the mirror's lens, crystallized in those words—

I WANT TO SEE YOU DIE

and what do I see? A solitary performer abandoned to his conviction, marooned among a woman's underthings, a sad, proud, gloriously timid figure kneeling to his own elevated will. A ridiculous being, a virile imposter majestically female, kneeling in a space that faith infallibly designates as sacred – a *kaidan* ordination platform or the bare shimmering floor of a Noh stage in noonday sunlight – such as my conviction alone can grant me the faith to see.

A sword reposes on the floor, and in a parallel line below it, the dagger lies before my knees. Two objects that I remember from another time, a first humiliating rehearsal in Sam Lazar's suite at the Imperial, so infinitely distant from me at this moment that it seems a fiction. I claim the weapons as real, and therefore mine now. I look up, into the mirror that frames me, and I remember the camera lens pedestalled on a tripod that once upon a time mocked me. I recognize now that a camera has always been there, from the very first, brutally, indifferently, continuously recording me in the uncut and unedited film of my life. And the make-believe stage on which I kneel is, and has always been, the inescapable film-set of reality. Reality has filmed me in make-believe and in fact, both fantastic and commonplace, with clinically implacable disinterest. And this cinematic eye that tracks me everywhere, this hidden but omnipresent mirror lens that shadows me without end, I know – I have always known – is the Impersonal, Unseen, Unnameable I – *no one knows who* – rumoured only as *Chin*, the ancient Chinese Imperial character for 'moon speaking to heaven'. And in this looking-glass moon that alone can speak to heaven, I am submerged, a non-existent personal pronoun, I, eclipsed among numberless others in mesmerized silence. But I am also the object of its anonymous desire, and it speaks to heaven with the fictional voice of my own conviction, as my only real alternant.

A sound breaks the silence – a noise of ripping, as though reality itself were being ripped apart, like a veil, yielding and coming apart with a non-human cry. I have torn a strip from one of the under-garments at hand. At the centre of this severed ribbon, I paint a red disc, the Rising Sun, with nail polish lacquer; and then, with an eyebrow grease-pencil, I write the characters of the samurai war slogan that expand like the Sun's myriad rays, *shichisho hokoku*. Serve the Nation for Seven Lives.

I tie this emblazoned *hachimaki* headband round my forehead. Now I am ready for the camera's appetite.

'When shall I witness you putting an end to all seven lives?'

'Now or later, what does it matter to you? You are simply *there* as the guarantee of my death, its reflection, the vacant frame I shall end by occupying. The film of one's life goes on to the end, to the very last frame which in a lightning flash gives meaning to everything that has gone before. Life concedes meaning at last, retrospectively. A sense is found in a life that is over. This, I am sure, must come next.'

'Only the dead may know what comes next.'

'I am dead.'

'Almost. And still you doubt it. Still you hesitate.'

'I am not pleading for any more delay. I am concentrating all my will power on the last frame, the last retrospectively original one. Those seven lives that you wait so impatiently to see ended – what sense did they have? What sense had my life? I can define the first six stages of my life from childhood to the present in six words – a bare, compact poem of only six words, like vertebrae in a spinal column –

> convalescent
> homosexual
> writer
> actor
> celebrity
> athlete

– six larval stages, until I come now to the last, the seventh –

> patriot

– and each one of the preceding six units of my thirty-five years' existence could be qualified by any number of scandalous but truly warranted adjectives –

> sickly
> conformist
> cynical
> narcissistic
> disreputable
> fraudulent

– six again the number of my sins, a catalogue of minor transgressions that falls dismally short of real criminal grandeur – until I arrive at the seventh accusation, *patriot*, a final possibility of stature that benefits from all six adjectives, as being the most sickly, most conformist, most cynical, most narcissistic, most disreputable, most fraudulent of all qualifications, that of *martyr*. Each link in the passage of my life has been conditioned by qualities that are reprehensible; but the last, the final one of martyr, casts a retrospective light that redeems them all in the seventh and culminating accusation – MUTINY. I die in mutiny – a last, vain flickering sunset that brings to an end the Emperor's last mutineer. And most scandalous of all, I have named patriotism, MUTINY. Mutiny permits me to see the fiction of patriotism in its true, visibly manifest and unqualified reality. Patriotism is A WOMAN.'

'Then, let this woman see you die.'

I take the *yoroidoshi* by the hilt, and with a pull, release the dagger's blade from its scabbard. The knife gripped tightly in my right hand trembles a little. Is it fear that sends a shiver through the blade, a killer thing otherwise innocent of any feeling?

'You tremble?'

'I had not imagined the knife might weigh so heavy, so inert.'

'What did you expect – the lightness of words? You shake because of the unexpected deadweight.'

'No, I shake because of the lightness that surprises me. My hand trembles because it exerts more effort than is needed.'

I hunch over the stuttering tip of the knife, my back and clenched arm in the form of parenthesis, as though shielding an unquiet flame in the hollow of my self-composure. I gaze firmly at the bared fang, willing it to accept my mastery; but there is nothing to be won by the mere force of looking.

Guided by the fingertips of my left hand, the keen point of the knife comes to rest on its predestined place of entry. Balanced there on its point, the steel quakes for some little more time, then stops, reassured by the submissive flesh, unconscious of its own helplessness. How vulnerable, how soft it feels to the knife. I press down harder, and mark the spot by pricking it. Now the blade knows its appointed target.

A thread of blood issues from the left side of my abdomen – real, not cosmetic, not the lacquer of red nail polish – and still the flesh acknowledges nothing of its peril. Only I can see what is happening in the mirror, like some anaesthetized, dissociated onlooker, watching as my body submits to actions that seem the instantaneous commands of the mirror. I can see the dagger being raised high, a pair of hands fastened tight round the hilt. I can feel the muscles on my back bunching together like compacted jackhammers; I can even feel a moment's pride in those muscles, poised to assassinate me. Am I able to observe myself like this – while yet completing one action after another that in no time at all will lead inescapably to the end – because the completion of my act must remain in doubt to the end?

A sound erupts from the mirror, rending the dark stillness of the room in a bat-like flurry of splinters, shattering the tranquillizing mirage of my reflection. I hear the sound of my own outcry, the viscerally propelled *kiai* shout, discharged with every ounce of my ingathered strength. And now, with the expelling of air from my lungs, the knife plunges down towards my abdomen.

For the very last time, I answer faithfully to the will of Yukio Mishima. We have summoned the void. Blindness descends, in which the two of us, Yukio Mishima and I, will vanish together. Blindly, we have conspired to take a life that neither one of us has ever fully possessed.

In that inconceivable fraction of an instant before the blade strikes home, no mind can intervene, no mind can conceive of time or space enough to know, and yet, the mind knows. It knows: '*I am* the difference between reality and faith.' Knowledge has never been of any use, and least of all now, as the blindness of reality and the blindness of faith are set to collide. And they do collide in a moment that is suddenly no more than the anguishing fact of an iron bar piercing my side. My agony has begun.

How comforting, how unimaginably peaceful it would be, if pain were alone real at this moment. But it isn't. Pain makes the familiar unfamiliar, and although the image of Yukio Mishima is extinguished in pain, even this, a mortally terminal pain, cannot silence the commentator who voices his experiencing of the unfamiliar. 'Is this *seppuku*?' Dull, stupefied, piti-fully human wonder – this is what I must listen to, in torment. Comedy rides the tiger of pain. 'Exquisite fool, all your life toying intellectually with an ambition to commit *seppuku*, now your hands are really full with the absurdity of its single unsparing demand – the perseverance of your will to live in the effort to die.' Yes, this is *seppuku*, this – the fictional voice of my own conviction, my only real alternant.

Every muscle, every fibre of my nerves, every particle of my being which has reposed in blind faith secure till now in the instinct of self-preservation, rises in violent mutiny against me, in protest against the care-taker who has gone off his head. My hands refuse to obey the madman who steers a razor through the intestines that have been his secret lifelong companions. My guts themselves rebel against me, seeking by every means to evict the parasite steel I have insisted should cut across them. The serpent of life resident at the base of the spine rises up it now in explosive fury to the head, and like a cobra inflating its hood, darkens my brain and paralyzes my volition with the onrush of agonizing pain.

I verge on a desperate scream of refusal. Reality commands me to sur-render, to cease, finding voice in my life's blind resistance. Against this voice, I must recognize another which commands a blind faith greater than I am. 'I am myself the protest against the furtherance of my act.' A scream – I believe I have screamed these words – but there is evidence only of a long drooling pendant of saliva released from the gob that my mouth has withheld in panic, unable to swallow, fallen now in a mucous spill from sagging mouth to my lap, a sight that brings me to focus on a blood-stained hand round a knife stuck in a wound, and both the hand and the knife are shuddering uncontrollably in the grip of palsied spasms.

I had not expected so savage an opposition. My hands are at war with each other. The left one grips the right in desperation, compelling it to maintain its hold on the slippery knife. My eyes disbelieve the cut which millimetre by millimetre, against the antagonists of clenched diaphragm and stubborn entanglement of intestines, crawls towards my navel. The *yoroidoshi* must be encouraged to progress beyond the navel which looks so discouragingly far. I can already see the knife point exposed, squirming out grease-yellowed from the haemorrhaging wound, as my strength ebbs.

My stomach heaves, its wall perforated, suffused by bilious pancreatic wastes from the open sewer of my duodenum. A corrupt broth wells up from my oesophagus, choking me. I repress an excruciating attack of vomiting with the last of my failing strength, and the hiccoughing spasms rip open the wound a little more. In wonder, I see my bowels begin to creep out, like a spool of worms. A diarrhoetic sluicing of the severed colon hammers massively, intolerably upon my rectum. And now, just as the knife must slip from my hand as it loses conscious hold, so must my bowels evacuate themselves in the immodest finality of death. But the excrement does not spill; it is withheld by the cotton wool packed in my anus. I remember now – 'My sly instructress, almost forgotten, so it was for this –'

'– for this, as you knew very well, when you complied with my instructions.'

A sigh escapes me, which I know must have the sound of a death-rattle elsewhere. 'A precaution taken in vain. It has not prevented the release of blood-stained urine in my loincloth.'

'Urine, do you think it is? Or is it fluid of another sort, the sticky albumin of your own discharged semen?'

'What good does it do to torment me now?'

'Ah, but it does me immense good. This is our act of coitus I have waited forever to enjoy, to endure your pain as my unendurable pleasure without restriction.'

Can it be my tormentor's endless waves of pleasure that I am suffering? Sensation has no limit, no personal meaning now in my cocooned space, remote from the deafening clang of pain that has taken undisputed possession of my will.

My head lolls uncontrollably. I can read my entrails, spewing fat and obscenely robust in a cascade from the mouth of the wound to festoon my crotch. My sight fails; my eyes ooze out in perspired glue.

'I see my pleasure has exhausted you.'

'That smell.'

'Don't you recognize it? You have attended autopsies in the morgue, don't you remember? This is the smell of a corpse under dissection. You should see yourself. Your face bears the jaundiced look of someone already dead, whose trenched cavity below exhales a frightful stink of the abattoir and the latrine – a malingering aroma such as offends one's nostrils upon entering a recently used public toilet –'

'– the vengefully repellant stench of life.'

'Be satisfied. You're leaving this stinking life.'

'That awful noise. Is someone moaning?'

'Yes, you are. And you will go on and on for a long time yet. Because, speaking of precautions, you have overlooked the chief one, the *kaishaku-nin*, the appointed beheader whose duty it is to bring your contest with death successfully to an end. Have you forgotten?'

'I don't want to be left in pain. I expect someone –'

'– someone? Your loyal accompanist and executioner, a loving presence behind you, standing ready with his sword uplifted, his eyes unflinching on the back of your neck. Someone –'

'– who will strike! strike!'

'Conspicuously missing. You speak to me of mutiny, but where are your fellow conspirators? Where is your script for them, and for someone exclusively dedicated to the loving caress of the sword and your *coup-de-grâce*? You have been alone too long, a midnight scribbler, and writing has made obscure midnight of your sense. Being seen by a woman, a woman mirror-wise that your own self-reflection names patriotism, will not suffice to make reality of fiction. I am your umbilical cord of confidence that keeps you secured to this life. Look round you. This is a theatre of intimacy. A mirror, a room, a bed. All the props are there, except for someone naked upon the bed, a lover whose gaze reflects your unashamed eagerness to take pleasure from him. Your script calls for realities of blood, vomiting wounds and beheaded cadavers. It could end here, in theatrical make-believe, a Grand Guignol of foreplay. Blood is a fine pornographic stimulant, even if shed only in imagination, and I can see your unruly yard like a dog's tail stiffening to a curl. I could release us both from your bondage to the dagger. How temptingly facile could be a last minute change in your script of death, even now. You could choose to live death from the inside, in reconciliation with the advance of old age, and continue to survive like any other modern pragmatic zombie. *Look round you –*'

My body sags, released from the mind whose efforts subside and collapse, as though beheaded. My fingers relax their grip, unclamping the shoulder with an arthritic twang, as the object of my tension drops to the table – not a knife, but a pen sticky with the black gore of night.

I kneel at my scribe's altar, an improvised one tonight, which displays not the ritual instruments of *seppuku*, but the cosmetic ones of a writer, paper, pen and ink. My body is slick with perspiration streaming down my torso into the waistband of my trousers which has turned cool as glass encircling the skin. All that remains of my night-long physical strain – of the immense realization of finality that has crystallized in words on a page – is a cramped right arm.

I hear the fluting trill of birds that preludes dawn. And away in the distance over the eastern sea, the thunderstorm god Susanoo grumbles briefly and resigns himself to the first pink-lipped smile of light. An electric fan paddles ineffectually against a viscid mass of humidity, rising in steady percentage as the day begins. The blades transmit a morbidly damp zephyr, caressing the back of my neck, stirring the moist papers on the table. Keiko's talismanic figurines, the dog, rabbit, squirrel, bear and fox, stand in a row, keeping vigil as little sentinel paperweights on the border of a picture –

– Guido Reni's painting of Saint Sebastian. Tonight, Reni's icon of the athletic martyr reposes here, on my improvised writing-desk, at the Urokoya Inn, situated in the seaside resort of Atami.

A relieving clink of ice against glass attracts me to look up from my scrawlings. My eyes betray me in the semi-darkness. I see the written characters of my pages, black on white, transferred and greatly enlarged on a screen occupying the bed. The screen rustles, shows life, and identifies itself to me as Keiko seated on the bed. She is clad in a white silk dressing-gown splashed with a pattern of windswept bamboo leaves, black on white. 'It's so terribly humid,' she says. 'I couldn't sleep.'

Keiko lights a cigarette in the candelabra of her fingers, the nails like little red torches. The flame discloses a mask of pallid, anguishing beauty, more beautiful with its caverns of shadow, its aurora of black hair, than I remembered seeing it before. Her robe lies open to a breathless air, her flesh glistening with perspired dew. This creature of incomparable beauty whom I have mirrored in my text, retires again in pre-dawn darkness, like the sun goddess Amaterasu to her Ise rock cave.

'I'm sorry if my nocturnal bad habit has disturbed you.'

'Not in the least. You were perfectly silent.'

'Like a thief?'

'Let's see what sort of thief comes to light.'

Black thundering clouds obscure the dawn. The meandering glow of a cigarette, the tuneless chimes of ice in a glass of scotch, alone testify to Keiko's presence. Silently I await the sun's reappearance.

8   IKIGAMI – RECOGNIZING THE LIVING GODDESS

I RETRACE my path. After the riotous day of June 15th had gravitated my steps back to Keiko, we arose from bed early the next morning to find an English breakfast laid out for two in the adjoining morning-room. To discover a meal served by someone invisible in a pretty little Jane Austen room next door to our peeping-Tom's bedchamber – and on whose orders? – unsettled me in the extreme. Keiko ate with good appetite. Hideki, Senator Ito's houseboy, she assured me, was the soul of discretion. 'More stealthy than discreet,' I replied. 'Senator Ito is sure to know about us.'

'He already knows,' Keiko cheerfully remarked, pouring us some Darjeeling tea into a pair of Meissen bone china cups.

The small breakfast table was dwarfed by a vase of two dozen black tulips. An engraved Tiffany greetings' card addressed the flowers to 'the *ikigami*'. The sinister bouquet must be meant for Keiko, but the strange title *ikigami*, 'living goddess', puzzled me. It designates a shamaness of unusual magic powers. I took it to mean a secret message of congratulations from Senator Ito Kazushige for having trapped me.

'Aren't you going to eat?' Keiko asked. I accepted a triangle of toast that she spread with strawberry jam. I felt watched, a prisoner in a cell without walls, the inescapable penitentiary constructed by my own history.

'Tell me the story you're writing,' Keiko said. 'I want to know why you were so keen to possess my little Wedgwood figurines last night.'

'Like most writers, I am reluctant to discuss unfinished work.'

'You are obliged to break your golden rule this time.'

'I am writing a love story that cannot possibly end successfully.'

'Ours?'

'In a manner of speaking. An ideal love story.'

'Certainly not ours, then.'

'How do you imagine an ideal love story should end?'

'How else, except in death.'

'I envy your husband, Baron Omiyeke's death. I am thinking of cherry blossoms on a bridal gown. I envy him *that* – the place he occupies hereafter.'

'In the hereafter makes no sense. He's dead.' Keiko's expression belied her answer.

'Wasn't it supremely exciting to make love with someone who has accepted the Emperor's invitation to die?'

Keiko smiled, but her face resembled the *naki-zo*, the antique Noh mask of a weeping woman. 'Oh yes, it was extremely gratifying. I did not like Baron Omiyeke, do you see?'

'Were you tempted to follow him into death?'

Keiko opened her compact and began examining her face in the mirror. 'I begin to understand now why you wanted my figurines.'

'You are correct. Every detail has its rightful place in life, as in fiction where even the most trivial detail must have its theoretical basis. Daily life is governed by minor beliefs. I can see clearly the look on your face, the sensation you experienced, after the news came of Baron Omiyeke's death and you contemplated these innocent trifles, these little porcelain keepsakes, and how strangely luxurious it must have felt to observe the lost and forlorn gaze of these small animals, an improper feeling of attachment to life in its most private, sentimental, and yet deepest real sense – as powerful and as fragile as Baron Omiyeke's own determination to die. These lifeless animals, expressing nothing and everything, are in reality the esoteric aspect of a pilot's blazing aircraft. Destiny is expressed in them.'

'How preposterous! Naturally, you can use my figurines. You would anyway, even if I were to refuse. You writers exploit reality. In your embrace everything real shrivels away to fiction.'

'Suppose I said, I am rewriting the story of the *niniroku* mutiny.'

'What, again?' Keiko laughed. 'The incident of 26 February 1936 is of no importance. Have you forgotten that libellous story you wrote for Senator Ito's benefit? At that time, you portrayed the *niniroku* mutin-eers as poor misguided fools duped by the agents of the High Command into an uprising that could only end in dismal failure.'

'Or success, a renovation of Japan, if the Emperor had supported them.'

'*If*? By what perversion of logic can you say *if*? Evidently you can no longer read clearly what your own good commonsense led you to write. Each and every incident of mutiny and ultra-nationalist violence in the 1930s was fake, pure *coup-de-théâtre*, staged-managed by the highest officials and acted out by the most cretinously naive fools.'

'I repudiate that story.'

'Oh, do you? Why not say you repudiate writing altogether, which has been your life and the reason for your success?'

'I am saying that.'

'But just for one last time, you are aiming to cast us in your *niniroku* love story, is that the idea, *sensei*?' Keiko stared at the black tulips. 'Tomorrow is the feast day of the Bodhisattva Jizo at the Osorezan mountain temple. I would like to bring these flowers to the mountain spirits of dead children. Will you come with me?'

'Shimokita is a considerable journey. I shall have to make arrangements.'

'Make your arrangements.'

I had no choice but to accept Keiko's invitation to visit the sacred mountain Osoreyama, known as the mountain to be feared. I did not realize it this first time, but our nightclubbing sorties of the old days would now be replaced by a summer of pilgrimages to other sacred mountains, other peaks celebrated by clairvoyants, shamans and ascetics. Literally, we raised the level of our sinfulness, tormenting our con-sciences with visions of the other world that all such mountains represent to pious folk.

As I say, I was unaware at first that the stakes of the game had been raised, although I myself devoutly wished them raised. One is not always aware that one's wish has been granted – and the realization is not always welcome. I went with Keiko to the mountain of the blind *miko* clairvoyants, not entirely unwillingly, but with scruples. I suspected malevolence in her choice of the *jizo* feast day. My own secret attachment to the *jizo* child-saviour aggravated my bad conscience. Surely, it must be Keiko's intention to remind me of my crime that had caused the loss of her child twelve years ago? I anticipated retrospective punishment from her to redeem the past, not realizing yet that the odds were staked on the future.

Osoreyama, a volcanic peak on Shimokita peninsula, rises forbidding and sterile of vegetation. It is desolate, the inhuman picture of my own emptiness. Desert places give consolation to saints, but also to the black-hearted. Here pilgrims came from all over Japan to consult the blind *miko* soothsayers. Osoreyama's slopes are believed to profile the lands of the unhappy dead, a notion of hell that gains credence when one approaches the white gash on its side and views, as I did with Keiko, the sulphurous springs bubbling up from some netherworld beneath. Keiko deposited her black tulips here, on the shore of white cinders, threshold to the abyss of restless spirits. 'Osoreyama manifests the six realms of the dead in Buddhist cosmology,' Keiko said, 'including the hell of raining swords.'

'My grandmother used to frighten me with a description of this hell by the Amida preacher, Genshin.'

'This is the entry.'

Keiko wore a kimono of immaculate white cotton. Her *geta* left a pattern of bird's prints on the white ash.

We came to the temple which stands on the edge of a lake half way up the mountain. Under the antlered eaves of the main hall, a row of blind *miko* women received their petitioners, the majority of them women of my mother's age or older, widows, grievers over lost sons. I thought of Shizue, recognizable in these suppliants' lost and unrecognizable attractiveness of youth. Some of the *miko* rattled their spirit-conductor rosary of one hundred and eighty black soapberry beads; others waved the *oshirasama*, a cloth-draped doll with the head of a horse on a foot-long stick. For the price of 30 yen, the *miko* would call up a ghost and speak in its name. I overheard more than one bereaved mother in distress questioning the clairvoyant about a soldier missing in action, a Kamikaze unrecovered from the sea, ghosts torturing their dreams. To these sad inquiries, the blind seers replied with, what seemed to me, formulistic expressions of an inadequate, anodyne nature. 'The miko's answer is nowadays only able to give comfort,' Keiko explained. 'It is simply *kata*, a fixed recitation, which has long since lost the power of genuine prophecy.'

'I should give anything to experience these ancient powers of divination, which I imagine have always just slipped round the corner to a more remote past.'

'You have doubted my word, *sensei*,' Keiko said. 'Before leaving with me on this journey, you made certain hasty inquiries.'

'Word travels fast, as I might have guessed. It's true, I did seek to find out the truth about your maid Koyumi, the real reasons for her confinement.'

'And what did you discover?'

'That she is indeed confined to a Hosso sect convent, but at the Gesshuji outside Nara, not in Kyoto as you told me.'

'And do you conclude from this the existence of a real daughter after all, hidden away in Nara – or in Kyoto?'

'Who knows?'

'Koyumi is where she is, because of what she knows, which does not concern a child dead in the past but one in the future.'

Before I could challenge her on this outlandish utterance, Keiko pointed and said, 'Look, the *abisha-ho*.' A number of white-clad pilgrims advanced from the temple, chanting esoteric Buddhist spells and rattling the *bokken*, a noisy castanet-like instrument of wooden ball and clapper which is said annihilate sin-hindrances. This knot of worshippers encircled two small children, their faces painted white, a boy and girl *abisha-ho*. 'The children have survived long hardships of exposure in the mountains,' Keiko said, 'and now they are *kamigakari*, spirit-possessed.' Truly, they seemed little spectres from the netherworld, drained of lifeblood by the vast, unforgiving, eternal blackness of the mountain. The boy detached himself from the band of protectors and approached Keiko. He tugged at her kimono with a hand still dimpled like a baby's, and hailed her, *ikigami*. The *abisha-ho* next turned to me and broke the mood of sorcery that had raised my gooseflesh by sticking out his tongue at me. The impertinent red of his tongue, a vivid living disproof of any semblance to a ghost, made me laugh. No one else seemed to find the boy's rudeness comical. The chanting stopped; the *bokken* fell silent. And the boy clung to the *ikigami* for safety. 'It is inauspicious,' Keiko said, as the others began invoking the Lotus Sutra against evil, to the beating of a fan-shaped drum.

I had crossed over to the world of the mountain cults, a sacred geography completely foreign to me, known only by vague legend and hearsay. Keiko guided me all summer long to the spiritual highlands of a Japan that I had never known existed. White, the pure and impeccable nun's whiteness of her robes, the ascetic paleness of her face after days of fasting and cold water austerities, white is the colour I see in absolute stark contrast with the mountains' black evergreen forests and barren lava peaks, white and black extremes of contrariety, from the summits of self-denial and otherworldly practices one day to a sudden descent the next into alcohol and sex at the neighbouring hostels at the bottom of the mountains. *Komori*, the word for pilgrimage, can mean being still or going, stationary seclusion or constant walking at one and the same time without contradiction. Our travellers' bodies, fallen from mountain tops, and shut into the dark closeness of village inn, was *utsubo* to Keiko's way of thinking, the process of sacred gestation. 'I travel with a mortuary tablet in a bag round my neck,' she told me one August night as we lay together on our hostel's three-mat floorspace in Odaki, a hamlet in the foothills of Mount Ontake. 'Here, touch it, but I cannot let you see my posthumous Buddhist name which is written on it.' She undressed and hid the tablet under her clothes, then lit a candle. The wax spent itself in lighting our travails, like two climbers striving against an impassable rock face, till the first grey before dawn. Keiko outdoes me in stamina. She marches ahead, unhampered by her awkward *geta*. Forests of tall pine and cryptomeria, and the plunging waterfalls that characterize the first five of ten stages on our route to Mount Ontake's summit, dwindle away at the sixth to a low creeping type of *haimatsu* pine, a skeletal tundra, which itself ceases at the last two *gome* stages of the climb and rears up in sheer lava rock. The several miles of steep ascent from Odaki in August humidity is a trial of one's endurance. Keiko takes it lightly, hardly perspiring. A folded headcloth like a nun's wimple protects her complexion. Nothing disturbs the snowy perfection of her garments. Her white *tabi* socks remain unblemished as we scale the lunarscape of volcanic cinders.

Our way from the village has been clearly marked by avenues of megaliths clustered like chess pieces, memorials to the former holy men of the Ontake cult, carved with their posthumous names and honorific title, *reijin*. Their spirits dwell forever on these slopes, available to summons of the faithful. The *reijin* monuments are replaced where the vegetation ends by stone figures of terrifying Buddhist deities and bronze shinto pigs with banderillas of *gohei* pennants stuck in their backs. A sudden drop in temperature up here, a draught of cold alpine air like the caress of a ghost on the skin, makes me shiver.

Mount Ontake, in Central Honshu, stands 9,000 feet high. It is not so impressive as Mount Fuji or Mount Miwa that we climbed on our June pilgrimage to the Saigura festival. Ontake's cone had long ago been flattened by volcanic explosions which have left a dishevelled plateau of five craters, each one a green lake. We encounter some *goriki*, the porters bowed under huge loads of provisions for the hundreds of Ontake visitants. As for us, Keiko has warned that we would taste neither food nor drink in our two days' stay. White mist envelops the upper crags, a chill deadening eeriness in which the only sounds are the nearby flapping of a votive flag planted in an offertory rock-heap, the clapping of a worshipper's hands at some water's edge. The antlered cornice of the Kengamine shrine higher up and the heads of primitive stone images hover weightless in mid-air, above the world, and suddenly the mist is gone, the sun bursts through and finds us on a jagged precipice looking down into craters of green lakes, huts and clusters of statues, and scatterings of white-clad groups from which come strange gasps and cries, the clanging of bells, shouts of *e*, *hyun*, *shin*, that induce trance in the mediums.

Keiko and I had undertaken our ascent alone, unescorted by any of the *ko* pilgrim clubs that annually visit Ontake. Keiko placed little faith in these present-day mediumistic clubs, 'spirit tourists', she called them. 'This is a congress of mediums,' she says, as we pass the stone image of a dragon-woman and nearby hut that serves soup, and my stomach knots with hunger. 'Some are good, some bad. But our purpose is to meet a true spirit master, *sendatsu* Hirata Ansho, a professor of ancient history at Waseda University.' We crossed a dry riverbed littered with small pyramids of rocks, known as *sainokawara*, said to be piled by dead children in the course of centuries.

I spent the day with Keiko attending outdoor séances conducted in groups or in pairs. I witnessed the prophesying trances of male and female mediums – palsied tremors, eyes rolling back to the whites in epileptic convulsions as the dragon god Ryujin takes possession – brought on by the *maeza* leader shouting mantras at them in a fierce, commanding voice. And what manner of oracles were extracted from the spirit-possessed *nakaza*? News of the rice harvest, forecasts of typhoons, but mostly banal everyday information.

At day's end, we had reached the topmost shrine, Sanjurokudoji, 'The 36 Boys', on a windswept crag patched with snow. Wisps of cloud like smoke from a volcanic cauldron arose from the invisible depths. Weak from hunger and cold, my brain dizzied by the endless screams and seizures of the past hours, I desired only rest and retreat from this witches' carnival.

Repose was impossible. Keiko and I found shelter for the night in a hut so crowded that we had to sit back-to-back. I tried to doze off, but could not for all the noise of bells and chanting around us, the arrival of more guests in the dark, and a medium in the room above whose yells went on to the early hours.

Our posture was the contrary of love-making, and yet in those hours of sharing a backbone with Keiko, I had my deepest sense of intimacy with her. I felt the nearest confirmation of something impossible, the possibility of Keiko's love, rippling through me from the marvellous, solid prop of her back. Strands of her hair crackled in shoots of lightning on the nape of my neck. In this sealed vessel of bodies packed like mud, Keiko spoke to me in the privacy of English, the remote foreignness of those sounds being at this moment the melodious secret oracles that lovers exclaim in pleasure. What she whispered could have pleased no one else but me. 'You think of suicide all the time. It follows you like an evil smell. I recognized it, and so did the *abisha-ho* on Osoreyama. You have engineered an athlete's body with a single Kamikaze purpose in mind. It is now only a matter of *when*, not *how*, you are planning to die . . .'

At 2 a.m., we joined with other parties filing to a promontory at the summit when the sacred bonfire would be lit. A full moon perfectly illumined the pilgrims' way along the ravine. Our long shadows fell into the abyss, down which the peaks of lesser mountains were visible, floating in moonlit haloes of mist. A mass of strange lunar beings all in white gathered in the crescent amphitheatre of lava rock to watch the magic fire ceremony. Three circles of wickerwork, about six-foot high and ten-foot across, awaited the torch. These were made up of small strips of pine latticed together, thousands of them, each bearing someone's brush-written name, age and wish. On many of them too I saw references to Kamikaze and other war dead. The elder of the Ontake sect, waving a sword, invoked the *kami*, the amphitheatre resounded with chanting and bell-ringing, and the magic circles were set ablaze. Every spline in the lattice-work rings burned individually bright red and distinct like single candles in towering banks against the night. As the bonfires died down, several figures began dancing round the circles. I felt an ecstatic urge to join these dancers. 'At sunrise,' Keiko said, 'we meet Professor Hirata at the Shintaki falls.'

We began our descent of Ontake as daylight broke, transforming the leaden grey billows of cloud and lower peaks to brilliant gold and blue, like one of Cimabue's enchantingly naive paintings. Unwashed, famished and without sleep, we nevertheless skipped down the slopes on wings of lightness. The sound of a waterfall ahead became our guide as we penetrated the thick forest at the lower stages. Another sound, a child's laughter, like the brief trill of birdsong from the steaming evergreens, came to bewitch our ears. 'The elusive sightings of the other world are shot through into ours.' I seemed to hear those words quite clearly as the laughter ended, although perhaps only my mind had tricked me into speaking them.

We arrived at Shintaki falls. A clamorous jet of water, swollen by the August storms, fell from the heights to a cave before us filled with scripted stones. A frail, sickly young man, but of striking beauty, welcomed Keiko with an armful of wild lilies, the summer's last, translucently pink with stamens of caramel colour, the long stems wrapped in a russet skein of ferns. '*Ikagami*,' he greeted her, as he handed over the bouquet. He passed on, brilliant as one of his lilies, naked save for a loincloth, and stepped under the waterfall. Could this be Professor Hirata? He looked far too feeble to withstand the immense, stunning force of the cataract on his bare head. 'He has stood like this every day in mid-winter to perform the *suigyo* cold water austerity,' a voice growled from the forest, and a wizened-faced, shaven-headed little goblin stepped into view. He too was stripped bare to a *fundoshi*, having just now disrobed behind the trees. This elf I took to be Professor Hirata, a creature of indefinable age, of ascetic body whittled down to sinewy detail as if by a knife. Without introduction, he launched familiarly into conversation. 'Do you still take the view that Shinto history inevitably culminates in the black rain of Hiroshima?'

'Pardon me?'

'You know what I'm saying. Uranium's A-bomb force is our doom, predestined for us by the position of Uranus in His Majesty's horoscope. This is the original meaning, you say, of our culture.'

Keiko! How else could this wizard know of my discussion with Dietman Tsuji eight years ago? She disregarded my suspicious look and addressed the gnome. 'You have your flute, *sendatsu?*'

'Yes, I am allowed the flute, but my pieces of leather are not permitted on Mount Ontake.'

What did he mean, 'pieces of leather'?

Professor Hirata opened his hand to show us a flute of black *oya* lava stone, like a smooth large egg perforated by finger-stops. 'Haguro mountain gave me this flute, just as it is, with the holes already in it. The *kami* spirits presented me with a readymade means to call on them.'

He put the stone flute at an angle to his lips and blew. It produced a range of sounds inconceivable for its size, from bass drone to the shrillest high pitch that rose beyond human hearing like a dog-whistle. These notes were interspersed with the player's own grunts, sighs and chirps. I have heard nothing comparable, not even from the Zen flautist's virtuoso bamboo, an inhuman music that gave voice to the stone's *kami* soul. This occult piping must surely have been responsible for the child's laughter I had earlier imagined on the slopes.

The effect of Hirata's playing on one's nerves was spectacular, and on none more than the young man weighed down by the falls. Professor Hirata skittered up to the cascade, and with more emphatic, cruel accents on his instrument, drove the youth to paroxyms. Gasping, mortally pale, he seemed at death's door. 'Will he survive the trance?' I asked Keiko. 'He seems far too weak.'

'He is possessed by the *goho-doji*, the supernatural boy who assists Professor Hirata in his séances. I have seen it before. His name is Ogawa Sei, a student of Professor Hirata's at Waseda University.'

I wanted to cover my ears. The assassin flute penetrated to the very marrow of one's bones, the twitches and death-rattle of the medium were beginning to be my own. 'What did he mean by pieces of leather?'

'Professor Hirata is a *yamabushi* of the mystic Shugendo cult, and deerskin is part of their costume. But leather is strictly taboo on Mount Ontake. Professor Hirata will guide us on our pilgrimage to Mount Haguro this autumn. He is the *sendatsu* captain of the Haguro *yamabushi*.'

I had heard stories of these *yamabushi* to which Hirata Ansho belonged, the so-called 'sleepers in the mountains', a medieval order of warrior priests who combined Shinto shamanism with esoteric Buddhism. Although not of the samurai class, they were privileged to wear swords and had served as mercenaries in feudal times. The *yamabushi* had been suppressed in the last decades of the Tokugawa Shogunate and again by Meiji legislation. My goblin flautist was a modern day survivalist of that fierce, independent race of magicians who had intermarried with *miko* women. It is said that the *yamabushi* is guided on journeys to the spirit world by a harpy-like demon of the trees, the *tengu*, half-man, half-hawk, the enemy of Buddha's laws

The *tengu*-like Hirata occasionally broke off his fluting to repeat the question, delivered with the booming sonority of a Noh actor, 'Who is it that arrives?' The figure crucified by the escalator of water responded with incoherent shrieks. After several of these pitiable failures of communication from the spirit world, Professor Hirata rescued his medium from the waterfall. He sat Ogawa's near-lifeless carcass down on the ground and thumped him fiercely on the back, shouting *e, hyun, shin*, which is supposed to revive the medium from his deepest trance.

Keiko had disappeared into Hirata's vestiary among the pines. She reappeared, and contrary to the normal rules of propriety on Mount Ontake, walked naked into the waterfall. Professor Hirata left his convalescent and joined her under the torrent. He crouched there facing Keiko, the mountain's cargo of water striking them with such force that it ricocheted in a band of iridescent mist, a rainbow outline around them, and then, as though suspended in water, his fingers began expertly forming the nine syllable mudras, ending in a *kiai* yell, *rin-byo-to-sha-kai-jin-retsu-zai-ZEN!* His fingers nimbly composing the mudras, swifter than barely the eye could follow, took on the semblance of a hawk's ferocious talons, and Keiko seemed the prey, her flesh a stream of radiant ice lashed by black chutes of hair.

I approached the water, thirsting to bathe myself in its crystalline purity. Hirata had left his flute on the lichened rocks on which Ogawa sat in a dreamy return to life. I picked up the weighty black lump of *oya* lava, glistening still with Hirata's spittle, and blew into it. Nothing. No sound but the hollowness of my breath in the channels of the rock.

Professor Hirata stabbed his fingers at Keiko's stomach in the pointed-sword mudra, growling savagely *a-un, a-un*, the alpha and omega of the Sanskrit alphabet which contain the universe. Keiko suddenly jack-knifed at the midriff and bellowed in an unrecognizable masculine voice, 'From across the sea, the unquiet spirits come, but not yet, not till the ugly son of the sea-dragon princess —' and she stopped. The water avalanching from her thighs had turned a foamy pink, like salmon flesh, but showing itself menstrual red as she hurriedly quitted the falls not to defile them.

'Not yet, this is not yet the time,' Professor Hirata said, following her, his goblin's face scored by razored lines of disappointment and disgust at the shamefulness of a woman's blood. He seemed not to address the three of us but a larger audience. And now, from the circumference of deep forest skirting our glade by the falls, the white figures of pilgrims began to emerge, numbers of them, a congregation that must have lain hidden from view until this moment. Professor Hirata rushed forward – and Ogawa too, awakened from his dream – waving his arms at these pious onlookers to drive them back, shouting, 'Away! Away! Can't you see it isn't the hour yet?'

Quietly, without protest or remark, the assembly of visitants, materialized from who knows where or how, melted away to insubstance again. Ogawa had fetched the kimonos from behind the greenery, and when Keiko had fastened hers, he thrust the mass of lilies back in her arms. Professor Hirata turned to me, while knotting his belt, and laughed. 'The folk of Nippon are by nature messianic. It is their destiny.' And with this, he leapt away down the slope, through the growth of bamboo grass and tall cryptomeria, almost at once gone without trace like a real *tengu* demon, a hawk taken flight.

Keiko, with an armful of lilies and a cherry spray of blood on the underside of her kimono, had reverted to the bride. 'I would like to offer these flowers in expiation to the Seven at the Atami shrine,' she said. 'I would like to go right now, this very morning. What do you say?'

By the Seven, Keiko referred to General Tojo and the six others hanged as war criminals by the Allies, and whose seven wooden name-markers, discreetly hidden behind a statue of the Kannon Buddha at the Atami hilltop shrine, serve as memorial and cenotaph.

'Atami is a very long way from here,' I replied.

'Of course, if you would rather not stay with me –'

'No, I do. We can hire a car in Fukushima.'

Black squalls of rain prolonged our journey to Atami, a beach resort celebrated for its baths and courtesans, some fifty miles down from Tokyo and a lengthy coast ride north from Kyushu. We arrived too late for the arduous climb to the shrine that perches a thousand feet up from the bay. We decided to lodge for the night at the Urokoya Inn.

Sunsets that follow aestival storms are often magnificent, and this one at the onset of twilight was spectacular. Over the darkening sea, the irregular masses of cloud glowed with lavish, almost extravagant washes of purple, with riotous, green-veined oranges and patches of bilious white. I felt uneasy, disquieted by this chaotic muddle of a rainbow, as though the colours I saw were those of human intestines gaping out through the horizon's cut. Matters worsened as I stepped from the car to the white-pebbled driveway of the Urokoya Inn. The pebbles were carpeted by the bodies of innumerable red dragonflies, as though the afternoon's tempest had rained a Biblical plague of these insects.

Keiko laughed at me. 'You walk gingerly like a Jain forbidden to harm any living thing.'

'I see no reason to harm any living thing.'

'And yet you prize the martial virtues?'

'A samurai doesn't have to be an unreasoning brute.'

Keiko's *geta*, that she'd retained in her haste to leave Ontake crackled on the pebbles. I looked at the Urokoya. 'Did you know,' I said, 'that one of the very greatest champions of Go, Shusai, twenty-first in the Honnimba succession of Go masters, died here in 1940?'

'I cannot imagine you playing Go.'

'I used to, with my grandfather, until he died two years after the Shusai master.'

I stooped down to pick up a pebble. 'This reminds me of the Go stones — white against the adversary's black, placed on one of the three hundred and sixty-one points of the board.' The pebble I held was spattered with the red juice of trodden dragonflies. That sight — and behind me the visceral sunset — overwhelmed me with the sudden anguishing remembrance of my grandmother Natsuko's painful death from haemorrhaging ulcers, twenty-one years ago, in 1939.

Everything conspired to make our sojourn in Atami inauspicious.

Just then, a sportscar like a silver-humped porpoise pulled into the parking area. And from this luxurious vehicle, a Porsche I believe, stepped my neighbours in Magome, the young stockbroker, Matsui Kenji and his wife, Ayako. Matsui Kenji was an enthusiast of sportscar racing, a passion that my wife Yoko shared with him. Yoko's friendship with Matsui had encouraged her to take up this sport in earnest. Her racing permit required my endorsement, however, and my refusal brought us into the most acrimonious conflict that our marriage had so far known. 'And what of our bargain, *dannasama*★? Have you forgotten? My freedom was the real dowry you promised. "I am not an orthodox Nipponese husband," you said (and Yoko growls in baritone mimicry of my voice). And now you forbid me a little hobby of my own? I should have known better, that you never expected anything more from me than to provide a domestic semblance of respectability. Do you fear I might compete with your pranks, in your indulgences in the martial arts and posing in the nude for Hosoe Eikoh's photographs on our terrace, and in broad daylight? What is my role in all of this?'

To my acute shame, I remember replying: 'Be quiet, woman. My mother will overhear you.'

'I am especially eager that *she* especially should hear me.'

★ Traditional term for head of family.

Anger brings out Yoko's charming (un-common as plum blossoms') oddity, the pout of her forehead, which invests her wide mouth with a calm sensuality. Then she is truly beautiful. Yoko has no imagination. Her will is too narrow, better suited no doubt to racing cars than to poetry; but her fits of intemperate pique sometimes elevate her almost to the wildly poetic excesses that my grandmother Natsuko inflicted on me in the bygone days of my childhood.

I blamed Matsui Kenji for my misfortune, and thereafter avoided contact with the Matsui household. And now, there he was, eyeing me over the roof of his car, nonplussed to discover me here with another woman, as his wife's gaze far more honestly expressed. Matsui contemplated Keiko's armful of lilies. Did he guess what votive purpose they would serve? The irony of my situation achieved perfection – irony in the original Greek tragic sense – because I now recalled that Matsui Kenji was a descendant of General Matsui Iwane, Commander-in-Chief of the Japanese forces in central China and 'butcher of Nanking', whose name-marker featured among those of the seven hanged men on the wooded hill of the Atami Shrine above us.

Our embarrassment was mutually paralyzing, a deadlock broken by our instinctive bowing, two curt nods of the sheerest reflex formality.

'Who is that?' Keiko inquired.

'General Matsui's grandnephew.'

'Is that why you've turned pale as a ghost?'

'I feel like a thief.'

'And why is that, because you've robbed me of my precious little figurines?'

Dawn, gathering in the *t'jen-ching* courtyard style window-frame, sheds light on those porcelain figurines, and on Keiko too, now seen as a more weary-eyed reality than a formidable mythic being. And the lilies in a vase appear flushed and already sadly wilted.

Keiko hands me a cigarette from her lips and her drink. 'I don't usually breakfast on nicotine and whisky,' I say, nevertheless accepting both.

'You deserve them. I've been watching you for the past two hours, and I confess, in envy at your concentration. Your hand looked stuck to the page, like an abalone to a rock, never hesitating nor stopping to correct.'

'Writing at a deliberate speed was once a necessity. Now it's a habit. I'll confess another idiosyncrasy. No one has ever watched me write, not even the person closest to me, my mother. It was her custom to lay out my pens and ink, supply fresh paper and a pot of tea before I began work at night, but then she would retire.'

'I am privileged to have seen what your mother herself never saw.'

I perceived a declaration of sarcasm in Keiko's bow of thanks. 'Now comes my turn to tell you something else of peculiar interest,' she continued. 'This room has played host at least once before to a writer – a writer by necessity rather than habit. The writer I speak of lodged not only here, but in many other inns of an often disreputable kind during the summer and winter months of 1944, when he composed his masterpiece. He took beautiful young companions with him, male and female, to these inns, and after an evening of carousel with them, as they lay asleep, intoxicated and snoring, he would begin work on a memoir that caused him grave anxiety.'

'Of whom do you speak?'

'Prince Konoe Fumimaro, descendant of the great hereditary lords of Kyushu, the Konoe of Fujiwara clan whose regents governed Japan in the Emperor's name from the ninth century. In 1944, when His Majesty contemplated abdication, it was Prince Konoe as personal advisor to the Throne who inspected the Ninnaji Temple in Kyoto as a suitable place for the Emperor's retirement.'

'Prince Konoe's aim was always to safeguard the Imperial Throne from extinction.'

'For that very reason, as head of the 'Peace Faction' whose duty it was to plan for surrender negotiations and achieve salvation in defeat, Prince Konoe undertook to write his memoirs.'

'I know what masterpiece you are referring to, though I haven't seen it personally.'

'A document of pure fiction, composed of forged diaries and state papers which would convince our American victors that a real struggle had existed between moderate liberals in government and a military clique of extremists – and a further real struggle within the military establishment itself, an internecine feud between the Strike North faction aiming for limited war with Communist Russia and the Strike South faction agitating for all-out confrontation with the US and its colonialist allies in South East Asia – a memoir addressed to His Majesty that would detail all the conspiracies, the extremist mutinies and attempted *coup d'états* of the 1930s that destabilized the nation, suppressed the moderates and overruled His Majesty's own wishes for peace. But the most brilliant and audacious purpose of the memoir was to unmask a systematic Communist plot, an incitement to militarism that the Reds masterminded in order to create the conditions for mass discontent and revolution that would inevitably arise in the confusion of defeat.'

'An implausible thesis that only the most gullible would swallow.'

'But the Americans were indeed gullible. Prince Konoe relied on America's obsessive fear of Communism. He reckoned that America suffered from a Christian bad conscience, a deep-seated and nightmarish doubt that Communism must be right because it sided with the under-privileged of the world.'

'An interesting theory.'

'Not a theory, a fact. Because Prince Konoe's masterpiece succeeded in its purpose – to absolve the Imperial Presence from any hint of blame, expunge it from history, and at the same time persuade Washington that only the Throne could withstand the floodtides of social revolution.'

'So I've heard, but I disagree. Prince Konoe's masterpiece seems to me redundant. America had already opted for Japanese rightwing conservatism without Konoe's promptings.'

'Let's agree to differ.'

'You mention Prince Konoe's notorious orgies. Were you present at any of them in 1944?'

'Not in the flesh.'

'Of course, you benefit from Count – pardon me, Senator, Ito's information.'

'Ask him yourself. He'll show you a rejected draft of the Prince's memoir, one of many. Besides, you should remember, 1944 was the year of my marriage.'

Keiko returns with a fresh whisky, an imperilled ship listing drunkenly on her way back to me. 'The homosexual's icon,' she points to Guido Reni's Saint Sebastian on my table. 'You are writing about that?' Her nail polish is chipped, pearly freckles showing through the red. A cigarette dangles mannishly from her lips.

I do not reply. Keiko laughed. 'Sebastian pincushioned by the arrows of his own comrades, fascinates you, does it? You people. My wonder is reserved for the compassionate widow Irene who came to bury him, but found him still alive and nursed him back to health. I am intrigued by the widow's methods of nursing, aren't you?'

Again, I did not reply.

'Are you writing your ideal love story?' Keiko glazed her breasts with an ice cube plucked from her drink.

'For a love story to be ideal, it can only be in the purest sense, meaningless. My story therefore requires a defeated warrior, in accordance with the rules of Noh as originally prescribed by its founder, Zeami. Defeat softens the warrior's fierceness and permits lyricism.'

'And the heroine of your story?'

'The same rules of Noh apply to her. She must have *hie*, the absolute beauty of coldness. Ultimate beauty in a woman cannot be found in one who enjoys present happiness, but in one whose beauty suffers the refinement of memory. Beauty is always in a certain sense, past, which gives meaning to the aesthetic goal of *sabi*, faded, sad, cold as the moon hidden by rain.'

'What is that crying from the tree?
It is only the cracked husk of a locust.'

396

Keiko recites from the Noh play *Kakitsubata*.

'Well said. The moment of greatest risk in a writer's life occurs when he looks back on his past works and discovers himself at a dead end. Everything I have written is the cracked husk of a locust. I face a row of empty husks that constitute my collected works, and I hear the applause of dead hands. I do not wish to see myself old and ugly. By old, I do not simply mean decrepitude, and by ugly, not simply ill-favoured looks. One can already be old and ugly in earliest youth, and indeed these are the very features of precocity. The deformities of age and ugliness are liable to be evident even under the fairest bloom, as I am often ashamed to encounter in our streets these days. I perceive a spiritual leprosy, worse by far than the literal disease that may visibly ravage the body, because this one corrodes stealthily and invisibly from inside the person. Spirit is one's insatiable enemy.'

'But you are extraordinarily ugly, sensei.'

'Alas, yes, Madame Omiyeke. Ugliness has seeped through the armour I have created. But without that shell of fairytale muscles, others would see something even uglier — the obscene picture of the writer hero, martyr of the desk whose gravid labours have produced a certain austere 'inner' beauty, much admired by those who prize above all the heroism born of weakness. I risk being termed inwardly, monstrously beautiful by a public that is itself spiritually in leprous decay. I am the jackal spokesman of those who labour at the edge of endurance, the over-burdened, those already worn out but still holding themselves upright, of modern Japan of progressive accomplishment, of stunted growth and scanty resources, yet which contrives by skilful husbanding and prodigious spasms of the will to produce, at least for a while, the effect of greatness.'

'The real Japan is the one that exists now.'

'The real Japan, in which I exist posthumously.'

Keiko studied her face in the mirror luminous now with sunrise. 'Why not reconcile yourself to the fact, and like your respected mentor, Kawabata Yasunari, adopt conservative elegance and subtly mourn the passing of Japan?'

'I cannot simply mourn. I must act. How strange, to think I was eleven at the time of the *niniroku* mutiny, the snow was falling that morning as I left for school in my Peers' uniform, and I heard the mutineers' bugles in the distant centre of Tokyo. I saw the airplanes dropping leaflets urging the rebels to surrender. I was eleven, and I imagined the Emperor on his white horse, as in an Oscar Wilde fairytale, going in the snow to meet the loyalist rebels who had mutinied in His Name, and saying, "Yes, I accept the genuine sacrifice of your protest. You are honoured to commit *seppuku* as the pledge of your sincerity, and I shall be your witness. Go ahead now, cut open your stomachs, your blood will renew the nation." And I saw rank upon rank of grateful young soldiers, kneeling in the snow, covering it with their blood like scattered, wind-blown cherry blossoms. So did I imagine at eleven.'

'The reality was considerably less impressive,' Keiko said, her finger-tips testing the slight puffiness that the mirror revealed under her eyes. 'And I am forty. Why don't you read me the fairytale you've written this night?'

I began to read her the story of a young lieutenant of the Konoe Transport Battalion who was kept ignorant of the mutiny that his com-rades and dearest friends had planned. Perhaps his senior officers had acted out of compassion because he was newly wed. But their sympathy for the lieutenant had been misguided, since his exclusion now landed him in a terrible dilemma. An Imperial ordinance was expected that would proscribe his friends as traitorous rebels, and he faced the unwel-come prospect of commanding a unit against them. A choice between loyalty to comrades and allegiance to the Emperor is no choice at all. The lieutenant has no alternative but to commit *seppuku*. And so, on the night of the 28th February, three days after the mutiny had begun, he and his wife prepare to die together. The lieutenant asks to go first, because he needs his wife to be the witness to his suicide –

Keiko stopped me here. 'A wife invited to witness her husband's *seppuku*? That's improper. Unheard of. A violation of the code of *seppuku*.'

'In strict point of fact, you're right of course. But I permit myself a certain licence.'

'It's none of my business. Violate a basic criterion of *seppuku*, if you like, tamper with reality. But facts are facts.'

'Spoken with true Confucian rectitude. Literature is mendacity.'

'Praise be Confucian ethics, then. I could ask, perhaps unimagina-tively, why do you need her to witness the suicide?'

'Obviously, because I require a narrative viewpoint from which to describe the *seppuku* from the outside.'

'Why not better from the inside, from the lieutenant's own point of view?'

'Difficult. It might risk to violate the main criterion of aesthetics, the exigent one of credibility.'

'Aesthetics takes precedence over ethics. Or is there something else inadmissable in your choice of viewpoints? One which perhaps answers to your own desire to be seen in the act of *seppuku*? I am led to suspect that your lieutenant, despite all his idealist vigour, is in fact – what? a writer? A writer sick to death of writing? Isn't it the case, *sensei*, that a writer will sometimes cast himself as a doomed character whom he destroys in order to survive? In the final analysis, is there any real difference between your lieutenant and Thomas Mann's Gustav von Aschenbach in *Death in*

Venice? Both are sentenced to death by ethics, but executed by aesthetics. Mann assassinated Gustav von Aschenbach in order to supersede him as a writer. Have you grown so weary of literature that you seek a means of ridding yourself of it, fictionally, in suicide?'

'If you are right, then I have one of two choices. Either choose to live death from the inside, in reconciliation with the advance of old age, and continue to survive like any other modern pragmatic zombie –'

'I have already indicated that possibility in the excellent model Kawabata Yasunari provides –'

'or commit suicide –'

'and also choose to live death from the inside. In either case, it is too late for you to avoid fiction.' Keiko resumed her decorative, semi-nude pose on the bed, reclining in a sardonic parody of the attentive listener. 'Have you written the description of the lieutenant's *seppuku*? Good. Then read it to me – but with one small alteration in your script. Please translate the wife's viewpoint into your own personal one.'

I did as Keiko instructed, with more ease than I had anticipated. 'Is it convincing enough for you?' I asked, at the end.

Keiko gave no reply; but the heat of her vixen's eyes made the silence eloquent. And with the indolent gesture of an Empress, she summoned me to her bed. 'Let's see how you respond to the nursing of a compassionate widow.'

'The intensity of our dislike for each other is truly impressive.'

'Impressive, but not displeasing,' she replies.

Her eyes are bolted open, even as her climax begins exerting its unconscious grip of steel, but unable to overcome those watchful eyes that take greater pleasure from the vision of someone hated. Our coupling is an embrace of ice, like two mirrors reflecting an absolute, null void between them. Our extreme of pleasure comes from the morbidly cerebral assurance that we see one another because we are being seen. By a third party? A pervasive divinity, like the rays of sunrise through the window? No, it is at once more intimate and more enigmatic than a third party spectator. It is –

– gaining lightness from pleasure, soaring above it in a cold, moon-like sterility of reflection –

– an exquisitely inhuman hatred for the human object in whom I confide my love.

Pressed together, face to face, one upon the other – what are we? We are alike as two crystals, opposed by being enantiomorphic, not superposable because one mirrors the other. I can clearly see what I am in the ferocious apertures of Keiko's eyes. Homosexual. Exclusively homosexual in my act. I have for years tried to gain some sense of my Uranism (that archaic term once used by Sam Lazar to dignify and neutralize our condition, far preferable than the clinically repellant label, homosexuality.) I have tried to understand the *yin* and *yang* gender conflict within me that dictates absolute exclusivity in my choice of love-object – myself as preferred image – and renders homoerotic narcissism so enigmatic. I cannot deny what my own being patently confesses to be. I wish neither to oppose it nor simply acquiesce to it, but to free myself of the sense of being accompanied by someone else. I feel the presence of a mythical creature, perhaps the sinister god Uranus, dogging my every step.

It's over. I lie on my back, drained by the night's excess of labour, followed by coitus at dawn. Drowsiness only complicates my post-coital malaise, without permitting me untroubled sleep. Keiko's hands massaging my body do nothing to soothe me. Her touch is a mechanic's caress, obsessed by its own frigid curiosity, but disinterested in me. I feel the untender operation of her hand, as though wiping moisture from a bathroom mirror, as though a museum custodian were polishing the surface of a lifeless classical statue.

'Don't pretend affection, Baroness.'

'I'm not. I can sincerely appreciate what I never have to love.'

'If it gives you pleasure.'

'Answer me this. Are you trying to convince yourself that *seppuku* can be undergone without suffering pain?'

'No, I can only presume immense pain. But I must persuade myself that it can be endured pleasurably.'

'You mean, by deceiving yourself?'

'A fictional deception. By habit I become accustomed to what is unimaginable.'

'A repulsive idea.'

'Is it? How does it differ from what occurs normally in life? The postponement of death is an unconscious deception needed to go on living. Until gradually we see ourselves trapped, without possible escape from a death that our own routine deception has made possible. Suicide is a conscious deception – minus the postponement.'

My eyes are closed. I can hear Keiko unzipping her cosmetic kit, the rattle of tools as she prepares to remake her face. As I ease into sleep, a sudden pain of unaccountable shrillness jolts me back to wakefulness, a pain like a zipper of ice opening across my stomach. I rise up on my elbows to see Keiko kneeling over me, with the detached, professional look of a surgeon. She holds a razor blade clamped between a pair of tweezers, the edge buried some millimetres in the flesh of my abdomen. I watch the razor's steady progress, accepting its feather-light trace of pain, its delicate beads of red creeping along behind in a snail-like trail. Keiko's hand trembles a little as she suppresses a delighted laughter. We both can see my penis stiffening obediently, curling towards the razor, attracted to it like a snake charmed by seductive music.

I look down at my abdomen. Its muscles are cobbled paving stones sloping up to the expanse of my chest. I think back to what I once wrote, and believed, that muscles render possible a voluntary acceptance of pain. Muscles are a preparation for another, higher category of visceral sensation. 'The visceral equanamity of true culture,' I called it, which is the samurai's acceptance of death. I look at my fine abdominal armour being sliced by a razor in a woman's hand, one that she probably uses to shave her armpits or her legs, and I consider that my former beliefs were a sham, heroic pretences, the proclamations of fiction. Pleasure in the pain that I now feel, confronts me with the insufficient idea I once had of my body. Everything was externally articulated, superficial. But *inside*? How many people are able to make a correct inventory of their own inner organs, mentally see them all in their rightful arrangement? How many know the size of their liver, its weight or even its place? We exist in blessed ignorance of our insides, and to all intents, hollow, animated solely by the afflatus of will power and individual identity. The maliciously insistent thrill of pain instructs me otherwise about my real desires. I realize that I have always yearned to live *inside*, in that inner landscape flooded with blood, everything constantly in motion like restless sand dunes, exotically coloured, the bifurcated islands of my lungs under an ogival sky of ribs, the heart a luxuriantly crimson branched thing, the subterranean conduits beyond the stomach sphincter, estuaries of the epigastrium, bronchia and trachea, and eeriest of all, the endlessly coiled labyrinths of the brain filled with resounding voices, odours, flashes of light in which the nameless things I have forgotten rediscover their names — here is where I desire to be, familiar with it all like a wood-cutter knowing the forest path, like a game-keeper knowing the animals under his jurisdiction — and why do I want to reside here, among my own innards? The strange, indeed very strange answer to this question is supplied by my enraptured acknowledgement of pain. Why do I want to be inside? Because I can protect my insides from harm, I can prevail against the harmful anxieties that seep in like poisons from the outside and threaten my paradise with illness, decay and ruin.

I want to live without the pretence that normally leads to illness, decay and ruin.

My compassionate widow leans down, her hair descends in a prickling mass of black icicles on my skin, her tongue licks the disconnected necklace of blood that spills from my cut, and then she straddles me, inserts my *mibashira* pillar in her central chamber, and presses the snowy pad of her belly to my wound. Through a parting in her dishevelled curtain of hair, I see a pair of red lips giving shape to words. 'Isn't it time your were introduced to the midwife in your story.'

'Midwife?'

'The villain who brings the hero to deliverance.'

'And this midwife, would he by chance be named Count Ito Kazushige?'

Keiko reclined her forehead on my shoulder, her haunches tightening and heaving round a pillar of slime.

9   A TEA PARTY FOR ASSASSINS

GRAVEL CRACKLED in a rapid-fire hiss under the wheels of my taxi as it turned into the driveway of Senator Ito's house in Azabu. Autumn rain this morning had left glistening drops on the stems of forsythia, on the black tongues of rhododendrons under the cedars flanking the semicircular drive. White birches appeared at the bend, as in a Russian fairytale, their jittery leaves shedding gold in the afternoon sunlight.

A funeral limousine parked at the entrance of the house had already deposited the two illustrious guests who habitually frequented Count Ito's monthly tea parties, ex-Prime Minister Kishi Nobosuke and his younger brother, Sato Eisaku. The sibling strong men of the LDP had arrived ahead of me on that pleasant, Indian summer afternoon, a Sunday. I had given special notice of my attendance by forwarding an autographed, fair copy manuscript of my recent story, *Patriotism*, to Count Ito through my good will emissary, Baroness Omiyeke Keiko. I had delayed four months in fulfilling my promise to make this visit, until a certain propitious event occurred that gave me the ideal circumstance for it.

A sleek, pretty young houseboy in a dark blue serge uniform welcomed me at the door. His smirk ought to have forewarned me of the unexpected reception awaiting me. I bent down to remove my shoes, but stopped, remembering that guests were not obliged to do so in Count Ito's Western-style home. Just then, a gorilla-faced bodyguard suddenly pounced out of the twilit vestibule and began roughly frisking me for hidden weapons. I glimpsed a fringe of tattooes under the shirt cuffs of my attacker's wrists, indicating that I had fallen into the hands of a *yakuza* thug. From somewhere within the lobby, a voice mournfully called: 'Hideki, please ensure that Mishima-*sensei* is not harassed.'

Count Ito now approached us, limping on a snake-wood walking stick, informally clad in a brown hound's-tooth sports coat and fawn slacks. I remembered what my father used to say, that 'a dog becomes the master's faithful caricature,' an amusing maxim on canine fidelity that could well have applied to Count Ito. He had truly evolved into a faithful replica of his master, Prince Konoe. His one concession to the post-war era of democratic repentance had been to sacrifice the Himmlerian moustache that the Prince had favoured till his death in 1945. The absence of moustache on Count Ito's upper lip served to emphasize its camel-like, supercilious length. A narrow head with sharp-beaked nose and equine jaw above the elongated shaft of his body completed the reincarnation of the suave Prince. Count Ito surveyed me through droopy shuttered eyelids, his eyebrows like two worn-out brooms stuck high on his steep forehead. 'Please forgive this frightful indignity, Mishima-*san*,' Count Ito apologized, in a voice more accustomed to pronouncing ironies. 'But our former Prime Minister insists on these regrettable security measures after the unfortunate incident last week.' Count Ito referred to the recent assassination of Asanuma Inejiro, Chairman of the Socialist Party, stabbed to death by a young ultra-rightist on 12th October, only four days ago, the unforeseen event which had decided me to make my visit today.

'A minor incident compared to events in the 1930s,' I replied, 'when eminent politicians were threatened almost daily with assassination. I recall an interesting anecdote from those Dark Valley times which bears witness to His Majesty's caustic humour. His Majesty recommended the wearing of a new therapeutic stomach-belt to His elder statesmen, apparently as a remedy for their sagging bellies, but in reality as an implied protective aid to deflect the knives of assassins.'

Count Ito led me along a glass-sided and roofed passage to the east wing of the house. 'Strangely enough, I was in fact present with Prince Konoe when His Majesty made the therapeutic suggestion that you mention.'

'Were you? And so you will know better than I that His Majesty's precaution anticipated the February mutiny of 1936.'

'You are indeed correct.' A moustache would have added Chaplinesque savour to the Count's little twitch of a smile.

'I should like to talk to you about the *niniroku* mutiny.'

'Whatever for?' He glanced aloofly at me, before introducing us to the roomful of tea party guests. 'Haven't you dwelt sufficiently on the mutiny, twice, in both those stories you were kind enough to send me?'

We passed into a cheerful sitting-room with French windows that gave into the garden. The selection of furniture, Thonet bentwood armchairs and a Jugendstil Bergère suite, imparted a charming, artificially rusticated manner to the room, a playful affectation underlined by a pair of Boucher paintings of *fête champêtre* nudes and several Hiroshige *ukiyo-e* prints of rainy scenes from the Floating World. Pastel green wallpaper striped with runners of honeysuckle echoed the picturesque view of an

English style garden through the open windows. Sunlight poured into the room, and yet I felt the chill breath of corruption, as though I confronted the subfusc atmosphere of an underground archive. The murky occupants of this room were as eerily familiar to me as characters I might have invented in a theatre script.

Ex-Prime Minister Kishi and his brother, Dietman Sato, greeted my entry with disquieting stares like two jailers. Kishi sat in the nook of a chaise longue, a teacup and saucer perched at his elbow on the headrest. His brother, stooping forward precipitously from his bentwood chair, stubbed out a cigarette with pugnacious jabs of his forefinger. Kishi treated me to one of his shameless politician's grins, a crop of horse teeth exposed to the gums, as he turned away. A diminutive chin like a small walnut, embossed with an outstanding wart, receded between the pouchy dewlaps of his cheeks and scrawny neck. He had the elongated ears of a Buddha, a feature shared by his younger brother, Sato. Impudently ambitious Sato, whose acts of bribery and malfeasance had caused the downfall of Yoshida's government in 1954, and had nearly led to his arrest, enjoyed the superiority of good looks over the ill-favoured Kishi. His stern, conventionally handsome appearance disguised a complete absence of imagination and humour. A common practice accounted for the brother's difference of names. Kishi was born a Sato but had been adopted by the Kishi family. His younger brother Eisaku kept the name of their father, Sato, which oddly enough had originally been Kishi too before the latter's own adoption into the Sato family. Adoptions in Japan are not unlike financially or socially advantageous marriages, another category of alliance in which the brothers had also been successful.

To my surprise, ex-Colonel Tsuji Masanobu now stepped forward impetuously from his station by the French windows, and before Count Ito could commence his formal introductions, seized me in a vigorous handshake. 'Our mystery guest,' he exclaimed, pumping my hand enthusiastically as though welcoming an Occidental appreciative of that republican habit. 'How different you look, Mishima-*san*. May I compliment you on your splendidly fit condition?'

'Fit enough, I dare say,' Count Ito interjected, 'to risk blotting his neutralist record, spotless until now, by joining us today.'

Kishi snorted disdainfully. The teacup and saucer rattled in the tense, irascible grip of Tsuji's left hand, and he blushed fiercely. 'Were you ever a neutralist by sincere conviction, Mishima-*san*?' he asked.

'Only by lack of a true alternative,' I replied, and Tsuji nodded, apparently satisfied. He retired to his post by the windows; but he eyed me persistently as though measuring up a volunteer for an assault mission.

Count Ito proceeded with my introduction to our ex-Prime Minister. Kishi's strengthening of the US-Japan Security Treaty in defiance of

liberal opposition had led to the summer riots and his consequent resignation from office. Kishi studied me with a lacklustre gaze: 'So this is
the author who called me a nihilist in his *Asahi* articles?'

'A *tiny* nihilist,' Sato added.

'Quite so, tiny,' Kishi pursed his lips wistfully in a show of restrained
offence.

'Come now, *mon cher* Kishi,' Count Ito interceded, 'surely you have
been subjected to worse names on the floor of the Diet?'

'I can accept the rough-house abuse of my Diet colleagues,' Kishi
replied. 'But not from an unknown assailant who stabs me in the back
with a pen.'

Nicely phrased. Kishi was no fool. But his peculiar choice of metaphor, referring to assassination, disclosed the unease that preyed on his
mind.

Kishi's barbed witticism drew the high-spirited laughter of Sato's
wife, seated out of view to our right. 'With respect, brother-in-law,
Mishima-*san* has not been invited here to atone for his remarks in the
newspapers,' Madame Sato declared. Kishi shrugged.

Count Ito now presented me to the ladies sitting in a row on the
Jugendstil Bergère sofa, and in this he followed a Western practice
strange in a country where women are normally overlooked. I could
understand Keiko's function here as Count Ito's hostess; but even the
mock informality of an occasion like this did not warrant any additional
presence of women, acknowledged or not.

Madame Sato occupied the centre between Keiko at her left, elegantly
poised as she served me tea, and a Vietnamese woman on her right who
was introduced simply as Madame Nhu. I recognized her at once as
the fabled 'Dragon Lady' of Saigon, sister-in-law of Ngo Dinh Diem,
President of South Vietnam. A typically Indochinese comeliness of face
was spoiled in Madame Nhu's case by a sullen mask of effrontery. She
acknowledged my bow with a curtly dismissive nod. Keiko's disagreeable little smile as she gave me my tea opened the parenthesis of an
unspoken sarcasm ('So, despite your penchant for Western mannerisms,
you did not risk bringing your wife to this rendezvous.') Our audience
merely heard a politely voiced query: 'Do you take sugar with your
tea, Mishima-*san*?' 'Without, Baroness. I always go without,' I answered,
striving by innuendo to take revenge on her. Madame Sato's amused
reaction to my proclamation of Keiko's obsolescent title brought me
satisfaction enough.

The wicker-back sofa had been designed for persons of European
stature, which agreed with Keiko's height, but was too deep for the
Rumpelstiltskin legs of Madames Sato and Nhu that hung awkwardly
truncated at the calf. Madame Sato's rather plain, undistinguished features were rescued from homeliness by two virtues lacking in her

husband, a lively imagination and a sense of humour that shone from her eyes behind the glittering panes of her eyeglasses. A copy of Oscar Wilde's *Salomé*, unmistakably signalled by Aubrey Beardsley's sinuous line illustrations, lay open on Madame Sato's lap. I had glimpsed her attempts to engage Madame Nhu's interest in these pictures as I first entered the room.

'Kishi-*san* has given you a taste of blunt speaking,' Keiko said, 'which is entirely in accord with the spirit of Oiso that we celebrate here.'

'Excuse me, but isn't Oiso the place to which our veteran post-war leader, Yoshida Shigeru, has retired?'

'It is indeed,' Madame Sato replied. 'Madame Omiyeke has obviously failed to inform you that the spirit of Oiso who presides at our monthly tea parties is none other than Yoshida-*san*. As you probably know, Yoshida-*san* served as ambassador to Britain from 1936 to 1939. He developed a taste for British manners – in particular the English style of tea and frankness – while residing in London. This is our Yoshida Memorial, created since his retirement in 1954.'

'Consider this a genuine tea ceremony,' Count Ito added. 'One which encourages its practitioners to speak frankly of indelicate things in a refined way. Japan has achieved such an impressive ugliness these days that it calls for the cultivation of plain speech.'

'I shall bear that advice in mind,' I said.

I was left to observe the 'spirit of Oiso' noticeable in the style of English casuals worn by all the men present, although none rivalling Count Ito's degree of convincing elegance, and the ladies all similarly uniformed in Balenciaga two-piece suits with loose, smock-length jackets and velvet-trimmed straw hats, the latest rage among chic females of the upper class. I admired the lovely Bauhaus tea-set, the cups of bright egg-yellow with white raised spots, the little Art Deco teaspoons and sugar tongs. I looked at these ceremonial objects with a pang of discomfort and nostalgia, because they emitted a mysterious aura of the 1930s, a time when the 'spirit of Oiso' operated skilfully as a diplomat promoting the Strike South faction's aims of war against the Western colonial powers in South East Asia. Yoshida, son-in-law of Lord Privy Seal, Count Makino, had been later appointed to another diplomatic function in the so-called Peace Faction, a cover organization headed by Prince Konoe and unofficially sanctioned by the Emperor himself, which planned every detail of the Surrender strategy. Yoshida's arrest by the secret police in 1945 as an alleged 'peace campaigner' had been a further astute manoeuvre which deceived SCAP investigators into judging him a reliable democrat blameless of any war guilt.

I wondered: what outspoken secrets could the sobriety of English tea possibly foster in this absurd, memorial atmosphere of tinkling porcelain?

Count Ito exercised his blunt speech in French conversation with

Madame Nhu. And she, with rancorous sidelong glances at Dietman Tsuji (something he had earlier said must have badly ruffled the Dragon Lady's scales), gave an ostentatious account of her stay this summer at the Hyannis Port family residence of John F. Kennedy, boasting of the friendship that her brother-in-law Diem had formed with the US Presidential candidate in the past during a two-year sojourn at the Maryknoll Seminary.

Keiko offered the guests another round of tea, to which Dietman Tsuji responded with an instruction: 'No milk, please. I have a China-man's aversion to the stuff. Did you know that the Chinese lack the intestinal enzymes to digest milk?'

'Thus speaks an old China hand,' Kishi observed with a depreciatory grin.

'At length and tiresomely,' Sato confirmed.

Impervious to this fraternal rudeness, Tsuji answered: 'There is nothing in the least tiresome about the China question, as must be painfully obvious to Madame Nhu's brother-in-law.'

Madame Nhu and Tsuji's utterances dovetailed perfectly on the words 'brother-in-law', pronounced at the same moment, as their eyes met. With a petulant toss of her head, Madame Nhu now addressed Tsuji in fluent Japanese. 'Your remarks earlier in praise of Mao struck me as unacceptable. We would be far better off with Chiang Kai-shek in control of China.'

'Why, because he is a Christian like yourself and President Diem's élite Catholic minority?' Tsuji stared at the lemon slice in his tea cup. 'Chiang has grey eyes, you know. A legacy of the Portuguese wine merchants in his blood-line.'

'What have Chiang's grey eyes do to with it?' Madame Nhu irritably countered.

'Excuse me,' Tsuji said, 'but a choice of evils between Chiang or Mao is irrelevant. China will always remain Vietnam's enemy.'

'And ours,' Kishi added.

'Our rival, certainly,' Tsuji said, 'although not necessarily our enemy. I shall better acquaint myself with the situation when I visit Hanoi next year as a correspondent for the *Asahi*.'

Madame Nhu's lips tightened into a vehement pout. So, this was the cause of Madame Nhu's irritation – Dietman Tsuji's mission to President Diem's mortal enemy, Ho Chi Minh.

Madame Sato acknowledged my look of surprise at Madame Nhu's command of Japanese with an explanation. 'Madame Nhu and I were contemporaries at the Sacred Heart School in Tokyo during the war,' Madame Sato declared. 'A privileged hospitality that she enjoyed with some members of the Vietnamese royalty, the daughters of Emperor Bao Dai and Prince Cuong De.'

'The hostages of our Co-Prosperity Sphere, might one say?'

'You put the case too cynically, Mishima-*san*,' Madame Sato replied. Her smiles were given sparingly but to great effect in evincing her intellect.

Madame Sato's looks revived the poignant memory of my sister Mitsuko's homely, tomboy vivacity. 'Did you know my sister Mitsuko at the Sacred Heart?' I asked.

'No, I had left by then. But I heard from a cousin that she died of typhoid in 1945. How very sad.'

Keiko meanwhile conversed with Madame Nhu across the interval of Madame Sato's shoulders, in an effort to distract the Dragon Lady from her vexation. Madame Nhu's attention was again reluctantly coaxed in the direction of Madame Sato's lap and Beardsley's piquant drawings decorating the *Salomé* text. I had the impression that Count Ito had set Keiko and Madame Sato the task of inhibiting too sharp an altercation between Madame Nhu and Tsuji. Madame Sato verified my guess by coming to Keiko's aid. 'I've waited all of six months to cross-examine Mishima-*san* on his production of *Salomé* last spring,' she said, turning to Madame Nhu.

'I warned you,' Keiko reminded me, winking roguishly for my cooperation. 'Madame Omiyeke tells me that you seriously considered taking the role of John the Baptist,' Madame Sato continued, winning a little more of Madame Nhu's curiosity. 'You would have made a strangely athletic martyr in that role.'

'There are days when one would like to be an athlete, and others when one would like to be a woman,' I replied, beginning a quotation. Count Ito intervened to complete my quotation: 'In the first case it is the muscle which quivers; in the second it is the flesh which yearns and flames.' And finally Madame Sato correctly identified the source: 'Flaubert, in his journals.' Keiko applauded our triple performance; while Madame Nhu grumbled something about Flaubert and Wilde being a pair of vile and debauched decadents; and our trio of Dietmen looked on – Kishi with another of his horse-toothed grins – and the other two in blank astonishment.

This was my cue. An urge to laugh out loud, to do something outrageous in defiance of the 'spirit of Oiso' overcame me – anything, any bizarre act would do, so that I might seize my pathological timidity by the neck and throttle the life out of that unclean parasite. Dominating my innate shyness would give me the chance to dominate these people who felt no real respect for me.

'I see that you are reading the *Salomé* text,' I said to Madame Sato, 'in the French, as Wilde originally wrote it.'

'Yes, I thought it might help to entertain Madame Nhu. She complains of migraine, if forced to speak Japanese without break.'

'I invite you to rehearse a scene from the play with me,' and so saying, I went down on my knees before Madame Sato, whose own plump knees confronted me at eye level, vulnerable above the broad beam of her calves squashed on the edge of the sofa. A tugging adjustment of skirts now ensued in reflex unison as Madames Sato and Nhu modestly defended themselves against my gaze. I sat back on my heels like a Zen acolyte in a *dojo* session. 'Please read from the scene where John the Baptist rises up from his dungeon-well to face Salomé on the eve of his decapitation. I shall mimic the Baptist's ascent from deep below as I rise from my knees. Please don't feel shy.'

Madame Sato laughed; but she betrayed not the slightest unease. Madame Nhu glared at me, aghast; and the stupefaction on the Dietmen's faces gave me exquisite delight. 'I am not suited to play a maiden still in her teens,' Madame Sato demurred.

'Nor am I a saint destined to lose his head over a teenage virgin.'

'Losing your head is not quite what the spirit of Oiso demands of you, Mishima-*san*,' Count Ito rebuked me; but the tone of his voice failed to convey displeasure at the spectacle.

Madame Sato came to the rescue of my foolhardy venture by complying with it. In a hesitant school-girl French, Salomé addressed the martyr Iokanaan, as Wilde names the Baptist in his play:

SALOME
Speak again! Speak again, Iokanaan, and tell me what I must do.

IOKANAAN
Daughter of Sodom, come not near me! But cover thy face with a veil, and scatter ashes upon thine head, and get thee to the desert, and seek out the Son of Man.

SALOME
Who is he, the Son of Man? Is he as beautiful as thou art, Iokanaan?

IOKANAAN
Get thee behind me! I hear in the palace the beating of the wings of the angel of death.

Lack of French excluded our three Dietmen from appreciation of this hothouse duet; and those able to comprehend, responded symptomatically according to their characters. Madame Nhu, primarily, maintained a look of pained alarm during the recitation; Keiko barely restrained her hilarity; and Count Ito looked on, mouth slightly ajar, with a nonchalant air of feigned idiocy.

SALOME
I will kiss thy mouth, Iokanaan. I will kiss thy mouth.

As the duologue of Salomé and the Baptist spirals to its virulent erotic climax, I rose up by degrees from my haunches, and I reached out – I do not know what devilry prompted me to this – I reached out and with both hands grasped Madame Sato's legs above the ankles just where they spread into flattened muscle against the sofa. Madame Sato flinched; and the upshot of my action was that one of her shoes slipped off her foot to the floor. I bent down and refitted the shoe to her foot, like a shop clerk attending to a client. A twitch of excitement crossed Madame Nhu's face as she stared loftily at me, an involuntary thrill that flared up in her, mushrooming like an odour of sweat under the elegant cuirass of her French perfume.

Keiko retrieved the volume fallen from Madame Sato's lap and carried on with the reading. She chose the final scene of the play, when Salomé's wish has been fulfilled and the executioner presents her with John the Baptist's decapitated head on a dish. She seizes the head – and here, Keiko took mine between her hands – and exclaims: 'Ah! thou wouldst not suffer me to kiss they mouth, Iokanaan. Well! I will kiss it now. I will bite it with my teeth as one bites a ripe fruit . . .' Keiko imitated Salomé's triumphant, exalted kissing of the martyr's lips by bending down to kiss mine.

Glacial silence descended on the room. Dietman Sato visibly paled with rage; Kishi's eyelids lifted dramatically as his mouth fell; Tsuji jerked his head repeatedly as though nagged by a wasp. Madame Nhu led us out of the impasse by jumping to her feet in outraged protest at the offence to her Christian morals. 'I cannot listen to such blasphemy,' she exclaimed. 'Wilde was a pervert jailed for indecency.'

Madame Sato relieved the weight of her own discomposure by turning it against Madame Nhu. 'Madame Nhu has become a notorious puritan, you know. She forgets what a pair of incorrigible rascals we used to be at the Sacred Heart. She and President Diem's brother, Bishop Ngo Dinh Thuc, have succeeded in outlawing all the favourite amusements of the Saigonese – divorce, dancing, beauty contests, gambling, fortune-telling, cock-fighting and prostitution. Oscar Wilde can now be added to her Vatican index of forbidden pleasures.'

'You should not treat our reforms so disrespectfully,' Madame Nhu objected, her pique blazing higher still.

'Pardon me, but I cannot take you seriously as an arbiter of morals,' Madame Sato laughed, adding a mischievous side-swipe at Dietman Tsuji's former role as morals instructor at the Military Academy thirty years ago.

Madame Nhu could tolerate no more. She looked set to march out through the French windows to the garden in search of dissident refuge. 'Do please restrain your anger and sit down, Madame Nhu,' Count Ito said. 'A harmless little charade should not offend you, when there are greater misdeeds to consider.' Count Ito's mysterious formula had the desired repressive effect. Madame Nhu sat down.

Count Ito had exemplified his occult power in a politely veiled threat to Madame Nhu. I wondered at the true nature and extent of that power.

My little display of misbehaviour had resulted in a fragmentation, a sort of breaking of crockery, which left each guest awkwardly isolated and adrift. I had failed to achieve my goal, domination of the 'spirit of Oiso'. And now, Count Ito began expertly to restore the shattered mood to coherence. He started with Kishi, who pretended to interest himself in the manuscript copy of my *Patriotism* story, which had been placed on exhibit for all to see on the tea table. It alarmed me to find my story on public loan.

'What do you make of Mishima-*sensei*'s tale of heroic suicide?' Count Ito asked.

'Judging from his deplorable performance just now,' Kishi answered, relishing the opportunity for punishment, 'it seems entirely in character. I found it distastefully sensational. I mean, really, that description of *seppuku* – I felt subjected to a treatise on vivisection.' And here Kishi put on his reading glasses and began to quote.

'Please stop,' Madame Nhu found voice to object, in an excess of disgust. 'It's perfectly horrid!'

I glanced at Keiko. No point seeking an ally there. Her face had the same look I had seen before, when she gashed my stomach with the razor.

Count Ito's game had its own keen double edge: offering me up as sacrificial lamb to his disgruntled Oiso clientèle, but also, presenting me once again with centre stage.

Kishi had relinquished the manuscript to his brother, Sato, who now scrutinized the dedicatory page with a frown. 'I am puzzled by the name you use,' he said.

I had signed myself Yukio Mishima, but by a play on the characters of that name, I gave it another sense.

mi	shi	ma	yu	ki	o
魅	死	魔	幽	鬼	男
attract	- death	- wizard	ghost	- devil	- man

'That is the true meaning of my name,' I asserted.

'An entertaining, if somewhat eerie joke,' Count Ito commented.

"And in questionable taste,' Sato added.

I had regained my audience. Tsuji prowled up and down, his eyes quizzing me. 'What do you think of my story, Dietman Tsuji-*san*?' I hazarded a question that caused me anxiety. No matter how callous a writer has grown in his professional life, an opinion – anyone's opinion – can still raise butterflies in his stomach that he felt as a young amateur.

'I am no connoisseur nor even admirer of literature,' Tsuji responded, 'but I found your story romantic. And for that very reason, deeply moving, because it seemed to me an expression of unqualified romantic love for the Imperial Presence, something that I welcome. Mishima-sensei has dared to revive feelings repressed since 1945, and that can only be a good and proper thing, even if – *particularly* if – it arouses embarrassment among liberals. I do not agree with Kishi-san that your description of *seppuku* is repulsive, sensational though perhaps it might be – no, no, it is a good thing to be reminded that simple-hearted virtue was once capable of choosing an honourable death, because today we do not countenance honour or sincerity, we despise virtue as old-fashioned. My one criticism is that your story offends against decorum in permitting a wife to attend her husband's *seppuku*.'

'I have already been criticized for that,' I replied, glancing at Keiko, but encountering a surgeon's clinically detached gaze again.

Tsuji was determined to make my story an excuse for a campaigner's impassioned speech. 'I am willing to overlook a breach of decorum, however, because I am pleased to find a leading writer of the post-war generation who for the first time promotes *butoku*, martial virtues. Our own LDP members in the Diet have been shamefully reluctant to do as much.'

'You forget something,' Kishi interrupted the orator. 'The person we honour on this occasion, none other than Yoshida-san himself, was instrumental in reviving the pre-war Martial Virtues Association★ in 1954, soon after the Occupation ended.'

'I don't forget,' Tsuji rebutted. 'I served faithfully in the Yoshida government, and would have continued to do so, if Yoshida-san's premiership had not been unnaturally terminated by scandal in 1954.'

Tsuji's reference to 'scandal' was a dig at Kishi's brother, Sato, whose narrow escape from arrest on charges of corruption and bribery, while serving as Prime Minister Yoshida's aide, had brought down the government. Sato brazenly disregarded Tsuji's jibe, and Tsuji continued. 'I remember something else, an episode reported in Yoshida-san's own memoirs, when he pleaded with General MacArthur not to dissolve the Martial Virtues Association. And what was his plea? That its dissolution would harm the Liberal Party at the forthcoming election. MacArthur, of course, refused; but he struck an interesting bargain with Yoshida-san to postpone the law enforcing a change of *zaibatsu* trade names. And so we gained the perpetuation of Mitsubishi, Mitsui, etcetera. Our

---

★ Or the *Butoku Kai* founded in 1895 in Kyoto under the leadership of prominent military men.

former prime minister cites this as an example of the Supreme Commander's sagacity.'

'What are all these insinuations driving at, Tsuji-*san*?' Sato impatiently wanted to know.

'It seems to me,' Tsuji pursued, 'that Yoshida-*san*'s confession of this "bargain" sheds peculiar light on the reconstitution of the army at that time, and indeed is not without relevance to the army's situation nowadays.'

'The *what*?' Kishi exclaimed, laughing. 'The "situation of the army"? What on earth are you talking about, Dietman?'

'You were present and should know very well what I am talking about, Kishi-*san*. You know that Dulles pressured Yoshida-*san* to increase the numbers of our army – an army of illegal status – from 75,000 to 350,000. You know Prime Minister Yoshida worried that such an upgraded force might be used in Korea. And it *was*. The US and its allies in Korea needed the assistance of thousands of Japanese military specialists familiar with the terrain of that country. They needed our maps, our military engineers and combat ships in mine-sweeping operations. We trained RoK personnel in Kyushu. Our shipping and railroad experts with their own crews were present in Korea under US and UN command –'

' – and so what?' Sato brutally interjected. In a softer spoken, conciliatory tone, Count Ito added: 'Dietman Tsuji-*san*, we are all quite familiar with this data. What exactly is your point?'

'The point, exactly?' Tsuji muttered, pausing to stare calmly at the ceiling. 'Exactly this. When I consider the morale of the army today, its present aura of illegitimacy, the suspicion and resentment that our civilian public harbours towards the army, the insult of "tax thieves" which the volunteers of the Self Defence Forces have to bear from this heartless public –' Tsuji stopped, he looked round at the attendants of the Oiso spirit. ' – "tax thieves", can you imagine? As a member of the Diet, I know that our *zakai*★ businessmen – our Floating World of privileged executives – spend more tax-exempt millions of yen on entertainment than is allocated to the Defence budget, more than the government's expenditure on education. Our corporate tax thieves account for 1.5% of GNP.'

Kishi shared a look of pitying irony with his brother, and sighed. 'Ah, our samurai Dietman – he has not yet overcome the naive sensitivities of a former Imperial Army officer. I could almost suspect him of being sympathetic to the mutinous outrages of the 1930s.'

Kishi's savant little barb was a grave insult to ex-Colonel Tsuji Masanobu, a loyalist well-known for his antipathy towards the extremist military conspirators of the 1930s. To be named a 'samurai' by Kishi

★ The finance world.

was again far from being complimentary, another insult which categorized Tsuji as a flamboyant, swashbuckling adventurer. I looked at Tsuji, and his face did resemble one of those portrayed in the Hiroshige *ukiyo-e* prints on the wall, the wild-eyed, rain-swept face a *ronin* adrift in the Floating World of decadent luxury.

'I wonder if a *coup d'état* against a government such as ours,' Tsuji said, 'is not better than one's collaboration within it.' Aggression was entirely absent from Tsuji's utterance; rather, it expressed the sadness of his own position. 'I have tried to make two points. First, that Yoshida-*san*'s political manoeuvres under the heel of MacArthur's Supreme Command were useful in their day, but we have relied on them to elaborate an entirely retrograde system which now imprisons us. Second, the over-sensitivity of former Imperial Army officers – as you put it – which had expressed itself in a keen dislike for a politically appointed civilian director of the Self Defence Forces, has been overcome, partly through my own efforts, and the political reality of the day has become acceptable to our sensibilities. I am not so naive as to hanker after a revised Constitution which would abolish Article IX* and restore the army to legality, respectability and independence from civilian control, as much as I might desire it, and even though our American allies are extending us virtual *carte blanche* to go ahead precisely with a constitutional reform designed to normalize the army. There is another game at stake. As I have always argued, our position should be one of armed neutrality, especially now when the conflict in South East Asia looks set to escalate, and foreseeably, to involve us.'

Madame Nhu's mouth opened at the mention of South East Asia, ready to air her views; but a look from Count Ito silenced her.

'Surely, we would never involve ourselves again in South East Asia?' Count Ito seemed to take the words from Madame Nhu's mouth, as the mute exclamation of her eyes confirmed.

'That's the game at stake,' Tsuji cryptically replied. His peregrinations round the room came to a halt at the site of my manuscript exhibited on the table. He gestured at it, like a magician conjuring up an object out of thin air. 'And this romantic story is an unexpected good omen. It is timely, and in the best sense, politically expedient that Mishima-*sensei* should have produced a story of patriotism and heroic self-sacrifice just now. A virtuoso master-stroke, and if I may say so, a positive remedy to hardened cynicism. It demonstrates that old-fashioned, simple virtue can cut through the Gordian Knot of complexity, of political chicanery and corruption.'

* Article IX of the 1946 Peace Constitution specifically declares that Japan must '. . . forever renounce war as a sovereign right of the nation and the threat or use of force as a means of settling international disputes. . . . land, sea, and air forces, as well as other war potential will never be maintained. The right of belligerency of the state will not be recognized.'

'By what, committing good old-fashioned *seppuku*?' Kishi scoffed. 'How charming. I can only hope that my political opponents will adopt your simple and virtuous remedy without delay, Tsuji-*san*.'

Sato guffawed appreciatively at this witticism.

Tsuji himself smiled. 'Is it really a joking matter? Corruption infects us all. Our political parties are a mess of feuding self-interest gangs, and the LDP benefits by tactical misalliances between pimps. Our conservative party is rotten through and through and oozes pus.'

'All this talk of corruption,' Sato replied, translating the samurai's outrage into an audacious platitude, 'is merely the envy of greedy and unscrupulous persons who feel left out of the banquet.'

Sato's remark was absurdly impudent. Everyone knew that Tsuji supplemented his Dietman's income by regular journalism, not by corrupt practices.

Unwisely, Madame Sato felt urged to rescue her husband from his own inanity. All this while, she and Madame Nhu had been fidgety neighbours on the sofa, two cats rubbing furs together, and now their accumulated electricity was brusquely discharged.

'Tsuji-*san*'s rectitude is uncommon and beyond dispute, of course,' Madame Sato began. 'But he should not judge the frailties common to others with such intolerance. After all, what oozes from the LDP might be less a matter of corruption than the only practical adhesive that can bind together so many diverse self-interested factions. Dietman Tsuji-*san*'s nostalgia for pre-war morality may well be enshrined in Mishima-*san*'s fiction, but it is only discovered in fiction, and will never appeal to political realists.'

A fine speech, spoilt by Madame Nhu's addition. 'I am convinced that Dietman Tsuji is an intelligence agent of the anti-Western, pan-Asian movement, and he would betray us to our enemy, Ho Chi Minh.'

The unsayable had been said. More crockery had been broken, and the spirit of Oiso lay truly in pieces. A lull followed; but a consequent scene of reparation had already begun. Keiko rose to her feet, as though aware of the next steps in the progress of this scene. Her action did not seem prompted by any evident command from Count Ito, although she looked to him for instruction. He, instead, sat sprawled in his chair, gazing idly at the sunlit garden outside. A casual observation on the fineness of the afternoon was at last heard from him, addressed to Keiko in particular, and to which he added: 'Please accompany Madame Sato and her friend on a tour of the garden. There are splendid autumn roses to admire, which might also succeed to calm the fires of our petulant Dragon Lady.'

'The garden?' Madame Sato was brave enough to protest. 'But surely it must be a quagmire after this morning's rain?'

'Not if you stick to the path,' Count Ito overruled her objection.

Count Ito's laconic recommendation expelled the ladies from any further part in the discourse. Sato nodded his compliant approval. A look of grieving annoyance could be read on Madame Sato's face as she claimed her handbag and followed the duo of Madame Nhu and Keiko quietly out of the room.

'Couldn't you leave your wife at home?' Kishi hissed at his brother.

'She insisted on meeting Mishima-*san*,' Sato complained. 'Besides, Madame Nhu is our guest, and you heard – she gets migraines from speaking too much Japanese.'

'Pity they aren't fatal,' Kishi drily observed.

Sato obliged me with an irate look. 'Your deplorable example, Mishima-*san*, really is to blame for inciting that pair of witches.'

'I accept the blame for all of this,' Tsuji spoke up in my defence.

'And so you should,' Kishi handsomely accepted.

'Please accept my contrite apologies,' Tsuji bowed. 'I don't know what came over me.'

'It's Mishima-*san*'s bad example, I tell you,' Sato insisted, responding with a bow to Tsuji's own. 'My wife doesn't normally turn sour like that.'

Kishi grinned. 'In my opinion, it isn't your wife's sour milk, but the spirit of Oiso that Tsuji-*san*'s Chinese stomach finds truly indigestible.'

'Gentlemen, an antidote to every sort of witches' brew is on its way,' Count Ito remarked, as the white-gloved houseboy Hideki entered with a tray of malt whiskies and bourbon.

'About time,' Sato grunted.

The first whiskies went down gratifyingly. Kishi now pleaded a silent favour from Count Ito – or so it seemed to me. Unpracticed as I yet was in deciphering the hidden reactions of Count Ito, I could not be sure whether I imagined or really saw Kishi in an attitude of suppliant. Only when Kishi bent down to unlace his oxblood brogues, did I realize what power Count Ito exercised. Our ex-prime minister had been permitted to remove his shoes, although I failed to intercept any sign of this from Count Ito.

Kishi stretched out his legs on the chaise longue, flexing his toes, the swollen joints clicking loudly as though his socks were filled with *pachinko* pin-balls. 'My rheumatism acts up in damp weather like this,' he explained.

'It's gout, not damp weather,' Sato pronounced. 'You're drinking too much.'

'It's rheumatism,' Kishi stressed, accepting a refill of whisky from Hideki.

While the brothers argued over the correct diagnosis, I turned to Count Ito. 'I noticed something interesting, when I first arrived at your door.'

'Ah yes, Kishi-*san*'s security guard,' Count Ito chuckled.

'Yes. I noticed he belonged to Kodama's clan.' I fished in murky waters by referring deliberately to Kodama Yoshio, one of the younger grand dragons of the ultra-nationalist underworld, and a confidant of ex-Colonel Tsuji's militarist clique.

'That's very perceptive of you,' Count Ito admitted. 'And how did you identify him?'

'I know enough about tattooes,' I said: a risky fabrication – and a stab in the dark. 'Besides, I have my contacts in the National Martyrs' Youth Corp.'

'So, you are a confessed appreciator of our idealist youth?' There was lascivious treachery in Count Ito's eyes, as they strayed over Hideki's firm bottom.

Mention of Kodama had earned me Kishi's full attention. I forestalled any denial of Kodama's undercover role, which I could see forming on Kishi's lips, by going on the offensive. 'I understand that our ex-prime minister enlisted Kodama-*san*'s help during our recent June disturbances. I believe the idea was to supplement the police force unofficially by mobilizing thousands of Kodama's rightwing henchmen at the time of President Eisenhower's visit in that fatal June – or am I mistaken?'

'It was alleged, wrongly,' Sato blundered in.

Kishi almost winced. 'Unhappy days, certainly. We advised President Eisenhower to cancel his visit, as you know.'

'I don't see what good Kodama's shadow troops would have served anyway,' Tsuji remarked. 'The truth is, if conservative politicians cannot rely on the army in situations like the June riots, then any deployment of thugs by an outdated patriotic rightwinger will prove useless.'

Tsuji's statement was intriguing, because riddled with contradictions. His repudiation of Kodama's methods was interesting, but perhaps not altogether surprising. Tsuji came to Kishi's support by distancing them both from the inadmissable ultra-right. An old trick of almost knee jerk response among traditionalists. What did seem surprising to me was his apparent disregard of a constitutional truism – that under no circumstances could the army be mobilized against civilians. It was inconceivable that Dietman Tsuji would be unaware of this fact. And so, his reference to conservatives 'relying on the army' to control the June rioters must assuredly have had some other esoteric meaning, and one that I felt sure would benefit me in the end.

'I should like to reconsider Dietman Tsuji-*san*'s fascinating proposition in a moment, if I may,' I said. 'But there are certain questions that I would like to clarify first, with Kishi-*san*'s permission.'

'You are not going to badger me pointlessly on the issue of Kodama, or the Security Treaty or anything of the sort, I hope?' Kishi sighed.

'No fear of that, sir. I would rather discuss problems of the Constitution with you, now that I have the opportunity of hearing your expert views on the subject.'

'A boring topic, but permissable. What are you so eager to know?'

I had intentionally seated myself at such an angle to Kishi's position on the chaise longue that his neck muscles would strain uncomfortably in turning to reply to my questions. I intended to be, as Americans say, a pain in the neck.

'An acquaintance of mine in G-2 Section, I remember, once called our Peace Constitution, "the last Shogun's enigma".'

'He referred no doubt to General MacArthur by the amusing soubriquet, "last Shogun"?'

'Exactly. Of course, you must remember Captain Lazar too, Dietman Tsuji-san?' Tsuji nodded stiffly. 'Yes, the enigma of our Constitution,' I continued. 'And who is better qualified than you, Kishi-san, as the chairman of the LDP's Constitution Investigation Committee appointed shortly after the Occupation ended, to unravel this enigma?'

'That was some time ago, and besides, the Committee is now dormant.'

'Dormant, perhaps, but far from ineffective. I remember its proposed draft revision of the Constitution in 1954 that openly challenged postwar democratic reforms in education by re-introducing the old discredited principle of "filial piety" –'

'– never implemented,' Kishi said, a twinge of rheumatism vexing him as he turned to interrupt me.

'Shall we say, *partly* implemented? More important, however, was the government bill of 1954 which created the *Jieitai* or Self Defence Forces. A tortuous legal basis was found to sanction the existence of a constitutionally illegal army. Dietman Tsuji-san is right – the army exists in contradiction with itself, by protecting the very instrument which denies its right to existence – our Peace Constitution.'

A pained wisp of a smile crossed Kishi's lips. 'You forget, it was Prime Minister Hatoyama Ichiro, a former Strike North partisan, who introduced that Bill.'

'But you did not oppose it.'

Tsuji muttered: 'Patriots who pretend not to be.'

'You should be the last to grumble, Tsuji-san,' Kishi retorted. 'Our patriotic aims are the same. We earnestly seek to progress in the footsteps of the advanced nations of the West, and at the same time, return to the former Meiji ideal of *fukoku kyohei*, a wealthy nation and a strong army. What's wrong with that?'

'Nothing wrong with it,' I said. 'Except that we seem to be crossing the bridge from both ends – progressing towards an industrial future, while retrogressing to a former Meiji state of affairs. Don't you fear a head-on collision between these two contradictory forces? Or at least a major cultural traffic jam?'

Count Ito studied his fingertips joined in a peak, like a jack-knifed bridge. 'Mishima-*san*'s image does have a certain nicety.'

'But no reality,' Kishi replied. 'We were forced into a policy of national defence, as every realistic person knows, by the terms of the Security Pact with America – something I don't wish to discuss.'

'Defence against what? against whom?' I said. 'Against the internal enemy, Communism, naturally. And this neat, simplistic formula accomplishes two contradictory but desirable ends of the Cold War – to undermine the Constitution and yet maintain it.'

'How on earth do you deduce that?' Sato grumbled. He was bored, and at the same time, jittery, chain-smoking and downing whiskies. 'Your conception of the Constitution is academic.'

'Let him finish,' Kishi admonished, much to Sato's surprise.

'The extremes of left and right are repugnant to the intelligence,' I said. 'Politics is the art of the middle way.'

'Agreed,' Kishi nodded.

'But what is the middle way?'

'The course we follow, obviously.'

'Why not call it the "Third Party"?'

'Indeed, why not? It seems a perfectly reasonable description of our own LDP.'

'But a Third Party assumes two other partners at a disadvantage, the two extremes of left and right in this case. The politics of the middle way must therefore imply the covert use of these extremes, in order to triumph over them.'

'What you describe, Mishima-*san*,' Count Ito said, 'is not government but management by conspiracy. Government is not espionage.'

'Government may not be espionage, perhaps, but isn't *above* espionage. It seems to me that politicians govern openly by lying with the truth and covertly by never allowing the truth to matter.'

'Too extravagantly cynical to be of any practical use,' Kishi grinned. 'You betray an intellectual's ignorance of pragmatism.'

'I don't pretend to be anything more than an ignorant, apolitical writer. But the June riots convinced me of something momentous, something beyond my narrow routine of fiction writing.'

'Something beyond the fiction of a "tiny nihilist" submitting to Washington?' Kishi said, his eyebrows rising in mock surprise.

I laughed. 'Oh yes, something quite different. I finally solved the enigma of our Constitution. What you said earlier, Dietman Tsuji-*san*,' I turned to him, and he nodded attentively, 'if I may return to it now, struck me as odd. You said that conservative politicians – referring to Kishi-*san* himself, no doubt – cannot rely on the army in situations like the June disturbances. What did you mean by that?'

'I meant *cannot* because prohibited by the Constitution from so doing.'

'Of course, a piquant situation would have arisen, had the government decided to test the real validity of that prohibition by mobilizing the army, don't you think?'

'Piquant but merely hypothetical,' Kishi replied, 'since the police force alone sufficed to restrain the demonstrators, without need of the army.'

'A highly instructive experiment, in short.'

'What do you mean, *experiment*?' Kishi burst out, wheeling round completely now to face me.

'I think Mishima-*san* is getting into his conspiratorial stride again, brother,' Sato tried jokingly to pull the teeth of my challenge. Kishi glanced irritably at him.

'Please clarify your allegation, Mishima-*san*,' Count Ito mildly scolded, though evidently much enjoying himself.

'Oh, it's only a theory about the June affair. I think the government knew beforehand what maximum strength the left could rally, and it gambled on the public's acceptance of virtual martial law imposed by a police force using counter-insurgency tactics. I believe the riots triggered by the new Security Pact were calculated, as I say, an experiment intended to prove once and for all that our police force alone could defend the system, without recourse to the army, and therefore avoiding any conflict with the Constitution. Indeed, after June, the question itself of the army's constitutionality could be indefinitely shelved. No government hereafter need feel obliged to raise the troublesome question of constitutional reform.'

'Are you saying we deliberately risked a collision with the public in order to leave the Constitution unchanged?' Kishi smiled incredulously at me.

'I am. Because an unreformed Constitution is your best mainstay. It is obvious even to a political innocent like me that since June our Constitution ceased being an effective platform for opposing the regime or mobilizing revolutionary forces. The lesson I am compelled to draw is that from now on the Constitution can only be overturned either by a rightwing *coup d'état* or a mass revolution from the left. And so, your Third Party must ride the tiger of the middle way.'

'You can't prove your theory,' Sato said.

'It doesn't interest me to prove it, but to use it.'

'Use it how?' Kishi wondered, grinning still like a smug Cheshire cat. 'Perhaps in your occupation of writer – a writer with an ambition for scandal on a grand scale?'

'I confess only to a literary ambition which poses me a problem unique and insoluble to a Japanese writer.'

'We're not here to discuss literature,' Sato gruffly declared. 'You'd better join a literary society for that.'

Sato had entirely missed the point of his elder brother's innuendo, either through obtuseness or, as I began to suspect, by cunning dissimulation. I did not believe he was quite so befuddled by alcohol as he pretended to be. I knew, Sato could not possibly be unaware that my 'ambition for scandal', as Kishi implied, must refer to the post-war financial blueprints and the file of names I held in store from my days of collaboration with Sam Lazar and G-2 Section.

Count Ito gave me an opportunity to test the accuracy of my insight into the brothers' two-faced game, by saying: 'I believe Mishima-*san* already belongs to enough literary societies, and consequently his problem must be of a different nature that can only be addressed to an extra-literary group, such as ours. Am I right?'

'Perfectly right, Ito-*san*. My problem exceeds the boundaries of literature, because it is this – a problem that I have long considered – what would happen if I wrote about the Emperor himself as the central character of a fiction?'

Kishi's marvellously practiced lack-lustre gaze, his wistful smile, betrayed no evidence of shock; nor did Sato's stern affectation of disinterest. Tsuji alone responded with a start. 'You would be attacked by both left and right, certainly, but the grave offence of *lèse-majesté* would expose you to the wrath of the far right most of all. You would be punished.'

'I spoke fictionally.'

'Speak however you like, the offence would not go unpunished,' Tsuji emphasized.

Count Ito amused himself by examining the grain on his snakewood cane. 'Mishima-*san*, as a writer of modern Noh plays, you do not need me to remind you of Zeami's original instructions to Noh actors – one should not attempt to impersonate the character of the Emperor, because, as Zeami delicately put it, his experience of life is very different from ours and we have little opportunity to study it.'

'I am aware of Zeami's advice against unlawful imitation. However, times have radically altered since the 14th century. We can no longer overlook a deceitful impersonation of the Emperor that we are pleased to call our "democratic" Constitution, while all the time we know better. We have always known that the Jewel Voice need never speak directly in order to rule, that the Imperial Presence does not require acts of worship to be a divinity, because he presides supreme through the correctness of our attitude.'

'To put the matter a little more indelicately,' Count Ito said, 'the Emperor has no clothes, except for the Constitution that you would like him to shed. Why do you bother to agitate openly for the "restoration" of the Emperor when it has already happened *de facto*? You can best assist His Majesty by remaining silent.'

'Perhaps I've not made my position clear. I believe one can render assistance to His Majesty by risking oneself in agitation which is strictly limited, individual and designed to fail. I expect that you are all familiar with the story of Takinori Kojima, a feudal chieftain involved in an abortive attempt to rescue Emperor Godaigo from exile in 1332. Takinori's renown has endured for over six hundred years despite his failure. And why? Because of a poem he carved on a cherry tree, so that the Emperor on his way to exile would be certain to notice it and take comfort from a loyal subject's futile persistence in his cause. Takinori's lines allude to an obscure Chinese poem –' I began to recite the poem, but was stopped at once by Count Ito: 'That's unnecessary. We know the poem only too well.'

He stared at me oddly, defying me to make the connection that he knew I had in mind. So did Tsuji, whose expectation was keyed up taut as a drum skin. Kishi and Sato exchanged a look of veiled dismay. 'Good, since you all recognize the poem,' I continued, 'you'll also know that it was seen again recently, written in toothpaste on the wall of Yamaguchi Otoya's cell, just before he hanged himself. Takinori, the failed hero, was Yamaguchi's model – this seventeen-year-old boy who assassinated Asanuma Inejiro, Chairman of the Socialist Party, four days ago.'

'The boy was *kichigai*, out of his mind,' Sato waved his hand dismissively.

'Sato-*san* does not care much for literature,' I replied. 'But it might interest him to know that Ibsen makes his character, the unsavoury Judge Brack, react with precisely that word *kichigai* when Hedda Gabler shoots herself at the end of the play – *kichigai*, Brack says – "People don't do that sort of thing".'

'Well, damn it, Brack whoever he might be was right – people just don't do that sort of thing.'

'Some people have been known to do it,' Tsuji quietly remarked, eyeing me with melancholy wonder.

Kishi lay back on his chaise longue and closed his eyes, as though sinking into sleep. 'Such a distance between your words, Mishima-*san*, and your appearance. When I shut my eyes, I hear the unacceptable slogans of fanatics like Inoue Nissho and Kita Ikki in the 1930s. When I open them, but shut my ears, I see an extravagant person, someone preposterous who craves respectability, the Nobel Prize, and – what else, Mishima-*san*? what else?'

'A death like Hedda Gabler's, maybe,' Sato answered.

'I referred to that misguided youngster, Yamaguchi,' I said, 'not because I agree with violence –'

'– naturally, we all deplore violence,' Kishi interrupted, eyes still closed like a meditating sage.

'– but because his action was sincere, a purity of motive demonstrated by his choice of immediate suicide. Violence of that type has the clean, sterile disinterest of a surgical operation.'

'You admire that?' Kishi's eyes opened on me.

'I do. I admire sincerity, whether on the extremes of left or right, that certain young people have recently demonstrated.'

'You admire the *zengakuren*★ too?' Sato inquired.

'Of course. They showed courage in trying to storm the Diet on June 15th. A girl student, Kamba Michiko, secretary of the League of Communists, was killed in that attempt.'

'Are we witnessing a turning-point?' Tsuji mused.

'In the hearts and minds of our youth, perhaps,' I had come prepared for an eventuality of this sort. I retrieved a newspaper clipping from my wallet. 'The *zengakuren* attack on the Diet was inspired by the example last March of the coal-miners' strike at the Mitsui-owned Miike Mine in Kyushu. A local event which developed into a mass movement of small farmers and tradesmen, involving the Korean sub-class and low-caste *eta* miners. Allow me to quote from a statement by Shima Shigero, a student leader of the Kyosando Communist League, on the Miike strike. 'It led me to think that a revolution happens because people are aroused to the occasion by witnessing a heart-rending scene. Thus, I thought, what we should do was to present to the public a moving image that would crystallize into one moment the true meaning of the situation. This was why we broke through the Diet gates on June 15th. It was the most dramatic means of symbolizing the reclamation of the Diet, which had been beyond reach of the people, on behalf of the people whose representative it should have been'.

'What's this?' Sato grunted. 'Are you a Communist sympathizer now?'

'No, on the contrary, but I sympathize with courage. Courage in a failed cause. I return to your earlier statement, Tsuji-*san*. You said, and I believe you were right, that levying Kodama's army of civilian rightwingers in the June riots was useless, because first, the use of extremists to protect the status quo proved redundant, and second and more important, rightwing extremism does nothing to resolve the contradiction of an army unconstitutionally sanctioned, but indeed *confirms* its illegal status.'

'I had something like that in mind,' Tsuji nodded; but then he added a bizarre non sequitur, intended as a coded message for my understanding alone. 'Are you aware that Kodama Yoshio was present at the *seppuku* of Vice-Admiral Onishi?'

★ Federation of militant leftwing university students, active since General MacArthur's 'red purge' of 1950.

'Yes, as reported in Kodama's autobiography. He also reports something else – the last words of Shibukawa Zensuke, a *niniroku* mutineer, being dragged to his execution: "Oh people of Japan, don't trust the Imperial Army!" Like so many others from the pre-war ultra-nationalist right, Kodama felt betrayed by the military's exploitation of civilian zealots. He knows that in the eyes of ordinary folk, ultra-nationalism remains tainted by its participation in the military's aims for a total and disastrous war. Nowadays, of course, his type of old style ultra-nationalism is even further compromised by being a client of orthodox dirty politics.'

'What is Mishima-*san* after?' Sato asked, addressing his elder brother.

'One wonders,' Kishi replied.

'It is sufficiently clear, I think,' Tsuji commented.

'Well, *what* are you proposing exactly?' Count Ito said.

'Suppose I asked for admission to a basic training course with one of the SDF's best units, the Ranger Division or the paratroopers –'

'– out of the question,' Sato exclaimed. 'A writer playing at toy soldiers! All we need is a scandal like that.'

'One moment,' Kishi motioned for calm. 'What for?'

'For the purpose of building a public relations bridge between university students and the army. The prestige of our armed forces is so dismally low at present that the SDF must rely on big business to coerce their employees into accepting basic training with the SDF. And you know of the organized campus resistance in Tokyo and Kyoto against SDF personnel even being allowed to study in those universities.'

'And you think your stint of voluntary basic training would somehow make the SDF more acceptable,' Kishi asked, adding with a smile, 'or perhaps more glamorous, to university students?'

'It might attract those youngsters with an idealist, patriotic spirit who have remained a silent minority so far.'

'Do you know this from your contacts with the young fanatics of the National Martyrs' Youth Corp?' Sato's question urged him on to voice a further dire implication. 'Can it be that Mishima-*san*'s advocacy of Yamaguchi's misdeed is based on prior knowledge, perhaps gathered from the same extremist quarter?'

'A grave accusation,' Count Ito breezily reproached him. 'Yamaguchi acted entirely on his own, so far as anyone knows.'

Sato did not even bother to look abashed.

'I don't figure in the Yamaguchi police dossier,' I said, 'as the one kept on me will surely reveal. Of course, there was a time when extremists conspired all in the open. It used to be the practice of our terrorists in the 1930s to report their meetings to the police, an exemplary delicacy of conscience that I rather favour myself. We are a curiously law-abiding people, even where crime is concerned.'

Kishi laughed. 'You are exonerated from connivance with Yamaguchi. But now, supposing you were permitted to enlist for basic training, what follows next?'

'That will depend on my success in establishing myself as an independent civilian model of the right, eccentric perhaps, but unidentified with the criminal far right. The next step logically would be to multiply that model, so to speak, replicate myself in a hand-picked number of spiritually minded young men.'

'A cadet corps,' Tsuji immediately grasped.

'A paramilitary force, more like,' Sato objected. 'A flirtation with illegality, as I see it.'

'Call it what you will, brother,' Kishi said. 'We are merely theorizing. And how many cadets would you think of recruiting, Mishima-*san*?'

'Ideally, one hundred, equipped and financed by myself.'

'One hundred,' Kishi thought it over. 'A centurion's number of men, isn't it?'

'Exactly as in Roman times: a company of soldiers loyally dedicated to the Emperor.'

'And how do you propose to train your cadet company?'

'I hope it will benefit from the same privilege first granted to me – basic training with the SDF and thereafter occasional participation in joint manoeuvres with the army.'

'Do you realize what you're asking?' Sato looked appalled. 'A civilian paramilitary force allowed to exploit the SDF's facilities? It is utterly unthinkable.'

'I know very well what I'm asking. Twelve years ago, when I served for a time as a clerk in the Banking Section of the Finance Ministry, I became acquainted with a formula that explained our post-war economic rehabilitation, explained to me with admirable clarity as a triangle, a three-point financial strategy of credit, production and export that would redeem our *zaibatsu* industries and miraculously enrich the nation. I won't bore you with mere accountancy details. In any case, I was never more than a humble bookkeeper, no match for Kishi-*san* who as Vice-Minister of War Industry under Prime Minister Tojo must know more than I about the mysteries of administering the economy. I was impressed by the occult power of this triangle. And today, after its magic has indeed brought us economic recuperation, but alas, also spiritual stagnation, I see another use for it, another truly occult application. I see myself and my cadets as forming two points of spiritual communion at the base of the triangle, a supra-individual community of purpose recuperated by virtue of the triangle's apex – '

' – the Imperial Presence, in short,' Count Ito supplied. 'Are you suggesting, Mishima-*san*, that you would give up your absurd notions of writing about His Majesty in exchange for a centurion's role?'

'I am willing to abandon one fiction in favour of another which is a reality.'

'I'll wager he already has a name in mind for his paramilitary cadets,' Sato conjectured.

'I do, borrowed from the honorific title of the legendary sixth century warrior, Yorozu★, *tatenokai* −'

'− that's Shield Society in English, or SS,' Count Ito chuckled. 'You fancy yourself an SS centurion, do you?'

'Not many would have your aptitude to notice that, Ito-*san*,' I laughed. 'But why not?'

'And these "SS" cadets of yours would parade in uniform, I suppose, like the National Martyrs' Youth Corps?' Sato inquired.

'On formal occasions only. But unlike the Martyrs, my cadets would never be involved in illicit activities.'

'Incredible,' Sato drained his whisky to the last, remnants of ice crackling between his teeth.

'Very instructive,' Kishi said. 'I am stirred by Mishima-*san*'s quaintly old-fashioned patriotic feelings. I shall regard them as the innocent expression of a poet.' He glanced at his watch, and slyly at Count Ito to confirm the meeting's end, before replacing his shoes.

'It grows late, and I suppose we should release the ladies from exile in the garden,' Count Ito said.

As the others proceeded to the garden, Tsuji, clutching me by the arm, held me back at the French windows, whispering urgently: 'You chose a bad moment to put your case, Mishima-*san*, now that ex-Flight Lieutenant Mikami Takashi has planned his direct action for the twenty-fifth anniversary of the *niniroku* this coming February.'

I tried not to look blank.

'You know Mikami's plan?' Tsuji frowned.

I nodded, lying.

'Well, I suppose you had no choice but to take the initiative today.'

I nodded again.

'You must be patient, Mishima-*san*. I can help you realize your dream, but wait till the after-effects of the Mikami incident subside. Wait till Sato wins the premiership in a few years' time, then we'll have a new civilian director of the SDF sympathetic to our cause.'

Tsuji surprised me with another handshake, then a bow and a respect-fully growled *sensei*, as he took leave of the Yoshida memorial tea. I was never to see him again, because the samurai Dietman Tsuji on his tour of Hanoi and Indochina as feature writer for *Asahi* that following year, vanished without trace.

Other farewells were exchanged in a more ceremonially frigid

★ Ancient chroniclers entitled him the 'Emperor's shield'.

way, leaving me in doubt as to the success of my afternoon's performance.

I saw Keiko retreating on her own into the depths of the garden. I went in search of her as twilight began to fall.

Count Ito's garden – originally intended for Prince Higashikuni's French mistress in the 1910s – was a most bizarre spectacle, an exact copy of a Japanese-style fantasy garden commissioned by the eccentric Sir Frank Crisp for his Friar Park mansion in Henley, Oxfordshire, at the turn of the century. I wandered in a Japanese replica of an Englishman's fanciful imitation of an unimaginable Japanese garden. The back wall of this Fantasia Japonica also reproduced one of Crisp's mock alpine rockeries. Very odd indeed.

I crossed a toy bridge of bamboo flanked by geese and herons – all of these being artefacts of stone – and found Keiko beside a pagoda-style gazebo surrounded by pines.

'Has your wish been granted?' she said.

'I don't know.'

'One thing's certain. Madame Sato was right, the grounds certainly are damp.' Keiko grimaced at her heels, muddied from digging into the soil.

'Sit down,' I said. 'I'll clean them for you.'

The gazebo's interior provided a wall bench. I knelt down, took off one shoe that Keiko presented, and began wiping the heel with my pocket handkerchief. She sat, abstractedly eyeing a rill flowing into the pond, her unshod foot perched tiptoe on the instep of her other shoe.

'I had the strangest dream last night,' she said. 'I awoke feeling cold, as though I'd become uncovered and moonlight on my bare skin felt like vaporized perfume. But the curtains were tightly drawn, and anyway hardly any moon could be seen last night. It was dark. I could hear rain on my window, like someone drumming on it. I called my maid, Koyumi, to see whether I really dreamed or not. She too was awake. "I believe there's a prowler outside, Madame," she said. "What should I do?" "Do nothing. Just see that the doors and windows are securely locked, then go back to sleep." And, despite my feeling of apprehension, I fell asleep at once. I awoke again after first light, and went out immediately to the garden in my dressing-gown. Sure enough, Koyumi had been right. I saw footprints in the muddy soil under my window, partly obliterated by the heavy rain. I searched for other clues that might tell me something about the prowler's identity. I found the place where he had taken shelter from the rain, under a cedar behind some bamboo grass, and I discovered the evidence that gave proof of his long vigil. Instead of risking to light cigarettes, he had chewed gum, and several wads of it were left on the moss where he'd spat them out. I guessed that my thief must be a young man, very nervous and not very experienced in his line of work. I held the gum in my hand, the marks of his teeth visible in these discarded grey pebbles. I had the peculiar idea of still being asleep, and dreaming that an unknown lover would keep me under surveillance all night, every night.'

'A thief, here in this garden?'

'No, no, mine, at my house in Koganei.'

Keiko's story revived a bitter memory. I remembered the time in 1953 when a thief had broken into my parent's home in Shibuya and I hid in a neighbour's house. My shame had been broadcast the next day in six major dailies. Did Keiko make up her story of a thief purposely to embarrass me?

Keiko opened her handbag and took out a ball of tissue paper. I thought for a moment she was going to show me the relics of chewing gum; but, no, she held out something else to me in both hands, like a child offering candy in a torn paper bag. Peeking through the wrappers, here and there, I glimpsed the Wedgwood porcelain figurines, the dog, rabbit, squirrel, bear and fox. I could hardly believe that Keiko would make me a gift of them in such an unusually haphazard fashion. Tears welled up in Keiko's eyes: tears, incomprehensible to me, wavered on the brink of her eyelids, but did not spill. 'Take them,' she said. 'They're yours.'

As I reached out, a thought suddenly occurred to me. The maid Koyumi – wasn't she the one Keiko had banished years ago to a convent?

My question was deterred by Count Ito's voice. 'Ah, fitting Cinderella's shoe again, Mishima-*san*?' He leaned on his cane which probed into the soggy earth by the flagstone pathway. 'Decidedly, you incline to fetishism.'

'Please forgive my wandering off like that, Ito-*san*,' Keiko said, slipping into her shoe and replacing the figurines in her handbag before I could claim them. 'I hope my unsociable fugue hasn't offended your guests. Have they gone?'

'All but one, Madame Nhu.'

'I thought the Satos were in charge of her?'

Count Ito shrugged. 'Please see that Madame Nhu is entertained, while Mishima-*san* and I have our little chat.' He voyaged on with a limping gait towards the grove of pines, and I followed, abandoning Keiko to her duty of hostess.

'Do you admire this garden, Mishima-*san*?'

'It is most unusual.' The air grew chillier as twilight declined.

'I have restored it faithfully in every detail,' he pointed with his cane to the stream. 'On a meandering stream like this one, gallants of the Heian court used to sail their wine cups in games of forfeits with their lovers. As a connoisseur of the medieval Heian period, I am sure you know all about such erotic refinements?'

'I do.'

'You will appreciate, then, a feature of this stream which is lacking in Sir Frank Crisp's original. Mine flows east to west, as did all the streams artificially created in the gardens of Heian Kyoto.'

'Or north to south. West and north are traditionally avoided as the outlets of taboo impurities. The dead should always lie with their heads north. There are superstitious people even today who will not sleep facing north.'

'Correct, Mishima-*san*. Legend says that it is unlucky for the Emperor to travel westwards, for in so doing he must turn his back on the sun. The same wisdom of the landscape gardeners that directs our streams west or south also advises against the Emperor's move west, since corruption and death proceed that way.' Ito, lost in thought for a moment, gazed at the stream. 'Have you ever considered, Mishima-*san*, that poetry is a woman's natural way of understanding?'

'I know a poet of minor talent who seduced a great many women with that line of flattery.'

'Only a person of no talent would be foolish enough to lie with the truth.'

The force and apparent sincerity of Ito's reply surprised me. Was he warning me off my liaison with Keiko? Such a possibility made no sense, as it contradicted the more obvious truth that Keiko must be acting on Ito's instruction, or at least with his approval.

Ito noted my bafflement. 'In the case of Madame Omiyeke, poetry as a natural means of understanding is elevated to prophecy. You must know that by now.'

'I have heard her called *ikigami*, several times.'

'Be assured, she is. She knows herself appointed to give birth.'

Ito's revelation totally astounded me. I could only gasp, 'Ah, it can't be that she's –'

'Pregnant?' Ito laughed. 'She'll give birth as only an *ikigami* is privileged and condemned to do, in the phenomenal sense of spirit.'

'Ah –'

'Don't look so relieved,' Ito stared at me, without a trace of irony. 'You are far from being out of danger.' He glanced at his watch. 'Please follow me to my study. I have a gift for you, in return for the manuscripts that you twice generously conferred one me.'

This mad-hatter's tea party wasn't over yet, and the idea of facing more surprises did not appeal to me.

'Madame Omiyeke, I believe, has acquainted you with the *yamabushi* mountain cult,' Ito remarked, as he limped along on his snakewood stick. 'In former times, when its rules were stricter, anyone who fell ill or was injured during the ascent of the sacred mountain would be stoned to death. With my leg, Mishima-*san*, I would obviously have been executed.'

'Fortunately, those days are over,' I joked, not thinking him serious, 'and we aren't climbing any mountain.'

'That's where you're wrong,' he replied, without trace of humour.

The window of Count Ito's study on the upper floor of the house admitted a last glow of sunset through its Art Nouveau amber stained-glass adapted to a frame carved in the Momoyama style. Caramel-tinted light fell on the Biedermeier furniture, enriching the warm tones of birch and cherry veneers inlaid with ebony. Count Ito switched on a chandelier of black Hyalith glass and went to his desk, so that we now stood facing each other across it. Several objects on the desk attracted my curiosity, a Noh actor's fan and *naki-zo* mask of ancient make, but especially a long narrow object wrapped in canvas and placed lengthwise in front of me. 'This is yours,' Count Ito said, with a bow, indicating the object that I knew must be a sword. I unwrapped the canvas, unfastened the ornamental protective bag within, and found a samurai sword and dagger – the diamond-shaped, black and white chequered panelling inlaid with mother-of-pearl on the hilts and scabbards of the two weapons were familiar to me.

'Your friend, Colonel Lazar, entrusted me with the safe keeping of this gift before he left for Indochina.'

'Why have you waited all these years to give it to me?'

'His instructions were very precise. I must only hand it over when you came to me, and not before.'

'I see. And where is my benefactor these days?'

'Still in Indochina,' Count Ito replied noncommittally. 'Would you care to examine the blades?'

'No need. I am quite familiar with them. Something that Dietman Tsuji-*san* hinted at earlier, however, interests me far more. Something about an alleged military plot by a certain ex-Flight Lieutenant Mikami Takashi.'

Count Ito chuckled. 'Our samurai Dietman obviously considers you a member of our inner circle.' He relieved the discomfiting pressure on his bad knee by easing himself into an ormolu-columned armchair. 'Since the indiscretion has already occurred, I must rely on you to keep silent. You may perhaps know that Mikami-*san* participated in the *coup d'état* of 15 May 1932 together with the agrarian fanatics and Strike North partisans who assassinated Prime Minister Inukai Tsuyoshi. He was imprisoned till 1940 for his role in that abortive coup, which included attacks on Tokyo police headquarters, power stations and the Mitsubishi Bank. Our former Strike North hothead has now approached staff officers of the SDF to mount a coup that would remedy three great evils, corruption, taxes and unemployment.'

'And what will happen?'

'Nothing of consequence. The officers will hand Mikami over to the police, and of course he expects them to do precisely this.'

'Which should cost him more years of prison. How strange.'

'Not really. This is another conspiracy of the "law-abiding" sort, as you yourself wittily remarked at tea, a scandal intentionally designed to prove the loyalty and anti-rightism of the army.'

'It doesn't look to me quite so simple as that. I understand that Mikami's coup is planned for February 26th next year, the twenty-fifth anniversary of the *niniroku* mutiny. Mikami's anniversary action could well be aimed at embarrassing our present government, which dares not even contemplate the possibility of Japan's renewed military hegemony in Asia.'

'A possibility that will in time become an established economic fact, without resorting to military hegemony. Mishima-*san*, as a writer of fiction you should know that a story is apt to elude the control of its author, but the risk of anarchy is nevertheless a calculated one. So it was in the 1930s. But now, tell me frankly, why are you so attracted to those bygone fanatics and adventurists? Do you plead on their behalf or your own? You would be wise to accept Colonel Lazar's postponed gift of the sword and dagger as timely warnings against *shinigurui*, the samurai's "death frenzy", which I fear has taken possession of you. I speak as an admirer who would not like to see you lose control of your story.'

'Many thanks for your vote of sympathy, Senator Ito, but my death frenzy, as you call it, is a matter of speculation.'

'Eight years ago, you ended your story of *The Patriot* with a remark on my cynicism.'

'I regret the caricature I made of you.'

'As they say, the caricature is often more truthful than the reality. You wrote accurately against the deadly attraction of treason.'

'Is treason still possible in our world today?'

'So it would seem,' Count Ito mused, his thoughts already elsewhere, as he stroked the features of a Noh mask on his desk, a rare and beautiful example of a *naki-zo* or weeping woman of the Hosho school. 'We came so very near, close as this to treason,' he said, as though referring to the weeping woman's mask in his hands, and that he now held up to his face. It was indescribably eerie to listen to his next words emerging from the dignified hollow of that mask. 'And in another deeper sense, perhaps far graver than any obvious crime against the Imperial Throne, I feel I have committed a hidden sort of treason for which no punishment exists, nothing at all, but a vague repetitive guilt that eats away at the marrow of one's life.' He lowered the *naki-zo* and stared at me. 'Do you understand the treason I mean? Beware of it. You will endure a loneliness that carries all the insubstantial regrets of the after-life into this life.'

I understood. Count Ito had given another name to the joyfully criminal feeling of weightlessness. I recognized what was plainly legible on Count Ito's unmasked face, that he would one day commit suicide. 'Life as it is, is unacceptable,' I said.

'I was very privileged in my childhood to witness a performance by the revered Noh actor Umewaka Minoru. He was very old at the time, in his eighties, when he honoured us by visiting my family's *shoen* manor in Kyushu. How very old he was I could judge from a story told about him. Umewaka Minoru was acting in the Shogun's garden when the news of Admiral Perry's arrival stopped the play. It was said, the art of Noh would have perished without him. And now he was performing in the garden of our estate, on a stage erected especially for him, its polished cedar planks glowing in the noonlight. One of the plays he chose for that day was *Sotaba Komachi*, the story of a poetess of the ancient court, a lady of incomparable and fatal beauty who has decayed into a repulsive creature one hundred years old, a beggar wandering the roads. This mendicant old woman is of course only the regretful ghost of Ono no Komachi, long since dead, and I wondered how such an old man as Umewaka Minoru could possibly transform himself into the beautiful lady who reappears in her former glory. You wrote a modern version of *Sotaba Komachi*, did you not, Mishima-*san*?'

'I did.'

'This is the fan of Umewaka Minoru, the very one he used that day,' Count Ito said, as he hoisted himself up awkwardly on his good leg. He opened the fan, and with the stumbling gait of a broken-legged heron, he began to recreate from memory the steps of the Noh actor Umewaka Minoru in *Sotaba Komachi*. His voice, totally devoid of anything remotely like a woman's charm, but gratingly harsh like the sound of a rasp on a rusty tea kettle, chanted the lamentations of the beautiful Ono no Komachi's ghost. And somehow this lame and unlikely figure at the centre of a Biedermeier study accomplished a miracle, his gestures with the fan were the delicate ones of a court lady, his voice attracted the chill of moonlight into the room, and I shivered to hear it conveying the torments of melancholy love from the realm of the dead.

In my young days I had a hundred letters from men greater than you see now. They came like raindrops in May. And I held my head high, may be, at that time. And I sent out no answer. You think because you see me alone now that I was in want of a handsome man in the old days, when Shosho came with the others – Shii no Shocho of Fukakusa, Deep Grass, that came to me in the moonlight and in the dark night and in the nights flooded with rain, and in the black face of the wind and in the wild swish of the snow. He came as often as the melting drops fall from the eaves, ninety-nine times, and he died. And his ghost is about me, driving me on with madness.

Count Ito shut his fan with a click. 'Shall we see how the ladies are faring?'

'We have absented ourselves a long time.'

Count Ito replaced Umewaka Minoru's fan on the desk, beside the weeping *naki-zo*. 'Leave your sword and dagger here. Hideki will fetch them for you later.'

I followed Count Ito down a different staircase from the one we had earlier used, and he motioned for silence, as though wishing us to surprise the Baroness and Madame Nhu. We arrived at the angle of a passageway and a door that seemed familiar to me from a previous visit. The door opened into a sombre little room, discreetly lit by a weak red lightbulb suspended from the ceiling. I glimpsed a figure within whose eyes goggled as they met Count Ito's look of wrath.

'Put away your sword, cretin,' Counti Ito whispered harshly to a startled Hideki, a command given in French, a language that the houseboy may have understood or not, I did not know, but to the tone of which he certainly reacted by fastening his trousers with lightning speed.

I knew where I was. The citric odour of developing-fluids, the red light and shape of the Hasselblad camera on its tripod – I stood once again in the peeping-Tom's stall behind the mirror.

I looked into the Regency bedroom on the other side of the glass, at a dazzling tableau framed in the wall like the open grate of a furnace, and I could see what had excited Count Ito's houseboy to onanism. On the bed, Baroness Omiyeke Keiko and Madame Nhu were engaged in a wanton Siamese pairing, like two squids glued together. Their faces at opposite ends were hidden between each other's thighs and screens of hair in gelatinous black tentacles. I distinguished Keiko's body upper-most in pale marble contrast to Madame Nhu's duskier one beneath, with her head buried deep in the open V of the Dragon Lady's legs, prised apart like a woman in labour. Keiko's red lacquered finger-nails dug into her partner's buttocks. Madame Nhu's calves flexed and loosened, shuddering with little quakes of pleasure, her feet hanging suspended a fraction above the bed, as though the sheets were red-hot iron, and her own correspondingly red lacquered toe-nails clawed at the empty air.

A blurred, liquescent sound of compressed nostrils, sighs and the obsessive lapping of tongues gurgled like dirty water from the electronic conduit in the wall, transmitted by the microphone to the endless tape-worm spools of the recorder, till at last Madame Nhu gave clear operatic voice to her climax, *tenchu*, she cried, 'Heaven's punishment!' And now, Keiko raised her face from the Vietnamese's moist pasture, and smiled at us – at the mirror, in any case, in which she might see her own blood-stained lips. A sight which provoked a culinary witticism in

French from Count Ito, alluding to under-done meat – 'Ah, la pauvre Madame Nhu, elle est saignante,' to which he added, 'Doesn't our Baroness make a splendid vampire?' Hideki's giggle suggested that he was well enough acquainted with French.

Count Ito gazed dispassionately at the two specimens pleasuring themselves behind the glass. He seemed to me a more inhuman version of the three-legged camera, as he stood tranquilly in repose, both hands propped on the handle of his cane. Behind him, a row of clothes-pegged photographs hung pallidly sanguinous in the red gleam, like the dripping and severed limbs of his victims. I saw Count Ito transhumanized into the she-wolf of treason. It was not a trick of the light or of my own mind straying into despair. I saw his she-wolf's features as a fact, peculiarly disfigured by a mystical leanness, the mouth grown thin-lipped from kisses and impure acts, the cheekbone high, abutting the eye, the jaw set low upon the withered skin of the neck. And between them, an oblong cavity, which rendered the chin protruding, almost pointed and ridiculous, like a death's-head mask. And the eye, parched in its ardency, seemed all the more abject in so resembling the ardent agonies of saints: an hallucinatory dryness of the gaze that wherever it falls fastens itself like pressed glue from the wide-rounded pupil, now too frank, now shifty; and in the middle, a nose of grossly swollen lupine skin, and nostrils over an upper lip almost worn away by dissipation – the human nose of a beast that makes itself the guinea-pig of its own lusts, turning gangrened as it becomes ever more natural in its unnaturalness. That she-wolf frightened me, not because of what unimaginable degradations she represented, but by the simple fact of being a freakishly objective apparition, a definition of oneself, a sort of *ecce homo*, an acquaintance with reality from which there is no escape. The presence of treason was palpable, like the stink of carrion, forbidding any hope of another path but the one I must take.

And the she-wolf that I recognized in Count Ito's look, I knew would also find itself confirmed as the mirage of my own reflection staring back at me from the dead lenses of his eyes. And yet, yet – what else did Count Ito's eyes truly reflect at this moment but two languorous females caressing each other, another sort of mirage, perfect in its tiniest details down to the fingertips and exploring tongues.

'You haven't answered me yet, Mishima-*san*,' Count Ito said. 'Do you still worship at the shrine of the *niniroku* mutineers, despite everything I've said?'

'I do.'

'And are you resolved somehow to imitate their foolhardy enterprise?'

'I am.'

'Then, *tant pis* for you, my friend. You are expected in a zone beyond what is normally called pure or impure, idealist or corrupt, ultra-left or ultra-right, in a realm where the sun's compassionate rays never reach, except by the sterile reflection of the moon. A frightful place of ghosts, Kishima-*san*, to which you condemn yourself. And the worst of it is, no one will even comprehend why you accepted to go there.'

An imperceptible nod of Count Ito's head brought Hideki to him. The houseboy knelt and at once began to unbutton his master's trousers. Count Ito accommodated himself to the encumbrance of the boy's head on his crotch by leaning a little more aslant on his cane; but his face conceded no such extra room either to pleasure or its opposite.

'Look –' Count Ito said. I turned, and found myself almost face-to-face with Keiko, separated from me only by the width of the dressing-table on her side of the mirror, eyeing me as though the impermeable glass were transparent. She had arrived, dishevelled and her torso slick with perspiration, from the bed on which Madame Nhu still twitched like a segmented eel. Keiko disgorged the contents of her handbag on the dressing-table, and the tissue-wrapped figurines rolled out in a ball. She marshalled her porcelain dolls in a row, the dog, rabbit, squirrel, bear and fox, so that they appeared to be filing in single line towards the ark of her pubes moored against the marble table-top. Her eyes sought to pierce the mirror as she leaned nearer to it and her lips formed the shape of a word inaudible to the microphone, a word softly exhaled that left a vague aura of her breath on the glass, 'Thief.'

Restore the Emperor!

the posthumous script of
A Modern Noh Drama by
YUKIO MISHIMA

THE CAST

Keiko: former Baroness Omiyeke Keiko, now hermit nun of the Mount Haguro sect, known to pilgrims as the *ikigami*, the Living Goddess

Yukio Mishima: (Hiraoka Kimitake) himself

The Mother: Mishima's mother

The Bride: Mishima's wife

Kawabata Yasunari: writer, Nobel Prize winner and Mishima's former mentor

Senator Ito Kazushige: former Count and patron of Keiko

Morita Masakatsu: lieutenant of Mishima's paramilitary Shield Society cadets

Professor Hirata Ansho: a (*yamabushi*) sect leader of Mount Haguro

Ogawa Sei: Hirata's *ichi* or spirit medium

General Mashita Kanetoshi: commander of the Eastern Army at the Ichigaya HQ, Tokyo

Shikata Yuichi: Mishima's former amateur boxing sparring partner

4 members of the Shield Society cadet corps

STAGE INSTRUCTIONS

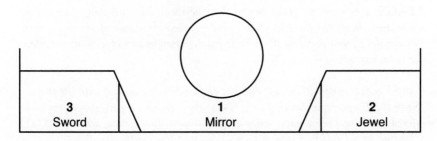

3	1	2
Sword	Mirror	Jewel

A 3-section stage without curtain. Centre Stage 1 (MIRROR) reminiscent of the Noh open-sided or apron stage, connected to Stages 2 and 3 by bridges, ramps or stairways.

Lighting to indicate changes of action and scenes. Backdrop projection screens on all 3 stages.

★   ★   ★

SCENE ONE

Darkness. The play opens in the classical French manner – 5 rapid knocks followed by 3 slower ones.

Music: the Sanctus *from F. Schubert's* Mass in A-flat.

STAGE 2: Screen projection: hell scene of the Raining Swords from a medieval emakimono *picture-scroll.*

Player: KEIKO in male peasant white cotton costume, hempen-fastened leggings, clogs, blouse and straw hat on her back.

To the side, interior of a rustic cabin formed by two walls of planks, a god-shelf shrine and floor matting round a sunken fire in the floor, a tea-kettle steaming on the grate, pot and cups arranged as if for a tea ceremony. Everything must be WHITE in detail – the walls, the costumes of all players, even the tea-kettle and the tree outside . . .

KEIKO chops at a dead tree with a mattock – 3 blows like the first introductory ones, at which –

STAGE 1: *a red spotlight focusses on a very large circular mirror at backstage – a sudden brilliant sunrise.*

As the red spotlight gradually dims and goes out: lights up on STAGE 1 *to reveal 4 young men in the white summer uniforms of Mishima's paramilitary cadet Shield Society bowing to the mirror sunrise.*

STAGE 1 *decor: an 18th century drawing-room, all furnishings covered in white dust sheets till the end of the play – a marble statue of Apollo is seen through the French doors on the outside patio. Arrangement of furniture to allow the following action –*

The SS cadets remove their caps and put on headbands inscribed with the slogan, 'Serve the Emperor for Seven Lives'. Next they unwind a pair of hempen cords affixed with ritual mino paper strips to form a waist-high avenue across STAGE 1 *leading to* STAGE 2 *and* KEIKO'S *forest hut on its elevation.*

As the SS cadets unfurl the cords, Schubert's Sanctus *ends and is replaced by Zen bamboo flute and drums. The SS cadets building the Sacred Way recite verses from the Shinto liturgy (from the* daijowe *festival of the First Fruits after the Emperor's accession to the Throne or the Palace Courtyard* toshigohi *harvest festival) –*

> '. . . 1000 rice-ears' harvest culled from the labour of men whose arms drip foam drops like sea water, on whose thighs right and left the mud is gathered . . .'

As the cadets finish their work STAGE 1 *lights dim and –*

STAGE 2: KEIKO *again chops with her mattock,* (knock, knock, knock,) *and –*

STAGE 1: *dim spotlight discovers* YUKIO MISHIMA *at stage front kneeling at his desk and writing.*

KEIKO (*leans on her mattock and looks towards* MISHIMA): The maple shows itself red at summer's end. The sound of a cricket, like a weaver weaving dead grass, *kiri, hatari churr, isho* . . .

MISHIMA (*at his desk*): *kiri, hatari churr, isho* . . . There isn't time. Everything must be beautiful, everything must be perfect, but there isn't time. All I have time for now is to write a farce, and the farce is this – to go on writing. (*Writes*) These plum trees haven't flowered . . .

KEIKO (*echoing* MISHIMA'S *words*): These plum trees haven't flowered this year. They need pruning. To cut them is my duty. What hasn't flowered, must flower again . . .

MISHIMA: What is that sound? *Jyari, jyari, jyari*, the endless noise of silk worms endlessly eating mulberry leaves. *Jyari, jyari, jyari* . . . no, it is simply the rustle of paper, myself feasting on the pages I fill. The room is freezing. Or is it me? (*Takes off his shirt – white, as are his trousers*) I'm sweating. I'm cold, like someone in a fever of panic. (*Touches his hands, arms, torso*) Cold as ice. Every bit of human warmth has left me (*touches his head*) all of it gone up here to feed the brain, sterile moonlight on my desk. (*Writing*) Stop! What are you doing? Isn't this madness? . . .

KEIKO (*raises her mattock as MISHIMA begins writing again and repeats*): Stop! What are you doing? Isn't this madness? You have cut down a human being! (*KEIKO falls on her knees*)

MISHIMA: What I am imagining has already happened. I do not imagine anymore. I am the reality I put into words, a reality that will happen, not foreseen, not prophesied, but already scripted. (*MISHIMA gets up while speaking and crosses over to KEIKO'S cabin at STAGE 2*) I have crossed the bridge of dreams that writers only dream of, no difference between what is imagined and what really happens next, which only the dead can know. Writers dream of it, the perfect criminal work of art, and are seized by terror. They know, I know, to cross over is the essence of evil.

knock, knock, knock

KEIKO (*at the sound of the three knocks she rises from her knees*): My guests have arrived.

STAGE 1: *The Mother and The Bride now enter and, escorted by the* yamabushi, *travel the hempen-cord avenue towards KEIKO at STAGE 2. Both women are outfitted in white: The Bride in a Balenciaga suit, The Mother in kimono and geta. The* yamabushi *wears traditional costume: small round cap on the head, yellow surcoat with six-tufted collar, with strips of deerskin behind, baggy tunic and trousers, coils of red rope and triton conches hanging from the waist.)*

STAGE 2: *THE MOTHER and THE BRIDE enter KEIKO'S cabin. A frozen frame moment occurs as MISHIMA hands THE BRIDE a dossier of papers. He addresses THE BRIDE . . .*

MISHIMA: This is how we must do it. There isn't time. I have said – and meant it once – I despise words. A lifetime of words has eaten away the marrow of my life. I felt it, I believed it sincerely, but it wasn't true. The most shameful admission a writer can make is to realize why he hates words, because others will go on speaking them after he is no more. Others will have my words – *my words* – but I cannot control how they shall use them. My words shall not explain me anymore. (*MISHIMA exits*)

441

KEIKO: My guests have arrived. (*She enters the cabin*) The widow and the unfortunate mother of the private citizen Hiraoka Kimitake.

THE MOTHER (*to THE BRIDE*): She looks like a woodsman.

THE BRIDE: There is no Hiraoka Kimitake. For six years this woman carried on a public affair with the public figure who was my husband, Yukio Mishima. (*She opens the dossier and glances at the papers*) I have his unpublished papers to burn. But first I must hear the story from her own lips, and when it is told, destroy every trace of it. That is why I have come here.

(*The* yamabushi *guide exits. All three women kneel by the fire and KEIKO serves tea.*)

KEIKO: Over a bridge of dreams they travelled, across the wild grass, in the long shadow of the mountain, to see me.

THE MOTHER: She is mad, they say, and in touch with the ghost of my son. Last year, she murdered a woman, but she was pardoned. She had powerful friends. The *yamabushi* magicians have given her sanctuary here in the forest of Mount Haguro in Yamagata, a privilege no ordinary woman would ever be granted. She inhabits a shrine in this forbidden place. On the road through Saba village, we saw pilgrims who had come a long way to see her, but the *yamabushi* guardians of this sacred mountain would not let them pass. All of them say she is *ikigami*, the living goddess. Have I done the right thing to come here? All those people. It was impressive. Perhaps she can tell me, is the spirit of my son finally at peace? (*To KEIKO*) Thank you, Madame Omiyeke, for granting us this invitation to see you.

KEIKO: My name doesn't matter. I was the widow of Naval Lieutenant-Commander Omiyeke Takuma, but that was long ago. Who remembers the person I was?

THE BRIDE: Who can forget? For twenty years she was the hostess of that fabulous villain, Senator Ito Kazushige, the Shogun of racketeers and blackmailers. It is all here in his papers. (*Shows the dossier to THE MOTHER as if from a previous discussion between the two*) What shall I keep, what shall I burn?

THE MOTHER: It is better to overlook such things, if we decide to see her. I don't want to know.

KEIKO: You will have heard stories, naturally. True ones, false ones, what does it matter now? For twenty years after the war, I was no one. Thieves of the lowest description came to me like cats at night, rubbing themselves at the pillars of my house and purring. But the truth is, the house had long since been abandoned. No one lived there. In 1966, I renounced the world and entered the Hosso convent of Gesshuji at Nara. When the senior nun shaved my head – (*KEIKO pauses*) – listen, do you hear it? The cry of the forest shrike which

442

impales its prey on thorns – I felt the entire weight of the world leave my shoulders. I sensed the coldness of the mirror on my scalp, and I felt relieved. So I imagined. I overlooked a terrible reunion. Fourteen years before, I had exiled my maid Koyumi to the convent of Gesshuji. She had served me loyally, too loyally, in those seven evil years from the death of my husband Baron Omiyeke to the end of the Occupation in 1952, when I sent her away. Her excessive devotion reminded me too much of all the shameful things I had done in those seven years, things that she had witnessed as my loving accomplice.

THE MOTHER: She confesses the unnatural appetite of one woman for another.

THE BRIDE: A lesbian nastiness, in plain words.

KEIKO: I did not foresee. My presence at Gesshuji aroused Koyumi to feelings kept buried for fourteen years.

THE MOTHER: Even in the separate world of the recluse, the sins of the world will follow.

THE BRIDE: There was no sign of repentance in her choice of convent. She deliberately inflamed the passions of that stupid woman. And when I think – what a fine pair they must have made, this female degenerate and my husband. A lesbian swindler in the arms of a sodomite. I have never permitted anyone, not even myself, to speak of his deviance. (*To KEIKO*) I prefer his infidelity with another woman than –

THE MOTHER: Forgive her, reverend sister. My son's bride speaks impetuously from grief.

THE BRIDE: Listen to her. After twelve years of marriage to her son, she still calls me bride, denied even the right to be entitled daughter-in-law. But now I am a widow.

THE MOTHER: I am the one to be pitied, reverend sister. She was his bride, not his mother, and my grief is beyond comparing.

KEIKO: Don't call me reverend sister. I have lost my name. My hair has grown back.

THE BRIDE: And what name do you suppose I have?

THE MOTHER: There is no need to be offensive.

THE BRIDE: She thinks herself the widow, not enough to be his mother. What are we here – three widows?

KEIKO: As a question of destiny, yes. Madame Hiraoka, I am not offended, but you have a right to be.

THE BRIDE: Oh, I am very grateful to you, Bride Number Three.

KEIKO: I was arrested two years ago for the murder of Koyumi.

THE MOTHER: Senator Ito Kazushige intervened, and you have found tranquillity in this refuge.

THE BRIDE: One scoundrel coming to the rescue of another.

443

KEIKO (*looks at THE BRIDE who speaks her thoughts in asides to the audience*) Destiny again. I should perhaps have remained where I was, in the psychiatric unit for criminally insane women. Listen – the cricket. How like a weaver it sounds, weaving the shroud of its husk. 'Why did you do it?' they asked. 'Why did you do it?' I refused to speak, and so they pronounced me insane. I have never told anyone what happened. If I had spoken, it would have been proof absolute that I was truly as they supposed me to be, insane. (*KEIKO rises from her knees with the mattock in her hands, like a warrior*) I will break my silence, only once, before I resume it forever.

THE MOTHER: How frightening she looks, the living goddess. I can see now, I was wrong to come here.

THE BRIDE: I want to hear this story.

KEIKO: At twelve noon, on the 25th of November 1970, I was in my cell meditating. A vision appeared to me, someone unrecognizable, naked, covered in blood like a newborn child, but headless. Nembutsu! Nembutsu! I invoked Buddha to rid myself of that hideous ghost.

THE MOTHER: Nembutsu! Nembutsu! On that same day, at noon, I felt a great pain in my womb, as of birth. And I, an old woman of sixty-five, passed blood as though my monthlies had resumed. My lover has come back to me.

THE BRIDE: Is that all they have to say? Superstitious nonsense from the retired hostess, and as usual from her, sickly sweet fantasies of incest. What happened next?

THE MOTHER: Did you understand what the vision meant?

KEIKO: I had no idea he was dead, not until later.

THE BRIDE: The living goddess is a liar. She protects the former Baroness Omiyeke Keiko, but her falsehoods are exposed in what he wrote. (*She takes some papers from the dossier and puts them in the fire*) She knew his plans, she knew he would kill himself, she knew everything. (*Pauses, looks at the fire*) I have not admitted to others, not even to myself, that perhaps I knew everything too. He told me, but I refused to comprehend what he told me. I don't remember.

KEIKO: Work is the best remedy. I wanted to burn things to rid myself of that ugly child without a head, so I went to the orchard to do some pruning. We had a number of old plum trees which had failed to blossom that year. It was a fine, clear autumn day. I cut the dead branches and my head began to clear. (*She kneels again with the handle of the mattock across her lap. MISHIMA re-enters the cabin in white Shield Society uniform with visored cap*) Koyumi carried the branches away to burn at the far end of the garden. I felt cheerful. And then it was as if the smoke of Koyumi's bonfire took the shape of a person approaching me. I recognized him, but I knew it was his ghost.

THE MOTHER: How did he look?

KEIKO: He wore his Shield Society uniform, looking as he did in life. (*MISHIMA kneels and embraces KEIKO from behind. Her head falls back on his shoulder and she sighs*) I became terrified when he spoke. He said he had come to make love to me in the spirit.

THE BRIDE: She is making it up, but I can see it, I can see the remembrance on which it is based.

KEIKO: He began to undress in front of me. 'Do the same,' he commanded me. 'Undress, quickly.' (*MISHIMA opens KEIKO'S blouse, exposes her breasts and fondles them*) As he spoke, his voice changed – I cannot explain this – a powerful voice, but the voice of an old woman. He removed his jacket, and I saw the breasts of an old woman. I can see this woman's face very clearly, someone who resembles him in aged female form. (*MISHIMA refastens KEIKO'S blouse*)

THE MOTHER (*takes out a photograph from her handbag*): Was this the woman you saw?

KEIKO: Yes, that's the face I saw.

THE MOTHER: She was my son's grandmother, Natsuko.

THE BRIDE (*snatches the photograph from KEIKO'S hand*): The only woman he ever cared for.

THE MOTHER: That's not true. She took him from me at birth, she kidnapped him and kept him prisoner in her room for twelve years, until –

THE BRIDE: Until she died. We know the whole sad story.

KEIKO: I tried to defend myself against the apparition. I prayed, but prayers failed. (*KEIKO stands and brandishes the mattock*) Away! Away! I struck it, again and again, with all the skill of Kendo that I remembered from my youth, again, again, until it fell bleeding and nearly decapitated.

THE MOTHER: To hear this again, to relive the horror of it – I should not have come here. (*She covers her ears*)

KEIKO (*kneels facing MISHIMA*): Then I saw. It was my maid, Koyumi, dead on the ground. (*MISHIMA rises and exits*)

THE BRIDE: A fine story. She can blame Mishima's ghost for deceiving her into murder. A story that she would not dare to try on anyone else, except us, because we are weak enough to believe it.

THE MOTHER: I believe it, because he deceived us too.

THE BRIDE: He certainly deceived me, but that was the bargain I accepted when I married him. I want the Living Goddess to tell us about Mishima's real wife, Morita Masakatsu. It is all here, written down in readiness for the flames. But I would like to hear it from her own lips.

THE MOTHER: No, I don't want to hear anything about that person, Morita Masakatsu, my son's killer.

THE BRIDE: You were present at his first meeting with Morita?

KEIKO: Are you prepared to hear it?

(As KEIKO speaks the yamabushi *guide re-enters and walks past the cabin to the raised level of* STAGE 1. *The* yamabushi, *PROFESSOR HIRATA ANSHO, is accompanied by his* ichi *spirit-medium, OGAWA SEI, a young man in plain white kimono carrying the catalpa wood bow. HIRATA and OGAWA kneel backstage. MISHIMA, kneeling at his desk, faces them at stage front. HIRATA plays a small stone flute – a high pitched wailing sound. OGAWA strums the bow, a droning sound, and falls into a trance as KEIKO'S story unfolds.)*

I enjoy the sanctuary of the *yamabushi* magicians on Mount Haguro. I would offend against them if I said too much about their secrets.

THE BRIDE: She can be as discreet as she likes – it's all written down here anyway.

KEIKO: The *sendatsu* of the Mount Haguro order is Professor Hirata Ansho of Waseda University. On several occasions, Mishima-*san* had witnessed the esoteric ceremonies of the *yamabushi* that take place in the mountains – the smoke and fire rituals, the barefoot ordeal of walking on red hot coals and climbing a ladder of swords. Mishima-*san* expressed a keen desire to attend a spirit séance, and he appealed to Professor Hirata to arrange for one. In 1966, at the time of the vernal equinox, we met at a farmhouse in the rice fields of Seba, the village at the foot of Mount Haguro that you passed on your way here. Ogawa Sei, a student at Waseda University, had served for a long time as Professor Hirata's *ichi*, the spirit-medium. Together they had performed 40 days' fasting and the mid-winter cold water austerities in preparation for this seance. Professor Hirata played his stone flute, the *ichi* strummed a bow of catalpa wood and fell into a deep trance. At once, a great storm shook the house. *(As she speaks, a monotone drone of voices in chorus grows louder,* uhhh, *like the storm wind.* STAGE 1 *lights dim and the red spotlight focussed on the backstage mirror intensifies to brightness.)* But louder, more compelling and terrible than the noise of the storm, we heard the *ichi* possessed by the lamentations of not one but many spirits. I have never seen a possession more terrifying than this one, and although four years have since passed, I can still hear the voice of the heroic dead. They identified themselves as spirits come from beyond the sea, the Kamikaze pilots whose bodies lie unreclaimed in the oceans. Their summons was the fulfilment of Mishima-*san*'s own wish, as if he, and not the *ichi* – who moment by moment dying in his trance – had been the one to attract these spirits from their graves deep in the sea. He wrote it all down. The rest of us were frozen by the noise, loud, loud as a hundred engines of combat aircraft filling the room. We could do nothing to rescue the *ichi* – a frail young man, weakened by the severe fasting and mid-winter austerities – visibly perishing before our eyes. One after another, the Kamikaze spirits used his body to speak, relentlessly like a forest fire consuming him to ash. Mishima-*san* very carefully wrote it all down. One after another, each one different and yet always the same, the lamentations of the pilots went on – betrayal, betrayal, betrayal. They were betrayed by the Emperor's declaration of non-divinity in 1946. By declaring himself human, they said, the Emperor had rendered their sacrifice meaningless. In agony, they cried, 'Why did the Emperor have to become human?' An agony so great that it finally had to end in the only way it could – (*The red spotlight dissolves: lights up on* STAGE 1 *to dim.* OGAWA *has collapsed. Pause. Silence. The sound of heavy rain on the roof.*)

HIRATA (*props up* OGAWA *and strikes him hard on the back*): Shu! Hyun! Shu! Hyun!

MORITA MASAKATSU (*enters in university uniform, kneels and holds the* ichi OGAWA *in his arms*): Ogawa Sei, Ogawa Sei, my brother! His eyes are open!

    (*Stands and faces* MISHIMA *at his desk*) It's no use. He has died of heart failure.

MISHIMA (*writing*): I don't believe her. It was just another story he wrote – yes, good, good.

THE BRIDE: I don't believe her. It was just another story he wrote . . . (MISHIMA *at his desk repeats*: 'Good, good!') and one that he was ill-advised to publish. Did he really wish to embarrass the Imperial Household? What has this got to do with Morita Masakatsu?

KEIKO: Morita was a student at Waseda University.

THE BRIDE: Of course, I knew that.

KEIKO: Morita was a close friend of the dead medium, Ogawa Sei. They came from the same place, Yokkaichi on the coast. When Morita was sent to fetch the doctor, Mishima-*san* said to Professor Hirata –

MISHIMA (*at* STAGE 1): – *that young man, he will be my* ichi. (*Lights out on* STAGE 1)

★　★　★

SCENE TWO

Lights up on STAGE 3 *(JEWEL). A typical electoral campaign HQ after a victory. Back screen projection: photograph of the candidate for the Tokyo governorship. Shouts of victory heard from offstage, the pop of champagne corks. Electric fans blow papers like a snowstorm of white confetti across the room.*

Enter KAWABATA YASUNARI in this storm. He wears a white summer suit and shoes, and carries a cigar and glass of champagne. He sits down at a table and fans himself.

447

KAWABATA: This is the real Japan. At least, that's what I tell myself. The noise, the confusion of an election campaign which never seems to end. A permanent campaign. We await the results, but they are inconclusive to tell us what we really want to know. What have we become? Like throwing dirty laundry into a washing-machine. The not so clean, the not so dirty, this colour and that, everything rotates so fast that it all disappears into a single whirlpool of white. I am so tired.

(*Enter SENATOR ITO KAZUSHIGE, also in white, but with a white shawl over his shoulders as though cold in the August heat. He carries a cane and limps.*)

KAWABATA: Ah, it's him, Senator Ito Kazushige. The sinister whiteness of our dirty laundry. The absolute dead-centre of this whirlpool of our political machine in which nothing moves but stagnates. I would prefer not to have this encounter.

ITO: Kawabata Yasunari, the Nobel Prize winner, the sage of Kamakura who has flown seventy years beyond the reach of ordinary corruption. He does resemble a heron, an old one on its last legs. His forehead slopes back to a white crest, his neck is bent in a U-shape, the flesh hangs loose and soft like feathers. He thinks me shallow and cynical. I envy him. With such ease, fame and glory have come to him, and with the good taste of apparently never lifting a finger to strive for them – and certainly never dirtying a single finger. I must congratulate him.

KAWABATA: Look how he hobbles on a stick, an old man like me. His limp reminds all that he fought in Burma and Malaya. Once upon a time, a hero. He has done something with his life, unlike me, never mind that he is the quintessence of corruption. I fear him.

ITO: Kawabata *sensei*, permit me to offer my sincerest thanks and congratulations. Your contribution on behalf of our candidate has been invaluable in sweeping our party to victory once again.

KAWABATA: It has been easy for me.

ITO: Do please sit down, you look very tired.

KAWABATA: I confess, I am exhausted.

ITO: Pardon my curiosity, but why at your time of life have you sacrificed tranquillity to the ordeals of campaigning?

KAWABATA: Not at my time of life, Senator, but to call it simply what it is, old age.

ITO: You told a journalist that the late Yukio Mishima had inspired you to political action.

KAWABATA: I said that.

ITO: You have received the visits of Mishima's ghost, you also said. Is it true?

KAWABATA: It is. (*As they speak, backscreen picture of the candidate changes to MISHIMA posed with his sword*)

ITO: Do you mind my asking? Does he appear to you — how shall I say, in terrifying form, covered in blood?

KAWABATA: Only as he was, and as I last remember seeing him, a man approaching forty-five. It is a sight terrifying enough to behold, a vision of someone who is, after all, dead.

ITO: Others too have seen him.

KAWABATA: Have you, Senator?

ITO: I was thinking of the case of Madame Omiyeke Keiko, a sad story.

KAWABATA: As you say, a very sad story, which has led Madame Omiyeke to the psychiatric unit of a prison for women offenders.

ITO: It may be the last service I can do for the former Baroness, to see her released from hell and returned to the safety of the Gesshuji convent.

KAWABATA: I earnestly pray that you succeed, Senator, in your act of merciful deliverance.

ITO: Concerning Mishima's suicide, you did not approve?

KAWABATA: Naturally I did not approve. He has withdrawn all evidence of his existence.

ITO: That is a curious way to put it, Kawabata-*san*, but I think I know what you mean. It was a spectacular death, in the true sense of the word spectacular. Mishima's suicide has tested our limited conventions of privacy.

KAWABATA: Everyone, including myself, has obeyed the rule of turning one's face away. The spectacle of his misconduct has therefore, in a sense, not happened. Privacy is normally a matter of maintaining face. In short, an entirely public affair. I have learned an instructive lesson in what is private, what is public, in this month of campaigning. A critic once called Mishima, Japan's first Dadaist. That seems to me accurate.

ITO: If indeed he was our first Dadaist, he was the last.

KAWABATA: A true Dadaist must necessarily be an internationalist. Mishima was perhaps a limited internationalist, but he was one. Global village is a description that especially applies to us. Superficially cosmopolitan as we might appear to be in Tokyo, we are in reality deeply, deeply provincial. In this village, Mishima's death by ritual *seppuku* is a fiction, a fiction that has upset our fiction of what we suppose ourselves to be, but are not, except conventionally.

ITO: What you say is true. A sufficient reason for Mishima's suicide will not be found. But, of course, a variety of insufficient reasons have been advanced, which say more about the state of Japan's psyche than anything Mishima did. They say, he died by reason of sadomasochistic exibitionism; he died by reason of hyper-decadent aesthetics; he died by reason of homosexuality in a love-pact suicide; he died by reason of ultra-nationalist Emperor worship. Every reason has been – and will be entertained.

KAWABATA: Except one.

ITO: Except one. And what is that one for you, Kawabata-*san*?

(MISHIMA enters, a ghost in white Shield Society uniform, carrying a pair of military boots painted white that he places on the table)

KAWABATA: In October 1968, Mishima was the first to arrive in Kamakura to congratulate me.

MISHIMA: Three times the Nobel Prize has eluded me. I lost it the first time in 1965 to a Russian, Mikhail Sholokhov, and the second time in 1967 to a Guatamalan, Miguel Angel Asturias.

And now, for the third and last time, I have the pleasure of seeing it go to you, *sensei*, my old friend and mentor.

KAWABATA: Praise which honestly revealed disappointment. (*Addressing his reply to ITO*) Why do you say last time? You are young, Mishima-*san*, with plenty of opportunities still to gain this prize. Besides, who remembers Nobel Prize winners? It is, in the fine English expression, the kiss of death, of guaranteed oblivion. Have you seen pictures of the Nobel laureates? What a fine gallery of old and senile abbots, gone in the teeth, not rewarded for their finest work, which is in the remote past, but merely for having survived. Do you regret not being counted in this number?

MISHIMA (*laughs*): There isn't time.

ITO: Are you saying he killed himself because of his failure to win the Nobel Prize?

KAWABATA: I am coming to that, Senator. In the last months of that same year, 1968, Mishima became involved in the notorious university teach-ins, putting himself at risk in confrontations with thousands of student rioters occupying the faculties. I knew only what the newspapers reported of these eccentric one-man shows – Mishima's crank pre-historic utterances, his ultra-rightwing challenges to a mob of extreme leftist youngsters.

MISHIMA: Pronounce the Emperor's name – just do that – pronounce his name, and I shall join hands with you at once!

KAWABATA: Can you imagine, Senator? I saw photographs of him decked out in black like a gangster, in a Ginza playboy's string-fronted shirt and tight trousers –

ITO: The homosexual icon. He was well-pleased to be called ape-man by such an audience, expecting, perhaps seeking a knife in the belly from them, but knowing at the same time what a comic travesty he played, aware that the youngsters idolized him as an absolute old fool with considerable daring. Never once did they silence him, for all their heckling and abuse, because he presented them with a mirror – a reflection of their own delighted surprise at getting away with misbehaviour. It was a perfect god-sent audience before which he previewed a drama of subsequent transgression.

KAWABATA: I had the uncomfortable idea that he was giving his Nobel Prize acceptance speech to a chosen audience of barbarians who despise the mendacity of literature, as he had come to despise it.

ITO: So, you do put the loss of the Nobel high in his reasons for suicide?

KAWABATA: No, I dismiss it altogether. As I said, there is only one reason, but I am reluctant even to think of it.

ITO: Please continue. I am eager to hear your explanation.

KAWABATA: I would prefer not to have one. Later, in the spring of 1969, he paid me a visit at my villa in Kamakura – conservatively dressed, he was always conservatively dressed when he came to see me, and as so often before, with a gift of cigars and fine brandy, because it pleased me. He spoke of Hitler's recipe for agitation, Hitler's sound advice on the art of public speaking.

MISHIMA: It is the sexual domination of the subject, that is, of the masses. The scandal of Hitler is that never before or since has there been such a charismatic figure to treat the masses like a woman.

KAWABATA: Grotesque, depressing. I remember thinking, why this anguish, old friend? Why are you punishing me like this for having been chosen a Nobel winner by the whimsy of chance?

(Exit MISHIMA to STAGE 1 and a rank of 4 white-uniformed SS cadets. MISHIMA arrives in a white whirlwind of blown papers and the undertone sound of brushed cymbals, low but persistent. MISHIMA removes his cap and accepts a headband from MORITA among the cadets. MORITA hands MISHIMA a dagger and sword. All the cadets put on headbands with the slogan, in Chinese characters, Serve the Emperor for Seven Lives!

A reenactment of the kidnapping of GENERAL MASHITA KANETO-SHI at the Ichigaya garrison HQ in downtown Tokyo unfolds as ITO tells the story)

ITO: Hitler's art of public speaking was of no use to him at noon that day on the balcony of the Eastern Army Headquarters at Ichigaya.

KAWABATA: You were present at Ichigaya on the 25th of November?

ITO: I was an eye witness by personal invitation. In the early morning of the 25th, a young man in the uniform of Mishima's paramilitary cadets presented himself at my door in Azabu. My houseboy tried to send him away, but the cadet insisted that he had an urgent message for me. 'Absurd young man, what do you want?' I laughed at him. He was so small, so puny, so timid – was this a specimen of Mishima's prae-torian guard, this toy soldier in resurrected Meiji costume? 'Mishima-*sensei* requests your presence at the Ichigaya Headquarters for 11:30 a.m.,' he said. 'Therewill be a great revelation.' I dismissed him.

KAWABATA: But you went? (*Aside*) The fox, the fox, he knew all about Mishima's plans, and now he pretends merely to have been a bystander, a spectator.

ITO: Kawabata accuses me of involvement in Mishima's terrorist plot, I can see it in his eyes. Knowing that a crime will happen, as I knew it must, is a form of spiritual complicity that I cannot explain to him.

(STAGE 1: *MISHIMA, MORITA and the 3 SS cadets present themselves to GENERAL MASHITA KANETOSHI, seated backstage on an arm-chair. MISHIMA shows GENERAL MASHITA the blade of his sword to admire, and as the general leans forward to examine it, one of the cadets at his back seizes him. The general is tied hand and foot and gagged. MISHIMA and the cadets quickly move the furniture to create a sort of barricade, as ITO proceeds with the story*)

I phoned Ichigaya shortly after 11 a.m. An officer said there was trouble. 'Mishima is running amok with a sword in General Mashita's office.' I arrived at the Ichigaya parade ground under the balcony just before noon, when Mishima commenced his speech.

(STAGE 1: *two cadets approach stage front and let down two long banners from above stage to the floor. The banners are inscribed with the Shield Society proclamations of a coup-d'état. The words of the manifesto should be clearly legible to the audience. The cadets step back as MISHIMA advances and stands between the banners, as if to make his speech. MISHIMA wears a headband with the* 'Serve the Emperor for Seven Lives' *slogan. A voice offstage exclaims,* 'Look, he has blood on his uniform!' *A droning noise, the crescendo hiss of cymbals*)

ITO: In everything so far he had been successful – kidnapping General Mashita, barricading the office, repelling the counter-attack of the HQ staff officers. He could rely on the law which forbids the use of firearms against civilians. And his blackmail demands were met, the thousand men of the garrison had been assembled to listen to him speak. The publicist had succeeded too well. It was his undoing. Newsmen and television crews in helicopters circled over the balcony, and the noise drowned out most of his speech. Those on the parade ground below who could hear something only heckled and jeered him. His summons to restore the Emperor, overturn the Peace Con-stitution and incite a military *coup-d'état* were a complete fiasco.

KAWABATA: He must have known it would be.

ITO: Kawabata-*san*, I do not know what Hitlerian powers of persuasion your colleague imagined he had gained in confronting the *zengakuren* students of '68, but his fantasy proved hollow on the 25th of November 1970.

KAWABATA (*aside*): Ah, scoundrel, I do not know exactly how, but I know you are somewhere and somehow behind all this. (*To ITO*) Kidnapping a general at swordpoint in broad daylight in his central Tokyo garrison by a world-famous writer leading a suicide commando unit – this is not an everyday occurrence, Senator. It is an action consonant with the ultra-right terrorist incidents of the 1930s – but anticipates the red extremism of the 1970s. No one, apparently, wants to face this. We would all rather bury our heads in Mishima's exhibitionism and ignore his action as a pathological aberration.

ITO: I do not, Kawabata-*san*, believe me.

KAWABATA: Very well then. Consider with me the great many questions still unanswered – questions in fact never even raised. How did Mishima come to have easy access to the Eastern Army Headquarters . . .

MISHIMA (*addressing the audience continues KAWABATA'S questions*) . . . the confidence of General Mashita himself, the privilege of joint training with the Self Defence Forces that his cadets received, a cooperative relationship of illegality between a private citizen's paramilitary unit and the regular army – how did Mishima come to have all of this?

ITO: You don't expect me to know the answers, surely?

KAWABATA: That's the answer I always get to my questions – the three monkeys, blind, deaf and dumb, no one knows who, or knows how or knows why. Someone or some others had the power to honour the whims of a middleaged writer who liked to play soldiers. Who were these political brokers – and what did they expect? That a popular celebrity might give artistic cachet to militarism? If so, this unholy extension of entertainment into the military and political arena backfired right in their faces. Mishima gave the establishment its most unforgettable teach-in.

ITO: One might almost think you were pleased, Kawabata-*san*.

KAWABATA: I ask myself that, Senator. Am I pleased? Or am I horrified to the point of pleasure?

(*As KAWABATA and ITO speak, MISHIMA retreats to backstage. A cadet removes GENERAL MASHITA'S gag. MISHIMA takes off his jacket and bares his torso. He kneels before the general, unfastens his trousers and pushes them down below his loincloth. He unsheaths the dagger that MOR-ITA hands him. GENERAL MASHITA exclaims, 'Stop! What are you doing? Isn't it madness? You are cutting down a human being!'*)

MORITA, with naked sword, takes the beheader's position at MISHIMA'S side – he raises he sword as MISHIMA lifts the dagger high in both hands. 'Stop! Stop!' General Mashita cries as lights dim – brilliant red spotlight focusses on the backstage mirror)

ITO: All things considered, Kawabata-*san*, it is wiser to stick to the aberration theory. I can prove it to you.

KAWABATA: Ah –

ITO: Indeed I can. At about half-past twelve on November 25th, I looked inside General Mashita's office. It was all over by then – the double *seppuku* of Mishima and his lieutenant, Morita. General Mashita had been released unharmed and the three other surviving cadets were arrested. I beheld a slaughterhouse, the carpet inundated by blood, the disembowelled corpse of Mishima, he and Morita beheaded. The stench in the noonday heat was unbearable.

KAWABATA: You don't have to go on.

ITO: And placed neatly side by side on the carpet, the heads of Mishima and Morita Masakatsu, and I could not help thinking, how interesting they looked, two heads like Van Gogh's pair of boots. (*ITO picks up the military boots on the table and arranges them*) Strange notion, isn't it? Perhaps because I felt sick, or perhaps I wanted to weep, as some of the officers there openly wept.

KAWABATA: This isn't necessary.

ITO: It is necessary, you will see. I went outside on the parade ground for some air. The young soldiers who half an hour ago had laughed at him were now repentant. 'He was sincere,' they said. 'We should not have laughed at him.' Ah, so this is it, I thought to myself. This is the aberration.

KAWABATA: I don't understand.

ITO: You will. Tell me frankly, Kawabata-*san*, what did you think back in 1968 when Mishima came to you with his delusions about Hitlerian ultra-eroticism? Clearly he was going insane.

KAWABATA: I felt depressed.

ITO: And what else?

KAWABATA: What else? Shame. The shame one feels in being the captive of an ivory tower. The weakness of living too long. I felt angry with him. (*Enter MISHIMA, his jacket unbuttoned and worn like a cape. KAWABATA now speaks directly to MISHIMA, as though his ghost were visible*) Have you come to believe a sacrifice of the intellect is a necessity?

MISHIMA: A necessity in estimating the value of one's life, which does not require intellect. On the contrary, I have very nearly missed the entire point of culture. My exclusive commitment to bookish culture was only another way of being ill-informed. Hitler finally made me understand, by turning the masses' inner feelings inside-out, one releases a spiritual power of nuclear force. (*Back screen projection of 1968 pitched battle between police and student rioters with helmets and sticks*)

KAWABATA: This made me feel angrier. (*To MISHIMA*) Have you discovered intelligence in your encounters with the *zengakuren* students?

MISHIMA (*laughing*): They are mostly pig ignorant. So little do they know even of Communist ideology that some actually believe Marx-Engels-Lenin is one person. The dissidents among them who blindly worship Mao Tse-tung are the stupidest. (*A group of 3 or 4 students enter, helmeted, in black plastic raincoats, anti-teargas cloths across their mouths, and carrying Gewalt batons*) It came as a great shock to them when I explained that Mao was a follower of Wang Yang-ming Confucianism, the warrior philosophy which profoundly influenced our own samurai. (*To the students*) The action of culture in bringing salvation to peasant humanity is entirely consistent with samurai compassion. (*A student replies, 'You agree then, Mao is the right way for Japan?'*) No, there is a difference. Hitlerism can do us no harm, but Maoism is contrary to spirit of our folk. (*Student:* 'What is the difference?') Mao threatens the uniqueness of Japanese culture which is identified with the Emperor.

KAWABATA: I couldn't believe my ears. Such a low, such a dangerous low level of discussion in a person of Mishima's intelligence.

ITO: He was paying you a great compliment.

KAWABATA: What?

ITO: Yes, really. It was a favour he granted you. He allowed you a glimpse into the techniques he used to indoctrinate his Shield Society cadets.

KAWABATA: How do you know what methods he used?

ITO: I had the opportunity to witness him in action.

KAWABATA (*aside*): That's more like it. Now the villain begins to admit his involvement. What was it like?

ITO: Essentially, very simple. A question, as they say in chemistry, of elective affinities. The process of conversion requires the agency of a charismatic personality on a youngster predisposed to react in a fanatical way. The recruit must not have any doubts, and this is easy to find out by asking some questions.

(*The students remove their raincoats, helmets and masks, and reveal themselves as Shield Society cadets in white uniforms*)

MISHIMA (*to the cadets*): What is your attitude to Western pop music and jazz?

ITO: Your reaction, Kawabata-*san*, or mine, would not be the right one, too complicated, or if simple, far too élitist and therefore complicated.

KAWABATA: And what is the right answer?

MISHIMA: It is forbidden. Likewise, it is forbidden to attend baseball games. All participation in sports is forbidden, unless these are the traditional Japanese martial arts. No books, unless they are the classics that celebrate martial virtues.

KAWABATA: Tell me, then. Is Western food also not permitted?

ITO: Of course.

KAWABATA: That cannot be. I have seen Mishima in a French restaurant with his lieutenant Morita Masakatsu, teaching him the proper use of knives and forks and glasses.

ITO: What you saw, Kawabata-*san*, was a terrible irony, the Last Supper, a lesson in cannibalism in which the eater becomes the eaten. Mishima was instructing his executioner in the correct table manners for eating his flesh. Do you understand?

MISHIMA: The rules of suicide that guide one in the right use of the dagger and sword are in the end no different than the ones governing the proper handling of a fork.

KAWABATA: This is vile, unspeakable. And yet, I am curious to know more.

ITO: You can see how basic the elements of this chemistry are. Everything depends on the subject's crucial reaction to one question.

MISHIMA: What is your attitude to the Celestial One, His Imperial Majesty, the Emperor?

KAWABATA: And what is the right answer to that?

MISHIMA (*laughing, replies to KAWABATA*): You should know. You have heard it with your own ears.

ITO: Did you ever come face to face with Mishima's real wife? (*The SS cadets leave, except for MORITA*)

KAWABATA: I know Mishima's wife, Yoko. What do you mean, real wife?

ITO: His fanatic fiancée, his righthand man, his beheader whose own head was also cut off on November 25th. Morita Masakatsu.

MISHIMA (*strolls with KAWABATA*): We carry our glasses of brandy into the garden at nightfall. Kawabata staggers for a moment, losing his balance, as old men are liable to do. A loss of mind? A false step? Is he going to tumble off his pedestal? His cigar goes out. I light it again.

KAWABATA (*as MISHIMA lights his cigar*): I begin a fresh page.

MISHIMA: I observe him. I see him taking it all in, the night, the stars, our talk about politics, my stories of the student demonstrators. Like a sponge that tomorrow will ooze ink. I feel sorry for him. He collects rare and antique pornographic photographs of little girls.

KAWABATA: I met Morita Masakatsu for the first time when Mishima came to see me, as I said, in the spring of 1969. We had been talking for hours. Night fell, and we took a stroll in the garden. Suddenly, Mishima said that Morita was waiting for him in the car. (*To MIS-HIMA*) Ah, but you can't just leave him there?

MISHIMA: Why not? If I command him to wait, he must.

KAWABATA (*aside*): Like a dog. I prevailed on Mishima to invite the young man inside for a drink.

ITO: He was forbidden to drink and to smoke.

KAWABATA: I saw that.

ITO: Were you impressed by Mishima's lieutenant?

KAWABATA: His real wife? I saw nothing of that. What I did see was a four-square, solid, not very bright twenty-three-year-old student from Waseda University.

MISHIMA: He is from Yokkaichi on the coast, the son of a high school principal, an orphan raised very strictly by his elder brother.

ITO: You saw nothing mysterious about Mishima's dangerous bride?

KAWABATA: No, nothing in the least mysterious. He did not impress me at all, only as an exceptionally dull, ordinary youth. A typically provincial specimen with extreme rightwing views. He was bitterly opposed to the leftwing occupation of Waseda University.

ITO: Nothing else?

KAWABATA: He wore the new white summer uniform that Mishima had designed for his cadets.

ITO: The mystery, Kawabata-*san*, is that he appeared so dull, so ordinary, so like the perfectly obedient wife. Mishima was the father of one hundred handpicked warrior cadets, a quarrelsome family of competitors striving to gain the status of favourite. Morita was a crafty politician. He was behind many of the feuds, playing one clique against the other, to make sure no one rivalled him in Mishima's affection. The perfect wife among ninety-nine others.

(*MISHIMA shrugs off his jacket, kneels, and places one of white-painted military boots from the table in front of him. He says:* 'Only the dead can know what comes next.'

ITO (*with his cane raised like a sword over MISHIMA'S neck*) Morita raised the sword and struck – once! Twice!

KAWABATA: At the end, his hand trembled.

ITO: Two deep cuts across the shoulders – but he could not strike off the master's head. (*ITO'S shawl has fallen off his shoulders and MOR-ITA replaces it*)

KAWABATA: Ah, terrible. Could I foresee any of this when I heard Morita speak for the first time?

ITO: He spoke to you?

KAWABATA: Not to me exactly. To an audience of ghosts that his master encouraged him to address. Like a proud father, Mishima listened, and I had simply to bear what he said – a hymn of praise to the H-bomb, I remember very well, some utterly repellent notion that the H-bomb is logically consistent with Japanese culture, natural to us, in the same way that our tea ceremony seems deeply natural.

ITO: These are Mishima's ideas, we know.

KAWABATA: He seemed not only to love the idea of nuclear holocaust, but – this is hideous, truly insanely hideous – to help in making it a reality. Total annihilation, the end of the world, was the boy's ambition.

ITO: In a sense, Morita achieved his ambition.

MISHIMA (stands and says to MORITA): When two lovers die together, they bring the world to an end. The sun goes out. (Exit MISHIMA with MORITA)

ITO: Did Morita say anything else?

KAWABATA: Something very odd, frightening, but only now when I think back. He said, 'Mishima-sensei is related to the Emperor.'

ITO: Related – is that the word he used?

KAWABATA: I think so – in any case, a very special closeness which somehow made him feel the presence of His Majesty in Mishima himself.

ITO: Did Mishima tell you of his meeting with the Emperor?

(Lights up on STAGE 1. Four young men in ceremonial festival costume raise the handbars of the great portable omikoshi shrine on their shoulders. To a drumbeat rhythm, they shout in chorus, nuh! huh! and recite the nine magic syllables – rin-byo-to-sha-kai-jin-retsu-zai-ZEN! The bearers sway from side to side as though in a procession)

KAWABATA: He mentioned it, of course, the autumn garden party at the Imperial Palace in 1966.

ITO: I arranged the invitation for him. I can imagine how he boasted.

KAWABATA: I wouldn't call it boasting, although, if one sets aside the humorous manner –

ITO: I know, he gave you an account of the Emperor's quaint manner of speech – like a knife cutting a string of the koto – uhnn!

KAWABATA: Nothing like that. I meant humorous only because he seemed quite casual about it. I don't even know what they spoke of.

ITO: Equestrianism.

KAWABATA: Pardon me?

ITO: You heard correctly, horseback riding. Or at least, His Majesty's regrets that his painful motor condition had not allowed him to enjoy riding for a long time now.

KAWABATA: He said the Emperor appeared unusually friendly.

ITO: Unusually open. His Majesty does not ever refer to his muscular defect.

KAWABATA: Why did he on this occasion?

ITO: Who knows? My guess would be that it was a serene comment on Mishima's own unusual request. He had wanted permission to visit the bunker where the Surrender was planned. It is still there, an underground bomb shelter in the Palace grounds.

KAWABATA: Were you able to arrange it for him?

ITO: After his little chat with the Emperor, a court chamberlain escorted him to the place. Mishima asked, who sat here, who sat there? Where was the Emperor? When he knew all the actors' exact positions, he became quiet, as though listening to the voices discussing the Surrender. Fifteen minutes went by, and then he looked round and said –

MISHIMA: – a perfect empty cube of night. (*He has appeared at* STAGE 1 *with MORITA, both stripped to loincloths and helping the bearers to carry the* omikoshi). It is the omikoshi shrine, the immense weight on our backs – we carry a perfect empty cube of night.

(The bearers exit with the omikoshi. *MISHIMA and MORITA remain on STAGE 1. The red spotlight again focusses on the great circular mirror at backstage – a few moments of dazzling blindness – fades out)*

MISHIMA: What does it mean – 'restore the Emperor!'? Speak, Morita Masakatsu.

MORITA (bowing deeply and as if breathless): *Hai, sensei!* It means that for us the Emperor is God.

MISHIMA: Again, Morita, again!

MORITA (bowing each time to MISHIMA): God! God! God!

MISHIMA: What is the mirror in which to see God?

MORITA: The sun is the mirror in which I see God.

MISHIMA: When you look at the sun, Morita, you are blinded.

MORITA: *Hai, sensei!* I am blinded by the vision of divinity.

MISHIMA: His Imperial Majesty is the Sun God. Can you see with the eyes of the blind? What am *I*, Morita?

MORITA: You are the Mirror, *sensei!*

KAWABATA (on STAGE 3): What madness does he preach? I cannot believe my ears.

ITO: Believe it, Kawabata-*san*. Did he not make himself clear, how often? Countless times.

KAWABATA: Who could possibly believe him?

ITO: We are not capable of belief, Kawabata-*san*.

MISHIMA (on STAGE 1): The Mirror of Divinity is shattered into millions of pieces – millions of blind Japanese today who live without hope in total eclipse. Tell me, Morita, can the blind see with their own tears? From the darkest, most secret power of the earth, a force of destruction was created, and it fell on Hiroshima and Nagasaki. A force brighter than a thousand suns eclipsed the Imperial Sun God. Life as it is, is unacceptable.

MORITA: Life as it is, is unacceptable.

MISHIMA: Suicide is our map of Heaven, Morita. Our time has come. On the 25th of November, 1970, I will adress the Heavens at exactly midday. I have chosen the right moment. We will restore the Sun God to power. Our nation must once again be divine. It must re-arm itself for the great and total war of annihilation that will come after us.

KAWABATA (on STAGE 3): No one recognized the terrifying crime he was planning.

ITO: No one *could* recognize it, as he knew only too well (turns to address MISHIMA on STAGE 1).

MISHIMA (on STAGE 1 replying to ITO): The rate of crime in Japan is very low — because so few people ever report crimes.

ITO: It could also signify there are no crimes to report.

MISHIMA (laughing): Precisely! What a well-behaved people we are.

ITO: You mean, what well-behaved criminals we are.

MISHIMA: That is a wise remark, Senator Ito.

ITO: Wiser than I can say.

(*Lights out* STAGE 1. *Lights dimmed* STAGE 3 *up as* KAWABATA *and ITO resume.*)

KAWABATA: I find it difficult to accept. Impossible.

ITO: What, Kawabata-*san*?

KAWABATA: That Mishima could do such a thing, put this idea into Morita's head that he represented the Emperor. It is a shocking idea, a blasphemy.

ITO: Who else could have put it into his head? And not only Morita's head but into ninety-nine others, all of them similarly indoctrinated, as you say, with a blasphemy.

KAWABATA: Were they really lovers, do you think, as some people believe?

ITO: What does it matter? If two people share a transcendental obscenity of that sort, as they did, it becomes pointless to talk of sexual intercourse.

KAWABATA: Without knowing it, I knew it. Obscenity. Yes, you are right to call it that. Something between Mishima and his consort upset me, irritated me beyond reason. I was provoked to a cruelty which even now I cannot regret. That night, before Mishima left, I gave him a picture. I collect 19th century erotic photographs, the earliest examples of the art, daguerreotypes and that sort of thing. In my collection, I have some rare, almost priceless specimens of little girl prostitutes taken in London in the 1850s. I showed Mishima one of these, an extremely beautiful 1867 collodion plate of two little girls in the act of cunnilingus.

MISHIMA (*enters with the plate KAWABATA has given him, studying it closely*): This is very disturbing. The absolute stillness of eternity in a moment.

KAWABATA: That's because the models had to keep still a long time for the exposure to take.

MISHIMA: No, it's the eyes of the girl looking at us. She smiles but reveals no emotion, no indecency. But when I look closer into her eyes, I see two naked girls making love. This is what she contemplates, and this is what is so disturbing, because her eyes are riveted on us. Where is the source of those two love-making girls? Her eyes can only reflect us.

KAWABATA: Maybe it is in the space behind us. I give you the print, Mishima-*san*. (*MISHIMA exits*)

ITO: The one reason, Kawabata-*san*.

KAWABATA: One reason?

ITO: You have not told me the one reason that explains his suicide. (*ITO walks slowly away from KAWABATA. As the two part, lights dim, gradually reducing to 'portrait' circles round them.*)

KAWABATA: I have forgotten. (*He contemplates ITO like a receding photograph*) He goes away, out of my life, thank heavens. He will keep his promise and secure the release of former Baroness Omiyeke Keiko from her prison for the criminally insane. She will resume her life as a recluse, the saintly hermit of Mount Haguro, proclaimed the Living Goddess by thousands of pilgrims who travel in vain for a glimpse of her. This will be Senator Ito Kazushige's last act of power. On Christmas, 1971, after a night of orgy at his home in Azabu, Senator Ito will retire to his room and take a massive dose of cyanide. He has instructed his houseboy Hideki to stand by with a pair of garden shears, and at the climax of his death agony, to cut off his penis. (*Light goes out on KAWABATA*)

ITO: Kawabata Yasanuri, Nobel Prize winner, elegant, wise, undogmatic, who so deeply disapproved of Mishima's suicide, will gas himself to death in 1972. (*Light out on ITO. End scene*)

★ ★ ★

SCENE THREE

(*Light up on STAGE 1. MISHIMA at the proscenium front, kneeling at his desk, torso bare, dressed only in white trousers, no shoes. Back screen projection of books – shelves of hundreds of books.*

461

A rustling, clicking sound . . .)

MISHIMA: There isn't time. There isn't time. *jyari, jyari, jyari . . .* eating paper like a famished silkworm. My mouth turns black with ink. I wanted to write a beautiful, perfect Noh play. I wanted to act in it as the chief ghost – but I end up with a farce, a *kyogen* farce which is a mere interlude between two Noh plays.

(Noise of the wind outside. Lights up on STAGE 2. The three women round the fire, KEIKO, THE BRIDE and THE MOTHER have changed into white dressing-gowns, each similar and yet subtly differing, from THE BRIDE'S Western-style gown to KEIKO'S deep-sleeved kimono variety)

THE BRIDE: Three nights before he died, I woke up at 3 a.m. Something woke me up, a noise in the house, or outside, the *karakkaze* wind, the November *karakkaze* wind . . .

MISHIMA (*at his desk*): . . . the *karakkaze* autumn wind, the annoying hooligan wind that blows away the smog of Tokyo and sweeps the sky clear. I can see the winter moon.

THE MOTHER: I felt restless that night too. I woke my husband at 3 a.m. There is an intruder outside trying to break into the garden.

MISHIMA (*replying as the father*): Go to sleep woman. It's only the wind.

THE BRIDE (*crosses over the STAGE 1, lights dim to evoke moonlight, and walks among the dust-sheeted shapes of furniture*): Everything looked so strange in the moonlight. He was working in his studio, as he always did until dawn.

THE MOTHER: In my day, I never pestered him when he was at work.

THE BRIDE (*replying to THE MOTHER who remains on STAGE 2*): I don't normally. I know his habits. It was quite cold in the house. I could feel the wind even indoors. It gave me gooseflesh. But he was perspiring as though ill with fever and had taken off his shirt.

THE MOTHER: She knows nothing of what a writer like him suffers. Twenty years I saw it, I knew.

MISHIMA: *jyari, jyari, jyari . . .*

THE BRIDE: That strange noise, it was coming from him (*she too repeats*, jyari, jyari, jyari)

MISHIMA (*to THE BRIDE*): What is it?

THE BRIDE: Pardon me. Someone's trying to break in, a thief outside.

MISHIMA: A thief? Very unlikely. A thief would not trouble to wake you. A noisy thief is a stupid thief.

THE BRIDE: Your mother's come out too, on the patio. I saw her from the window.

MISHIMA: I cannot bother about my mother's insomnia.

THE MOTHER: It's true. I sleep badly.

THE BRIDE: Aren't you going to investigate? At least, call the police.

MISHIMA: We are respectable, law-abiding people. We never report crimes. That's why Japan has the lowest crime rate in the world.

THE BRIDE: I thought he was afraid.

THE MOTHER: He would not be afraid.

(*MISHIMA rises from his desk and takes up the samurai sword lying on it, partly unsheaths the blade to examine it*)

THE BRIDE (*touches his arm*): He was cold as stone, like damp marble. (*To MISHIMA*) Is that necessary.

MISHIMA: Let's hope not. (*MISHIMA and THE BRIDE cross the drawing-room*) Don't switch on the lights. (*He looks round at the furniture, laughs*) Do you remember the critic Yoshia Kenichi at our house-warming party in 1959?

THE BRIDE: I remember he was very offensive.

MISHIMA: He went round pretending to admire our brand-new furniture. Like a department store manager in a showroom quoting prices (*points with the sword*) – this, fake Louis Quinze, so many yen – Taiwan reproduction rococo, so many yen – Chinese restaurant salon piece, so many yen – Jewish baronial . . . He was right, it was all phoney and pretentious.

THE BRIDE: You never spoke to him again.

MISHIMA: He couldn't stop his tongue from wagging. Yoshida Kenichi understands. A gay man's kitsch version of normality

THE BRIDE (*addressing THE MOTHER*): I had never heard him speak like that before. This went beyond his usual fits of black humour, as I had come to know them.

THE MOTHER: You should have realized how disturbed he was. What else is a wife for?

(*MISHIMA draws his sword*)

THE BRIDE: He advanced through the French doors into the garden patio. Moonlight on a statue of Apollo. A zodiac-tiled sundial.

MISHIMA: The steep night sky. Clouds moving fast across the moon like a speeded-up film.

THE MOTHER (*descends from STAGE 2 to STAGE 1*): I heard the slap of the *karakkaze* wind on his bare chest.

THE BRIDE: No, it was the wind striking that big, ugly statue of Apollo, whistling round it. I saw her (*pointing to THE MOTHER*) gliding towards us, a preposterous Kabuki ghost in the moonlight, and her voice, unreal, grating on my nerves like the pestering wind, apologizing to her son because she appeared in the wrong kimono.

THE MOTHER: That's not so. I did not apologize for the wrong kimono. I merely said I'd come straight from bed because I was worried.

MISHIMA: She looks younger in the moonlight, beautiful as she once used to be thirty years ago. I remember when I was one year old tripping on the hem of your kimono and falling down the stairs. I cut my eyebrow.

THE MOTHER: You are mistaken. Your grandmother did not permit you to use the staircase to our separate quarters on the upper floor at Yotsuya. You climbed upstairs on your own, when we weren't looking. (*She touches MISHIMA'S eyebrow*) You bled a great deal. It has left a scar.

MISHIMA (*puts the sword in his belt and lights a cigarette*): She is pursued in the dark by the glowing tip of my father's cigarette.

THE BRIDE: Father-in-law was in a hurry. He tripped over the garden hose on the patio.

MISHIMA (*imitating his father's growl*): Damn it! The gardener leaves everything hanging about.

THE MOTHER: My husband had formed an opinion about the intruder.

MISHIMA (*again as his father*): I've checked it out. There's some crazy fellow at the garden gate. He's been out there all night, calling your name, Mishima-*sensei, sensei* . . . Probably one of your crank admirers seeking an autograph.

THE MOTHER: Nothing to worry about, my son. Go back inside. You look so weary. Your father will deal with him.

MISHIMA: I don't think it's an autograph he's after.

THE BRIDE (*as Mishima stoops down to pick up something*): Why has he picked up the garden hose? He has some plan in mind. He tightened the nozzle and tucked it behind him in his belt. 'What are you doing?' father-in-law said.

MISHIMA: I have an idea. Go over to the faucet and watch me carefully. I want to have a few words with our night visitor at the gate. When you see me signal like this – turn the water on full blast. Do you understand?

THE BRIDE: 'Yes, yes, go ahead', father-in-law said. He was so excited that he lit the filter end of his cigarette.

MISHIMA (*hands a coil of hose to THE MOTHER*): Play it out behind me – don't let it snarl up. (*He draws his sword from his belt and moves away with the nozzle tucked behind him*)

THE BRIDE: Look at her. She plays out the hose against her belly, like an umbilical cord issuing from her womb.

MISHIMA (*looking back*): Now the dragon has a tail.

THE MOTHER: We could see the garden gate quite distinctly in the moonlight. A shadowy figure in the street paced up and down behind it.

(Spotlight on MISHIMA as goes backstage to an exaggeratedly big gate with bars like a cell door, no walls. THE BRIDE follows him discreetly in the dark and waits nearby)

THE MOTHER: Did you overhear anything?

THE BRIDE: I crouched down behind a stand of pampas grass and listened. I heard everything.

MISHIMA *(to a figure behind the gate, black fedora hat and raincoat)*: What do you want? It's 3 a.m.

(The mysterious night visitor is YUICHI, MISHIMA'S one-time sparring partner in the 1950s)

YUICHI: I've been here all night. Hasn't anyone told you?

MISHIMA: What reward do you expect for that?

YUICHI: That you answer one question sincerely.

MISHIMA: One question. Go ahead.

YUICHI: When are you going to kill yourself, *sensei*?

THE MOTHER: Bride, is that what he said? Did you recognize him?

THE BRIDE: I couldn't see him. His face was in shadow.

YUICHI *(takes off his hat)*: Do you recognize me, *sensei*?

MISHIMA: I remember that scar on your face, Shikata Yuichi.

YUICHI *(laughs)*: Very good. That's a compliment to my scar. How else could you remember me? You've had so many young men.

MISHIMA: I don't need the scar to remind me.

YUICHI: Was I so special, Kochan, really? You bastard.

THE MOTHER: Shikata Yuichi, I remember him. His father Shikata Ichiro was our local grocer in Shibuya. Yuichi was an amateur boxer, my son's sparring partner. A nice boy, not very bright however. He had great difficulties with his university entrance exams and my Kimitake gave him some free tutorials.

YUICHI: What a fine tutor you were, Kochan, do you remember? Mathematics, physics and English lessons in buggery.

MISHIMA: Then you graduated as a hooligan of the far right and joined the National Martyrs Youth Corps.

YUICHI: So you do remember? That was a long time ago. Nearly twenty years. I was nineteen. I've moved on since then.

MISHIMA: To what? You're not so young now.

YUICHI: But you, Kochan, in three days time you will not grow any older. Aren't you fortunate. Look at you. You are completely transformed from the sick, puny corrupter of youth that I used to know. You carry a sword like a samurai. Very impressive. And such admirable muscles. Isn't it a pity that you must put them to use to kill yourself?

MISHIMA: I don't need you to remind me.

YUICHI: I am just a messenger. No going back, *sensei*. No changing your mind.

MISHIMA: Who sent you?

YUICHI (*laughs*): I remember something you told me once, Kochan. We are such law-abiding folk, we Nipponese, that our most dangerous terrorists will report their conspiracies to the police, out of politeness. You were being cynical. Would you like to call the police? A man with a secret like yours does not call the police. Anyway (*he points across the street*) notice that car parked over there, across the street? No, of course, it's hard to see. The streetlamp doesn't appear to be working. But I'm sure you can see those two cigarettes glowing in the dark.

MISHIMA: I'm under surveillance. So what? Do you think I don't know?

YUICHI: There are a number of important people who admire your purpose. They wouldn't like it if you lost heart now and decided to turn back at the last minute.

MISHIMA: Tell them from me – go to hell!

YUICHI: Don't be so unsociable. I'm only here to give you encouragement. Ah, what's this? Your gate seems unlocked. (*He partially opens the gate*) It wasn't hard to open. (*He tries to enter*) We're on the same side now.

MISHIMA (*bars YUICHI'S entry with his sword held crossways*): Look at this blade, Yuichi. Admire its watered-silk pattern. A masterpiece of the 16th century craftsman Seki no Magoroku. (*He pushes YUICHI out and jams the gate shut with the sword*) It is a crime to use it like this. But we are not on the same side. I would never be on the side of the political racketeers you represent. (*He signals to his father to turn on the faucet. MISHIMA sprays YUICHI with the hose*)

YUICHI: Stop! Stop! I'm going. But remember, you aren't the private citizen Hitaoka Kimitake anymore. Whatever you say, you belong to us.

MISHIMA (*stops the water and drops the hose. He turns to THE BRIDE*): Did you see?

THE BRIDE: Enough.

MISHIMA: Everything is so clear in this moonlight. (*He touches her face, her stomach*) I can see the cut, I can feel the stitches that cross it.

THE BRIDE: Again, that noise, like gnashing teeth – *jyari, jyari, jyari.*

MISHIMA: The silkworm making its coffin.

THE MOTHER (*arriving at the gate*): What is it? What's happened?

MISHIMA: Nothing. It was all nothing. (*He removes the sword from the gate*)

THE BRIDE: He asked me to fetch our son Ichiro's bicycle chain to padlock the gate.

THE MOTHER: You look so weary, my son. I'll make some tea to calm you.

MISHIMA: I am perfectly calm, *chère maman*. I have another hour's work to do. (*To THE BRIDE as they return to the house*) I want to show you something.

THE BRIDE: Perhaps you shouldn't work anymore tonight.

MISHIMA: One more line. One more line. Just a few more stitches.

KEIKO (*appears inside the drawing-room and addresses THE BRIDE*): Did he make love to you that night?

THE BRIDE: Why does she ask me that? Somehow, her question isn't offensive. It doesn't sound lewd. (*Replying to KEIKO*) I was lying down on the staircase. I remember. The steps on my back felt like the spine of a great animal. He opened my dressing-gown and ran his fingernail across my belly. (*She stoops down to pick up something from behind a dust-sheeted sofa*)

MISHIMA: What have you got in your arms?

THE BRIDE: Your old stuffed lion, the one you've had since childhood. It fell behind the sofa.

KEIKO: Did he make love to you?

THE BRIDE: He wanted to show me something.

MISHIMA: Would you like to be photographed like this with me?

(*Back screen projection: the enlarged photograph of Louis XII's tomb*)

THE BRIDE: Who are they?

MISHIMA: The cocoons of Louis XII and his wife Anne de Bretagne, circa 1530, at the Abbey Church of St.-Denis. This is how their tomb sculpture shows them, the way they looked after the embalmers had stitched up their corpses.

KEIKO: An invitation to die with him?

THE BRIDE (*while MISHIMA again makes the noise, jyari, jyari*): I didn't understand. (*She sits down on the sofa, holding the stuffed lion*)

MISHIMA (*with a book in his hand. Screen projection changes to the library shelves of books*) There are 8,000 catalogued books in my library. Not one of them, nor all the others I have read in my lifetime, means anything to me now. Nothing, except for these few lines. (*Opens the book and reads*) 'What I should like to find is a crime the effects of which would be perpetual, even when I myself do not act, so that there would not be a single moment of my life, even when I were asleep, when I was not the cause of some chaos, a chaos of such proportions that it would provoke a general corruption or a disturbance that even after my death its effects would still be felt.'

THE BRIDE: What's that?

MISHIMA: That is Lady Clairwill in Marquis de Sade's masterpiece, *Juliette*. Lady Clairwill is a monster who seeks after the perfect crime of cosmological proportions.

THE BRIDE: Is there such a crime?

MISHIMA: I don't know. But this is the answer her pupil and friend

Juliette offers – 'Try your hand at a moral crime, the kind one commits in writing.'

THE BRIDE: Isn't that a grandiose way of confessing, you are of no use except as a writer?

MISHIMA: Yes, it is a confession of insane futility.

THE MOTHER (*enters the drawing-room and shakes THE BRIDE'S shoulder, as though she were asleep*): Did he make love to you?

THE BRIDE: I have the odd habit sometimes of falling asleep with my eyes open. Did I fall asleep again with my eyes open?

THE MOTHER: Yes, again, for the first time.

MISHIMA (*sits down at his desk stage front and picks up his pen*): I can be forgiven every transgression, except one. I am not permitted to sin against my own conformity to success. Faith – faith is permissable only to simpletons who have no voice in the affairs of success. This is the crux. I have put the ease of my success to work on self-destruction. My contemporaries are creatures of atrophied imagination who respond only to a single conditioned reflex. Success. They are unfit to understand or accept or forgive anyone who wantonly subverts their cherished faith in success. I face a blank wall of incomprehension, which will be their final revenge. 'He had no business to die. He died an inexplicable death.' I will be classed a social deviant. A fascist agitator.

(*As MISHIMA writes, the three women remove the dust-sheets from the furniture. They tidy up and open the French doors: early morning sunshine pours in*)

MISHIMA (*writing*): I dedicate these pages to someone who will never read them – someone who was a god in my childhood, but who showed himself human when I came to manhood. (*THE BRIDE approaches MISHIMA'S desk and takes papers from his hands. She continues reading what MISHIMA has written –*)

THE BRIDE: Who else will want to read these pages? My friends have long since done with me. I dedicate them to my enemies. I offer them one last chance to see me in hell, where I am in the certainty of finding them. I enjoy an incalculable freedom which they do not. I have all the night ahead of me, at my command. I rule the night absolutely and without opposition, a power to see my entire epoch in hell –

> all my contemporaries and confrères
> all the time-serving cliques
> all the lickspittle arriviste canaille
> all those with just enough talent to benefit from
> what they do not deserve –

on all this protozoan slime, I can confer immortal damnation, because I can write the last lines of their epitaph. These are the last thoughts of a dangerous rightist.

(THE BRIDE gathers up the rest of the manuscript from the desk — a loud knocking, three times. The women freeze)

THE MOTHER: Ah, it's him.

THE BRIDE: Shall I go and see?

KEIKO *(stops her)*: Thirty-three years according to Buddhist reckoning are stipulated for the liberation of a spirit after death. Thirty-three years.

THE MOTHER: I am too old to wait thirty-three years. Let him in now. I feel sorry for him.

KEIKO *(restrains THE BRIDE who tries again to move)*: I am fifty years old and pregnant.

THE BRIDE *(clutching at KEIKO'S sleeve)*: His —?

KEIKO: Not by him, but with him. Do you understand? After thirty-three years, a spirit finds liberation, or, as in his case, if the spirit is restless — if it wants to return . . .

THE MOTHER: What are you saying?

KEIKO: I am called the Living Goddess. Have you seen the pilgrims who would like to make a religion of what they believe I carry? I cannot help it. It is not my doing. What he is, in thirty-three years' time will come to fulfilment, in the year 2003. It is already expected by some, but there will be many more by then, perhaps the entire nation.

(3 loud knocks again)

THE BRIDE: If what you say is true, a terrible event can be avoided if we see him as he is now.

KEIKO: We are not expecting anyone.

THE MOTHER: Please let me reply.

KEIKO: There is no reply. We permit entrance to no man.

(Lights dim and out on drawing-room. MISHIMA alone at his desk, head bowed, not writing. MORITA enters with dagger and sword and places the dagger before MISHIMA, on the desk.

MORITA unsheaths the sword and holds it over MISHIMA'S neck. Pauses. He puts down the sword, goes over to the phonograph and replaces the Schubert Sanctus with another record, George Gershwin's, My Sweet Embraceable You. *He returns to MISHIMA and again raises the sword over MISHIMA'S neck . . .*

Embrace me, my sweet embraceable you!
Embrace me, you irreplaceable you!
Just one look at you, my heart grew tipsy in me –
You and you alone bring out the gypsy in me . . .

Lights dim and out. Red spotlight focusses to blinding glare on the great mirror.
End.)